The
Lynn
The Fighting Strength

☆

"The Fighting Strength tells the real story about the life of the combat nurse in Vietnam.... Hampton was there—the reader can feel it, hear it, and see it within the pages of this uncommon book about an uncommon person in an uncommon war zone."
—*Wisconsin Bookwatch*

☆

"A resilient and caring individual, Hampton has written a forceful affirmation of America's traditional values."
—*Publishers Weekly*

☆

"Compassionate, dynamic and a very good read."
—**Donald E. Zlotnik, author of the** *Survivor of Nam* **series**

☆

"Lynn Hampton is an incredible person, a heroine in the truest sense. The images of her book consumed me, helping me imagine the daily horror that so many experienced in Vietnam."
—**Brad Frey, editor of** *Letters from 'Nam*

☆

"Lynn Hampton has been an inspiration to hundreds of vets. I highly recommend reading her book. It is candid...[and] has taught me a lot about a part of the war I was not familiar with."
—**Reverend John Steer, Director of United Veterans and Family Support, Inc.**

THE FIGHTING STRENGTH

MEMOIRS OF A COMBAT NURSE IN VIETNAM
LYNN HAMPTON

WARNER BOOKS

A Time Warner Company

In memory of
Bill Abernethy, Richard Cole,
Johnny Hays, and Richard Hood

This book is dedicated to the many in whom there were marvelous glimpses of the image of God. And to the POW activists, our best patriots, engaged in battle today for the honor of America against the biggest "City Hall" in the world and monumental forces of evil.

WARNER BOOKS EDITION

Copyright © 1990 by Lynn Hampton
All rights reserved.

Cover design by Don Puckey
Cover lettering by Carl Dellacroce
Cover photograph by Black Star

This Warner Books edition is published by arrangement with Daring Books, P.O. Box 20050, Canton, Ohio 44701.

Warner Books, Inc.
1271 Avenue of the Americas
New York, NY 10020

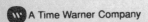 A Time Warner Company

Printed in the United States of America

First Warner Books Printing: November, 1992

10 9 8 7 6 5 4 3 2 1

ACKNOWLEDGMENTS

A special thanks to my mother, who prayed me through Vietnam, and who, like the best of mothers everywhere, believed and encouraged me to write when the chances of failure still far exceeded those of success. To my sister, a virtual one-woman fan club. To my father, for always being there. And to my aunt for sound advice and editing. To John and Donna Steer for encouragement, and the best kind of friendship in the world—that given by God.

I would also especially like to thank Joan Almand for her help in getting started. And Carol Duplessie for hours of typing, retyping, editing, and cheerful and personal interest. A special thanks to Cliff Dudley for advice and help, but especially friendship. To Paris Curry, and all those at the Orlando Vet Center, especially Norman Jones, for interest and encouragement.

It was the best of times, it was the worst of times, it was the age of wisdom, it was the age of foolishness, it was the epoch of belief, it was the epoch of incredulity, it was the season of Light, it was the season of Darkness, it was the spring of hope, it was the winter of despair.

Charles Dickens
A Tale of Two Cities

TABLE OF CONTENTS

1 Beginnings   *1*

2 Birth-Control Cookies   *10*

3 If This Was the ''Nitty-Gritty'' of Life . . .?   *18*

4 Only His Mind Away   *22*

5 Light Banana Yellow   *28*

6 Life Goes On   *32*

7 ''To Conserve the Fighting Strength''   *36*

8 Built on Sand   *44*

9 The ''Saga'' of Gary Owen   *54*

10 Ward 13, I Think   *58*

11 Somewhat Like Riding a Bicycle   *70*

12 Children   *74*

13 The Zoo   *82*

14 VC   *90*

15 Red Alert   *101*

16 Saigon   *107*

17 ''Whatever Happened to Baby Jane?''   *118*

18 ''Die and I'll Kill You!''   *129*

19 Ships That Pass in the Night   *132*

20 Dak To and Darvon   *140*

21 A Little Insanity Goes a Long Way   *145*

22 The Day Before Tet   *155*

23 Tet   *160*

24 Good-bye   *170*

25 Another Martian   *174*
26 Deliverance   *182*
27 Help, Murder, Police!   *193*
28 The Orthopedic Bathtub   *201*
29 Later   *207*
30 "Its Wavering Image Here"   *221*
Epilogue   *226*
Index   *241*

PREFACE

Some time in the afternoon the plane took off from Bien Hoa airbase. I looked down and thought, *How strange it is to be leaving a place I know I will never see again*... I was able to identify a few of the compounds and buildings below. I thought of people there who were, and would always be, dear to me. The words of Mark*, my friend, spoken at Tuy Hoa when we sat on the beach or in the club talking for precious hours, sounding the depths of our souls with the breeze blowing from the South China Sea, came to mind: "Don't ever look back." And I knew I wouldn't—at least not in the way we had understood. Times and places in our lives have value in themselves just for what they are. Whatever good there may have been... and there is always good, is fixed forever in time and space and hearts, and nothing can ever detract from it. Life goes on... best to go on with it and not wish for things to be the way they were... or not to have been the way they were.

I looked down on a deceptively pretty land and saw rice paddies and trees, little villages and mountains. I thought about how cheap human life was down there and yet, at the same time, never more precious. I thought about how war brings out the worst in people, but also the best—and I knew I had seen "good" more clearly and in a different way than ever before.

Years later, when I understood things better, I *would* look back, in a way Mark and I would have thought acceptable, and realize that in spite of heartache and anger and frustration, there was also a certain peace...

For many of us who were there, our perceptions of the particular hell of Vietnam very quickly became distorted: numbed, if you will, so we could get the job done. Helicopter door-gunners nonchalantly read comic books, nurses dealt cheerfully with mayhem. Burned patients were "crispy critters," quadruple amputees "basket cases." "It don't mean nuthin." This was our context and we functioned well in it. Rambo-type "blood and guts" stories are more likely to come from those writers of fiction who were not there. Although "numbed," my nurse's heart knew those guts and blood belonged to someone real, someone who was precious to others. Morbid curiosity will not be satisfied here. And a stereotypical Army nurse will not be found.

*Not his real name

Beginnings

> "The only real security in life
> lies in relishing life's insecurity."
>
> M. Scott Peck, M.D.
> *The Road Less Traveled*

"May I have your attention, please! Flight #103 for Honolulu is now ready for boarding at gate #6."

I turned to Lynne and Marie, two nurses I knew from Fort Campbell and said, "Well, this is it," as we scrambled to gather our belongings. We'd been pretty calm up until now, talking about our families, and leave time, and the "psychedelic" paint jobs on the new Braniff planes—but now we could *really* sense the excitement. Someone's radio blared, "Sittin' on the dock of the bay," as what seemed to be several hundred total strangers in green uniforms converged on the big jet—all going to Vietnam—just simply getting on a commercial jet and going off to war!

San Francisco—city of the sixties—of the "flower children." The city seemed fresh, interesting, and innocent . . . most of us barely knew what it all meant. Later, when we returned, it was just hippies and drugs and war protesters. Nothing fresh or innocent about it.

The flight was breathtakingly beautiful. The sky had never looked so mysterious; the plane seemingly in a race with the afternoon sun.

After what seemed to be an eternity, we landed in Hawaii:

lovely, balmy Hawaii and took off almost immediately for the Philippines. The sun finally beat us and it was dark when we landed in the Philippines. I think I first realized how really tired I was in that crummy little waiting room in the Philippines. I felt like it was all closing in on me in the stifling humidity, but soon we were refueled and on our way again . . . next stop, Vietnam. By now, after eighteen hours of flight, there was not a spot on my body that was not in pain. *Vietnam will seem good after this,* I thought. But pain was soon forgotten in anticipation of what was ahead. "Hang loose," a friend had said, so that's what I was doing to the very best of my ability.

I was still hanging loose when the pilot announced we had just crossed into Vietnam. And I hung *pretty* loose as the plane suddenly went nose down in its "dive-bomb" descent over Bien Hoa Airbase. A PFC in the seat behind me said, "Wow! I didn't know a commercial plane could do something like this." But the pilot was apparently an "old pro," explaining that we were less likely to get shot down this way. "Bien Hoa, Vietnam, straight ahead," he announced rather happily, as hand luggage fell from the overhead racks and the sky began to light up like noonday from the flares suddenly going up everywhere. They drifted and descended slowly on little parachutes. They were awesome; eerie to look at. I looked at my watch. It was 2:00 a.m., March 2, 1967.

Lynne, apparently realizing in a new way the seriousness of what we were doing said, "Do you realize there are people down there who would kill you if they got the chance?" Of course, we all knew it, but coming to some kind of *realization* of it was difficult, although becoming easier with every passing moment!

"I can't recall having an enemy in my entire life," I mused. She thought about it for a second or two and decided she hadn't either. I had often thought that *surely* people must be basically good. Actually, most of us were too young to be afraid and too crazy, if at all possible, not to have a good time. But our ignorance would be bliss only a little longer.

In moments we were on the ground and the plane came to a screeching halt. When the door opened, for a moment I

thought of hell. The blast of heat which hit us was almost more than one could bear.

Even at two in the morning, in the dark, it seemed things were quite well-organized. I'm not really sure what I expected, but I recall being somewhat amazed at so many permanent buildings and so much electric lighting. We waited in line for something, and finally ended up in the 90th Replacement Detachment in Long Binh—a whole busload of nurses.

They led us to a room full of bunk beds. No more was said—we knew what to do with them. "Take your pick, ladies, we will brief you in the morning."

My body seemed to sigh as it stretched out on that wonderful, flat surface. My mind began to wander. A memory from boarding school days filtered in, of a pleasant spring afternoon in my senior year immersed in one of Dr. Tom Dooley's books about communist atrocities in Southeast Asia. He told the story of an old woman, one of many refugees, who tried to escape to freedom. Communist soldiers had shattered her collarbones with the butt of a rifle, yet on she struggled, stooped and broken. As I recalled Dr. Dooley's road packed with fleeing refugees, I remembered my heart crying, "Why doesn't somebody help them?"

And, strangely, another memory from my boarding school days in Tampa filtered in. We were rejoicing with Cuban girls and wearing black and red armbands when Castro took over from Batista. I remember their truly bloodcurdling stories of Batista's atrocities.

At that time, none of us had known Castro was a communist. We all thought he was a hero. But within a few months, those same well-to-do girls would be refugees, too, with very little left but their freedom.

By now it was a half-conscious memory: a confused awareness that in supporting the corrupt Batista government, the United States had helped drive Cuba into Castro's clutches—funny to think of it now.

I thought about my twin sister, Leigh. Memories of boarding school couldn't be complete without her. We were so close, but so different— and not the type who couldn't stand to be apart. Yet I missed her now as sleep quickly overtook me.

As with everyone, certain things in my early years combined to determine how I would view life as an adult. My childhood was full of love and security, so I felt little need to rebel as did many of my contemporaries in what I considered to be rather self-destructive ways. Nevertheless, I *always* reserved the right to my own opinion.

My father owned citrus and cattle and had attended Harvard; my mother had taught school; and as a child, I loved summertime the best. I could get out of all those horrible, confining winter clothes and play in the thick, lush grass of our big Florida lawn. There were ixora bushes with flame-red blossoms, flower beds, and palm fronds rustling in the breeze. Even now, I can recall the pungently sweet, exotic smell of those huge, cream-colored palm blooms that always seemed to stir something in my soul.

I especially loved it at high noon—the world was so intensely bright. A moist heat would rise from the thick grass, and insects would begin a buzzing which continued into a lazy drone through my nap time. There were mocking birds and red-winged black birds with their distinctive, melodious, "laid-back" call, and butterflies. The grass grew so fast I could almost see it, especially from my vantage point right down in it. There was a "saturation" of life—a wild profusion of it. I *ran* almost everywhere I went—*life!*

When I was five, an aggravation entered my benevolent world, one that would cause me to form one of the most basic principles in my philosophy of life and eventually bring me to volunteer for nursing duty in Vietnam.

My mother was, in a sense, "Super Mom." If she had a flaw, it was in her overprotectiveness of me. I remember well the time I complained that I had a sore throat and was hot. Mother called the maid and gave instructions to put me to bed at once.

The doctor was called and strongly suggested I be taken to the University Hospital in Atlanta. They were both convinced I had rheumatic fever. "Mrs. Hampton," the doctor said, "don't let Lynn do anything physical, it could damage her heart."

I knew it couldn't possibly be true—they were mistaken. I couldn't bear the thought of staying in bed when spring had arrived and my annual love affair with life was just beginning. I remember their chasing me across the yard as I ran for a tree. Surely if I could climb it, they would see how healthy I really was. I made it to the tree, climbed up and sat on a limb, knowing I would eventually have to come down and grieving in advance for my loss of freedom. Why were they putting so much effort into making a healthy person sick?

The very next day, Sister was pushing me down the hall in my brand new doll buggy. "Faster, faster," I screamed. Suddenly the buggy caught on something and out I flew. No big deal, but you would think the world had come to an end. Everyone was crying but me.

We readied to go to Atlanta. Mother had this beautiful, yellow silk blouse covered with polka-dots which I insisted on wearing as a dress to the hospital. My grandmother was appalled, but I won out, and now I was the MOST fashionable person to hit the Jacksonville train station. I still had on my fancy blouse when they put me on the examining table. They were all coming to hold me down because I was fighting for my life. I mean I really gave them a fight against all the needle tests. I fancied later that they were back there saying, "Boy, that stylish kid sure can fight!" I still thought I was wonderful.

And to this day, I thank God for a family who raised me to feel good about myself. One of my earliest memories is of my father picking me up as a baby and pacing the floor with me. I think he did it a lot. I can still remember him patting me a little too hard on the back with his big, gentle hand, and saying a few words that seemed to mean everything in the world. Even at such an early age, he made me feel important and special. My father still is one of the most honest, moral, and gentle men I have ever known.

My mother loved people and hospitality. I grew up listening to the wonderful stories she told of growing up in a small town. Her friendships were her most valued possessions.

By the time I was five, I was utterly *fascinated* by people. They had something that I suppose is best described as *charm*, and I would lie awake at night pondering it. What caused it? Where did it come from?

After five weeks of hospital treatment for rheumatic fever, which turned out to be a simple case of tonsillitis, I became convinced they were trying to make an invalid of me. At one point, I tried to escape from the hospital and fell down a rocky hill, skinning my knees and elbow. I felt sorry for my mother—she looked so worried—but I didn't know how to tell her that even with the accident, the whole thing had done me a world of good.

I didn't understand all the ramifications myself, but I knew in the depths of my soul I could never live my life in fear and I would not live it cautiously. As all children, I had a sense of wonder and excitement about life. To accept overprotection—to shrink back from life in neuroticism, would be to live it unworthily.

Our high school was probably average, but there were things about it I didn't like. It was overcrowded and there was a sense of being herded like cattle. One or two of the teachers were disagreeable and unpleasant and, over all, the odor of dirty bodies lurked in the corridors. When my parents decided to send me to a Catholic boarding school, my reaction was more than anything else a sense of relief, although we were Episcopalians. It was a wonderful school. My first memory is one of fresh floor wax. It smelled so clean! There wasn't one dirty fingerprint on a wall anywhere, and everyone looked, acted—*and smelled*—civilized! There was an air of serenity and discipline—sanity. The school was small, and each girl was seen as an individual and free to be her own person, and the Sisters were committed to investing their lives in ours. Close friendships developed and there were, of course, the shenanigans—the stuff of which Walt Disney movies are made. There always seemed to be something "fun" going on, but always against a backdrop of goodness and propriety and human dignity.

In the Glee Club, we sang lots of Rodgers and Hammerstein and Lerner and Loewe. I especially remember "My Fair Lady," "The King and I," and "The Sound of Music." When we sang about "girls in white dresses with blue satin sashes," we were those girls. On special occasions, we wore white dotted swiss with full skirts and blue satin sashes.

In chapel, we weren't allowed to lean back on the edge of the pews while kneeling. The Sister in charge of etiquette said, "Can you imagine a lady like Jackie Kennedy doing something like that?'' I tend to believe that the good Sisters, with their typical flair for expertise, succeeded exactly according to plan, imparting in our hearts and minds a wisdom for living I have found unequaled anywhere—''Life is serious, should be lived with a sense of dignity, and is best 'taken with a grain of salt.' '' They understood that we needed to be prepared to cope with all of life's contingencies; and a sense of humor would be vital in our approach to life.

When I left the academy* for a large, secular university, one of the Sisters told me, ''If you go to a secular university, you'll come out an atheist.'' My reply was something to the effect that if my belief in God couldn't stand up to the best and worst the world had to offer, it would be worthless anyway! We both had our points.

In college, I studied nursing and all the psychology and philosophy I could squeeze in. People and life fascinated me more than ever, yet I found the academic atmosphere oppressive. Modern philosophy especially depressed me. I worked hard and made good grades, but was continually assailed with feelings of hopelessness.

There were discussions in class as to whether or not there were any ''absolutes,'' and the general consensus seemed to be that there were only ''shades of gray.'' Some actually thought it was valid to wonder if there was any way you could know for sure whether or not you were a figment of your own imagination, if indeed anything was real! Descartes', ''I think, therefore I am,'' was supposed to be profound!

While all this may have seemed ''quite intellectual'' in the philosophy classroom, across the street in the psychology building, we did *at least know* that people with true reality problems were stark raving crazy. But I had doubts about psychology, too. Pavlov was called the ''father of modern psychology,'' yet to anyone taking the time to investigate, he could be considered nothing more than a Russian sadist who tormented and terrorized thousands of dogs in an attempt to discover methods of controlling human beings! Sigmund Freud seemed little more than a sex maniac. How petty and degrading were their concepts of man! I

*The Academy of The Holy Names, Tampa

had to ask myself if we were progressing forward or backward, and feared that I would become an educated fool.

I was encouraged by my instructors to stay in school and get a Masters Degree in psychiatric nursing, but I was tired of school. Psychology and philosophy notwithstanding, my desire to understand people had not been satisfied, and I longed for the nitty-gritty of life.

Before graduation from nursing school, we were required to talk with a counselor about our plans for the future. Mine had changed drastically in the past month, and I was feeling more than anything "at loose ends." When she said, "How would you like to go to Vietnam?" I had remembered Dr. Dooley's road packed with fleeing refugees and wanting even then to help them. I thought of Americans fighting there and of how often our country ended up fighting for the freedom of others. They probably needed nurses.

I realized the counselor was explaining the mechanics of becoming an *Army* nurse. Vietnam was one thing, but it hadn't occurred to me that I would have to join the Army, and for a brief instant found myself wondering if I was "the type." And, of course, the dangers and unknowns were very real; yet at an early age, I had understood that there was true sickness involved in clinging to safety.

The next day, I visited the Army recruiter in town and found it was *quite simple* to join the Army with a guaranteed assignment to Vietnam. I told him, "I'm not really interested in being in the Army, but I will join if you can promise I will go to Vietnam." He had an expression on his face like "Oh boy! We've got a live one!"

Soon I found myself seated in the football stadium at graduation on a balmy Florida afternoon. I thought about the sum total of everything I had just spent so much time and effort trying to learn, and knew it was best to leave a good bit of it behind. It was one of the best and most important decisions I could have made. Where I was going, I didn't need the meaninglessness and despair of modern philosophy, although I would find soon enough that it was certainly not confined to the insane asylum of the classroom, and many had indeed brought it with them.

I found myself falling back on the love of life and the

values I had held even as a child. I thought of my childhood desire to understand the mystery, "the puzzle" about people, and regretted that I had not studied literature instead. Poets seemed to have a feeling for what it meant to be human which psychologists had missed all together—a grasp of something so intangible, but so real; *the main thing—the heart*, and the wonder of life.

For some reason, I had done poorly in gerontology and had actually "sweated out" the last few weeks of the semester, living with the possibility that I might not graduate. But those weeks of suspense only served to make the moment that much sweeter.

Free! The full force of the reality of it hit me ... "I'm free of school now!" Only then did I realize how really stifling it had all been. Suddenly, it felt as though a little underground spring of the joy of life had just broken through somewhere inside. It bubbled and tickled me, and there was a smile on my face from gladness deep within.

After the ceremony, I took off my cap and gown and shoes and went running and leaping across the football field to meet my family. I still remember the dress I was wearing—light blue, gauzy, with a Peter Pan collar. It kind of floated as I ran, and I felt like I was floating, too.

On the way home in the car after dinner, my sister's boyfriend (he had a British accent and wore a cravat) presented me with a beautiful, seafoam-green, lace bra and sang me a song he had made up to the tune of the "Ballad of the Green Berets"—all about the green "bera." (I didn't even know what a Green Beret was.) I was a little embarrassed; nevertheless, I thought it was delightfully silly. Things had been *far too serious, far too long!*

It had been a long day. The song had the effect of a lullaby, and before he could finish all the verses, I put my head on his shoulder and fell asleep. It was a time of innocence and calm before the storm. I felt loved and secure in my new insecurity, and had a good feeling that America was what I thought America had always been.

2
Birth-Control Cookies

So in September, 1966, I found myself at Fort Sam Houston, Texas, at the Medical Field Service School going through what they called the "Army Nurse Corps Officer Basic," more an eight-week orientation than anything. Fort Sam Houston was pretty in the late summer, quite hot, and compared to my preconceived notions of "Basic," everyone seemed quite civil. We were treated with respect, and I was especially thankful we didn't have PT (physical training).

We went to classes about the Army and learned how to wear our second lieutenant uniforms—and they did their best to try to teach us how to march. Although most of us were going to Vietnam, in fact, we wanted to go; we just couldn't get excited about marching. We often sang, "Mickey Mouse" as we traipsed back and forth across the parade ground, praying that the person in back of us would be paying attention when the person in charge said, "Halt." Marching could be dangerous business if someone behind you got too carried away on her Mickey Mouse!

There were doctors going through the school, too. Most seemed rather bitter (an understatement) at having been drafted, and wore their hats sideways. No one seemed to mind. What were they going to do to punish them—send them to Vietnam?! But in spite of Mickey Mouse and the sideways hats, I'm sure the Army wasn't worried. They'd had enough experience with professionals to know that when the chips were really down, most would come through like professionals. All in all, there was a good spirit about our class. We were a little dumb, patriotic, cooperative and naive!

The thing I noticed most about the doctors was that a good number of them dispensed with their wedding rings, yelled, "Yahoo," and started going through the nurses like Sherman through Georgia. It was a time of broken hearts. It got so bad that one of the doctors stood up in class one day and said, "Please, they're just out of school, they don't know anything, *please*..." 1967—times sure have changed. Of course, we didn't think we were naive. We thought we were "registered nurses and second lieutenants." I thought, *That will never happen to me*. I don't know why I thought it wouldn't.

Basic became more serious as we began to study combat casualties. Looking back, I must say they probably prepared us as best they could for what was to come, but some things just can't be "simulated." Many things we would need to know were very faithfully drilled into our heads. It had a way of giving casualties a "framework" into which they could later be "logically" fit; perhaps *too* logically.

They *swore* to us that the goats had been anesthetized before they shot them; I suppose they had. Anyway, after they were shot we got them, or what was left of them. We did emergency tracheotomies, debrided wounds, anything we might have to do to soldiers under similar circumstances. I'll never forget the first time I stabbed a goat in the throat with a pair of scissors. Air *rushed in*, reminding me of a vacuum cleaner which had just been switched on! Somehow I thought it wouldn't be so simple on a person. I'd seen doctors have trouble performing a "trach" with all the right instruments, with three nurses and another doctor to help.

We'd get all dressed up in our fatigues and go to "the field" and have drills on what to do for this kind of wound, and that kind, and a combination of this and that. Which patients to take first and which to leave—triage. We practiced starting I.V.'s on one another and wondered where the goats were when we *really* needed them.

We had three-day field exercises like "let's all go out with a map and compass and get lost." I had never even been camping before. It was dumb, but kind of fun, and funny to see how serious a few were about it. (I really think they did it just to give us a break.)

And there was "How to eat standing up in the rain with a mess kit."

Then the break was over and it got serious again—serious but somewhat unreal, the "Vietnamese village," complete with booby traps. We learned about punji sticks with pou-pou in pits, and trip wires and tunnels—and never *ever* to trust a Gook (Vietnamese)*—and that guerrilla warfare is different; it almost seemed they were trying to convince themselves as they went along.

The men who taught that class were wearing jungle fatigues and had all been to Vietnam (at least to Saigon or Long Binh). I kept searching their faces to see if I could get some kind of a "personal" clue as to what it was *really* like, but they avoided eye contact and seemed to be wearing masks, so I quit searching their faces and went back to concentrating on punji sticks.

We had firing practice with .45s, which are really too heavy for most women to hold straight out in front of them for any length of time, but we were hitting the targets a good number of times. Just as we were finishing, one sergeant yelled at me, "If you ever have to use it, you'd better throw it!" I remember telling him that if I ever had to use it, I intended to prop it up on something! I thought at the time he probably talked like that because he thought it was the thing to do; he seemed almost inordinately upset over how we were doing. But as we left, my roommate said, "You know, I felt he really cared what happens to us," and another nurse said, "I do, too." I think he did.

---

*Even nurses, although with less brutality, were taught they weren't human.

Our final baptism into "things really military" was gas masks. If I remember correctly, we had to take them off in a tear-gas-filled tent and then run out. On my way out, I tripped over one of the tent ropes, as did the next three nurses after me. We all flew through the air and landed sprawling, but it was so good to get out of there that we didn't even care.

At graduation, we marched and kept our rows straight; everything was sparkling and the band played, "This is My Country." Some were leaving straight for Vietnam, but most of us had "interim assignments." A lady general or colonel gave a speech which sounded pretty good and looked at our uniforms and said, "Very fine." She was rather masculine. I thought, *Poor thing, I'm afraid maybe she's been in a little too long*. Were we ready for Vietnam? Who knew? We supposed we were as ready as we would ever be!

Fort Campbell, Kentucky, "Home of the 101st Airborne," was my interim assignment. It was fall of '66 and gray and gloomy when I arrived and began working in the Intensive Care Unit, but I liked it—ICU was special.

I had a room in the BOQ, which my mother thought was "scandalous," but which was no more scandalous than a room in a hotel. To get to it, I had to go through the "Little Club," more precisely, the Little Officers' Club, and hardly ever made it to my room without being sidetracked. The Little Club was undoubtedly a dive, but since I didn't know what a dive was, I just thought it was a cozy place to go for lunch and meet with "the group" after work to drink beer and talk for hours. Although none of us ever got to be close friends in the "lifelong friend" sense, there was a feeling almost like family. There were nurses, guys who were going to Vietnam, and those who had already been.

I had always thought there was an art to drinking—have maybe two, have a good time, but don't get drunk. Yet at Fort Campbell it quickly became an art and a science . . . these guys were experts, and had the "prop-blast diplomas" to prove it. I had thought college students could drink; I hadn't seen anything! Of course, *the important thing was to keep partying* without ending up under the table. I found I could look someone straight in the eye, keep up a steady stream of conversation, and switch beers so he would never know it—my full one for his almost empty. You might say we were all intrepid partiers! We were all kind of silly; I suppose it was youth still trying to have some youth . . . glad to be alive and celebrating. Many times I laughed until I nearly fell out of my chair.

Sometimes the men would all jump off the tables and do PLFs (Parachute Landing Falls), and sometimes the nurses would do them, too—starched white uniforms and all. There was a mystique about the airborne. I think we all thought it was rather wonderful, and there was an excitement about the 101st getting ready to go to Vietnam. If there was anything "wrong" with Vietnam, no one seemed to have told anybody at Fort Campbell. Those who had already been, seldom talked about it; it was something more or less taken for granted. You could look at someone's uniform and "size him up" in about half a second—a good deal of his life would be right there, written on his clothing with his medals and various insignia. It seemed strange for an entire, life-changing year to be reduced to a few doodads on a uniform, and as little as it was talked about, that's what it often seemed to boil down to.

Within a week after I arrived, I'd been propositioned by total strangers so many times it was getting ridiculous. New arrivals, it seemed, were fair game until some sort of an understanding was reached. One day on my way back from the PX, someone waved from across the street and ran over like a long-lost friend; I'd seen him at the Club maybe once or twice. The gist of the conversation was that he "was madly in love and going to die if we didn't go to bed."

I thought I was pretty cute, but *die*? Yet, remarkably still somewhat naive, I was trying to figure out how to tell him to bug off gently. (I didn't think it was nice to hurt someone's feelings!) I had a bag of Oreos I'd bought in the PX, and not really even thinking, I held the bag over and offered him a cookie. He took one and then another and then said, "Bye" and left—apparently having forgotten all about dying. Really!

I told some of the other nurses about it, and we all thought it was such a scream that we decided to carry a few cookies in our pockets at all times and try it out some more. We called them "birth-control cookies," and it turned out to be such a big joke that the bartender at the Little Club stocked them behind the bar. That way we didn't have to carry them, we could write a "prescription" to be filled at the bar by anyone getting a little out of hand!

One day, one of the helicopter pilots and some others said, "How would you like to go auto-rotating?" I didn't know what it was, but they all said it was great fun, so another nurse and I could hardly wait. They said, "Oh good, you're just going to love it, we all do."

Nothing seemed too unusual at first, except that it was getting pretty cold—we were flying high. "Auto-rotating," it turned out, means they cut the engine and let the helicopter fall until the air pressure causes the blades to begin rotating. You *fall* for quite some time without power. Naturally we screamed. But not to be outdone, we finally managed to say, That was great, do it again, *please*." So we did it again and again. Everything back then seemed like a big joke, especially sometimes the Army. We were all going to start a new unit—instead of crossed rifles, its insignia was going to be crossed swizzle sticks—rather astute, I thought.

A few members of the group thought we were getting flabby sitting around in the Club all the time, so we started running—in the pitch black dark, full speed ahead, screaming. We would all join hands; I don't think I got very much actual running in, my feet didn't seem to touch the ground from the time we started until we finished. And it was supposed to be important to scream (I always thought just to be as uncivilized as possible). I couldn't do it; I just *knew* that if I ever screamed I would fall down.

The Intensive Care Unit was also the Recovery Room and Coronary Care Unit. We were always the first to know about accidents and their sometimes intriguing causes, but I think maybe the main reason ICU seemed special to me was because we did a truly excellent job. We had some terrible motorcycle and automobile accident victims—terrific head injuries who were comatose for weeks, yet most of our "hopeless cases" walked out of the hospital a few months later. Every time the 101st jumped there would be injuries, some quite serious. One guy had gotten the static line around his neck. While it was happening, he "knew" it was hanging him! He ended up with a horrible-looking burn, something several degrees worse than a rope burn, and very thankful to be alive. We all rejoiced with him.

I remember our worst head injury . . . his chest had been crushed, too. By the time we got him off the stretcher into bed, several of us were covered from head to toe with blood spraying out of his tracheostomy. It was the first time this had ever happened to me. I felt if I moved it would make it worse—smear the blood somewhere else, maybe . . . so, I was helplessly watching some of it run in my shoe when this wardmaster, who had been in Korea and at times had to run for his life, looked straight at me and said, "You'd better get used to it." That patient died; they never even operated—nothing to work with.

There always seemed to be this sense of "preparing" for Vietnam; I knew I would be at Fort Campbell only a matter of months. The new Special Forces corpsmen all worked in ICU for experience with serious injuries before going to Vietnam. I suppose we were all somewhat like sponges trying to soak up every bit of knowledge and experience we could. There was a feeling of honorable people preparing for an honorable thing.

Emotionally, I suppose, we were all trying rather desperately to desensitize ourselves before we got there, as if that might make it easier to cope.

The "experts" told us, "Things will go better for you if you don't get in the habit of complaining. When you get to Vietnam, Lynn, remember to *hang loose*, hang loose about everything . . . and don't get hung up on food. Make yourself believe that it isn't important, and don't complain unless you've had lima beans and ham for a month."

They were back from Vietnam, professional-soldier types— some of the best partiers, divorced, the nicest guys. My first Christmas away from home was spent at Fort Campbell; it was snowing and we were sitting in the Little Club. My time was really getting short, and I was finally understanding that they were more serious with all their advice and running than I had thought.

That Christmas wasn't lonely, but there was a feeling of loneliness because of those who stayed. It was my first hint of another side of what it means to be a soldier. There was a solitariness about them.

"What's in the box?" I had just stopped by the mailroom and had a huge box from home.

"I don't know. I'll bet it's something wonderful, though."

"Here, *I'll* help you open it," he said, whipping out a big fancy survival knife. And before either of us knew what had happened, a massive amount of popcorn was all over the floor and we still didn't know what was in the box. (My mother had used popcorn, lots of it, to pack the mysterious gift.) Just then, my next-door neighbor came through with a huge white dog, who began immediately gobbling down the popcorn. I could almost hear the dog saying, "You rang? At your service!" He was certainly a big help with the mess.

The gift turned out to be a Christmas tree, decorated with photographs of friends, many of whom had gathered at our home on Christmas Eve for as long as I could remember. Each photograph was in a hand-decorated frame. We all breathed out a "Wow," very reverently.

I wrote home and thanked my parents for being who they were, for the things they had taught me . . . things that really mattered in life. Later, several stopped by to take another look at the Christmas tree. It had the most remarkable impact on us.

Sometimes it seems like only yesterday when the door to the Little Club would fly open and our coziness would be momentarily interrupted by a blast of cold air and snow, and in would come someone with much of his life written on his clothing.

I had scarcely two months left at Fort Campbell. Some of those good memories were yet to be made, as I found myself up to my eyebrows in the "nitty-gritty of life."

3

If This Was the "Nitty Gritty" of Life...?

Friend after friend departs;
Who hath not lost a friend?

James Montgomery
Friends

There is a vulnerability about being a brand-new second lieutenant. You know that, from a military point of view, you know practically nothing, so you go from one day to the next in a kind of precarious confidence, trusting that if you just wear your uniform and keep your mouth shut you'll get by. I still had trouble saluting. It seemed I never did it quite the same way twice. I always expected someone to turn around and stare at me as if to say, "What was that she just did?" It was a bad time to be faced with a "military" crisis.

One fateful day, I went innocently off to lunch after an uneventful morning, never suspecting that within the next 45 minutes the bottom would fall out of my world. When I returned, the other nurse on the ward was preparing to go to lunch, and as he passed me on the way out the door, he handed me the keys to the medicine cabinet and drawled in a heavy Southern accent, "I gave the medications." The problem was I thought he said, "*Give* the medications." Technically, I was supposed to give them when I returned from lunch. He had actually given them early, an acceptable practice, which only added to my confusion, and from the way we kept records, it wasn't always clear if they had been given or not.

One of the patients was a general who had had a heart attack. He was a nice person and was doing fairly well. He liked to talk and joke with us. Every time I gave him medicine, he questioned me about it—pill by pill—and I knew I had better have a satisfactory answer. Only the day before he had said, "What would you do if I refused to take it?" Without even thinking I heard myself saying, "Well, it's pretty simple—you can either swallow these pills or prepare to get jabbed in the rear end . . . *Sir*." He thought it was funny, and we laughed. After that he stopped questioning me about his medicine, and when I handed him the second dose of the same medicine he had taken only minutes before, *he*, of all people, didn't question a thing. He simply swallowed it down!

The next patient, a PFC, was to receive a penicillin shot. Well no one in his right mind is going to take two penicillin shots in a row without an argument. "Oh, no!" he protested, "I'm not taking another one. That male nurse just gave me a shot fifteen minutes ago." I stared at him—numb with shock as I suddenly realized what had happened. I had just given the general an overdose of drugs!

Nurses don't panic . . . much! I calmly walked to the desk and phoned the mess hall. My second attempt at dialing was a little more accurate and I got the Emergency Room. The doctor on duty there was nonchalant about the problem saying, "I really don't know what could happen to him, but I'll be up after a while to check him."

The reaction of the male nurse when he returned from lunch seemed somehow more in keeping with the situation. He said, "Good grief! Do you realize what you've done? You've made a medication error involving a *general!* You'll never hear the end of this one!" He was a first lieutenant and seemed to know all about these things. His attitude seemed to be, "It won't be easy, but you *may* live through it." And I thought he appeared slightly amused as he added, "We better call the supervisor."

The supervisor arrived, then with a worried frown called the chief nurse, who bustled in shortly in somewhat of a "tizzy" with forms in triplicate to be filled out. It appeared they were more concerned with the possibility of "fallout" from the error than with the state of the general's health. I felt sick at heart. That nice man had taken his medicine because he trusted me, and now he might die and all these people could think about were forms in triplicate. It all seemed terribly callous.

It was four in the afternoon when I finally left the ward, having spent the entire afternoon explaining what had happened and filling out seemingly endless forms. I wanted to lie down somewhere and die, but couldn't stand the thought of being alone. I ended up in the Little Club with "the group," and a beer in front of me, trying to lose myself in the conversation.

I was trying to choke back tears and choke down the beer all at the same time, and it wasn't working. One of the guys, Mac, picked up his chair and brought it down to the end of the table where I was sitting. He sat with his arms propped on the back of the chair and said, "I've never seen you when you weren't happy. What's wrong?"

Mac was one of the zaniest people I had ever known, lots of fun to party with, but now he was dead serious. Having dealt with the problem all afternoon, I really preferred just to forget about it, but if Mac cared enough to ask, I could tell the story one more time. "Oh, Mac, you'll never guess what I did; just leave it to me!"

The words were tumbling out of my mouth, end over end, *fast forward speed*, "I gave General Smith* an overdose of heart medication. He could conceivably die, and nobody seemed to really care! They wanted *paperwork*! I've been filling out paperwork all afternoon."

I finally finished, and after a moment of silence, he put his hand on my shoulder and looked at me with his dark brown eyes. "Lynn," he said, "I'm going to tell you something, and I don't want you ever to forget it."

He was so solemn and stern he almost frightened me. I tearfully stammered, "Y-yes?"

---

*Not his real name.

"Lynn," he repeated, "Generals don't crap Hershey bars."

I stared at him with my mouth open. "Wh-What?" Then the pricelessness of the statement struck me and I started laughing. What ridiculous profundity! What an idiotic, wonderful thing to say—and what an effect it had on me! It was as good as a helpful slap in the face! I thought it was at least as profound as "I think, therefore I am!"

Suddenly the joy of life was back, bubbling inside again. We laughed until our sides hurt, and when I could finally get my breath I said, "Mac, you're crazy, but I'll always love you for that and I'll never forget it." I never did.

Before the year was out, while in Vietnam, I heard Mac was dead.

4
Only His Mind Away

Light breaks where no sun shines;
Where no sea runs, the waters of
  the heart
Push in their tides.

Dylan Thomas

"Believe me, Sarge," puffed the doctor as he struggled to hold the man on the bed, "we're all going to feel a lot better in just a minute." There were two Special Forces corpsmen on the ward just "passing through" again on their way to Vietnam. One of the other corpsmen, struggling with the man's leg said, "This is exactly like in the movies when the calvary arrives just in the nick of time. We really needed you guys for this hand-to-hand combat. Great reinforcements!"

SGT Kelly* heard it and it made him fight harder. I stepped on the corpsman's foot and whispered, "Would you stop talking about fighting—now he thinks we've called in the cavalry and the Special Forces."

The sergeant we were struggling with had seen me whispering to the corpsman and was now convinced there was a conspiracy! And to top it all off, the doctor added, "I gave him enough of that stuff to kill a horse. Something ought to happen soon."

We didn't even know the sergeant was an alcoholic until

*Not his real name.

he began having DTs* in the hospital. Kelly was regular Army and almost up for retirement. He had had a lot to drink every day of his life for many years until he found himself in the hospital after a heart attack. All of us liked him—he had only been on the ward a day or two, but was the kind of person you felt you had known for years.

The morning SGT Kelly went into the DTs, I arrived on the ward to find the entire staff gathered around his bed. One of the doctors—a huge man, was sitting on top of him. My first thought was of cardiac arrest and that the doctor must be doing cardiac massage, sitting astride him the way he was. But as I got closer to the bed, I realized SGT Kelly was fully conscious and the doctor was talking to him for all he was worth, and obviously not having an easy time of it. Actually, the doctor looked somewhat like a man in a rowboat trying to make it through the heavy surf! There was at least one corpsman on each arm and leg. Everyone was perspiring. SGT Kelly had gone into the DTs, thought he had been captured by the enemy, and was putting up the fight of his life. I thought, *They're going to kill him for sure. How can someone with a heart attack possibly survive all this?*

The sedative finally calmed him down and kind of incapacitated him physically, but he never did go to sleep. He wouldn't. Kelly was "resisting the enemy" the best he possibly could. They got him tied to the bed and all morning, two corpsmen stayed with him, talking about all kinds of things, trying to get his mind off his alcoholic withdrawal delirium.

Around noon, when he seemed better, the corpsmen decided to untie one hand, thinking it would help him to feel a little less "captured." It was time for his medication and as he seemed to recognize me, I decided to act as though nothing had happened. Someone said, "You look so sweet and all-American—he'll take it from you." I should have paid closer attention to the gleam in his eye. With one quick motion, the freed hand lashed out and an ounce of sticky red liquid splashed me full in my face and dripped down the front of my uniform. He seemed delighted with

*Delirium Tremors.

himself for having inflicted some damage on the "enemy," and except for my discomfort, I couldn't help being a little proud of him, too. He certainly was putting up a valiant battle. Although a delusion, his position as a POW was very real to SGT Kelly, and I had to admire him for his persistent refusal to be defeated.

We had been taught in nursing that in the case of DTs, it was sometimes advisable to "go along with" someone's delusion. For instance, if they thought there was a snake on the wall, you could hit it. (That is, you could hit it if you could locate it!) Often they would see you had "killed" the snake and feel a lot better. DTs have to run their course, so there is really very little which can be done to help the person get back in touch with reality during this time.

It was becoming apparent that SGT Kelly was suffering more mental anguish in his conviction that he was a POW than the average drunk who sees snakes and rats on the wall. Since in times past I had successfully "killed" quite a few imaginary snakes and rats, I decided to go along with his delusion, thinking perhaps there was a way to alleviate his anxiety. Perhaps if SGT Kelly were to be convinced that he was in a hospital and would receive better treatment than in a prison camp, it would help. I pretended to be the enemy and said, "This is a hospital. We don't mistreat prisoners here, we have our ethics, believe it or not. We may not like you very much, but you will receive adequate treatment," and hated myself. (In less than six months, with quite a bit more pain, I would remember those words.) SGT Kelly looked around and said, "It is a hospital, isn't it? I must have been wounded pretty bad; I don't remember a thing about it." It may have helped for a while, but within an hour or so, he was back to resisting the enemy for all he was worth.

He was disturbing the other patients, so we moved him into a private room across the hall from the nurses' office. As we pushed the bed through the door he said, "Oh, no! Solitary!" From then on, we tried to achieve a balance between leaving him alone in "solitary confinement" and "tormenting" him with care and medication. To him, one was as bad as the other.

Now SGT Kelly began talking to an imaginary buddy who had joined him in the "prison camp." I heard him tell his buddy, "Sooner or later everybody breaks under torture. If you've done your best, don't feel bad when it happens." There was a tenderness in his voice that would break your heart. Later Kelly said, "When it gets to the point where I think I can't stand it any more, I'm going to try to stand it just one more second, and one more after that, and then one more." My heart ached for the pain he was experiencing . . . just as real as any physical pain. I don't think I have ever suffered quite the same with any other patient. There was absolutely nothing we could do to give him any relief. It was agonizing and continuous.

The world is full of people with DTs—it was nothing new to me. They all become Houdinis: masterminds of the impossible. They will fight you, escape their restraints and fall out of bed. They are convinced you are "out to get them." But there was something different about SGT Kelly. He went the extra mile. And while DT delusions may be common, few drunks believe they have fallen into the hands of those who would torment them endlessly.

SGT Kelly's conversations with his buddy were too much for me. Enough is enough. "This has gone far enough," I finally told him angrily. "I heard that. You haven't been tortured and you know it!"

"I know," he said sadly, "this is a hospital. You told me that before. But just because you call it science, it doesn't change the fact that it *is* torture." And to him it was. His eyes reflected a calm resignation to his "fate," yet an attitude of "I have not yet begun to fight" undergirded his words.

An hour or so later, I looked up from some paperwork in the nurse's office to see a little river of blood flowing out of his room and down the hall. I dashed into his room and found he had managed to free one hand from the restraints and disconnect his I.V. tubing. The needle was still in his vein and the tubing attached to it was hanging off the bed. It was literally draining the blood from his body!

We didn't like putting him in restraints . . . it simply reinforced his delusion of being a prisoner, but he would have had his delusion anyway and he needed to be controlled for his own protection. The cuffs were padded, but because he never stopped trying to free himself, his wrists and ankles were taking a terrible beating.

As the sergeant began to recover, he was very apologetic for having given us such a hard time. It seemed to take him a while to get up the nerve to ask what he had done and if it was "too bad." When I told him he thought he was a POW he said, "I always wondered how I would do." I told him I thought he deserved a medal!

In the years following, I was often reminded of him. In a way, I had entered his delusion. It was so real to him that it became real to me, until I wanted to scream at him and tell him to "snap out of it!" There was only a fine line between captivity and freedom for this man, and the line was in his mind.

Kelly seemed almost like a herald of things to come in my memories of Vietnam. In a few short years there would be many POWs as in our other wars, miles away from freedom and *even today*, simply political and economic expendables left over from a war of political and economic expediency.

Yet something about him often reminds me, too, that down through the centuries it has not infrequently been the most ragged, wretched and tormented—those who have been almost totally "dehumanized"—who have exhibited excellence of character, loyalty, courage, and trueness of heart which both Pavlov and Kissinger* couldn't seem to figure out in their lifetimes.

"And the world will be better for this, that one man scorned and covered with scars, still strove with his last ounce of courage..." (Peter O'Toole as Cervantes, "To Dream the Impossible Dream" a song from *Man of La Mancha*; the play and movie from United Artists, 1972; music by Mitch Leigh, lyrics by Joe Darion)

---

*A reference to his having said to Alexander Haig that soldiers were "dumb, stupid animals."

"If the government of North Vietnam has difficulty explaining to you what happened to your brothers, your American POWs who have not yet returned, I can explain this quite clearly on the basis of my own experience in the Gulag Archipelago. There is a law in the Archipelago that those who have been treated the most harshly and who have withstood the most bravely, who are the most honest, the most courageous, the most unbending, never again come out into the world. THEY ARE NEVER AGAIN SHOWN TO THE WORLD BECAUSE THEY WILL TELL TALES THAT THE HUMAN MIND CAN BARELY ACCEPT. Some of your returned POWs have told you that they were tortured. This means that those who have remained were tortured even more, but did not yield an inch. These are your best people. These are your foremost heroes who, in a solitary combat have stood the test. And today, unfortunately, they cannot take courage from our applause. They can't hear it from their solitary cells where they may either die or remain for thirty years."

Aleksandr I. Solzhenitsyn
June 30, 1975

5
Light Banana Yellow

In Kentucky when it gets cold, the air can become unbelievably dry. If you add radiator-type heat to that, which is what we had in the BOQ (and if you are from a humid state like Florida), it can become unbearable. I may not *really* have been suffering, but I thought I was. My sinuses burned and my entire body felt "creepy." Bottles of lotion weren't helping. I suppose I had never really had dry skin in my entire life. A pan of water on the radiator did just enough good to make me long for the humid air of home.

One night I was sitting in the bathtub, momentarily lost in another world, watching the steam rise and fill the room. I blew at it, and it made little swirls. It reminded me of when I was a child and my sister and I would run the shower full blast, fill the bathroom with steam, then open the door and watch it literally pour into our bedroom. We would pretend it was "Brigadoon," from the movie. You could fan it and do ballet-like dances through it.

I had noticed the BOQ never ran out of hot water. No matter what time of day or night you needed it, there always seemed to be plenty. I thought, *why couldn't I leave the shower running just a little one night?* The idea represented such blessed relief that I didn't stop to consider another thing. And it *was* blessed relief—I slept like a log.

It must have been the sound of the combat boot kicking the door open which woke me up. I was sleeping with my face toward the door, and my eyes flew open just in time to see a boot and a leg right in front of my face. It was such a shock that I was frozen to the spot. I wanted more than anything in the world to close my eyes and pretend I was still asleep, but curiosity as to what might happen next prevented it. The door hit the wall with a loud "kabang!" It was Jake*, my next door neighbor, in complete uniform, including helmet, looking neither to the left nor to the right, heading straight for the bathroom.

He turned the shower off and left without so much as a hello, closing the door behind him. A drop of water fell from the ceiling and hit me in the face.

For a minute I had that horrible sinking feeling you get when it's time to say, "Oh no, I've really done it this time." I was aware that there was something comical about it, but I couldn't figure out what it was. Actually, the whole thing was comical, but right then I wasn't quite able to appreciate it. And then I knew what it was. It was the helmet! He was dressed that way because he was on his way to work, but it made me imagine that he had donned uniform and helmet to wage war against my shower.

There were at least a dozen places on the ceiling where moisture had collected and drops were about to fall. No wonder I had slept so well, it was better than a rain forest! And the paint was beginning to peel here and there. There was no hot water that morning: it was freezing cold.

That night, I ended up in the Little Club and ran into my nextdoor neighbor. Jake smiled and went on as though nothing had happened. I was thankful he wasn't holding a grudge, we were pretty good friends, but I was too proud to apologize. According to me, he had gotten all the satisfaction he deserved when he kicked my door open. It must have seemed that way to him, too; he never mentioned it the

---

*Not his real name.

entire time I was at Fort Campbell. I never will forget that helmet!

During the course of the evening, I told Barry, a 1st Lieutenant, what had happened and how bad I felt about the paint peeling. He said, "Don't worry about it, it was probably going to peel anyway." But I said I couldn't help it, I felt responsible.

Then he said, "You know what? We just got a whole shipment of paint in. I could send some of my men over to paint your room for you. I don't think they would mind at all."

I said, "Oh, how nice. What color is it?"

Barry said, "Well, it's soft yellow." Then he got kind of a faraway look in his eyes, took a sip of beer and said, "Light banana yellow," as though summing up something important. He was obviously in another world. "Do you know what that reminds me of?"

"No, what?" (I was wondering if the paint was light banana yellow before or after the banana was peeled.)

"When I was in Vietnam, I went to get my first sergeant out of a whorehouse, but he wouldn't leave. So I sat down outside to wait for him. There was a statue of Buddha there and someone had left a bunch of bananas in front of it. I got hungry, so I ate the bananas. Just when my sergeant was coming out of the whorehouse, the police came along and took me away for eating Buddha's bananas. Can you imagine that?"

"No!" (I was thinking, *How exotic! Vietnam! Whorehouses! Where else in the world could you hear such an interesting story?*) It didn't seem bad at all, it seemed kind of "romantic" to me then.

He said, "It makes you wonder about things, doesn't it? I wonder if there is any real justice in life?" That night, we decided surely there must be, but apparently not in every circumstance, and it was probably best not to expect it. That way you wouldn't get bitter or disillusioned. We talked about respecting the culture of people in other countries. (I would recall *that* conversation many times in the year to come.)

We talked about religion and wondered why, with all the

different religions of the world claiming to have the truth, so many people simply believe the way their parents or even their ancestors did and never seemed to question anything. We wondered why so much about religion seemed so superficial. Were there any clear-cut answers about God— did He care about us? There were many of life's profound questions left unanswered that night in the club—among the empties, and my room was left unpainted. I received orders for Vietnam before they could begin.

The next day, Lynne, one of the other nurses, came to my room after work looking very serious indeed. She had just received orders for Vietnam, and my name was on them, too, mine and Marie's. I couldn't quite figure out why she was so upset. We all knew we were going . . . why ask to go and then be upset?

My last conversation on my last night in the Little Club—I remember it well: "Lynn, you've got to promise us something."

"Tell me what it is first."

"You've got to promise you won't fall in love or get married while you're in Vietnam. *It's just not normal over there* and you won't understand until it's too late."

"How can I promise you that? You're asking the impossible!"

I understood more than they thought, but much less than I knew.

6
Life Goes On

"Eating must go on."

Mrs. Floyd Wiggins
(my mother's maid)

I opened my eyes to bright sunlight and a screen door. There were Vietnamese women walking on a red clay road just outside the door. They were wearing black "pajama" bottoms and white tops; some wore *ao dais*, the long, paneled, split skirts worn over pants, and had conical hats just like in pictures I had seen. They were talking and laughing. I just lay there watching them for a while. They walked differently than Americans. I thought perhaps they took longer strides, but it also seemed to have something to do with the way they moved their hips.

Some of the other nurses were still sleeping, but most were already up wearing housecoats and rubber flip-flops, with towels on their heads—fresh from the shower. Some rummaged through their luggage in a manner typical of those trying to live out of a suitcase. It was rather a pleasant scene, filled with the camaraderie of strangers in a strange place, trying to get along. There was a lot of talking, but in hushed tones so as not to awaken those who were still sleeping. There was giggling. It seemed more like a summer camp than Vietnam.

Perhaps one of my most accurate first impressions was of

the Vietnamese civilians. They hardly seemed aware that a war was going on around them, nonchalantly going about their business. Of course, they were enjoying relative security at Long Binh, and most had lived with war for as long as they could remember. A little later it wouldn't seem so strange. Nonchalance and a kind of numbness to it all came rather quickly and, after all, if you don't get killed, life goes on.

The next day about 40 of us were flown from Bein Hoa to Tuy Hoa, a small town on the coast, in a C-130 cargo plane. The hospital at Tuy Hoa was new; in fact, it wasn't quite finished, and we were to be its first nurses. The trip was uncomfortable, very hot and stuffy. We all sat on the floor.

The last leg of our journey from the landing strip at Tuy Hoa to the hospital was made in a Chinook—a giant helicopter, which was an improvement over the C-130. By the time we disembarked, it seemed things weren't going to be half-bad after all—there was something of a celebration in progress to greet us!

I mostly remember the sea of friendly faces greeting us. And I remember how very blue the South China Sea was, the smell of salt air, bright sunlight, sand, and the heat—*always* the heat. There was another smell, too, from the burning of human waste. The best way to describe it may be to say no one who ever smelled it is likely *ever* to forget it!

That night we all went to a welcoming party. I managed to have a very good time. I was dancing with Colonel Munnely from the Artillery battalion and he said, "That's a waltz. Do you like to waltz?"

I liked to waltz better than most anything and so did he; so we did—most of the night. It was like experiencing a little island of civilization in the midst of *something else*. It's still a special memory, and I would later realize how much just a little touch of civilization, or at least civility, could mean.

On the way home that night, we passed a field where only hours earlier some Koreans had killed quite a few VC. They had mutilated the bodies—chopped off their testicles and stuffed them in their mouths. Someone from 4th Division said, "Don't let things like this get to you. The Koreans just know that the VC understand terror. This is one of their favorite tricks, too.''

Then somebody else started talking about how there had actually been wars in times past in which soldiers on both sides felt something like respect for one another since they were all ''in the same boat.'' Then some of them laughed a little uneasily and a little sadly. There was no doubt about the VC ''understanding terror,'' yet later I did feel something close to respect for them. The night air was cool, and I shook all the way back to the hospital. Welcome to the real Vietnam! Later, such things would seem commonplace.

The hospital compound was enclosed with concertina wire and there were two small villages, Phu Heip I and Phu Heip II, very close on either side. Rumor had it that there were VC in the villages, but *nobody bothered them because they never seemed to cause any trouble*. It seemed somewhat weird to us, and the chief nurse, LTC Swarther*, told us (with some pride, we thought) that she was on the Viet Cong's list for kidnaping.

The hospital itself was composed of two rows of freestanding buildings perpendicular to the beach. One of the rows was of wooden ''tropical'' buildings, each being a ward. Most were general surgical wards, one Pediatrics, one Orthopedics, and there was a prison ward for VC. Across the way was a row of quonset huts which contained the Emergency Room and Admitting, the Operating Room, X-Ray and Lab, Surgical Intensive Care, and Medical Intensive Care.

The nurses' quarters were in tropical buildings close to the beach. We called them ''hooches,'' and we each had our own room. They were very small, with just enough room for an Army cot and locker, constructed of natural, unpainted wood, but our own.

The officers' club was a quonset hut even closer to the beach, and the only place where there was a breeze. After work, I used to like to sit on the front step of the club hooch and look at the South China Sea until the sun went down.

*Not her real name.

Sometimes there would be junks with lights bobbing in the distance. There would be children from the villages around, which made it nice. Those who weren't exhausted from the day's activities (and many who were) usually ended up in the club at night.

I was assigned to the Medical Intensive Care Unit. The first weak or so was spent trying to get the hospital ready for opening day. All the quonsets had to be painted inside (a rather pretty, mint green) and there seemed to be no end to the last-minute preparations, so we all pitched in with the painting and other chores. (The enlisted men who had arrived several months earlier had been building the hospital and were at the point of exhaustion.) We put up so many Army cots that every finger on every hand in the hospital must have been pinched at least once, and blew up so many air mattresses it's a wonder anyone's lips were ever normal again. But it was fun, and everyone worked hard to make it the best hospital possible. Finally, some of us began to realize that our arrival had been welcomed so wholeheartedly for a different reason than we had thought. We were extra bodies that could do some work, and lighten the heavy load just a little.

7

"To Conserve the Fighting Strength"

"*AAH!* . . . *AAH* . . . *YEEAH* . . . *NO!* . . . *NO!*"

"It's okay, it's only a dream, everything's okay." I was kicking the cot, jumping back and trying not to fall down while simultaneously doing my best to communicate that everything was indeed okay.

3:00 a.m., Medical Intensive Care, another screaming nightmare.

"Oh . . . I'm sorry, Ma'am . . . I didn't hurt you did I?"

"*No*. You didn't hurt me, I know to get out of the way. Are you okay now?"

"Sure . . . Have you got a light?"

I fished in my pocket for my cigarette lighter, lit his cigarette, and walked back to the nurse's desk past rows of sweet, sleeping faces. These young soldiers tried to be so "macho," so totally intrepid—they would have "died" had they known I thought their faces looked *sweet*! They were so young, their faces still had the innocence of youth, and the nightmares seemed like growing pains from all the things that were taking youth away so fast. Yet even those with the worst nightmares and the most badly wounded seemed truly undaunted by anything.

"AH! . . . AAH . . . NO!"

Sweet sleeping faces one minute, and screaming nightmares the next! This time he woke himself up and appeared out of the darkness at the nurse's desk at the far end of the quonset, looking bedraggled and asking for another light and some coffee.

"What is it?"

"At first I thought it was just this one guy stepping on a mine. But it was an ambush—mass confusion—leaves and branches were falling on us. I never even saw *one* of them, not even *one*—I never do. I've only been in-country about a month."

"Me, too, just about a month."

"His legs were messed up real bad . . . I looked right at him. *He tried to get up!* Like an animal that doesn't have sense enough to know that when his legs are hurt, it can't stand up. He was out of his head. He tried to grab his legs—to try to make him feel better, I guess. But they were real gooey, there was really nothing for him to grab onto. I didn't know guys screamed so much when they got hit—it shocked me real bad at first. His face is stuck in my eyes . . . just like an animal, trying to get up . . .

"This one guy was my friend. It seemed like it lasted forever, but I think it was over pretty fast. We were on our faces in the dirt right there together. I thought everything was okay, but when I got up my hand slipped out from under me . . . it was in the brains of my friend."

"Murder!" I exclaimed.

"We must have hit a couple of them; we found some blood trails. I hate Gooks—nasty little things. Those ones who wear Bermuda shorts with their hair sticking out all over don't even look human . . . dead or alive."

"You can't go by looks—especially over here; it's not what's on the outside that makes us human, anyway," I tried to rationalize the situation.

"I guess not. We've been humping the boonies since I got here, stumbling around in that fucking, excuse me, jungle. That's all we do—hump the boonies, try not to step on anything . . .

"The other day, this one guy almost got killed by red

ants. Every leaf out there could have been covered with them as far as I know. They only get on one side; you don't even know about them until it's too late. We were all just crashing through the fucking, excuse me, jungle, and he starts screaming and dancing around. They had to med-evac him . . .

"When you're out there in it, it seems like you'll never get out . . . like your face will be sweaty and red-hot forever, and you'll never get a drink of good water again in your life . . . or even a breath of air . . . a lot of them didn't . . .

"That's how I got dysentery. I knew better than to drink out of that puddle—we all did—it was filthy, but it didn't make any difference—it was water, and that's all that mattered. After that, we were just poopin' and crashing through the jungle! If 'Charlie' was out there, he probably smelled us and went the other way. I threw my underwear away. I needed to throw everything away. Well, good night."

"Good night." By then, two more patients had appeared out of the darkness and were sitting with us at the nurse's desk. Neither one of them looked a day over seventeen. Their eyes were typically bloodshot from malaria.

The day before, they had been shaking with chills and fever so bad that the cots nearly fell over and they thought they were dying; now they were in a hurry to get back to their units. It was truly remarkable how many were in the same hurry. As much as they hated it, as much as they suffered through every minute of every day . . . early 1967 was still a time of high morale. But mostly they felt loyalty to their friends, and the more understrengthed in man-power their units were, the less chance everyone had of making it out alive.

I had never really like the motto, "To Conserve the Fighting Strength" which we saw on banners and signs in hospitals in Vietnam. I understood it, but it seemed too "utilitarian" or something . . . somehow it seemed to fall short of humanity, and it always gave me a mental image of someone recycling dented tanks through a garage. I often wondered how it would make someone feel who had been wounded too seriously to have their "fighting strength conserved" to see that motto over the door of the hospital as they were carried in. I had even thought at times that something like "Competent, Compassionate and Clean" might be more reassuring, and wished they had been able to come up with something a little more "caring." It seemed to go without saying that we were conserving the fighting strength.

Although from a "military" point of view the motto was fine, it later symbolized for me a truth I believe I was able to glean from my three years in the Army. It seemed that as soon as someone began to take their Army career "seriously," before long you could see something lacking in their care of patients. They would either make themselves look a little foolish playing "the officer" and lose some essence of nurturing; or, in extreme cases, some would sacrifice the quality of care or even patient safety for the sake of their "career." But for the most part, the medical services had a reputation for being rather "non-military," which was essential to perform our service to the fullest.

I left the nurse's desk, hung a bottle of I.V. fluid, and returned to a conversation I had already heard too many times before: "Man, that's nothing, I was in-country two days before they gave me any ammunition—I had a rifle and no ammunition!"

"That's not as bad as knowing they're out there, coming for you, and you can't shoot until they attack. We could see them crawling around out there and he kept telling us it was 'against the rules.' Now that's stupid! We fired anyway, told him they fired first—he didn't even know the difference. Does that seem right to you?"

"No, it *is* stupid," I agreed with them.

It was surprising how many of the soldiers thought all officers naturally knew a lot about war, or whether something was right or wrong. Actually, most were getting their education along with the men.

Something which bothered almost everybody was the civilians. It was hard to say which was more distressing— the civilians who weren't civilians, or the ones who really were! We had all heard about smiling little boys with hand grenades, but what about whole villages?

Suddenly the conversation was over, interrupted by an all-too-familiar knocking sound. Someone was having a chill and the cot was about to fall over.

At night I was often alone, without a corpsman, so the patients pitched in to help . . . they knew the routine well. Fevers spiked to 104 degrees or higher "without even trying," called for *aggressive action*.

While I was getting the thermometer and aspirin, they were stripping off his clothes, wetting him down with ice water from head to toe.

"Oh, no! Please. I'm freezing to death!"

"Now, be brave." SPLAT.

There is something truly pitiful about someone having a shaking chill and begging you not to put ice-cold water on them! But we put it all over them from head to toe—towels soaked in it with fans blowing on them. And usually three aspirins instead of two. Sometimes they would be so hot I almost expected the water to sizzle. But no one's fever ever get out of control on our ward!

I drew some blood and sent it to the lab so they could identify the strain of malaria. The organisms didn't always show up in the blood, but after a while I thought I had an "intuition" about the exact best time to "catch them." I probably didn't. And we continued putting sloppy wet towels on the shaking, red-faced body. Finally his fever went down, I started a letter to my mother, and the patients went back to bed.

"Good night, Ma'am. You watch that Gook over there real close, he's more than likely VC. You let out one peep and we'll kill him for you, don't worry."

"Good night."

> *Dear Mom,*
> *I'm on night duty again . . . The other afternoon I thought the engineers behind us were blasting with dynamite. All my patients laughed at me because it was mortars. It was so embarrassing . . .*

Memories come back now like scenes from old movies . . . of SGT Wilson, the wardmaster, my favorite . . . cutting my hair for me. He was black, and a barber, and maybe a little bit of a father figure . . . down-to-earth, pleasant, and he understood things.

Of MAJ Gorman, the head nurse, tall, thin and somewhat tense . . . returning from the MACV briefing on the Tuy Hoa area, saying she was scared. Of LT Fox, another nurse, we called her, "Foxy." And of a skinny male nurse who told dirty jokes that weren't even funny. It didn't matter to him that you didn't want to hear them.

Of Dr. Brown, the ward doctor . . . a nice person and a good doctor . . . of us playing Chinese checkers behind the nurse's desk. He would come on the ward in the morning and say, "Get your book, let's save lives," and he would give orders to send patients home—as many as he could. Often they didn't want to go.

Of a patient with jungle rot, sitting on the side of his cot, looking at what was left of his feet . . . shaking his head and saying, "I didn't know they were this bad, I haven't had my boots off in two months."

Of Qua, the fourteen-year-old Montagnard from Ban Me Thuot . . . carried in on a litter in his tiger-striped fatigues and bright red undershorts, telling us how many VC he had killed . . . and recuperating with a coke in one hand, a *Playboy* in the other, and a big, honest smile on his face.

I began to crave honesty in relationships and personal honesty as never before. It seemed especially important in Vietnam, where the patients were popping in and out of the "land of body bags and booby traps."

There seemed to be an "unwritten law" which most everyone understood without saying: "You don't mess with anyone else's morale." Cheerful, pleasant and considerate were the things to be. If you had a problem, you kept it to yourself. Iron Bottom didn't understand. Poor Iron Bottom—she was one of the supervisors, and she made rounds seemingly with the weight of the world on her shoulders and not taking it well *at all*. And she just didn't seem to have much respect for the feelings of others, especially the wardmasters—NCO's who consistently did good work. I think we all took it rather philosophically, though; after all, how could you possibly have a traditional Army hospital without at least one "Iron Bottom?" She kept us in line.

One day kind of ran into another until there was a blur of chills and fever, of amoebic dysentery, scrub typhus, plague. Dr. Brown with a syringe and needle trying to aspirate a buboe, or sweating over a cut-down.

At night there was a steady drone of voices in the dark ward, with the nurse's desk lit only with a flashlight. ". . . I killed a woman the other day, if I'd stopped to think about it I'd be dead now . . . Everything was gone, I mean his balls, and everything . . . The gooks were so hopped up on dope that they were still coming on stumps! What a sight, gooks charging on stumps . . . It's hard for me to believe, see, my mind just can't grasp it, I'm alive because a couple of my buddies are dead. They died for me. I didn't even know one of them. They died for me . . . There were guys fighting with tourniquets on their arms and legs, with half their faces blown off . . . Do you believe in God? . . . I think so, do you? . . . I don't know . . . Do you think there are any absolutes? . . . We were lining these Viet Cong bodies up, and he came up and started congratulating us on the count. It was all I could do to keep from asking which one he was going to have stuffed and mounted . . . I went to college to get some answers, and they taught me there weren't any. I left and went into the construction business . . . We gave all the kids in this one village shots and worm medicine and the pregnant women, vitamins. The next day the V.C. cut off the kids arms to teach them not to take anything from Americans. And they cut some of the babies out of the mothers and hung them in trees . . . It was a different kind of ambush, some of the children were booby-trapped with grenades . . . Believe me, they have a bunch of stuff in Cambodia . . ."

The press rarely mentioned these everyday Viet Cong atrocities, while our soldiers were being called "baby killers" at home. To me, America was no longer worthy of her sons—only boys, but heroes in my eyes.

I was aware of embarking on a time of closeness to others I had never experienced before. At first I felt a little sorry for the patients all lined up on their cots, with no privacy—

and us watching them day and night. We watched them and they watched us—twelve to fourteen hours a day. I was a little uneasy for about the first 30 minutes, and then I started liking it. We were just all there together. I did feel like an observer in a way, but a casual one. I don't remember anyone being self-conscious. Actually, it seemed to be a health-producing arrangement, with everyone offering support to everyone else. It could be quite touching. Sometimes I would look out over the ward from the nurse's desk and wonder if they really realized that they were in the business of dying. I wonder if I *really* did. It was something I couldn't think about for very long—after all, I was in the business of "conserving the fighting strength."

> Dear Mom,
> This war would be hell if they weren't even shooting . . .
>
> Love always,
> Lynn

8
Built on Sand

"And every one that heareth these sayings of mine, and doeth them not, shall be likened unto a foolish man, which built his house upon the sand: And the rain descended, and the floods came, and the winds blew, and beat upon that house; and it fell: and great was the fall of it."

Jesus Christ
The Bible, King James Version

SGT Wilson and I were standing outside the front door of Medical ICU and he was showing me some sandals that had belonged to a VC. They were made from tires.

Some air strikes were going on just behind the mountains, and even from several miles away it felt like we were having an earthquake. He was telling me how many thousands of dollars they thought went into killing just one VC. I said, "SGT Wilson, why can't we win this war?"

I had never seen him look so serious, but all he said was, "I don't know."

The chief nurse, LTC Swarther, appeared, seemingly out of nowhere, and asked me if I would like to work on the surgical wards. I didn't know if she meant permanently or temporarily, but she said it in a way that made me think she needed help, so I said, "Sure."

She said, "Well, go on over and get started."

LTC Swarther was headed in the same general direction, so we walked part of the way together, trudging through the deep sand ruts. It seemed to be quite a struggle for her.

Almost from the day we arrived, she had been something

of a conundrum to me. About half the time I wasn't sure I understood what she was talking about. I knew the enlisted men didn't like her. LTC Swarther had been there since Thanksgiving and was very fat. They called her, "the pumpkin on wheels." I felt sorry for her—she seemed to be trying awfully hard, or at least struggling awfully hard.

Suddenly LTC Swarther was saying,"You have no idea how lonely it is at the top." It wasn't at all lonely at the bottom; I was thankful I was a second Lieutenant. As we neared the surgical wards, she went her way and I went mine. I was glad. It was a beautiful bright blue and golden day—no time to be bothered by such nonsense as being "lonely at the top."

The air strikes continued; a Chinook flew past the hospital and down the beach with an artillery piece suspended beneath it, and some dustoffs landed with casualties. Although the mid-morning heat felt as though someone had just opened an oven door, I felt good about leaving the air-conditioned, mint-green confines of the Medical Intensive Care quonset.

As I neared the door of the first ward, a panful of discarded bath water barely missed me and splashed over my boots. The nurse throwing it out hadn't seen me coming. She must have been in a hurry—we usually threw it out the back door of the wards.

The patients on the first ward were mostly Vietnamese civilians, a few ARVN's and it looked like bedlam from a distance. There was weeping and wailing, some having just awakened from extensive wound debridement with huge gaping holes where smaller ones had been. It was like being wounded twice! A mama-san was sweeping and a cloud of dust filled the ward. A nurse moved slowly through the murkiness changing reams of bloody bandages while family members helped with baths, sat holding their heads, or lay exhausted and sleeping under the cots. Children were feeding those who could not feed themselves, and a lizard bounded noisily off the walls as several Vietnamese dashed about trying to catch it—anything edible in Vietnam was a prize . . . that lizard didn't have a chance!

Almost without exception, the Vietnamese were friendly and sensed that we were trying to help. It was hard to be sure because, more than anything else, the Vietnamese were survivors who knew without any doubt whatsoever that the name of the game was survival. They were not encumbered by the simplistic idealism all the young Americans brought with them. They didn't have the illusions, but then neither would they crash when the illusions were suddenly gone and the only thing left was survival, like it had always been.

Life goes on, make the most of every situation, help the Americans by day—the VC by night. It was a good way to get killed by either side, but maybe the only way to stay alive—*their predicament.*

An even greater problem lay in their long history of cruel oppression by the French and the fact that the United States had sided with the French. Many of the Vietnamese who longed for freedom and independence would never be able to believe it would come from the United States—no matter how many Americans died for them.

The Vietnamese who were sympathetic to America were often the victims of VC terrorism. It could be unbelievably gruesome. One of their favorite tricks seemed to be to cut off children's hands; also disemboweling, which caused a slow death of excruciating agony. The ARVNs could be cruel, too. It was a cruel country.

The Navy began shooting from the sea and the Air Force napalmed the hills to our north. The VC tried to mortar a pontoon bridge about two miles down the road and hit a village instead. We were swamped with casualties, and three of us went to help out in a makeshift Pre-Op. It seems almost unbelievable to me now that we could cover several wards and Pre-Op too, but we did. It was just part of it. After a while, you could get yourself all "revved up" in a physical and emotional "high gear" that was truly remarkable.

I started out working with another nurse. I can see her face, but I can't remember her name. We were going from patient to patient.

"Thank God (to myself), minor fragment wounds." Quickly, on to the next . . .

"Thank God (again to myself, even more grateful for two in a row), minor fragment wounds." On to the next . . .

A doctor was working to my right, one body over. As he said, "Get something and clamp this bleeder for me," a large dressing, heavy with blood, "plopped" on the floor. Blood was pouring from a thigh that appeared to be mostly mush. I tore open a suture set and, while the doctor held the bleeder in his fingers, managed to clamp it. There was another bleeder, too, smaller. Blood seeped up from it fast, filling the mass of raw "hamburger" and occluding our view—blot and look, blot and look. We knew exactly where it was but couldn't see it. Finally he clamped it.

"Okay, now hold this for me. Good, now cut."

"Where? Here?"

"Perfect, maybe a little further from the knot. Good . . . now this one."

He tied off another one, "And one more."

The doctor was already applying a pressure dressing. "How's his B/P?"

"B/P 70/50, pulse 112." (Not too bad, considering.)

"Where's that blood?" On to the next . . .

"Have you got some vaseline gauze? Let's get a chest tube in him! How's his pressure?"

"B/P 90/60." We were ripping into supplies. "No sooner said than done!"

The sucking chest wound was one of the "biggies." They had talked about it so much at the Medical Field Service School that it was a virtual "giant" looming in the great unknown. It did look pretty bad, but something about it seemed strangely "logical."

The patient was sitting up, resting his head on my shoulder and gripping my arm "for dear life," and I was trying to hold him up. His head was hot—sweaty—steaming. I was sort of "carried away" by the intensity of his suffering, by osmosis!

Leg wounds for me were the worst. Maybe because everyone's legs always looked so strong and then they were just ruined, little more than hamburger with the white of bones. Terrible pain. It's strange, even though I was "steeped" in wounds for almost three years, I've had difficulty remembering what they were actually like. Where were the beginnings? How did they end?

Then there was the little boy, maybe four years old. He looked so calm in the midst of all the goings on. He had some fragment wounds of the chest, very tiny wounds. There was hardly any bleeding. His face was so peaceful. "Doctor! Quick! Over here—he's on his way out!"

Those damned fragment wounds. They looked like nothing, but they were killing him. We were ripping open the pack for a cutdown, holding his little arm still, but he wasn't fighting, he wasn't even crying. He had the sweetest little face. I've never seen a doctor do a cutdown so fast. By the time the bottle was hung and the tubing connected, we were in business, and a corpsman was running with him in his arms through the sand to O.R.

I don't remember who the doctor was. I don't know what happened to the little boy. He may have died in surgery or before. He was only one of many who sped through my life that year, who changed it and were gone. I cared more about him for that moment than I had ever cared about anything in my life, and then he was gone and there were others. Some went to Japan, some went back out in the boonies, some died, some came back through, some made it home . . . and, in the end, we seldom knew.

I was ready for my next deceptive fragment wound sometime later, though (almost). At least I never again took them for granted.

"Nurse! Nurse! My head, it's splitting!"

"These fragments all look superficial. Turn your head. I think you're going to be all . . . Oh, my God!"

His ear was full of blood. A fragment in his ear! Who knew how far in—we couldn't see it. Rush him to x-ray.

The rest is a blur of I.V.s and cutting off blood-soaked clothing; of morphine and getting them ready for surgery and picking up those "heavy" dressings. So many were just beginning the long, black journey into sheer agony: months and years of it. I would have to deal with that later. Right now I had the relief of stabilization, of hanging that second bag of blood . . . B/P 98/60, B/P 100/60. It looked so good. It was the whole world—nothing else existed.

It was several hours later when we finished, but the shift wasn't over—back to the wards. I ran to the hooch to change my clothes. It had to be done, yet I felt guilty taking the time to change. I tore off my bloody fatigues and threw them in a heap on the floor. That afternoon we had fought flies and death with perhaps equal success in a dirty, wretched little place resembling a hospital less than any place I could imagine. But I didn't see it that way at the time—the "matter-of-fact" attitude was in me, too! Already the heat seemed like nothing; the flies seemed like nothing; the wounds, too.

Later we watched the helicopters firing red tracers and laughed over a report on the radio that all the nurses from Tuy Hoa had been evacuated because it was under attack. The news media! So often they seemed oblivious to the truth.

In a few days, I found myself on a MEDCAP (Medical Civic Action Project) in a small village in a very barren, parched area. It was little more than a few hooches clustered around the most putrid well I have ever seen or smelled. The people we saw were covered with sores, although we didn't see many adults. Everyone always said when only the children came it meant it was a VC village.

And soon the children *were* coming, the older ones carrying the younger ones. These weren't the eight to ten-year-olds whom you really had to watch—they were younger—sometimes a three-year-old bringing a little baby. There was such simple trust on their faces. I thought of scenes in doctors' offices in the States where children would scream and pitch fits when it was time to see the doctor. But these children knew they needed help and they were coming for it—VC village or not.

It was the same old story: poverty-related, filth-related diseases. Sores, infections, the thin limbs and swollen bellies of protein deficiency, often with its deadly adjunct—diarrhea, serious vitamin deficiencies, worms, anemia, ear-aches, coughs, fevers, syphilis, tuberculosis, boils, burns, hurts, etc., etc. Lots and lots of misery.

It was always pretty much the same, although the scenery changed and sometimes the doctor would do minor surgery or pull teeth. There were sweltering markets with big baskets of smelly, dried fish and rice and fruits. And mama-sans squatting with beetle-nut black teeth, wrinkles, black pajamas, and conical straw hats. They always seemed friendly, but I could look them straight in the eye and still know that I didn't know what they were thinking.

When we left, I usually felt like I had been at the scene of a high-speed accident with a box of Band-Aids; we had barely scratched the surface and the roots ran so deep. Then it was back to the hospital.

We visited orphanages, too. Many of the babies in one were obviously half-American. If that orphanage is still standing, some of my youth and innocence are still there with it. I felt something come over me as though someone had pulled down a shade, or maybe what happened was the shade flew up.

How could people just go around leaving their own children hither and yon to fates such as this?

I can still see it without even closing my eyes—rows and rows of little iron cribs with grass mats and babies with that desolate look of neglect—babies who might live but, because of emotional deprivation, might never fully know the joy of being human. They didn't even have anything soft to lie on. There was a statue of the Virgin Mary over the door, and a little group of thin, tired nuns. They were doing their best; there were just too many babies.

I thought about a big display of contraceptives in the PX (a mountain as big as a man!) which I had accidentally backed into and knocked over only a week before. Another nurse and I had been so embarrassed, we had run out of the PX without picking them up. If it had happened only a week later, there's no telling what I might have done—maybe carried them all outside and put the display back up where everyone could see, and given a speech!

A veterinarian friend and I often laughed about $26,000 the government spent to retrain some scout dogs to understand Vietnamese! That was over and above the $300 per dog already spent just to purchase them. The dogs were turned over to the ARVNs with dog houses and a year's supply of dog food. The ARVNs ate the dog food, stored their Hondas in the dog houses, and then ate the dogs. I suppose the real shame was that they didn't eat the dogs first; by the time they finished the dog food, the poor dogs were skin and bones.

Some soldiers I knew who went into the tunnels after the VC said that they had tons of our medical supplies. They were stolen by our "friends," and sold to our enemies! It was so common it was almost a joke—admittedly a bad one.

Not as funny were the tales told by some colonels I knew of the whole-scale corruption which was a way of life in Saigon. Our soldiers often went without basic necessities in the field—food, for instance; yet VC and NVA bodies were frequently found with American C-rations. The high-ranking officers in Saigon were well aware of what was going on and could have put a stop to much of it, *but they didn't want to make waves that could possibly affect their careers!*

It wasn't hard for me to believe after one of my patients was raped all night by two corpsmen and another nearly murdered, and the chief nurse threatened to "ruin my Army career" if I didn't keep my mouth shut. I was pleased to tell her that I didn't have an Army career.

I made out two separate incident reports. I found out later they had been destroyed. I brought this up with the I.G. later, distraught about the whole episode. He was very surprised and said he knew nothing about these incidents. So, I got a big, mean friend of mine to threaten the health of the corpsmen who raped the patient, if they tried anything again. (There was eventually a congressional investigation of this hospital.) Real discipline at the 91st was almost nonexistent; what they had was rule by fear and anarchy.

All was not well at Tuy Hoa. Although most of us really appreciated how much we had it made compared to the guys in the field, we soon began to realize that many of the corpsmen would gladly go to the field just to get away from the hospital. It was "common knowledge" that if we ever had a ground attack, the hospital commander wouldn't live through it (and 1967 was early in the war to hear about officers being killed by their own men). They said it had something to do with "a little understanding" they'd had early on about the importance of his career and them being treated like animals. So they worked past exhaustion to build the hospital in record time.

There was also a doctor who was so arrogant, I'm sure he never realized how close he came to getting killed. He was truly sadistic; a large blonde man. He would swagger onto the ward and my heart would sink, and a hush would fall over the patients. Almost every day, I reasoned with some of them not to kill him—not for his sake, but for theirs. And every time we had a red alert, I would wonder if the colonel was about to get killed. It could get to you after a while. Some of us began to believe that the hospital, and even the war, were there for the benefit of the CO and the chief nurse.

In spite of it all, most everyone was trying their hardest. Yet here was an entire hospital, discombobulated to say the least, because of some utter nonsense about Army careers. It's still very hard for me to find words to express how I felt. I suppose about the closest I can come is to say that I felt involved in something ultimately indecent. In more ways than one, the hospital at Tuy Hoa was *built on sand*.

Although some were truly dedicated professionals and many others were serious about serving their country, I began to see the Army as just another giant, self-serving bureaucracy (with military trappings) that was quite self-defeating and too dumb to realize it.

I had made something of a joke of saying "the middle of a war was no place to be playing Army," but the realities I was facing every day made me begin to think it might have been an astute observation. Why couldn't we just get the job done? I loved my country and the things I thought it stood for, and I was determined to give it my best. Yet in the days and months to come, I would discover that doing my best wasn't a simple thing. It would involve struggling with the system as we struggled through the sand at Tuy Hoa.

We finally got wooden sidewalks at Tuy Hoa. One night, during the rainy season, in the middle of a blinding storm, I lost my way, ran smack into someone, and asked if he knew where the sidewalk was. He said, "You're on it, Ma'am," and gave me a "We Try Harder" button!

I had several "We Try Harder" buttons while I was at Tuy Hoa. Somebody would give me one and it would fall off in the sand, and someone would give me another one. "We Try Harder" always meant a lot to me because so many were trying so very, very hard, and guys were giving their lives (what more could they give?). Yet it seems significant to me now that, in the end, the buttons were always swallowed up by the sand.

9
The "Saga" of Gary Owen

This is the place. Stand still my steed,
    Let me review the scene,
And summon from the shadowy Past
    The forms that once have been.

The Past and Present here unite
    Beneath Time's flowing tide
Like footprints hidden by a brook,
    But seen on either side.

Henry Wadsworth Longfellow
from *A Gleam of Sunshine*

Around ten in the morning on my first Saturday off, I heard the new field telephone in the nurses' quarters ringing. I was delighted to hear that the call was for me. It was Major McGinley with the 4th Division, whom I had met at the party our first night at Tuy Hoa. He invited me and another nurse, Marie, to visit their base camp and have lunch.

The only problem was the chief nurse had recently announced that the nurses could no longer leave the hospital compound without specific permission from her. Thinking she would be less likely to turn down the major's request than mine, I asked him to ask her for me. He called back in a few minutes to say everything was all set, permission had been granted.

I was busy looking around their base camp and thinking, *Is this what a base camp is like? Poor things*. But they ed rather proud of it. I suppose it *was* a great improve- over being in the field, and once again I realized how e really "had it made" at the hospital.

After lunch the major said, "Are you ready for a surprise?" We went outside and there was the cutest little horse I had ever seen. He was "round" and shiny, and had big brown eyes. And there was something about him which made me think right away that he was probably very gentle. I said, "Oh, you dear little thing." The major said, "You can ride him," and I thought, *That's easy for you to say.* I wasn't sure I wanted to ride a horse without a saddle and only a flimsy-looking piece of rope tied loosely around his nose. But he was too small to look menacing—if he ran away and I fell off, it probably wouldn't hurt. The more I thought about it, the more it seemed like it would be great fun.

He helped me up, and I sat there for a minute getting used to the idea. Someone took my picture. Then he said, "Go ahead," and gestured toward a piece of wide expanse of beach stretching in the direction of the hospital. I had no idea how to communicate with that horse, but I nudged him a little with my feet and he seemed to know what I meant. Away he went.

I was wearing shorts that someone donated for the occasion, and cheap canvas shoes. His coat was as smooth as velvet against my legs, and he felt soft and squishy through the shoes. He was very obedient. He really wanted to please. We rode together for quite a while; sometimes we would gallop, but mostly we just walked. I kept saying, "Oh, you dear little thing."

I forgot all about being in Vietnam. For a few minutes I was in another world, or perhaps it was just the world in general. There seemed to be a timelessness about it. It reminded me of the discussions in my old philosophy class about "absolutes." I believed in moral absolutes and they were serving me well, as they had served many before me, and would serve others to come in the hard tests of life.

I had already witnessed some in groups of partiers on the beach at the hospital, their self-respect swept away as if by the waves, but truly by their own "shades of gray." So spaced-out or drunk that they didn't move to throw up; lost virtue, empty eyes in rebellious faces. How glad I was that if you *chose not to be*, you didn't have to be only a "child of the sixties!'' I was acutely aware of a sense of well-being and an inner strength forged from the knowledge that some things never change.

When I returned, they told me how they had come to own the horse. A VC pony from the Central Highlands, they ''captured'' him after a fight, gave him a tranquilizer shot, and brought him back in a Chinook. They called him ''Charlie,'' which seemed like a sacrilege, so we named him ''Gary Owen'' after an old calvary tune. We even whistled a few bars in honor of the occasion, and after that bit of silliness, he seemed sufficiently Americanized!

The major said, ''Would you like to keep him?''

I said, ''Oh, how sweet!''

We decided to continue partying at the officer's club at the hospital. They tied Gary Owen to the back of the jeep. We had to go slow, and it was dark by the time we arrived.

My memory is a little foggy on it, but it seems to me that they led Gary Owen into the club to introduce him to the hospital commander and ask if it would be possible for me to keep him.

The commander of the hospital didn't like the idea, and mentioned something about keeping an animal at a hospital being a court-martial offense. I never really knew if it was or not. The chief nurse at Long Binh had a dog almost as big as Gary Owen. The major said, ''Don't worry, we'll think of something. Let's have a beer and worry about it later.'' It seemed like an excellent idea. So we left Gary Owen tied to the jeep.

A little while later, someone went out to see how Gary Owen was doing and came running back in to report that he had been stolen. The club was full, and most everyone present agreed that it was *treachery* to steal a horse from a nurse.

In the weeks following, many people became involved in the search for Gary Owen. Rumor had it that someone from the engineer battalion behind the hospital had done the dastardly deed. It was like some kind of a detective mystery with ''many chapters,'' and ''intelligence reports.'' Finally, Colonel Munnely, with whom I had waltzed half the night, discovered he was at Vung Ro Bay, very comfortable and well-taken care of. It seemed best to leave it at that.

The chief nurse wanted to know why I had visited the 4th Division base camp without her permission. I think it was because the major never asked her. Only later did we find out that the reason special permission was needed was because of increased enemy activity in the area. A week or two later, the same group from 4th Division was ambushed on their way to the club one night. They arrived late, and when they started talking about it they said, "Guess what happened to us on the way to the club tonight?" They seemed nonchalant in a way, telling us about it, yet talking among themselves at the same time. Actually, it seemed more like guys talking over a Saturday afternoon touch-football game in the backyard than anything else. They had killed three VC.

Major McGinley had just been promoted to lieutenant colonel, so it was something of a promotion party for him. Before leaving the club that night, he wrote out a deed to Gary Owen, just in case I might be able to use it. Shortly after that, they all left for the central highlands. I never saw any of them again.

Looking back, I marvel at our attitude. I would probably get more excited over someone slipping in the bathtub now than I did then over ambushes. It all seemed so "normal" somehow. Often people "commuted" back and forth in helicopters, to and from the war, not much differently than men with briefcases going on business trips. Sometimes they came back, sometimes they didn't.

10
Ward 13, I Think

> Every parting gives a foretaste of death; every
> coming together again a foretaste of the
> resurrection.
>
> Arthur Schopenhauer

July 1967. I had been in Vietnam almost six months and
most of my illusions were long gone. Once we were open
for business, it was booming, and covering four or five
wards could be the proverbial "merry-go-round." Yet the
patients were so great. Sometimes I wondered if anything
could get them down. Many soldiers were recuperating and
coping with problems they would have for the rest of their
lives; they had strength. I sensed a sort of unspoken,
mutual agreement with them. "I won't let it get me down if
you don't let it get you down." It was a sharing of strength.

Nowhere was that sharing more evident or more needed
than on Ward 13, if I have remembered the number correctly.
When I was covering four or five wards, it was usually the
last one I got to because I started at the other end of the
hospital and worked my way toward the South China Sea. I
don't remember why; it must just have been the way we did
it.

Finally getting there was like jumping off the merry-go-
round and feeling lightheaded. There had already been so
much activity, so many facts to assimilate about so many
patients that I often felt rather incompetent by the time I

made it to Ward 13. It always took me longer to decipher and initial the doctor's orders, and the paperwork would be dragging. I would feel pressed to get it finished and get on with things.

One afternoon, I was about halfway through giving everyone their twice-daily, huge penicillin and streptomycin shots. They were all badly bruised from getting so many shots, but this one guy was so bad that I just couldn't find a safe, unbruised place to give it. When I told him he would have to have it in the thigh, it freaked him out. He said, "Oh, no! Please! I don't care if you shoot me in the bruises, my leg muscle is too hard. *Please* shoot me in the butt." By the time he finished begging, half the ward seemed interested in the outcome.

I couldn't figure out if it was against my better judgment or not, and if it meant *that* much to him, what the heck, it was his butt. I was just about to give him the shot when I imagined jabbing the needle in all those bruises. Although I had found one small, half-suitable spot, I didn't think I could go through with it. I wiped the spot I had chosen off with alcohol again to stall for time. I reminded him that this couldn't go on indefinitely anyway; he was going to have to get used to the idea of getting them in the thigh. I had a feeling everyone was watching and waiting with bated breath. His butt looked so pitiful and he was lying there— waiting for it! A tear fell out of my eye and hit the guy, right where he was supposed to get the shot! I was mortified. I was so embarrassed I couldn't even look up. I felt that the entire ward had seen it and they were going to talk about me when I left. Of all the things to cry about in Vietnam; of all the things to cry about on Ward 13! I was so put out with myself! When I finally gave him the shot he said, "That didn't hurt a bit, honest, I didn't feel a thing." he was protesting a little too much.

The next afternoon when I started giving the shots, one of the patients said, "Here comes the ace tail-gunner of the 91st," and many swore up and down that they hadn't felt a thing.

And I said, "Well, I certainly didn't feel a thing either!"

They weren't your usual nineteen year olds; they understood about tears. For a long time they called me, "Ace." It helped.

Iron Bottom wasn't doing well at all. She was distant, apparently lost in her own world of many problems. To us, Iron Bottom was "the enemy," but it was more in the way that a traditional Iron Bottom would, naturally, have to be the enemy. She could make you feel guilty if all you had done was tell her how many patients were on your ward. She always *suspected* us of wrongdoing, and expected to catch us at it any minute.

But Iron Bottom was not a true villain. I have a feeling she was suffering because she really cared. I always thought that if you were dying, Iron Bottom wouldn't let you do it. And I think she was the assistant chief nurse. At Tuy Hoa, that was probably enough to account for *anything*. But she could hurt your feelings, and she was especially hard on the wardmasters for no apparent reason. They were always kind and very patient with her, and I admired them for it—especially the one on Ward 13.

One morning she came in, was her usual "endearing self," and the wardmaster maintained his famous, admirable self-control. As she was leaving the ward, I sat down in my chair and, in anticipation of the good feeling I was about to have when she was finally gone, started to lean the chair back on two legs. At the same time, as calm as you please and as matter-of-factly as could be, the wardmaster said, "What she needs is one this long and about that big around."

For a second, I didn't know what *it* was (the size was so deceptive). Then, just as I was exclaiming, "Wow," I lost my balance and started to tip over backwards, naturally accompanied by a scream and gales of laughter. (I had to admit she needed something!) Iron Bottom looked back as though she was thinking, *I know they're up to something, I just haven't caught them yet!* (If Iron Bottom walked in today, I would be glad to see her. We went through a lot, and surely by now she must have figured out that we weren't "up to something.")

One evening one of the patients (he had the nicest face) came to the nurse's desk and said, "If I pinned my jump wings on your shirt, could you wear them?"

I was already wearing some buttons which technically we

weren't supposed to wear, but they were important. Patients would give them to us, and it meant we were cheering for them. They needed to feel we were cheering for them...most people back home certainly weren't. Just imagine, they were out fighting a war—a war with special horrors, and few even cared. They needed to know somebody thought they were wonderful.

I had the "We Try Harder" button which the nameless, but considerate soul had given me that night in the dark when I couldn't find the sidewalk. And, not to be outdone by the 173rd, someone in the 101st Airborne had given me one of their buttons. But jump wings were a little different than buttons. My mind never worked really well on Ward 13 anyway, and all I could think to say was, "Oh, how sweet, but I'd better not. I know you have to earn those. But if you want to pin them on my undershirt, I'll wear them next to my heart."

It was developing into a really special occasion! It *was* a special occasion.

I had just come on the ward and had seen Iron Bottom darting in and out about three wards behind me on her rounds. The patient had his jump wings in his hand, and it didn't seem to me that it could possibly take more than a second or two for him to pin them on me (*he* wanted to pin them on). He was tall, so I stood up so he wouldn't strain his back bending over.

He was having trouble with the little plastic clasps, and I was hoping he wouldn't drop one in my shirt. Then I started getting a little worried about Iron Bottom walking in. It was such a totally innocent situation that I hadn't given it a moment's thought, but what would she think if she walked on the ward and found him "fumbling in my shirt?" I certainly didn't want to make him nervous or spoil the moment, so I was keeping calm and being brave. By the time he got the first clasp on and was working on the second, I was having flashes of Iron Bottom getting closer and closer to the ward.

The flashes were like movies—giant screen, living color, sound effects. Here she comes, red hair and all, closer and closer, looking very military indeed—major's oaks leaves "gleaming" in the sun. Accompanied by what else but a big base drum—BOOM *BOOM*, BOOM *BOOM*, BOOM *BOOM*.

To make matters worse, my back was to the door. BOOM *BOOM*, BOOM *BOOM*, BOOM *BOOM*. Finally I said (quite calmly), "I think Iron Bottom may walk in any second."

He said, "She just did." He had just gotten the second clasp done.

Somehow I had peace that honest, straightforward intentions and real innocence would be their own defense, and I was determined not to let something simple and nice deteriorate into something complicated and ugly. Maybe Iron Bottom could make me feel guilty for taking the census of the ward incorrectly, but not for this.

Iron Bottom not only looked very military indeed, but very puzzled and said, "*What* is going on here?"

I said, "It has to be *absolutely* the sweetest thing that has happened to me all week. Look," and I showed her the jump wings.

She smiled and said, "Oh," asked how many patients were on the ward and left. Triumph!

When I left the Army, I threw my uniforms and ribbons away, but I still have those jump wings. I hope he made it.

So many things happened on Ward 13. It was on Ward 13 I was overcome with the heat. I still can't believe it happened to me, a person from Florida who loves the heat. But if you got busy and forgot to drink a lot of water, that heat would get to anybody. Sometimes the nurses would feel it happening to them, go to the Emergency Room for an I.V., and then go back to work. I remember a terrible headache and feeling dizzy, and pressing my sleeve against my arm thinking, "That is *so warm*." There was something about it I almost liked; I think I was fascinated that clothing could be hot. It was a very dry hot. I barely made it to the Emergency Room, and had to spend the rest of the day in bed. I often wondered how on earth anyone could fight a war in such heat. I think it killed a good number of men.

There were two patients right in front of the nurse's desk who had, to say the least, extensive fragment wounds of both legs—gunshot wounds, too. They were all sewn up with wire sutures, up one leg and down the other. And they were both "as fresh as paint."

At this point in medical history, suture removal was still part of the "doctor's mystique," although it is simple enough for anyone to do and nurses did it routinely in Vietnam, along with the many of the not-so-simple things doctors also do.

I had just begun removing one guy's sutures. I think I was on the first one when he said, "Ouch! You hurt me!"

I thought, *What kind of a thing is that to say?*

I was only on the first suture, and already he was saying "Ouch! You hurt me."

The suture lines were jagged and the sutures had been in a little too long and were embedded in the flesh, encrusted with scabs. One thousand, nine hundred and ninety-nine sutures to go—his legs were looking longer! It wasn't going to be the simple task I had anticipated. After a few more difficult ones he said, "Here, I'll take them out. You go do something else."

The soldiers were just like that, always helping us through something. He turned out to be better qualified than I was anyway, having had over two weeks to do nothing but sit there and contemplate his legs, he was intimately acquainted with each and every scab! Of course, the other guy had to do his, too, so the first one showed him how. They spent most of the afternoon picking out sutures.

I can't really say why it seems important to tell about those two instead of others who were in worse shape. Maybe because of the way he said, "Ouch! You hurt me," which has stuck in my memory all these years. More probably because they were so typical of so many of the patients, including the ones in really bad shape—always bouncing back. It was the attitude. It was heart. They really were giving the whole thing their best shot. I suppose that's why it hurt so bad to see how these young men were treated when they got back to the States.

In the final analysis, it's still difficult for me to say which was worse—the ones who came in terribly messed up, or the ones who finally went back out. Back out to what? They were the ones who, after several weeks, I really knew. We all finally got to the point where we avoided close attachments; nevertheless, "something happened." There was a closeness among us which I have never experienced anywhere else. I'm sure it's responsible for the awful ache I think will always be there inside. Yet it was a precious thing—worth the price.

So many things happened on Ward 13.

One evening I had just arrived on the ward and was "running in slow motion" through the paperwork again when one of the patients, Mark, a lieutenant who had impressed me as perhaps just a little bit of a smart mouth said, "How would you like to have an affair?"

I didn't want to have an affair—it sounded sordid to me; I wanted to get my work done. So, like a real priss I said, "Please. Don't harass the nurses."

I can hardly believe it now, but somehow I had failed to notice how nice looking the lieutenant was.

He must have "regrouped" and rephrased the question without my noticing, because that night after work, we sat outside the ward talking for hours. Afterwards, I thought Mark was the most beautiful person I had ever met, and was totally and hopelessly smitten.

I soon realized he had not meant "affair" in the sordid sense at all, he was lonely and wanted companionship. Of course, neither one of us could have foreseen what kind of relationship might develop. Maybe it was different than what either of us expected. All I know is that even in the last hours of my life, I'll be able to look back and still remember it as the most precious friendship of my life.

Mark had some fragment wounds in his leg and, although it was stiff, he was getting better. There must have been a hospital regulation against patients swimming, because I remember us sneaking down to the beach. I was walking ahead, watching for anyone who might mean trouble, and he was following about 20 yards behind, hobbling. I don't know how he managed to salvage his fatigues, the same ones he was wounded in, but he was wearing them. That was really a mistake for anyone trying to be inconspicuous—

they were such a mess, all wrinkled. We must have been quite a sight.

We did make it to the beach, though. And we did have the doctor's permission. Good "old" Dr. Fitchett. He *was* a good doctor, and he thought swimming would be good therapy. It was excellent therapy—but we were hardly interested in therapy.

Dr. Fitchett gave him permission to go to the officers' club too, and suddenly our humble little club became the most romantic spot on the face of the earth. There was an orange and white parachute suspended from the roof, some potted palms, and the breeze from the South China Sea. We had a tape player but not many tapes, so the same songs were played over and over. I only remember one; it goes: "They say there's a tree in the forest . . ."

Somehow we managed to find hours and hours to spend together. Something very close to a lifetime was crammed into a couple of weeks. Mark was with the 173rd Airborne. They were always into something, and lieutenants were notorious for being a "dime a dozen" in combat. Although it hung over both our heads, we did manage to forget, sometimes. We never talked about the war. The only thing he ever said was, "You know what? War *really is* Hell."

Although I realized he was alluding to his own revelation and was definitely making an understatement, I replied, "I *know*." It's one thing you don't have to tell a doctor or a nurse in a combat zone.

He was a good partier of the sort I liked, and strong, and so thoroughly gentle that I felt all the good things of civilization had somehow culminated in his personality; yet subtly—in ways not even he was aware of. There were so many of them, I grouped them all together into one "big something" which I thought of as *excellence of soul*.

We talked a lot about our families. His sounded so wonderful. He often mentioned how much his father loved him and seemed to think "the sun rose and set on his son!" He'd say, "I just can't understand it." And I would reply that I could. I suppose I loved him, in a way, like I loved God—just for all the good things about him.

And I was so glad that our relationship was platonic!

My faith precluded anything else. I believed sex was only for marriage, and sacred, and apparently Mark did, too. Everything seemed so perfect for those happy weeks. My world must have had an orbit all its own. It didn't even seem like the same Vietnam.

I don't remember much else of what we talked about, but we sat for hours, sounding the depths of our souls with the breeze blowing from the South China Sea. For me it was, "How do I love thee? Let me count the ways," and "moments of glad grace," and pink and peach and lavender sunsets all rolled into one. Our relationship was so comfortable; I felt I had always known him. I loved him better than life a hundred times over, and I loved life with a passion. I always toasted, "To Life." He had always toasted, among other things, "To A Short War," and something about it even then broke my heart.

It was a beautiful "lifetime." One night, near the end of it, he said, "Don't ever look back." There was a whole philosophy that went with it. And later, when I thought about it, I always thought about how our time together seemed suspended in space and time, and there was a feeling about it like, "Don't touch it—let it be."

One afternoon in particular, it seemed time *was* standing still. Sometimes, when you have so very little of it, time has to stand still. The ward was bathed in brilliant sunlight. I had taken just a moment to sit on Mark's bed and watch him add some columns of numbers—of all things, and I was impressed. (That's just how things are when you're smitten.)

Sitting on the edge of his bed wasn't *too* much of an indiscretion, although one of the supervisors seemed to think so. We often sat on patients' beds. It was either that or suffer through all their treatments kneeling on the cement floors.

There was an old Vietnamese man on the ward in the bed next to Mark's. He was a village chief, and the VC had tried to castrate him with a machete. How they missed was a miracle, because they certainly succeeded in hacking him up, with huge gashes. It was the kind of thing people would look at and exclaim, "Oh, my God!"

There was something very likable about that old man. He

suffered through all the pain and indignities of such a thing with a marvelous, quiet dignity. It was the way of the older Vietnamese, and it aggravated some Americans to distraction. I'm not exactly sure why. This old man felt deeply—he just suffered well.

He had a wispy beard which I was sure must have taken him 50 years to grow, and was just beginning to feel a little better when one of the corpsmen cut if off. He was giving shaves, and apparently got carried away.

I wasn't sure what the beard meant to the old man personally, but I knew those beards were symbols of honor to the Vietnamese. It was kind of like attempted castration all over again. It was so sad—more quiet dignity.

The same day his I.V. infiltrated, and his veins were so bad that after two unsuccessful attempts at restarting it, I called for one of the doctors. There was just no way I was going to hurt that old man one more time. Mark watched and said, "I can't believe you can't start an I.V."

It may just have been "par for the course" on Ward 13, because I hadn't missed on my first try since I had been in Vietnam. All I knew was it was one miserable day, and Mark was about to leave.

Before he left, he gave the old man his rubber flip-flops so he would have some shoes. I never would have thought a pair of flip-flops could mean so much, but it was a very healing thing. I can still remember how it made me feel—sort of like there was hope for humanity after all.

And then I was standing in the door of the ward, trying to tell him good-bye, and it wasn't working because I was just standing there almost paralyzed. I suppose I *was* paralyzed. Finally, he kissed me on the forehead and left. I watched him walk away in his awful fatigues thinking he had to be the most beautiful person I had ever known, and feeling like he had just died—or maybe that I had. But then I was aware of something else, the tiniest ray of hope. I felt quite certain I would see him again.

A few days later, I was promoted to first lieutenant. Before she pinned the bars on, COL Swarther removed all my buttons. I thought how much I preferred my buttons to the new bars. And it seemed she was enjoying removing my buttons! As she was pinning the bars on she said, "Now isn't this wonderful—a first lieutenant!"

I blurted out, "No, actually it's the end of an era."

I was determined to keep my priorities straight—people first, Army career nowhere.

After the ceremony, I put the buttons back on and received a letter from Mark with another "We Try Harder" button. The first one had fallen off somewhere in the sands of Tuy Hoa.

> *Dak To, VN 10 Aug. 1967*
> *Dear Lynn:*
>
> *Enclosed is the "We Try Harder" button I promised you. Also have enclosed my first-lieutenant bar for you. Could not send you two because I never did get back to Bien Hoa where the other one is on my cap. We came forward in helmets. I hope you will decide it is "wonderful and good" to be a first lieutenant and wear it on your fatigue blouse.*
>
> *Spent a crazy couple of days hitch-hiking rides all over Vietnam, but am now back with my battalion. They switched me from "A" to "C" company, which means I'll have to learn about a whole new platoon of men. Haven't met them yet, but will in the morning. . . .*
>
> *. . .I'm sure the 91st has breathed a sigh of relief that the patient in dirty fatigues has ceased to flout their regulations and gone away. I hope your reputation has not received too grievous a blow, and that all of the fat majors have ceased looking askance at you. Do give my warmest regards to Foxy.*
>
> *Must also take this opportunity to thank you for your excellent care and morale-building therapy. Whenever I can get my "91st" lighter to work and light a cigarette, I'll think of my best days in Vietnam. . . .*

So much of Vietnam was horror, death and destruction and unmitigated mayhem. Yet life did go on for us too, and rubber flip-flops, a teardrop, some buttons, one thousand ninety-nine sutures, and jump wings are still fresh memories and, ever so gratefully, they are still fresh with a sense of life's wonder.

The flip-flops were given not in a condescending way, but as one ordinary, decent person to another. The tear was for much more than a few bruises. The buttons said I thought they were wonderful, and they thought I was, too. And the guys with all those sutures will always represent the others to me—they had heart. The jump wings will always remind me of an afternoon when one human being reached out to another in a special, nice way. I suppose all those simple, little ordinary things weren't so small after all. No, the wonder of them was not small.

11
Somewhat Like Riding a Bicycle

> Better a dinner of herbs where love is,
> than a stalled ox and hatred therewith.
>
> Proverbs

My only thought as I ran for the latrine was, *This is going to be terrible—and I'm afraid I've forgotten how!* But actually it was somewhat like riding a bicycle—you just don't "forget" how to throw up (amebic dysentery is a very violent disease). When about an hour of "violence" had abated, I threw my fatigues on a chair, dressed for bed, and lay down on my cot feeling weak, but confident that *surely* the worst of a temporary inconvenience was over.

A friend happened by and said, "You look awful. Don't you realize you have a fever?" I don't think I "realized" much of anything. The next thing I knew, the chief nurse was there saying something about getting in an ambulance that was waiting at the door of the hooch. I was reaching for my clothes when she said, "You don't need clothes, you're sick." It seemed like a very strange philosophy to me—you always need your clothes. Before I knew what was happening, she spirited me out of my room and into the ambulance—wearing a pink nightie. *It was too embarrassing for words.* I thought, *Doesn't anyone around here have any sense of propriety?*

I remember sitting at the desk in Admissions, very

conscious of my nightie, with some guy asking all the routine questions, including "next of kin," wondering if anything at all could be done to preserve a little dignity besides, of course, trying very hard not to throw up. Finally, I was able to apply the "theory of momentary embarrassment."

I ended up on my old ward, Medical Intensive Care, in a little cubicle at the end of the quonset. About three days later, I ventured out feeling much better, clad in some blessedly modest patient pajamas of very heavy, blue cotton. One of the patients, who had *really* thought he was dying of malaria a few days earlier, looked well and happy, and greeted me with a cheerful, "Hi."

Things suddenly got busy on the ward, so I sat at the desk and did some paperwork for the nurse on duty. I suppose nowhere but Vietnam could you be a patient one minute and go to work the next wearing pajamas.

On my way back to the little cubicle, the guy who hadn't died and some others invited me to play Monopoly with them. Three or four of them were sitting on the only real hospital bed on the ward. I remember pinning a little piece of gold paper from a pack of cigarettes on my collar and saying, "If I get in bed with you guys, I want you to remember I'm an officer." It wasn't necessary to say it, if it had been I wouldn't have done it—it was just another big joke. So we sat on the bed in blue pajamas and played Monopoly, pretty much regressing into childhood for the rest of the afternoon. There was a feeling of relief in the utter simplicity of it.

One guy said that in addition to carrying all the things they had to carry in the field (usually weighing over 70 pounds), he also carried a case of Cokes. He just liked Cokes! Somebody mentioned collecting ears, and they talked about them for a while. I don't know why, but the few ears I saw never totally freaked me out like they did some people— maybe because they didn't quite look like what they were. I didn't want to get too close to them and I couldn't imagine why, if someone took one he would ever want two, but they didn't freak me out. They just seemed to be "part of it." The training alone brutalized an awful lot of people, and in a way, it was expected of them. But I saw a *lot* of decency, too, in spite of it.

That afternoon they needed someone to see the decency. They were being torn apart, and I was only vaguely sensing it. They were supposed to be the "good guys," the liberators, defenders of freedom . . . products of the Judeo-Christian American ethic which valued human beings and their inalienable, God-given rights. And they were truly fighting a terrible evil.

In a few days I was fine, and resumed working on the surgical wards. One afternoon, an old mama-san brought me a gift. Her little girl was on the pediatric ward, and she always seemed so appreciative of even the most routine care. She often swept the floor for us or helped on the ward any way she could. The gift was wrapped in white paper. It was a sandwich—a long, thin sandwich that reminded me of the Italian sandwiches I sometimes bought in Tampa. It could have used some olive oil and oregano, but I was just extremely thankful there wasn't a trace of Nuocmam (fermented fish sauce) on it anywhere.

The mama-san seemed old, but she probably wasn't much over thirty—Vietnamese women had a way of aging fast, their life was so hard. I could tell the sandwich was really something special. It was quite beautiful. The chief nurse had warned us repeatedly not to eat Vietnamese food, but since I had just had amebic dysentery and lived through it, it didn't seem to matter. I thought of the theory of gracious acceptance of gifts, and that it's not every day a Vietnamese gives you an Italian sandwich—a very generous gift from such poor people.

We sat down outside the ward and I tore it in half and we ate it. It was good. I knew the Vietnamese had all kinds of customs which seemed strange to us, and I wondered if giving her part of the sandwich back was the right thing to do. It felt like the right thing, and she was the kind of person who would understand even if it wasn't.

In a way I was sorry I didn't know enough Vietnamese to say much to her, but then, in a way, I was glad. Actions speak louder than words, and I know we sensed each other's good will. When I think of the horrendous way the war ended, I'm especially thankful for those special times of mutual, sincere good will. They kind of "stand alone" in the face of historical catastrophe.

As I tore the sandwich and smiled back at the mama-san's smiling face, I thought of a verse of scripture my mother often quoted, "Better a dinner of herbs where love is . . . ," and I was wishing that it *was* just "herbs." The sandwich contained some small strips of meat that seemed to have an unusually fine texture (maybe from a very small animal?). There had been bubonic plague in Tuy Hoa. They said the people had been eating rats—but for some reason, it hardly seemed to matter at that moment.

12
Children

The child's sob in the silence curses deeper
Than the strong man in his wrath.

Elizabeth Barrett Browning

The sublimest song to be heard on earth is the
lisping of the human soul on the lips of children.

Victor Hugo

I would walk on the ward and all the little arms would reach
out and those who could, would come running for loving,
and I never failed to wonder how on earth heaven and hell
could both end up under the same roof. Working on the
children's ward was simultaneously heart-rending and happy; carefree, and hopelessly depressing. They looked like
miniature soldiers who had been through a bloody battle.

I can still recall their faces, and who was in which bed. In
about the third bed to the right as you came in the back
door, was a little boy with a sweet face who reminded me of
the little boy with the fragment wounds that first afternoon
in Pre-Op. He was skinny, and as sweet as his face, maybe
four years old, and desperate to be loved. But then, they all
were. Some had parents who visited, who lived near the
hospital, others didn't. We never knew if they were orphans
or if they had been flown in from a distance and the parents
were back home some place. Maybe it was best not to
know.

One little boy about eight years old had to be the
homeliest child I had ever seen in my life. He was almost
ready to leave the hospital and he liked to help us on the

wards . . . a nice little boy. He looked something like that big cartoon duck, "Baby Huey." He was "egg-shaped," as though he had just hatched, with an egg-shaped body and an egg-shaped head. But he was precious, and so willing to help that we all soon forgot how ugly he was. he was our Baby Huey, someone special.

He often helped on the wards distributing trays and picking them up. The combination of oppressive heat and high fevers frequently made it difficult for the patients to eat, and there was often food left untouched. It must have been a terrible temptation for him to be so close to so much good food that no one wanted, day after day. One evening, it must finally have been too much for him. He cleaned all the trays on an entire ward—after he had already eaten supper! And looked more egg-shaped than he ever had before, more than I like to recall.

He couldn't walk. He couldn't move. We called the doctor. Finally, his eyes rolled back in his head and he had a convulsion. We put down an NG (stomach) tube. He remained unconscious that night. I don't know whatever became of him! And I don't know why I don't know. It was so easy to lose track of people, even special people. There were so many, and they came and went so fast, you just got hardened to it after a while. It seems unbelievable now that I could have cared about someone so much, yet feel as though I didn't. And he wasn't the only one.

I remember him lying there, all swollen up, with the doctor standing there wondering out loud if maybe he had some hidden problem which had caused the convulsion, and deciding to give him a little more time to see what might develop. Only minutes before he had seemed so happy. He knew how much we liked him; he was included. Then suddenly, there were even doubts he would live, certainly doubts that he would be normal again.

So here I am, years later praying, "Lord Jesus, please bless him. If he's still alive, bless him, and make sure he has plenty to eat. Lord, he won't be at all hard to spot . . . he probably still looks very much like a big duck."

They came in with gunshot wounds, spattered with fragments and blood. There were several rows of two and three-year-olds in front of the nurse's desk. Cuddly little ones who at first didn't seem to have been traumatized at all, or maybe it was just the "forgiveness" of little children. But then, just like real soldiers, they had their problems sleeping, too.

Most of the others ranged from about five to eight years old. The thing about children is they can't take "time out" from growing and living to be sick. Many of them still had a fantastic zest for life which children have. I found myself becoming very concerned that they not lose that sense of wonder, especially for the little things.

Sometimes we would have rubber gloves to blow up like balloons, with merthiolate or "Magic Marker" faces painted on. Sometimes we would have water fights. They started off harmless enough with syringes, but always escalated to the fire extinguishers—the pump kind with water, heavy as lead! We would be dripping wet from head to toe, shrieking and running all around the ward. The children would scream with delight, jump up and down, and try to help their favorites. I'm pretty sure I always lost miserably, but it was a little hard to tell—winners and losers both ended up drenched.

The children really loved it when we "accidentally" got them wet, and if you shot one on purpose, he was especially "honored," so we couldn't possibly leave anyone out! And it seemed someone always laughed so hard, they wet their pants. Sometimes you need to laugh that hard. It was glorious. It was important . . . more important than all the paperwork, *as* important as the treatments and medications.

Fortunately, Iron Bottom never walked in on the chaos. I doubt she could have coped. We were never afraid of someone walking in, although there were those who would have considered the goings-on "unforgivable." I'm surprised half the hospital didn't come running to check out all the noise. Afterward, we would have to sit down and gasp for breath. Our faces would be bright red and we would be about to pop from drinking water, yet still thirsty.

Iron Bottom did come in one day when we were distributing a box of chocolate candy Mark had left for them. I don't really know why she was against it (general principles, I suppose), but when she couldn't come up with a good reason for the children not to have the candy she said, "It might give them worms!" *Luckily*, they already had worms! I thought how convenient it was that they already had them . . . they certainly didn't have to worry about getting worms! And life could be good, candy, worms and all . . . at least for a while. Iron Bottom had just hung herself with her own rope.

By now, I was perceiving more than ever that war was also a life and death struggle for the preservation of "humanness." It had been very vague at first, and still was in the sense that I probably could not have verbalized it.

I felt more human with the children than anywhere else. Tears and laughter were more intense with them. I felt the joy of life bubbling inside, yet it hurt more with them and, in the end, being so involved in their suffering probably made me feel more dead inside than anything else. However, I also think they helped me hang on just a little bit longer.

I was vaguely aware of becoming hardened to all the suffering, and as well as I can remember, felt something like "embarrassment" about it, although that was vague, too, and I didn't give it an awful lot of thought. Emotionally, I was primarily concentrating on the job to be done.

Iron Bottom and the candy that day was almost the "last straw." The dignity of each individual soul was being attacked from every direction at once, not to mention the strange assault from within.

I wrote Mark and mentioned it, and a few weeks later received a letter:

> *Dak To, VN*
> *26 Aug 1967*

Dear Lynn,
   Was pleased to receive your letter and know you are still raising hell with everyone at the 91st. As if my candy would ever give anyone worms.
   Am in the middle of a two-week operation right now up in some ungodly mountains. Leg has

*given me no problems, so I count myself among
the cured. Another startling success for the 91st.*

*Have a man named Hunt in my platoon who
was at the 91st three times already. He liked it
almost as much as I did, and he never even swam
in the South China Sea.*

*A day out here goes pretty fast, but I can't seem
to accumulate very many of them. It's still nine
months and days. Perhaps I'll never go home. But
if you keep drinking to a short war and get all
your friends to, perhaps I will yet.*

*Hope you are enjoying your newfound rank and
status as a 1st Lt.*

*To A Short War,
Mark*

There was a little girl in the first row of cots on the
children's ward, right in front of the nurse's desk. She had
third-degree burns over most of her body. All things considered, she was doing fairly well. Except she wouldn't eat,
and she was a brat . . . a real brat, about six years old. My
heart went out to her, not only because she was so hideously
burned, but because I knew what it was like to be a brat,
having been pretty much of one myself.

It was critical for her to eat. She had to have her nutrition
for the healing processes to operate properly. We tried
everything. The interpreter came, time after time. Some of
the mama-sans brought food from home. The mess hall
cooked rice. But she was incorrigible. I knew a confrontation was coming. It was like two speeding locomotives on a
collision course. And, as badly as I didn't want it to happen,
I knew it was going to . . . she would *not* eat!

I believe in spanking children—spanking, not beating.
But someone else's child, and a burned one at that? The
idea was revolting. Yet when the time was right, I didn't
hesitate. Her bottom was one of the few places not burned,
that, and part of her back.

It scared her pretty badly, and nothing could have convinced me that I was not going to burn in hell for eternity

for a few minutes afterward, but it worked wonders. And it bonded us together in a way I will probably never understand, and certainly could never begin to adequately explain.

Shortly after that, we started letting her stand up for a few seconds several times a day. Poor little thing, she would stand there and shake like someone with malaria having a chill. It frightened her, and it was a terrible strain on her body. She needed desperately to be held, but there was no place to touch her—a terrible form of isolation, especially for a child. Something in me was crying out to hold her as much as she was crying to be held. Finally, one night when everything was quiet, I got her up and got her balanced on my lap on her bottom, and it was pretty comfortable.

I believe there was a big, high-backed rocking chair on the ward, but I don't see how there could have been. They weren't army-issue. It may have been only a straight chair. But you don't have to have a rocking chair to rock. We rocked and rocked, many nights. And talked, and sang songs. Neither one of us understood a word the other was saying, but we were very busy communicating.

We sang, "Good morning, good morning, the best to you each morning. With a K E double L, O double Good Good, KELLOGG'S best to you." And "Jesus loves me, this I know, for the Bible tells me so," probably the most profound theological statement anyone ever made. And "Slow down, you move too fast, got to make the morning last . . . doodle do do, and feeling groovy." She was smelly and oozy, and she gave me a rash on my legs.

I remember saying, " 'The time has come,' the Walrus said, 'To talk of many things: Of shoes—and ships—and sealing wax—Of cabbages—and kings—And why the sea is boiling hot—and whether pigs have wings.' " It wasn't just nonsense, it meant something. It seemed to symbolize what I was hoping for them, " . . . of shoes—and ships—and sealing wax . . . don't lose your sense of the wonder of life . . . Of cabbages and kings . . . especially for the ordinary things, they may be all you ever have . . . be able to be children while you are children." I wondered if she had already lost it. We studied each other's faces, and there seemed to be a spark of it left. I held on for both of us.

So many of the children of Vietnam were so very, very old. I couldn't realistically hope for much more. Things were awfully basic, and life was very much in the here and now. Maybe even such a simple hope was unrealistic, and to hold them back from early maturity would have done them a disservice. They had to grow up fast to survive. Yet I couldn't help hoping that just for now they could be children.

The children were all thrilled that the little girl could get up and be held (that's just how they were). Although they often clamored for attention, even some of the younger ones understood she needed a little extra time. That first night, they "oohed" and "aahed" for quite a while as we sat and rocked.

I would sit there, rocking back and forth or sometimes rubbing the little unburned place on her back until she went to sleep, with the night sounds and echoes of war, frogs and artillery, and damp air all around us, thinking *Maybe someday it will all be worth it. Communism is worse than war, slavery is worse than war.* I was thankful for the damp air, feeling that it was better for her burns (any little thing to help). She was pretty messy, and the smell was sickening. I can still recall it and it makes me nauseous even now, but it wasn't the first thing I remembered. The first thing was her face, how she seemed to "struggle" for every moment, and when she could ever get to sleep, it would be "almost peaceful."

I would think about Mark. I remembered standing in the door of the ward feeling paralyzed, the kiss on the forehead, "Goodbye," and watching him walk away in those awful, wrinkled fatigues, feeling like part of me had died. For those few weeks, he had been my life. It had been good enough to last a lifetime. He *had* to make it. He had to live. I prayed. I trusted. Trust came easy around the children; I just "copied" them. I thought about how he always drank to a short war, and how he had said, "Don't ever look back." I felt I was racing full speed ahead.

I would look out over the ward full of sleeping children. They had all been hurt so badly. But at least for now they were "all right." Nobody was having a bad dream. They were getting better. There was hope. Just like the real soldiers, they were recuperating, some coping with problems they would have for the rest of their lives, they had their strengths. Maybe all the suffering would be over soon. There was an awful lot to be said for drinking to a short war—and still a lot to be said for toasting "To Life."

13
The Zoo

> Life is real! Life is earnest!
>   And the grave is not its goal;
> Dust thou art, to dust returnest,
>   Was not spoken of the soul.
>
>> Longfellow
>> *A Psalm of Life*

It was the Surgical Intensive Care Unit at Tuy Hoa. We who worked there called it simply, "The Zoo." Max Cleland* wrote of it in *Strong At The Broken Places*:

"It was sometime the next day when I woke up. I was told I was going to the naval hospital in Danang for an overnight stop, then to an army field hospital further south. I slipped in and out of consciousness as I moved from plane to plane. After a trip in a C-130 cargo plane down the coast, a helicopter transferred me to a small army hospital in the Vietnamese village of Thuy Hoa.

"It was little more that a hut—and it was steaming hot. Two small air-conditioning units vibrated vainly against the heat. And the stench was almost unbearable. There were about 30 patients in the hut. I was the only American. The intensive care unit was used for both allied and enemy casualties. On my left was a silent North

---

*Max had lost both legs and his right arm to a grenade.

Vietnamese prisoner, to my right a glaze-eyed Viet Cong.

"At night, the hut temperatures plummeted to an icy cold. The swing in temperatures raised my continuing fever. At 4 a.m., following my arrival, the attendants decided to try to bring it under control with an alcohol rubdown. Convulsing with chills, I thought I was about to die.

"Morning brought a little relief in the form of fresh air. This was possible only during the cool, early dawn hours when the end doors were opened for a few minutes to dilute the stench.

"None of the pain I experienced was as intense as when a doctor decided to change all my dressings at the same time shortly after my arrival. Just touching the bandages sent agony flooding through me. Both thighs were as open as a slab of raw beef and my arm still had the bone sticking out of it. After a shot of Demerol, the doctor pulled away the blood-encrusted bandages one after another. It reminded me of a movie I had once seen when a cowboy was given a bullet to bite and a slug of whiskey while his trusted buddy amputated his leg.

"Despite my continued agony and the frequent drifting in and out of consciousness, I soon realized how strange this hospital was. The medical staff walked around like zombies and seemed far removed from what they were doing. Then I began to understand why. They had become casualties for the war just as we had. After breathing blood and death for months, they were victims of 'psychic numbing.'

It had been particularly affected one of the day-shift nurses. One morning I had been helped painfully onto the bedpan by an attendant. But he was gone, and I was ready to get off.

"The day-shift nurse was with another patient across the ward. I called to her for help.

" 'Do it yourself,' she said angrily. 'I'm busy.'

"Supporting myself with my left arm, I somehow inched off the pan.

"By Easter Sunday, April 14, 1968, the infection in my body was full blown. Six days had passed since the accident but my legs and arm stumps were still raw and open. My lungs were filling with fluid, and my windpipe had to be suctioned every few hours to keep the fluid from drowning me. When my fever reached 102 degrees, I felt that either it would break or I would die in this miserable hut.

"When a Vietnamese nursing aide took my blood pressure, he was alarmed that it had dropped so low and reported this to the physician on duty. An order was placed for blood plasma.

"Unfortunately, the nurse I had shouted at from the bedpan was responsible for setting up my I.V. feeding. Through an oversight she failed to turn on the mechanism that would allow the plasma to drain into me when she left to attend to another patient. Burning with fever and my strength ebbing fast, I called out to her: 'Come over here and turn this dammed thing on.'

"Her head shot up and she wheeled on me: 'Shut up and take a tranquilizer.'

"The hell I'll take a tranquilizer,' I spat. With low blood pressure and fever, I didn't think I could stand one.

"The nurse stood, hands on hips, and froze me with one of her looks.

"I fell back on my pillow and reached for the tranquilizer. Someone eventually turned on the I.V. feeder, but my fever soared higher. Other attendants aimed electric fans at me. Finally, they gave me an aspirin.

"I floated in and out of consciousness throughout the nightmarish experience. Desperately grasping for something to hold onto, I fantasized a congressional investigation into this hospital. 'I'll

have this whole hospital blown right off the map,'
I dreamed.''

As sick as he was, Max was certainly a very observant person. His description was so accurate that as I read, it seemed for a few rather frightening moments that I was there again, and actually jumped up to run out of the room—just to get away from it. I found myself standing on the front balcony looking out over the most tranquil lake you could ever imagine, with the most exquisite turmoil going on inside me. For perhaps the first time, I realized how very much the hospital at Tuy Hoa, and especially the Zoo, was in many ways a microcosm of the war itself, complete with all its distressing ramifications.

Max had intensely captured the spirit of it, or maybe loosed it in me. Whatever it was, the place did seem to have a spirit all its own . . . mostly malevolent. It was the land of body bags and booby traps—for sure. It was the land of dehumanized humanity (on both sides), the land of the ''Ugly American'' and of a confused and rebellious younger generation against an older, morally bankrupt generation. It was the land of ''the predicament,'' of the ugliest grossness and evil.

Human lives hung in the balance there, fighting for life, surely hoping somehow the pieces could be put back together again, although often there weren't many pieces left to work with. It was quite often a solitary fight, many of the patients being Vietnamese, isolated by the language barrier and aware of American resentment. Yet the drama of each life played out there might fill a book. It should have been a sacred place, but mostly it was a place of cold, efficiently-applied technology with little heart. And sometimes, the heart was there but not the technology. No wonder they call it, ''psychic numbing.'' Yet somehow, even that seems like an understatement. Body, soul, and spirit-numbing would be more like it.

My time at the Zoo began with a catastrophic event in the history of a patient on one of the surgical wards, an American. I walked on the ward that morning to find him having the most violent convulsions I have ever witnessed in my life. We rushed him to Intensive Care, and in the days following, an almost unbelievable story unfolded—frustrating, maddening, a maelstrom of events drawing me closer and closer into the Zoo, no matter how hard I tried to avoid it.

One of the nurses who worked in the Zoo was a friend of mine—in fact, Cathy was the first person I ever heard call it that. She had told me with tears in her eyes, "Do you know what they call it? They call it the Zoo—that's right, the Zoo."

It had something to do with a rather prevalent attitude that the Vietnamese were somewhat less than human, even more so with various parts missing . . . a collection of subhuman "freaks," I suppose. I knew she was often upset, even distraught over working there. "What is this about people not being human, anyway?"

She seemed about to break down. "I thought calling them 'Gooks' and 'Slopes' was just a joke at first, but it's for real, isn't it? I can understand hating them, sometimes I hate them—but they *are* human. What I really hate is the Zoo!" And she stormed out on her way to work.

To make matters worse, one of the doctors, whom I later named the "Sniveling Creep," was in the habit of waiting until the nurses were more or less helpless, incapacitated in sterile gloves in the middle of a dressing change or sterile procedure, and then pinching them on the bottom, etc. He and one of the nurses there were also "bosom buddies," and it seemed to adversely complicate relationships on the ward. It was one place I wanted to stay away from.

Every afternoon, Cathy would give me a progress report on the patient who had gone into convulsions, since he had been on my ward. He was in critical condition, and it seemed to help just to be rooting for him. Then, suddenly, he took a turn for the worse, and she doubted he would make it. The Sniveling Creep had ordered ten liters of I.V. fluid for him in twenty-four hours instead of the usual three or four. And, in spite of repeated questioning by the nurse on duty, he had insisted the order be carried out, even though the patient's urinary output was falling significantly below his intake. He went into pulmonary edema and almost died, drowning in the excess I.V. fluid. I wondered how much more he could take—certainly not very much; it seemed like a miracle he had lasted this long.

Then, unbelievably, the doctor began blaming the nurse who had questioned the order in the first place, and apparently getting away with it. It was a terribly ugly situation, horribly traumatic for the nurse, even though she had done everything humanly possible, repeatedly voicing her concern about the patient's condition, each time having to face the anger of the doctor. She ended up across the way, working on the prison ward, taking care of VC. It was almost as if she was being punished.

A few days later Cathy told me this doctor was continuing to blame the nurses for the patient's poor condition, forbidding all but his favorite nurse from going near him. They were pulling nurses from the other wards to take care of him at night. She advised me that if I was asked, to try and get out of it because the doctor was looking for a scapegoat.

All the nurses were scared, realizing that if the patient died, whoever was on duty at the time would have hell to pay.

Sure enough, the very next day, COL Swarther asked me to "special" the patient that night. We were walking through deep sand ruts again, in blazing heat. I remember my heart beating fast and my face feeling extra hot as I refused. I didn't know if I could refuse or not, but I decided to give it a try. I was really honest with her about it. "Putting my foot down," I told her I knew everything and had no intentions of becoming a scapegoat for the doctor, and tried very hard to give the impression that if anything happened to either me or the patient, Congress would never hear the end of it. It was a matter of survival and I knew it. Survival . . . it was something many of us were learning about, each in his own way.

I was mostly bluffing, I think, feeling I really had no choice, and was astonished at how easily she fell for it. I was beginning to understand how things worked, and was marveling at the revelation. *It was true* . . . they might as well have dispensed completely with, "To Conserve The Fighting Strength" and erected a huge sign to replace the hospital motto with, "Don't Rock The Boat—Under Any

Circumstances.'' Up to now, I had regarded the chief nurse as something of a puzzle, a rather weak character, but nevertheless someone who was surprisingly a silent benefactor at times, for reasons I will probably never understand. She seemed to have a certain amount of faith in me. Even now, as she asked me to special the patient in Intensive Care, I sensed her trust.

Actually, I felt horrible about refusing to care for a patient—especially an American. Under normal circumstances I would have been more than glad to do it. In a way, I was even sorry to let the chief nurse down—this whole thing had to be hard on her too. At the same time, I was sensing that although I now had COL Swarther's ''number,'' she also had mine. I had reached the point where it made no difference to me if the boat was rocked or not—either theirs or mine. In the past, I had made something of a joke out of saying that the middle of a war was no place to be playing Army, but it was no joke that some of their little games were hurting people, and I wanted no part of it.

I realized, up to a point, my attitude could be used for leverage; it had just gotten me out of a tight spot. What I wouldn't fully realize until later was that I was now a confirmed trouble maker, regarded as dangerous. But there was something about not giving a hoot about your ''precious'' Army career which set you free from all their mess, free to do what you knew was right, almost like ''floating '' above it all. I think it aggravated them to no end, although I meant no harm. The thought of solving even the most simple problem instead of covering it up seemed to strike terror in some hearts. But I wasn't responsible for their cover-ups or errors. It evolved into something rather ''automatic.'' You eventually fell into either one category or another. Either they could intimidate you, or they couldn't. And if they couldn't, then you bothered them. No matter if there wasn't, or never had been, anything big at stake . . . no matter if all you ever wanted was just to do your best.

Although I had managed to save myself from the schemings of the Sniveling Creep: I would not have to special *this* patient; I was unable to avoid being swept into the Zoo. The chief nurse told me she had no choice, I was to begin night shift there *immediately*. The male nurse from Medical Intensive Care would special the Sniveling Creep's patient. I thought they were two of a kind—it would probably work out fine! As far as I know, it did. And, as far as I know, no one ever stood up for the nurses who were having such a bad time.

I walked to work my first night, thinking about the nurses who had been pinched on the bottom, etc. I couldn't understand how anyone would just stand there and take it. Although I was a peace-loving person and consciously held the philosophy of "live and let live," I thought, *if that creep pinches me, I'm going to kick him where it counts!* And, for the very first time, I liked the idea of wearing combat boots! And then, because I had a mental image of what it might be like with instruments and dressings and trays flying, I also imagined hearing him shriek! In a very cool, intellectual sort of way, I liked the idea.

I recalled my days at Fort Campbell and how much I had enjoyed working Intensive Care, and was acutely aware of my feelings of dread for the Zoo. I wondered if I would end up kicking the Sniveling Creep, and how much trouble it might cause if I did. Theoretically, nothing should ever come of it—after all, the powers-that-be would be trying ever so hard not to rock the boat! I had not yet begun working at the Zoo, but already its threadbare nerves had touched me.

14
VC

"For my enemy is dead, a man
divine as myself is dead."

Whitman

I began working in the Surgical Intensive Care Unit (the
Zoo) in early September '67, the day after elections. I
particularly remember election day because we received a
lot of civilian casualties when the VC tried to sabotage the
elections. One was a pregnant woman who had been shot in
the abdomen. She lost the baby. She also lost the hope of
having any more children, an awful lot of blood, and a leg.
And she had some other relatively minor fragment wounds
all over her body. There were others in bad shape, too,
filling the Zoo with more mangled bodies. She ended up in
the first bed to the right of the nurse's desk.

On the other side of the desk was a Viet Cong. He was
little more than a skeleton, and his head looked like it had
been shaved, although I had a feeling his hair was like that
because he had fallen on hard times. He had been trapped in
a tunnel for a long time. What hair there was, was a
moth-eaten gray, and he had that distinctive look of accelerated aging, as though a victim of the Holocaust had been
lost in a time warp.

He had a long incision down the middle of a grossly
distended abdomen, and the distention was putting quite a

bit of strain on the sutures. They were pulling loose, and looked "weepy." There was a tube in his nose (a nasogastric tube, called "NG" for short) going to his stomach, which was connected to a suction machine. It was supposed to be relieving the abdominal distention, but it could hardly have been much worse. He drifted in and out of semiconsciousness, writhing weakly in misery and moaning.

He was the first VC I had seen so close, and I wondered how I would feel when I looked at him for the first time. I'd lost some friends (hadn't we all?); I think I was ready for just about anything. But after one look, I found I didn't hate him. Obviously, he was no longer anyone's enemy. I felt pity, and thought he might die, although we had a real knack for pulling through all kinds of hopeless cases.

I was the only nurse on duty. There was one corpsman. The male nurse from Medical ICU was there, sitting with the American who had almost died, but he wasn't speaking to me, apparently still angry at me for turning down his proposition! There were several other Americans, thankfully past the stage in which you feel compelled to worry about them (as though it was some essential part of the therapeutic regimen). One had lost a leg, another had extensive chest wounds, another a stomach wound. There were some in casts, still bleeding through the plaster, already smelling of infection.

Across the nurse's desk was an ARVN officer who had just had a very delicate arterial graft in his upper arm. The rest of the patients were mostly civilians. With everyone and everything new to me, and feeling that I was in "enemy territory," it would have been a memorable first night even if nothing extraordinary had happened. And although the better part of the night was spent caring for those many patients, the horror that eventually surrounded the VC has caused me to forget most of them and remember him.

His stomach tube failed to work properly from time to time during the night, but I had been able to keep it going simply by rotating it a little or irrigating it. Sometime after midnight, as I began to work with the NG tube the corpsman said something like, "This is what we usually do to make it work," and pulled and pushed it roughly in and out of the VC's nose (four or five inches) several times. The VC gagged and opened his eyes in a wide, horrified, glassy stare which may have looked something like my own by then.

I said, "You can't be serious! That's terrible! Don't you ever let me catch you doing that to anybody, ever again!"

He said he was sorry, in a way that gave the impression he was "only trying to help," an impression he had given all night.

A little later, as he was checking the tube again, I realized he had always done so with his back to me, blocking my view of what was going on. I wanted to see what he was doing, and as I neared the VC's bed he said, "This thing just isn't doing right."

I only had to work with it a minute and it began draining better than it had all night, but the corpsman said, "It's not draining fast enough," and pulled it completely out of the VC's nose. He gagged and retched violently.

What on earth was going on? Was he spaced out on something or what? The head nurse had said that he was *dependable*. I couldn't believe he had the nerve to do it right in front of me. If he was spaced out, he still had his wits about him enough to realize how angry I was; he went to get a new tube before I could find words to adequately express my exasperation. As he walked away, he seemed fine, even stopping to see about a patient who had moved almost imperceptibly as he passed by. All I needed was a problem like this on my first night. I decided to bring it up with the head nurse the next morning, as my shift was almost over.

The corpsman was holding the VC in a sitting position as I tried to put a new tube down. Just when the tube was most likely to penetrate a lung, he laid him back down, and it did. By then the VC was exhausted, and I wasn't sure the whole thing wasn't going to kill him right there and then. There had been so much manipulation of the tube that his nasal passages were bleeding. I finally got the tube down, the VC survived more gagging, and the corpsman kept up his "helpful" act.

I think I must have been in a state of shock. It had been a busy night, twelve hours non-stop, most filled with the uneasy feeling of being undermined. I kept thinking, *Surely I'm wrong, surely he hasn't been tormenting that wretched soul with that NG tube*, but in my heart I knew he had.

Memories of the sergeant with the DTs at Fort Campbell came flooding back, and of my saying, "This is a hospital. We don't mistreat prisoners here, believe it or not. We have our ethics." And I realized for the first time that as I cared for the VC, I had been vaguely aware of a prayer not even breathed, truly a hope against hope, that if we showed him mercy maybe *somewhere* an American prisoner would receive a little mercy at a time when just a little might mean a lot. All I could think was, *Dear God, it's not our job to kill them.*

Things always seem a little more hopeful when the sun comes up. I went through periods of thinking I had been mistaken, and was looking forward to the day shift arriving. However, my awareness remained filled with the sights and sounds of a gray skeleton with a huge, painful stomach, retching with what could easily have been his last ounce of strength, and of a blood-streaked stomach tube. I felt nauseous.

The sight of the head nurse walking on the ward put more of a damper on my glimmer of hope. From a distance, she looked like a fat man. Up close, she was a major—"rude, crude, and unattractive," with bright red, smeared lipstick and a very short hairdo reminiscent of some unkempt greaseball of the fifties.

As the major walked toward the nurse's desk, I realized I couldn't tell her what had happened or confide my suspicions about the corpsman. I felt she wouldn't believe me or even care. She already thought he was just fine, and there was no doubt in my mind that she didn't like me at all. It wasn't exactly a personality clash yet. We were both trying very hard to be tolerant, but I think we both also knew things were shaping up for a battle.

One of the doctors had come in with her and listened as I gave report. As I was leaving the ward, I felt compelled to try to get a little help for the VC, so I asked the doctor if he would mind looking at him right away, adding, "He really did have a hard night."

But instead of calling him, "the VC," for some reason I called him, "the old papa-san." Perhaps subconsciously I had hoped it might cause the VC to be seen more as a human being, but maybe it was just habit. After all, there really wasn't any difference anyway. We couldn't tell the difference because there wasn't any! But it was a *big* mistake on my part.

When the head nurse heard it, I thought she was going to have a fit. Her face turned red. She sputtered and then yelled, "*That*, I'll have you know, is not a papa-san, *that* is a VC!"

It struck me that she had had much more time to watch him suffer than I had, yet still, for all practical purposes had not been moved by any appreciable sense of mercy. After having "served" twelve long hours in the Zoo, I felt an overwhelming urge to put in a word for humanity. I said, "*That* is also a human being," and walked out.

As I trudged through the sand, I felt we had been tormenting something very close to a corpse, something with less value than a dog that might have been hit on the road and left to die. It had been horrendously gross.

There was a gnawing pain in my stomach, but thoughts of the mess hall and of eating only made me nauseous. I went to the hooch and tried to sleep, but the combination of scorching heat and distressing thoughts made it impossible. I knew what had happened was *relatively* minor, yet it was also the tip of an ugly iceberg.

I thought, *Is there any difference between communists' values and Americans'? I thought we were supposed to care about the individual person.*

I had read the book *The Ugly American* in high school and although I usually had a pretty good memory, I couldn't remember what it was about. I thought I remembered something about an old woman whose back was bent from sweeping all her life with a short-handled broom, and that was about it, except that there was something about Americans screwing up in foreign countries.

I tossed and turned and perspired, and tried so hard to remember amidst thoughts of wanting to break the electric fan which was intermittently blasting me with hot air.

Finally I gave up, certain that I would never read *The Ugly American* a second time to satisfy my curiosity. I had already met them.

It's not that I had any love lost for the VC. They made it easy for you to hate them, but better to hate than to dehumanize. It was dehumanizing *us* more than it was them. It frightened me. I didn't want it to happen to me, and I was already aware of the loss of some feelings.

It started with just trying to get through the days of suffering. Wounds had begun to seem "logical." If the diagnosis was "traumatic amputation, right leg," then it was logical for it not to be there. If the left leg wasn't there, than naturally the diagnosis would be "traumatic amputation, left leg," and it would be logical. When people shoot at one another, someone is bound to get hurt. This was, after all, a war. You did what had to be done, and feelings only got in the way. It wasn't because you didn't care, it was because you *did* care. It wasn't because you weren't human, it was because you *were*. I failed to understand this and felt bad about it for years after the war.

More tossing and turning. More blasts of hot air. The sound of dust-offs coming in—two, maybe three. I knew the VC were the "bad guys," cold-blooded terrorists to their own people. The end justified *any* means to them; nothing was too heinous. But then, it seemed nothing was to us anymore either. It's not that our soldiers were "baby killers," it was the attitude of our government. I believed with all my heart that if South Vietnam could have something even akin to "democracy," it would be better than communism. Why just yesterday, they had attempted to hold an election and we saw what happened. *Yet*, I was dealing with something kind of earth-shattering to me; something most of us in Vietnam came face to face with in one way or another . . . a knowing that America just wasn't quite what we all thought America had always been. And there was a shaking almost as if by the shoulders, and a scream from somewhere deep inside, wanting to know why, *why* if we are going to be no better than they, are we fighting?

At the time, I had no way of knowing how many others were hearing the same scream, or how long it would torment us, sometimes half-muffled, sometimes stifled, sometimes not. Or how many others were feeling the shaking of our world falling apart.

I must have drifted off for a minute, and my thoughts got all mixed up: with politicians who wanted a war but seemed to have a questionable attitude about winning it, and with mangled bodies and blood soaked bandages. With being a member of an expendable generation, and sweet sleeping faces—and screaming nightmares. With an older generation obsessed with clinging to "traditional values," but apparently quite often unable to remember why, or to live out those values with much integrity. With materialism and apathy and pettiness and selfishness and Army careers and don't rock the boat—and people hurting. With *clergymen* piously debating whether or not God was dead! Hypocrites. Why didn't they get honest work selling shoes! With losing blood and legs and babies, not to mention lives and minds. With "the predicament" and the cheerful greeting of a smiling eight-year-old on a water buffalo, "Fuck you." With human dignity and the Zoo, and the Major and the Sniveling Creep.

And with an afternoon on the beach that seemed very long ago, riding Gary Owen—my kingdom for an absolute! Then back again to a supposedly civilized, "professional" American nurse without mercy—and the finality of the way she had called the VC "*That*."

Confusion. Anguish. Anger. Disgust. Grief. I recognized it to be one of the true low points of my life. I knew it was a crisis; however, I'm sure I failed to understand much about it or to realize what a serious and valid crisis it was, or how universal.

I did realize I wasn't going to get any sleep, so I got up and sat on the front step of the hooch and watched the South China Sea. It was late afternoon! Another nurse, Patty, was on night duty and sat down beside me and we started talking. She said, "The club is open, let's go have a beer. I think you need one."

At that moment, I had no desire to go to the club and drink beer. She went without me. I wanted a drink of water, but couldn't get up to get it. I felt I might sit there for the rest of my life.

Cathy happened by, and I told her I suspected the corpsman of tormenting the VC, and about how the major had reacted when I asked the doctor to take a look at him. She said, "Oh, you really have to watch him. He hates Vietnamese."

Why hadn't anyone told me? Then she said, "We don't call it the Zoo for nothing!"

Patty returned from the club with a six-pack of beer, opened one and handed it to me. We sat there for a while talking and drinking it. It was good. For the first time in my life, I felt full-fledged rebellion rising up in me, a defiance which actually seemed to give me physical strength. And the beer was so wonderfully cold that, for another first in my life, I found it quite easy to go past two or three. I didn't care if I got drunk or not, and Patty kept handing them to me like she thought it was an excellent idea.

Finally I stood up and went weaving down the hall. Momentarily, a single word flashed in my mind concerning my condition . . . decadent. I hated what I had done to myself, and then I didn't care.

My friends decided maybe I had "overdone" it, and put me in the shower. I gasped for breath and thought, *What friends! How considerate to get you drunk and then put you in the shower!* And then I was saying, "I'm okay now, really I am. I'm fine."

So we all sat back down on the front step of the hooch. Actually, none of us were "fine," but you *might* say we were okay—just a little tipsy.

The crisis seemed to have gone away. It was all stuffed back down, somewhere inside. I'm sure we all sensed how dangerous moments like that could be. Two nurses had already been admitted for emotional problems. It was a very good year for bananas—they had to be "nipped in the bud." It was neither the time nor the place for distressing thoughts, or a crisis. Not the time to "scream, faint, and throw up all at once," no matter if it was sometimes the only truly appropriate thing to do. No time for grieving, either over a lost friend, or a lost stranger.

Patty said, "We have to be brave."

I said, "Yes, and cheerful, not to mention kind."

Cathy added, "All things to all people, we're combat nurses, you know."

"It sounds more like the Girl Scouts to me," I replied. "What am I doing in the Army anyway—I didn't even *like* the Girl Scouts. I remember the first hiking trip I ever went on. I got a tick in my belly button. It was the *last* hike I ever went on."

"The problem with you is that you hang *too* loose. Don't you realize where you are?" Cathy snipped.

"Just following the advice of friends."

"Do you realize that the security of this hospital is deplorable?"

"I never thought about it. What good does it do to worry?"

"Haven't you heard the patients on the wards talking about all the large units in the area?" Cathy chided me.

"I haven't been on the wards."

"Well, believe me, we're sitting ducks. The only reason we haven't been mortared is because they haven't felt like it. What would you do right now if some VC burst in here?"

"I think we'd sit right here and die. I can't even walk and we don't know how to fight. What do you think *you* would do?"

"We shouldn't give up without a fight."

By then, she was wearing her helmet, as though to prove her point, and was demonstrating how we could use a broomstick to jab a VC in the stomach. We were dying laughing, and she was dead serious. We said, "What makes you think some VC might burst in?"

"Who do you think those sappers were who got through the other night?"

"You can't really say they 'got through,' they caught them before they did any damage." I replied calmly.

"They were only *yards* from this very hooch! *Ten yards at the most!*"

And then Cathy continued with a plan to string some cans with pebbles in the door of the hooch to warn us when they came in. We decided it would just trip the first nurse who came in the door. It was funny, and we were carried away by the silliness of it all to Ward 13, to reassure PFC

Somebody that he needn't worry. After all, if we were going to be all things to all people, we couldn't have patients losing sleep over the security of the hospital, which was reportedly what he had been doing.

He did have a point. The surgical wards had no sandbags. There was only one bunker—the one for headquarters! And the hospital did seem to be sitting there in all that sand, asking for trouble. It turned out he wasn't the only one who was worried.

By then, it must have been nine o'clock. The lights were out on the wards, but most of the patients were still awake. I don't remember where we found the brooms, but we each had one. We found PFC Somebody and informed him that he could "Sleep in peace because if anything should happen, we have these '*sweapons*' . . . not to worry."

"Sweapons?"

"Yes, 'sweapons.' In other words, if push comes to shove, we can always beat them off with these brooms. There's plenty for everybody. Your fears are *absolutely* unfounded."

Poor thing. On top of everything else, now the nurses had gone nuts. (It seems to me that we were all wearing our helmets by then.) He looked bleary-eyed, and thanked us very kindly; another sweet person. His face was so young but it looked so old, so serious. There was, I thought, an expression of resignation (I'd seen it before), probably to his place in the scheme of things—something like, "(Mine) not to reason why, (Mine) but to do and die." Nothing made much sense anyway, and there wasn't a whole lot he could do about it.

I know now, and in a way I knew then, it was sad beyond telling. Back then it was cut off before it could be appreciated, "Stuff it all back down and keep going," something like the emotional equivalent of "Take two salt pills and drive on," I suppose.

They weren't all as "old" and sad as PFC Somebody. Many were still caught up in the illusion, thought it made sense, believed in what we were doing. At that time, morale was really quite high.

So we took it upon ourselves to "reassure" some of the

other patients too, going from cot to cot. Bless their hearts, they were such dears. I'll never forget their faces, trying so hard to understand what we were telling them, and then understanding.

As we left the ward they were laughing, telling some of the patients we had missed what was going on. They thought it was hilarious that we had called hand-to-hand combat "if push comes to shove." A few were laughing so hard they could hardly get the words out. Silliness is so contagious. As we were leaving some said, "Good night. Thanks for caring."

We were a little more sober on the way back to the hooch, and decided it would be best to sneak back in the shadows rather than "marching" with our sweapons right past headquarters as we had on the way to the ward! It's a wonder one of the guards didn't mistake us for some more sappers and shoot us. We couldn't have done a very good job of sneaking.

People have asked me, and I've often wondered myself (although for years I didn't allow myself to think about it), "What is the truth about Vietnam? What really happened? Why?"

I think maybe the closest I came to understanding some of it was on a singularly scorching hot day in September of 1967. We were all placed in a no-win situation.

15
Red Alert

We had had them before—"red alerts"—warnings of immediately impending enemy attack. On the surgical wards we
turned out the lights and put the patients on the floor. There
were no sandbags for those wards; however, we were told
there would be, someday, as soon as the already overworked
enlisted men could get around to it. Since there were no
telephones either, we always got the message from a red-
faced, out-of-breath runner. The quonsets did have sandbags, which offered a little more protection, and there was a
field telephone in the Zoo.

As I walked to work that evening wearing flack jacket and
helmet, struggling through the sand under the added weight,
I wondered if I might look something like a mushroom. I
certainly felt like a mushroom. As I walked, I thought how
really primitive the Zoo was, yet this was "Intensive Care."

It was obvious there was increased enemy activity around
the hospital (explosions, mortars, small arms fire), but I
doubt that most of us understood the extent or seriousness of
it. We never received any comprehensive official information. If you didn't get it through the grapevine, you missed
out. And I was "hanging loose," being nonchalant. Noncha-

lant was the thing to be in Vietnam. Everybody was nonchalant... "It don't mean nuthin."

It wasn't until later that I learned there had been a massive assault on Tuy Hoa, and that the nurse who had said we were "sitting ducks" had gotten her information from a reliable source. (She *tried* to tell us.) All I knew at the time was that, in the words of the guy who called three times to warn us instead of once, "They don't come any redder. You'd better be prepared for anything."

The Intensive Care Unit was also used as a Recovery Room or "Post-Op," and there was a stream of new patients coming through; however, most of the "old regulars" were still there. The VC was there; the American still hovering near death with the male nurse from Medical Intensive Care; the woman who had lost her baby and her leg; the ARVN officer and Vietnamese civilians; plus a few other Americans.

There seemed to be a real subculture in the Zoo. You would hear the Vietnamese speak only a word or two from time to time, but there was a feeling that those few words said a lot. They definitely knew what was going on, and communicated. I was convinced that the ARVN understood more English than he let on.

Around nine that night, the phone rang and the voice on the other end informed me that we were having a red alert. Since we had sandbags and all the patients were seriously ill, I only dimmed the lights. A few minutes later, the phone rang again. It was the same voice, informing me again that we were having a red alert. I said, "You just called, remember, Surgical ICU, ten minutes ago?"

He said, "Yes, but this is a *very red alert*."

I thought, *What a kook. Whoever heard of a very red alert?*

About the same time, a red-faced, out-of-breath runner appeared at the door, gasped, "We really are having a *big* one this time," and disappeared. He made me think of Paul Revere.

There were two corpsmen that night. They left to get their rifles. (I couldn't help wondering if it was going to be the hospital commander's last night!) The corpsman who hated the Vietnamese seemed delighted that he might get a chance to shoot some "Gooks," although I thought I had sensed a softening in his attitude, and had not caught him tormenting anyone else.

The doctor on duty came striding through the ward looking worried, "surveying the situation," in flack jacket, helmet, and .45. He struck me as the kind of person who wouldn't have hesitated, it necessary, to handle the emergency wearing *only* helmet and .45! He said, "We're having a red alert, you know," as though he thought the patients ought to be on the floor. I told him we didn't usually put ICU patients on the floor because of the sandbags. Nevertheless, he left me with the definite impression that I should seriously consider it.

The corpsmen returned with their rifles. It looked like daylight outside with the white light of many, many flares. The phone rang for the third time. The guy on the other end seemed pretty excited, but I was getting a little exasperated. We weren't being mortared, and each time he called he only said, "We're having a red alert."

Then I would have to pump him for information as to why it was different from any other red alert. I felt I needed some more information to go on. He said, "They don't come any redder. You'd better be ready for anything."

I decided to put the patients on the floor. If we waited until the last minute, it might be too late to move so many and we might hurt some of them. Better to be safe than sorry.

There were some patients who couldn't be moved for any reason except "mortars coming through the roof." One was the ARVN with the arterial graft. His arm was in a cast, but even with the cast, it was risky for him even to move in bed. In fact, his cast was sandbagged. The American who was still very close to death couldn't be moved, and there were a few others. For them, we would just have to wait and "play it by ear."

I can't *really* say that putting all those patients on the floor was a "monumental task," but that's the description that comes to mind. We quickly put blankets, sheets and pillows on the floor, and then began lowering the patients down. Most had at least two I.V.'s apiece, plus there were casts and drains and tubes and machines and catheters, and raw, bandaged places to be careful of. Most were well aware of what was happening and why. I can still recall the sensation of arms around my shoulders as they tried to help us lift them down. We let them help because of the time factor. I was shocked at how light some of them were. The Vietnamese were small anyway, and with legs missing they were surprisingly light. Throughout the night, the male nurse sat with his patient and, I thought, smirked.

The ward was dimly lit, and we were whispering, as though not to awaken anyone, although everyone was awake! Being "all closed in," in the quonset with the air conditioners running, gave a feeling of isolation from it all. There was kind of an eerie peacefulness about it, heightened by the contrast of what was going on outside. Having the patients on the floor was, at least, symbolic of safety. And it was symbolic of caring.

One of the American patients said, "Listen . . . Puff the Magic Dragon."*

For a second, I had an impression of the ward as a well-run, mythical children's nursery with a sleepy little boy mumbling something about some dragon in a fairy tale that had suddenly become a little too real. But we all knew if "Puff" was out there, it was serious!

The corpsmen had a tendency to become preoccupied with the goings-on outside. I really couldn't blame them. I wanted so badly to take a peek myself; there just wasn't time. But it seemed like a good idea for them to know what was going on. I consciously blocked out everything except what had to be done. We worked steadily all night. By the time we got word that the danger had passed and got everyone back to bed, we were running about 30 minutes behind schedule, which really wasn't too bad—you could run 30 minutes behind *without* a red alert.

I was trying to catch up on some last-minute charting

---

*Puff was a C-47 transport plane with Gatling guns that could tear up a football field in seconds. (He) sounded like a big cow mooing.

when the day shift arrived. As the head nurse, the major, voiced her disapproval of my "lack of efficiency," I said something to the effect that I thought we had done remarkably well considering that we had to put the patients on the floor for the red alert.

The major looked at me with an expression close to contempt which, combined with her usual boorishness, was really quite something and said, "We're sandbagged. We *never* put ICU patients on the floor."

Then she elaborated for a while on the line they'd been giving us about "*even if a mortar round hits the roof, it would just roll off!*" Somehow, I could never quite believe that one! And I had never heard anyone say that you *never* put ICU patients on the floor.

She had, however, succeeded in making me feel like I had done the worst thing in the world. I suppose it was just the way the major said it. I felt terrible and wondered it I had made an error in judgment. But I knew, even then, that my conscience felt pretty good about it. Perhaps, in the end, that's all that really matters anyway.

The next morning after work, the interpreter intercepted me on my way to the hooch. She had a message from the Vietnamese patients in the Zoo. It was that they knew the major was angry with me for having put them on the floor, but that they had been terrified and felt helplessly stranded in their beds, and really appreciated it. They wanted to thank us for going to all the trouble to put them on the floor, and they had all agreed that "the major wouldn't have bothered."

I thought for sure the ARVN officer was probably responsible; he seemed so much more aware of what was going on than the others. But it turned out that it was the woman who had lost her leg and her baby. It meant a lot to me, because she was so totally miserable, yet she had thought of me.

I have a memory of walking with someone on the way to the hooch, thinking what a beautiful, quiet day it was, talking about the red alert. I commented that you would never know anything had happened from the looks of things. And they said something about the engineers behind us taking some damage. But I'm not sure if it was this red alert or another one. I asked a friend from one of the neighboring units about it in the club a few days later. He said, "You've heard of the proverbial 'yellow hordes,' haven't you?

That's all he said. I knew he was serious, yet we were all so nonchalant, and several days had passed by. It seemed longer; other things had happened since then. The really important thing was *the moment*. Maybe the moment was the only thing—"It don't mean nuthin."

16
Saigon

He that lacks time to mourn, lacks
   time to mend.
Eternity mourns that.

Sir Henry Taylor
Phillip Van Artevelde (1983)
Part I, Act I, Sc. 5

Sheets draped over legs in traction, and pulleys and sandbags and casts, and frames with trapezes were highlighted
in my peripheral vision by the light from my flashlight as I
traced around the expanding red and greenish circle on a
cast with my pen and wrote, "2200 hrs.," and the date. We
marked the bleeding through casts that way so we could
have some idea of what was going on inside. *Surely tomorrow they'll window this cast,* I thought to myself, but was
glad for the time being that I didn't have to look at what was
inside. There was apparently a large wound at the knee, and
with the smell and green drainage, he had to have a
Pseudomonas infection.

Some dust-offs were coming in with casualties, but I was
only vaguely aware of it. That sound had become about as
common as the steady drone of lawnmowers on a Saturday
afternoon at home, or the nightly artillery and mortars.

The patient was lying there, staring straight ahead (about
like he had been doing several hours earlier), in spite of a
pain shot and a sleeping pill. Quite frankly, his behavior was
bugging me. I had asked him what was wrong earlier, and
he had stared at me like he was looking straight through me.

Since he obviously had a pretty nasty wound in a place which could leave him disabled, I had assumed he was worried about it and had tried to reassure him. Why wouldn't he even talk to me? This was getting serious. Nobody else acted like that to me.

Nobody else acted like that. I wouldn't really understand it until years later. At the time I was too close to it, and it was my problem as much as anyone else's.

I said, "Do you need another pain shot? Is there anything I can do?" He only stared through me again and shook his head slowly, "no." Then he started to say something, but looked away. He was grieving; he was overcome with grief! I had seen it so rarely that it was the last thing to occur to me. I found out later that he was the only one left out of his platoon.

In August, I received a letter from home which said Bill Abernethy had been killed. It was unbelievable—one of the finest young men from my hometown. The second one now in a matter of weeks; first Richard Hood, now Bill. He had stopped by to see me not long before. I recalled Johnny Hayes' father trying to reassure my mother about my going to Vietnam by saying that Saigon was "the Paris of the East," and everything would be okay. I could see myself standing there with them at a party, with my heart going out to them because they were trying to be cheerful and brave, and something inside me was wanting to scream, "It's a war, don't you understand? It doesn't matter that Saigon is the Paris of the East!" And then I realized something inside them was probably screaming it even louder. Yet what could they do but try to be optimistic? (Soon Mr. Hayes' son would be dead, too.) And then there would be Richard Cole. One day I caught myself saying right out loud, "Why does it seem that war always takes the best?"

The news had been a terrible shock, and the reality of it invaded my awareness from time to time and made me feel bad, yet no one's death affected me like it should have. Grieving was a luxury indulged in by only a few. We refused to allow grief to invade our emotions, lest we lose our ability to cope with each new day of tragedy. (I know now that I shouldn't have been so worried about the patient who *was* indulging in it.) I kept feeling that I was speeding ahead with the events of each day. I was somewhat aware of an attempt to keep my emotional equilibrium, but it didn't matter to me if I understood it—all I knew was there was a job to be done and I had to concentrate my energies on doing it. I had never been at a loss for tears in my life, but I seldom cried in Vietnam. Fifteen years later, I cried about Vietnam for the first time. I think it helped, but it was *a little late*.

I had arrived on the Orthopedic ward one dusty, fly-infested afternoon to find the corpsman doing a skin graft. He was putting little pieces of punched-out skin into one of the most nauseating looking wounds I had ever seen. He said the doctor had told him that he didn't expect the grafts to "take" anyway. It had seemed so haphazard to me, and so filthy.

The personality clash with the head nurse in Surgical ICU was full-blown, and I had moved back to the surgical wards. Although the chief nurse was friendly to my face, for all practical purposes, we fell into naturally opposing camps.

It seemed there was always that unique, troubling sense of unrest at the 91st. And there was a feeling that if you had fallen into the opposing camp, just about anything might happen to you. I suppose it was the subtle "rule by fear," with that special "catty" touch that women in authority can sometimes add to a situation.

I wanted a transfer, but everyone said it would be impossible; others had tried unsuccessfully before me. I had heard that the 93rd Evac at Long Binh was a really good, well-run hospital and that the chief nurse didn't even have a derogatory nickname. It sounded too good to be true.

I went to COL Swarther and told her I was miserable, that I hated all the goings-on, and that I was usually a humble person, but quite frankly I was too good for a place such as this and I wanted a transfer! (If that wouldn't shock her into action, I figured nothing would. I felt like it was another matter of survival.) She must have thought I was nuts! The colonel said, "How would you like to go to Saigon?"

I didn't know if she meant permanently or temporarily, but it sounded good to me. So she sent me on a three-day trip "running errands" for her.

I went to the airstrip and caught a C-130 down the coast to Cam Ranh Bay and then found a chopper that was going to Bien Hoa. It was so absolutely wonderful to get away from the hospital, and I thought hitching all those rides was fun, but I saw an awful lot of caskets.

I spent the night at the hospital in Long Binh. It was raining "cats and dogs," there was red mud everywhere, and it was humid and steamy. I went to a party in the chief nurse's room that night. She had a big, black dog, and in other ways impressed me as an honest-to-goodness, normal person . . . not exactly "another one of the girls," but apparently not suffering from delusions of grandeur, either. All of the nurses I talked with said they liked it there.

I went to sleep that night thinking, *Please, dear God, get me transferred here.* There was artillery being fired over the hospital from some place fairly close by. It would boom and then make a reverberating, whirling sound as it passed over. The stability I sensed at the 93rd and the "super reality" of the loud artillery was comforting somehow. I fell asleep feeling that there was hope, and there was a sense of *outgoing artillery—all's right with the world.*

The next morning the sun was out somewhat, although the whole world appeared to be dripping from the rain the night before. There was a jeep and a driver waiting to take me to Saigon, where I was supposed to deliver a letter to the chief nurse there.

We drove south past rice paddies, clusters of banana and palm trees, and little houses. The road near Long Binh was busy with motorcycles and Lambrettas (we called them "Italian mine sweepers" because they were always hitting mines and getting lots of civilians hurt).

After driving for what was beginning to seem like hours to me, the traffic disappeared and there was dense jungle on either side of the road. Just as suddenly the driver, who was black, was saying, "We're lost."

I had always rather disliked comments about black people's eyes getting as big as saucers because I thought they were bigoted, but his eyes *were* as big as saucers. I said, "But we can't be *truly* lost, because we're on a road and it has to go somewhere."

He repeated, "We're lost." By then, he was probably thinking he had never seen a white woman with eyes that looked so much like saucers!

We decided to keep driving for a little while longer to see if the road came out anywhere recognizable, which was probably a mistake, but then nothing behind us had seemed recognizable. And there was not so much as a papa-san on a bicycle to ask directions . . . just dense, steaming, dripping jungle.

Finally, we came to a place called Camp Red Ball. Everyone seemed surprised to see us. I think they said it had something to do with the post office, but I have always wondered why a *post office* would be in the middle of nowhere. They gave us directions to Saigon and told us to be careful because there had been lots of VC activity the night before—in the area we had just come through! The driver and I looked at each other with our saucers, swallowed hard, and set out for Saigon again. I was wondering what exactly were we supposed to do to be careful. The driver said, "I wish I had another flack jacket." I was wishing I had several flack jackets. We were sitting on ours!

We made it to Saigon and immediately got stuck in one of the most remarkable traffic jams I had ever experienced, but I was so glad to be out of that "VC-infested" jungle, it was a welcome relief. The driver wanted to stop for a minute at a shop, and while it seemed like he was taking forever, a little boy about seven years old and I stared at each other. I think I still had VC on the brain, because all I could think about was the stories I had heard about children throwing grenades at Americans. It was the first time I had *really* been afraid of a child in Vietnam . . . there was something about him that seemed different; I never did figure out what it was.

The next thing I remember is waiting for the chief nurse in her apartment. I think we found her at the hospital and she sent me there with the key to wait for her. The driver went back to Long Binh.

It was about eleven in the morning and it was hot, but there was still that feeling of morning freshness lingering in the air. I was sitting on a couch in the center of a large room with a high ceiling, typical, French-influence, tropical, dilapidated architecture, with large windows and shutters. There were the most wonderful city street noises from just outside the window. It seemed ages since I had heard them, although it wasn't really... only six months.

The chief nurse arrived and read the note from the chief nurse at Tuy Hoa. As she read, her face became quite serious. She looked up from the note and asked me if I had written orders to do what I was doing. I didn't, but obviously the chief nurse had sent me with the note; she was standing there reading it. When I answered, "No," she appeared extremely concerned and said, "You are in serious danger. Stay here and wait for my driver to take you to the airport—and *don't* go near the window."

How could I possibly be in danger? I didn't feel like I was in any danger. There was such a feeling of unreality about it; I couldn't seem to get a grip on what she had just said, and she had made the statement in a way which made me feel quite certain that even if I asked for an explanation, she wouldn't give me one.

So, I found myself sitting on the couch in the center of the large, dilapidated, tropical-French-influence room again, waiting for the driver and listening to the street sounds, and wondering what on earth was going on. *Why shouldn't I go near the window? What could possibly be "out there?"* Suddenly, I remembered some nurses at Tuy Hoa who had been given permission to leave the compound and then were reported AWOL. Talk about paranoia! Did the chief nurse in Saigon have some special understanding of the chief nurse at Tuy Hoa? She had seemed genuinely concerned about my safety, yet obviously unwilling to involve herself any further. I'll always regret that I didn't insist on an explanation. I'll always wonder what the danger was. For a long time, I had felt COL Swarther was probably "out to get me" in some way or another. And yet, I do realize that there are often explanations for things which we have failed to consider, even when we think we have considered them all. There's a chance she could have thought I needed a "change of scenery," and honestly didn't realize there could be a problem. Anyway, I will never know. (Maybe she *wanted* the MPs to get me!)

I was sitting in the Ton Son Nhut airport waiting for a plane and talking with a colonel, and enjoying all the people and the fact that nothing had "gotten me" so far, and happened to mention I was disappointed over having to leave Saigon without getting to see it. The colonel said, *"I'll show you Saigon,"* and I forgot all about "something getting me." You can't be paranoid forever. We had the best time!

We drove down the wide streets with walled homes and large shady trees, and we drove down busy, crowded streets. We saw Tu Do Street and the Presidential Palace and the American Embassy. We stopped at a hotel for something to drink. I think we were sitting on a veranda, but maybe the dining room just seemed like a veranda. The colonel was a nice person. I kept thinking, *Amazing, I've run into two apparently normal people in the last 24 hours.*

I felt a little out of place in my fatigues, and after six months of wear they looked pretty bad. I thought men could get by with going to nice places in fatigues, but I felt uncomfortable. So I pretended I was wearing my light blue linen dress with the A-line skirt and apple green trim, and sandals I had bought for R&R. I had no idea that the closest I would come to wearing them in Vietnam was that afternoon in Saigon, in my imagination.

I wondered how Saigon must have looked before the war. Much of it was beautiful, even though it was filled with reminders of the war . . . street urchins, prostitutes, soldiers, sandbags, beggars without limbs, and an abundance of black-market sidewalk vendors. Finally I thought, *It doesn't matter that I'm wearing fatigues. It's a war, and it doesn't matter at all that Saigon is the Paris of the East.*

I caught a C-130 from Ton Son Nhut to Cam Ranh Bay that night, and had dinner in the Air Force officers' club. I had not been aware there was anyplace that fancy in Vietnam.

I think it gave me something rather like "reverse culture shock," but I sure did enjoy my steak, lobster and champagne in spite of it! That night I slept on a real bed instead of an Army cot, and the sheets were crisp and they smelled good!

It was a room that the Air Force nurses used who were flying with patients to Japan. There were two nurses using it that night. We wanted to stay up and talk, but we were too tired. Most of their patients were in terrible shape: burns, triple and quadruple amputees, plus just "average" amputees, head injuries, paraplegics, guys who had lost their sight, and everything else you can think of. They were both depressed, and they were so tired, they could hardly cope.

I made it back to Tuy Hoa the next afternoon, feeling I had flown "all over Vietnam." Everywhere I went I saw shiny metal caskets in stacks waiting to be sent back to the States.

I wondered if I would be AWOL when I returned, but I wasn't. And I didn't detect any unusual behavior from the chief nurse, but having been in "serious danger" was often in the back of my mind.

Tuy Hoa had always seemed like "the end of the earth" to me, but amazingly, friends often found their way there for a visit, and when they did it made all the difference in the world. I was walking to the PX one afternoon around mid-September when a jeep stopped to give me a ride. Everyone in it was with the 173rd. I asked if they knew Mark and someone said, "Oh, you must be Lynn Hampton." *Mark was doing just fine!* And they were friends of his. Two battalions of the 173rd had just arrived at Tuy Hoa, but not his. I knew I'd be seeing other friends though, and suddenly a jeep full of strangers were friends and I had the afternoon off, so we went straight to the club to celebrate.

I always felt it was sort of a sacred trust to party well with friends who were just in from the field . . . there was such an intense need for a little bit of joy in life, and to escape. There was important reaching out going on, to try to feel like a normal human again; it was no small thing.

One friend of mine from Fort Campbell, a captain, had had some kind of trouble and had almost lost his company.

He was the last person I ever would have thought could have a problem like that. And a lieutenant who had been an excellent trumpet player had been shot in the hand and his fingers would be stiff for the rest of his life. So much had happened to all of us since our carefree, confident, illusion-filled days back at the Little Club. *They* looked different, and made me wonder if *I* did. But for at least one night we were *almost* the same as we used to be.

I had a beer and then broke out the iced tea; there was very serious partying going on, and I knew I could never keep up with them. I also broke out a tin of bourbon balls my mother had sent in a care package . . . little confections loaded with chocolate and bourbon, *definitely good for the soul!* They were lovingly packed with paper doilies between each layer! And I saw a friend from home whose mother had been worried about him. Thankfully, he looked fine, so I could send a good report.

Between my trip to Saigon, and seeing friends, and hope for a transfer, there *was* reason to celebrate. I realized I still had quite a bit of the joy of life to share. But then "disaster" struck. I wrote home:

Tuy Hoa

Dear Mom:

The biggest news is that the 173rd just arrived in Tuy Hoa. I've seen friends from Campbell, and I've seen Brian Keefe several times. You can tell Mrs. Keefe that he really and truly looks great.

I've been working about fourteen hours a day and partying the rest of the time—like I always said, 'Work hard and party hard.' Although things are slowing down quite a bit because we've been moving a lot of the patients out to make room for the 173rd. We've always had patients from the 173rd, but seeing all those empty beds just waiting for them is terrible—it makes me weak and sad. But I'm glad I'll be here if any of my friends get hurt. I watch for them every day, and then we celebrate life at night—every moment of it seems so precious. They haven't made contact with any sizable force yet, but everyone seems to think that it's only a matter of time.

The bourbon balls were great, although I didn't get to eat many (a hint to send more immediately). I shared them with some friends. I was so tempted to be selfish—they were so good, but they are out there fighting the war, so they deserved to have them. A few days later I ran into the same group and they said they had been finding doilies in their pockets for days! We all got a good laugh out of it. But they told me something awful. They said they were pretty sure that—Mark would be coming to Tuy Hoa in November and that their base camp may even be moved here. With that I had a fit and tried to cancel my 1049 (request for a transfer) but it was too late. Oh, dear!

Love always,
Lynn

On Thursday, September 28 at 10:00 a.m., my transfer came through, only the second one from Tuy Hoa and in record time. Saturday morning I was in Long Binh at the 93rd Evac, feeling like a weight had been lifted off my shoulders.

I was assigned to Ward Four. It was a large ward—four quonsets in the shape of a cross with the nurse's desk in the center (four desks, actually). Two of the wings were for combat casualties, one was for venereal diseases, and one was psychiatric. Although it was rainy and muddy and ugly, one word exemplified Long Binh . . . *sophistication*. The ward had a refrigerator to store their thermometers in so they wouldn't get ruined in the heat (120 degrees is quite a bit hotter than the highest fever!). And the patients had cots with mattresses (and so did I). And someone had just given one of the nurses a hard time and the supervisor actually backed her up! I felt like I had "died and gone to Atlanta" (that's what Southerners do!).

Typically, I "forgot" about my friends at Tuy Hoa, and the 173rd and the terrible empty beds. I was concentrating all my energies on the here and now and the job to be done. It was great for getting the job done; I certainly wasn't looking back, but it seems that I was always speeding ahead like that, caught up in it all and leaving things unresolved.

17

"Whatever Happened to Baby Jane?"

> "..... every coming together again
> a foretaste of the resurrection."
>
> Arthur Schopenhauer

Although it was rainy and muddy and steamy and ugly at Long Binh when I arrived, I don't remember it that way. I remember a sunny Ward Four; maybe because from the day I arrived I fell in love with it, and the love affair grew until the day I left, and the rainy season didn't last forever. There were dear souls with true hearts working on that ward and even though it was often unbelievably hectic, there was real teamwork and an overall feeling of satisfaction . . . of things being done right.

Jean, the head nurse, had just made captain. She was attractive, with long dark hair piled on top of her head. Her hairdo made wearing her baseball cap nearly impossible, which I thought was wonderful. Even more wonderful was the fact that someone was always threatening to court-martial her for it, but it didn't seem to be a serious thing at all. I hated those ugly hats!

None of us were what you could call friends, yet eventually there was a very deep "knowing"—the kind of knowing that only comes from working with people under pressure, and an appreciation of each other.

The first few days I was there turned out to be sort of a

testing period to see what we were all about. Jean liked to have all the patients bathed, their beds changed, and their dressings changed before breakfast. I preferred to let them sleep. I think she thought I was inefficient, and I thought she was mean, but we worked it out. (Sometimes they got to sleep.)

One of the corpsmen made a smart aleck remark to me about something. I had been waiting for just the right moment to try something another nurse had told me about. She said, "If you ever want to blow an enlisted man's mind, say to him with a very straight face and in a sweet little voice, 'Would you please lock your heels?' "

He was the first one I ever tried it on, but not the last, because it was instant revenge for a loose lip. There was immediate communication, immediate understanding. I was among "patient-care purists" who weren't into playing Army any more than I was. (Neither one of us could have done much to hide the twinkles in our eyes!)

From that day, the joking started, and it was still going when I left. There was never any doubt that everyone was doing exactly what they were supposed to be doing. We were "all business," however, a casual observer might not have been able to tell at first glance. I always thought it was good for the patients too, to be in a relaxed, happy atmosphere. They really needed it.

The patients would usually have a radio playing, and it seems we were always hearing, "Slow down, you move too fast, got to make the morning last . . . and feeling groovy." I started feeling "groovier" than I had in a very long time. Long Binh was such a relief after Tuy Hoa . . . everyone was so civil. And yet the war was always with us. I think we were all aware that our joking was an attempt to keep our morale up. If something was too horrible to contemplate, we joked. If we were too tired to take another step and patients were still coming, we joked, and took many more steps. As time wore on, I was somewhat reminded of the guys from Graves Registration, except that we weren't weird or morbid. It's just that joking was better than letting it get you down. The shoe fit, so we gladly wore it.

A few weeks after I arrived in Long Binh, a letter from Mark caught up with me, forwarded from Tuy Hoa:

1 Oct. 1967

Dear Lynn:

Many things have happened of late—some good, some bad and, as a result, I find myself still fighting the war.

Two battalions from the 173rd are at Tuy Hoa or the environs close by, so you needn't worry about the safety of your hospital for a while. I had thought that our battalion would also be going, but they didn't send us.

About two weeks ago, received a pleasant surprise and was sent back to Bien Hoa to take over as executive officer. Really thought that the war was over for me and could become a rear-echelon soldier. But you can never tell about these things.

A few days ago, received orders assigning me to a new unit they are starting at Bien Hoa. A Long Range Reconnaissance Patrol company, more commonly called LRRP's. So it's back to the war.

Right now I am at Nha Trang observing the training at the special forces recondo school here. We'll be taking our platoons through it one at a time starting next week. I am not very happy about it because they have forced marches, runs, PT and a lot of other miserable stuff that I thought was left long behind me.

I guess getting off the line in this unit will be a joke. I'll probably be with it until I DEROS back to the States. If you hadn't warned me about my own advice of not looking back, I might be tempted to. Being XO was such a good job. But I'll carry on in that good old airborne fashion, and perhaps even "try harder." Wow! Sometimes I just about make myself sick.

Hope things are better for you at the hospital.

*Keep an eye out for my name on your patients'
roster. I'll surely be back now. In fact, I might
even start carrying my own zippered plastic bag.*

*Take care—of yourself and the patients. Say
hello to old Fichett for me.*

To a shorter war,
Mark

Bien Hoa! His new unit was going to be at Bien Hoa!
Only a few minutes from Long Binh. I thought for sure I
had been living right. It was just too good to be true.

Although it was obviously more dangerous than being
XO, I breathed something akin to a sigh of relief. That job
might not have lasted anyway, and at least a smaller unit
would be a little more autonomous, less at the mercy of
someone's mistake or the whims of some glory seeker. I
didn't know much about it, but I had been in Vietnam long
enough to have learned not to trust. Tragically, Dak To, the
largest battle of the Vietnam War, where the 173rd alone
would lose more than 300 men, was only a month away.

One afternoon a few weeks later, I was looking through a
newspaper from the States at the nurse's desk. It was the
only time I saw a newspaper the entire year I was in
Vietnam. I don't remember what city it was from; by then,
"the world" seemed so far away that it wasn't even very
interesting. And the ward was quiet for the first time since I
had arrived in Long Binh.

Suddenly *Mark* was standing behind me and I knew it
before I ever turned around, yet when I looked at him I
couldn't believe it—and the newspaper was shaking in my
hand! It was a sunny afternoon. To me, the rainy season
stopped almost immediately.

We went to the club that night and celebrated. It felt like
we had never been apart. The club at the hospital always
played lots of *The Mamas and The Papas* tapes. I can still
hear Mama Cass Eliot's clear sweet voice singing, "You
have to make your own kind of music, sing your own
special song." We certainly were doing that! (Later, it
became almost my personal "theme song" because I was
becoming more and more aware of whatever it was about

Vietnam which tended to make loners out of people.) But, for the time being, we weren't loners by any stretch of the imagination!

For my remaining four and a half months in Vietnam, fate seemed to be smiling on us. I saw Mark a lot, whenever he was in from doing whatever it was he did. We seldom talked about it; the war was a million miles away, and quite unimportant when we were together.

For me, so much of the good about Vietnam was at Long Binh, although you never could really escape the bad; they were always right there together in sharp contrast. It was truly "the best of times and the worst of times."

The psychiatric wing of Ward Four was something of a unit unto itself, with its own specially-trained corpsmen and a male nurse during the day shift. However, the ward nurses gave the medications and were in charge at night. There were two psychiatrists who were pretty nice fellows, and not the least bit kooky like the psychiatrists I had known in school. They had a little cubby hole of an office at the end of the quonset, barely big enough for an examining table, over which hung a stomach tube with a funnel attached. I was never quite sure what it was there for—maybe easy access in case of attempted suicide by overdose, or perhaps a deterrent for any thinking person who might be contemplating it . . . or maybe a decoration?

Most of the psychiatric patients were led in, dazed, filthy and ragged from the field, sometimes with leeches they were unaware of around the tops of their boots. They would be guided to a cot where they began several days of "sleep therapy," which was just that . . . sleep induced by drugs or the patient's own exhaustion. Most of them would probably have slept without drugs for several days, almost everyone in from the field did. They would finally wake up long enough to drink something and maybe to eat, go to the latrine, and then sleep for hours and hours again. Finally, they would have a little time to talk with one of the psychiatrists and, after a few days, would be back in the field again.

Sometimes they would talk with the nurses. Although the particulars varied, the problem was always pretty much the same . . . too much Vietnam: death and killing and horror and exhaustion; just worn out and worn down by it. And, of course, there were always the unanswered, unanswerable questions about Vietnam.

The stories which seemed shocking my first few weeks in Vietnam, were no longer even unusual. The "horrors of war," although not unimportant, can become repetitious after a while. There are just so many things that can happen to human bodies . . . brains spilling out, guts spilling out, human limbs on trees, guys hurt really bad, confused, dying and calling for their mothers. It's the price of freedom, like Thomas Payne's famous "Heaven knows how to put a proper price upon its goods; and it would be strange indeed, if so celestial an article as *Freedom* should not be highly rated." Most went to Vietnam willing to pay it. I ran into very few who simply looked around and said, "Eek! A war, let me out of here!" but after a while most of us started wondering if we were going to get what we were paying for.

So they slept, and told their stories and went on their way. Someone had understood. But we had all understood anyway, and there was nothing anybody could do about it. Sometimes I would watch them leaving and think, *It's not easy being cannon fodder*. They faced it like men, and I became aware of a growing contempt for politicians through the ages making young men like these just so much bullet bait.

Quite a few of the patients had been emotionally ill from childhood, somehow managing to make it to Vietnam before anyone noticed. The tragedies of their childhoods would break your heart, yet I was often impressed by the courage they displayed in simply facing life from day to day, let alone Vietnam!

Mostly, it was just Vietnam. If I had never seen it anywhere but in their eyes, it would have been enough for me.

The patients on the urology wing usually had gonorrhea (lots of gonorrhea), sometimes syphilis or lymphogranuloma venereum: a disease causing huge, painful lumps in the groin which had to be lanced. Every now and then there would be someone in the agonizing throes of kidney stones, and some were wounded in areas that qualified them for urology, but primarily, it was a VD wing.

It has always kind of bothered me to run into people who seem to think just because medical personnel know about the human body and different diseases, they have somehow sunk, at least part way, into the depths of human experience. I think it would be surprising for many to have seen, in Vietnam of all places, the professional and dignified way such a thing as VD was managed. I was about halfway through giving medications on the urology wing one day when it suddenly hit me, *Here I am, standing 'knee deep' in VD and not thinking a thing of it!*

When I first arrived, we didn't even have running water to wash our hands, just basins. It was probably somewhat of a health hazard with so much infection on the ward and open wounds, too. But by then, dirt had definitely become relative. It seems much worse to me now looking back than it did then. We just got used to it after a while. Later, Sgt. Howdyshell got us some jerry cans with spigots on them. It was such an "innovation" that they got to work and installed them throughout the hospital! It always bothered me, too, that in an area as civilized as Long Binh, the hospital (of all places) was so primitive in comparison. But then, priorities in Vietnam often seemed strange to me. It wouldn't always have had to be that way; luxuries abounded, if the powers-that-be had been interested in "procuring" them.

One luxury we did have was a television set, and every evening the patients watched "*Combat.*" At first, I couldn't believe my eyes. What was it . . . some kind of a freaky "busman's holiday?" Later, it made me a little sad as I realized something important was going on. Day after day they watched Vic Morrow and his heroes fighting their way through Europe, making progress. It was John Wayne and the movies all over again, something nice to think about even though we all knew that "John Wayne and the movies" were somewhere in Never-Never Land.

Christie*, one of the nurses I had flown over with, had

*Not her real name.

been transferred from Vung Tau to Long Binh, but I hardly ever saw her. She was working in the next ward over, which was Intensive Care. I ran into her one day on the sidewalk after lunch. One of her patients was a "basket case," had lost both arms and both legs, and hardly got any rest; it was just continual suffering, yet he was expected to live. And then she was talking about a prisoner on the ward, saying something that sounded like she had killed him, or was thinking about it. I'm not really sure, because by then I was momentarily "going blind" from the impact of what she was saying. And then she was saying something like she wouldn't hesitate to do it again if she thought the ARVN's were going to turn them loose to kill more Americans. She didn't say why she thought they might; she must have heard something. (I always thought they were more likely to shoot them than turn them loose!)

And then I was thinking, *Why am I standing here going blind? If I thought they were going to get loose and kill Americans, I would try to kill them, too. Why sit around waiting for them to do it, like they are doing in Cambodia?* Her face looked so cold and hard. I only saw her a few times after that, never for any length of time. We were different people now, only a few short months later. I did see her one night at a movie. Movies were shown outside, and there were some benches that felt like they were falling down because the ground was uneven. I got there late and was balancing on the end of one. I don't remember the movie, but it may have been *The Russians Are Coming*, which made me angry because they made the Russians out to be nice guys, while Americans were here getting all shot up with AK-47s—little entrance wounds, *big* exit wounds. It seems they showed that movie in Vietnam a lot—our own government!

But there was a news segment I will never forget. It showed Israeli soldiers during the Six-Day War. As the Wailing Wall was being liberated, they were running for it and weeping and praising God. I wanted to weep and rejoice with them, but I couldn't. I just sat there balancing on the end of my bench, shaken to the core of my being.

They had obviously won over insurmountable odds. Just as in Biblical times, *God had fought for Israel*. Something earth-shattering *was* happening! I think it did me more good than any church service I had ever attended. History seemed reconnected, and to me, something had happened like it should have . . . for a change. I wondered if God was with America. Maybe I should have wondered if we were with *Him*!

But I didn't have time to think about it much. Things got so busy for a while that I didn't even write home. My mother just about scared me to death when she threatened to have my name put on "the blacklist of the Red Cross!" Actually, I was running out of things to write home about. How do you tell your parents about a war . . . I mean, *really* tell them? Who would want to? And the "newness" had worn off; no more pages filled with what things looked like, etc. (And every spare moment was spent with Mark!)

After a while I began working the night shift quite a bit and the pace was a little slower, but sometimes nights in Vietnam could be more hectic then days if you had very sick patients; and a lot of the fighting was done at night.

Ward Four was closest to the nurse's quarters, so when dust-offs came in with casualties, the nurse on nights had to run to the hooches and wake up the operating-room nurses. *Speed was of the essence*. They only had seconds to throw on some clothes and go to the bathroom before working all night. If they missed that one chance to go to the bathroom, they just might have to "live with it" for who knew how long.

Many a night I remember running full speed through the dark, taking the short cut, *convinced* that I could jump the drainage ditches, and then falling in one! The landscape around the 93rd was marred with them: huge ditches about four feet wide and just as deep. It was always such a surprise, but the only damage ever done was my skinned knees and hurt pride. It made me feel terrifically incompetent, and there was no way I could hide what had happened because the knees were all out of my fatigues. It was something else to joke about, though. Even though I was getting a little sensitive about it, everyone else thought it was hilarious. The corpsmen started calling me, "LT Strac," strac being a term used to depict someone who was really sharp and "with the program." After a couple of months, I got to where I could jump those ditches *almost* every time. It got to be kind of a personal challenge. And it was no small thing for those nurses to have a few extra seconds to go to the bathroom! It's a good memory now.

Then there was Baby Jane, half-Vietnamese, half-American, eight or nine months old . . . one of the children from the orphanage. She was at Long Binh when I arrived and had been pretty sick, sick enough to have her spleen removed. And she had clubbed feet.

The movie, *Whatever Happened to Baby Jane?*, hadn't been out too long, and sometimes I wondered if we would ever think of her years later and say, "Whatever happened to Baby Jane?"

She was sort of the ward mascot, and she was very important. I knew it then, but now I think she was even more important than any of us realized. In a situation with a baby like that, you really have to forget about being a nurse and become a mother. You can't hold back anything, or the child won't develop properly. So we were all mothers . . . even many of the patients. It wasn't the easiest thing to be doing in the middle of a war, but it was one of the best.

Jane was doing something good for all of us. I'm convinced that it was much more than sentimentality over a cute baby. It has taken me years to learn enough to really understand it and for history to unfold a little more. Things we were only sensing with confusion then, have become much more obvious. She gave us an opportunity to make a statement about the value of one human life and we really put everything we had into it.

So, in the middle of a war in which Americans and Vietnamese treated each other as less than human, a very sick, discarded Baby Jane was precious and loved and nurtured. "*Combat*" wasn't real but Jane was, and very much in the here and now.

About two weeks before Jean was due to return to the States, she was standing by Jane's bed (the first bed on the urology wing, right beside the nurse's desk). She said, "I love her, and I'm not leaving without her." And *she meant it*.

There was little doubt in anyone's mind that when she left, Jane would be with her; however, we were all interested in seeing how she was going to do it, because getting through miles and miles of South Vietnamese red tape in two short weeks wasn't going to be easy. Jane just sat there looking cute, unaware of the momentous occurrence taking place in her life.

"Miles and miles of South Vietnamese red tap" turned out to be a piece of cake! All it took was a doctor to verify that she needed treatment in the States, *and a big enough bribe*!

By the time they left for the States, Jean's parents had sent word that they were delighted and standing behind her, and a service organization was already making plans to help with the expense of repairing her feet. It was a happy ending and a new, hopeful beginning. After all Jane had done for us, it seemed only right.

As much as they all meant to me, I haven't kept up with anyone from Vietnam. I don't even remember when COL Jamison, the Chief Nurse, left. (I hope someone in the Army had the presence of mind to give her a medal!) But once in a while I remember and think, "I wonder whatever happened to Baby Jane?" And I've thought that there are others, scattered all over the United States who, from time to time, have remembered and wondered the same thing. I'll bet Jane's doing just fine!

18

"Die and
I'll Kill You!"

Whomp . . . whomp . . . whomp . . . whomp went the med-evac rotors.

Whomp . . . whomp . . . whomp . . . whomp . . . *gurgle, gasp.*

"I'm a nurse, I'm right here with suction, I'm watching every breath you take. Don't worry." It was frustrating yelling comforts to a dying soldier under the relentless beating of the chopper blades. This one was gurgling and gasping for air through the slit in his throat.

His body was like a fat mummy, probably twice its normal size in thick bandages—the face was charred: twice its normal size *without* bandages. The patient seemed to have been reduced to nothing more than a monumental effort to breathe. He opened his lashless eyes momentarily in acknowledgment of what had just been said, then closed them again in abject misery, gathering what strength was left to blow a huge, thick, green glob out of his tracheostomy. *Slurp* went the improvised suction. The smell was pervasive and utterly nasty—the kind you somehow get all mixed up with taste. Whomp . . . whomp . . . whomp . . . whomp . . .

There were two of them, burned to crisps; even their lungs. And they would die, but not fast. I wondered how they had been burned, if they realized this was probably the end, if they had gone to Vietnam feeling that nothing bad would ever happen to them. Now they couldn't even communicate. They were dying, drugged and helpless in a world of pain.

I remember my mother having said once, "Medical science always learns a lot about burns in war time." Whomp . . . whomp . . . whomp . . . whomp . . .

Far too much! I thought.

A few minutes earlier I had been taking it easy, enjoying my dust-off ride south to transfer some patients from one hospital to another, looking at the scenery and talking with the corpsman. I'd had a busy morning. One nice thing about Vietnam was that nobody ever begrudged you a few minutes to take it easy if you could. They knew it wouldn't last long.

It soon became apparent that I was the only one on the chopper taking it easy. The crew was definitely "on duty," scanning the radio frequencies, preoccupied with responding to calls. I realized that I had thought about it all quite simplistically—take the chopper, pick up the patients, transport them to the hospital. But they were dedicated to speedily removing casualties from combat areas, and their minds were obviously on it like steel traps.

Before I knew what was happening, the corpsman was tapping me on the shoulder and yelling to my face, "Do you mind if we take a few extra minutes to pick up some casualties? I don't think it will be too dangerous."

I yelled back, "No, I don't mind." I always felt like nothing bad would ever happen to me.

There was more talking on the radio; a tense, rather worried atmosphere. I felt that they resented my presence. Nothing personal, just a complication. The corpsman was tapping me on the shoulder again, pointing out their smoke, when they changed their minds.

By the time we got the patients loaded, the guys in the chopper seemed impatient, to say the least. There was more conversation on the radio.

Both patients had two I.V.'s apiece. Since I.V. fluids for burn patients must be very carefully regulated, I had just finished checking their charts, computing the I.V.'s in drops per minutes, and counting each one drop by drop. I looked up to see the corpsman turning them all wide open!

I said, "Wait! Stop. That I.V. was perfect. What did you do that for?"

What happened next is as vivid to me as if it happened only this afternoon. I can see the corpsman standing there near the patient's feet; I was closer to his head. I can see the olive-drab canvas on the litter, and hear the I.V. bottles jiggling, and the whomp, whomp, whomp of the rotor blades, and how he raised his voice because of the noise. He was tall and thin and looked very young. He said, "I always turn all the I.V.'s wide open."

But it was the expression in his eyes, even more than the blood on the floor and his boots or what he said, which caused me to really understand. They told a story that all the words in the world could never tell. They were utterly serious and kind of wild.

I could have given a "mini-lesson" on I.V.'s, but the only thing that seemed truly appropriate to say was, "Oh." He didn't *need* a lesson. After only sixteen weeks of training, they did a super job—*"forcing" guys to live!* Dealing with stabilized patients was just totally out of his context.

We all had the greatest respect for the dust-off people. Everyone said you had a better chance of making it after being wounded in Vietnam, all things being equal, than if you had been in a traffic accident in the States. When seconds counted, they didn't lose many. When I got off the chopper, I'm sure they were glad; they didn't need complications. And I left with something more than respect for them, not so much for "minds like steel traps," but for hearts and souls like steel traps. I'll always remember that corpsman and his utterly serious, wild eyes. More than anything, I suppose they were saying, "Die and I'll kill you."

19
Ships That Pass in the Night

"So on the ocean of life we pass
and speak one another..."

Longfellow

There was heavy fighting somewhere and we had been so busy the day before that I was exhausted and decided sleep was my first priority, so I had gone to bed without supper. The next day, I overslept and missed breakfast and was too busy to stop for lunch or supper. When I finally left the ward that night, I had been almost two days without anything to eat. I was starving and the mess hall was closed.

I knew it would be useless to try to sleep feeling so hungry and decided to stop by the officers' club to see if I could get something to eat there. I climbed wearily onto a barstool, asked the bartender for food, and sat there in somewhat of a daze. I was scarcely aware of the full-bird colonel beside me until he took out a little book of poetry and began reading aloud. It was beautiful poetry, music to my soul. The bartender returned with half a bag of soggy potato chips and a beer, mumbling something about beer having nutritional value.

The beer and potato chips weren't helping very much but the colonel, who seemed like a decent sort, continued reading, and I was beginning to feel a little better. After a few minutes, he closed the book and asked casually, "How would you like some bologna?'' ''Bologna!'' I could cheerfully have given ten years of my life for bologna at that point.

''I'd like some very much,'' I assured him. ''I haven't eaten for two days.''

''Well, come on,'' he said, ''I have some right outside in my jeep.''

We left he club and walked over to where his jeep was waiting, his driver lounging, apparently half-asleep in the front seat.

''This will be fun,'' the colonel grinned as he helped me into the back seat. ''Just like a picnic.'' But the bologna *wasn't* in the jeep, and the last half of my sitting down was more of a *falling down* as the driver gunned the gas pedal and the jeep raced out of the hospital compound. I couldn't believe it! I had apparently fallen for the ''old bologna line.'' (I didn't even know there *was* an ''old bologna line.'')

With all the sincerity I could communicate, I told him I didn't want to go anywhere, but my words fell on deaf ears. At first, I was more angry than frightened. I was going to stand up so the driver could hear me telling him to stop the jeep, and to lend credibility to my threat to jump if that didn't work. But the attempt to stand up didn't work! My stomach felt as if it was turning to mush, all the strength seemed to drain from my arms and legs, and I felt light-headed as fear and the colonel's strength momentarily overwhelmed me. He was holding both my arms with a grip that left no room for doubt concerning his determination. Quite calmly, as though giving neighborly advice he said, ''Don't.'' Obviously he meant, ''Don't struggle, I'm stronger than you.'' I could see the logic of it; it would have been futile. But I could still protest.

I opened my mouth to say something, but nothing came out. Instead, tears shot out of my eyes and rolled very obviously down both cheeks. I thought, *Oh no, this is no way to convince him that I'm dealing from a position of strength!* For sure I was going somewhere I didn't want to go, and there was nothing I could do about it.

When he saw my tears, the colonel relaxed his grip somewhat and said, ''I give you my word, I really do have some bologna, you'll see in just a few minutes." Could he seriously believe I was still thinking about bologna? If I wasn't mistaken, I was being kidnapped. Yet I believed him. True, he had tricked me, but now he was giving his word and it made a difference.

Apparently the whole thing had been planned in advance, and I had to give them credit, they *had* pulled it off with finesse. The driver had done his part with uncanny timing—I hadn't even heard him start the engine. And I suppose I was thankful that, as kidnappings go, it was quite civilized.

I was hanging my head in silent anger. Even if I did believe him, I wasn't going to act happy about the situation. I regretted I didn't have so much as a purse to hit one of them with, and it occurred to me that one of those little collapsible umbrellas would be nice at a time like this. I had a mental picture of myself whomping the driver over the head with it. But then I remembered that "an officer never carries an umbrella." Where had I read that? Probably at Fort Sam Houston amidst all the information we had tried to assimilate in eight short weeks. No clue had been offered as to just *why* an officer never carries an umbrella—it was just seemingly a bit of trivia which stuck in my mind while something important was probably forgotten. Next, I imagined myself pressing a button and causing the umbrella to open in the speeding jeep. It would be kind of a slapstick thing with lots of confusion.

Just thinking about all this had cheered me up, and my intuition was telling me this was something of a boyish prank. And it *would* be good to have something to eat after all. I was getting the impression they were both trying not to laugh out loud, which was what I was trying not to do. I looked at the colonel with the straightest face I could manage under the circumstances and said, "That bologna sure better be good!"

We drove for fifteen minutes, finally arriving at a building where, on the second flood, a party was in full swing. I began to wonder if my "kidnapping" might be the result of a bet (it looked like it might be a wild group), but if it was, no one was letting on that they knew. I thought it would be embarrassing to arrive at a party against your will, so I tried to act as though nothing out of the ordinary was happening.

It turned out to be a fun party and there was plenty of food . . . including bologna! I think I ate most of it. But when it was time to leave, we discovered the colonel had passed out and the driver didn't have the keys to the jeep. Someone looked out the window and said, "You'd better find those keys. The last jeep just left." They searched through the colonel's uniform and everywhere else we could think of, but the keys were nowhere to be found.

"What am I going to do?" I wailed, "I have to be at work at six in the morning and it's almost midnight now. I'd like to get some sleep!"

"Well," suggested someone, "We could always call for a dust-off. They'll be glad to take you to the hospital."

"This is serious," I said. "I don't want to waste a lot of time talking about transportation. Surely there's something around here we can use."

"Look for yourself," said the guy at the window. There was nothing in sight but the colonel's jeep.

Finally, two of the guys who had been conferring about the situation said, "We can get you back. There's a shortcut through that field . . . almost a straight shot to the hospital. We can walk it."

"That sounds like a *terrible* idea to me," I moaned.

"It's the *only* idea," one of them answered adding, "Nothing to it!"

One of them was in some kind of recon unit and the other was wearing a Special Forces patch, which reassured me somewhat. I thought, *Well, they are supposed to know all about tramping around in the terrain at night or whatever it is they do*. I reasoned to myself that, after all, it was supposed to be a "safe" area, whatever that meant. They had their rifles with them. This would have been out of the question at Tuy Hoa!

"What if we should just happen to run into a VC out there?"

"We'll kill him," one of them said.

I felt like saying, "Well, please see that you do," but didn't. The other one said, "Look. We know what we're doing." He sounded so arrogant in a good sort of way, it would have been hard to doubt. But it was black as pitch and my eyes had not yet adjusted. I had to say, "Wait a minute, I can't see."

The next thing I knew, I found myself between them, being propelled into the dark, feeling at any moment I might run into a brick wall. But soon my eyes had become adjusted to the darkness and we walked along talking for quite a while. And then it seemed as if we had been walking for a very long time. I thought, *Right! Nothing to it. A straight shot to the hospital—only fifty miles straight ahead!*

I hadn't thought of it before, but suddenly I realized there was a chance some Americans might shoot at us, but when I mentioned it, they said, "Don't worry." Still, it was after midnight and I knew the general attitude was that anyone out wandering around after midnight was probably up to no good. They were likely to shoot first and ask questions later. I'd heard people say, "If they're dead, they're VC." Not a half-bad philosophy when it's either you or them.

I remember having placed my life in God's hands on the way over in the plane. I had done it with total trust and I was still trusting. I had always thought the sense of benevolence I usually just took for granted was because I had had such a good life, but now I noticed that it seemed more real than ever before. I felt safe and happy. I remembered something I had read years before . . . something about "after finding the hand of God, I trod gladly into the night." It seemed singularly appropriate. I was blissfully trusting that "goodness and mercy would follow me all the days of my life," when all at once the one on my left simply dropped out of sight. One minute he was there—the next he wasn't! We stopped suddenly and found him at the bottom of an old crater (it *was* a very dark night). The hole was deep— deeper than he was tall, and we had quite a struggle getting him out. With a lot of pushing, pulling, tugging and grunting, we finally managed to get him back to ground level. The whole thing was so hilarious, I started laughing helplessly.

"Shhh!" one of them commanded. I wasn't sure if it was because we shouldn't reveal our position to some "enemy," or because the man in question was feeling a little out-of-sorts at being the object of my amusement. But I was getting too tired to want to talk anyway.

I thought we *were* very quiet. We had been walking for several hours, and I began to feel as though we had entered another world, passing over some invisible line into silence and darkness. There was nothing around us for miles, although there were some lights in the distance. I began to envision the three of us as sailboats gliding quietly through the night on a smooth sea.

I had a friend in college who was talking about "ships that pass in the night," lives touching each other and moving on. I had sometimes thought, *That's Vietnam for you—lots of ships that pass in the night.* Suddenly I was seeing a parade of faces—people I had known in the past months; people I would probably never see again, yet would never forget.

It occurred to me that this was the first time since I arrived in Vietnam that I had had so much time alone to think. There was hardly ever any time to be alone, and when there was, I was sleeping. I thought about some of the horrible things war does to people. By now, I had my own collection of unforgettable memories: burned children, guys with arms and legs blown off, the old man who wasn't quite castrated, the VC who reminded me of a dog carcass. Yet there was something else, there was another reality... not just in my eyes, but in my heart. I had had the rare privilege of seeing some very good things in people. Not big, impressive things—just human things, very decent things.

I could see patient after patient, most with long rows of sutures. Some were such characters—nothing ever seemed to get them down. I remembered the guys who had removed their own sutures, and those who were in a hurry to get back to their units. Others were just nice, unself-consciously minding their own business, playing the hand life had dealt them with a quiet dignity void of any complaining or self-pity. I realized I owed much to those who had paid so dearly with their flesh and blood. And I was thankful for the atmosphere of real courage and optimism which prevailed where I worked.

I thought about the nurse at Tuy Hoa who had helped me write my request for a transfer, and remembered she had said that macaroni salad reminded her of everything that was good and pure in the world. I thought she was probably right . . . it reminded me of families and picnics on the Fourth of July. I thought about the wardmasters and corpsmen at Tuy Hoa who, in the face of ugliness and disrespect, had done such a good job and had "kept on keeping on" even when morale was at its lowest.

I thought about the corpsman on the helicopter with the serious, wild eyes who always turned everyone's I.V. wide open, and I could see the face of the patient who pinned his jump wings on my undershirt. I thought about Mark who had the elusive qualities I had named, "excellence of soul." I could see the patients on Ward Four with Baby Jane. Sweet, inspiring violin music might as well have been playing!

I thought about the ones so overcome with grief they could hardly talk and all the good things they must have seen in their friends who died. I remembered the ones with awful-looking feet who could have screaming nightmares one minute and sweet, sleeping faces the next. And the fevers, and the chills, and how brave everybody was. And it seemed my heart would burst for love of humanity.

You can get used to almost anything. The sky was beginning to lighten, and it seemed like the most normal thing in the world to be walking along in the darkness of a Vietnamese night through an endless field. Someone said, "It's 0500."

"Oh, my God, hurry!" I urged, although I couldn't have gone any faster if my life had depended on it.

We walked through the gate of the hospital compound just as the sun was coming up—five minutes before 6:00. They had, indeed, known what they were doing. We walked straight to it. I know I thanked them, but later wondered if I had thanked them properly; they had gone out of their way to help me. I had less than five minutes to get to the ward.

My boots were a fright. I stopped in back of the ward to try to clean them up a bit. It was the second and last time I appreciated those boots. I didn't have a single blister even though we had been walking for almost six hours.

I sat down at the desk, got out my lipstick and perfume from the bottom drawer, and tried to look normal using them. I felt as though my body was still in motion, but surprisingly, I felt a lot better than I had when I left there ten hours before. I wondered if it was the brisk walk in the cool night air, but decided it was probably the bologna . . . and good thoughts.

When the nurse on duty sat down to give report, I said to her, "Don't ask me why, just tell me the truth—how do I look?"

She looked at me quizzically and said, "You look fine."

It occurred to me momentarily that I didn't know the colonel's name and didn't even know where I had been. Not that it mattered. I was suddenly too busy to give it another thought.

At about ten that morning, the colonel arrived on the ward to apologize. His remorse was genuine. He told me they just never could get any nurses to party with them. I really did understand. There were so few of us, "our social calendars were usually booked up months in advance." To make amends, he offered to get me anything for the ward I wanted, so I sat down and wrote out a list.

I wondered later why no one thought to hot-wire the jeep. Maybe everyone had partied a little too much. There was a "craziness" about that night . . . yet, years later, answers to all the important questions—Who am I? Where did I come from? And where am I going?—would come clear and I would remember that strange night and understand.

20
Dak To and Darvon

> O Lord! that lends me life,
> Lend me a heart replete with thankfulness!
>
> William Shakespeare
> *King Henry VI*

On the evening of November 22, I walked past the mess hall on my way to the nurses' quarters. The aroma of turkey dinner cooking filled the still night air and brought thoughts of home and family and the meaning of it all to mind. Tomorrow would be Thanksgiving Day. I remember thinking how glad I was that Thanksgiving was an American thing . . . how "right" it seemed.

Early the next morning, we got word that casualties would be coming in . . . lots of casualties. Some new patients had already arrived during the night and before long, the ward began filling up with more.

Around midmorning the supervisor, a male nurse, came through talking with patients. The conversation seemed to be mostly about Thanksgiving and turkey. I was busy changing dressings and didn't pay too much attention until I heard the supervisor say he didn't see much to be thankful for, being in Vietnam instead of at home, but those words struck me with such clarity I remember doing a "double-take." A few mouths dropped open in disbelief and one of the new patients said, "We do. We didn't think we'd live to see today and a lot of our friends didn't." They were with the 173rd Airborne Brigade and they had been fighting at Dak To.

As the day progressed, a picture of the battle of Dak To began to take shape. Knowing they were terribly outnumbered, they had gone after the NVA anyway, three regiments well dug in, in bomb-proof bunkers in the mountains around Dak To: Hill 875; *a suicide mission*. A terrific battle ensued which must have lasted for about four days. One patient said they had heard a general on the radio giving orders not to fall back for any reason. (Even *John Wayne* in *The Green Berets* fell back!) Air strikes were finally called in, but the bombs missed the NVA and hit our troops instead. Two companies had been virtually wiped out.

A sergeant came through the ward talking with patients and looking for men from his company. He said, "Every hospital between Dak To and Saigon is full, I've been through all of them. There are only two men left out of my company."

I gave him some juice and he drank it like he needed it desperately, but wasn't even aware he was drinking it. He sat there by the nurse's desk for a few minutes and left. What else was there to be said?

After seeing their wounds, the term, "fresh casualty" sounded like a sick joke. The stories continued. If we had been blindfolded, the stories alone were enough to make you want to scream, faint, and throw up. Helicopters were unable to get in . . . no supplies. Casualties could not be evacuated. Men died who would have made it even after a day, even after two, even after three days . . . *four*. Without water. Without morphine. Living and dead alike were rotting. Tales of horror beyond belief. Helpless, they had heard the screams of wounded men being tortured and killed by the North Vietnamese.

At noon, when Thanksgiving dinner was served . . . turkey with all the trimmings; some were obviously in awe of what was happening to them. Not long before, they had considered themselves as good as dead; now they were having turkey and it was Thanksgiving. It was probably the most meaningful Thanksgiving any of us had had. (They say you have never really rejoiced until you have rejoiced with someone who has just escaped certain death. It is true.) It was overwhelmingly obvious that life, "only" life is cause enough for celebrating. Yet it was somber, and sort of "numb." There was a sense that we had witnessed something "infamous."

Late the following day, Mark telephoned. He'd been trying to get through all day. Only weeks before, he had been with the 173rd. I was sure it had to be an answer to prayer that he was transferred. I was so thankful that such a beautiful person had been spared, the realization of it was almost more than I could stand. He wanted to talk to some of the patients who had been at Dak To. He had heard a good friend, a classmate, was killed there.

That evening he arrived and we went through all the wards, talking with everyone who had been there, hearing all about it. It turned out his friend had not been killed after all . . . not even wounded! They told us he had done a super job of getting things organized and had rescued many of the wounded, pulling them back sometimes without a weapon.

It was such marvelous news, unexpected good plucked from bad, it was a little hard to grasp. I felt a bittersweet joy I can't describe.

Sometimes in the evenings after supper, the wards could seem so peaceful. Especially that evening.

When it was all over and I was finally alone, I wanted to cry but couldn't. My emotions had run the gamut for two very long days and were thoroughly spent. I lay down, I thought for only a minute, and awoke the next morning fully clothed, boots and all, wondering what had happened.

No one noticed at first, but in a day or two it became obvious one of the patients was in a great deal of pain, yet had never asked for a shot. He wouldn't even take Darvon, an analgesic somewhat stronger than aspirin. The thought of it actually seemed to make him feel sick . . . you could see it on his face. He had done a good job of hiding it, but something like that can't be hidden forever. I said to him, "I know you're suffering. You haven't fooled me for a second," and stood there looking friendly as if to say, "I'm not leaving until you tell me something."

He didn't mind talking about it. He said, "I just can't

bring myself to take anything. Every time I think about asking for a shot it doesn't seem right, and when I think about Darvon it *really* almost makes me sick.''

Then the whole story came out. He had been ''acting medic'' at Dak To because all the corpsmen had been killed. He had been there for days with a lot of guys who were very seriously injured. They had run out of bandages and water and morphine. All that was left were 2 × 2-inch gauze squares and Darvon. He said, ''Every time we got people on the LZ to dust them off we'd get mortared. I patched up the same guys three and four times just trying to get them out.''

He said, ''Darvon is real strong, isn't it?''

Everything about him was begging me to say yes. I said, ''*Oh yes, Darvon is real strong.*'' That night I cried—the only time I cried in Vietnam.

It's very strange. I can't remember if he ever took anything for pain or not. When I first started trying to remember, I thought he did. If it was a matter of talking him into it, he probably did. I've always been able to talk just about anybody into just about anything (and it would have been sincere). But I have the feeling I may not have tried. He wasn't playing some kind of a ''martyr-complex'' game. People with martyr complexes are usually somewhat superficial, playing for sympathy or to impress themselves or others. This was honest and deep. I think I may have decided to respect it and let him do what he felt he had to do. (One of the advantages of being young and strong is that you heal fast . . . physically, anyway.) For sure he was suffering, but physical pain (as bad as it was) was the least of it.

He needed so much to be done with it, to put it all behind him, but with memories like that, it was too soon. He was still fighting the fight and keeping faith with those he couldn't help (although he probably helped them more than he realized).

Darvon for him didn't stand for the relief of pain, it represented suffering. Maybe he had to experience for himself what it had been like for the others. Maybe if he could make it through being wounded with nothing for pain, he could look back on it and believe it wasn't as bad as it had seemed, or feel reassured that it was at least bearable. Who knows?

We talked quite a bit, but I can't remember his face. It's funny what you do remember. I remember seeing him on his way to the mess hall with two other patients a few days after his wounds were closed. He was using crutches, but he looked so strong and full of life on his way out the door. I remember that, and the back of his head, and my awareness of what he'd just gone through.

I wrote home distraught, and later received a letter from home which said the battle had been reported as a "victory." None of us then could have imagined that in the end, after years more of seemingly endless fighting and after future battles were fought and won, they would *just give it away*. I think I will never understand.

21
A Little Insanity Goes a Long Way

> "It was startling to me to find out that we had no military plan to win the war— It was a real loser."

> U.S. Secretary of Defense
> Clark Clifford, 1968

I saw a film the other day of combat in Vietnam—a "search and destroy mission." Afterwards, someone asked me what I thought of it. I had never seen combat in Vietnam, but I had heard it graphically depicted time and time again, and experienced something about it second hand from those who were tired and dirty and hurt—*for nothing*.

They all got on helicopters which landed in the middle of nowhere—with tall grass blowing. They fought their way through impossible-looking jungle for hours in heat that could literally kill, or sometimes through water chest-deep. Finally they were shot at, they shot back. A few VC were killed, a few wounded. It may have been a matter of days, I don't know, but they eventually got back on the choppers and left. There were more VC where those came from and more Americans where those came from. Nothing was accomplished, but the process was repeated over and over again *ad infinitum* for years, and years to come.

In addition to waking up one morning and coming to the conclusion, "This is stupid," there seemed to be an insanity about Vietnam you could catch by osmosis if you weren't careful. I think it all really caught up with me after Dak To.

I certainly had not gone to Vietnam in a flurry of flag-waving patriotism, it was more with a naively-calm sense of assurance that the United States was there to fight Communist aggression in Southeast Asia. But then, why were we put in a position of not fighting to win? Why were those in charge of the whole thing apparently "content" with the endless, fruitless killing? Looking back, I remember hearing an awful lot of talk about understanding guerrilla warfare, but I don't think most Americans, including our military experts, really understood it. The little guys in the rubber sandals made out of tires understood it. And I'm sure the North Vietnamese thought we were a bunch of naive fools. They were right, and we demonstrated it for the whole world to see. The only ones trying to fight to win were the American soldiers, America certainly wasn't. And after a while, the soldiers, sensing it, found themselves fighting just to survive. Maybe that's where the "insanity" came in, when each person realized it (some arrived knowing it). But, of course, the real insanity was in those who thought everything was okay.

In any case, Vietnam had an attitude of "anything goes," often the crazier the better. Maybe it was because we sensed the hopelessness of it, maybe it was rebellion. I was barely aware of it in myself, but I know I finally came to an attitude of having loyalty mostly for our own, which was almost nonexistent for anyone else.

For a while, there was a general on our ward. The doctors thought he had cancer of the prostate, and he was in the last bed at the end of the urology wing. His bed was screened off, so he was fairly isolated. I felt sorry for him—the lowest ranking patient on the ward at least had the support of all the others. He was there around December and January; we had some pretty busy times while he was there.

He wanted to keep his .45. Patients weren't supposed to keep weapons, but I didn't care if he kept it and, after all, he was a general. So we put it in the bottom drawer of the nurse's desk. He was afraid of being captured.

Sometimes I fantasized about it. I wondered if something happened and he needed it if I would have sense enough to know. I could see myself running to give it to him and falling down right before I made it, or really being a nurse about it and carrying it to him calmly on a little tray even though the ward was about to be overrun by hordes of VC. I might as well have been silly about it; after all, if you gave it much thought at all, what could possible be sillier than a general defending a hospital with a .45!

I wondered if he "knew something." And I wondered what it might be like to look up and see some VC coming in the door. I always thought they would come in the north door, like the doctors and the supervisor usually did. And I remembered the sergeant at Fort Sam Houston telling me if I ever needed to use a .45, it would be best for me to throw it!

Naturally, many at the hospital were in a state of semi-tizzy over having a general for a patient. I was thankful to have learned my lesson well about generals, at Fort Campbell! I think it may have helped us give the general better care. We *tried* to see him as a person, not a general.

The general had high-ranking visitors almost every day, and the supervisor was overly concerned about the cleanliness of our ward, even though our ward was always clean (clean, at least, for Vietnam). She *was* a nice person; I liked her. The pressure must have been getting to her because one day she walked on the ward looking extremely upset and said, "There was a piece of paper on the ground outside and I had to pick it up!" Horrors! All I could think to say was, "Yes, but our patients are well-taken-care of." And the commander of the hospital started talking about "beautifying" the grounds with potted palms. I suppose you would have to have been there to really appreciate the situation. The only thing which could possibly have beautified the grounds was a bulldozer. Otherwise, he seemed fairly normal.

Then one day, another general came to visit. We knew about a week in advance and received orders to polish things we didn't even know we had. Since the psychiatric patients were the most able-bodied, they ended up doing most of the work.

The big day finally arrived. The ward shone and the patients were proud of a job well-done. The general entered with an entourage, wearing starched jungle fatigues. I don't know why that impressed me so; it just never had occurred to me that jungle fatigues could be starched. Apparently no one thought to tell the general that most of the patients on the urology wing had venereal disease, and he appeared to be congratulating them! I was really enjoying it. I had missed Bob Hope, and thought *this had to be the next best thing!*

Except for those in sleep therapy, the psychiatric patients were all lined up in front of their beds, standing at attention. The general was making his way to their wing when the commander of the hospital whispered that they were psychiatric patients. He shook his head, "No," and left the ward, leaving them standing there with their faces falling. The rest of us were standing there more or less paralyzed in disbelief. I think my mouth was open.

A million thoughts were racing through my mind. I wanted to respect the general, but I was dumbfounded. I even tried to make excuses for him to myself. After all, some people are uncomfortable around psychiatric patients. But I think we all knew it was a *deliberate* snub, meant to communicate that he thought they were cowards, or something. I was thankful some of them had slept through it.

One night at about eight o'clock the same week, one of the psychiatric patients went bananas. It always happened so fast. I looked up from some paperwork to see a pile of corpsmen and patients on top of him, and ran to the medicine cabinet to get the usual big shot of thorazine. No matter how many people pitched in to help, it was often a very unnerving matter of trying to hit a "moving target," and wondering if you were going to end up bending or breaking the needle and really hurting the patient.

In the midst of the chaos, attempting to cope with the moving target, needle poised in mid-air—STOP FRAME. I knew that *I knew*. This guy wasn't crazy. He was reacting *normally* to Vietnam. He really knew what was going on. The rest of us somehow just hadn't quite let ourselves experience the intensity of the realization.

In a split second, I saw my chance and injected the thorazine, leaving the moving target crumpled at the bottom of the heap, sobbing out the anguish of us all. The patients and corpsmen were patting him, telling him it was all going to be better in a minute. But it wasn't going to be better in a minute, or even a year. I walked back to the nurse's desk with the empty syringe, feeling extremely abnormal. I thought about how many of the patients looked when they came in: ragged fatigues, filthy, eyes staring blankly. And I recalled the general in his starched jungle fatigues and wondered who was really in touch with reality, and who wasn't.

And, although it was all beginning to "catch up with me" around this time, I remember December and January as two of my happiest months. I got to see Mark a lot. It was all catching up with him, too. It was around this time he started saying, "You win a few, you lose a few, some are rained out, and *some were never scheduled*," and, "Money makes the world go round." And then one day, my precious friend, graduate of West Point that he was, who had naively drunk "To a short war," while I persisted in toasting life, just up and said, "You know what? This whole thing stinks. I just don't give a shit anymore." I felt about the same way. He was pretty depressed, but neither one of us were the type to be morbid for too long. I just got crazier.

One night in the club, he took out his pen and wrote on a ticket, "Illegitimo non carborundum est." It was Latin for "Don't let the bastards wear you down." I knew then and there that they certainly weren't ever going to wear me down, or anyone on my ward if I could help it. I still have the ticket.

His LRRP unit had a base camp in Bien Hoa, only about a fifteen-minute drive from the hospital at Long Binh. I have some very good memories of visiting there, and of driving back late at night in a jeep with a machine gun mounted on it. (Funny, I don't remember noticing the machine gun except on the way back.) I was always very much aware of the ditches on either side of the road with dirt all piled up. I always thought the conditions seemed perfect for an ambush. I never did know if I was shaking from fear or because I was cold.

It was around this time some of Mark's men fell out of

the McQuire rig (the canvas sling on the end of a long rope used to extract men quickly from the jungle by helicopter). I think some had fallen because of serious injuries, but in the case of others, it was a mystery. It seemed so terrible to me—someone falling just as he was about to make it out alive. I wished more than anything that I was an inventor and could think of some kind of an improvement, especially something to make it safer for the ones who were injured. We talked about it a lot, and I racked my brain (we both did), but couldn't come up with anything.

Mark tried many different ways, many different times to tell me he thought his chances of making it out of Vietnam alive were practically nil, but I wouldn't even consider it. I never worried. I *knew* even if everyone else in Vietnam got killed, somehow *he* would make it. So he would go out on ambushes and LRRPs, and in a few weeks he would be back and we would have some time together.

Every minute with him was magic. He was a sweet, funny, bright soul in a very dark place . . . an excellent soul. I'm sure there were things about him I didn't understand, but there was a deep beauty I did understand, and that was enough. I've often wondered about the elusive qualities of one person which can strike a chord in us when others can't. I'm sure it's one of the great mysteries of life—and who would have it any other way?

The general remained a patient on our ward for quite some time, and the state of "semi-tizzy" was getting to all of us. And although the insanity at the 93rd surrounding the general was relatively minor compared to the full-scale, political insanity pervading Vietnam, it *did* symbolize that insanity: priorities askew, death and maimings and heartbreak—some for reasons too petty to contemplate. And "fanny kissing at its finest" just wasn't our mission. Our first priority was *patient care*, and we guarded its purity with fierce jealousy. Compromise wasn't in our book, although we were quite cooperative when first things had to come first.

We needed something special. We needed somehow to make a statement concerning our position—one leaving no room for misunderstanding. So we had big "Ward Four" buttons made up in town which we each wore proudly every day. They were big enough for our motto to be read easily by anyone passing through. It was emblazoned across the top of the buttons—*Illegitimo non carborundum est.*

There were too many beds on our ward—more, we were quite sure, than were originally intended. They were on the urology wing, and the result was that the cots were so close together you could walk between them only with great difficulty. Theoretically, it was a health hazard—but what the heck, Vietnam was a health hazard! Technically, they were much too close together for Army regulations. The patients were jammed in one another's faces; they hated it. So we devised a plan.

For the sake of the supervisor, who was basically a very decent person, I regretted it. I knew it would "throw her off" for a while, but the benefits far outweighed the disadvantages. One night when we weren't busy, we removed the two extra beds. One of the corpsmen spent the entire night with a bucket of paint and a stencil fixing new numbers over each bed. We made a new patient census board for the nurse's desk that you couldn't tell from the old one, and practiced our innocent poker faces until the sun came up.

The big test would come when the supervisor made rounds and tried to get the patient census and number of empty beds to jive. It was fun—even the suspense was fun! We knew there would be trouble if we were caught, but it just added to the excitement. We never doubted our success! The poor supervisor left confused and too tired to care. And it was our secret, good for our patients and good for our morale . . . a little fun and craziness.

Christmas came. Christmas in Vietnam. What can I say? It came and went. I remember carving some little soap animals for a manger scene on the ward. SGT Howdyshell made a sleigh with reindeer out of a bedpan and some urinals. It was darling, suspended over the nurse's desk. It was a reminder of the time one of the psychiatric patients, who had been locked in the psychiatrist's office for safe-keeping, went a little more bananas than usual and threw a bedpan out over the partition. It flew out over the ward just like the "sleigh." There was a Christmas tree with pretty lights giving a warm glow to the ward at night; a glow that caused homesickness like you wouldn't believe.

I was especially lonely. Mark scheduled his R&R for Christmas, went to Hawaii, and then caught a plane home to see his family. I loved and respected him for it when I found out. He knew he might never see them again.

The best New Year's Eve party I ever attended was in Vietnam. Well, maybe not the best, but the craziest and most memorable. No, the best. It was at the LRRP unit with Mark. At midnight, all the officers shot flares, lots of flares, several different colors—red, white, green. They were in tubes about a foot long. You held the tube in one hand and hit the bottom of it with the other. I loved the feel of whomping it with the palm of my hand. It was like New Year's and the Fourth of July all in one.

We had all just gone inside and sat down when there was a sound that made my blood run cold. There was no doubt for any of us that something terrible was wrong. One of the enlisted men appeared at the door and said they had gotten some Claymore mines turned around backwards and had fired them at themselves; several were wounded. I felt an obsession to stop the bleeding, so I jumped up and started to run out. But Mark stopped me. I don't know why, maybe because I was wearing a pretty dress. He said, "You can't go out there."

I said, "I don't know why not. *I'm a nurse.* Don't you think I know what to do when someone is bleeding to death?"

But by the time I finished my speech, he had sat me back down in my chair and walked out the door like it was all in a day's work. After a while he came back.

The next morning I arrived on the ward to find all the guys who had shot themselves with the Claymores. No one was too seriously injured, but they sure were embarrassed! I thought then that if it had happened in the States, it would have been in the news as a tragic accident. Here, we joked and laughed about it; in Vietnam it was just part of the normal insanity. But in our hearts we all knew they were very lucky to be alive, and in one piece.

My time in Vietnam was getting short, and I was starting

to feel panicky. Mark had several more months to go and I didn't want to leave him. I wanted to be there in case he got hurt. I went to see the chief nurse about extending. She said it wasn't a good idea, "Too much stress." She had been in Korea and her hair turned gray there. It didn't seem like too much stress to me. "I am doing fine," I protested and considered calling the President of the United States to ask for his help! (My mother had always said, "If you want results, go straight to the top." She probably would have.)

Meanwhile, the LRRPs were still falling out of their McQuire rig. Mark and I were in the club one afternoon talking about it again. I said, "For crying out loud, can't you tie them in it with a piece of rope or something? I'll bet I wouldn't fall out of it." One thing led to another, and before I knew what was happening, he had arranged for me to give it a try, thinking it would be good for morale for a nurse to go up in it. I thought it sounded like great fun . . . I *knew* I wouldn't fall out of it.

When the day arrived, Mark was in the helicopter and one of the other officers was on the ground with me. We did it together.

It *was* great fun. To this day, when I hear a helicopter I get a feeling of anxiety because it reminds me of dust-offs coming in with lots of patients; but that day, was pure excitement. I liked the sound of the helicopter and the wind blowing my hair. While we were hanging suspended under it, hundreds of feet off the ground, I leaned way back and waved at the guy in the door (anything for morale!). They said he almost had a heart attack. I never told anyone, but I almost had one, too. For a second, I felt I had leaned back too far and was about to fall backwards! But everything was okay, there was an arm around me. He smiled, and I tried very hard to act as though nothing had happened, and then forgot all about it. I suppose it was all a part of the philosophy of "hanging loose."

One night, Mark and I were sitting on the couch in the nurses' lounge. It was getting kind of late and no one else was around. For some reason, he got up and walked over to the refrigerator, opened the door and looked in. He must not have seen anything interesting because he closed the door and then, very casually looked in the freezer which was right beside the refrigerator. He said, "Wow, look at this." The freezer was full of steaks, big steaks.

We sat back down on the couch and in a few minutes he said, "I wonder who they belong to?"

I said, "Oh, some colonel probably gave them to one of the nurses."

He said, "My men are out fighting the war, and we don't get steaks." I had often felt bad about the men fighting and not getting much of anything good to eat. Sometimes it was 1940s vintage C-rations, and not enough of those. He looked at me and I looked at him; we never said a word. We just got up and walked over to the freezer and started loading the steaks on the jeep.

Captain Price had left, the best head nurse anyone could ask for. Now I was head nurse. Not long after that, SGT Howdyshell got orders for another unit. He received them one afternoon and had to leave the next morning. There was no time to get a party together or anything. I went to the NCO Club with him that night. Nurses weren't supposed to go there, but it was all quite on the up-and-up, just a way to say goodbye to a good man who had done an excellent job.

Tet was just around the corner, and how I would miss them! But everyone else was on the ward—all the dear souls who worked hard and cared so much. If you had to go through Tet, there couldn't have been a better group. The new wardmaster, SGT Byrd, seemed a little overwhelmed by some of our craziness, but he was trying hard to adapt.

22
The Day Before Tet

"How frequently the last time comes and we do
not know."

John Waller
The Meaning of War

Toward the end of January 1968, two "very interesting"
patients arrived on the ward. They were from Bien Hoa
airbase, and were appalled to discover the ward didn't have
hot water (we didn't even have *running* water!). They
assured me they knew an Air Force colonel who had a water
heater and were "almost certain" that if I'd go see the
colonel, he would give it to me. Scrounging had become a
way of life for most of us, and nurses could get almost
anything they wanted, but in anyone's book, a water heater
was a prize!

Getting patients cleaned up could be a real problem. It
wasn't at all unusual for guys in the field to go several
months without a bath. Some had been in rice paddies
which contained human as well as animal excrement. There
was always the feeling that they wouldn't *really* get clean
until they were able to go to the shower. Using little pans of
cold water, it's surprising they did as well as they did. (I
don't remember any of us "worrying" about it too much,
though.) For those who were extensively injured or unusually
weak, we tried to warm bath water in "jerry cans" outside
in the sun. By afternoon it would be hot, but there was a

disadvantage in having to wait for it, and there wasn't much of it.

We really did need a water heater. It would have been nice for all the patients—and they certainly deserved it. One of the corpsmen was an electrician and said installing it would be simple, so my mind was made up.

The afternoon I had planned to see the colonel, the supervisor came through the ward and told me the MP's didn't want the nurses hitchhiking all over the place anymore. No explanation was given, but I should have put two and two together then.

We never received any "official information" on how the war was going. (At times, it was as if they were deliberately keeping information from us. During Tet, they never told us when there was a red alert, they always said, "Our alert status had changed," and everyone knew it meant we were supposed to run to the bunker.) But for some time, there had been rumors from the Vietnamese that "something big" was going to happen on Tet, the Vietnamese New Year. At first, I had thought our hooch girl was saying that Tet was something big, but that's not what she meant. I believed the rumors. I had heard them too often to disregard them, but I think I may have temporarily forgotten that tomorrow was the beginning of Tet. And I simply got the impression the MP's thought it was a bad idea *in general* for the nurses to be hitch-hiking (although it always seemed perfectly safe). And everyone thought the Bien Hoa-Long Binh area was very safe. Anyway, by then the "life-goes-on" attitude was fully ingrained, and I was prepared for Tet in that I was going to try not to be surprised by whatever might happen. It never occurred to me to alter my plans to be ready for Tet, and the lure of the water heater was just too much.

There was a little place right outside the hospital gate where there were always some MP's. I didn't really want to do something they said not to, so I asked them for a ride over to the airbase to see the colonel about the water heater. It stood to reason that if *they* gave me a ride it would be okay, and I wouldn't get in trouble.

After we got there, I found out the MP's couldn't wait for me. When I asked, "How am I supposed to get back?" they said, "Oh, you won't have any trouble catching a ride this time of day, there's all kinds of traffic on that road." (Instead of putting two and two together then for sure, and realizing it wasn't the local MP's, but probably some higher, better-informed source who didn't want the nurses hitch-hiking, I thought, "*C'est la vie*.")

The colonel was sympathetic to the need, but he wasn't exactly in a hurry to get rid of his water heater. I could tell right away it was going to be a challenge. I can't remember any of the conversation, but from time to time I was aware I was doing a good job, and congratulating myself. As badly as I wanted that water heater right away, it was difficult to appear calm and unhurried, as if I had all day. And I was anxious to get it as soon as possible in case there was any trouble catching a ride back to the hospital. *Finally*, he said, "Yes."

It took a while to get to the warehouse and get the heater loaded on a jeep. And then the guy with the jeep told me he could only go as far as the road which ran past the airbase. When I saw the road, I started getting a little worried. It must have taken longer than I had thought, and the "traffic" was not at all what it had been earlier, *to say the least*. I remember standing on the road beside the heater feeling very much alone, and beginning to feel panicky. (Even then, hundreds of VC were infiltrating the area!)

After an hour, a big truck came along. I was so happy to see it, I didn't pay too much attention to who was inside. The driver said they would be glad to give me a ride, but they weren't going past the hospital. By then, I wasn't up to taking a chance on something else—it was late afternoon! I thought about Mark's base camp—just down the road. If I could get that far, hopefully he would be there and they would have a jeep they could spare for a few minutes. The truck was full of troops with 101st Airborne patches on their fatigues. It brought back memories of Fort Campbell that seemed "long ago and far away," even though I had been there less than a year before. When we got the water heater in the truck and I had a chance to look at them, I regretted they had come along when they did. I had never seen human beings in such bad condition—at least not so many at one time. They were filthy. They were covered with dirt on top of dirt, overlaid with a layer of dust. Their helmets were caked with mud, and when I looked at their boots I hated to think what must have been inside some of them. And they looked so tired—their eyes were sunken, with dark circles—they looked dazed.

I wondered where they had come from and where they were going, but all I could say was, "I'm so sorry, you look so tired. If I had known, I wouldn't have asked for a ride. I'm trying to get this water heater back to my ward so the patients can have hot water." Someone said, "We don't mind. Maybe some of us will end up using it." And a few of the others smiled like they agreed. Those smiles really meant a lot to me, because I knew there was so much effort behind them.

There is an "aura of wretchedness" about war. Naturally, in a hospital you are *aware* of what they have gone through, but you can be well aware of it and still fail to fully understand that aura. It didn't linger very long once the civilization of hospitals or base camps was reached. It was there with fresh casualties in the shock and pain of being wounded and of seeing friends die in revolting ways, and the confusion and excitement of it all. It was there in the truck that afternoon. There's a terrible feeling in the pit of your stomach which goes along with it. I think maybe I wanted the water heater to help wash off the "aura of wretchedness" as much as the dirt.

By the time we got the water heater our of the truck, a small group had gathered to see what was happening, including Mark and his commanding officer, a major. I knew most everybody. It had been a very trying afternoon, but suddenly finding myself among friends caused me to feel I was about to make it, and everything was going to be all right.

Well, I *was* among friends but, a water heater is a water heater. I began to perceive that right then and there, I was about to lose it! After all, what was there to keep a friend (In those circumstances, even a friend would have taken it!) from just walking off with it? An emergency seemed to be shaping up; if I wasn't mistaken, the major was coveting my prize. He could have been teasing me, but something told me he wasn't. By then, I was in no mood to be messed with; just talking the colonel out of the stupid thing had been bad enough.

It seemed the major was working up to try pulling rank on me, which was ridiculous, but with a water heater at stake, I supposed anything was worth a try. I finally blurted out, "You can't do that, you're just being a smart mouth." I think it shocked him a little, but it worked. It put things in proper perspective and made it a little more difficult for him to walk off with it. The afternoon seemed fraught with perils.

We got the thing loaded on a jeep (for the hundredth time), and started out for the hospital. As we neared the gate, it occurred to me that all I'd been doing *all* afternoon was "hitch-hiking." I knew the MP's wouldn't be a problem, but I was a little worried about running into my supervisor. I was tired, and I wasn't up to another hassle. There was a piece of canvas over the water heater, and I got in the back of the jeep and hid under it. Mark must have thought I had taken leave of my senses. (I think I may have forgotten to tell him about the supervisor and hitch-hiking, etc.) He kept saying, "Would you get up from there?"

We made it to the ward without incident and since we were a little short on space, the water heater ended up on the examining table in the psychiatrist's office, covered with a sheet.

All hell was fixing to break loose in a few hours. I never did know how much of a surprise it was to everybody—I think it was a pretty big one. It was one of the last times I saw Mark. It may have been *the* last time—I've tried so hard to remember, *but I can't.*

23
Tet

Tet, the Vietnamese New Year, 1968:
Communist forces launched a mammoth,
all-out offensive against over 100
cities in South Vietnam, and every
major American Compound.*

"There it is again. Do you smell that?"

"PeeYoooo! What is it?"

"What is it and where is it coming from? There is
definitely something rotten on this ward."

For days, we had cleaned and searched and cleaned some
more. Since many of the mattresses were badly stained,
every time there was an empty bed we put the mattress in
the sun, but the revolting smell kept popping up at us like a
Jack-in-the-box to taunt us, no matter what we did.

The morning before Tet, a patient had come in with the
worst case of jungle rot I had ever seen. The skin was
peeling off his feet in long strips so badly that just washing
them was a delicate operation. I was down on the floor,
washing his feet, despairing that he would have any feet left
in another week, when there it was—that awful smell again.
But this time it was stronger; I knew I was on to something.
I dropped the towel and sniffed, and then did everything but

*(Even the North Vietnamese admitted they were defeated after Tet;
however, unbelievably, our news media was joyfully preaching the "Gospel"
of our defeat!)

yell, *Eureka!* "Oh, it's worse than we thought. PeeYooo! I found it! Somebody come here."

And, to the patient, "Get your feet up off the floor—the stench is in the floor. Our floor is rotten! We've got to clean this place."

In spite of regular mopping with disinfectant, apparently months of blood and drainage from infected wounds had seeped into the porous cement floor, and stains from the red clay had helped mask the problem. Sniffing like hounds, we put Mama-san to work with a brush and more disinfectant; then, to make doubly sure, she mopped and scrubbed again with a different disinfectant.

I told SGT Byrd I thought we should be scrubbing the floor like we did at Tuy Hoa. There we had a water truck empty a tank at one door of the ward and we would scrub with brooms and sweep it through and out the other door. He thought it was a good idea, too, so we had ordered a water truck for the very next day. After all, stinky floors on a surgical ward seemed scandalous . . . things had to be made right.

The truck, unfortunately, had just emptied its tank in the same door the two psychiatrists had simultaneously entered, and they didn't seem very happy about it. I think the water had covered the tops of their boots; it was pretty deep when they first dumped it. We were all working hard, trying to finish the floors as quickly as possible, and had forgotten about the water heater on the examining table in their office. A few seconds later, one of the corpsmen came out of the office laughing. Apparently the psychiatrists had mistaken the water heater (covered neatly with a sheet) for a body. (It wasn't hard to get "bodies on the brain" in Vietnam.) Poor things, they were having a hard morning; I think it freaked them out, but it *was* funny.

We were still laughing when an ear-splitting explosion rocked the ward, then a sound like tinkling glass. Patients dove for the floor, I.V.'s were pulled out, sheets were soaked as patients sloshed around in water. For a while, it was total chaos. The VC had blown up the ammunition dump down the road. Someone said later, "We started the holiday out in style, with a clean floor and a bang."

There were a few more relatively "minor" explosions after that, but Tet was such a noisy time I can't remember if it was the ammo dump or something else.

We got busy restarting I.V.'s, changing everyone's dressing *again*, and cleaning up the mess. The commander of the hospital came through to see how we had fared. Everyone was okay—wet, sore arms, a few bruises, but basically okay—no broken bones or eviscerations. Soon we heard the sound of dust-offs coming in. The psychiatrists were nowhere to be seen. I'm sure they must have left to help with triage, but it kind of felt like those who understood us best had finally given up on us, or maybe concluded we were all stark raving mad and fled in terror.

A baby was brought in unconscious with a gunshot wound through the head. The baby was dying. The only order on the chart was concise—"Observe." There was obviously no hope. The baby was accompanied by a five-year-old sister, the only living relative.

The little girl sat quietly with the baby for several hours while we admitted a steady stream of casualties. She must have been in a state of shock, but when lunch was served we put a tray down in front of her and she ate; the Vietnamese: bearing unbearable sorrow but surviving, always surviving.

Early in the afternoon, the baby stopped breathing. Another nurse and I went through the motions of trying to resuscitate, for the little girl's sake, so she could remember we cared and the baby's life was important.

The nurse's name was Donna. She had just arrived in-country and was so pretty that when the wiry little general with the 101st came through giving out medals, he always got her to pose in the pictures. And it was Donna who told me about Mark: "He's *married*."

What? For a second my world went a sickening, bleached-white. The ammo dump might as well have blown up again—in my face! The heart-crushing impact hit my mind with devastating clarity. Yet my Vietnam-numbed emotions handled the shock and horror as easily as they were handling the Tet Offensive of 1968.

Why on earth hadn't he told me? Tet was no time for

personal problems, I couldn't spare even a moment to think about it. But one answer appeared strangely clear amidst the chaos of Ward 4. I had been wondering why our relationship didn't seem to be progressing normally. I was not an aggressive person, and had been waiting for Mark to set the pace, determined not to be possessive. Here was the answer.

Things had happened so fast—a relationship neither one of us could have foreseen—for him, on the perilous and lonely brink of eternity. Out of respect for his wife, and me, it couldn't have gone any farther.

I loved him so much, I would gladly have died for him, but the last thing in the world I wanted was to be in love with a married man. I didn't want to sin (and I owed myself better than that). In a way, I knew I would always love him, but that love changed in a heartbeat. I was totally numb as I replied, ''Well then . . . it's over.''

In less than thirty seconds the conversation was concluded, as we rushed to admit some new casualties coming in the door. ''Fare well, dear friend,'' was suddenly, and forever, ''Farewell, dear friend.'' Dear friend. It was over.

A doctor pronounced the baby dead and said, ''When you take the baby to Dispositions, take the little girl there, too. They'll know what to do with her.''

I thought, *Only a month to go and I'll be home, and by this time tomorrow I'll be in Bangkok.*

I was planning to meet friends and had scheduled my R&R late in my tour to have something to look forward to.

Things seemed to be slacking off a little, and I decided to take the little girl to Dispositions myself.

I wrapped the baby in a towel, took the little girl by the hand, and walked outside. The afternoon was bright-hot, dry, strangely still. With the exception of dust-offs coming in and others hanging suspended in heat waves, not a soul was in sight—they were all inside working like crazy! This was going to be more than a hard day!

Great billows of black smoke were rising from the ammo dump and from other areas around Long Binh. There was a sense of desolation as well as destruction. The scene reminded me of those weird modern paintings which always have something out of place and try to scream at you from the canvas that life is utterly meaningless and man will eventually exterminate himself—and that will be that.

I felt empty, kind of like feeling nothing, intensely. For some reason, it was like the end of the world. I was ready for Tet, I wasn't surprised; though none of us knew then that this was "the Tet Offensive of 1968." It was the same death and carnage—only more of it.

I looked down at the little girl trudging along beside me, and thought perhaps I understood. Although the day had rapidly deteriorated from chaos to gangbusters . . . a whirl of pain, shock, blood, vomit, death, dirt and paperwork; from time to time I had looked at the little girl and wondered what must be going on in her head—unable to really communicate with her, and knowing that aside from a few inadequate kindnesses, there was absolutely nothing we could do to help. Had she seen her mother killed earlier in the day? What must it feel like to be five years old and all alone in the middle of a war? I thought it must feel like the end of an empty world. The short walk to Dispositions with the baby and the little girl had to be one of the longest in my life.

We finally made it. I realized I didn't smell too good. The psychiatrists weren't the only ones who had had an "eventful" morning; before noon, I had been thrown up on twice. Dispositions was gangbusters, too, but there was an unexpected touch of civility which I appreciated. They knew we were coming, and there was no confusion over what to do with the little girl. It was a timely reminder to me of how important those little touches of civility could be, especially in the worst of times.

When rushed for time, civility could require great self-control or, at least, presence of mind, but it helped us all make it through. Sometimes we would literally be running between patients, but when we arrived it was time to act like they were the only ones in the world. During Tet, it was often stripped down to a resolve to at least look at the patient *once* as though I *realized* he was an individual. There were times when even that was impossible, and a few times toward the end when exhaustion made focusing a struggle, but it was a worthwhile endeavor to be civil that I look back on now with satisfaction.

Someone took the baby out of my arms and to the back room. Now, I suppose I had "bodies on the brain," but it seemed like I saw them *stacked* in the back room and, even now, have a memory of bodies not in the back room but in pigeon holes to the right of the counter (I don't know why)—all neat, the proper disposition.

There was no hug "Goodbye" with the little girl as there had been with other children; no room to try communicating, "It's all right to cry." Maybe it wasn't yet. Maybe neither one of us could afford to feel too much . . . there was more surviving to do first.

There was a patient next door in the Emergency Room who had been wounded in or near the bladder, not far from the hospital, I gathered. He had lain in a ditch all night playing dead with the VC all around him, and about to scream because of an agonizing desire to urinate. They were putting a catheter in—blood and urine shot out all over everything. The rest of the scene was chaos.

Patients were lined up on the sidewalk, as they would be for days, weeks to come. Some seemed to patiently reflect the old standard Army attitude about almost everything— "Hurry up and wait," even when you're wounded. Others were actively suffering, almost in a world of their own.

"Ma'am, Ma'am, nurse!"

I finally realized one of them was calling me. I was hoping he didn't want anything too complicated; I had to get back to the ward. He was one of the active sufferers, and I thought for sure he was going to ask me to get him some morphine. All he wanted was something to put under his head.

On the way back to the ward, I helped a corpsman push a gurney to X-ray at breakneck speed. He almost ran me down with it, yelling, "Help," as it careened down the sidewalk. I have other memories of pushing gurneys at breakneck speed during Tet, but I don't remember the patients on those gurneys, or the beginnings or ends of the wild trips. In fact, I only specifically remember one other patient from Tet besides the baby and the little girl.

He looked so young, all bleary-eyed from the anesthesia . . . just waking up because the ward had become something of a giant Recovery Room and Intensive Care ward. Definitely a square peg in a round hole, and we both realized it the minute he said, "What happened?"

An emergency appendectomy. His tiny, trauma-less incision stood out in sharp contrast to all the combat casualties around him!

Five minutes later, I was back on the ward (the floor was a mess) thinking, *I'll bet I miss my R&R*, but then realized I really didn't want to take it anyway. Tet was certainly no time for nurses to be going on R&R.

That night, there was heavy gun fire near by, and gunships firing red tracers at some VC who seemed so stubborn to me. I kept thinking, *That ought to get them*, but they kept firing back at the gunships and at our troops on the ground. Sometimes the tracers looked like ray guns in the movies.

The battle was very serious indeed—the gunships worked for quite some time. It didn't occur to me then that if they failed, there was nothing between many VC and the hospital.

Men with M-16s patrolled the drainage ditches which were like old friends to me now; I almost felt that they were being violated. No one would be taking the short cut tonight—too risky. They might be mistaken for VC, or maybe even run into some. But then, from the looks of things, the OR nurses would be up anyway.

That night, one understatement followed fast on the heels of another, as time after time the supervisor ran down the hall *calmly* stating, "Our alert status has changed," a "suggestion" we run to the bunker! Unbelievable!

The bunker was musty and had spiders in it. I kept wondering if it had been properly maintained or if it might fall in on us. When I first arrived in Long Binh, I had looked at all their bunkers and thought, *How typical—we needed them at Tuy Hoa and didn't have them, and they have them at Long Binh and we'll probably never need them*. I was wrong.

The last time the supervisor came down the hall "hinting" our alert status had changed, I was so tired and fed up with being treated like babies (I really think they thought we would panic), I ended up doing something rather childish. At that point, I think I was more perturbed with the supervisor than I was with the VC. It would have been so gratifying if just once she had said, "Run for your life . . . it's a red alert!"

I thought to myself, *Maybe our "alert status had changed" for the better. There's nothing incoming around here but patients, and if we don't get some sleep, we're not going to be doing a very good job on them.*

I stayed under my bed with my flack jacket and helmet on. I was falling asleep and kept thinking, *In just a second, I'm going to get up and get my pillow*, but I fell asleep before I could.

The next morning, I woke up stiff as a board from sleeping on the cement floor bent backwards in a flack jacket, and momentarily thought something had happened and I was paralyzed. It was a split second of guilt.

Back on the ward, it was gangbusters again. There were days when the wardmaster did little more than "direct traffic" of incoming and outgoing patients. I finally started seeing the ward as something of a three-ring circus. SGT Byrd reminded me of an English Bobby—kind of an English Bobby clown, although it was serious. Being head nurse, I alternated between ringmaster and someone in white tights, tutu, and nurse's cap spinning wildly from a rope in the center of the "Big Top," while others balanced, juggled, and performed on the tight wire various procedures.

I think I began seeing it as a circus because of the patients on the urology wing with stomach wounds. (Anyone with VD was shipped out immediately to make room for casualties; in fact, no one who could travel stayed long.) Usually, patients with stomach wounds would have stayed in Intensive Care for a few days, but now all the wards were taking Intensive Care patients. There were so many stomach wounds, we ran out of suction machines almost immediately. We were using "Asepto" syringes instead: rather large, bulb syringes. Needless to say, they weren't very satisfactory. The bulbs had to be squeezed so often that they reminded me of the men in circuses who balance spinning plates on sticks, and by the time the last plate is successfully balanced, the first one is teetering and about to fall.

Thank goodness, we did manage to get all the patients with stomach wounds lined up in a row near the nurse's desk. I could be admitting and discharging patients at the desk, jump up and squeeze the syringes, do a little more paperwork, squeeze some more, and keep them going. No wonder it reminded me of spinning; naturally, the tutu and tights just went with it. And, with SGT Byrd directing traffic (with "fancy flourishes and flings"), it all just fell into place.

One evening just as my shift was ending, we had another large influx of patients. I decided to stay and help the nurses who had just come on duty. Two hours later, we were still admitting patients and the supervisor had not yet made it by on her rounds. She finally made it, looking very tired (God only knows what she might have just been through), and seemed somewhat confused. Not being satisfied with the patient census when the shift had ended, she kept insisting on an accurate count of patients on the ward *now*. We counted them several times for her, but more kept coming in to complicate things.

Neither of us could think; I felt like my eyes were crossing. We had work to do, and I *needed to squeeze those bulbs*. A corpsman walked by and I said, "Do you want to get those *plates*?"

I couldn't believe I had said it, we were all just so exhausted; I kept thinking I would be okay if I could just get up from the desk and move around . . . maybe give some pain shots. *But even more incredible—the corpsman understood what I meant and began squeezing the bulbs!*

I finally gave the supervisor a number that satisfied her; I didn't know for sure if it was accurate or not, and was quite beyond caring. Just as she was writing it down, through the door behind her appeared three more litters. I didn't say a word. If she wanted to add them to her grand total on the way out, it was her business.

We didn't see the doctors for days. They were operating and didn't even have time to put any orders on the charts. The nurses wrote the doctors' orders, got any lab work or x-rays, and did what we thought they would do if they were there. It worked out pretty well.

What was Tet like? Perhaps it was best described in the words of a nurse who said, "I think they're trying to bury us in bodies, and it doesn't seem to make much difference anymore if they are alive or dead."

Or in the words of a corpsman, "If we make it through this one, someday we're going to look back and say it was a *big* one."

There was such a boyish innocence in the way he said it.

During Tet, my mind seemed to expand into a giant computer processing endless facts for long periods, "one jump ahead of" the complications which were more numerous and more dangerous now, and organizing a vast, unwritten list of things to do that my body amazingly followed through on like a well-oiled robot. A three-week adrenalin high put the world in slow motion for months afterward, rearranged priorities, and simplified life. The water heater was one of those priorities. I have no idea what became of it—we were too busy even to think about it.

Then it was over, a screeching halt, and I was waiting for an airplane to take me home, sitting across from a captain who was asking, "Where were you during Tet?"

"Long Binh."

"Long Binh. You had a ground attack by a VC regiment, you know."

"No, I didn't know."

He seemed to know that I didn't know before he said it . . . strange. Maybe Tet was something like running in the Derby with blinders on. To this day, working calmly in big messes is easy for me.

24
Goodbye

Last nights are always so complex. This one was no different, probably the worst. Feelings of relief and sadness; goodbyes; confusion and disgust over the war, yet maybe still some belief; finished and unfinished business; the screeching halt after the chaos and intensity of Tet were all crowded by last-minute details and excitement—and thoughts of home that I barely dared yet to think about.

I hadn't heard from Mark—had hardly even thought about him during Tet except when I realized that Bien Hoa was being hit to think, "Fare well, dear friend," almost in an attitude of "every man for himself." Now he was out on an ambush, expected in just before I was due to leave. I kept thinking if he made it back before I was finished packing, I would just throw my suitcase in the trash, forget about packing, and spend what little time was left with him. Now I was panicky; I had called his unit several times but he still wasn't back. I finally had to leave not knowing whether he made it back in one piece or not. It was over anyway; I knew it, as final as death itself, just like the screeching halt after Tet, with no chance for a goodbye. But isn't this what I had wanted? Well, yes, *but not like this*.

And there was another vivid memory—it felt like a storm, but it really wasn't—it was the prop blast from the dust-offs. It was night and there were bright lights, maybe from the helicopters, and men were running in the storm—running with a litter, running for the hospital. They didn't realize it was too late, the guy on the litter was dead. Probably seconds before there had been hope, now it was gone. As hard as they must have tried, life was snatched away. It wasn't even really unusual—but somehow it "stuck."

But my last thought on my last night in Vietnam was typical, I think, in its practicality. I had a top bunk and there was a ceiling fan *very close* above me. I thought, *Wouldn't it be ironic if we were mortared on my last night?* I was very much afraid that if we were, the ceiling fan would fall and cut my legs off. I fell asleep thinking about it.

Waiting for the plane the next morning was a drag. The excitement of the last night had worn off, and there were some realities to face in the daylight—the unfinished business. I hated it, yet if there is anything typical about a war, it must be unfinished business.

Sometime late in the afternoon, the plane took off from Bien Hoa airbase. I looked down and thought, *How strange it is to be leaving a place I know I will never see again.*

I was able to identify a few of the compounds and buildings below. I thought of people there who were and who would always be dear to me. The words of Mark spoken at Tuy Hoa when we sat on the beach or in the club talking for precious hours, sounding the depths of our souls with the breeze blowing from the South China Sea came to mind, "Don't ever look back."

I looked down on a land that was deceptively pretty, and saw rice paddies and trees, little villages and mountains. I thought about how cheap human life could be down there and yet, at the same time, never more precious. I thought about how war brings out the worst in people and also the best. I knew certainly I had seen both more clearly and the good in a different way than ever before.

Years later, when I understood things better, I *would* look back, in a way Mark and I would have thought acceptable, and sense a "completeness" about the good that would always be there, and realize that in spite of heartache and anger and frustration, there was also a certain peace.

Finally my thoughts turned toward home, *really* turned toward home, and I got excited— it was going to happen! I thought about my dog, Trinket. He was getting old, had shared most of my life; he wouldn't be able to contain his joy at seeing me. My family—how good it would be just to hug them and hold them tight and catch up on the entire year. What was the "real world" *really* going to be like? I wanted to take a bubble bath for an hour, and polish my nails, and go shopping in a department store that smelled like perfume when you walk in the door . . . and forget about fatigues and combat boots and *baseball caps*.

I worried that what I called the "real world" might not seem like the real thing after all, compared to the life-and-death kind of reality I had been experiencing for the past year. I wondered if I would be able to enjoy all those things as much as before and, strangely, hoped that I wouldn't. They reminded me of the colonels from MACV in the big officers' club in Long Binh who never talked about anything but luxuries, and seemed to think *they* were fighting the war! Although they were always buying the nurses steak, I was finally so turned off by them that I stopped going to the club. There was something almost sickening about dealing with the consequences of the war every day and then being exposed to that stuff.

I was thankful I had made it out of Vietnam without hating anybody for long. But I was aware of a very deep, complete, and absolute contempt for people and things political.

Before landing in San Francisco, I got out my overnight case to put on some make-up and a piece of paper fell out. It was a letter from the staff of Ward Four. Momentarily as I read it, I was back in Long Binh with all of them . . .

> *"The staff of Ward Four want to express their appreciation to 1st LT Hampton, ANC, who has served in the capacity of our head nurse. LT Hampton's constant good humor, wit, and undying energy has been a morale booster for those of us with her. Fearlessly she has gone to the front of*

*the battle and fought for the best interests of Ward
Four... 'LT Strac' has truly shown us how to
accomplish the task, even in the midst of utter
confusion and chaos...has weathered many
harassing moments from PFC's and her fellow
constituents, including off-beat insubordination from
her EM...braved the treacherous terrain between the ward and the nurses' quarters at
night...Yet never succumbed to wounds inflicted
upon her person on these perilous patrols (I
always knew they thought it was "wonderful"
when I fell in the ditch!)...Wherever she may
go, we know she will always reflect the motto of
Ward Four, 'Illegitimo Non Carborundum Est.'
Although strict military courtesy and bearing sus-
tained many wounds, the high quality and atten-
tiveness toward patient care and needs was never
neglected. In all sincerity, our loss is Fort
Campbell's gain...''*

We'd done it, *I had done it*, made it through the year,
through Tet, patient care had triumphed, integrity had been
kept—*no fanny kissing at its finest*—just *our* best. We had
real teamwork. It sort of undergirded me as we walked
through the crowd of obscenity-screaming hippies in the
airport. It was that eight-year-old boy on the water buffalo
all over again—he seemed to be everywhere.

It frightened me. For the past year, even when the VC
were around, at least there had been people with M-16's and
machine guns. Now there was nothing—not so much as a .45
in the entire group! They looked like they wanted to kill us.

Just when it seemed like a good idea to keep moving, I
dropped one of my packages and tripped over it. I had to
stop and pick it up and get all organized again, right in front
of them. I tried to keep from laughing, but I couldn't. It
reminded me of the Vietnamese. I reminded myself of some
old mama-san cooking dinner with a fire fight going on. *Life
goes on,* I thought. *If you don't get killed, life does go on.*

25
Another Martian

Men the most infamous are fond of
  fame,
And those who fear not guilt yet start
  at shame.

Charles Churchill

Home was exactly the same as it had always been. My family was the same, seemingly changeless. It felt stable and good. I was welcomed back as though I had perhaps been on an extended trip around the world, understandably exhausted, but otherwise fine. And I *was* fine. Nothing missing, a blessing we thought about and realized many families didn't have.

I finally got to take that hour-long bubble bath. My mother had remarked at how good I looked when I got off the plane. I was amazed; my ankles were swollen and I felt like a wreck. When I got out of the bathtub, however, I found she had thrown all my underwear in the trash and gone to town for new. I was a little huffy—*my* underwear were clean, just kind of a funny orange color from the red clay in the water at Long Binh. Then I slept until about noon the next day.

I awoke to the sound of birds singing and a lawnmower— no dust-offs! Our maid was running the vacuum. The "real world" was soft and sweet. I lay there for a few minutes savoring it. I almost fit back in.

Although they asked, "How was it?" I was unable to

communicate what it had been like. I wanted to share my experience, but ended up feeling like I was keeping some kind of secret or, more accurately, that I was simply the possessor of a secret. I finally realized that whatever was shared about Vietnam was shared *in* Vietnam, and gave up trying. I was pleased with myself at how normal I thought I appeared as I tried to "hang loose" in my own home, determined to adjust.

I don't remember much about the next two weeks except they were both wonderful and a little miserable. The whole world seemed to be in slow motion. When the time came to return to Fort Campbell, I was ready. I couldn't wait to get back to work.

Everything seemed so simple; life was so simple. Within fifteen minutes after arriving, I had unpacked and was sitting in the chief nurse's office volunteering to start work immediately. She declined my offer adding, "Everyone who comes back from Vietnam is a troublemaker."

I thought I was still the farthest thing from a troublemaker the Army had ever seen. How could somebody who only wanted to do her best be a troublemaker? I was a little wound-up, a little wild, but to the roots of my heart still a terrific square. I thought for sure it must show—maybe that was the problem (a threat). I chalked it up to a bad day and tried to forget about it.

Before the week was out, I began to get the idea I was in for some real trouble. I was standing in the foyer of the hospital talking with the chief nurse. "It's a real shame," she said, "that I stayed here and worked hard, and you're getting all the glory."

I was shocked—shocked at what she was saying, but also that she wasn't ashamed to be saying it. I felt sort of embarrassed for her and thought, *If I felt like that, I think I would be keeping it to myself.* Then, I thought, *What is it anyway, and who would want it? What exactly did she think was "glorious" about Vietnam?*

It reminded me of playing with a little bead of mercury as a child—just couldn't quite pin it down. Of course, I had a general idea of what she meant, but wondered how on earth anyone could have been in the Army long enough to be a LT Colonel and have the stomach for such pettiness.

Having made her statement, she was walking off down the hall. I wanted to scream after her, "Don't you think the price is a little high?"

I could almost hear it reverberating in the halls of the hospital. It needed to reverberate and, having been screamed, to lodge in the walls there forever. In my imagination, I saw her turning around and with an expression of total incomprehension saying, "Price?" (All the faces of all my patients seemed to have flashed across a giant screen in my mind!)

By then, I was ready to fling myself on the floor and have a fit. I really don't know why I didn't. It was the beginning of eighteen months of continual, rather amazing harassment which became so ridiculous that I was almost impervious to it. This turned out to be my best defense—and offense (I'm sure it bugged her no end that she never got to me). I wasn't even trying to have an offense at first; I couldn't help it if I had an even temperament. And, as long as I had been in the Army, somehow it still hadn't quite sunk in yet about people being bitchy for the sheer pleasure of it. It was extremely naive of me, and I think she truly hated me for it.

A few days afterwards, I was called to her office as though I was in deep trouble, only to be told that I could not wear my Montagnard bracelet with my uniform. It was no big thing to me, I was wearing it more from habit than anything else. I always said it was given to me by "an old Montagnard," but that's not where it came from. (A little jewelry did seem to help the uniform.)

I took the bracelet off and, wouldn't you know, dropped it and it rolled under her desk. Naturally it was out of reach. Finally, I was down on my hands and knees stretching for all I was worth and still unable to reach it. The door to the office was open and she said, "Get up quick! Someone might think you're down on your knees to me." *Was she serious?!* I thought.

This woman's delirious!

I was getting tickled and it was making me weak. Vietnam *had* made me a little less likely to be intimidated and, at that point, it wouldn't have bothered me a bit to fall on the floor, laughing hysterically. I knew I was only seconds, and a quickly waning will, away from collapsing under her desk in laughter—it had just occurred to me that maybe she had been in trouble before for making people get on their knees to her!

Just in the nick of time, I reached the bracelet, miraculously regaining my composure, jumped up and said, "I GOT IT! DON'T WORRY!"

All I wanted to do was get out of there fast. I wondered how anyone could ever really understand what makes people crazy. I put the bracelet in my pocket and remembered the day I got it—Tuy Hoa. And then I remembered a day in the mess hall at about the same time, trying to drink some sickeningly sweet red Kool-Aid and looking at the colonel and the chief nurse across from me, thinking they wouldn't be any harder to understand if they were Martians, with their "Army careers" and a hospital full of unsolved problems. I thought, *Oh, my God, another Martian.* She might as well have been from outer space.

I was working on the orthopedic service. Most of the patients were from Vietnam—the ones we shipped out fast and had bad dreams about—nasty, grossly-contaminated compound fractures; stubborn bone infections that could go on for years; a few paraplegics; amputees; extensive skin grafts; large areas just shot or blown away; guys who were in traction or body casts or on frames—forever, it seemed; badly-damaged tendons and ligaments and nerves—you name it. Some of them smelled so bad, and there was no place they could go to get away from themselves.

They oozed, and you could look into gaping holes and see the displaced bones, some sheared off to almost nothing. They were eerie, not shocking like fresh bloody wounds that seemed quite "healthy" in comparison, but weird with their grayish, rounded edges trying to granulate in, yet continually thwarted and eroded by infection. Still, they were the best patients in the world. They made me feel I was in the right place . . . very little complaining, surprisingly optimistic a lot of the time, patient with what I thought were glaring inequities. Things most people would have thought were basic . . . the flies, for example. The screens on the ward must have been pretty old, and sometimes the flies were unbearable. The wardmaster did the best he could to patch them, but I thought we needed new screens. When I mentioned it to the chief nurse, you would have thought I had just committed treason. Maybe I was just being naive again, but I thought they deserved better.

The hospital wasn't *really* there for the patients; how stupid of me to have thought that it was. Later, when the scandal about the VA hospitals broke, with tales of paraplegics throwing their food on the floor so the rats would eat it and hopefully leave them alone, I wasn't surprised.

Although the staff was dedicated and hard-working and some of us became friends, there was never the closeness or the absolute trust and almost intuitive functioning I had known in Vietnam. One of the problems there was drug abuse which was fostered, really even "encouraged" by the hospital administration.

The first time I reported a corpsman for "bouncing off the walls," it was handled as a minor disaster, but not in the way most normal people would have expected—the boat was rocking, the danger wasn't to the patients—*I was the danger!*

Heaven forbid that a problem be admitted and solved! "Distinguished" Army careers were being jeopardized! Murder! I was the worst troublemaker out of Vietnam lately! Most of the time, the corpsmen weren't even taken off duty; everyone just got excited and that was the end of it, except I was in a little deeper.

The chief nurse had her cronies. One was a retired major. A calm, rather sweet-appearing character who was, nevertheless, determined to keep the boat "steady as she goes" —they could bounce off the walls 'till Doomsday and she would still be maneuvering around it with unflappable expertise, maintaining the status quo, manipulating, appearing to be doing something and doing absolutely nothing.

One supervisor was fighting alcoholism and losing. I suppose it hit pretty close to home to have someone around who believed people shouldn't come to work incapacitated. One day, after she had staggered down the hall, she threatened me if I got her in trouble. Of course, there was very little I could do to get her in trouble. What was I going to do—report her to the chief nurse? She was in such bad shape that she said it right in front of a sergeant as though he wasn't even there, who offered to back me up in spite of the fact that he had a wife and family to think about (they could play pretty rough at Fort Campbell).

Kentucky was having a glorious spring, lush vibrant green, and lots of violent thunderstorms. Sometimes I would wake up at night and momentarily think I was still in Vietnam. I had a few really gross dreams, and then I would go to work and *it* would be gross. There was a civilian aide who had come from Germany, and her translation of flesh was, "meat." It just about did me in. I would go grocery shopping, up one aisle and down the other, and when I finished the cart would be empty and I would have to start all over again. I had no appetite. All I bought for a while was strawberry ice cream and miniature egg rolls! Added to what I had lost during Tet, my weight dropped below 100 pounds.

Vietnam and Fort Campbell and the glorious spring and I sort of rushed onward together for a while. I wasn't looking back, Vietnam just came along with me—almost seemed to be there waiting for me when I returned.

Although the routine of the ward carried us along almost like a stream and morale was pretty good, there was a vague sense of depression, a feeling that the patients were second-class citizens: a little forgotten, somewhat forsaken. These guys hadn't died in fact, but many had given their lives as they knew them and as they had hoped life would be. Sometimes it closed in.

In Vietnam, we said, "they went bananas," a good enough term as any for paroxysms of anguish beyond expression except by fits. I think this one man's chart said he had an anxiety attack, but it meant little if nothing in actuality. What happened was that at 11 P.M. he realized he was stuck there in traction and his family needed him, and no one would even give him an idea of how much longer it would be. I think the night might have been a little blacker than usual and he couldn't see past it. And the system had gone a little too far in its "subtle" statement that he really didn't matter all that much. So, in the middle of report, when the shifts were changing, he screamed out against it and threw things and banged his traction.

I promised him I wouldn't rest until he got some answers and then, since I was a little "numb" myself from Vietnam, asked if he would mind keeping quiet until we finished report so the nurse on duty could go home! He minded. I could understand; it must be pretty hard to bring a rip-roaring anxiety attack to a screeching halt. "But would you please just stop screaming in my face so I can think?"

"Okay," he said. He was sorry, he knew I needed to think.

"How would you like to have some medicine to knock you out?"

I could almost hear myself saying, "*nice* medicine," that's what we always did, not that it ever solved anything, but it wasn't half-bad in a pinch.

Orthopedic doctors have a tendency to forget their patients aren't bones. I had a terrible time the next day getting the doctor to appreciate the gravity of the problem. He said he wasn't a psychiatrist, and couldn't seem to understand he didn't have to be one if he would just order a consultation. The psychiatrist was a pretty nice guy, I went out with him once, but he had just gotten a hair transplant and when the patient saw how preposterous the new transplant looked, he had another fit and refused to talk to him! Darned if he was going to bare *his* soul to a guy with an armpit growing on the top of his head! I called the chaplain.

I was talking to Jim in the Little Club, saying I was sorry I had come back to Fort Campbell. "It's not that I expected it to be the same as before, I didn't, but I didn't expect it to be this bad either."

Plus, now that all of the 101st was in Vietnam, most of the good, wild partiers were gone. There was a new unit, training for *riot control*! The place had gone to the dogs!

Jim said, "Your eyes look sad."

Talk about huffy! My eyes were not sad! How could he possible say such a thing? I denied it, but he looked at me as if to say, "You can't fool me."

I wasn't trying to fool him. I finally said I supposed they had looked at a lot of sad things—what did he expect? But I wasn't sad, I was *just fine*.

He said, "You're not going to be happy for a while anyway, unless you're doing something requiring superhuman effort. Why don't you join the Parachute Club?"

He'd been to Vietnam twice and was getting ready to go again. I suppose he was trying to help me the best way he knew. I understood what he was getting at, but I wasn't so sure I wanted to take up sky diving!

Then I remembered having watched the Parachute Club jumping the year before, how blue the sky was, and all the pretty-colored parachutes, and how the idea of it seemed so utterly fantastic. The more he talked, the more it became an actual possibility.

"Do you suppose I really could? Are you serious, or is this a joke? I've always been terrible at sports, don't you think I might kill myself?"

"Believe me, I know what I'm talking about. It's the best way in the world to get your mind off things. You can do it. I'll get you the number to call, a SGT Kramer..." Famous last words.

Friends who help the best way they know. What would life be without them?

26
Deliverance

> From ghoulies and ghosties and long-
>   leggety beasties
> And things that go bump in the night,
>   Good Lord, deliver us!
>
> Scottish Prayer

Before I could call Sergeant Kramer, I began to receive all kinds of advice on how to best approach him. In fact, the Little Club was turning into a veritable "smoke-filled room." Strategy. "Don't do anything until we get this strategy figured out. Sergeant Kramer had something of a reputation.

"Why don't you wear that little dress with the flowers and try to look real pitiful, maybe he'll have mercy on you!"

"No, she should wear her uniform, he might have some respect for her rank."

"Are you kidding?"

I was beginning to get a picture of a crazy man who ruled the Parachute Club with a "rod of iron," thought nothing of eating lieutenants for breakfast and picking his teeth with their bones, and even bumped slowpokes off the road with his car if they got in his way!

"Don't worry. He's going to turn you down flat anyway."

The big day finally arrived. After all the careful planning, I can't remember if I wore the dress or the uniform. The "strategy" was sort of an attitude, and although we had *rehearsed* things to be said, I was so scared I forgot it all before I arrived. And I was running late! I drove around the block again, trying to get my wits together, trying to get up my nerve to go in, grasping for something that would save me—perhaps a thought. I felt so alone, the strategy had deserted me, all but, "Now remember, you run two miles *easy.*"

My sister had seen a movie once about a very successful stripper who apparently attributed her success to the fact that she always had a gimmick. She had decided to see if it could be applied to everyday life, and swore that it worked. She was always saying, "You've got to have a gimmick."

I thought it was kind of silly, just something to have fun with, but suddenly I could hear my sister saying, "You've got to have a gimmick."

"A gimmick, a gimmick. What would it be? Something new and different." My mind would barely even work.

Parking the car made me think about this friend telling my mother about her driving test. (She was a terrible driver and didn't even know it.) She said when she finished the test, the officer patted her on the shoulder and said, "Now, you be careful."

And she said to my mother, "I thought for sure he was going to tell me I was just a dandy little driver."

I made it over the threshold without tripping. SGT Kramer seemed to be a reasonable man; we were talking. Actually he was appearing to be a very nice man and I had overcome my first impulse to say, "Don't kill me! I just have to ask you something!"

My mind did seem a little "blown," but I noticed some of the strategy was automatically coming out of my mouth . . . "A gimmick—you've got to have a gimmick."

I remember very little of the conversation. He asked me if I ever ate anything and I panicked, suddenly ashamed of the egg rolls and ice cream! I blurted out, "If you'll just give me a chance, I promise I'll be a dandy little jumper . . . (Was it a gimmick? I didn't know.) . . . and don't ask me if I can run two miles because I can't!"

He said, "Okay." *Okay!*

The following weeks were spent learning all about sky

diving, running around in many, many circles doing PLF's*
off a platform, packing parachutes, hanging in a harness
from the ceiling practicing emergency procedures and doing
more PLF's off the platform. (I thought mine were excellent!) SGT Kramer left shortly thereafter, which may have
saved my life. I think he would have made me so nervous
that I might have had an accident (although he was always
just as nice as he could be), and everyone said the reason
they had an "almost spectacular" safety record was because
their training was so good.

There was a good group in the Parachute Club, and we all
got along fine. Most everyone was married, and it gave us a
certain freedom for some nice friendships. They teased me a
little at first, but it was meant in good fun. The only time it
got to me was the day I went with Mike Sullivan to the
storeroom to get my jumpsuit. He said, "Here, have a red
one, the blood won't look so bad on it."

So I took it, just in case. Vanity, you know. It definitely
got to me, but I put on my poker face and pretended it was
nothing at all. Something about Vietnam made poker faces
easier; I often marveled at my own self-control.

My first jump. I remember looking out of the airplane
and seeing a river. We flew over it, then turned and flew
back over it while I was making my way to the wing. I
hated even to see a mud puddle before jumping, and it was
surprising how many there always were. I wanted to tell the
jumpmaster, "Don't you see what's down there? Eeek,
water, be careful, don't slip!"

It didn't seem to be bothering him at all, which to my
way of thinking at the moment seemed very strange indeed.

I remember the way the plane smelled—like old leather
and rubber which might be getting a little soft (or a little
hard) from the sun or time. To this day, that smell, or the
memory of it, increases my heart rate. "Go!" and I blasted
off the wing into the blue sky. There was hardly time to
think about anything. The first few jumps were made with a
static line that opened the parachute automatically. Violence
quickly followed by a miracle blossoming overhead, a

*Parachute Landing Falls.

perfectly-formed, orange and white miracle. I thought, *This is many things, but it's **not** disappointing*. I was hooked.

I talked to myself all the way down. "You did it. You actually did it! See those trees? *Away* from the trees. What about the target? Turn right, oh, how neat, it really works! Turn left. The wind, where is it coming from anyway? Oh, this is so neat I can't believe it.

I was so excited that I couldn't figure the wind direction; and hardly even wanted to try.

"Try to miss the trees, *forget the target, miss the trees*."

I did miss them, barely, and swung around a little hard when I needed to be concentrating on a smooth, straightforward landing. For all of my previously "excellent" PLF's, I ended up with some embarrassing grass stains in the wrong place, and was glad that I had landed behind the trees and no one had seen just how unceremoniously. Even though it was a little "shocking," I was pleased with myself.

Summer settled in over Fort Campbell with a pleasantness reminiscent of "baseball, hot dogs, apple pie and Chevrolets," in spite of my troubles at the hospital and the training for riot control. (I just couldn't get over it—Americans training to fight Americans.) Every weekend became a picnic filled with bright blue skies, pretty-colored parachutes, friends, and something *truly, utterly fantastic!* During the week, I packed my parachutes in the lazy warm twilights of Daylight Savings Time, white buildings and green grass, and on the weekends flung myself into the sky with reckless abandon. (It sure beat flinging myself on the floor every time I ran into the chief nurse!) It required total concentration—my friend had been right, "The best way in the world to get your mind off things," sweet deliverance actually. The joy of life started bubbling in my heart again—maybe not quite the same as it had before, not so much like a child, but fully knowing the bad and the good. Yet mostly, I think, just from a little *relief*.

There was something rather spiritual about the jump itself, something really good. I've often thought it had something to do with the letting go, or courage, or faith. But after the parachute opened, it was pure adventure! That's when I always wished everyone would disappear and

I could be totally free to do my own thing. I hadn't caught on to canopy control (something of an understatement), but hitting the target didn't interest me that much, anyway. I think I was a balloonist at heart. What I really wanted to do was go as far as possible for as long as possible, or to spin down in endless, long, spiraling circles. I would run with the wind even while the others were yelling advice from the ground. Later, I would pull my ripcord a little early to give myself more time in the air. I never told anyone; I was afraid they would make me stop. They just kept writing in my logbook, "TFTM," for "Too Far to Measure," in the space for distance from target, and reassuring me that everyone catches on sooner or later.

I usually landed so far away, no one had any idea of the adventures I was having. I often landed standing up, which you weren't supposed to do at first, but I couldn't help it. I floated down so easily it just happened. If anyone did see me, I would fall down afterwards to make it look good— maybe it just looked stupid.

Corn fields are interesting (and very beautiful) to land in . . . the stalks seem to rattle for an eternity before you hit the ground. Then it's hard to find your way out. I missed a herd of cows once, but didn't see the fence in time. I bounced off the top with my feet, and thought I was absolutely wonderful for the rest of the day.

For all my fear of water and efforts to avoid it, I finally even had to face that. A good-sized pond . . . I saw it coming and the more I tried to miss it, the more I went straight for it. I was screaming, "Water, help, water, help, help!" but they couldn't hear me. It's amazing how fast you can get out of boots, helmet, harness, etc. when you are totally panicked. I skimmed over the pond, holding my feet up so they wouldn't get wet, and landed on the far bank.

The sand was soft and damp. It took me forever to find all my stuff, and it was *so* hot. I cried all the way back, thinking I would never make it—parachutes aren't exactly light. But when I made it back to the others, I couldn't remember what it was that had been so awful to cry about.

There was one guy who almost always landed in a tree, and his wife *always* got mad at him as though he had done it on purpose. After I saw what it took to get out of a really tall tree, I was very careful around them.

I always jumped first, so everyone started calling me the "wind dummy" (maybe they knew what I was up to all along)! But I think I would have died if they had changed it and made me watch everyone else going first. I think I would have felt like I was being left behind.

Although sky diving was great for getting your mind off things, it didn't do much at all for the feeling of being "revved up" all the time. I think I must have known I was pushing myself, but I couldn't seem to stop. I thought nothing of working all night, driving a hundred miles, jumping all day, then driving back and going back to work. It was that old familiar attitude—you could do anything you had to because it really didn't matter how you felt, it didn't matter at all. There was a great freedom in the realization of it. Only once did I even consider that I might be overdoing it.

It was my third jump, late afternoon. When I pulled the ripcord, the handle came out of the pocket, but *that was all*. It was stuck! A conversation I had overheard about "hard pulls" flashed through my mind. By then, my fall was out of control. I shouldn't have tried to stabilize it but did, which didn't work. I decided to try pulling the ripcord one more time before going for the reserve. (It must have looked absolutely ghastly from the plane and from the ground.) With my mightiest tug, it finally came out—just as the altitude-activated, automatic opener deployed the reserve. I was falling with my back to the ground when it happened. Suddenly, in the sky above me there were two parachutes— one orange and white, one white; terrific pain (I wasn't at all sure I hadn't broken my back) and ecstasy. The only thing which could have looked any better would have been *three* parachutes! I knew it was a miracle they weren't entangled, and when I saw how close to the ground I was, I couldn't believe it. There would have been no time at all to try to work with a malfunction even if something *could* have been done. It could easily have been a streamer anyway. *Seconds* later I landed, very near the target—the closest I ever came to hitting it—*seconds* from death!

The plane landed about the same time I did, and nothing less than the Spanish Inquisition got out. The entire world was strewn in nylon—parachutes all over the place.

The question, "What happened?" wasn't the least bit pertinent. The answers, "Nothing," "Everything," "I don't know," and "All of the above," applied equally. Except that, momentarily, "*Nothing*, nothing at all happened," made an awful lot of sense. "I pulled and pulled, and *believe me*, nothing happened." And then, of course, *everything* . . . wasn't it obvious that *everything* had certainly happened? I said, "I don't know." Actually, I didn't.

"Why aren't you crying?"

Not only had I apparently just failed my multiple choice, Mike Sullivan thought I had committed the unpardonable emotional problem. I said, "I don't know."

It made perfect sense to me, but I suppose two "I don't knows" in a row did sound pretty poor. Actually, if I had had the strength and another parachute, I think I would have jumped again. I didn't feel much of anything—the *nothing* intensely feeling. Somehow, it didn't seem the least bit unusual. I couldn't understand why Mike was so concerned about it. Years later, when I heard about "psychic numbing" for the first time, I remembered that day, and a few others.

It was hot, so I took off my jumpsuit—and remembered about it being red. And then I wished I had left it on, but it was too late. I was wearing shorts underneath, and one leg had bruises obviously made from suspension lines. Of course, everyone noticed, but they didn't say a word; they didn't have to. If looks could have killed, I would have been a goner. I had a split-second, *vivid* mental image of myself hanging upside down with one foot caught in the lines. I was sure everyone else had "seen it," too. I knew I'd had it, but by then was feeling so much remorse that I didn't care. I shouldn't have jumped, being so tired; I had definitely "blown it," and it wasn't a nice thing *at all* to do to your friends. Mike said, "You're grounded until you go through all the training over again."

I thought, *I deserve it*. I loved jumping so much it was almost the worst thing he could have said.

On the way home someone said, "Did your life flash before you eyes?"

I said, "No, I wanted some leverage to help me pull the ripcord so bad that a door frame with my foot on it flashed before my eyes."

It never did really bother me how close I actually came to getting killed. I guess I saw so much of it that death meant almost next to nothing.

I felt terrible for the next two weeks. I was convinced everyone hated me, and although they weren't acting like it, I didn't blame them. My back hurt, but I was afraid to ask one of the orthopedic doctors to look at it . . . they knew *far* too much about broken bones. I finally confided in my friend, the ward psychiatrist. He understood. I said, "Just tell me you think it's going to be okay."

He felt it and said he was "pretty sure nothing was too badly damaged."

I started the training over again, but my heart wasn't in it. I was hanging in a harness from the ceiling one evening, supposedly to go over the emergency procedures, when they turned out all the lights and left. I thought, *They do hate me, they really do, and this is their chance to get back at me and they've taken it.*

I had visions of hanging there all night and being found the next morning, asleep in the harness. Then I thought for sure it must be a joke and yelled, "Help," and thought they would come back any minute, but they didn't and I felt foolish. There were tall windows with little white panes, and outside the night was a very peaceful, very quiet, very lonely midnight blue.

I opened my reserve parachute and let it fall to the floor, then climbed out of the harness and started down it. My heart was so heavy; I had lost all track of time. I fell the last five feet, and landed sprawling with a thud.

The lights went on. And suddenly everyone was there, enjoying *the show!* A Coke bottle had fallen over and was spewing its contents, but it didn't matter . . . I understood. It was their way of letting me know all was forgiven; things were back to *normal!*

On my next jump, I got an "Unsatisfactory" comment in

my logbook, but it wasn't nearly as unsatisfactory as the last one! After that, they actually improved to "Good," and "Very Good," and there even a few "Excellents."

There was a captain who jumped with us for a while. I don't remember his name, but one day I remember him saying that if jumping didn't scare you pretty bad, there was something wrong with you. *That* scared me, because jumping hardly scared me at all, but then I wondered why *he* was doing it if it scared him so bad. Surely nothing was wrong with *me*. I remember him saying it, though. I think his wife must have been sort of a "Women's Libber." She was always trying to tell me that I was proving something. I had to be the last person in the world who was proving anything! I always felt they had very graciously allowed me to "intrude."

Cold weather came, and jumping became miserable. We finally had to stop and simply wait for spring. By then I had met Tom and was glad to have all my time to spend with him. I admired and respected him, and loved being with him—we had some really great times. We talked about marriage, but something was wrong. I loved him in a way, but not enough. And I still hadn't gotten over Mark from Vietnam. I told Tom and he said it didn't matter, but it did.

Looking back, I can see now that I was doing a lot of insensitive things, and I didn't even know it. I wrote a letter to Mark in Vietnam to say goodbye. I don't remember much about that letter, but I have a feeling it was terrifically callous; I guess it was a form of self-protection. I cared a lot about people and had always been very sensitive to others; it was so unlike me. Needless to say, things didn't work out between Tom and me.

I never received an answer from Mark. Several months later, a man from his unit was admitted. His legs were really messed up bad. He told me Mark was okay and he had already left for the States. It was the last I heard of him.

Things were getting worse at the hospital. What I had identified as a serious drug problem was really a monumental drug problem . . . I didn't know the half of it! I knew of six corpsmen who were coming to work under the influence not only of marijuana, but sometimes of LSD. It was getting to be a constant hassle.

Sometimes I thought the only friend who really understood the magnitude of it all was Sergeant Johnson, the NCO in charge at night. He had been in the Army almost 20 years, and was one of those wise, professional soldiers who knew everything that was going on—all at once.

I had been to the hospital commander, who had been sympathetic. He even told me he was convinced my problems with the chief nurse stemmed from petty jealousy, but the drug situation had not improved. I feared for the safety of the patients.

I told Sergeant Johnson I was going to write my congressmen if things didn't improve soon, but he encouraged me to hold off until I was out of the Army (September, '69) because they would "crucify" and discredit me, and nothing would be accomplished. He said he had been threatened with a court-martial. Every time I told him I didn't think I could possibly wait much longer he would say, "You've got to. This is a big problem and it's going to be around for a long time because that's just how the system works. You'll never be able to fight it as long as you're in it." *Even now* in case of war, the experts are planning for 30% of our soldiers to be immediately incapacitated from drug abuse!!

One night, he told me that a lot of narcotics had been found missing from the Recovery Room/ICU. The nurse on duty was a new second lieutenant, and she had mentioned to him that the pain shots she had been giving didn't seem to be having any effect. Many of the patients were experiencing severe pain. He tasted the narcotics and found they were only *salt water.*

The next night, he filled me in on the outcome. The incident had been reported to the chief nurse, who ordered the second lieutenant to keep her mouth shut and continue giving the saline as though it was pain medication! If she didn't cooperate, her husband (who happened to be an enlisted man) could expect orders for Vietnam. She refused, and when she arrived at work the next night, found that the saline had been replaced with brand new narcotics. Sergeant Johnson went to the pharmacy to see how the paperwork had been handled, and found that it hadn't. There was no record anywhere of narcotics having been sent to the Recovery Room.

The expression "Bouncing off the walls" isn't just an expression. Many did, literally, complete with sound effects. It *was* a monumental problem. About that same time, while I was working nights again, I heard what I thought was a patient on crutches with a cast trying to make his way to the latrine, an "accident looking for a place to happen." There was bumping and banging like you wouldn't believe. I jumped up and rushed into the hall to try to prevent the poor guy from breaking his other leg and, to my surprise, found the supervisor (and major) literally bouncing off the wall! The next day, she called me at home and promised to "Get me good."

I wasn't too worried. Surely, I wasn't the only one who knew what was going on. She apparently walked around like that quite openly, and reported to the chief nurse at the end of the shift. And she was hardly in any condition to be "getting" anybody. I put in a request for a transfer, feeling that the problem was so widespread and so much a part of the system, there was little hope of ever getting it straightened out. It was denied.

I thought spring would never come. At least when we were jumping, there was some relief from it. I felt so sorry for the patients, and sometimes wondered if I could possibly make it until September. Little did I know that horror, and a form of hope, was just around the corner.

Surprisingly, when I look back on that time at Fort Campbell, my most vivid memories are not of the bad things—horrible wounds, flies, second-class citizens, harassment, training for riot control and an increasingly uneasy feeling about the war—*not to mention* those who bounced off the walls, including the supervisor! (And from things that go bump in the night, Good Lord, deliver us!) I have vivid memories of bright blue sky, pretty-colored parachutes, friends, and something truly, utterly fantastic. *Sweet deliverance*.

27
Help, Murder, Police!

"Pride goeth before destruction..."

Proverbs

I got promoted every year whether they hated me or not. Now the Army had just made me a captain.

A few days later, two patients had pooled their resources and given me a beautiful gold cross. I felt a little bad about it because ever since I had gotten back from Vietnam I had been saying, "God, are you really there? If you are, please let me know."

I suppose that since America had turned out to be not quite what I thought it had always been, I was wondering about God, too. And I think I was blaming Him for letting things happen. *I realized that it was going to make a critical difference in the way I lived my life and I wanted to know—one way or the other, I just wanted to know if He was real.*

To make matters worse, although I had been raised in church, I had never really known Jesus; I didn't even know it was possible! In short, I was a cultural Christian, very sincere, yet still a Christian in name only. I had been baptized, catechismed, confirmed, trained, ceremonied, and bored to death. I had written to my mother and told her not to bother praying for me, that it wouldn't do any good. But

I was wearing the cross because the patients meant a lot to me, and saying, "God, where are you anyway? If you're there, please give me a *sign*."

There were entire wards of trainees. Poor things. They would get really bad upper-respiratory infections with high fevers, sometimes strep throats and pneumonia, and sometimes meningitis. Everyone called it the "Big M," and I think it was supposed to be a secret. (Don't rock the boat again!)

I suppose trainees are known for being pitiful, but since I returned from Vietnam, I thought the more pitiful the better—it would help them survive later. I remember really shocking myself one day as I passed by one studying Vietnamese. I said, "You don't talk to them, you shoot them!"

Of course I believed in talking to them and thought it was an excellent idea that he was studying—I just wanted to make sure he realized what it was all about. He was looking at me in utter disbelief when a corpsman came running down the hall yelling, "Captain, PVT Smith is in the latrine committing suicide."

I rushed into the latrine to find blood everywhere. PVT Smith had a nosebleed and had given up trying to stop it. He was now sitting on the floor sobbing. For a split second, I couldn't remember what to do for a nosebleed, but what he was trying to say was, "Help me!"

Things always seem worse when you are sick, but this boy really thought he would never make it through basic, let alone Vietnam. He didn't believe in the war. It churned up an unexpected surge of my own frustration and anger and doubt, all sharply focused on that one life on the bathroom floor; complete with misery and blood. I knew I had to tell him the truth. So when we got the nosebleed stopped, we had to talk. He had been trying to communicate unsuccessfully for at least ten minutes! We just sat there on the bathroom floor, leaning against the wall by the sinks, and talked.

I said, "You can simply get killed fighting and never know what hit you, or you can end up paralyzed from the neck down for the rest of your life. You can end up burned to a crisp, even your lungs, but you won't die fast. You can step on a mine and get your legs blown off. Do you realize you can get your penis blown off? Or your arms. You can lose your eyes or be a vegetable for the rest of your life, or fall in a pit and be impaled, or the VC can carve you up after a fight and leave you to die. You're going to see your friends die and hear them screaming. And I have reason to believe that one day of humping the boonies can be worse than all of basic put together.''

You could have heard a pin drop. His eyes looked like he was ''seeing'' it all, but I knew he really wasn't—I was. I was hoping he hadn't seen me shudder. It was the second time I'd done it since I started talking—a deep, gut-level shudder. I wanted to hold my stomach, but just kept on talking instead. ''I've come to the point where I don't blame anyone for going to Canada. I don't blame them for not wanting their lives thrown away. I think we've got something worse going on over there than what provoked the Boston Tea Party—by a long shot. But I have to tell you, I don't have any respect for the ones who are going to Canada, and I wonder if they respect themselves. But for crying out loud, don't kill yourself. This is no time to be committing suicide—you've got to think about *surviving*, and don't you *dare* go over there if you don't feel good about yourself.''

He was looking at me as if to say, ''Can I get you another soap box?''

By then I was holding my stomach and added, ''You'd better sign up for ranger school, and if you don't feel good about yourself after that, *then* you think about Canada.''

God only knows what he ever did! I've often wondered—and whether he lived through it. These were some hard things to think about, *at seventeen years of age*.

We talked about life being grim, grimmer than you could ever imagine, but I couldn't help saying that I felt that no matter what happened, I believed there was good in it somewhere, but maybe ''good'' in a totally different way then most of us expected. His face brightened a little as he considered this. I hope it helped.

* * *

I was living off-post in a duplex, and it was in need of a few basic repairs. I had mentioned it to the landlord several times, but after months of "promises," nothing had been done. A friend had said, "Why do you put up with it? Go to the housing office on post and file a complaint; they can make him fix it." So that's what I did.

In a room full of secretaries, where everyone could hear, the sergeant who handled complaints made an appointment to inspect the duplex the next day. He had a sweet-looking face, but the next day, about three seconds after I let him in, there was no doubt that there was nothing sweet about him—he was stark-raving crazy, and extremely weird! He said, "The lock on your door isn't working very well. I came by early this morning before the sun was up and started to come in."

There was an icy coldness in his voice and in his eyes which I had never seen in anyone else before—my blood ran cold and the rest of my body felt like Jello. *Don't panic. Whatever you do, don't panic—this is life and death right here and now!*

I couldn't believe it, but he sat down and took his boots off, watching me like a hawk. I was afraid even to back up a few inches toward the door. Some kind of internal "automatic transmission" shifted me into intuition . . . and I had no doubt whatsoever that I had to act like I didn't realize he was dangerous. I felt if I broke down or even showed the slightest hint of fear, he would freak out and hurt me. The first time he turned his back, I was going to be out the kitchen door and down the street screaming, "Help."

But he never turned his back! I kept talking and talking, wondering how much longer I could possibly keep it up, trying to maneuver toward the door. But when I moved only a little toward the door, he moved, too. Twice he had his hands around my throat "demonstrating how dangerous it was for the lock on the door not to be working properly." I just kind of hung there on my tiptoes, keeping calm, acting like I didn't have sense enough to be scared. At one point, I reminded myself of a mixture between a Raggedy Ann doll and a dog with its tongue hanging out, and almost laughed. But, even hanging there, I felt that I had some control—

because my fear wasn't showing, I suppose. And I felt a sense of benevolence very strongly, and knew I was communicating it. I said, "You're frightening me. I promise I'll get it fixed right away," but in a tone of voice that didn't sound frightened.

Then he glanced at the floor and picked up something. It was the gold cross. I thought I had lost it. He said, "Is this yours?"

I said, "Oh, yes, I thought I'd lost it. Give it here."

He gave it to me and then said, "Well, I guess I'd better go," and sat down to put his boots on. He said it so convincingly that I believed him. I thought, *I did it. I psyched him out*.

I didn't actually think, "I certainly am wonderful," but that's how I was feeling—yesterday I contemplated suicide with someone and life won, and today I psyched out a sociopath! So, instead of taking my chance to run, I sat down on the couch, and for a moment relished the same satisfaction lion tamers must feel when all the big cats are finally on their pedestals. Pride—definitely the wrong kind.

He sprang across the room like a freight train, had me by the throat, and sat on me before I could think, *Oh, no!* I was so shocked, and the most horrible wave of helplessness passed over me—I was struggling and it wasn't doing the least bit of good. I could breathe, but there was a terrible pressure in my head and I was dizzy. I thought I was going to scream, but only choked.

I thought, *This just can't be it—no, not like this*, yet I was beginning to think maybe this *was* it.

I don't know why, but I held the little gold cross up right in front of his eyes. He said, "Get that thing out of my face."

I sputtered, "I will not either, it's going to save me," and shoved him with the other hand.

To my utter amazement, and his, too, he flew across the room (about six feet) and hit the wall hard! I was off and running.

Running through the snow to my neighbor's across the way was just like those slow-motion dreams again. For all I knew, he was right behind me, but I couldn't spare the extra time to look. I was shaking so bad from the cold and from fright, and still trying to scream and choking.

My neighbor came to the door right away, and thank goodness realized something was terribly wrong . . . I think I was pointing. He pulled me inside and ran out after the guy, stopping him just as he was getting in his truck. I just sat there at his kitchen table, shaking, watching him writing something down.

I must have shook for fifteen minutes; I couldn't seem to stop. When my neighbor came back in, he asked me if I was all right, but while I was still trying to say, "Yes," he said, "No," and started pouring some bourbon in a Coke. I was really afraid the first sip wasn't going to go down, but it did, and I was glad to have it. Then he gave me a big hug and held me tight. I didn't know him very well, but he had seemed like a nice person, a lieutenant. I can't remember his name. He had the sweetest dog, a big dog, and someone had shot it in the stomach and left it in the forest to die. When I thought about it I almost cried. Finally I stopped shaking, and he called the MP's.

The MP's said since it happened off post, we should call the sheriff in Clarksville. The sheriff said that since everyone concerned was in the military, we should call the MP's. It was a big hassle. I don't really know how the CID (Criminal Investigation Division) got in on it—something like a military FBI. Two really nice guys. They thought it was attempted rape.

He was cold-blooded enough for it to have been murder, rape and mayhem! They all tried to talk me out of pressing charges "for my own good." They said that, amazingly, things like this usually go badly for the victim, but I was determined. I felt he was so dangerous that it was worth trying to get him locked up. But before anything could be done, they sent him to prison at Fort Levenworth for a prior conviction on several counts of assault and battery and assault with a deadly weapon. No one knew why he had been loose before sentencing, working in the housing office, of all places! He had already been diagnosed as a psychopath!

Somehow, quite a bit of trust developed between me and the CID guys, which I realized later was rather remarkable because they were a little "paranoid," an occupational hazard that eventually wore off on me, too. They were distraught over the drug situation at Fort Campbell, and convinced that the main source of it was the hospital. And they had been unable to get any cooperation whatsoever from hospital headquarters. Did we ever have something in common! When they asked me to help them, I didn't hesitate; in fact, I had a letter to my congressman stamped and ready to go the day they asked. I tore it up, thinking there was more hope working with them.

It made me feel like a spy sneaking around with the suspense of getting caught. They needed information from places I had no reason to go, some out of filing cabinets— that was the most scary. I just hung loose and was pleasant, and walked right in and got it.

Sometimes I followed people and watched them. Sometimes I had to talk to people and ask just the right questions so they didn't suspect what I was getting at; often it took two or three conversations just to work up to one question.

After a while, I was no longer afraid of getting caught and just thought it was exciting. No one had ever said what to do if I did get caught, but I already knew I would tell the truth. I could just imagine the berserk reactions I would get to witness when the chief nurse and the supervisors realized their little mess had been infiltrated by the CID. I thought it might be well worth anything I might have to go through just to see it! Although I was beginning to relax and enjoy it, I was thinking about sneaking and details so much that I was getting slightly paranoid too, to the point of sometimes wondering about SGT Johnson and even the CID! And I hated the feeling. It *was* fun in a way, but I really wasn't a sneak at heart.

For the first time in a long time, there was real hope. They knew who had stolen the narcotics from the Recovery Room; had even found an empty morphine container on the roof of his trailer. They tried to track down the "switch" in the pharmacy, but I don't know that they ever did. Only later did it occur to me that somewhere in the pharmacy there may well have been saline in narcotic containers that would eventually find its way back to the wards!

I often thought about the way that guy just flew through the air and hit the wall. I mostly thought it was adrenalin, but there was always "something else" about it, kind of a "knowing" somewhere inside that it was *God*. Not that adrenalin isn't wonderful stuff, but I just didn't shove the guy hard enough to make him fly across the room. And I would think about the little cross and saying, "I will not either, it's going to save me," and the two patients who gave it to me. From the way things worked out, I think they had prayed for me. I still didn't know what to do about God. I had a long way yet to go; there were perils ahead, worse in a way than what I had already been through.

Life. It is grim . . . but there's still an awful lot of wonder in it!

28
The Orthopedic Bathtub

"If the shoe fits, wear it."

Unknown

Another glorious Kentucky spring arrived, and with it more thunderstorms: now less frequent reminders for me of the guns halfway around the world where things weren't the least bit glorious. Not that it was necessary. Any dreams they prompted were always met upon awakening by the instant realization that for many at that moment, reality was far worse than any nightmare could ever be. And, anyway, more vivid reminders were constantly with us, arriving from Japan. From Japan were long flights home of wounded and crippled men: multiplied agony beyond any one person's comprehension.

There was a sergeant with a rather extensive leg wound. He arrived from Japan with a cast, and with old, dried blood and dirt from Vietnam. Not so long before, I might have been critical of the care he had received. Now I only thought of the nurses who cared for him. "Poor things, I know what they must be going through," and actually felt *satisfaction* that the sergeant was alive, in fairly good shape, and in no immediate danger of losing his leg, although it was infected. Dried blood and dirt were nothing on a body that had made it home intact and would eventually be all right. Now we could deal with the dirt.

Corpsmen scrubbed, and scurried back and forth with basins of water. The curtains around the bed scarcely contained the activity with bulges that reminded me of the old classic line about a fat lady's skirt looking like two little boys under a blanket fighting. And yet it was only a bed bath, a "birdbath," no match really, for the filth of Vietnam.

There was one patient we teased unmercifully about smelling like a rice paddy. I'm sure we carried it too far. And yet a few days later in surgery, they found rice in his cast! It only served to prove us right, yet it seemed to make him feel better, as thought it proved the real "culprit" was, after all, the rice paddy!

We joked a lot about the dirt, and more or less lived with it. It's just not like men trying to be macho to talk very much about how badly they want to take a bath, and yet they *really* did.

One day I was looking through a hospital supply catalogue and was amazed to find that portable plastic bathtubs were actually available that could be used in bed. Of course, the cost for one was several thousand dollars; I had no hope that at Fort Campbell my patients would ever get to use one. Nevertheless, the idea was such a marvelous one that I couldn't help getting excited. Ta dum . . . in walked the chief nurse . . . it *had* to happen that way—fate works like that for some reason. She said, "And what are *you* up to this morning?"

I said, "Look at this, isn't it wonderful? I had no idea they made things like this."

Instead of saying, "I hate your guts," she managed, "*We* don't order supplies," but they were one and the same. And she bustled off down the hall.

I didn't realize it at the time, but the patients weren't the only ones who had baths and tubs on the brain. Only later, when I was out of the Army and traveling in Europe, did I realize how deeply a year of dirt without a tub had affected me. Every time I saw a fancy sarcophagus (and some not so fancy), my first thought was it must be a bathtub, a wonderful big bathtub. Of course, then I realized it was a sarcophagus and felt sick and thought about Vietnam and death and hated them. But my first impression, no matter how many I had already seen, was always of a bathtub.

In that frame of mind, I suppose what happened next was only inevitable. And, as bad as most pride is, there is also a good kind of pride, and I must say that I have the good kind about what happened next—sort of a "job well done." The chief nurse had hardly left the ward before I *knew* it would be the simplest thing in the world to improvise one of those tubs, and I was going to do it and every patient on my ward who wanted to was going to get to use it to his heart's content. I suppose I had gotten so used to improvising in Vietnam that if the shoe fit, it would have seemed like a crime not to wear it!

I talked the idea over with COL Sturkey, the chief of orthopedics, and he liked it. (To have approached the chief nurse with the idea would have doomed the project to failure before we even got started.) And he "understood" about the chart for the "orthopedic bathtub," abbreviated, "Ortho-tub," since we were being very sneaky indeed and since it probably looked a little more professional than an order to put the patient in a rubber dinghy (life boat), full of water!

That night in the Little Club, I found some Air Force pilots who passed through from time to time and stayed in the BOQ. I asked them if they could get me a dinghy without too much trouble, and explained the whole thing. They laughed at first, but then the logic of it caught up with them and they said, "Oh, that really is a good idea—so simple, and inexpensive, too. Everything about it seems perfect." So they promised to bring one back with them when they returned in a week.

The next week they did return, but without the dinghy. But they were so optimistic and excited about something, I could hardly wait to hear the news. "We have the most wonderful news. We don't have the dinghy with us; we had to clear the whole thing with our CO, who thought it was such a great idea that he wants to fly it down and present it to you on the runway and have a ceremony!"

I thought I was going to die. Here we were with this

clandestine plan going, and the guy with the dinghy wants to have a ceremony!

I held my face in my hands for a few seconds with my mind racing for a gracious answer and finally blurted out, "What on earth are we going to do? I really love your CO for the thought, but things aren't the least bit normal here. I think the chief nurse hates me, and something like this would blow her mind. If the doctors weren't behind me, I wouldn't dare risk it."

Then we all decided they would have to convince their CO that sneaky is preferable to flashy *any* day, and a lot more fun, too. So the problem was solved before I fainted. They were sure their CO would think sneaky was more fun, and he did. (And, of course, it really was!)

In fact, the whole thing turned out to be fun—and, in my professional opinion, just what was needed to make the ward more therapeutic. The patients would strip down except for a towel, and getting them in it would be funny and "embarrassing" (except that we weren't really). Some could make it over the sides with it fully inflated, then legs in traction or casts could rest on the soft rubber sides. It was a perfect size, a one-man dinghy, and they had a nice soft headrest, too. But before they got to do too much resting, we siphoned water from a giant garbage can on a cart all over them. It was great for washing hair and laughing and screaming . . . being people instead of "patients," regimented on a dull ward all day "forever and ever, amen" it seemed. Sort of a breaking out of the mold. It was good. And although we never named the dinghy or christened it, for me it was always sort of the "SS Illegitimus Non Carborundum!"

Even badly incapacitated patients could use it. We deflated it and slipped it under them as gently as putting on clean sheets, then blew it up by mouth—and tried not to be quite so rowdy with the water!

With the spring, First Sergeant Solis arrived, back from Vietnam, with his wife, six kids, and King, the German Shepherd. He had been with the Golden Knights Parachute Team, and took over as president of the Parachute Club when LT Sullivan left. (Jumping was still a big factor in saving my sanity up until the day I left the Army.) He took one look at me and said, "If we don't look out for her, she's going to get killed."

I didn't mind. I certainly didn't want to get killed, although I had very much liked being somewhat free to goof off. None of us ever questioned anything he said; he was an *expert*. And he really did look out for me, to the point that I got rather dependent and didn't pursue sky diving when I left the Army. Dependent and sky diving just don't mix well at all. But we were buddies, and there were some very good times. When I managed to forget the hospital, it was a good summer, filled with lots of parachute meets where I found that my problems with canopy control were largely a matter of motivation—if I had to, I could. I'll always remember Sargeant Solis's smiling, backward somersaults off the wing!

And 1SGT Solis will always be tied in my memory with the anguish of one patient who had stepped on a mine. It had quite literally blown off his rear end, totally. Horrendous expanses of brownish-gray, nasty, smelly, bubbly skin grafts reminded me of driving through Texas . . . *expanses*. He was stuck on a frame that was turned every hour, but which gave him little relief, and actually seemed more like a torture rack than anything else. And then there were the large, raw expanses from which they had shaved the skin grafts.

And then there were the flies, back again for the summer.

The other patients, no matter how bad off they were, could at least swat at the flies, but he was stuck on his frame, unable to protect himself at all from them. He was on the brink of losing his mind. I called hospital supply for a mosquito net and told them it was an emergency. They wanted paperwork. And then they wanted time to process the paperwork! Never mind the hell that the patient was going through, or that we had to have a corpsman with him all the time—guarding the skin grafts from flies!

I called 1SGT Solis at his unit on post and said, "Help, help, emergency! I have to have a mosquito net right away."

Fifteen minutes later, he appeared at the door of the nurses' office with a mosquito net. I'll never forget it—the patient was so grateful.

Such a simple thing—*gratitude* for a last resort that we

never should have had to resort to in the first place! Soldiers were given the impression that if they got wounded, their country would see to it that they got "the very best of care . . ." There was such an emptiness to so much that was said back then. All that talk about a "Great Society," a society that wasn't even providing the basics for its soldiers *after* they had offered the supreme sacrifice . . . a sad symptom of a country in serious trouble.

It was a very real part of the special hell that was Vietnam. We felt our country crumbling beneath us long before we ever lost the war. Crumbling in its commitment; crumbling in the values which made us great and good and gave us strength; crumbling in a president who admittedly cared too much about the opinions of men, and in so many leaders who put their own careers first and everything else far behind. Veterans witnessed the crumbling from the inside out when the chips were down, individual by individual by individual, and we experienced the consequences more than most.

That summer, the patients used the "orthopedic bathtub," and little by little, the skin grafts began to "take" on the patient under the mosquito net. In September, my three years with the Army were up. It wasn't much of a decision to leave; I could see little future in it for me. Although I had done my best, it had required that I fight the system almost every step of the way to do it and to keep any semblance of integrity.

I drove away from Fort Campbell's green grass, white buildings, and summertime reminiscent of "baseball, hot dogs, apple pie and Chevrolet" and so much much more determined to race onward with life. For years, about the closest I ever came to summing up my experiences as a soldier in Vietnam and back out again, was once to compare the prevailing philosophy of "Don't rock the boat" with the "SS Illegitimus Non Carborundum," and to think, *I suppose they had their boat and I had mine*.

29
Later

"Don't look back. Something may be gaining on you."

Satchel Page

Like most everyone else at the time, I pretty much locked the door on Vietnam and threw away the key. My sister had a good job as a nurse at Emory University in Atlanta. It sounded so good I decided to join her for a while. But the Army popped out at me one last time in the form of the chief nurse from Fort Campbell, seeing a last chance to screw me up and taking it. She sent an unofficial, unauthorized, and apparently very uncomplimentary reference to Emory. Before they had said, "Just let us know when you want to start work—start anytime," now they wouldn't reconsider me for employment even after I finally got to the bottom of it all. It must have been quite a report. Although, after considering the source, I realized it had to be the supreme compliment.

Getting to the bottom of Emory's "about face" concerning me, wasn't too easy; however, armed with $11 and my mother's Shell card, I set out for Fort Campbell and a confrontation.

Nobody knew anything—I had never seen so many "innocent" faces. The commander of the hospital did immediately write me a letter which recommended me for

207

practically anything! And the chief nurse, bless her heart, sympathetically volunteered that a Captain So and So at the end of a very long hall might be able to help. He turned out to be a psychologist or sociologist, and encouraged me to feel free "to talk about it" *anytime*. He also added (I always thought just to let me know I was defeated), "It will take a lot more than a credit card and $11 to get to the bottom of this."

I said, "Talk is cheap," and prissed out, on my way to getting to the bottom of it. Before the month was out, my congressman had somehow *convinced* the chief nurse that it wasn't very smart to continue lying about it!

So I go a job at another hospital and locked the door, one more time. My new job was boring . . . a 30-bed, medical/surgical ward, staffed by others who seemed more bored than I was.

The nurses mostly talked about recipes and cakes. People were getting blown away in Vietnam and their conversation was about *cakes*. It wasn't their fault, but I could hardly stand it, although I probably couldn't have verbalized my feelings. After all, Vietnam was far behind me. I wasn't looking back, not me.

So I moved back to Florida and applied for a job near home. The supervisor said, "Oh, you were in Vietnam. You should be just perfect in the Coronary Care Unit, we really need someone."

I said, "Okay," and wondered if you had been to Vietnam it meant that heartache and death were automatically supposed to follow you for the rest of your life.

I didn't like that job, either. Although it wasn't boring, I sensed the same lack of caring in the staff as I had in Atlanta.

The last straw was added one day when one of the doctors mentioned he thought it was time to "pull the plug" on a patient's life support. One of the nurses walked over and kicked the plug out of the socket in a way that seemed to say, "It's nothing at all to me, I'll be *more* than happy to do it."

I came to hate that job, the death, the attitude. I suppose

Vietnam was behind my hatred somewhere—although I never consciously thought about it.

The day my year was up, I quit.

I began to feel I had seen enough medicine and nursing to last me a lifetime. The profession certainly wasn't what it was cracked up to be. I finally realized I actually hated hospitals; I could hardly even bear to visit sick friends anymore.

I doubted seriously that I would ever work in nursing again; life is too short to spend it doing something you think you hate, although it seemed to come naturally to me. One thing sort of led to another, and before I knew it I was totally involved as an agent with our local Humane Society. I was on call 24 hours a day to pick up hit animals, and we were hot on the trail of some dog fighters, and well on our way to closing down a pet shop which dealt primarily in misery.

By then, I was already well on my way to losing faith in humanity; medicine and nursing being the main culprits. War *can* sometimes be morally justified and I had expected man's inhumanity to man in war, but I didn't expect it in our own hospitals. I no longer had any misgivings about man being basically good. Even the best humanity had to offer, the "helping professions," were teeming with sadists, the greedy, and the incompetent.

But the animals; they were innocent. I thought they *deserved* help. And very few were coming to their aid. I picked up those hit dogs with a vengeance. No distance was too far, no hour too late, no situation too dangerous—even the police called me for help. I splinted broken bones with rolled-up paper plates; I muzzled them only when absolutely necessary; I could rush them to the veterinarian before they knew what happened to them. I hit trees, bent my fenders—but I was fast. And the big ones always threw up in my car. Mercy was all I cared about, I was obsessed with it. And there was something about rescuing those mangled, bloody little bodies that satisfied something deep inside . . . and their innocent faces, their eyes, trusting. *Betrayed trust.* My heart was breaking, but there was something strangely "comfortable" about it—kind of an old familiar rut. Surprisingly, I had absolutely no insight into this at all, at the time.

In 1975 I watched the fall of Saigon on TV, horrified, but not really surprised. Just a little more *betrayed trust*, but then, I had become used to it.

As North Vietnam broke its word (naturally) of the Paris Peace Accords and invaded the South, Congress turned its back now on an ally in desperate peril. However, in reality, Congress had long since turned its back. Without spare parts, and with only four rounds of ammunition per soldier, the South Vietnamese fought in vain to hold off the largest armored invasion since Hitler's tanks rolled into Poland!

This had been no "civil war," but a well-planned conquest of an entire region by communist forces. And the "masters of deceit" had fought the war and won it on American streets, college campuses, and in congress, without ever firing a shot!! And a nation that had lost its vision and love of freedom, lost its first war, and honor it had yet to regain. For in their haste to get out of an unpopular war, our government knowingly left behind hundreds of POWs.

As hundreds of thousands of Vietnamese were murdered, tortured and fled their ancestral lands in leaky boats, no students or press protested in America. As the communists committed genocide in Cambodia on the grandest scale history has ever seen, their "useful idiots" in this country fell predictably silent. And Jane Fonda, quite possibly one of the most heinous traitors in American history—if you ask any Vietnam veteran, would soon be made rich by Americans with nothing more important burning in their souls than their physical appearance.

For me, Vietnam was ending the same way it had started, with long lines of refugees running for their lives and *terrible suffering*. But this time, the heart-felt cry of a naive high school girl, "Why doesn't somebody help them" didn't come. There was no hope, no help. It was defeat and it was final; and, after all, I had "thrown away the key." I simply put Vietnam out of my mind.

I moved to St. Augustine. As I was unpacking with the TV on, I heard this very strange voice say, "I believe in miracles because I believe in God."

I thought, "That must be a real weirdo from the sound of that voice; I'm going to look and see if the body is as strange as the voice."

It was! It was Kathryn Kuhlman.

I was still having real problems with God. I'd gone about as far as I could go with humane work; I just couldn't stand seeing so much suffering any more, and I couldn't understand how a good God could allow innocent people and animals to suffer so horribly. Not just the neglect and injuries, but the millions upon millions of cruel and useless laboratory experiments, and so much more. Everyone I knew in the Humane Society agreed we were fighting a losing battle on many fronts. And yet, I suppose I was still seeking; at the end of my rope, burned out, totally fed up with people . . . and their cruelty. Shades of Vietnam!

To make matters worse, I had been in the occult for several years—about enough time for it to catch up with me, which it *always will*.

I had naively thought that anything supernatural was of God. But I found out there are two sources of supernatural power—God and Satan. Although Satan's power is much less, he does possess real supernatural power, and is more than glad to demonstrate it to those unsuspecting souls like me who might happen to wander through while "seeking God."

As interesting to me as the occult was to begin with, it was around this time that I began experiencing severe anxiety and fears—the most hideous fears. There was no peace *at all* in my life. When you mess with Satan, he makes sure you pay the price.

And Kathryn Kuhlman, who "believed in miracles because she believed in God," looked and sounded like a first-class kook! *Big help*. God, *where are you?* But then, she had some apparently normal-looking people on her show who claimed to have been healed by God. They even had medical reports and x-rays. Something about it intrigued me. I had tried everything else; I decided to check it out.

I went to one of her meetings, driving 200 miles to get there.

I saw miracles with my own eyes. There was indeed something to it. *Kathryn Kuhlman was no kook.*

Still, all was not well. I dreaded the nights because they were times of torment, of stark raving terror. The only way I could sleep at all was with a death grip on a crucifix that the nuns at boarding school had given us at graduation—*blessed for a happy death.* I was beginning to think I might *really* need it! And I awoke every morning with the same death grip as when I fell asleep, if I did fall asleep.

One night, I awoke to find a "Yogi" standing at the foot of my bed. It was real—no hallucination. I'm not really sure how I know, but I do. And such a sense of evil pervaded the room that it cannot be described. I screamed and jumped from the center of the bed into the adjoining bathroom. I couldn't have held out much longer; the lack of sleep, if nothing else, was really wearing me down.

I went to a simple little church. They said it was "Full Gospel" which meant that they believed the whole Bible. And the pastor showed me a few basic truths that no one in all those years had happened to mention:

"For all have sinned and fall short of the glory of God" (Romans 3:23).

"For the wages of sin is death" (Romans 6:23).

Nobody had ever just flat out told me I was a sinner before. I had always thought I was a good person; I had even thought I was a Christian. But once I heard the truth, it was the most blessed, liberating thing anyone had ever said. I *was* a sinner, and I felt I was dying. It explained the torment I felt.

"Jesus said, 'I am the way, and the truth, and the life; no one comes to the Father, but through Me.'" (John 14:6).

All the "other ways" I had tried to find God hadn't worked, they had gotten me deeper and deeper into spiritual trouble.

"That if thou shalt confess with thy mouth the Lord Jesus, and shalt believe in thy heart that God hath raised Him from the dead, thou shalt be saved. For with the heart man believeth unto righteousness; and with the mouth confession is made unto salvation," (Romans 10:9 & 10).

Suddenly Jesus was so real to me that it almost "hurt."

What a reality! And He was *my* Lord. You know when you've been born again, because its more real than anything in the world and *peace* comes with it, not torment.

A few minutes later, as I was praying with some of the people in the church to be baptized in the Holy Spirit*, I spoke in a language I had not learned and fell to the floor under the Power of God. Someone caught me, and it felt like falling up instead of falling down! What a glorious experience—peace and joy and light and love *flooded* my soul.

That night I slept like a baby and awoke the next morning still engulfed in the love of God—it felt like an actual blanket of love about six inches thick! No more nightmares, no more demonic visitors, no more terror. Then Jesus started teaching me how to wage spiritual warfare through His Word. Later, when the demons tried to come back, I fought them off easily, and slept, *"safe in the presence of my enemies."*

Jesus began restoring my faith in humanity . . . giving me a love for people better than I had ever had before—and *not just for the deserving*; that's God's kind of love. And He assured me that animals are important to Him and in His special care!

In 1978 when I heard about the Boat People from Vietnam, my heart went out to them. *Refugees again!* By the thousands, willing to risk everything to be free, and dying at the hands of pirates and on the sea, often to be turned away if they reached land. I would cry, and beg the Lord to send me to work in the refugee camps.

I heard about a group based in Switzerland who worked in the refugee camps, but you had to go through their three-month school first . . . a "Discipleship School." They had a fine reputation and I set out with high hopes. I was so willing to cooperate and so trusting that I didn't even realize until half-way through the school that they were using

*Something quite scriptural that still happens today. Acts Chapter Two. Christianity is what the Bible says it is, if you just believe the Bible!

brain-washing techniques, and had gotten into some very serious false doctrine concerning authority and submission.

I dreamed every night that I was escaping, and I suffered through it, but I finished the school—I was still holding out hope of working in the refugee camps. But when it was over, I felt like a zombie. It reminded me of something my mother used to say, "The hard school of experience, fools will learn in no other."

She was right. It was a hard school, but I had learned and the Lord had allowed it. I believe He allowed it as an actual example of the things He had been teaching me.

I had thought I finally understood about all the suffering in the world. God literally made men free—free even to sin and hurt one another if they so desire. *Freedom*, the second-most precious gift after life itself. I had seen men fight and die for it. I had seen children suffer in a struggle for it, and now I desperately wanted to help those who were risking everything for it. Yet I had never lost even a little of my own freedom. I knew it was precious beyond telling, yet I still needed the experience of this school to really feel it for myself.

Now, as the bus sped toward the airport, I heard myself saying right out loud, "Free at last, free at last, thank God Almighty, I'm free at last."

I didn't care who heard me! Never again would I blame God for man's suffering. God gave the *priceless gift*; man causes the suffering.

When one of the leaders of the school found out that I had been in Vietnam, he said, "Oh, come tell me how you plan to go to the refugee camps to make restitution."

He was taunting me and it really hurt; I was reminded of the hippies in the San Francisco Airport! I must say, I exhibited admirable self-control; I didn't say anything because there was nothing I could have said in love at the time! But now I can, and it needs to be said, "I didn't see any smart-mouth Swiss over there fighting Communism!"

Americans have been the most generous people on earth with material resources and the lives of sons and brothers and husbands and fathers for the freedom of others. Vietnam may have turned out to be a big mess, but most of us who went, went for a good reason. *Vietnam*. It seemed to follow me like a curse and jump out at me when I least expected it!

So I ended up in Haiti, riding donkeys into the mountains doing "mobile clinics." Saw *a lot* of suffering—never blamed God. The lesson stuck.

But as much as the Lord had helped me, even with Vietnam, and as much as I tried to never look back, it was "gaining on me." An entire year of stifled emotions and unresolved conflict can't be pushed back down and simply forgotten forever. That's why it does gain on us, and keeps popping up from inside where most of us squashed it down years ago—because, to get the job done, we had to ... the frustration, the anger, *any emotion*, all the suffering apparently for nothing, the *games*.

Haiti looked a lot like Vietnam; even the missionary who picked me up at the airport said, "I think Haiti looks like Vietnam!"

Then I hit another snag, the real clincher—politics. I'm sure it must be inevitable, a certain amount of politics in anything, even churches, but my Missions Board was seeming more and more political as time went by. They had promised a mobile unit which was reneged on (for political reasons) the moment I arrived. And they had promised "all the medical supplies I could use," but month after month, nothing materialized. Little children were suffering while grown men played *games*. *Again* ... more faces, innocent, *trusting*.

I practically went berserk. I suppose you can stuff it all back down just so long. I wrote a letter to my Missions Board that I'm not too proud of, but which they needed to hear, packed up and left Haiti.

I began thinking about Vietnam all the time, everywhere, even in church. I had dreams—dreams of feeling sick from the smell of blood (which was really strange since that never happened in Vietnam), and weird dreams about the Vietnamese.

I started writing; it made me sick—physically, something close to nausea with a headache. As I struggled with buried conflicts, still unresolved and seemingly unresolvable, with unanswered questions, with the overwhelming sense of betrayal, and just plain old pain, a feeling of isolation settled in over me. It was subtle in a way, and yet so real I could almost sense a barrier between myself and everyone else.

There seemed to be a huge disparity between what I knew had occurred and my perceptions of it at the time. I tried my best to break through to the reality of it, but couldn't. I suppose *bewilderment* best describes what it felt like— bewilderment with anxiety. And I didn't know what I was anxious about. My nerves just felt absolutely shot.

A friend from way back in my Humane Society days called me two or three times to say she had seen something on TV about nurses from Vietnam having "delayed stress." She kept saying, "I think you've got it, don't you think you ought to get some help?"

And every time, I replied that I was "*Just fine*, that I had gotten through Vietnam fine, and was still fine." I thought I was. I had never even heard of "delayed stress."

After a while I stopped writing; creativity ceased. I heard about the Vet Center in Orlando, that they had a rap group. So I attended the group, at first simply thinking it might help me get back to writing. I still didn't think anything was wrong with *me*, even though I felt terrible!

For weeks I hardly said anything in group; I couldn't get enough of a handle on what was going on inside me to talk about anything. Sometimes someone else would say something that would seem almost overwhelming and I would think I was about to cry, but I never did. It is still almost impossible for me to cry in front of others. Just a little "leftover" from a time when, if the world was falling apart, I had to hold it together.

I continued to feel like a "fish out of water" everywhere I went. My Christian friends prayed, but didn't understand; I think they thought I was backsliding. Fellow veterans understood about Vietnam, but often had no understanding of where I was coming from as a Christian. It all added to the feeling of isolation.

It was a dark night of the soul (about a year), but not so much of the spirit. The prayers helped, the rap group helped, and Jesus was there through it all *like a rock*. My faith actually increased . . . not blind faith, but "*because I know in Whom I have believed''* better than ever before, during this dark night.

I finally recognized one of my biggest problems was "psychic numbing," the cause of the disparity I sensed in trying to write about Vietnam. (I had pooh-poohed it when I first heard about it!) I have only recently realized that I still have some buried anger yet to deal with—I'm glad it's not a surprise to Jesus! And only after I had begun working at the Vet Center as a counselor did I finally get up my nerve to ask one of the psychologists if he thought I had "delayed stress." He answered, "Not only *did* you have it, you *do* have it: a classic case!" And I wondered if I had just bought the latest "package" they were selling these days! I have often thought that "delayed grief" described it better.

Although many veterans do have "delayed stress" (PTSD) and need counseling *that it has taken years to obtain for them*, I have come to regard the "selling of this latest package" with some caution. In some cases, it has become such a "bandwagon" that in all the hoopla about it, the public has lost sight of the fact that the majority of us did not return from the war as "emotional wrecks" but better, stronger people for our experiences—even *with* PTSD.

I get a little distraught with those who preach the "Rose Garden Gospel." The Lord never said we weren't supposed to be human, and humans sometimes hurt. He *promised tribulation—and His peace in the middle of it*. "The peace that passes understanding"—you can't understand for the life of you why you've got it!

One thing I learned from the rap group is that many Vietnam veterans are still having a great deal of difficulty with trust. *I wonder why?* (Please don't miss the sarcasm in that question.) Often, they will only trust another Vietnam veteran. And although problems with trust can seriously discombobulate a person's entire life, I think I've come to the point where I can say with confidence that it could turn out to be one of the best things going for us. In my own case, I know it made me seek God in a way I might not have. I kept going until I found the truth; not content just to take someone's word for it, or with something that wasn't logical, or with someone else's watered-down, secondhand religion. Although I am still grateful for even a *nominal* Christian heritage . . . it got me through Vietnam better than most. And I finally found the only thing which can ever totally satisfy the human heart—a fresh, real experience with Jesus Christ. And I found He isn't some quick and easy panacea—He's *the* answer to life!

I think there is hope in knowing that, scattered throughout the United States, there is at least the remnant of a generation who know firsthand that something was terribly wrong with the road this country was beginning to take in the sixties. No doubt it's still a confused generation, groping for answers but, thank God, at least still groping . . . and acutely sensitive to honesty. And, as one Vietnam veteran put it, "I can honestly say that I loved America passionately and profoundly."

It seems important to me to try to evaluate what it was that made America great. A man once said, "America is great because America is good."

But what brought us so quickly to become a nation which one day could consider the inhabitants of another country less than human . . . and the next, callously declare its own unborn children non-human? I'm convinced it's because we have forgotten who we are and where we come from.

It seems pertinent to me that in the Old Testament, every time Israel began slipping away from God, she also began having "problems on the battlefield"—like losing! And I've often wondered about integrity in leadership. The Bible talks about the fear of God being the beginning of wisdom, but what is the fear of God? It's not an unhealthy terror! *It's the hatred of evil; it means caring more about what God thinks about you than what man thinks.* So simple . . . and so obvious when it's missing.

I've wondered why America has traditionally been a champion of freedom. It's not that we are by law a Christian country, it's that we are by law a free country, free because enough people knew God personally to understand the value of freedom and that it is a right backed up by the authority of God Himself; that it is indeed worth fighting for. The

Constitution of the United States is a profoundly "Judeo-Christian" document in its content and morality.

If Vietnam was anything, I think it was a clear warning of trouble in the very fiber of who and what we are becoming—on the most personal, private level and on up through the ranks of our legal, government and executive branches. I would hate to see us have to go to war today; I'm not even sure that we have what it takes anymore to resist enslavement. I can only pray we will really turn back to God and to the Biblical truths which once made us special and strong and good, and that if we ever begin slipping away again, it won't happen in the middle of a war.

Guilt is a problem among Vietnam veterans. There is "survivor's guilt." "Why me? Why did I live when all of those good guys died?" And some, at least, have found that God had a specific purpose for their lives. I wouldn't hesitate a moment to say that He has a specific purpose for all our lives, if we'll only turn them over to Him . . . *sell out 100% to Jesus, and watch what happens!*

Some are guilty over things they did that they know were wrong. God says, *"Come let us reason together. Though your sins be as scarlet, they shall be white as snow. Though they be red like crimson, they shall be as wool"* (Isaiah 1:18).

Only God can remove guilt. Psychiatrists are traditionally stymied by it. But Jesus specializes in it—no penance necessary, no gimmicks needed. There is hope; and whatever caused the guilt, God isn't shocked.

Some are guilty over things they shouldn't be guilty over at all. Killing in battle is not murder; the Bible makes that more than clear. In fact, King David, *"a man after God's own heart,"* was a soldier and he had his *"mighty men of valor"* and they *"did exploits for God"* (2 Samuel 23:8-39). War was probably no less nasty then than it is now.

When the Vietnam Veteran's Memorial in Washington was dedicated, one of the reporters said something like, "Well, they finally got their monument; they built their own monument and held their own parade."

My first impression was that it was sad and unjust. But then immediately I thought, "No, it's only right." Even those who watched the war every night on television don't know the truth—maybe especially those. Only the veterans themselves really know. *But we do know* . . . for what and to whom.

We experienced the all-out assault on human dignity; the games and the politics; we saw the mutilations and the terrorism, and felt our country beginning to crumble beneath us—not to mention war itself. We also know the good that was there:

> "Not in the clamor of the crowded street,"
> Not in the shouts and plaudits of the Throng,
> But in ourselves, are triumph and defeat."

Longfellow

30
"It's Wavering Image Here"

> So nigh is grandeur to our dust,
>   So near is God to man,
> When Duty whispers low, thou must,
>   The youth replies, I can
>
> Ralph Waldo Emerson
> Voluntaries, III

In the back of my Bible I've written, "Memories of yesterday can destroy all tomorrows." *To live in the past is to walk in darkness for sure*. We do have to go on—and forgive and forget. But I wouldn't want to forget all together. And there does seem to come a time when it's good to remember—to take just one look back. The surprising thing is that at times I found myself missing it, or something about it, and wondering what it was that I missed in all the dying and killing and hurting and stupidity and insanity—and the whole tragic affair. *People*. Because Vietnam is also a time and place made precious by some who died and some who lived, and many who did their best and tried their hardest.

Vietnam did some pretty bad things to people besides killing and maiming them—the brutality and the senselessness of it. But it did something strangely beautiful too. It had a way of stripping off things that weren't real and leaving most everyone somewhat naked before themselves and everyone else, bringing out the best and the worst—often simultaneously. And I finally realized that in the place where I first feared the loss of humanness the most, I found more than I had known existed.

I don't know who Alfred North Whitehead was, but he wrote something interesting. He said, "Youth is life as yet untouched by tragedy... When youth has once grasped where beauty dwells—with a real knowledge and not as a mere matter of literary phraseology—its self-surrender is absolute." I think many of us experienced youth's self-surrender and sensed that strange beauty, even though, at the time, our feelings about it all may have seemed quite mysterious. Because as bad as Vietnam hurt, you still couldn't deny there was "just something about it."

I remember that night in the little club at Fort Campbell right before I left for Vietnam, wondering why, if God is God, there wasn't something earthshattering happening somewhere. Well, there is. Real miracles still happen. And God still talks to people. It's just that God is like anything else of value—He doesn't come easy. *But when you seek Him with all your heart, He will be found of you.*

Almost immediately after I found Him in 1976, He began showing me about people being made in His image. It's not some far-out, theological thing you can't see. It's real, and as down to earth as "shoes and ships and sealing wax" and "cabbages and kings." There is no great gulf fixed between the spiritual and the natural. God's mark is certainly on nature—"*the heavens declare the glory of God... and all the earth His power.*" But, more than that, His mark is still on man, fallen and undoubtedly rotten, and in desperate need of a Savior, but nevertheless made in His image. *When we forget God, forget where we are from, we lose that sense of human dignity! And things get really gross.*

In a way, it was right to have felt that people are basically good—man was made first in God's image. *That's why people have charm,* and beauty; that's why there is human dignity. That's why we have real heroes! That's why people have all the good things we see in them—attitudes of kindness, justice, courage, benevolence, lots of things, even little things. That's why we sometimes like "sinners" better than "saints." All men are created in God's image; sometimes you can see more of it in a sinner. The Christian is "just forgiven, not perfect." I've known many a *real* sinner who had a deep sense of personal integrity and honor which I have failed to see in some preachers. We dare not be arrogant.

Jesus allowed me to see His face once. I was reading my Bible and trying to understand about the madman of Gadara and all the pigs that ran off the cliff and drowned. Suddenly, I was "there." It was just like a movie going on inside. It was a terrible thing to witness. A filthy, naked, demon-possessed man and a huge herd of pigs stampeding over a cliff. There was grunting and screaming and choking, and a cloud of dust. Horrible! And it was a real tragedy—so many pigs were very valuable. But Jesus said it was done to show that the human tragedy dwarfs all others, that we have all fallen short of what God meant us to be. He said the pigs were less than nothing compared to that one disgusting man—*who had been made in God's image*.

And then I saw the expression in His eyes when He looked at him. I'll never forget it as long as I live. Everybody else was upset over losing the pigs, but Jesus looked like someone who had just found a huge emerald or diamond or something. To Him, the *man* was a treasure. I could never adequately describe His expression, but there was absolutely no condemnation, only intense love, and that look of just having found something priceless.

For a short while in my life, I had lost my faith in humanity. I no longer had any doubts about man's fallen nature. To hear someone say that man was made in God's image meant nothing to me. That's when the Lord gave me the vision and let me see His face. And waves of His Presence were flooding over me, and I finally understood what glory is—something that properly belongs only to God. And, at long last, in an instant of time, I understood the puzzle, the mystery about people. It's so simple, yet truly earth-shatteringly profound . . . we really are actually made in the *image of God*. Not some faraway God with a white beard, who, for so many years, seemed like an abstract idea to me, but a real person—a Father who reaches out to his children and communicates.

And then He caused me to remember my days in Vietnam

(of all things), when I had seen a balance of extraordinary good and bad. He caused me to remember the night I was kidnaped and had to walk back to the hospital in the dark, feeling that my heart would burst for love of humanity and the sweet, inspiring violin music that might as well have been playing. He caused me to remember when the plane took off from Bien Hoa airbase and I knew human life had never been more precious, and I had seen good in people as never before. He *can* give beauty for ashes.

Not long ago, I was reading a poem by Longfellow called, *The Bridge*. When I finished I said, "Oh Lord Jesus, this is it, isn't it? This poem kinds of sums it all up!"

THE BRIDGE

I stood on the bridge at midnight,
　As the clocks were striking the hour,
And the moon rose o'er the city,
　Behind the dark church-tower.

I saw her bright reflection
　In the waters under me,
Like a golden goblet falling
　And sinking into the sea.

And far in the hazy distance
　Of that lovely night in June,
The blaze of the flaming furnace
　Gleamed redder than the moon.

Among the long, black rafters
　The wavering shadows lay
And the current that came from the ocean
　Seemed to lift and bear them away;

As, sweeping and eddying through them,
　Rose the belated tide,
And, streaming into the moonlight,
　The seaweed floated wide.

And like those waters rushing
　Among the wooden piers,
A flood of thoughts came o'er me
　That filled my eyes with tears.

How often, oh how often,
　In the days that had gone by,
I had stood on that bridge at midnight
　And gazed on wave and sky!

How often, oh how often,
　I had wished that the ebbing tide
Would bear me away on its bosom
　O'er the ocean wild and wide!

For my heart was hot and restless,
　And my life was full of care,
And the burden laid upon me
　Seemed greater than I could bear.

But now it has fallen from me,
　It is buried in the sea;
And only the sorrow of others
　Throws its shadow over me.

Yet whenever I cross the river
  On its bridge with wooden piers,
Like the odor of brine from the ocean
  Comes the thought of other years.

And I think how many thousands
  Of care-encumbered men,
Each bearing his burden of sorrow
  Have crossed the bridge since then.

I see the long procession
  Still passing to and fro,
The young heart hot and restless,
  And the old subdued and slow!

And forever and forever,
  As long as the river flows,
As long as the heart has passions,
  As long as life has woes;

The moon and its broken reflection
  And its shadows shall appear,
As the symbol of love in heaven,
  And its wavering image here.

Henry Wadsworth Longfellow
America The Beautiful

When I got to the last verses, I remembered riding Gary Owen on the beach at Tuy Hoa. I was almost there again. I could sense that feeling of being one with the world, even while being in Vietnam with a war going on, and the sense of timelessness.

In the course of human events, terrible things happen. Another generation will go off to war if, for no other reason, than to stave off economic disaster. Many will die before they have time to figure it all out, or understand the remarkable good they will see in their buddies and themselves.

But God knows who they are, has the hairs on their heads numbered, knows them from beginning to end.

There *are* absolutes . . . *God and His word*. Life does not have to be meaningless for anyone . . . there is beauty on earth and remarkable good in people. The "image" is a wavering one, but, for sure, it *is* here!

Epilogue

In the summer of 1983, I was watching a Christian television program that was making an appeal for doctors and nurses for medical teams to help the refugees in Central America. I felt the Lord would have me volunteer, so I walked to the telephone and did. A few weeks later I received a letter: "Thank you so much for your interest. You are needed in El Salvador." My first thought was, "Oh no! Not another war. Guerrillas, Communism, complexities to match Vietnam, people burning to death in buses—no!"

But then I heard the still, small voice of the Lord whispering, "Don't ever stop fully casting your lot with the poor and suffering of this world. Have I ever failed to restore you soul *and more* when it gets you down?" He never has, so I ran through the apartment saying, "Yes, Lord, I will go; I'm happy to go."

After four medical teams with Feed the Children, I felt led to stay, and joined Paravida (a Christian Mission) in El Salvador where I lived for almost two years. The Lord told me only one thing in preparation for going, "*No man* is your enemy." And He gave me an awareness deep inside that my purpose was carrying the ministry of reconciliation.

Besides working in the refugee camps, the Lord began calling me and the group's evangelist into a ministry that wasn't new to me—into those hard-to-reach areas where few want to go. We went all over El Salvador. We had a card from General Blandone, the top general, authorizing us to go into any area and commanding the soldiers to help us. With the guerrillas, we trusted God. Often, we would take a bag of medicine and walk over the mountains into guerrilla-held areas, sometimes even at night. The guerrillas stopped us many times, commanding that we help the people only in their name, or that we bring them food and medicine. We always replied, "We can't help your cause, but we wish you no harm. We don't come in the name of the government or of any political party and we will not come in your name—only in the *name of Jesus.*"

They had always let us pass, except for one time that they planned an ambush for us. We lived through this, but a Catholic priest who lied about us—told the guerrillas we were with the CIA and encouraged them to kill us, was killed himself shortly after that. Churches are springing up and overflowing with joyful Christians in the midst of war and hatred in El Salvador and people are being reconciled to God and to each other. When the guerrillas there really find God, the first thing that happens is they want to stop being guerrillas. It has been our privilege to help some escape . . . a very dangerous practice, but well worth it in the sheer number of lives saved.

You will not hear the truth about El Salvador from the North American press. There is *much* hope for El Salvador; the people do not want Communism. They are scared to death that the United States will abandon them like we did the Vietnamese. And it looks like we may, just as many wanted to abandon the Contras and Nicaragua to Communism. Hopefully, their new government will truly represent *all* their people.

There is a tremendous revival going on in El Salvador. I am drawn to it like a magnet, probably because "where the Spirit of the Lord is, there is freedom." How strange to sense it so strongly there, of all places.

I had hardly noticed, but all traces of "delayed stress"

just disappeared. The Lord doesn't send us to do things that He himself doesn't equip us to do. In taking the ministry of reconciliation where it was needed most—in a different way, reconciliation was given to me in abundance, in my own heart.

In September of 1985, while in Central America, I became convinced that the Lord would have me return to the States to work on the problem of our POWs who are still held captive from the Vietnam War. I felt God was showing me there is more momentum now than ever before in this issue and that we have a special moment in history, given by Him, to either seize or lose forever. So I got on a plane and returned to the States.

Once again, it is the Vietnam veterans who are experiencing our corruption so acutely. The corruption of Nixon and Kissinger, who abandoned our POWs to Communist prisons; the corruption of petty, mid-level bureaucrats who have covered it up for so long, and the rumors of involvement of some of our highest officials in the SE Asia drug trade stand in our way today . . . as future generations are decimated by drugs, and our former First Lady tells them to "Just say no!"

We have come face to face with the fact that our brothers are Prisoners of Washington as well as of the Vietnamese . . . a Washington that can forget its own citizens if necessary, for political purposes.

There is hope. The Vietnam veterans are the first in two generations to fight to get their prisoners home. Twenty thousand were abandoned in Russia after WWII, and over three hundred after the Korean War.

My life in El Salvador was nothing less than a series of total impossibilities turned into victories by God. *I know what He can do.* Although we are fighting the biggest "city hall" in the world to get our POWs home—the United States government—we are not alone!

On July 4, 1988, trusting that if we fight well and don't give up, God will give us victory, I found myself on an airplane headed back for Vietnam. I felt certain I would be successful at something, although I wasn't sure what. I felt excitement and the peace of God. And I carried a heavy and sobering burden, knowing I would have a last-minute decision to make which might affect many, many others for years to come. I was returning with a group of veterans who had no idea what I was about to do. I had already agreed not to mention POWs. But then, this was a *covert operation*, to quote Ollie North, ''Of course I was lying!'' And I thought they were, too, at first.

As a comedy played on the movie screen at the front of the plane, I looked down at my wrist. It was the first time in years I was not wearing three POW bracelets—bracelets with the names of men abandoned in Laos almost twenty years ago, *never even negotiated for.* Men we have reason to believe are still alive, dreaming of home. Now I was wearing some cheap plastic bracelets, part of a ''dingbat, absentminded tourist'' guise that would later include pink shorts, pink Reebocks, and Panama Jack T-shirts!

This seems extremely stupid and silly to me now, but I had supplies with me just in case the underground church was hiding a POW, and we might be able to get him out. After all, the group I was going with was composed of four Christian veterans. Although the leader, Richard*, had said several times that we were not to mention POWs, I just couldn't bring myself to believe they weren't on a secret rescue mission. I couldn't believe they would completely turn their backs on Americans still held prisoner under the cruelest of conditions.

In addition to a collection of medicines appropriate to treat someone with any number of tropical diseases, I had special make-up to cover large scars, hair dye, and extra passports. I knew it was a long shot, childish, wishful thinking, and dumb, but I didn't care. I wanted to be prepared for a miracle.

Not only was I determined not to betray our POWs, I was equally committed to their families, many of whom I'd been arrested with (at the Wall on Veterans Day 1986, in a bamboo cage in Don Regan's driveway, planting a POW flag on the White House lawn). We'd worn holes in our shoes together (literally), futilely lobbying congress, only to finally realize that POW is a dirty word on Capitol Hill.

*Not his real name.

I joined up with the rest of the group in the Tokyo airport, and we spent a few days in Bangkok sightseeing and waiting for our visas, and I grew close to these Christian brothers, who were by now bringing back so many memories of Vietnam, twenty years later.

At the last minute, our tour switched airlines on us and we continued on to Vietnam, not on Air France, but via Air Vietnam! As the rickety, old, Russian-made plane without seatbelts rattled toward our destination, Vietnamese visiting their homeland for the first time since the war, wept openly in fear. I looked out the window and remembered a phrase from the movie "Rambo II," "back in the badlands!" Indeed.

I was preparing to infiltrate a communist country! No U.S. Embassy. They answer to no one and are cruel beyond belief. If caught, just as in the case of our POWs, they could keep me forever. *"Trust God and try to be brave; hang loose and be sensitive to whatever the circumstances may be,"* I told myself, and once again felt peace.

I arrived at Ton Son Nhut Airport in a T-shirt with clasping hands which read, "USA/Vietnam—It's Time." As we deplaned and walked across the tarmac in the blazing afternoon heat toward the terminal building, the Vietnamese wept harder, overcome with relief and the overwhelming emotions of setting foot again on Vietnam soil. The pain these people have lived through! I wept with them. How I wished there would be something we could do to help the Vietnamese people. I recalled all the nights on my face before the Lord, weeping and praying that He would send me to help the Vietnamese Boat People back in the 70's, then being sent to Haiti instead. Maybe Haiti had been sort of a "school" preparing me for now, honing my knowledge of tropical medicine and public health in the Third World.

I was snapped back to my senses when, through my tears, I came face to face with a uniformed customs officer. He looked "very NVA" to me! And I suddenly remembered Ted Sampley asking me a question that we both already knew the answer to: "What is the POW's worst enemy?" I had not hesitated to answer, "Time!" The POWs would have to come first. If I had learned anything from the

Vietnamese, it was the importance of not missing an opportunity! This one would not pass me by.

Then Ted had given me the instructions for "Plan A" on the pay phone we used for "sensitive talks." Ted is the leader of the POW activists: a highly decorated veteran, two tours, Special Forces—a tireless worker who would be a rich man if most of his time, effort, and money didn't go into the POW issue. Another one of those "dear souls with true hearts" who were tested and proven in Vietnam. If I was a POW, I would certainly be encouraged to know Ted was working to get me home. (I was encouraged *even now* to know that if anything went wrong, he would be working to get me back!)

Time seemed to go in slow motion as I flirted with the customs officer who was going through my purse, counting my money, and listing even my cheap jewelry. There were two $100 bills tucked in my pocket that I had not declared, to be used for "Plan A!" I felt no fear and looked him straight in the eye!

Out on the sidewalk we met Hinh, our Vietnamese communist guide. I liked her. She was poised, diplomatic, pretty, and seemed to be a basically decent person. She took us to the Tourism Office where we were introduced to the "Number Two Man." Richard asked how we should go about beginning a program to help the Vietnamese people. The Number Two Man told us we should give him our proposition in writing and he would see that it got to the proper authorities.

Richard sat down and wrote out the proposition. None of us saw what he wrote. The next afternoon, we all came out of our hotel rooms into the hall at the same time. Hinh was telling him the People's Central Committee was so pleased with what he wrote that they wanted to meet with us in person. His immediate response was, "Oh, I hope news of the contents of that letter doesn't get back to the States, it would make a lot of Vietnam veterans angry."

Though he might have had the best of intentions, this seemed like a very bad attitude to me, and I suddenly remembered something Richard had said to me earlier. He had said, "You are more than welcome to come with us to

Vietnam as a tourist. I will be in meetings with government officials and you can wait outside." I hadn't given it much thought before, but now I didn't like being involved in *something that was very pleasing to a communist government*, something I was implicated in and didn't even know what it was. Any doubts about initiating "Plan A" disappeared; I had my green light.

The next few days were spent sightseeing around Saigon (Ho Chi Minh City). We went to a Chinese temple in the Cholon district. We visited an orphanage and went through some tunnels around Cu Chi. I had been on Highway 1 into Saigon once before. It looked so different to me now— wider, smoother, with new trees and buildings not twenty years old along either side.

Plan A called for me to break away from the group, charter a taxi, and take about a six-hour drive to the southwest coast where an old French prison was located. There was sufficient evidence to show that American prisoners had been there as late as the early 1980's. Naturally, I doubted I would make it, even out of Saigon. I would probably be thrown out of Vietnam and could then cause an international incident to draw attention to our POWs, and keep the pressure on the U.S. and Vietnamese governments. I had notified an AP reporter in Bangkok that something might happen.

I had been "hanging loose," observing, getting to know Saigon, and trying to notice the faces around the hotel. The Vietnamese on the tour told us that we had more secret police eyes on us than "Carter has pills." Even our tour organizer told us our luggage was probably searched when we left our rooms, and that they were bugged. We were also followed when we left the hotel. I was beginning to feel very inadequate. How on earth was I going to pull this off when I was still afraid I would get *lost in Saigon*? Ted had said, "You can do it, all you need is a little Special Forces ingenuity!"

But I'm not a Green Beret, I'm a nurse, I thought, as I began making preparations for Plan A. *It will have to appear to be spur of the moment when it happens. I've got to be ready to do it the second I get a chance, in the next couple of days.* I was prepared to offer a cab driver $100 (from the money I had not declared), and I was all ready to appear "lost" in town. I had a city map and a country map, and my camera was around my neck. *When the time comes,* I thought, *I'll go to the market in back of the hotel and pretend to be lost.*

About noon the next day, my chance came. We were scheduled to visit a school for the handicapped. I and several others said we just couldn't face it. We had had a long, hot morning at a local orphanage. Just observing the children in their "sweatshop" jobs had been bad enough. It was the perfect time to credibly bow out.

I went to my room, threw my toothbrush and a few other items I thought might come in handy in prison in my purse (very proud of myself that it didn't look stuffed) and, instead of going to lunch with the others, ran down the stairs and headed for the market. Already I was being watched, but I felt good. After thinking about Plan A for days, it was a relief to finally get started. The suspense would be over soon—that was the worst part—wondering if I would succeed or fail.

I made it to the market, having stopped a couple of times to ask street vendors the way. I wanted the secret police to get into a very boring habit of always finding out that I was only asking directions. In the market I asked for hats, and bought one of many during the trip. When I left the market, I began asking directions to the hotel after pretending to get lost. Then I got in a pedicab and asked him to take me to a taxi. This was it! Now my heart was pounding! We seemed to be flying! I didn't dare look to see if anyone was following. I wondered if the driver behind me was watching me. Would the taxi driver be a loyal government employee, or would my hundred-dollar offer be more than he could refuse? I would soon know. As we rounded a corner, there it was, a taxi. There didn't seem to be many left in Saigon.

I had no idea where I was, but had rehearsed this moment in my mind so many times before that there was a definite sense of deju vu! I shook hands and calmly offered the driver $100 to take me to Rach Gia. He asked me to repeat my destination, so I showed him on the map. He thought a moment, looked at his watch, and said it was too late, that he didn't want to be on the road at night, but for me to return earlier the next day. I agreed. I showed him my $100 bill, to entice him to be punctual, and asked directions back to the hotel. I dropped one of my maps and made a "mini-scene" just so I would give the opposite appearance of stealth.

The next day it took a lot more effort to get away from the group without being noticed, but I found my way back and waited . . . and waited . . . but the cab never showed up. I returned to the hotel feeling like a failure. What to do now? I began to eat some M&M Peanuts I had brought with me and to pray, "Dear Lord, help me, I've failed. Here I am in a country that is holding Americans; surely there must be *something* I can do."

My purse was on the bed with some Vietnamese money beside it. *Dong*, they call it. The denominations are in green, red, and black with Ho Chi Minh's picture. I opened my eyes from prayer and my gaze fell on the money. It happened so fast! In an instant, I knew what to do! Just last night, someone in the hotel had asked if I wanted him to change money for me on the black market—three or four thousand Dong to the dollar, *depending*!!! I had two hundred undeclared dollars to work with—does anything circulate better than money?!

There is a $2.4 million reward put up by 22 U.S. Congressmen and Red McDaniel—a former POW, for any Vietnamese, Laotian, or Cambodian who will defect and bring a live American prisoner with him. It's their own personal money; that's how strongly they feel about our POWs. But every time they try to advertise the reward in southeast Asia, the United Stated Government blocks their efforts. The reward had never been advertised in Southeast Asia, *but it was about to be!* I could write it on thousands of Vietnamese bills and secretly distribute it throughout Vietnam!! "Thank you, God, thank you . . . for *Plan B!*" I even had a nurse's pen that wrote in red, black, and green ink. The message could be somewhat camouflaged on the Dong. While Richard and his group were busy "playing diplomat," I was going to be "Donging the Cong!" I liked it!

I located the Vietnamese with relatives who wanted American money, and that night I had too many Dong to count! I never did count all that money. It was all denominations— red, green, and black—thousands of bills. I just locked myself in the bathroom and started writing:

> 2.4 Million Dollars Gold
> For An American Prisoner of War
> At Any U.S. Embassy
> Call U.S. 202-544-4704

When we left Saigon a few days later by minibus to drive north to Hue, I was loaded with "messages" carrying the reward. There were marked bills stuffed in the lining of my purse, in all available pockets—even in my bra. I wanted to be ready for every opportunity! Fear seemed to be motivating me to think clearly. And, as bad as the fear sometimes was, I found I was also exhilarated. *If ever there was a righteous mission, to me this was it!*

The first marked bills I left were at a beach resort; I think it was our first rest stop. The gray stone hotel seemed bleak and deserted to me. But when we entered the restaurant there was a long table with soldiers, "Cambodian soldiers on R&R," we were told. I went to the restroom, which was used by men and women, and unloaded a large number of bills where they might be found by the soldiers.

Hinh, our guide, got sick and ran outside to throw up. I was very relieved because she wasn't there to see my hand shaking as I tried to get a glass of water to my fear-dried mouth. I picked at my lunch, straining to see who entered the restroom, and then wondering if they would come out yelling and search us all! Someone told me I didn't look very well, and I answered that I was hot. (But I was a lot cooler after getting those hot bills out of my bra!)

Several Cambodian soldiers went in, and came out with straight faces, then Hinh went back in. Fear made the blood seem to rush from my stomach to my head!! Would I be caught on my first attempt at laying out marked money? Somebody was talking to me, but I hadn't heard a word he was saying! Hinh came out, looking worse than I felt—thank God. She was too sick to notice *anything*.

We got back on our minibus and headed north again, toward Nha Trang where we were to spend a couple of days. It was a hot, dusty trip up Highway 1 with the afternoon sun beating on us. We stopped briefly to rest near Cam Rahn Bay and climbed on some huge rocks near the shore. I looked out over Russian ships. *If the Vietnam War was a mistake*, I thought, *why does Russia have Cam Rahn Bay?* Then I sat on the sandy shore and emptied my left pocketful of marked bills into a little hole in the sand. "Within a day or two, some truck driver will find them," I thought, "blowing all over the highway."

Back on the hot bus, Richard was overdoing his "gentleman" act with Hinh again. She was a classy girl, and I'll bet she saw right through him. Well, at least he was keeping her distracted for me.

By the time we arrived in Nha Trang it was late afternoon, and I had left marked money in three different places. I stood on the beach, surrounded by a large group of children, telling them every Vietnamese word I could remember; laughing, enjoying the cool air, wondering how long I would be free, and savoring every second of it. That night and every night thereafter, I was up almost the entire night, writing the reward on the money to be used the next day. I used a whole bottle of Visine on that trip, trying to keep up the appearance of being well-rested. Richard, who had only spent a couple months in Vietnam during the war, kept remarking about what a rigorous trip he thought it was, and what an "emotional roller coaster." I realized I could not afford the luxury of an emotional roller coaster. I had to be very level-headed, here and now!

That evening, two of the guys went for a walk in town, were followed, doubled back around behind the Vietnamese following them and he became so angry when he realized what had happened, he tore up a small tree!

At supper, Richard asked a former VC what he had done during the war. The VC responded that he had been a mortarman. Riachrd said, "Me too, but you'all were *much* better." *Spare me!* I thought.

The next day, I went to the market with one of the guys and left marked money in nooks and crannies everywhere! Then I pretended to be about to have a heat stroke. The only beverage we could find to buy was hot beer. It was terrible! And, while Rob* went looking for film, a Vietnamese woman let me sit in her shop while she went for ice. She was so nice—she plugged in an old electric fan and aimed it at me. She gave me a hug when we left and I gave her some unmarked bills—one thing I had was plenty of Vietnamese money!

"Having been overheated" gave me a few excuses to hang back and act strange, leaving marked bills behind. I was beginning to enjoy it—between fits of anxiety! Sometimes my attitude was that I didn't care if I got caught. My cause was a righteous one.

I left bills in the dark Cham temple in town, and had a "ton" of them in ziplock bags in my bathing suit when we went to the beach. I swam out a little way, dove under, and unloaded them, hoping they would wash ashore after we left for the States!

When we visited the Seaquarium in Nha Trang, I had a "field day!" The crowds of sightseers and opportunities to be alone allowed me to practically cover the entire area with marked bills. I had them rolled tightly with rubber bands. The bills were folded in on themselves so the reward offer might not be noticed for quite some time. What economically hard-pressed Vietnamese would ever turn them in? You could bet your life they would try to spend them—and I was!

I had so much Vietnamese money that my luggage was bulging. I hid it in my hotel room and worked at a fever pitch to write the reward offer on it and get rid of it. In Nha Trang, I began worrying that I would never be able to get rid of it all.

We moved on to DaNang, and that night before supper I noticed Richard seemed depressed. He confided that he thought we were being watched more closely than ever

*Not his real name.

before. I agreed; there was a very oppressive feeling in DaNang. I lay on the bed in my hotel room, wondering if I had spread the bills too thick, and had a couple of anxiety attacks. That night, I pitched a few rolls out of a window, but was afraid to do anything else.

On to Hue, which was beautiful and the best place ever for leaving bills. The Citadel, as well as other tourist stops, and the kings' tombs offered endless nooks and crannies. I ran out of bills, there were so many, and that night didn't even get an hour or two of sleep, I was so busy writing.

There is a buddhist temple in the Citadel where only men are allowed. I eased up to the door and pitched two rolls of bills in. I took a big chance on being seen because our guide and one of the guys were sitting under a tree right beside the door. But I couldn't turn down such a super opportunity! The fact that women couldn't enter would throw any suspicion off me.

We went back through DaNang and visited Marble Mountain. Talk about an opportunity! A huge dark cave with many, many small caves, crannies, nooks! I had a field day! Only once did I give someone who knew me marked money, and it scared me to death. But it was just another opportunity I couldn't pass up. *Nothing ventured, nothing gained!* I thought, as I gave him the money. I did it because I thought he wasn't really a communist but was able to work within their system. The perfect type of person to possibly take advantage of the reward.

The next time I saw him, I could tell by his eyes that he had seen the reward on the money. I was sure I was about to be arrested. I looked him in the eye for as long as I could, an eternity! Then I looked down. My heart was racing; I could hear it pounding! Would they keep me forever like the POWs? It was almost a relief to know that the suspense at least was about over. He turned and walked away. It took all the self-control I could muster to keep from shaking and gasping for breath! That night in the bathroom, marking more bills, I cried and thanked God for deliverance.

Back in Saigon, we had the meeting with the People's Welfare Committee. Richard began talking, saying, ''We want you to know that we have nothing but respect for your government . . . Before, Americans came here to kill and to destroy, and now we want to bring life." Then I knew for sure that my doubts about Richard were well-founded. How glad I was that I had initiated Plan B! I would have felt like I had betrayed all Vietnam Vets, otherwise! More people have drowned trying to escape that cruel government than died in the war! To me, Christians should stand against such evil, not give them respect and encouragement. I don't think any American went there to kill and destroy. We were fighting for their freedom. What a betrayal—not only of the POWs, but of the memory and sacrifice of our dead! I was so disgusted I could have vomited right there on the spot.

Richard finished his speech by saying, "We want you to know that we came here to submit ourselves to you." It was all I could do to keep myself from jumping up and screaming, "Not me! I won't submit myself to evil!" The only reason I didn't was because I didn't want to compromise Plan B—but I did refuse to have my picture taken with them.

After that, I spread marked bills with a vengeance. I no longer cared if I got caught. We went to the market behind the hotel about two days before leaving. I was stuffing bills everywhere. We knew we were being followed. My new attitude may have been too much; I think they knew by then that someone was doing it, but not who. I had even tucked some marked currency in the luggage of some Frenchmen!

I looked up and saw a very tall, ragged Vietnamese with one arm off at the shoulder, gesturing to me. He looked angry. He was begging, asking me for money. I thought he had probably been VC. I gave him unmarked bills: he was probably trying to trap me right there!

The day before we left we were sitting in the tourism office, with cups of tea. The Vietnamese were asking, "What can we do to make tourism better for Americans?" One of the guys piped up and said, "I would appreciate it if the secret police weren't so obnoxious. I was in the market the other day, and every time I bought something or gave a beggar money, they would snatch it away from me and look at it real close."

I sat there very calmly, not even rattling my teacup, feeling very prim and proper indeed, thinking, *Superspy! You did it! They think it's the guys!*

Back in the hotel, I had several anxiety attacks, wanted my mother, wanted a hamburger, and wanted *out of there*! The next 24 hours were the longest in my life. The suspense was terrible; so close to leaving for home, but *they know*! I made time pass by salting the hotel with the rest of the currency.

I had a few bills left over at the airport and was able to leave some in two different ladies' rooms where the maids would find them. We waited about an hour to get on the plane. The suspense was horrible. When I saw the plane I thought, *Freedom Bird . . . beautiful Freedom Bird!*

I sipped a little champagne as we waited to take off—more suspense—toasting to "Donging the Cong." The beautiful Air France plane finally took off. As we rose into the sky, a cheer went up. I didn't cheer; I quietly thanked God, it was still "our secret."

When I left Vietnam the first time, on the plane I remember thinking that my integrity had been kept, no *fanny-kissing at its finest*, only the best I could give. And, once again, I felt such deep satisfaction. I had infiltrated a communist country, gotten the reward into Southeast Asia, and did what I could. I had not betrayed our living POWs or the sacrifice of our dead. "Thank You, God . . . Thank You!" I breathed, and fell asleep.

INDEX

A

Abernethy, Bill, 108

Academy of the Holy
    Names, The,
    Tampa, 7

American Compound, 160

Atlanta,
  University Hospital, 4

ARVN's, 45

B

Ban Me Thuot, 41

Bangkok, 163

Batista, 3

Bible, 219, 223

Bien Hoa Airbase, 2, 33,
    120, 155–56

Blandone, General, 227

Boat People, Vietnamese,
    216, 232

Browning, Elizabeth Barrett,
    74

Byrd, SGT, 154, 161, 168

C

C-47 Transport, 104

C-130, 110

Cam Ranh Bay, 110, 113,
    238

Cambodia
  people, 237

Camp Red Ball, 111

Canada, 197

Castro, 3

Central America, 229

Central Highlands, 56

Chinese Temple, 234

Chinook, 45

Cholon district, 235

Christian Television, 228–29

Churchill, Charles, 174

Citadel, 238

Clarksville (KY), 201

Claymore mines, 152

Cleland, Max, 82

Clifford, Clark, 145

Cole, Richard, 108

"Combat," 124

Communism, 217, 228–30
    aggression, 146
    atrocities in SE Asia, 3
    forces, 160
    Congress, 211–12

Constitution of the United
    States, 221

Criminal Investigation
    Division (CID),
    199–200

Cuba, 3

Cu Chi, 234

D

Dak To, 121

Danang, 80, 240

DAP Reporter, 234–35

Darion, Joe, 26, 140,
    142–43

Dooley, Dr. Tom, 3, 8

E

El Salvador, 228, 229
    Paravide (a Christian
    Mission), 228

Eliot, Mama (Mamas and
    Papas), 121

Emerson, Ralph Waldo,
    224–25

Emory University, Atlanta,
    207

Episcopalians, 6

F

Feed the Children, 228

Fitchett, Dr., 65

Florida, 210

Fort Campbell, Kentucky, 1,
    13–14, 16, 17, 30, 89,
    114–15, 147, 157, 174,
    175, 179, 180–83,
    187–88, 194, 204,
    208–10, 222
    "home of the 101st
        Airborne," 13, 16
    Intensive Care Unit, 13,
        16
    Little Club, 15, 31, 182,
        205
    Parachute Club, 182, 186,
        206
    sky diving, 188
    PX, 14
    Sam Houston, Texas, 10,
        134, 147

France, Air, 232
French Prison (Vietnam), 234
Freud, Sigmund, 7

G
Golden Knights Parachute
    Team, 204
Green Beret, 234
Guerrillas, 228

H
Haiti, 217, 232
Hampton, Lynn
  army training, 10–17
  father, 5
  letters from Mark, 68,
      77–78, 120–21
  Mother, 4–5
  religious beliefs, 195,
      219–20
Harvard, 4
Hayes, Johnny, 108
Highway I (Vietnam), 234
Hill 875, 141
Hinh (Vietnam communist
    guide), 234
Ho Chi Minh, 236
Hitler, 211
Ho Chi Minh City (*see*
    Saigon)
Honolulu, 1
Hood, Richard, 108
Howdyshell, SGT, 124, 151,
    154

Hugo, Victor, 74
Humane Society, 213, 218

J
Jacksonville, 5
Jamison, COL, 128
Jesus Christ, 44, 215, 220,
    228
John 14:6, 215
Johnson, SGT (NCO), 193,
    202

K
Keefe, Brian, 115
"Kelly" SGT, 22
  alcoholism, 22–26
Kennedy, Jackie, 6–7
Kentucky, 203–4
Korea, 16, 33, 153
Korean War, 230
Kramer, SGT, 184–85
Kuhlman, Kathryn, 213–14

L
Laos
  people, 237
Lambrettas, 110
Leigh, Mitch, 26
Long Binh, 109–18, 121,
    124, 156, 163, 166,
    169, 173
  90th Replacement
      Detachment, 3, 12

Long Range Reconnaissance
    Patrol, 120
Longfellow, Henry
    Wadsworth, 54, 82,
    132, 222, 224–25
  The Bridge, 224–25
LSD, 193

M

Marble Mountain, 242
Marijuana, 192
Mark, 64, 67
McGinley, Major, 54, 57
Medical Civic Action Project
    (MED-CAP), 49
Military Police (MP's), 156,
    159, 201
Missions Board, 217
Montagnard, 41
  bracelet, 177
Montgomery, James, 18
Morrow, Vic, 124
Munnely, Colonel, 33

N

narcotics, 193
NCO Club, 154
Nha Trang, 237
  Seaquarium, 239
North Vietnam, 210–12

O

O'Toole, Peter, 26

P

Paine, Thomas, 123
Parachute Landing Falls, 185
Paris Peace Accords, 212
Pavlov, 7
Peck, M. Scott, M.D., 1
Philippines, 1
Phu Heip I, 34
Phu Heip II, 34
Poland, 213
Price, Captain, 154
POW's (Prisoners of War),
    212–13, 229, 232, 240
Proverbs, 70, 195

R

Rach Gia, 233
Rambo II, 232–33
Rodgers & Hammerstein, 6
  Music, 6
Romans 3:23, 212–13
  6:23, 214–15
Russia, 230
  Ships, 238

S

Saigon (Ho Chi Minh City),
    12, 108, 111–13,
    233–37, 240
  American Embassy,
    112–13
  People's Welfare
    Committee, 240

Presidential Palace, 112–13
Sampley, Ted, 230
Samuel II, 23:8–39, 221
San Francisco, 172
  Airport, 217
Schopenhauer, Arthur, 58, 118
Scottish Prayer, 185
Shakespeare, William, 140
Smith, PVT, 194
"Smith," General, 20
Solis, ISG, 205
South China Sea, 33, 58, 66, 207
South Vietnam, 95, 160
Southeast Asia, 237, 240
Solzhenitsyn, Aleksandr I., 27
Sturkey, COL, 203
Sullivan, Mike, 189–90
"Swarther" LTC, 34, 44, 45, 67, 109
Sullivan, LT, 204

T
Taylor, Sir Henry, 107
Tet, 156, 164, 165, 170
  Offensive of 1968, 164
The Ugly American, 94
Thomas, Dylan, 23
Ton Son Nhut airport, 113–14
Tuy Hoa, 33, 49, 51–53, 60, 73, 85, 112–14, 138, 161, 166, 178, 227
  hospital, 34–35, 38, 102, 124–30
  massive assault, 101
  personnel, 40, 85–89
  patients, 47

U
United Artists, 26–27
U.S. Army, 8
  91st, 109
  93rd Evac., 109, 116
  101st Airborne, 157, 162
  173rd, 65, 114–15, 120, 141–42
  C-rations, 50
  4th Division, 54, 57
  Medical Field Service School, 10
  Army Nurse Corps Officer Basic, 10
  PX, 50
  Special Forces, 16
U.S. Embassy, Vietnam, 232
U.S. Government, 237

V
Van Artevelde, Phillip, 107
Vet Center, Orlando, FL, 218
Viet Cong, 42, 95, 161
  atrocities, 66–67

Viet Cong (*cont'd.*)
  patient in hospital, 90–95
  regiments, 169
Vietnam, 2, 7–8, 10, 16,
    20, 30, 54, 58, 69,
    113–14, 186, 207–25,
    231–32
  Air, 231–32
  Christmas, 151
  Government, 235
  money, 239
  New Year, 156, 157
  people, 162, 218, 239
  terrorism, 46

veterans, 230
war, 230, 238
Vung Tau, 125

W

Waller, John, 155
Washington, 230–31
Wayne, John, 124, 141
Whitehead, Alfred North,
    222
Whitman, Walt, 90
Wiggins, Mrs. Floyd, 32
Wilson, SGT, 44
World War II, 230–31

Rory Managhan was back. He said he'd come for her but as far as Catherine could see, it was just another power-play in the bitter feud that raged between their families . . . it certainly wasn't love.

OUTCAST LOVERS

BY

SARAH HOLLAND

MILLS & BOON LIMITED
15–16 BROOK'S MEWS
LONDON W1A 1DR

First published in Great Britain 1985
by Mills & Boon Limited

© Sarah Holland 1985

Australian copyright 1985
Philippine copyright 1985
This edition 1985

ISBN 0 263 75063 9

Set in Monophoto Plantin 10 on 11 pt.
01-0685 – 54263

Made and printed in Great Britain by
Richard Clay (The Chaucer Press) Ltd,
Bungay, Suffolk

CHAPTER ONE

CATHERINE watched her brother's engagement party with a fond smile. He was the star of the evening and enjoying every second of it, as he twirled his new fiancée in his arms under the spotlight. Extrovert! she thought, grinning as she watched him tilt Lisa to one side like a handsome male film star, his wicked brown eyes filled with amusement. She'd always liked her brother—he was so easy-going, even though he was outrageously conceited. Luckily, she also liked the girl he'd decided to marry. Lisa was shy, reserved and took a long time to make friends with. But she was nice underneath, really nice, in the way that one knows she will never do anything to hurt or offend you.

'Poor Lisa,' James whispered beside her and she turned to look at him in the half-darkness.

'What do you mean, "poor Lisa"?' she queried with amusement.

James arched his brows. 'Imagine marrying into the Skelton family!' he drawled. 'A fate worse than death. Did your father have her thoroughly checked before he gave the go-ahead?'

Catherine laughed impulsively, shaking her red-gold head. 'You wouldn't dare say that if he could hear you!' Nobody would. Most people in this town were too much in awe of her father. She glanced at her brother again with a smile—of course, Stephen wasn't in awe of anyone. He was too busy enjoying life, and didn't really care much for being the eldest son of the family. All he wanted was a pretty girl, a beautiful car and a bottle of champagne.

never seen all your family grouped together
re,' James commented, looking around the
llroom at the well-dressed men and women, all
paying court to her father, Jed Skelton. 'Horrifying
lot, aren't they?'

She smacked his hand. 'Watch it—they're all I've
got!' She loved being part of a large family, it was
good to feel that there were always a lot of people
nearby and in all corners of England who knew and
loved her. That was one reason why she had come
back to Sleuhallen after her short spell of living in
New York. It made her feel safe, protected from
reality to be here, in the town of her birth. At least
here she would always have someone to turn to,
should she ever need help. But the outside world, she
had discovered, was pretty grim when it came to
people knowing and loving you.

'I must ask you,' James took her by the arm and
drew her close to him with a smile, pointing across the
room at someone, 'who is that funny little old lady
who looks so much like Miss Marple?'

Catherine followed his gaze to the slender white-
haired old woman and laughed, 'Funny old lady?
Don't be fooled! That's my Great Aunt Katie, and she
is not a lady to cross swords with!' She watched her
Great Aunt standing tall and erect, her elegant ringed
hands resting atop her black walking stick, diamonds
flashing at her throat. 'Even my father is scared stiff of
her. Nobody ever argues with Aunt Katie.'

James made a face. 'I'm glad you warned me. I was
thinking of asking her to dance. She looked so lonely
with all those diamonds weighing down her neck. Tell
me—is she horribly rich?'

'Horribly,' Catherine agreed with a smile. 'She's the
backbone of the family, always has been. If you asked
her to dance she'd rap your knuckles with that cane of
hers.'

James pulled a face.

Catherine glanced to one side as two small boys dressed in ridiculously formal suits ran past her firing imaginary guns at each other. They collided with a table and almost sent a cut-glass bowl of punch flying. Their mother, one of Catherine's cousins, came running after them angrily and smacked them both on the hand. Catherine smiled. It was a big family, full of life and enthusiasm, and she was glad to have that deep-rooted sense of belonging. It made such a difference to her life to know that she had an unbreakable foundation to fall back on.

'Little horrors,' James said with a grin, watching as their mother led them away by the ear. 'Thank God I never got married.'

Catherine paled, looking away. She had almost married, once. A long time ago. It had been so close to her she had almost believed it was a reality. But that had been when she was young and naïve, when she had believed in magic. She no longer saw romance in the sea and the stars, she just saw nature carrying on very well without her. She could remember sitting on a beach late at night in silence, listening to the waves and looking at the glittering sky. And she had thought the world was so exciting, so full. She had longed to rush forwards to meet it. Now she saw it as vast, frightening and far too big for her to take on. So she hid here, in this sleepy town of Sleuhallen, protected in the valley she had been born in.

The music came to an end and applause broke out, startling her.

'Here comes the proud father,' James said in her ear. 'Is he going to make one of his speeches?'

Catherine gave him a wry smile. 'What do you think?' she asked, laughing.

James raised his glass to his lips and downed the contents. 'I think I need another drink!' he told her.

Catherine gave him a warning look. 'Someone will hear you. You know how they're all in awe of him. It would get back to him in five seconds flat.'

'Money talks,' drawled James, as applause burst out when Jed Skelton slowly strode beneath the spotlight, and stood in between the young couple with his arms around each of their shoulders as he waited to speak.

Catherine watched her father's arrogant expression as he stood in silence, eyes barely flickering around at the friends and relations and hangers-on who surrounded him. He seemed so contemptuous of most of the people here, it was written on his tough lined face, and the long years of power and wealth had made his body stand with absolute self-assurance. Jed Skelton practically owned this town, Sleuhallen, and had made his presence felt to each and everyone who lived in it. He was the power behind the growing industry, the man who controlled livelihoods from behind the mahogany boardroom of Skelton Engineering, right in the heart of Sleuhallen.

He was her father, and she loved him—but she saw his faults clearly now. He was ruthless, domineering and there was a part of him that was almost iced over, although she didn't know why. She suspected it had a lot to do with Isabelle Managhan—but she couldn't be sure because it had all happened too long ago. That particular story was buried in the past, and her father never mentioned Isabelle's name in the house, nor would he allow anyone else to. The Managhan name was taboo in the Skelton household. It had been all her life.

But now she too had a reason for hating the Managhans. A damned good reason. The sins of the fathers had been visited on the next generations—and only now did Catherine understand the power of her father's hatred towards that particular family. Because only now did she share it.

'. . . Lisa will soon join the Skelton family,' Jed Skelton's dark cold voice rang out in the respectful and awed silence as he finished his curt speech, 'and we will accept her as a second daughter. Her friends will become our friends, and her enemies——' he paused, raising one long finger, 'will become our enemies . . .'

Catherine sipped her drink, looking away. Her father knew a great deal about enemies. How to hate them, how to destroy them and how to live with them. Catherine had learnt how to hate—but she had dropped out of the fight after that. It took too much out of you, to spend your life in a cold search for revenge—she had seen what it had done to her father, to her mother, and to the Managhans. Finally, she had seen it turn in her direction, and hatred of another generation had attacked her. She didn't want that to happen to another generation, she refused to pass on hatred to her children, when and if she had any.

'It still amazes me,' James said as they joined in the applause for her father, 'how a man like that could produce a son like Stephen.'

Catherine raised one pale brow with ironic amusement, 'But not a daughter like me?' she said dryly.

James laughed, eyes creasing at the corners. 'Paranoia sets in!' he remarked as the applause died down and conversation broke out again. 'You're more like your mother.'

Catherine gave him a wide smile. 'Thank you— that's a compliment.' She'd always admired her mother's poise and sense of style. Even now, when she was pushing fifty, her mother still looked like a fashion model from the pages of *Vogue*.

'Quite right,' James agreed, eyes flicking over her admiringly, 'You look extra ravishing tonight, if I may say so.'

Catherine had bought the black and gold ballgown

in London last month. It was startlingly original, and the sort of dress one would expect to see floating down a wide marble staircase in an old Hollywood film, with the feminine clouds of black silk taffeta, gold-edged, the off-the-shoulder neckline and enormous puffed sleeves.

She ran a slender hand through her red-gold hair, which fell in flowing curls to her bare shoulders. Eye-catching rather than beautiful, she had the kind of face one reads about in poems, with pale translucent skin, high delicate cheekbones and slanting green eyes that were ethereal rather than feline. Her father had always called her his little pre-Raphaelite angel, and consequently, Catherine adored Rossetti, Holman Hunt and all the other artists of the Brotherhood.

'Hi!' Stephen arrived beside them, grinning. 'Great isn't it? Have you seen the presents? My God—people have been so kind!'

Catherine laughed, pleased to see him looking so happy. 'You'll have to buy a bigger house to put them all in!' she told him, watching as he ran a hand through his black hair.

Stephen laughed. 'We'll never be able to get married now, or the whole town will go bankrupt!' He slid one hand into the pocket of his white dinner jacket, taking out a cigar which he held up for them to see, a wicked smile in his eyes. 'Even Dad's feeling generous, tonight,' he remarked drily. 'He gave me one of his best cigars.' And he lit it with a match, struck on the underside of a table nearby, which made Catherine laugh as she watched him.

Normally, Stephen looked like a homeless tinker, but tonight he was well-dressed, even handsome in the smart evening suit, his black hair brushed and silky. She had heard her father warning him last night not to arrive at the party looking like an Irish knife-grinder, and it had irritated Jed Skelton to hear Stephen laugh delightedly at the description.

'Lisa must be pleased, though,' Catherine pointed out. 'How is she coping? She looks a bit over-whelmed by it all. Did she realise what she was marrying into?'

Stephen frowned, nodding, 'Oh God, yes. I think it put her off for a while—you know how shy she is.' He flashed a quicksilver grin, 'But I soon talked her into it!'

Catherine laughed. She could picture that very clearly. Stephen had tremendous charm, a real gift with words. He could talk a blindman into buying a television set with no sound. If he hadn't been the only son of Jed Skelton, he would probably have made his way as a salesman, or possibly even a broadcaster.

'Be a pal, James,' Stephen said now, clapping a hand on James' shoulder with an air of camaraderie. 'Get me a refill! I'm dying of thirst, but this is my party and I refuse not to take advantage of it.'

James sighed, taking his glass. 'You've been spoilt rotten, did you know that?'

Stephen grinned, nodding.

James threw Catherine a wry smile, 'If it wasn't for the fact that your big sister would kneecap me, I'd tell you to shove off.'

Stephen drew on his cigar, watching James lope away towards the bar with three empty glasses in his hands. 'Nice guy,' he commented, looking back at Catherine, and she smiled, nodding in agreement. She liked James very much, he was tremendously good company, and she spent most of her spare time with him. She wasn't in love with him, she knew that, but then she didn't really want to be in love again. Although if it was possible to pick the man you would fall in love with, she would probably have picked James.

'I want a quick word,' Stephen said. 'Before James the Intrepid comes back.'

Catherine took a cigarette from her black velvet evening bag, fingering the slender gold chain as she put the bag back down on the shelf where it rested. 'Go ahead,' she told him, lighting the cigarette with a slim silver lighter and exhaling smoke in a steady stream.

Stephen frowned, eyes distracted. 'I've just been speaking to Billy Carter. He gave me some bad news.'

'Oh?' She frowned, eyes concerned as she studied him, 'What about? Not Lisa, I hope?' It surely couldn't be that, because he would hardly come over specifically to tell her.

Stephen shook his dark head. 'No, more serious than that.'

Catherine stared at him, suddenly uneasy.

The dark eyes fixed on her intently. 'Rory Managhan's back.'

Her heart stopped as she heard his words, but her mind raced frantically as she tried to take in what he had said. Rory? Back in Sleuhallen? It was unreal, she couldn't believe he was serious. Not after all this time—how long had it been since she had last seen him—two years?

Staring at her brother, her mouth open, she tried to pull herself together because she was aware she must look stricken, and she was. Rory Managhan was the one man she had hoped never to set eyes on again. But the last place she had ever expected to see him was here, in Sleuhallen.

'You're not serious!' she said, trying to look amused, but her voice sounded choked, even to her own ears, and there was a sudden wild look in her green eyes, the kind that can only be captured by a camera and make you turn away from yourself, because your eyes suddenly become windows, disturbing you with the force of your own emotion.

Stephen frowned, 'Of course I'm serious! Rory Managhan arrived in Sleuhallen today.' He drew on his cigar, eyes creased against smoke, 'He's been seen by a number of people.'

Catherine swallowed. 'Have you told anyone else?'

'You mean have I told Dad,' Stepehen said in a lazy drawl, and shook his head. 'Not on your life! He goes beserk at the mention of that man's name. God knows what he'll do when he finds out he's come back.'

Catherine looked away, pulses erratic. Stephen was right. Daddy had rarely mentioned the Managhan name, but when he did it was with a voice full of hatred and contempt.

She sighed, 'He'll find out eventually.' Looking back at her brother, she shrugged, 'You know how people talk here.'

He nodded. 'Yes, but that's not what worries me. I want to know what the hell he's doing here.' He laughed quickly, eyes thoughtful. 'It's twenty years since he left this town. I thought he was a confirmed New Yorker now. Why has he come back?'

Catherine held his eyes, her face pale. 'Revenge?'

Stephen made a face. 'You may be right. He's not just a nobody with a grudge now, though. He's bigger than Dad. He'll wipe the floor with the lot of us.'

Her shoulders slumped, but inside her heart was pounding unsteadily, her mind's eye conjuring up images of Rory. The dark hard-boned face, steel grey eyes and firm mouth. He was a man with impact, the sort of person you can't easily forget. Those sharp, threatening features were ingrained in her head for ever. Funny, she thought with a silent painful laugh, but I can never remember him as anything but a complete and utter bastard. But there had been days when she saw beneath the harsh exterior, a fleeting moment in time when he was tender, gentle and deeply sensual. But they were memories put aside now, long since buried.

'I suppose there's nothing we can do,' Stephen said now, and his eyes were distracted as he looked at her. 'The man's got good enough reasons to hate Dad.'

'Stephen!' she said sharply, frowning.

'Well, be realistic, Cathy! Dad completely destroyed his family, didn't he? I know Isabelle Managhan pulled a rotten trick on him, but she didn't deserve everything Dad did. He just doesn't know when to stop.'

Catherine sighed. There was some truth in what he said. Rory's mother had behaved selfishly, but had paid heavily for it. Isabelle had been engaged to Jed Skelton, but on the eve of her wedding had eloped with Jed's best friend, Damian Managhan. They had paid for the rest of their lives, and only Rory had been able to break the Managhan family out of the vicious circle of Jed Skelton's revenge. Now he was apparently going to go one step further and take his own revenge out on them.

Stephen studied Catherine, his face thoughtful. 'Has Rory been in touch with you since you left him?'

She swallowed on a raw spasm of pain. 'No,' she said in a low angry voice. 'No, he hasn't. I didn't expect him to, either. You know how badly it ended between us. There's no way we could ever speak to each other again.'

Stephen nodded with a sigh. 'So you don't suppose he'll try to see you while he's in town?'

Her heart was convulsive. 'I very much doubt it!' The thought made her want to run and hide. She hoped it didn't show on her face, because even though her brother knew exactly what had happened between her and Rory in New York, she couldn't bear to think of her feelings being exposed to anyone. She felt disorientated, needed to be alone to think, to calm down a little. But she had to put on a brave face for the sake of society, and that in itself took all her will-power.

'Here comes James,' Stephen said in an undertone. 'Are you going to tell him?'

Catherine felt startled. 'Of course not!' For a second she had almost forgotten who James was, and hated herself for not caring about him more. But although it was easy to find solace with a male friend who was good to you, she knew that just the mention of Rory Managhan's name was enough to drive everything else out of her mind.

Looking away from her brother, she frowned. If only she could feel indifference towards Rory, but however hard she tried, she knew it was impossible. He had scarred her in the way that one feels bruised and exposed when we place our trust in someone who hates us. Her father had broken the news to her in New York, and her whole view of Rory had been turned on it's head.

'Well done, James!' Stephen said cheerfully, taking the drink from him, 'Did you see Lisa on your travels?'

James shook his head, 'I'm afraid not. I was too busy battling at the bar.' He handed Catherine her drink and she gave him a forced smile, aware that it hurt her jaws to do it. In five minutes something inexplicable had changed her attitude towards him. She hoped it didn't show.

'I'll go and find her,' Stephen said. 'See you later.'

She watched him go in silence. Typical Stephen, she thought irritably. He'd dropped a bombshell on her and now left her to ride the after effects.

James slid one arm around her, pulling her into the crook of his shoulder which made her feel terribly uncomfortable. 'You're very quiet all of a sudden. Anything wrong?'

She shook her head, 'Of course not.'

He dropped a light kiss on her forehead and she felt herself shrink inwardly away from him. Stop it! she told herself, angry with her own feelings, but she knew it was hopeless.

'I want some time alone with you,' James whispered. 'You're always surrounded by so many people.'

'Am I?' she said, looking at him as blankly as she could. 'I hadn't noticed.' He meant her family, of course, but Catherine was too involved in her own thoughts to reply properly.

'Shall we go then?' James asked a moment later, and she nodded, glancing up at him with a rather absent-minded smile.

'Why not? Just let me say goodbye to everyone.'

They left the ballroom together in silence, going out into the car park where James helped her into his dark green Rover. They drove away in silence for which Catherine was grateful. She didn't want to talk, so she reached out and switched on the cassette player, relaxing as Bach's Brandenburg Concerto flowed out through the twin speakers.

The valley of Sleuhallen was breath-taking at night. Nestling between four steep slopes, the town was almost like a secret valley, hidden away from time and danger. The dark brooding moors were lit by moonlight, the old deserted mines rose up against a dark blue sky. The stark loneliness of the countryside touched her heart. From here, she could just see her family home rising up on the hills beyond. The white Georgian manor house had dominated the town for half a century, captured within a circle of tall pine trees that seemed to dance on the sweeping lawns of the estate.

The grey-slate town of Sleuhallen loomed before them, gold street lamps shining on wet roads. The houses were grey, bare, and very old, streets winding and narrow in places, a few dull lights were shining from front room windows of houses or shops. Everything was silent.

Somewhere Rory Managhan was waiting to take his revenge on the Skelton family. Where is he? Catherine thought, eyes scanning the valley, seeing nothing but a few hundred lights winking in the darkness, the outer edges of the town giving way to white farmhouses, fields and jagged black hills.

James pulled up outside her house and she looked up at the elegant white lines of it, the cool façade. Her father had built a small estate of ten or twelve houses in a cul-de-sac which was so secluded it often felt like another world. At the time of their completion, Catherine had been leaving for New York to study art, and her father had offered her one of the new houses in the hope that she would stay in Sleuhallen. Of course, she had refused with a carefree smile, thinking her life lay elsewhere. Well, she thought now with an angry laugh, we all make mistakes.

James switched the engine off. 'Any chance of a coffee?'

She gave him a smile, 'Would you mind if I said no?'

He laughed, 'Yes I would, but I can't very well argue about it!' He flicked his headlamps off deftly and gave her a curious look. 'You know I won't be back in Sleuhallen for at least a fortnight? I leave tomorrow and this is . . .' he grinned, '. . . your last chance!'

That made her feel guilty, which irritated her. 'Sorry,' she murmured because although she liked James, she refused to spend an hour or so kissing him in her own living room just to please him. Some people felt able to compromise themselves in order to avoid arguments. Catherine did not. She needed time alone to think, and an early night.

He nodded silently and looked out of the window for a moment before saying, 'What's on your mind, Cathy? There's something, isn't there? I noticed it after Stephen left—what did he say to upset you?'

She looked at him sharply, 'Was it that obvious?'

''Fraid so! But you don't have to tell me if you don't want to!' And he gave her a coaxing little smile with that last sentence that irritated her further, because it was intended to make her confess.

Looking him firmly in the eyes, she said, 'I'm aware of that, James.'

He blinked. For a moment he was silent, then he gave a light sigh. 'Well,' he said slowly, 'we'll leave it for another time.' But what he really meant was it's obvious we're never going to get anywhere together, so we may as well cool off for as long as it takes.

He leant over and gave a withdrawn kiss on the cheek.

Catherine felt guilt wash over her in waves. She got out of the car and waved at him with a smile before turning and walking to her front door. How irritating! Why can't I fall in love with James? she thought as she hunted in her evening bag for her keys. He's so suitable. He would make me terribly happy. The sort of man who's always there when you need him, a bunch of roses at the ready, a friend to go shopping with on Saturday afternoons. And he would die rather than hurt me. How boring, she thought with a sad smile.

Unlocking the front door, she went inside and closed the door, flicking the lights on with one hand, keys still clenched in one hand. She slipped off her sapphire mink coat, sliding it off her bare shoulders and laying it over the white bannisters.

Then she smelt it. Cigar smoke. It made her freeze,

muscles tensing. Someone's in the house, she thought, and every muscle on her neck tautened with fear and tension. It dawned on her in a terrifying cold-hot flush.

The silence was unnerving. Glancing behind her at the now locked front door, she wondered if she ought to just run outside where she'd be safe. The keys were still in her hand. Her heart pounded faster, sweat broke out on her forehead.

Pulses hammering crazily, she was unable to move or breath as she heard footsteps from the living room. Then the door-handle began to twist slowly like a scene from an old movie, and she just stared in silent, frozen panic.

The door pulled open. A man stepped into the hallway.

'Rory!' she whispered, eyes glittering in shock, her face suddenly white as her heart somersaulted.

He gave her a slow cynical smile. 'Hello, Cathy,' he said softly, and she stared at his face, feeling the years rush past as she looked into those cruel grey eyes. His mouth was hard, his jaw uncompromising, and his hard-boned face bore all the hallmarks of a Managhan.

She felt her heart thumping so hard she thought it might break out. Rory seemed to fill the narrow hallway, his presence overwhelming her as she stood in the frozen silence, drinking in everything about him. The lean body was still solid muscle and bone, and he was so much taller than she remembered. Had he always been this real? she wondered, or had her memory of him been fading recently.

Forcing herself to break out of the spell of shock, she flung her keys down on the telephone table with a loud thud, noticing as she did so that her hands were trembling.

'What are you doing here?' she asked. 'And how did you get in?'

The grey eyes watched her, cool and level. 'You left the back door open,' he drawled, and his voice was as familiar to her as his face. 'People do that in Sleuhallen, don't they? I'd forgotten.'

Catherine looked away. Forgotten? If only she had forgotten him—at one time she'd thought it possible, had even believed she had. Now she knew differently. Her whole body was reacting violently to the sight and sound of him.

Rory took a cigar from his cashmere overcoat. 'Don't you want to know why I'm back?' he asked softly, and bent his head, mouth clamping over the end of the cigar as he flicked open a gold lighter.

'I can guess.' She watched him, remembering those lazy movements so well that it was almost as though the last two years had been wiped clean and she had left him only yesterday.

The grey eyes flicked to hers. 'Can you?' He put the lighter away, his fingers long and tanned.

Her throat felt dry. 'My father told me everything, Rory,' she said, careful to mask her thoughts from him by keeping her face cool. He had always been able to read her like a book. 'The whole story.'

His face was suddenly grim. 'That much was obvious when you disappeared from New York,' he said with sudden harshness.

'What did you expect me to do?' she returned without thinking, then regretted it, biting her lip because arguing with him would only give too much away about her own hectic feelings on seeing him again.

Rory watched her coolly, waiting for her to continue. When she didn't he just shrugged those broad shoulders, muscle rippling beneath the well-cut black cloth.

'Well,' he drawled lazily, 'it makes no difference now. That's all in the past. What matters now—is the future.' His mouth crooked with a smile and his brows rose. 'Yours and mine.'

She whitened. Eyes a bright green in her pale face, she stared, heart pounding for a second. Then her mouth tightened. He was playing with her, making fun of her and she hated him for it.

Angry, she turned from him and walked into the living room.

'I see you've been helping yourself to my brandy,' she said with irritation, glancing at the half-empty glass beside the chair where he had been sitting.

Rory walked in lazily behind her. 'The Skelton hospitality is famed in the north of England,' he growled.

'Not towards a Managhan,' she told him, glancing over her shoulder. 'Or had you forgotten that, too?'

He laughed. 'How could I?'

Catherine threw him a cold glance over her shoulder, and took out the cigarettes from her bag. She needed the sharp taste of nicotine now and she was angry to realise that her hands shook as she tipped a slim cigarette from the pack. Exerting tremendous control, she forced her hands to keep still as she placed it in between her lips.

Rory walked to stand in front of her, flicking his gold lighter open.

'How very chivalrous.' she said acidly, bending her red-gold head to meet the flame.

Her eyes flicked to his face, met her own, and she felt her heart thud at the expression in them. Swallowing hard, she almost backed away from him. He seemed to fill the room with his presence, dwarfing her, and making her feel helpless, which in turn made her bitterly angry. How dare he affect me like this, she thought, folding one arm across her chest in defence, resting her elbow on her hand.

'Two years is a long time—I'd expected to find you

married.' Rory studied her through hooded lids. 'What happened? Haven't you met him yet?' A sardonic smile touched his mouth, 'Or are you still hopelessly in love with me?'

'Don't flatter yourself!' she said angrily, 'I'd forgotten you even existed.'

He laughed under his breath, grey eyes cool as he studied her. 'Liar!' he drawled smokily, 'People who hate never forget. I know that, Cathy. Hatred is the one thing that stays in your mind, whether you like it or not.'

She gave him a sharp sideways glance. 'Festers, Rory, is closer to the truth. It festers in you—I've seen it happen to my father, and now I can see it happening to you.'

He was silent for a moment, his mouth pursed as he studied her, and Catherine wondered if she'd hit home with that, because he obviously didn't like what she had said.

'And you, Cathy,' he said coldly, 'Why else would you leave New York so suddenly? Not even a brief note to let me know why. You just disappeared.'

She hesitated, not willing to reply, and finally looked away in silence because it hurt too much to remember that summer in New York, let alone discuss it with Rory himself. She stood staring at her cigarette absently, watching the paper burn in a thin brown circle.

'Reply came there none,' he snarled cynically.

Catherine shot him a cool look. 'What do you expect me to say? You surely didn't expect me to get in touch with you once I'd found out who you were, did you?'

'Not once Jed had had his say, oh no.' He laughed harshly.

She turned away from him, drawing on her cigarette, tasting the sharp flavour of the smoke, letting it ease the bitterness. Memories of New York came flooding back to her and she tried to push them out of her mind. He had never cared for her, not once in all those six months, it had been a sham from start to finish. Just a way to hurt her father, to get back at Jed Skelton, and that was what hurt most of all, the fact that she hadn't even existed where Rory was concerned. She had simply been a pawn with no feelings, no thoughts and no relevance. He hadn't even seen her properly.

'You're back for revenge?' she said in a low voice.

He inclined his black head.

Catherine tapped ash from her cigarette with trembling fingers. 'I suppose you won't tell me what you plan to do?'

He gave a short laugh. 'And have you warn Jed? Are you kidding?' he watched her with a cool smile, 'Oh no, Cathy. He's had this coming for a long time. Nothing's going to stop me nailing him once and for all.'

She looked round angrily. 'Are you any better? You used me in New York—didn't you? And now you're going to use anyone around you who can help hit back at my father.' She stared at him, shaking her head and giving a low sigh, 'No, Rory—you're no better at all.'

He was silent for a moment, studying her with narrowed grey eyes, and she wondered what he was thinking there was an expression on his face that was somehow out of character.

Then he shrugged broad shoulders. 'An eye for an eye,' he drawled lazily.

She laughed. 'Oh—quoting from the Bible now, are we?'

He gave her a sardonic smile. 'If the quote fits . . .' he drawled with light humour.

Catherine shook her head, red-gold hair shining, 'Wrong quote! How about—love your enemy? How about that one? That's a pretty solid quote if ever I heard one.'

'Practise what you preach.' he said bitingly, and she looked away, her cheeks flushing a little. What he said was perfectly true, she did not love her enemy, she hated him like poison, even though he made her heart thud too fast and the blood rush through her body frantically.

There was a little silence. Catherine heard the clock tick softly, a door slam in the house next door, someone calling up the stairs, a dog barking, and then silence again.

'Why did you come here, Rory?' she asked quietly, 'If not to warn me?' Looking up, her eyes fixed on his, 'Why?'

He blinked, black lashes flickering on his tanned cheekbones. 'I wanted to see you,' he admitted deeply, and his mouth crooked in a cynical smile. 'I was curious.'

Her pulses hammered. 'Curious? About me?' She gave a shaky laugh, 'You know what they say about curiosity!'

He gave a tight smile. 'And they could be right,' he admitted coolly, 'But for all I knew you were married—or fat—or both! Time does funny things to people.'

'Too right.' she muttered, green eyes angry, 'Look what it did to you. You could have stayed in New York—forgotten the past. But no—you took it out on me, didn't you.'

'No, Cathy!' he interrupted forcefully, 'That was your father. He dragged you into all this. He——'

'Oh, come off it!' she said angrily, walking across the room with a brisk agitated step, trying to put as much distance between them as possible, her heart pounding hard because Rory had always managed to make her feel tiny, insignificant. His presence in a room was overpowering, he dominated it, made her feel a deep awareness of him.

Rory watched her with narrowed silver eyes. 'You've still got him on a pedestal, haven't you Cathy? Still polishing his goddamn halo every day.' He laughed harshly, thrusting his hands into his pockets, 'When will you ever grow up!'

She spun, eyes hot with unshed tears. 'You lay off my father! I don't hate him, I've no reason to hate him.' She watched him angrily, 'It's you I hate. And you know damned well why!'

'No I don't,' he said coolly and was silent for a few seconds, eyeing her across the room. Then he slowly walked over to her, making her feel suddenly pressurised, afraid, so that she backed away a little as he came closer.

Rory stopped in front of her, eyes skimming her slender body. 'Tell me why, Cathy?' he said softly.

She swallowed. 'Don't be ridiculous!' she said rawly, trying to turn away from him.

Rory caught her arm, turning her back towards him and she struggled silently, so he took her face in one hand, the other holding her still, forcing her to look at him with wide green eyes filled with unshed tears.

'Tell me, Cathy,' he said under his breath, a sardonic smile on his hard mouth.

She wanted to hit him then, badly, but she didn't because she knew he was more than capable of hitting her back if she did.

'Let go of me.' She muttered instead through her teeth, his hand was clamped so hard on her jaw that she could barely speak, and her neck ached from being forced backwards.

His gaze dropped to her soft mouth. 'It's a long time since I kissed you,' he said absently, as though musing on the subject and that made her hate him even more because she felt so helpless, so insignificant.

'Why are you doing this?' she hissed, 'Just get out, Rory and don't come back. I don't want to play cat and mouse with you tonight—I'm too tired.'

'So long as you know the rules of the game,' he murmured, and bent his black head so suddenly that she couldn't get away as his hard mouth fastened on hers and he kissed her slowly, drugging her and making her heartbeat race dangerously.

Mind turning cartwheels, Catherine gasped and pushed him away as hard as she could, backing, almost falling over a chair which was behind her, her legs unsteady and her pulses hammering out of control. She stared at him like a cornered animal for a long moment, her hectic breathing audible in the white room.

Rory watched her with a cool smile of satisfaction. 'Don't look so scared, Cathy,' he said softly, 'I'm leaving now. I've found out all I wanted to know.'

Her lips trembled with humiliated anger. She was aware that her flushed face and terrified response had given away rather more than she had wanted to. The physical attraction between them was still overwhelming.

He turned on his heel in the silence that followed and walked over to the door of the living room while Catherine stared from the corner she had backed into, her eyes an angry green.

Rory turned to look over his shoulder as he opened the door. 'I'll be seeing you,' he drawled sardonically, and left the room.

She heard the slam of the front door, the sound of the car engine outside as it flared in the silent night, then he roared away from her house leaving her feeling as though she'd just been through a nuclear attack, her legs still shaky, her heart pounding. I've been nuked, she thought with a sudden burst of humour, and started to laugh, tears pricking her lids.

Damn him! she thought angrily, walking unsteadily over to the door and going into the little kitchen. Silence rang in her ears, thoughts buzzed in her head. She plugged the kettle in and started to make herself some instant hot chocolate.

She had come back to Sleuhallen because she had believed it was the one place Rory Managhan would never follow her to. The backlog of hatred towards him and his family was too strong in this town. She had thought he would never return. How wrong can you be, she thought bitterly.

But what did it matter now? she thought with a heavy sigh. He had left Sleuhallen twenty years ago, vowing revenge, and now he was back to fulfil his threat. Her father couldn't stop him. Catherine couldn't stop him. No-one, in short, could stop him.

But what did he have in mind? she wondered, her heart hurting. She didn't think she would be able to bear living in the same town as him. Surely he didn't plan to stay in Sleuhallen?

CHAPTER TWO

SHE didn't have to wait long to find out what was happening. The telephone rang early on Monday morning, waking her with a start. As she opened her eyes to stare across the cream silk pillows of her bed, she knew without question that it was bad news. Her hand shot out, eyes wide open now, and picked up the cream-gold receiver.

'Yes?' she said, feeling her heart beat increase, and hoping stupidly that she was wrong. But it was only six o'clock in the morning, and it would have to be bad news for anyone to ring her this early.

'All hell's broken loose.' Stephen's voice was crisp and clear, making Catherine shut her eyes, feeling helpless. 'You'd better get over here right away.'

She sat up quickly, her body tense. 'Rory?' she asked, and knew what the answer would be.

'I'm afraid so,' her brother said heavily, 'but I can't go into it over the 'phone. If this gets leaked, Dad'll have my guts for garters. We've all been getting it in the neck as it is.'

Catherine looked blankly at her reflection in the mirror, the sleepy tangle of red-gold curls, the green silk nightshirt she wore slipping off one soft-skinned shoulder, her long tanned legs drawn up underneath her.

'Has he been to the house?' she asked slowly, and Stephen laughed.

'I wish it was that simple!' he said drily, 'But it's a lot worse than just an unfriendly visit.'

She tensed, eyes staring. 'How much worse?'

Her brother paused, and she heard the line crackle

before he said, 'I'm sorry, I really can't go into it. But it's worse than any of us ever imagined. You could almost say it's a complete bloody disaster.' He laughed under his breath, but she knew he was very upset, 'I've never met the man, but from what you've said and what has happened today, I think he must be a complete bastard.'

Her mouth tightened. 'He is.' She ran a hand through her hair, and sighed, 'Give me half an hour. I'll be there as soon as I can.'

'Great.' Stephen sounded relieved, 'Bring your knuckle-dusters, you might need them! See you.'

The line went dead and she stared at the elegant receiver for a long moment, before replacing it on it's cradle. So Rory had moved already. He was fast, she had to admit that. No doubt he had planned it long before he set foot in Sleuhallen, long before he risked entering Skelton territory.

She got out of bed and went to shower quickly, the hard needles of hot water pummelling her tired muscles, bringing her alive as she twisted her naked body beneath them, and washed her hair in the steaming jets of water.

Catherine dressed in a white trouser suit, the jacket with big baggy sleeves that she pushed up to the elbow to make elegant and striking lines. The white trousers were narrow and slim-fitting, making her figure look like a model's. Bright blue earrings and an outrageous peacock-blue silk scarf tied loosely at her throat completed the casual fashionable elegance.

She didn't have time for coffee. Time for that when she got to the house. Slamming the front door behind her, she slipped behind the wheel of her red Ferrari Dino, a twenty-first birthday present from her father. She drove fast through the moorland and town of Sleuhallen, the Ferrari roaring as she took hairpin bends at dangerous speed.

Skelton House rose up on the hillside above Sleuhallen, dominating the skyline. The elegant white façade was kept clean white by her father's employees on the estate. The gardens were manicured into a long sloping lawn that rolled down before the house, and a circle of tall trees danced around the edge of the grounds like a fairy ring.

She screeched to a halt, throwing up gravel outside the front door and took the steps two at a time. As she unlocked the door, she saw Stephen in the hall coming towards her.

'I heard you pull up,' he said with a tired smile, 'Or should I say screech up. You really enjoy that Ferrari, don't you?'

She smiled. 'I've only had it for a year.' It had been second-hand when bought, and was eight years old, so driving fast wouldn't do it any damage. 'Where's Dad?' she asked, glancing around the enormous white and green reception hall.

Stephen nodded to the door on their left. 'In there. With his lawyers and some members of the Board. They're trying to talk him out of rash actions.'

Catherine stared, incredulous. 'Lawyers? Rash actions?' She studied her brother with a worried face, 'Stephen, just how serious is this?'

He eyed her for a moment. 'Come in the kitchen and I'll tell you all I know,' he said flatly, and turned to walk back towards the kitchen.

Catherine followed, noting that he was back to his usual appearance, wearing a bright blue shirt with a grey monkey-jacket, and blue baggy jeans. A blue tweed cap was perched at a wicked angle on his dark head, and he looked every inch the Irish knife-grinder.

The kitchen was long, bright and airy, sunshine streaming through the tall windows on one wall, lighting it up and bouncing off the smooth brown and green tiles. Stephen plugged in the coffee percolator, turning to look at her.

'How much do you know about Managhan's past?' he asked with a frown.

She looked away, sighing. 'Very little. Only what Dad's told me—and he just skims the surface, I'm sure of that.'

Stephen nodded. 'So you don't know anything about Rory's father—Damian Managhan?'

She shook her head. 'Well—only the little I've heard from Dad. But there are always two sides to every story, aren't there?'

Stephen laughed, brown eyes dancing. 'We're not likely to get anything out of old Damian Managhan! He's been dead for fifteen years! We could always hold a seance, I suppose.'

Catherine took a cigarette from her white jacket pocket, and lit it, exhaling smoke in a slow stream, watching it disappear into the dusty sunlight at the other end of the kitchen.

'What exactly has Rory done?' she asked her brother quietly, 'Why is Dad in there at this time of the morning with lawyers and board-members?'

Stephen looked away, eyes distracted. He pursed his lips, and Catherine felt suddenly very much afraid because she could see her brother didn't want to tell her, didn't know how to phrase it. A long silence stretched between them and she heard the coffee bubble noisily. Then Stephen bent his head.

'He's bought controlling interest, Cathy,' Stephen told her in a flat expressionless voice. 'He holds fifty-one per cent of the shares.'

Catherine felt the breath punch out of her, staring in stunned silence as shock waves flooded her body. Sitting totally still, she wondered if she'd heard him properly, because there was such a sense of total unreality about it. Sitting here in her family home, on a sunny morning, calmly discussing the fact that Rory Managhan, her father's most hated enemy, had bought their livelihood from under their very noses.

It was a long time before she could breath properly. The scene seemed to freeze in her mind like a grotesque tableau. She heard the clock tick, the paper burn on her cigarette. She sat like a statue, frozen, as though unable to move a muscle.

Stephen turned his head to look at her. 'Incredible, isn't it?' he said quietly, 'It's not our firm anymore, Cathy. It's his.'

He turned to take two cups down from the cupboard, closing the door with a hollow bang and putting them on the side. He poured coffee into them and handed one to her before perching on one of the kitchen stools at the breakfast area opposite her.

'But how?' Catherine finally spoke with an effort, 'How could it possibly have happened?'

Stephen looked at her and sighed. 'Great Aunt Katie sold him all her shares.'

Catherine whitened, hands gripping the kitchen table until her knuckles showed through. 'I don't believe it! You must have made a mistake!' Aunt Katie would have died before selling out to a Managhan. It was ludicrous.

He shook his black head. 'I wish I had. But the facts are there, and there's nothing we can do about it. Look at the share report if you want, it's all down there in black and white. Aunt Katie sold her majority holding to Rory Managhan at five o'clock on Friday afternoon.'

She just stared at him, incredulous. 'Why didn't we get the report sooner?'

'God knows. A foul-up over the weekend or something.'

Catherine stared down at her coffee. Aunt Katie knew at the party, then. Rory knew on Saturday night

when he came to see her. They had both seen her over
the weekend, had been in Sleuhallen. But they hadn't
spoken, hadn't told anyone what was happening even
though they knew that it was catastrophic. Damn him!
She thought angrily, he had obviously been planning
this for years. He must have worked on Aunt Katie,
trying to get the shares out of her, coming up with
endless good reasons why he should have control of
the company. She couldn't believe Aunt Katie would
just sell on impulse, on the spur of the moment. Aunt
Katie never did anything on impulse she was a very
shrewd old woman. But why had she done it?
Catherine could think of no explanation for it
whatsoever.

'Where is she?' Catherine asked her brother, 'Have
you spoken to her?'

He shrugged. 'Aunt Katie? No, she's vanished into
thin air. We can't get hold of her anywhere.' He
stopped, hearing movements from the other side of the
house.

'He's been like this since four a.m.,' Stephen told
her under his breath. They listened to her father
shouting in the hall among other raised voices, 'We
were all dragged out of bed as soon as he heard.'

'How did he find out?' she asked, frowning.

'Telex.' Stephen stretched his arms over his head
and flexed his shoulder muscles with a groan, 'I think
Managhan sent it—or one of his henchmen.'

Outside in the hall Jed Skelton's voice was raised in
icy fury. She listened, eyes worried, as he shouted
biting commands at his lawyers and the senior
members of the board. He was always so much in
control, she thought anxiously, but as this moment he
sounded on the edge of rage, and that was no way to
face Rory, she knew at least that much. Rory would
handle this coup with cool cynicism, and it would only
make it more enjoyable for him to see Jed Skelton

beside himself with rage. The thought made Catherine close her eyes, shaking her head.

'I should never have gone public!' Her father shouted outside, 'It was a monumental mistake! I shouldn't have listened to you! You just wanted to get a piece of my firm.'

Protests were raised angrily, and Catherine sighed, unable to close her ears to it all.

The telephone rang. It made her jump, staring at Stephen as he tensed too. There was silence outside for a moment. Then someone moved and the sharp bell stopped.

Catherine stood up, almost as though she knew it was Rory. Looking at Stephen, she walked slowly to the door of the kitchen. A moment later Stephen followed her, behind her now as she pushed the kitchen door open and went into the hallway.

Jed Skelton stood holding the telephone receiver, the central figure in a group of harassed looking men who listened attentively, papers held in their hands, ties askew, faces evidently worried. Of course they would be worried, Catherine thought soberly. Their jobs and livelihoods were at risk with this takeover from Rory Managhan. Rory had made it plain that anyone who was on Skelton's side was his enemy, which made almost every man, woman and child in Sleuhallen his enemy.

Her father's head was bent, silver hair glinting in the shards of sunlight that slipped through the top glass panel of the door. His tall wiry body was held as straight and unbending as the iron hewn from the ground.

'You tell Managhan,' Jed Skelton growled, his arrogant face dominated by blue eyes that were fierce in their intensity, 'I'll be there. Three o'clock this afternoon.'

He slammed the receiver back into place, staring at

it for a moment, then turned to look at the men he ruled over with an iron hand, surveying the army of lawyers, accountants and blood relations who had gathered silently around him in the hall.

'He's called a meeting,' he said grimly, 'for this afternoon. All the major shareholders will be there.'

Catherine glanced at her brother with worried eyes. Stephen held shares, which meant he would have to attend. Thank God father let me out of the firm, she thought, closing her eyes with relief. At least she wouldn't have to be there. She could just picture Rory at the meeting because she knew him so well now, and could read his mind in advance. He would be totally in control of the situation, and her father's rage would only make him smile that crooked, cynical smile of his, which would in turn make Jed even angrier.

She sighed, turning away from the family group and going back into the kitchen. Rory had kept his promise and come back to take his revenge just as he had said he would, fifteen years ago. But Catherine had an uneasy feeling that the revenge was only just beginning. She couldn't understand why, but something told her she would be his next target.

Sitting down at the breakfast area, she suddenly remembered what Rory had said on Saturday night, and her eyes widened with fear and excitement. What had he said—in a few days time you'll be more prepared to give? But what had he meant by that? Surely he couldn't imagine she would go back to him, start their affair again—especially after what he was doing to her family.

Her heart thudded faster, and she took a cigarette from her jacket pocket, lighting it and inhaling sharply, the smoke hurting her lungs as she drew it down. She looked at the glowing tip, frowning, and made a mental note to quit smoking as soon as this was over. Smoking was punishing her body, and one day her body would punish her right back for it.

She had to think, put herself in Rory's place. His life had been tinged with bitterness and hatred that stretched back into another generation. He wanted nothing more than to see Jed Skelton beaten once and for all.

But what did he have in store for her?

Mrs Tandy, the housekeeper, bustled into the kitchen, sniffing. 'You can put that out for a start,' she said, eyeing Catherine's cigarette, 'I won't have smoking in my kitchen when I'm getting Mrs Skelton's breakfast.'

Catherine obediently ground the cigarette out in an ashtray. 'Where is she?' she asked, 'In the dining room?'

'Aye, and cool as a cucumber, too.' Mrs Tandy attacked a carton of eggs from the fridge, cracking them into a cup by the stove. 'Your mother has more dignity than any other woman I know. Never lets on what she's feeling inside.'

Catherine smiled and stood up, going over to the stove to stand beside Mrs Tandy. 'I'll take it in for you,' she offered.

'You will not.' Mrs Tandy gave her an offended look, wiry brown curls bobbling above her dark eyes, 'I may be pushing fifty, but I'm not in my bath chair yet, madam, so you can stop treating me as if I'm incapable.'

Catherine leant against the kitchen surface, watching her whisk the eggs into a light creamy mixture in the saucepan. Mrs Tandy always made perfect scrambled eggs, which was the real reason she wanted to take them in to Catherine's mother. She liked to watch the smile on her mother's face as she gracefully accepted her breakfast. Worlds within worlds, thought Catherine with a sigh.

Stephen came back into the kitchen and walked over to where she stood. 'That smells good,' he said, peering over Mrs Tandy's shoulder. 'Is it for me?'

Mrs Tandy shook her head. 'It's for your poor mother. What she must be going through!' she sighed, and Catherine watched her with a smile. Mrs Tandy doted on Catherine's mother, and made it obvious that she did.

Stephen adjusted the blue tweed cap perched on his head, and beckoned to Catherine, putting one finger to his lips. She frowned, pushing away from the stove and following him to the back door, which he opened and went outside in the garden, Catherine following him in silence, while Mrs Tandy watched, eyes wide with curiosity.

Stephen closed the door, leaning on the handle and crossing his legs. 'I just rang Aunt Katie,' he told her quietly. 'She's not there. Or she's not answering. Either way, it's pretty ominous.'

Catherine frowned, folding her arms, the grass soft and springy beneath her feet. 'She's always been an early riser—maybe she's gone out.'

Stephen shook his head, looking out over the estate which was bathed in crisp morning sunlight, the rolling lawns which lead as far as the eye could see, to the circle of tall trees, and the hills of Sleuhallen beyond, all of it Skelton land.

'I don't think so. Besides, she doesn't usually take her morning stroll until around nine. 'It's early, even for Aunt Katie.'

Catherine looked down at her feet. 'So you think she's left Sleuhallen? Is that what you're saying?'

Stephen sighed. 'I don't know. I just don't like it, that's all.'

Catherine nodded in silent agreement, wondering where Aunt Katie could be at this time of the morning. Although, in all common sense, she realised that her Great Aunt would probably not want to talk to any of the family before the meeting.

Looking at Stephen, she shielded her eyes with her hand against the sunlight. 'Perhaps she'll come to the meeting this afternoon.'

He laughed, his smile ironic. 'I hope so. I'm not the only one around here who wants to know why she did this. Dad's been threatening to murder her all morning. He trusted her implicitly, you know that?'

Catherine nodded, silent as she looked out across the Estate. A cool morning breeze touched her face, lifting strands of red-gold hair across her eyes, and she pushed them back with one hand.

So Aunt Katie had disappeared into thin air, and Rory Managhan was about to bring thirty-five years of hatred and bitterness crushing down on everyone's head. It all seemed so unbelievable to her, as though it was a nightmare and she would wake up from it at any moment.

She had hoped she would never see Rory again, never have to look at his dark face and feel that inner conflict of love and hatred for him. It was too difficult to deal with, it pulled her in too many emotional directions at once, and Catherine just wanted to be left in peace. But Rory obviously had different ideas.

But what were they?

On her way home just before lunch, Catherine stopped in at Arundel's Art Shop, where she worked. She'd obviously have to take the day off and she could hardly cry off with a cold when both Mrs Caley and her son Rick had been at Stephen's engagement party on Saturday, and had seen her looking not only healthy but very cheerful.

Stopping the car outside Arundel's, she looked up at the white swinging sign with its black Elizabethan script. Even this small family-run business was owned by her father. Catherine had been manageress here for the last eighteen months, and was well-qualified for the post due to her year long stint at the New York College of Art and Design, followed by six months in Florence studying Renaissance Art under a professional artist. Back, then, Catherine had dreamed of becoming a professional artist, living in Paris in Montmartre and painting the Seine, the Boule Miche, and Parisian night-life. But she had grown out of that after Rory had forced her to, by bringing reality down on her head.

Pushing open the door of the art shop, the bell jangled over her head.

'Why, Catherine!' Mrs Caley smiled at her from the step-ladder on which she stood placing a porcelain figure on a shelf, and removing her son's choice of a modern gold hooped statue of an artist's impression of dance. 'We thought you weren't coming in.'

Catherine smiled back, closing the door behind her. 'I'm not. I just popped in to tell you I'll have to take the day off. Can you manage?'

Mrs Caley nodded her sleek black head. 'Oh, I should think so. Rick's been sneaking in too many modern pieces, but if I'm firm with him he'll do as he's told!' She laughed, putting the modern sculpture down on the floor. She and her son had a running battle over art style. 'Aren't you feeling well, then?' she asked, dusting her hands off, 'You look a bit peaky.'

Catherine hesitated. 'No, I'm fine. But something's come up, and I'm wanted at home for the rest of the day.'

'Oh?' Mrs Caley raised her head, curious. 'Really? Anything serious?'

'No,' Catherine opened the door again, keeping her voice casual. 'Just family problems—the usual stuff. I'll be in tomorrow, okay?'

Mrs Caley leant on the step-ladder. 'Of course,' she said with a little smile, but her eyes were very thoughtful, 'I hope it all goes well for you.' She watched Catherine leave, and waved, "Bye, love.'

Back in her car, Catherine sobered, driving on automatic pilot while she thought about the meeting this afternoon. She would have to change and shower before going to Skelton's. Rory would be prepared for battle, and she didn't want to face him without the best armour she could possibly find.

But as she turned into the small cul-de-sac road she lived in, she saw a long black Cadillac limousine parked outside her house, and her heart thudded hard as she realised who was in it. *Rory*, she thought angrily, her mouth tightening at once. Hands gripping the steering wheel, she parked carefully in her driveway, aware that he was watching her from behind the tinted dark windows of that long limousine.

Catherine got out of her Ferrari without looking round. Out of the corner of her eye she saw and heard the black door open, and a man stepped out into the cool spring sunlight.

The limousine door was slammed shut. Catherine turned her head, lifting her chin to observe him through wary green eyes.

'What are you doing here?' she asked coldly.

The hard mouth crooked in a cynical smile. 'I take it you've heard, then.' he drawled, lounging lazily against the limousine, studying her with a casual air.

She sorted out her door key, head bent. 'Yes,' she snapped, 'I've heard.' She turned to go to her front door, intending to go in without looking back at him.

But Rory moved faster. He was at her side before she could push the key in the lock.

'Not so fast,' he snarled against her ear and her pulses leapt as she felt his long fingers curl around her wrist. She tried to pull away but his hold tightened, and she winced as he suddenly crushed her wrist, forcing her to drop the keys into his outstretched hand.

Looking over her shoulder, her eyes were a cool green. 'Am I expected to bow to the conquering hero?' she asked, successfully keeping the tremor out of her voice. 'I take it that's what you're doing here? The new lord and master of Skelton Engineering.'

Rory watched her with darkening eyes. 'You know that's not true, Cathy.' he said, and his brows met in a frown, 'Why do you say it?'

She looked away, unable to reply. He was so close to her and his nearness was intoxicating. Averting her eyes from the tanned column of his throat, she saw the tight black waistcoat which emphasised his lean waist and hips, and she remembered how it felt to slide her arms around him. Her mouth dried. She shook her head, angry with herself, and looked away from him altogether.

Staring instead at the stone path, she said; 'You're every bit as ruthless as my father.'

'How kind.' His face was grim and unsmiling, 'But I'm not flattered. I know you've always been proud of him. But don't put me in the same category. They destroyed the mold when Jed Skelton was born.'

She almost laughed in his face, because for all his feigned integrity, she knew him better. The same characteristics were there—the ruthless streak that could lash out at any given moment, the dominance, the utter conviction in himself. There were very few people in this world like them, and it was cataclysmic that they should be involved in a head-on collision.

Looking up at him, eyes wide, she asked, 'Why are you here, Rory? What is it this time?'

He studied her carefully, his eyes hooded, 'I thought we could have lunch.'

'Lunch?' She was incredulous for a moment. Then

she laughed, shaking her red-gold head, 'Are you out of your mind? If anyone saw me having lunch with you I'd be labelled a traitor!'

It made him smile. 'And sent to the Tower forthwith?'

'Very funny,' she said, half-angry, half-amused. Flicking her glance away from him she shrugged, 'It's out of the question. You know that as well as I do.'

'Nothing is ever out of the question,' he shot back. 'Or haven't you learned that yet?'

She looked at him, her mouth firm, and knew she ought to have expected that reply. Rory was the sort of man who could not accept barriers. As soon as he saw a brick wall he either kicked his way through it or jumped over it. But he never under any circumstances walked away from it. She wished she had the same fighting spirit, the same refusal to give up. But it is inbred in people, and you can't just magically produce it like a white rabbit out of a hat.

Instead she said coolly, 'Haven't you learned anything about family loyalty yet? I would never betray my father—whatever the circumstances.'

The grey eyes hardened. 'Then you're a fool,' he said cuttingly and she felt her cheeks sweep with hot colour. He stood watching her, his height and strength making her feel insignificant, as though he could pick her up and put her in his pocket without effort.

No-one else makes me feel this helpless, she thought angrily, because she knew she could not defend if he chose to attack. With most people she felt confident, strong and independent. Rory made her pulses flutter, her body pound with rushing blood and her mind leap dizzy circles. She couldn't bear it.

Rory handed her the key back. 'Open the door,' he told her coolly.

She tightened her lips. Their eyes warred for a long moment, but in the end she backed down angrily, and

opened the door with a tight face, going inside and
watching as he followed her.

Catherine felt tense, unsure of herself as she faced
him because his presence shook her, and filled the
house with an unspoken threat that made her want to
run.

'You can't stay long,' she told him. 'I don't want
anyone to see your car parked outside.'

Sliding his hands in his pockets he murmured,
'Long enough for a glass of whisky.'

Catherine sighed, going into the living room, aware
of the burning gaze that followed her. The drinks
cabinet stood open still, the green leather-topped
wood shining in the daylight. She took a crystal
decanter and poured him a stiff shot of whisky.

It wasn't until she turned round that she realised he
was directly behind her. She jumped, startled. His
eyes bored down into hers. Catherine felt her mouth
dry. She hadn't heard him come in behind her, for
God's sake. He must have crept up silently, like a
wolf.

Their fingers brushed as she handed him the glass.

Catherine swallowed. 'Stop hounding me, Rory!'

A smile touched the hard mouth. He moved a little
closer. 'Am I hounding you?' he said softly, and she
watched his mouth move as he spoke, as though she
was hypnotised by it.

Angry with herself, she gave him a cold stare. 'I
should drop the sexual angle if I were you, Rory. It
won't work. I lost interest a long time ago.'

'Too bad,' he drawled, 'I didn't.' One long hand
shot out to catch her chin with sinewy fingers, tilting
her head up roughly to look at him and her hair
tumbled back over her shoulders, thick and glossy, her
lips parting in surprise. 'Why else do you think I came
back to Sleuhallen?'

That made the hairs on the back of her neck rise and

she hesitated for a long time before saying breathlessly, 'What are you talking about?'

'You.' The grey eyes pinned her to the wall. 'I came back for you.'

CHAPTER THREE

It took a long time for that to sink in, and she just stared at him in stunned surprise while her mind whirred until she was almost dizzy. It was absurd, it couldn't be true. He couldn't be serious. Not after all this time, not after two years. Admittedly, she had left New York without a word of warning or explanation. She hadn't been able to face him with what she knew because her anger had been too difficult to handle, her disillusionment too great. She had assumed he would guess the reason as soon as he found out that her father had flown out to New York the day before she left and had left with her on the following day. It had been cut and dried. After what her father had told her about Rory she hadn't been able to bring herself to even speak to him again And he had never made any attempt to contact her since that day. Two years was a long time—he could at least have tried to explain his behaviour. But he hadn't—there had just been a long silence, and Catherine had assumed that he didn't really give a damn, just as her father had assured her at the time. 'He doesn't love you, Cathy,' Jed had said coldly when she had protested. 'He's using you to hit back at me. You're an innocent pawn in a war that's been going on for as long as you've been alive. Longer, in fact.' And Catherine had believed him. Everything about Rory's rather inexplicable behaviour before she found out had added up to point to the truth in her father's words.

Looking at Rory now, she shook her head. 'I don't believe you,' she said huskily.

His face was grim. 'I'm deadly serious, Cathy. I came back to get you.'

That shook her, and she stared for a long moment before saying, 'But why? I don't understand you . . .'

'Don't you?' he cut in. He released her with a quick movement, and she swayed a little towards him, which made her flush hotly, looking away from his hard face. He slid his hands into the pockets of his trousers, standing in a strongly masculine stance, his body taut with tension.

Studying her with cool grey eyes, he said flatly, 'You agreed to marry me, remember? I'd even bought the ring. I thought it was clear cut.' His mouth firmed, 'But no. You walked out on me without a word of explanation. Disappeared from New York without even saying goodbye.'

She frowned, confused. 'But you must have known why! Surely you realised what would happen when I found out who you were? Rory, you knew what you were involved in—right from the start. But I didn't. I had no *idea*.'

'Oh, come on!' he snapped coldly. 'Don't tell me your family never mentioned my name to you? Not once? In more than twenty years?'

She shook her head, eyes sliding away from him. 'Only your surname. Managhan. But I didn't realise you were part of that family.' She lifted her head to look back at him, eyes seeking his, 'You were a New Yorker, a stranger. I didn't connect you with the Managhans of Sleuhallen. I thought it was just a coincidence.'

Rory laughed. 'Some coincidence! Considering I'm the only one left of the family—thanks to your father.'

Her eyes shot to his. 'You mean your mother's dead?' she asked under her breath, because she remembered that his mother had lived on the outskirts of town in a large white cottage, and every time she drove past it with a member of her family, they would stare at the drawn lace curtains, eyes narrowed with memories she could only guess at.

He sighed, shaking his head. 'No. She's still alive, and living in Sleuhallen. Where else could she go? Your father destroyed the life she could have led, took away every opportunity she ever had.'

Catherine bent her head, flushing hotly. 'He acts without thinking,' she murmured. 'He's too easily hurt and he hits back like a wounded animal.'

Rory gave her a grim smile. 'So do I.'

'Oh, Rory!' Catherine sighed heavily, looking at him with angry green eyes. 'Your situation is a little different to my father's—don't you think?'

'In what way?'

She slid her hands into the pockets of her jacket, looking down at the floor. 'Your mother was engaged to him. You know that. She eloped just before the wedding—and married your father.' Looking up at him she raised her brows. 'Don't you see? Your mother hurt him deeply. Not just his heart, but his pride and self-respect, too. She ran off with his best friend.'

'Was that any reason to destroy my father's life?' asked Rory coolly, 'Okay—so they pulled a pretty rotten trick on Jed Skelton. But they didn't take away everything he had. All's fair in love and war, Cathy. But your father pulled the sky down on the pair of them—and that's playing too rough.'

Catherine looked away, taking a pack of cigarettes from her pocket and extracting one, lit it, her fingers shaky. She exhaled jerkily, trying to think because what Rory said held some core of truth in it. Had her father been grossly unfair in what he had done? She had always accepted his word for what had happened all those years ago, had always believed his side of the story. But people saw things through their own eyes, and there were always two sides to every story.

'He didn't just break their lives,' Rory said quietly, 'he left them in smithereens. Even your Aunt Kate knows that.'

She didn't look up. 'Which is why she sold out to you.'

He nodded. 'She watched the whole thing happen. She's a formidable lady—every bit as tough as your father. But even she knows he went that little bit too far.'

Catherine felt totally off balance. It was too disturbing, there was too much to be said and too much to atone for. And for what? What lay in the middle of all of this? Her and Rory—a relationship that had never even existed except on her side, and one that was certainly not worth salvaging from the wreckage.

She gave a heavy sigh, shaking her head. 'It's all so pointless, Rory.'

'No, Cathy,' he said grimly. 'It has to be done.'

'It doesn't have to be done!' she said angrily, and faced him squarely now, her eyes glowing with her anger, 'You could stop now. Turn back, go home to New York. You could do it, Rory—but you won't will you?' Her lips trembled, 'Because you want to do it. You're enjoying it!'

Rory was silent for a long moment and she felt tension make her neck muscles lock together tightly as she watched his face. He gave nothing away with those features, only a dark brooding intensity as he stared at her, face implacable, unreadable, only the grey eyes watching her as she stood waiting.

'It's the only way I can get at you,' Rory said finally. 'Make you——'

'Are you deaf?' she interrupted angrily, 'Didn't you hear what I said five minutes ago?' Her eyes stared into his forcefully, 'It's over! Finished!'

'It isn't finished,' he told her coldly, 'you're mine.'

'Oh for God's sake!' she snapped, turning, trying to push past him to get away from him. The intensity that came from that lean hard body was beginning to make her so nervous she could hardly move, and she was fighting down the effect of his nearness.

His hand shot out. 'Don't walk away from me, you little bitch!' he bit out and she suddenly saw rage flash in the silver eyes, his nostrils flaring as he slammed her back hard against him, making her heart thud dangerously.

There was a long silence, she heard her breathing, fast and laboured as she leant helplessly against his muscular shoulder.

Then he sighed, hands running to hold her shoulders. 'Why do you make me flare up like that, Cathy? Don't you know what it does to me?'

Unsteadily, she twisted around to face him, her legs shaking. 'I'm not scared of you Rory,' she said bravely, lying through her teeth.

He looked at her coldly, mouth hardening. 'Then you should be. Because this time I'm going to win. Everything.' Then he turned on his heel and left her alone to listen in silence to his footsteps outside on the path.

Staring at the curling smoke from her cigarette, she saw her hand tremble and sighed heavily. If only Rory hadn't come back. She had thought she would be safe, here in Sleuhallen, had thought it was the one place he would never find her, because she had believed he would never return.

Catherine had returned after their affair in New York because she had needed the warmth and security that Sleuhallen provided. When you've been hit hard, you always run for cover. It's not so easy to stand on your own two feet and face the world alone when you've been hurt too badly to even think straight.

When she had first met Rory, he had eclipsed everything she had ever known before. It was like meeting her opposite half, her other self, and she had felt them merging in total understanding within an hour of setting eyes on each other. Stupidly, she had believed Rory felt the same. But obviously he hadn't. It had all been a game to him, a plan for revenge.

She had been at art school in New York, staying with her cousin Mindy, who was working as a fashion model in Manhattan at the same time. They were both the same age, and both ambitious in different fields. It had been natural for them to get together and share a flat in Greenwich Village.

Mindy was a live-wire and beautiful with it. She had had so many boyfriends that it had driven Catherine dizzy trying to count them all. She moved in the most fashionable circles, mixing with famous actors, photographers and film directors. Of course, Catherine had been delighted to step into that world every now and then, mingle with the rich and famous while Mindy fluttered around like a butterfly, catching everyone's attention but never holding it.

Until she met Rory Managhan. It had been a night like any other in New York that summer. Mindy had taken her to a high-society party, and Catherine had been whirled around for introductions, smiling and nodding as champagne was put in her hand and people forgot her name as soon as she moved on to the next circle of people.

Mindy had brought her face to face with Rory Managhan, and she had felt her whole body light up in response to his dark good looks, the heavy lidded grey eyes that seemed to stare right through her as though he knew everything about her. She hadn't heard Mindy's introduction, she had been too caught up in staring at him, eye-to-eye contact taking her breath away.

He had asked her to dance, and that deep drawling

voice had made her pulses throb in response. Silently, eyes holding hers, he had taken her hand in his and lead her to the centre of the room. One hand had slid to her waist, the other still holding her hand in long fingers, and he had started to dance slowly, never losing eye contact, their faces inches from each other as if in a dream.

A dream she had stayed lost in for the next six months. Rory had kept her by his side continually. Long weekends spent at his beach house on Long Island, making love to the sound of the waves outside, and lying silent afterwards, wrapped up in each other, talking until the dawn broke over the house while she lay, head on his naked chest, legs entwined with his.

She'd felt sometimes as though they didn't need to talk to each other, because somehow she always knew what he was thinking, and he seemed to understand her as well, in exactly the same way.

Memories flitted back now, like short scenes from a film, running on the beach with Rory, each dressed in casual rolled up beach clothes while his dog Scruffy ran on ahead of them, leaping and barking as his master threw him a stick while Catherine clung to Rory's hand, kicking her bare feet up in the edge of the sea. Shopping together during the day in New York, each holding a vast brown paper bag filled with food which they would never eat because they never seemed to be hungry once they got back to his New York apartment. Sometimes they just made love on the floor, and then slung on a dressing gown each, sitting cross legged together and gnawing on chicken legs at midnight, talking endlessly, discovering new things about each other.

Catherine's interest in her studies at college had fallen by the wayside. All she saw was Rory, all she thought about was Rory. Mindy stopped bothering to take her to parties because she spent every waking hour with him, and there was room for nothing else in her life.

Then the photograph was taken. They had been leaving a Fifth Avenue party late one night when it was taken. Rory, dressed in black evening clothes, white silk scarf flying back from one shoulder, had bent his dark head to kiss her passionately, lips at her throat while she half-turned in his arms, eyelids falling closed in breathless response, her mouth partly open, her white dress showing every curve of her slender body.

It had ended up on her father's breakfast table two days later, and he had been in New York within twenty-four hours of seeing it. He had told her, then, exactly what Rory's interest in her was. 'He's not in love with you,' he had said, and that was what really hurt because she had been so heavily in love with Rory that she had lost everything when she heard those words.

Incidents had buzzed back in her mind, making her see the truth in her father's words. 'This is Catherine Skelton, from Sleuhallen.' Mindy had said when she introduced her to Rory that night so long ago, and now Catherine could remember the quick upward shoot of his dark brows, the double-take as he looked closely at her before dancing with her. He had known who she was when he first saw her, Catherine had realised, and it had stabbed into her like a poison thorn.

He's not in love with you, her father had said, and Catherine closed her eyes now, feeling sick as she realised that he still wasn't and never would be. He was back for revenge, and he knew she was her father's favourite. Jed would be furious if she ever went back to Rory. Which was why, of course, Rory would do his utmost to make it happen.

Catherine sighed, rubbing her eyes tiredly. Once

bitten, forever shy, and Rory had almost savaged her to death. She would never go near him again.

He just meant too much to her, if the truth was known, and her love had turned to fear and hatred a long time ago. There was no way to turn back the clock, even if she wanted to—which she most certainly didn't.

Rory Managhan was dangerous—she intended to keep well away from him.

Prominent members of the family had been summoned from all corners of England, including Mindy Skelton who had been working in London modelling agencies for the last year. Catherine felt uncomfortable to see her again, even though she knew very little of what had happened in New York—only that Rory Managhan and she had suddenly split for no apparent reason. With any luck she would have the good sense not to mention it, because Catherine didn't feel able to handle discussing him again so soon after his reappearance.

By tomorrow, the entire Skelton clan would be here in the ten-bedroom mansion that rose over the valley of Sleuhallen. It was almost like an army being summoned to battle.

Mindy sat opposite Catherine and her mother now, after arriving in a cloud of perfume and diamonds and demanding to know exactly what was going on. With long legs and a cloud of dark hair, she looked like a spirited filly, and the wide glossy mouth that flashed a dazzling smile had often been in the pages of women's magazines, advertising toothpaste or lipstick. 'That's me,' Mindy would say, jabbing a red-taloned finger at a page her mouth smiled out from.

'Aunt Katie should get in touch,' said Anne Skelton quietly, a frown tugging at her brow. She sighed, glancing across at Catherine, 'It just isn't like her to disappear. She's always been the one to stand up to Jed.'

Catherine nodded in agreement with her mother. 'Perhaps she'll go to the meeting.'

Mindy said, 'Oh yes, I imagine she will. I expect that's where she was going when I saw her this afternoon.'

Catherine stopped short, turning her head to stare at her cousin. Mindy had seen Aunt Katie? 'You saw her?' she asked incredulously. 'But where?'

Mindy looked puzzled because she obviously didn't realise that no-one had seen Aunt Katie since Saturday night, at Stephen's engagement party. 'Well, yes.' Mindy flicked wide brown eyes at them both, frowning. 'I saw her just after lunch. On my way down here, just outside Sleuhallen—up near the White Bridge.'

Catherine and her mother exchanged quick glances. 'Who was she with? Was she alone?' asked Catherine quickly.

'She was coming out of Tinker's Cottage,' said Mindy, and frowned. 'With some woman—I've never seen her before. She had long black hair, very dark colouring. Almost Spanish, I'd say.'

Anne Skelton whitened, her mouth pressing tightly together, thin lines of strain etched at the corners. 'Isabelle Managhan.' She said softly, and the green eyes filled with memories that Catherine could only guess at.

Catherine looked at her mother with sympathy, but didn't voice her feelings because her mother was not a woman who had been born to weep, and she always kept her feelings under tight wraps. She knew she would be angry and proud if Catherine dared to express sympathy for her. Isabelle Managhan's presence in this town had always hurt her mother, Catherine knew that. She had seen it in her face a thousand times. Knowing that Jed possibly still loved her, Anne Skelton could only keep her thoughts and feelings to herself at the risk of offending her husband. Men are so selfish, thought Catherine angrily. Why had her father allowed Isabelle to go on living in the town? He must have known how deeply it hurt her mother to have to live near her, knowing he still thought about her. What a dreadful fate to wish on any woman—especially a man's wife. But then, Catherine thought again, men *are* selfish. And generally, their mothers have helped make them so. The hand that rocks the cradle will one day wish it had kicked it instead, thought Catherine with an angry smile.

'Is that who it was?' Mindy's mouth formed a round circle. 'My God, I've driven past that cottage more times than I can remember, but I never realised *she* lived there. I thought all the Managhans had left Sleuhallen years ago.'

Anne Skelton looked at her with a carefully controlled face. 'Isabelle has always lived at Tinker's Cottage. It was her parents' house before, and they left it to her just after she married Damian Managhan.'

Catherine looked across at her mother and saw her look down at her hands, bitterness in her eyes. She winced, sighing deeply. It was so unfair. A life wasted because of Jed's past love, Isabelle Managhan. And her mother hadn't even been given the chance to make her husband forget his other love, because Isabelle had always been here, within easy reach. Had Anne ever seen her, driven past her perhaps, met her eye—or spoken to her? Or had she turned her head as if burnt at the very sight of her? Worse still—had Jed ever spoken to Isabelle again? Catherine doubted that. He was too proud and unbending. He would happily walk past her in the street and consider himself the victor for ignoring her. Catherine frowned deeply. Even for Isabelle Managhan, it must have been tough. Jed had made her an outcast in her own home town. How on earth had she managed, knowing that the Skelton family were her bitter enemies? It must have made her life incredibly difficult.

Mindy was looking thoughtful. 'I wish I'd listened to my father's stories about them, now,' she said slowly, clear brown eyes staring into space. 'He used to talk about them all the time. But I was always too interested in the future. The past has never bothered me.'

'Until now?' Catherine said with a gentle smile and Mindy nodded, flashing a brilliant smile with those dazzling teeth.

'I like Uncle Jed,' she explained, head tilted to allow dark curls to trickle over her shoulder. 'Everyone says he's ruthless, but I don't think he is. I think he's just bitter—which is different.' She raised her head, studying them with unwinking eyes, 'I suppose that's something to do with Isabelle Managhan?'

Anne Skelton froze as if turned to stone, and she gave a tight smile. 'He . . . loved her,' she said quietly.

Catherine looked away. It must bring it all back for her mother, she realised. What a can of worms to open on someone, she thought angrily, and Rory Managhan was responsible. What if Isabelle Managhan came to the house to laugh at them all, throw her son's victory in their faces? Catherine shuddered, wondering what her mother would feel like then. Jed would have seen her then, spoken to her. Anne had lived with the ghost of Isabelle for long enough—now the living woman would be involved as a result of her son's revenge. Isabelle would be flesh and blood now, a memory no longer.

Mindy nodded, oblivious to Anne's discomfort at talking about it. 'Then why do you suppose Aunt

Katie was up there? Today of all days? Maybe that's where Rory Managhan is staying here. With his mother at Tinker's Cottage.'

'What time did you see her?' Catherine asked.

Mindy shrugged slender shoulders. 'About one o'clock. On my way down here from the airport. I was enjoying the drive—I haven't been North for seven years. I took a detour over the White Bridge and there she was, walking along the path with this woman.'

Anne Skelton frowned. 'Perhaps Isabelle and her son persuaded Katie into selling the shares in the first place,' she said thoughtfully. 'I think Katie was fond of Isabelle, many years ago. Before she ran off with Damian Managhan, of course.' She sighed, hands going to her slender neck to ease the aching muscles, 'After that—Katie took against her. Never spoke to her again.'

'But people change,' Catherine said quietly. Her mother nodded, eyes sad.

'As you say,' she said, her voice resigned, 'people change.' Eyes narrowing against the last rays of sunlight, she looked towards the french windows, 'Time makes it easier to forgive and forget,' she murmured. 'Perhaps Katie decided it had been a mistake, what Jed did to that family. Who knows? She so rarely tells anyone what she's thinking. I've never been able to read her mind.'

Catherine tilted her head, studying her mother. 'You think Rory went to see her, then? To talk her into selling the shares?'

Her mother looked back at her. 'I don't know, Cathy,' she said on a sigh, 'I just don't know.'

Mindy sat up straight suddenly. 'They're back!'

Catherine turned, eyes scanning the long stately driveway to the house. Yes, there it was, the long Rolls Royce humming slowly towards them, glittering under dying sunlight. Catherine stood up, her family all rising also as they moved almost as one towards the door.

Voices broke out in the hall, the front door was pulled open, and the assembly of friends and relatives who waited there were anxious, their faces filled with worry as they watched the Rolls Royce come to a halt on the drive, gravel crunching under it's wheels as it did so.

The door opened, and Jed stepped out, his face grim, his skin ashen. The blue eyes burnt fiercely, and Catherine's heart sank as she watched him. Something had gone wrong at the meeting. She could tell from the angry set of his shoulders. Rory had taken victory in both hands and hit her father with it, full in the face. She watched anxiously as Stephen stepped out too, silent, arching his back to ease tension and following Jed into the hallway.

He stood for a moment in silence, blue eyes flicking from face to face. Anne Skelton slowly pushed her way to the front of the assembly, eyes seeking her husband's as she waited for him to speak.

Jed looked at his wife grimly. 'He's won this time, Annie.'

Anne blinked, her skin paling.

Jed put his black leather briefcase down on the table with a thud. 'I don't want to list all the changes he's making,' he said in a cold angry voice. 'I tried to block his moves, but every man on that Board voted against me. When he motioned to change the name from Skelton's to Skelton Managhan, I saw their eyes shift away from my face. The motion was passed. It's his firm now, not mine. The bastard's won.'

Catherine felt her heart stop for a second in disbelief, and she looked away, eyes downcast. Rory had obviously gone into the ring with his fists hard and dangerous. He'd knocked her father into the corner and pushed him down. She felt the hatred spring up in her like a molten well. It made her heart hurt, she hated him so much.

'But Jed . . .' Anne was staring at her husband in disbelief. 'It *is* your firm. You built it up from nothing. Surely they wouldn't desert you now?'

Jed shook his head with a deep sigh. 'You didn't see them, Annie,' he murmured. 'Bowing and scraping their noses to the floor, trying to please him. It made me sick to watch them.'

Catherine turned away, unable to look at that proud leonine head bowed in defeat. Did Rory realise how much unhappiness he was causing with this insistence on revenge? It was true that her father had caused a great deal of unhappiness in the past, but two wrongs never make a right, and Rory was hurting too many people with this move.

'The only man on that board who was with me was Stephen. My own son.' Jed's mouth twisted in a bitter smile of self-mockery, 'I'd never have believed it if I hadn't seen it with my own eyes.'

Anne Skelton watched, her thin fingers absently twisting a rope of pearls at her neck. 'Is there nothing you can do?'

'Not this time.' Jed gave a cold laugh, 'But give me time. I'll think of something.' and he turned on his heel to walk down the hallway to the private study where he spent most of his evenings alone or with his wife, sometimes working until the early hours, his desk lamp burning until three or four in the morning, while she could see his silver head bent over his desk when she looked in on him.

Catherine watched him go with a heavy sigh. An excited murmur of voices sprang up in the hall as the study door closed, and the relatives who had arrived so quickly began to discuss what had happened, voices raised as they all walked quickly back into the drawing room.

She didn't follow them. She didn't want to hear it anymore. It had been an eventful day, too eventful and too upsetting. She didn't feel able to take anymore in just at this moment.

Someone touched her arm, and she turned, brows raised in enquiry. It was Mindy, standing beside her looking quite anxious, her dark eyes troubled as she said;

'Can't anything be done?'

Catherine sighed, feeling tired. 'I don't think so, Mindy. It's all cut and dried, isn't it?' She leant against the wall, grateful for the sudden silence in the hall, only she and Mindy stood there now, everyone else had disappeared.

Mindy slid her hands into the pockets of her silk dress. 'I can't believe it, you know,' she murmured, frowning. 'It doesn't sound like the Rory Managhan we knew back in New York, does it?'

Catherine whitened, looking away.

Mindy clucked her tongue. 'God, there I go again, putting my foot in it!' She ran a hand through her beautifully coiffured hair, 'Listen—can we go somewhere and talk? The atmosphere here is just too tense. Isn't there a café nearby or something?'

Catherine shrugged. 'In town, yes. But we'd have to drive there.'

Mindy laughed, dark eyes shining. 'Well let's go! I've got a whole load of questions for you—but you don't have to answer them all.'

They left the house a few moments later, going outside to get into Catherine's car. The shiny red Ferrari glittered in the sunlight as the wheels crunched gravel and they drove away from the Skelton House.

The fields and moors flashed past them, looking a little less forbidding this afternoon, the sun turning dark heather to bright purple, the grass from grey-green to bright meadow green, buttercups and daisies sprouting in the middle of fields.

Sleuhallen was busy, it was close to rush hour. Traffic queued up at the main road traffic lights, exhaust fumes choked the air. Shoppers ran from supermarket to baker's, stocking up at the last minute before the shops closed. Catherine parked the car in the main square and they stepped out into the cool but sunny afternoon.

'God, it's so long since I've been here,' Mindy said quietly as they walked across the square. 'It hasn't changed much. But then—places rarely do. It's people who change most.'

The church spire rose above the little shopping precinct, poking against a bright blue sky. It looked like a postcard, Catherine thought with a smile. The bookshop on the right was quite busy, the olde-worlde windows stacked with books. They walked across cobbled streets towards the café. Catherine felt the stares of passer's-by, but ignored them. It was such a small-town—no doubt they all knew what had happened up at Skelton's Engineering works this afternoon.

'Looks quite crowded,' Mindy commented, peering in through the smoky windows of the Spinning Wheel Café.

They went inside. The bell jangled. Heads turned, and all talking ceased for a stunned moment. Catherine felt herself stiffen under their curious stares. One or two people smiled at her in recognition and she smiled back, stiffly. Then they started to talk again. Catherine closed the door and followed Mindy across the crowded room to a small table, hidden away.

The waitress brought them two coffees in fat brown mugs. Mindy lit a cigarette, dark eyes watching Catherine.

'Have you seen him?' she asked abruptly.

Catherine nodded. 'Twice.'

Mindy studied her. 'Has he changed much?'

Catherine sighed painfully. 'He's harder, more cynical.' She frowned, looking down at the steaming coffee in front of her, 'And I think he hates me rather more now than he ever did.'

That surprised Mindy. 'Hates you? Are you sure?' The dark head tilted and she made a face, 'That's something I never picked up on in New York. He was always with you. It was the talk of Manhattan.'

'I remember!' Catherine gave a harsh laugh, memories flitting through her mind's eye. The party circuit, the sophisticates of New York, all watching like sleek jungle cats as Rory and Catherine's whirlwind romance flared up out of nowhere. What hurt most was knowing that Rory had been manipulating her every step along the line. It made her feel a fool.

Mindy was watching her and said abruptly. 'Why did you split up, Cathy? One minute you were the toast of New York, the next you just disappeared into thin air.'

Catherine swallowed hard. That was one question she didn't want to answer, but she could hardly refuse. Mindy would find out anyway, everyone in town seemed to know about the photograph her father had seen, the way he had flown straight to New York. Briefly, she outlined the story to Mindy, who listened attentively, nodding at polite intervals.

'I never realised though,' Mindy said when she had finished. 'It never clicked that he was one of the Managhans of Sleuhallen. It just seemed a coincidence.'

Yes, Catherine thought bitterly, she understood that only too well. It had been exactly the same for her. A coincidence, she had thought. Rory didn't believe her of course. He thought she must have known, and now he was going to make her pay for it.

'So what happens now?' Mindy asked, straightforward as ever, 'Rory must have said something to you about it.'

Catherine's hand shook as she put her coffee cup down. 'He said he's come back for me,' she said huskily.

Mindy stared. 'You're kidding!'

It hurt Catherine to laugh. 'I'm afraid not! But don't think there's anything romantic in that.' Green eyes flicked to her cousin. 'He's come back to hurt me, Mindy. I can feel it.'

There was a little silence, and Mindy studied her across the polished wooden table. Slowly, she flicked ash into the ashtray, diamond rings flashing on her slender hands.

'What are you going to do?'

Catherine shrugged. 'What *can* I do?' she said, feeling quite defeated. Rory was one of life's unstoppable forces, whirling around knocking everything and everyone in his path out of his way. Nothing could stop him once he had decided on a course of action. He could devastate if he wanted to.

Mindy was frowning. 'I upset your mother today, didn't I? She went as white as a sheet when I said I'd seen Aunt Katie. It was Isabelle's name that upset her, wasn't it?'

Catherine nodded. 'Isabelle Managhan ...' she murmured, and smiled, 'I've known that name since I was a little girl. For the first time it's becoming a real person, not just a legend.'

Mindy put her coffee mug down with a clunk. 'Isabelle Managhan and her son,' she commented dryly. 'Amazing, isn't it? The pair of them wreaking all this havoc. I wonder how they feel about it?'

Catherine gave her a bitter smile. 'I expect they're enjoying every minute of it!'

They left the café half an hour later after Catherine

had answered all of Mindy's questions about the family firm. Now it was no longer Skelton Engineering, though. Now it was Rory Managhan's firm, thanks to Great Aunt Katie. Why the hell did she do it? Catherine thought angrily. And where was Aunt Katie now?

Mindy didn't want to go straight back to the Skelton House, so Catherine agreed to take her for a drive around Sleuhallen. Her cousin hadn't seen the town and surrounding countryside for years, so Catherine drove across the valley, up into the black hills and along the mountain roads while Mindy spoke quietly about her life in London, the new friends she had made, and the exciting jobs she had lined up for the next few months.

As they drove along past Old Hallen's Wood atop the black hills, Mindy pointed across the moors with a frown.

'I remember that place,' she said, and her face broke into a smile. 'It's Old Hallen's Manor, isn't it? I used to play Double Dare there when I was little.'

Catherine looked across the sweeping hills to the manor. Hidden by trees she could only see the four Elizabethan towers poking up from a clump of trees. It was deserted now, rambling and tumble-down. No-one had lived there for over forty years. It was a ghost house, a shell.

'Let's drive up there!' Mindy said, excited now as they drove closer to the turn-off for the manor, 'I haven't been there for absolute years.'

Catherine smiled and indicated left. They had nothing better to do. The house was totally abandoned and no-one would object if they drove up, went into the grounds of the manor and wandered around for a while. At least they could escape the tension of the Skelton family.

Old Hallen's Manor came into view a while later. It

was breath-taking. The Elizabethan manor rose up before them in stately disrepair, four towers of dark red brick, the garden overgrown and clumped with weeds. A pair of iron gates rose very tall in front of the road, blocking the entrance to the drive.

Catherine pulled up. 'Do you want to go in?'

'Why not?' Mindy jumped out of the car, and Catherine followed her. They went over to the tall iron gates, and Mindy started to rattle them, trying to open them and get in. 'I used to climb over them,' she said with a wry smile. 'I'm too sophisticated for that now!'

Catherine laughed. The gates were creaking like mad, scraping the stone path and raking clumps of weeds that grew in the crack of the path. The manor was a complete ghost house now, she thought, staring up at the once-loved house that had been left to die.

The sound of another car approaching made Catherine turn her head. 'Who can that be?' she said under her breath, 'No-one evre comes up here.'

Mindy frowned. 'God knows.' She laughed, eyes dancing, 'Maybe someone who's been dared to sleep in Old Hallen's Manor for one night alone! What a gruesome prospect!' she peered through the rusty old gates, 'I'm sure it's haunted!'

Catherine froze as the long black limousine purred over the brow of the hill. 'Oh no,' she muttered, eyes wide. 'It's Rory, I'm sure of it!'

'You're kidding?' Mindy's head turned to stare too, watching the car glide towards them, sunlight glittering on the roof, flashing off the chrome at side and front. Slowly, Mindy let go of the gates and turned fully as the limousine slowed to a halt.

The door swung open. Rory Managhan stepped out. Studying them with cool grey eyes he said; 'What are you doing up here?'

Catherine moistened her lips. 'Just looking around. Mindy hasn't been here since she left school.'

'Mindy?' Rory frowned, black brows jerking in a frown. He studied the girl beside Catherine for a moment, eyes narrowed, then a spark of recognition leapt in them and he slammed the car door shut, a smile touching the corners of his mouth. 'I didn't recognise you. What are you doing in Sleuhallen? I thought the big cities were more your style.'

'I'm one of the Skelton Clan, remember?' Mindy drawled, raising her brows and giving him one of her sophisticated smiles, 'I got drafted back when the trouble started.'

He laughed wryly, 'Come in number nine,' he drawled and Mindy gave an answering laugh.

'Something like that.'

Catherine felt a stab of jealousy for some absurd reason because she wished Rory would talk to her in that light amused voice, all the hatred and bitterness suddenly vanished from his face as he smiled. But she hated him too, didn't she? Why should she care if he spoke to her cousin like that anyway?

Mindy studied him, and Catherine noticed, to her irritation, that Mindy's body had tautened immediately on seeing Rory, as it always did when she saw an attractive man. It was like radar, she thought angrily, looking at her cousin as she stood like the model she was, one hand on her hip, long dark hair rippling sensually down her neck. A pose she struck constantly in male company.

'How about you?' Mindy asked, brows raised, 'Why are you up here?'

Rory looked away for a moment, shrugging broad muscular shoulders. 'Oh, the same as you,' he murmured casually, 'I haven't been here since I was a boy.'

Catherine frowned, uneasy at the light thread in his

voice as though he was trying to evade the question, or even as though he knew something they didn't, and didn't intend to give it away by saying anything.

Rory caught her wary glance and his eyes narrowed on her. 'I would have thought you'd be at home,' he said coolly, 'giving tea and sympathy to your father.'

Catherine stiffened. 'Very funny. My father can look after himself. He doesn't need me to hold his hand.'

He laughed. 'How quickly you spring to his defence!' he drawled, barbed tone making her bristle with dislike. 'Saint Jed, martyred in the line of duty. It makes my heart bleed!'

Catherine felt her teeth clench, her eyes hating him. 'He's worth ten of you!' she said in a low angry voice, and was furious when he just laughed, the silver eyes watching her with lazy contempt.

'Worth ten of me?' he snarled lazily, black lashes flickering on his cheek as he added, 'He isn't worth a brass farthing.'

Catherine tensed, wishing she could slap his face, and wipe that sardonic smile off it, but she didn't dare, and not only because Mindy was present either. She wouldn't put it past Rory to hit her back and she didn't exactly like the idea of that either. He had absolutely no scruples when it came to women, or she didn't believe he had, especially from his rather blemished past record with her.

Mindy looked at Catherine with a worried frown. 'Maybe we ought to be getting back,' she murmured.

Catherine shot her an angry look. 'Yes. I think that's the best idea I've heard all afternoon!' and she gave Rory a contemptuous glance as she turned and walked back to the car with Mindy, opening the door and getting in behind the wheel.

Rory came over lazily, his lean body muscled and smooth. 'Give my regards to Jed,' he said laconically, resting one long tanned hand on the roof of the car as he bent his black head to look in through the open window.

'I'm sure he'll be delighted,' Catherine snapped, switching the engine on and revving it deliberately. The Ferrari had a kick like a thoroughbred mare when it was made to.

Rory laughed, silver eyes burning on her face. 'Tell him some people have been known to live with failure, after a while.'

Catherine's mouth was a bitter white line. 'Get out of my way!' she hissed, spinning the wheel, just as he moved back from the car, and roared away from the house at top speed, seeing his tall dark figure watching her drive away. Damn you! she thought angrily, making the Ferrari really give all it had.

Mindy looked extremely nervous, clinging on to the door handle as the sleek red car screamed round tight corners at a hair-raising speed. 'Must you drive quite so fast?' she asked quietly as they almost skidded into a sloping wall, 'I've only got one face, contrary to popular opinion, and I don't fancy going into the windscreen!'

Catherine sighed, and slowed down to a more sane speed, but did not reply, she felt too angry with Rory, even though he was miles behind them now, and they couldn't even see Old Hallen's Manor anymore.

They were silent all the way home, and Catherine pulled up in front of the big white Georgian mansion that was the Skelton home with a thud. Mindy got out before she could change her mind, unclipping her seat belt and almost falling out of the door.

Catherine watched her go. Then slowly, she too got out, walking on shaky legs to the front door which had been left open, and going inside. The hallway was deserted, the door of the kitchen open too and a draught wafted through the house, fresh and clean and silent.

From the study she heard raised voices, her mother and father arguing, and she walked quietly over, putting her ear to the door for a moment, heart thumping.

'That bitch Isabelle and her son!' Jed's voice rang out angrily. 'I should have thrown them out of Sleuhallen years ago!'

Anne Skelton saying anguishedly, 'You weren't to know. How could you possibly? Rory was only a boy when he left, a thin gangly boy!'

Catherine laughed painfully, she couldn't imagine anyone describing Rory Managhan as a thin gangly boy! Not by any stretch of the imagination could he ever have been remotely gangly.

Jed laughed then. 'God, Anne, if you weren't by my side I don't know what I'd do,' he said with a trace of bitterness.

'I'll always stick with you, Jed,' Anne Skelton said quietly. 'You know that well enough by now. You and the children are my life.'

Then there was silence, and Catherine felt herself smile because no doubt her father had taken her mother in his arms. She moved away from the door as silently as she possibly could.

She bumped into Stephen, who was racing down the main stairs two at a time, wearing his blue tweed cap which flew off as he collided with her.

Stephen gave her an irritable look and bent to pick up his cap, putting it back on his dark head at a jaunty angle. Sliding his hands into his pockets, he said;

'Back so soon? I thought you'd taken to the hills with Mindy.'

Catherine avoided his eyes. 'Well . . .' she said slowly, 'we got fed up with the hills.'

Stephen laughed. 'Pretty boring really, aren't they?'

he agreed, 'I'm off to Lisa's in a minute. Anything to escape this lot. Fancy coming along to play goosegog? You could always challenge her Uncle Tim to a quick game of backgammon. Great time-waster, back-gammon.'

Catherine gave him a dry look. 'Sounds like an exciting evening,' she drawled sarcastically, although she had spent many afternoons at Lisa's house, but only when Lisa's sister Andrea was at home. Andrea was an old school-friend, a little older than Catherine, but lived in Bristol, going to college there, so they didn't see much of each other.

The telephone rang.

Catherine froze, staring at it as though it might bite her. Her heart started to thud much too fast and she swallowed, scared that it might be Rory. But why should Rory ring her at all? And especially at the Skelton home on the day of his catastrophic meeting with Jed?

'Are you going to answer it?' Stephen leant against the bannisters, gazing wrily down on her. 'Or shall we draw straws?'

Catherine shot him a dark look and reached forward, pulses throbbing, to pick it up. Reciting the number quickly, she was astonished when she heard the voice at the other end.

'Catherine? It's me. Don't say my name out loud.' It was Aunt Katie, she realised, eyes widening and hand tightening on the pale receiver as she listened.

'Where have you been?' Catherine asked immediately, because they had all been so worried about her. Although Aunt Katie had sold out to Rory, she was still a very much loved part of the family.

'Never mind that now.' Aunt Katie brushed it aside with characteristic briskness, 'I want you to do me a favour.'

Catherine nodded. 'Anything.'

'I want you and Stephen to get in your car, and drive over to Tinker's Cottage right away. I wish to speak to you both, but particularly you, Catherine. Now—can you do that? Without telling a soul where you're going, or that I've rung at all.'

Catherine was amazed, she was stunned into silence for a few seconds while she thought quickly. Then she said slowly, 'But why——'

'Not now, Cathy love.' Aunt Katie said curtly, 'Just tell me if you can get here or not?'

Catherine sighed. 'I suppose so.'

'Good girl. I'll see you when you get here.' She hung up, leaving Catherine staring at the buzzing receiver in her hands and wondering why events always seemed to move so fast. Was there never time for any of them to rest and recoup their energies? Things just seemed to happen these days like bolts from the blue.

Turning slowly, she looked at Stephen who had picked up some of her confused tension and was watching her closely, his black brows drawn in a frown across his forehead.

'Who was it, Cath?' he asked quietly.

She moistened her lips, looking around to check that no-one was listening, especially Mrs Tandy, who had a dreadful habit of hovering behind doors, her ears almost out on stalks complete with radar equipment.

'It was Aunt Katie,' she whispered. 'She wants us to go to Tinker's Cottage right away.'

Stephen's brows shot up and he whistled under his breath. 'It's going to be one of those days!'

CHAPTER FOUR

TINKER'S Cottage lay on the edge of the valley of Sleuhallen. As they drove down from the hills towards the valley, she saw the old town laid bare before her, the thickly clustered grey-slate houses, lights glinting in the dusk which stole over the valley. As the industrial part of town faded, it gave way to fields, lush green slabs of land with white farmhouses dotted around them, sheep and cattle grazing on the hills around. Catherine drove slowly over White Bridge under which the stream gushed noisily over rocks and pebbles, and she parked outside Tinker's Cottage. She sat staring up at the white thickly painted stone, the black slate roof and two small chimneys which nestled in the centre, smoke curling in gentle wisps from them.

Pale yellow light spilled out into the front garden as a curtain was drawn back. Catherine's heart leapt as she saw a dark silhouette in the ground floor window. Broad shoulders, powerful arms and darkly carved features stared out. It was Rory.

What was he doing here? she thought angrily, eyes flicking to the drive way where the long black Cadillac limousine jutted out. Her heart sank, as if her aunt had somehow betrayed her by inviting her to Tinker's Cottage when Rory was there.

'Isn't that Rory Managhan?' Stephen said, eyeing the dark figure.

Catherine nodded without speaking. The curtain was dropped back into place, and she sighed, closing her eyes. Maybe he had been here since the meeting, and had been with Aunt Katie when she made that telephone call.

'Come on.' Stephen unlocked his door with a resounding click. 'We'd better go in.'

She watched him get out, her pulses hammering, and took a deep breath, getting out of her side too. The night was cool, the air smelt damp, and she locked her door with unsteady hands. Putting her keys in her white leather handbag, she slung it over one shoulder, gripping the handles with her fingers as if for reassurance.

Their footsteps click-clacked on the stone pathway. Stephen walked in front of her, unaware of the turmoil Catherine was going through at the thought of seeing Rory again so soon. She watched her brother lift the heavy black doorknocker and rap on the wooden door sharply.

Footsteps, recognisably Rory's, came along the hallway inside and the door was pulled open, a light from inside streaming out on to their faces as Rory appeared.

He stood framed in the doorway, dark eyes flicking to them, then past at the deserted road behind them. 'You're alone, then?' he said coolly.

Stephen nodded. 'Aunt Katie asked us not to tell anyone where we were going.'

Rory looked at Catherine with those steel grey eyes and she met his stare, chin lifted. 'You'd better come in,' he said with a ghost of a smile, and held the door open for them.

He looked dangerously sexy this evening, wearing black jeans and a black cashmere sweater which fitted closely to his muscular chest, showing the network of black hairs that curled on his chest at the neck of his shirt. He looked far too touchable. She felt an urge to reach out and run her fingers along the hard muscles in his arms, his shoulders.

Why did he always seem so unaccountably real to her? Larger than life, almost. Filling every room she stood in with him. As he turned his back on them she watched him walk away, and knew she'd recognise those shoulders anywhere, the set of his dark head—even the way he walked, like an animal, fast, graceful stride. Filled with energy, Rory seemed to burn like an electric power circuit.

The narrow hallway was cluttered and untidy, and the thick stone walls were painted white, just like the exterior. A door on the left spilled yellow light into the carpeted hall. Rory pushed the door open.

'Are they alone?' Aunt Katie asked as they went in, and Rory nodded. The old woman stood up, looking pale and tired by the brightness of the fire which leapt and spat in an iron grate.

'Why didn't you ring earlier?' Stephen went over to her, kissing the papery-skinned cheek she offered, 'We were all so worried!'

Aunt Katie laughed, gnarled fingers clenching and unclenching on her cane. 'And have your father bite my head off?' She shook her silver head, 'I'm no fool. Let him cool down first.'

Stephen studied her with a frown. 'But why invite us here? This may affect us, but it isn't really our fight.'

Aunt Katie flicked her grey-green gaze to Catherine. 'Isn't it?' she said softly, and Catherine looked away, realising she was talking strictly about her emotional involvement with Rory.

Rory closed the door with a sharp click, and Catherine looked at him quickly, feeling uneasy for some reason as he walked with slow grace into the centre of the room to stand beside her, hands thrust into the pockets of his black jeans as he eyed her in silence.

Turning back to Aunt Katie, she felt suddenly trapped, her eyes wary as she looked at them both.

'I never wanted this for you, Cathy,' Aunt Katie

murmured, standing framed by the fire looking rather like a sepia photograph, her clothes and manner echoing a bygone age. 'I didn't want you to get mixed up in all this bitterness. It was Jed who dragged you into it. He should have left you to run your own life.'

Hot colour flooded Catherine's face as she stared at her aunt, realising with dawning awareness that she knew everything that had happened between herself and Rory. When had he told her? she wondered bitterly, shooting a quick glance at him. A last ditch effort to get Aunt Katie on his side—and probably one thing that had swung the balance. He was despicable. He'd use anything, no matter how painful, to get his own back on the Skelton family.

'I've watched him for years.' Aunt Katie's heavy old brows linked in a frown, 'He's become so ruthless that he's prepared to destroy his own. He doesn't care who he hits out at—so long as he's the winner in the end. I can't let him go on like that or he'll ruin everything around him, destroy the whole family.'

Catherine looked away. 'That isn't fair. He only wants to protect what's his, not destroy it.'

'No, Cathy.' Aunt Katie fingered the cameo brooch clasped at her throat, 'He's gone too far this time. What he did to you and Rory was unforgiveable. I couldn't believe it had happened.'

Catherine shot a quick look at Rory, seeing him watching her steadily, and felt herself grow more angry with him. 'What have you been telling her?' she asked him under her breath.

The grey eyes held hers steadily. 'I didn't tell her a thing,' he said curtly. 'Your father got there before me.'

Her mouth tightened. 'That's a lie! My father told me he'd keep it all under cover. He didn't want anyone to know what you'd done.' She remembered that only too clearly. The journey home from the airport had been silent and tense, her father had sat by her on Concorde and had not spoken once all the way back from New York. He had felt as humiliated and bitter as she had, knowing that Rory Managhan had almost made fools of them both. She knew he would never have told any member of the family what had happened back in New York.

Aunt Katie rapped her ebony cane against the tiled fireplace. 'Cathy, he's telling the truth. Jed told me everything as soon as you came back from New York.'

Catherine stared, totally baffled for a moment, then looked away, unable to believe it. 'No,' she said huskily.

Aunt Katie sighed, silent for a few seconds, then she walked slowly over to sit in the flowered rocking chair by the fire, the wood creaking as she sat down. Stephen went to help her, but she waved him away with one frail old hand, frowning and he just stood back to watch her with a smile. Aunt Katie looked up at him, caught his smile, and her mouth curved wryly.

'I'm getting old!' Laughing gruffly, her finely chiselled head moved on top of her neck as though it didn't quite fit. 'It creeps up on you like this. Last year I thought I could go on forever. Now I know that I won't. I have very little time left.'

Stephen glanced across at Catherine, dark eyes concerned. 'Is that why you decided to sell out?' he asked quietly, and looked back at Aunt Katie, dark brows rising, 'Try to set the balance right while you could still do it?'

Aunt Katie nodded, sighing. 'I'd been thinking of doing it for a long time.' she told them. The grey-green eyes were thoughtful for a moment as she continued, 'I kept watching Jed, getting more and more ruthless, lashing out at everyone who opposed him. I knew he would have to be stopped, someday, even though I tried to keep out of it as much as possible. I didn't want to interfere.'

Catherine sat down too, slowly, staring at her aunt. 'But you were always standing up to him,' she said quietly, 'Even when I was little, I can remember that much.'

Aunt Katie frowned heavily. 'You can only intervene so much—and no more,' she said softly, and shifted in the rocking chair, hand behind back to adjust the cushions. 'I stepped in when I thought it was necessary, but left him to his own devices for most of the time.'

Stephen lit a cigarette, the smell of acrid smoke drifting through the room as he threw a spent match into the fireplace, and drew on the filter-tip, inhaling sharply.

Stephen studied his Great Aunt thoughtfully; 'But did you ever try to interfere when it all began?' he asked with a frown, 'With Isabelle and Damian?'

'Good Lord, no!' Aunt Katie looked grim, 'I didn't approve of what Isabelle did to Jed. That was wrong, and she deserved his revenge. But Jed doesn't know when to stop. He should have left them alone after the first year. But he didn't.' She shook her grey head, 'He just went on and on, until Damian died.'

Catherine watched Rory from beneath her lashes, trying to gauge his reactions. He had never spoken to her about his parents, and now he just stood listening, his face grim and unsmiling, eyes downcast, black lashes sweeping his cheeks. What was running through his mind? she wondered with a frown. It hurt to know she had never really understood him as well as she'd once believed she did. How naïve she must have been, back in New York. Believing that they fitted together like two halves of a two-piece jigsaw puzzle, when in fact they were almost strangers, each walking around with totally different thoughts in their heads that neither knew about. It had been a painful shock to suddenly see Rory zoom into focus as a stranger after she had spent so long believing they were in love with each other.

Aunt Katie looked across at Catherine. 'When I saw he was bringing his past into Catherine's future—I knew I had to stop him.'

Catherine looked round, 'That's unfair,' she said, rushing to her father's defence aware that she trusted him far more than Rory. 'He was only trying to help me. He didn't want to hurt me.'

'Perhaps not,' said Aunt Katie. 'But he did hurt you—didn't he?'

Catherine felt hot colour flood her cheeks, looking away desperately trying to conceal her reactions. 'No!' she said in husky denial.

Sighing, Aunt Katie shook her head. 'Oh Cathy. I've spoken to Rory at great length about this. He knows what you felt as well as I do.'

That made her suddenly angry, looking across at Rory to see him watching with a grim expression, and she couldn't meet his eyes. She felt exposed, helpless as though they had picked her thoughts out of her head and written them on the wall for everyone to stare at.

'How can any of you know what I felt?' she said in a low angry voice, 'You can't see inside me.' She stood up, her body trembling slightly, and turned her head away, trying to keep cool and controlled when she felt so exposed to them. How could they say these things to her when it had all finished so long ago? Why couldn't any of her family leave the past alone?

'Don't turn away, Cathy.' Aunt Katie stood up too, resting on her ebony cane and standing with her spine rigidly erect, holding her head up. 'It must be said.'

'Why?' Catherine said bitterly, 'Can't you leave the

past dead and buried? This has nothing to do with you—any of you.'

Rory's mouth tightened as he watched her. 'Doesn't it?' he said in a angry voice, 'It has a lot to do with me.'

'Very true,' she eyed him angrily, 'You caused it all. You should have left us all alone. Why did you have to come back here with your lies and your revenge?' She stared at him, eyes wild green, 'Why can't you just go away and leave us alone?'

He came over to her with quick strides, his grey eyes burningly angry at her outburst, and she almost flinched away from him, but forced herself to stand her ground, swaying slightly but lifting her chin in defensive reaction as he stopped dead in front of her.

'You of all people should know why I came back,' he said tightly, and she saw a muscle jerking in his cheek as he spoke.

'Oh, I know why, all right.' Catherine gave him a bitter look, 'You came back to destroy my family—and me with it.'

'Don't be stupid!' he ground out, 'I came back for you—I've told you that already. Why don't you believe me?'

Her pulses leapt at his words, but she fought them down, burning with anger at having her private feelings aired in front of members of her family. She didn't want to argue with him in front of them, she didn't want them to see how much she hated him for what he had done. It was too revealing. A dead give-away, she thought bitterly, staring at him. Her brother and Aunt Katie were watching this with widened eyes, amazed by her sudden explosive anger, because Catherine had always seemed so quiet and calm to them before, now she was standing, eyes flashing with temper at Rory Managhan, and Catherine knew exactly what they were thinking. It made her want to take her heart and hide it, away from their curious stares, away from the eyes of her family.

Looking at Aunt Katie in sudden desperation, she said, 'Surely you can see why he's doing this?'

Aunt Katie eyed her grimly. 'Only too clearly.'

Catherine flushed hotly. 'You're as blind as I was,' she said, her voice bitter. 'He's a clever talker—I know that only too well. He's made you believe his side of it—hasn't he?'

The old woman clicked her tongue with sudden impatience. 'Fiddlesticks, girl. I'm old enough to know right from wrong—I don't need to be told that your father is the one who's wrong. You'd see it too—if you'd only stop and think for a moment.'

Catherine looked at her, and knew that there was nothing she could say to change Aunt Katie's mind. Rory had persuaded her aunt into believing he cared, but Catherine knew better. He had known who she was from the moment they first met. Jed Skelton's eldest daughter. And he had made a concentrated effort to make her fall in love with him. So attentive, so charming, so exciting and all the time he knew exactly what he was doing.

That was what she couldn't forgive. The cold calculating side of his nature, deliberately playing on the emotions of an inexperienced, naïve young woman. Making her fall in love with him, while all the time he held back, watching her from behind those steel grey eyes, planning ahead, thinking of her family's reaction when they found out that Catherine Skelton was going to marry Rory Managhan. It was unforgivable.

'I'm not staying here to listen to this.' she said tightly, glancing at them all for a moment, before she pushed past Rory, ignoring his muttered expletive, and going over to the door, pulling it open fast and going into the hall.

Shivering, she noticed the contrast between the

warmth of the fireside and the cold hallway, damp stone walls seeming to press in on her. Going to the front door, she pulled it open, stepping out into the chill spring evening, the dusk beginning to seep across the valley, bringing a faint damp mist with it which hung over the huddled houses of the town.

Halting suddenly, she realised she had come with Stephen and she couldn't go anywhere unless he wanted to leave too. Damn! she thought angrily, turning her head to look back at the house while one hand rested on the handle of the sports car.

A sudden gust of wind whipped her red-gold hair around her face, and she dragged it back into place, pulling her jacket closer around her as the wind knifed through her breastbone.

It was two miles back to the Skelton house. It would be dark by the time she got back there if she left her keys with Stephen and walked. But Stephen was obviously going to stay in Tinker's Cottage to talk to Aunt Katie. His feelings weren't involved in this. Stephen was interested in every detail of the family feud that had raged for so long. She guessed that he'd stay with Aunt Katie for at least an hour to find out more about it. So she had a choice between going back into the cottage, walking home alone, or just waiting outside for a while.

Sighing, she looked across the White Bridge to the gentle slope of the hill that rose out of the valley of Sleuhallen. A tall oak tree stood there, wide stretching branches shading the lush green grass, and she thought perhaps she could sit up there for a while, smoke a cigarette and try to calm down.

Catherine walked slowly out of the front garden of Tinker's Cottage, across White Bridge where the stream gushed beneath, and up the gentle slope of the hill, sitting down beneath the shade of the oak.

The glowing red orb of the sun was setting behind

the jagged black hills of Sleuhallen. She lit a cigarette, staring at the sun in silence as the jagged peaks seemed to poke up into it's heart, making it ooze like a blood orange.

A dark figure came out of the cottage and Catherine's heart pounded faster as she recognised Rory. Looking up to where she sat on the sloping hill, he stopped short, hands on hips as his eyes stared at her. She prayed he wouldn't come up to the hill.

Her prayers were not answered. Rory began to stride across, his tall lean body moving with whipcord energy, black hair blowing in the wind, muscles flexing as he came closer to her. Catherine couldn't look away.

She had always found his body magnetic, hypnotically watchable. In New York she had spent hours staring at that dark chiselled profile, wishing she could touch it always, run her fingertips over the angular cheekbones, the contrasting texture of the softness of his black sooty lashes, the long straight bridge of his nose. It made her feel sick to remember how horribly in love she had been with him, knowing he had been coldly calculating every move. She felt humiliated, angry with herself.

'What on earth are you doing up here?' Rory stopped in front of her, hands on hips, legs apart, black hair rippled by the breeze.

Catherine did not look into his eyes. 'Smoking a cigarette,' she said flatly, exhaling and watching the smoke drift away into the breeze.

He eyed it with an impatient stare. 'You should give it up,' he said abruptly, 'God knows what it's doing to your lungs.'

She laughed. 'You smoke.'

Rory studied her for a moment, then laughed too. 'I'm a hypocrite!' he drawled with amusement, and she risked a quick glance at him. The grey eyes lit with laughter that made her heart stop, she looked away again, fighting down the attraction.

He studied her, face sobering. 'I thought you'd decided to do something stupid,' he told her, 'like walk home alone.'

She shook her head. 'I'm wearing high heels,' she pointed out and raised one foot elegantly to show him the white stilettos. 'I would have broken my ankle.' Apart from which, it would have been dark by the time she got home and Sleuhallen lanes were frightening at night, the cows and sheep becoming eerie monsters that made strange sounds as they trod the grass softly, their heads looming in black shadows over the slate-piled walls that surrounded the farmland.

Rory looked at her feet. 'Beautiful,' he commented, 'You always did have a sense of style.'

So did you, she thought, swallowing hard, but didn't say it. Instead she just quietly said; 'Thank you.'

Rory studied her in a long silence, standing towering over her, his eyes cool on her face. Catherine didn't look up at him, her eyes narrowed against the cold wind as she looked across the valley.

'Why are we talking about such pointless things?' Rory murmured under his breath.

Her heart twisted. She shrugged, face cool. 'I don't know.'

Rory's eyes brooded on her for a moment, then he sat down beside her, the dying sunlight making his tanned skin golden, highlighting the raven hair with threads of gold.

Catherine felt her pulses leap faster, intensely aware of his body so close to her, risking a quick look at the long legs, lean hips and tautly muscled stomach. He stretched out, resting on one hand, his body bent at right angles to the ground.

'How long do you plan to sit here?' Rory asked, glancing at his watch, 'It'll be dark in half-an-hour.'

She eyed his wrist and strong dark-haired hand. 'Until Stephen comes out.'

The grey eyes flicked to hers. 'You'll have a long wait,' he drawled, 'Stephen's talking to Katie. He wants to find out more about the past.'

Catherine laughed, a little harshly. 'I've had enough of the past to last me a lifetime.'

'So have I,' he shot back coolly. She looked at him, eyes narrowed because that thought hadn't occurred to her. It must be just as bad to have lived your life with the shadow of revenge and bitterness hanging over your head. Catherine just wished he hadn't felt the need to drag her into it all.

She looked away, frowning, plucking small blades of grass absently with one hand.

Rory eyed her. 'That hadn't dawned on you?' he drawled with a cool smile, 'That I've had a raw deal out of all this too?'

She raised her brows. 'You could have forgotten it, Rory. But you didn't. You kept it all alive, even when you had built a new life in New York—away from all this.'

Rory nodded his dark head. 'True,' he said quietly. 'And I did forget it all to a certain extent.' The grey eyes flicked to hers, 'Until I met you. You were the catalyst, Cathy.'

She frowned at him, frowning in disbelief. 'How can you say that to me?' she said under her breath, memories coming back to her with renewed anger, 'You only took an interest in me because you knew who I was. Jed Skelton's only daughter.'

Rory gave a harsh crack of laughter. 'You don't really believe that?'

'Yes I do,' she said, mouth tightening, 'You were so very seductive, weren't you Rory? You really swept me off my feet. Well, I've grown up a lot since then. It won't work again.'

His eyes flashed. 'No-one can fake that much passion,' he said tautly, and she felt her pulses leap crazily, hammering at her throat and wrists at the memory of those months in New York, the long hot nights of summer when she had fallen so heavily for him.

Her mouth went dry. 'You can,' she said bitterly, 'You're a complete phoney.'

He was silent for a tense moment, eyes broodingly angry. 'Would you like to test your theory?' his tone was hard, and she shot a quick look at him, seeing the anger in his eyes and wanting to take back what she had said.

'No, thank you,' she said in a shaky voice, and started to move away. His hand shot out grabbing her hair in a handful and pulling her back, ignoring her frightened gasp as he forced her back to lie pressed against the grass while he leant over her, face tight with anger.

'You're hurting!' she tried to get up but he thrust her down with the flat of one hand, dark shadow blotting out the sun.

'So are you,' he said through his teeth, and she stared at him as his head moved closer to hers, his mouth hard and disturbingly attractive.

'What do you mean by that?' she asked, hands fluttering to his powerful chest to hold him away.

'What the hell do you think?' he said bitingly, 'I suppose you think I like all the insults you keep flinging at me? What do you think I am—made of stone?'

She stared, thrown for a moment. Moistening her lips she said, 'I've only said what's true. Don't you like hearing the truth?'

'Not your kind of truth,' he shot back, eyes hard. 'I

thought you knew me. I thought you were mine.' His mouth twisted, 'I was wrong, wasn't I? You're branded Skelton until you die.'

Her mouth trembled. 'They're my family! If I can't believe them, who can I believe?'

'Me,' he said bitterly, grey eyes flashing, 'But you never will. There's only one way I've ever been able to get through to you, isn't there?'

His head swooped down and she caught her breath, pushing him away, her hands enjoying the feel of the hard shoulder muscles beneath her palms, 'It won't work Rory,' she said under her breath, struggling with him stupidly, 'I'm not your fool anymore. I know what's going on inside your head.'

He laughed huskily, and she felt his chest move as he did. 'Good, then you should know what's coming next!' and his mouth swooped to cover hers, kissing her insistently, lips hard and cruel while she twisted beneath him angrily.

Hitting out blindly, she tried to stop him, but he shifted to avoid her blows, hands gripping her wrists, face taut as he pushed her hands back on the grass pinning her down, lying on her to keep her still, her breasts thrusting up against his chest as she struggled angrily, her face hot.

'Kiss me.' he muttered against her mouth, and her pulses fluttered in momentary weakness, knowing she wanted badly to give in to him, and he sensed it, damn him, because he caught his breath sharply.

His hot mouth moved over hers, body pressing her down on the grass, and she clung to him, knowing she didn't want to get away from him yet, not just yet, because it had been so long since she felt him touch her like this, and since the first day she had seen him again, seen that hard mouth, those long hands and his lean muscled body, she had wanted to feel him next to her again, like a fever pounding in her blood that she couldn't stop herself from wanting, however hard her mind fought against the overwhelming attraction.

Dragging her mouth away, she murmured hotly, 'No, Rory . . .'

But his lips found hers again insistently. 'Yes.' he muttered against her mouth, making her groan, his tongue flickering inside her mouth to meet hers made her heart thud too fast as her fingers curled in silent protest and she gave in to him, her eyes shutting as heat flooded her body. She heard him murmur thickly, 'Oh yes . . .' as if she had spoken too.

The long fingers slid from her wrists, down her body, gliding over her soft breasts while she arched towards him and their bodies seemed to merge in one instant, heartbeats echoing together, blood pounding at her wrists and temples as she remembered in aching need the way he could turn her blood to mercury with just one touch, make her forget everything while she was in his arms.

Raising his head, breathing fast, he looked down at her with fiery eyes. 'God, Cathy, why won't you listen to reason?' he muttered thickly, and she closed her eyes, her mouth bruised.

She ran her fingers over the back of his neck, feeling the tight muscles beneath the skin, and longing to be able to hold him close, touch his naked chest again, feel his body next to hers entwined in a mass of tangled sheets.

'Oh Rory,' she whispered, lids closing as she buried her face in his warm neck, 'Why did you have to come back?'

He laughed huskily, and she felt his throat muscles move and throb against her mouth. 'I wish I knew!' he murmured, 'I was devastated when you walked out on me. I wanted to kill you.'

Catherine clutched him tightly. 'But you must have known why I went.'

His body tensed and he raised his head to look down at her, grey eyes hardening. 'Oh, I knew all right. Your bloody father flew out to get you, didn't he?'

'He saw the photograph.' Catherine murmured.

'The bastard,' Rory said tightly. 'It gave me great pleasure to watch him fall apart this afternoon. I've been waiting a long time to kick his teeth in.'

Catherine froze, a frown marring her brow. She didn't like hearing this. It was too much of a give-away of his thoughts. He was using her as a weapon against her father, and God help her, she only needed to be kissed once by that hard mouth to become a willing victim of his revenge.

Rory rolled on to his back, resting on one elbow as he looked down into her face. 'He came to see me—in New York.' Grey eyes flicked to her face grimly, 'Did you know that?'

Catherine shook her head stiffly, feeling hurt as she looked at him, knowing he was calculating another way of hitting back at her father even while he lay here with her in the silent evening.

Rory eyed her. 'He told me he'd found out what I was doing. He was going to pull all the stops out to prevent me marrying you.' His mouth tightened as he studied her, 'It worked, too—didn't it?'

'Yes,' she said stiffly, 'What did you expect? You made a fool of me. Once I found out what you were doing you didn't seriously imagine I would go along with it?'

The dark brows jerked together in surprise. 'I didn't expect you to believe him,' he said coolly.

Catherine flushed hotly, sitting up. She looked down at the valley, her mouth tight, feeling the anger of having been a fool, not just once but twice now, when she had given in to Rory again because she was so hopelessly attracted to him that she couldn't help herself, and that made her hate herself for her weakness.

'I'm going back now,' she said abruptly, standing up and brushing the grass from her skirt while Rory stared at her for a moment in stunned silence. Then he too stood up, slowly, getting to his feet with languid grace, eyes riveted in her face.

'But I thought——' he began slowly and she cut across his words.

'Yes, I know what you thought!' Her eyes flashed bright angry green, 'You thought you'd won me over with a kiss, didn't you? Well it'll take a lot more than that to make me betray my family to a man like you.'

He stared at her in silence for a moment, then gradually anger took over his features again, the grey eyes hardening.

'Family loyalty again?' he said bitterly.

'That's right,' she raised her brows, eyeing him.

He caught her arm, his mouth tight. 'You're all alike. Aren't you? Stick together till the end. It doesn't matter to any of you that other people are involved. All you care about is the family.'

Catherine stared, eyes wild green. He was speaking to her as though she had wronged other people in some way when in fact she was caught up in all of this against her will. How he could do it was a mystery to her, and it made her completely at a loss as to what she could say to him in reply. He had known in New York that her feelings were very much involved and he had exploited her innocence quite cheerfully and deliberately. To take a young girl whose illusions were all still very much intact and shatter them like that was unforgiveable. At some point in your life, you have to cry innocent tears when you see the illusions slip away, leaving the bare reality of life exposed for the first time. But generally it's a combined set of circumstances that makes it suddenly dawn on you.

Rory hadn't allowed her even that comfort. He had simply ripped her illusions from her in one fell swoop, and to stand here now accusing her of indifference to other people's feelings, was unfair.

'Are you any different?' she asked him simply.

Rory studied her for a long moment in silence, and she saw the thoughts running through his mind, his grey eyes moving across her face. Then slowly he let go of her arm, his hand going back to his side as he shook his dark head, mouth firming.

'No.' His lashes flickered. 'I'm no different. But I'm on the winning side this time, Cathy. And I won't let go. You'll all feel the weight of my anger before I'm through.'

She gave a painful sigh. 'We already do.'

Rory laughed. 'I'm just beginning!' and he turned on his heel, the wind whipping his black hair as he walked down the hill leaving her standing alone, rather shaken as she watched him go.

How quickly the mood between them changed. At one point back there she had felt herself begin to weaken towards him, and it had only been self-protective instincts that had pulled her back just as she felt herself drawn under his spell. Why did he always manage to make her feel like that when she knew damned well that he was the most manipulative man she had ever encountered. Surely by now she had enough sense to stay away from the fire. Their family loyalties divided them anyway, and always would. It would have been difficult for them both, even if Rory had sincerely been in love with her, she knew that. But knowing that he didn't actually care for her, only for her name, the Skelton name, made it all much more difficult to accept.

She had always thought it odd in New York that Rory never mentioned his family. Often she had asked him, tried to draw him out on the subject but he had simply said his mother was living in England but his father was dead. That was all. Nothing more or less, and his face would turn shuttered when she pressed him on the subject. So of course, she had left it alone, believing stupidly that he needed to have more time before he talked about them with her. Her mouth twisted in a bitter smile. Not so when it came to the subject of her family. He had listened then, attentively. So attentively that Catherine had found herself elaborating endlessly, telling him everything she could think of. Now she knew why.

Looking at the black hills of Sleuhallen, she saw the sun had finally died. Darkness was beginning to spread over the land. A few more lights winked down in the valley from houses and street lamps.

Tears stung her eyes as she looked down at Tinker's Cottage. Rory had never been hers, he had always been a Managhan first and foremost, her father's enemy, and he would never change. Taking a deep breath, she blinked the tears back angrily, her face bitter.

Slowly, Catherine walked back down to Tinker's Cottage.

CHAPTER FIVE

SHE woke next morning to see sun streaming in through her windows, and for a moment felt the excitement of a new day beginning. But then she remembered Rory. Her mouth tightened and she lapsed back on the pillows, staring at her reflection in the mirror opposite. The clock showed the time at eight and she sighed, realising she'd have to get moving if she was to get to work on time. Pushing back the bedclothes, she padded over to the bathroom to shower and dress before going to Arundel's. Snatching a quick coffee and a bite of lightly buttered toast in the kitchen, she went out into the crisp morning, getting into her car and driving away. It was cold this morning, and she switched the heater on full blast, listening to the irritating scrape of the back windscreen wiper as it dragged over slight frost.

The shop was silent when she arrived, and she walked through the rows of paintings and statues to the back where she could hear Mrs Caley making coffee. Catherine pushed the string beaded curtain back with a light rustle and gave Mrs Caley a bright smile.

'Why Cathy!' Mrs Caley was surprised to see her, 'We didn't expect you today.'

Catherine shrugged. 'I said I'd be in,' she pointed out, glancing around for a sign of Rick.

Mrs Caley watched her. 'Well, I know you said you'd be in,' she murmured, adjusting her glasses, 'But what with one thing and another . . .' she stopped in mid-sentence, looking uncomfortable for a moment, then patted Catherine's arm her face gentled with a little smile, 'But you're here now, and that's all that matters, isn't it?'

Catherine went over to the counter to start laying out the receipt slips ready for the day, and putting the float in the till. It was obvious that everyone now knew all about Rory Managhan's take-over, and although she had expected it to be common knowledge, she hadn't expected it to be quite so soon. A day or two's grace would have been more than welcome for her, especially after what had been said between them last night. She hadn't slept well. Thoughts of Rory had kept her awake, twisting and turning until the early hours, unable to stop thinking about him.

She worked steadily through the morning, although she found it more than usually difficult. Rory's name was on everyone's lips, and if they didn't actually mention him directly, they made sly innuendos or simply looked sympathetically at Catherine while she gritted her teeth and presented a good front. Usually she could relax here, sit reading an art book in silence while the odd customer browsed among the shelves. But today they had a lot of customers, all wanting to look at her as if she was a monkey in a cage.

Lily from the baker's next door came in at mid-morning to find out what she could. 'I saw him in that big black car of his,' she said with a sly smile, eyes caked with mascara and eye-liner, 'driving along Old Hallen's road at midnight.'

Mrs Caley clucked her tongue, pretending irritation with Lily, but Catherine saw only too clearly that she was just as interested. 'Away with you, girl. What were you doing up at Old Hallen's road at that time of night?'

'I was with Jack,' said Lily, red lips curling. 'And I saw a woman in the front seat with Mr Rory

Managhan,' she fastened Catherine with her knowing eyes and asked; 'Wasn't you, was it, Miss Cathy?'

'No,' Catherine snapped, walking out to the back of the shop and leaving Lily to raise her brows in a speaking glance to Mrs Caley. Let them think what they like, Catherine thought angrily, banging cups in the back of the shop as she made herself a cup of boiling hot coffee. They would anyway, whatever she did or said.

It was virtually the same story with everyone who came in that morning. All they wanted to know about was Rory Managhan. Catherine became more and more irritated as time wore on, and Mrs Caley's eagerness to gossip with the people who came in annoyed her even more. She could at least have the courtesy to wait until she was alone, thought Catherine, watching Mrs Caley with narrowed eyes as the woman whispered hurriedly to a woman in a red coat and hat, who stood at the far side of the rows of pottery. The woman turned and stared at Catherine for a moment, and Catherine looked away with a tight mouth.

Mindy dropped by at lunchtime and gave Catherine a sympathetic smile as she told her all about everyone's behaviour.

'Never mind,' she leant on the counter, bracelets jangling, 'Come out to lunch with me—I'll cheer you up.'

Catherine jumped at the offer, putting her coat on and leaving the shop, bell jangling behind her, and following Mindy over to where her little white sports car was parked nearby.

They drove to Forest Lodge on the outskirts of Sleuhallen. An old hotel on the edge of Old Hallen's Wood, it had a good restaurant and a breath-taking view of the valley. Catherine had often come here with her father and brother, especially on important business days. It was the restaurant where most of the deals in Sleuhallen were made over the cognacs and cigars.

Today it was crowded with businessmen and women, the atmosphere smoky and noisy, the sound of chattering and laughing floating out from the restaurant as Catherine and Mindy were escorted down the long corridor towards it by a rather impersonal waiter.

Entering the doorway, Catherine felt eyes flicker towards her, and a lull of voices followed her appearance as heads turned to watch her walk with Mindy to their table by the long french windows in the corner. They both sat down slowly, faces cool and remote as the waiters flicked napkins open on their laps while the other diners stared openly.

Catherine bent her head, eyes angry.

'Maybe this was a mistake,' Mindy said, eyeing her across the pink damask table-cloth. A single pink carnation stood in a long silver fluted vase in the centre of the table. A small china dish with pink ensignia sat beside the silver cruette set, holding slivers of butter on ice.

'They'll talk whether I'm here or not,' Catherine pointed out with a sigh. 'We may as well enjoy a good meal and put up with it. But I wish they wouldn't stare so much.'

Mindy nodded, dark eyes flashing round the room. 'Unsettling, isn't it?' she commented, 'I'm used to it in London and New York—people recognise me. But it's odd to be stared at down here like this. There's a different expression in their eyes.'

Cold sunlight glinted in through the french windows, and she glanced through them to see the dew still clinging to the lower branches of the thickly clustered trees of Old Hallen's Wood.

'Where did you go last night?' Mindy asked

suddenly and Catherine looked up with a resigned smile.

'Stephen didn't tell you then?'

Mindy shook her head. 'He was very close-mouthed about it all. Just said he'd been out to see some old friends with you.' Laughing, the dark eyes were shrewd, and her smile wry; 'But no-one believed him for a minute! We'd expected to see you at dinner.'

The waiter arrived with their first course, and Catherine sighed, beginning to eat, the smooth green flesh of her avocado curling on the polished silver spoon.

Mindy was watching her with raised brows. 'I take it you went to see Rory?' she said wryly, and Catherine gave her a quick smiling look, realising she wasn't going to drop the subject.

'He was at Tinker's Cottage with Aunt Katie.'

Mindy looked surprised, her eyes widening as she stared at her. Then she shook her dark head and leaned back in her chair to study Catherine, saying under her breath, 'Well, if that doesn't just take the proverbial biscuit. All three of them under one roof.'

Catherine frowned. 'I didn't see Isabelle. I don't think she was there.'

Mindy began to nod, but a sudden silence in the restaurant made her stop, frowning, to look over towards the doorway, and Catherine felt a sudden stab of unease, the hairs prickling on the back of her neck as she too turned her head to stare across at the wide glass doors at the far end of the red-carpeted restaurant.

'Well, she's here now,' Mindy said dryly. 'With the prodigal son.'

Isabelle Managhan stood beside Rory in the doorway, her spirited head lifted in defiance of the stares they were receiving. Still beautiful, thought Catherine with a sick pang of guilt, but her fascination was too great and she couldn't help staring at the woman who had caused all the pain and hatred in the first place.

Isabelle met her stare head on, the enormous brown eyes filled with pride, fringed by thick black lashes, her cheekbones high and aristocratic, a certain sensuality in the pouting red mouth. She had been ravishing in her youth, and had retained that sensuality, the almost Latin warmth that seeped from her curved body.

Whispering something to her son, Rory's dark head bent to hers, she nodded in Catherine's direction, and Rory's steel grey eyes flicked to her face before she could turn away. Now they were both looking at her and Catherine flushed hotly, looking down, her hand shaking as she reached to pick up her wine glass.

Slowly, they began to walk across the restaurant, the cynosure of all eyes.

'Oh my God,' Mindy said with dawning horror, 'They're heading this way.'

Catherine's mouth went dry, she felt sick and looked up, face hot with confusion to see Isabelle Managhan's graceful figure swaying towards her, dressed today in purple silk, regal colours, the thick Italian silk dress rustling as she moved.

They stopped at her table, and Catherine didn't feel able to look up. Out of the corner of her eye she saw Isabelle's long fingers, jewelled, resting on the dark sleeve of her son's arm.

'May we join you?' Rory's deep voice said, and Catherine forced herself to look up, only too aware that everyone in the room was now staring with open fascination.

Catherine shrugged, the words sticking in her throat.

Mindy quickly said, 'Of course.' She was just as fascinated as everyone else, and she wanted to know exactly what was happening between the two families. Mindy had long ago abandoned her roots, her family connections in Sleuhallen. But since the whirlwind of Rory's take-over, she had regained an intense appetite for family events, and the meeting of Isabelle Managhan and Jed Skelton's only daughter were too much for her to resist.

Chairs were brought over by the waiters, whose eyes were rounded and curious as they set the extra seats down on either side of Catherine's table while she sat with helpless anger, watching Rory and Isabelle sit down.

'My mother wants to meet you, Catherine,' Rory said coolly in her ear, and looked up through her lashes to see him bending his head towards her. 'The least you can do is return the compliment.'

Her face ran with hot colour, and she turned her head to Isabelle, aware that she had behaved rudely. 'I'm sorry,' she said, voice quiet, 'I didn't expect you to come over.'

Isabelle's lustrous dark eyes lit with warmth. 'How could I just ignore you?' she said, and the full rich mouth curved; 'I've seen you in Sleuhallen so many times, and wanted to speak to you. But I didn't dare until today.'

Catherine was surprised, and it showed in her face. She had never seen Isabelle Managhan until today, she had only heard people talk about the fact that she still lived in Sleuhallen, in the little white cottage near White Bridge. They had said she was beautiful, and Catherine had pictured her as rather younger, because one doesn't expect to see beauty in an older woman. But Isabelle's looks were still intact, she still glowed with some sort of inner magnetism, and the men who stared at her now did not just stare with curiosity, there was appreciation in their eyes too of her slender curved figure and delicately sensual face.

Isabelle read her thoughts. 'I've learnt to be invisible where Jed's family are concerned,' she said softly. 'He would never have forgiven me if I'd spoken to any of his children.'

Rory's mouth crooked in a sardonic smile. 'At least I've put a stop to that,' he drawled, flicking a cool glance in Catherine's direction. 'Jed won't bother you anymore. He's too busy trying to climb out of the mess he's in.'

Catherine shot him an angry look. 'There's no need to rub it in.'

Rory laughed, white teeth glinting. 'Temper, temper!' he drawled, and Catherine's eyes flashed, about to reply angrily when she was stopped by Isabelle.

'Please don't argue.' she said quickly, placing jewelled fingers on Catherine's arm, 'There's been too much of that for all of us. I'd hoped that Rory's take-over could bring both families closer together in the end.'

Catherine stared at her. 'You're not serious. You of all people should know how my father feels at the moment.'

Isabelle gave a rueful smile. 'Only too well! No-one needs describe Jed's temper to me.' She tilted her head, black hair piled up high on it in a mass of silken curls. 'But the anger will die down eventually. I hope he'll come round.'

Catherine wished she could believe that, but from the anger her father had displayed yesterday, she was quite sure that he would never forgive either Isabelle or her son, just as he had never forgiven Isabelle and Damian's betrayal so many years ago.

Looking at Isabelle she asked quietly, 'Did he ever forgive you and Damian?'

Isabelle looked startled for a moment, then looked down, lashes sweeping her cheeks. 'No,' she said softly,

'He never forgave us.' Sighing, she frowned, emeralds glinting at her ears. 'But it wasn't as simple as it seemed to everyone else—leaving Jed like that. It took a lot of courage for me to do it.'

'Why did you?' Catherine asked flatly.

Rory gave her a sharp sideways glance, his grey eyes angry as though he resented her asking that question, when it was the obvious question to ask. This had affected her life too, of course she would want to know the reasons behind Isabelle's catastrophic decision.

Rory seemed about to speak, but Isabelle intercepted his angry glance at Catherine and interrupted;

'No, Rory. She has as much right to know as anyone.'

Rory was still for a moment, then leaned back with a cool shrug. 'Okay.'

Two waiters appeared at their table, whisking away the uneaten avocado salads from Mindy and Catherine, their faces poker stiff, although Catherine noted that they hovered near the table continually in an effort to overhear what was being said.

'I left Jed because I knew it was impossible,' Isabelle said softly. 'Damian and I were in love, and Jed knew it—that's why he tried to force me into marriage so quickly. But I just saw disaster ahead for all of us if I went through with it.'

'So you left him the day before the wedding,' Catherine said, unable to understand her motives, 'Couldn't you have picked a better time to do something like that?'

Isabelle sighed, regretful. 'It's so easy for you to condemn me now. I should have chosen a better time, I know. But I had decided to make a go of it, to marry Jed and settle for him when I really loved Damian. But the more I tried to force myself, the more I panicked. In the end I just ran to Damian and told him how I felt.' She smiled, 'I was lucky he had the courage to defy Jed too.'

Catherine lit a cigarette, passing them silently across the table to Mindy when long tanned fingers closed over her hand and she glanced sideways to see Rory watching her, cool grey eyes steady. He took a cigarette from the pack, lit it, and smiled at her, eyes dancing suddenly with a warmth that made her heart turn over. He had tremendous charm. She looked away, her heart beating faster.

'Jed was never for me, anyway,' Isabelle told her. 'It was always Damian. We understood each other. We were alike as two peas in a pod. It would have been disastrous if I'd married Jed. We would never have been able to stick together.'

Mindy had been listening to all this with a sympathetic frown, her dark eyes fixed on Isabelle. Now she leaned forwards, studying Isabelle with curious expression, and asked;

'Do you have any regrets?'

Isabelle looked at Mindy and smiled. 'Very few. Regrets are so pointless, aren't they?'

Mindy laughed, nodding. 'I agree with that,' she said dryly, and flicked a quick look at Catherine. 'Don't you?'

Catherine shrugged without replying. It was more than she dared do to comment on regretting things in life because at this moment she regretted too much, and all of her regrets centred around Rory Managhan.

Isabelle watched Catherine's bent head. 'From what my son has told me about you,' she said softly, 'I would say you have many regrets.'

Catherine looked at Rory angrily. How dared he discuss her personal feelings with his mother? He apparently told everyone he met about her and their affair in New York. Aunt Katie knew all about it and from that remark she gathered that Isabelle Managhan knew as well.

'Only one,' Catherine said with cool emphasis, looking at Rory pointedly and receiving an equally cool glance back from him.

Isabelle laughed softly, and the brown eyes glittered with impish amusement. 'How interesting!'

Catherine flushed hotly, looking away. Relieved, she saw the waiters approaching with a silver trolley, a gas jet burning on it's botton shelf, a large silver dish in the centre of it which no doubt contained the roast beef she and Mindy had ordered.

The Head Waiter swished up beside their table, bowing his nose towards the floor as he stood respectfully in front of Rory, long black coat tails hanging behind him.

'Your table is ready for you, sir,' he said in obsequious tones.

Rory didn't look even look at him. Standing, he extended one long hand to his mother, helping her out of her chair, and sliding her hand to his arm to rest on it as she had when they first arrived.

'If you'll excuse us?' Rory inclined his head towards Catherine and Mindy.

Isabelle halted him, turning back to Catherine and giving her a warm smile. 'It was wonderful to meet you at last, Cathy,' she said, 'I hope we can meet again soon.'

Catherine felt uncertain how to respond, out of some misplaced family loyalty, she realised, because she had actually liked Isabelle very much and now she wasn't sure she ought to have done, which was quite ridiculous, her feelings were hers and no other influences should affect them.

Politely, she said, 'I'd like that,' and hesitated, but then gave Isabelle a genuine smile in return, which pleased the other woman—she looked at her son with raised brows as if to say I told you so. Rory just looked away, pretending boredom while his mother chuckled under her breath and pulled him away with amusement.

Mindy was silent, but agitated and impatient, as the waiters served the thinly sliced hot roast beef, spooning gravy on to the plates with pompous expressions as though presenting a work of art. Mindy waved away the potatoes they offered. She was a model, she couldn't afford to lose her figure.

When they were alone again, Mindy leaned over to say; 'What did you think of her?'

Catherine shrugged, non-committal. 'She wasn't what I'd expected.'

Mindy laughed, 'Well—what *did* you expect? Some mythical creature with six heads? I thought she was lovely. It's rare to find beautiful women who are nice too. I should know.' She shook her head, her smile wry as she leaned over, picking up her slim-stemmed wine glass and raising it to her lips, 'You should meet some of the women I have to work with. God, they're enough to make a scorpion turn and run.'

Catherine flicked her gaze across the restaurant to study Isabelle, seeing her smiling at Rory as she spoke to him, her slender neck tilted, one slim hand reaching out to emphasise a point with grace. Mindy was right, she was being unfair. Isabelle had been a complete surprise to her. But for so long now, Catherine had heard her name linked only with disaster, and people had always talked of the wrong Isabelle had done, the way she had left Jed on his wedding day to marry his best friend Damian. Of course Catherine had built up a pretty black picture of the woman, it was only to be expected.

It would have been perfectly understandable if Isabelle had gone to Jed and thrown her son's victory in his face. But she had kept a low profile during this whole affair.

She had obviously been wrong about Isabelle. Her heart thudded as she met Rory's cool grey gaze across the room. Was it possible she had been wrong about Rory too?

It was dark when she got home from work. Grey clouds sank over the valley of Sleuhallen in silent threat. The cream and gold living room was cold and silence rang in her ears as she walked in. Going to the fire, she flicked the switch, watching the electric bars turn orange with heat. Catherine put the television on. She needed noise around her.

No doubt her father had already heard of her meeting with Isabelle and Rory at lunchtime. She sighed, making herself some coffee. She couldn't face anymore family arguments, not tonight, which was why she had gone straight home from work rather than back to the Skelton House. Jed would only have grilled her about Isabelle. Not only that, it would upset her mother, and she didn't want her upset anymore than she already had been.

Rory never seemed to take that into account. He went around full of self-righteous anger, hitting out left and right and centre—but never seemed to see that innocents were being hurt too. This was no private war. Her mother had played no part in the downfall of the Managhans. Why should she have to suffer because of other people's past grievances?

Damn him! She thought angrily, because he was back at the front of her mind again, and she couldn't bear it much longer. She lit a cigarette, hands trembling and went back into the living room to switch off the television.

Hunting through her record collection, she saw *Carmina Burana* leap out at her. Perfect, she thought grimly, slipping it on the turntable, dragging harsh nicotine into her lungs.

The hushed chant of the music pressed in on her ominously, made her whole body tense in response. Devil-ridden music, dark and frightening voices matching her mood. Staring out of the window, she saw the wreaths of grey mist encircling the black hills of Sleuhallen. Dark rain-clouds pressed down over the valley.

A long black limousine purred silently to a halt outside her front garden. Catherine's heart jolted violently. Rory! Shakily, her fingers dropped the lace curtain back into place. Darkness was closing in now, the only light came from the orange street lamps.

The car door swung open. His dark lean figure stepped out, and grey eyes shone silver as he looked towards the house. Staring at that arrogant face lit by moon and darkness, she felt her pulses drum in response to his devastating good looks.

Mesmerised, she watched him walk with animal grace to her door. The three sharp rings made her jump. Edging into the hall, she felt her pulse beat in time to the crescendo of demonic voices chanting, as drums and cymbals crashed, the first climax of *Carmina Burana*.

The dark silhouette at her door made a shiver run down her spine. He rang the bell again, and this time, she walked towards it warily, drawing on her cigarette as she did. Putting the chain on the door, she opened it a crack and looked through it into his darkly handsome face.

'What do you want, Rory?' she asked in a low voice.

The grey eyes flicked to hers. 'Just open the door,' he said smokily.

Catherine was wary. 'Why?'

He watched her through hooded lids, lashes long

and thick. 'I'm not going to attack you, if that's what's worrying you,' he said coolly.

She hesitated, eyeing him, then slowly closed the door, slid the chain off, holding the door open for him to enter.

He looked devastating in the black evening suit. Her eyes were drawn to the tightly fitting waistcoat which emphasised his lean waist and hips. Her mouth went dry with sharp longing, and she ignored it, looking back at his face with a cool expression.

'You're not staying long,' she informed him politely.

'Nice to be wanted!' he murmured drily, and a half-smile touched his mouth as he closed the door behind him, taking a couple of paces forwards which instantly put her on her guard. 'Actually, I just wanted to have a quick word with you.'

Catherine raised her brows. 'About . . .?'

'My mother.' He slid his hands in his pockets. 'It's the first time you've met her, isn't it? I wondered what you thought of her?'

Catherine hesitated. 'She was . . . very nice.'

Rory smiled, eyes wry. 'That wasn't what I wanted to hear,' he pointed out with quiet humour.

She frowned, looking down at her feet. 'Well what else am I supposed to say?' she asked, mildly irritated because it was too early for her to make a snap judgment of Isabelle Managhan. For years she had been cast as a heartless, beautiful and mysterious woman—today she had appeared as a charming, warm-hearted lady. Totally opposing images which confused Catherine.

Rory watched her coolly. 'You used to be a lot more out-spoken, Cathy. I know you feel hard done-by, but there's no need for all this hedging. Why do you talk yourself into goddamned circles all the time?'

Catherine looked up slowly. 'Maybe because I'm confused,' she said, and there was a little silence which made her heart beat just a little too fast as they looked at each other. Now why had she said that?

Rory stood very still. 'Are you, Cathy?' he said softly, grey eyes serious now.

She felt herself colour slowly, but did not look away. The atmosphere between them had subtly changed now, and she didn't want to jeopardise the sudden softening of her feelings. It made her heart thud an expectant beat.

'I'm never sure,' Rory said, eyes never leaving hers, 'Sometimes you seem so self-assured.'

Catherine laughed shakily. 'So do you!'

It made him smile, eyes alight. 'Attack is the best form of defence!' he said lightly, and rubbed one long-fingered hand over his jaw, a self-conscious gesture that made her heart move.

Catherine looked down. 'Anyway ...' she said huskily, embarrassed at the spark of tenderness that had leapt between them, wanting to end it because she felt far too vulnerable. 'What was it you wanted to say?'

Rory's eyes darkened. 'Far too much,' he said softly, and her heart leapt crazily.

She couldn't look up, her skin felt heated, and this present mood between them made her want to hide because she badly wanted it to grow and develop, but felt too exposed to risk it.

Rory sensed her fear, and deftly changed the subject to a more neutral one in case she really did hide. 'Well,' he pushed his hands in his pockets again, smiling crookedly at her, 'Isabelle wants you to have dinner with us tomorrow night. At Tinker's Cottage. That's why I wanted to know if you liked her. It could be a disaster otherwise.'

Catherine breathed more calmly, smiling, a little shy now. 'Yes, I did like her,' she said, looking back at him, 'She wasn't what I expected at all.'

'I can imagine!' he drawled, and laughed. 'Let me guess—you pictured her as heartless and sophisticated?'

Catherine laughed too, nodding. 'Something like that!' she agreed, aware that her whole body felt warm and tensed in anticipation.

His brows rose. 'So—are you going to come? Tomorrow?'

She hesitated, frowning. 'It could be difficult. I would like to—but there'd be a problem if my father found out.' To say the least, she thought privately. Her father would hit the roof if he even suspected there were cosy dinners round at Tinker's Cottage with Rory and Isabelle Managhan. It would be viewed as treacherous behaviour at the very least.

He shrugged broad shoulders. Catherine studied him, seeing the way the leonine black hair brushed the collar of his jacket as he moved, the powerfully muscled arms rippling beneath the black jacket. Her mouth dried and she quickly flicked her eyes back to his face.

'He needn't find out,' Rory told her, 'I'll pick you up and bring you back—that way no-one will see your car outside the house.'

Catherine frowned, still worried about it, especially now that Rory was gradually turning it into a kind of conspiracy against her father. But she knew she wanted to go—especially if Rory was going to be in this sort of mood all the time. Knowing he didn't love her was hardest to take when they were at each other's throats. It made it easier to cope with somehow when she could forget calmly.

She took a deep breath. 'Okay.' She smiled quickly, and lowered her gaze. 'I'll come. What time will you pick me up?'

'Eight.' Rory said, and his smile was broad as he watched her, the grey eyes glittering. He looked about to say something else, his mouth parting for a second, but he thought better of it, and moved towards the door instead.

'Should I wear anything in particular?' she asked, worried in case it was to be formal, although she doubted that, but it was a possibility.

'Clothes might be a good idea!' Rory said, grinning, then shook his dark head, 'No, just wear anything. You always look beautiful, whatever you wear,' he said softly.

Catherine flushed hotly, smiling against her will, and looking away.

Rory opened the door, smiling at her before leaving. 'See you tomorrow,' he said. Then he left, closing the door behind him, leaving Catherine standing stupidly in the hall, biting her lip at her own ridiculous bout of shyness. Her heart sang as she took out a cigarette and lit it, hands trembling slightly. At least they didn't hate each other anymore, she thought, smiling to herself and sitting down on the stairs to smoke, staring at the floor as she imagined tomorrow night's dinner.

The telephone rang, jolting her, and she stood up automatically, going over to it and picking the receiver up, reciting the number.

'Hi!' It was Mindy. 'Where the hell are you when I need you? I've been getting it in the neck all afternoon. I thought you'd come straight here after work.'

Catherine frowned. 'What's up?' Her heart stopped with fear that Rory might have caused even more trouble for her family, and that would ruin the sudden truce they had apparently called without realising it.

'Word's out all over town about our little sojourn with Rory and Isabelle,' Mindy said drily. 'Jed's climbing the walls, Anne's beginning to look like Lot's Wife and Stephen just disappears over to Lisa's whenever arguments start.'

Catherine sighed, flicking ash into the ashtray on the pale cream telephone table. 'Are they really that angry?' she asked, worried. She had just had enough of the family arguments, she needed peace and respite. Deep down she knew that this sudden friendship with Rory would not last. It would soon blow up into hatred and fury again, but until it did, she could not bear to walk away from it.

''Fraid so!' drawled Mindy, 'I think Jed's calmed down a little now though. He's locked himself in his study.' She laughed, 'Maybe he's building a little cruise missile to nuke Rory with!'

That made Catherine laugh, eyes creasing. 'God, if he heard you!'

Mindy chuckled. 'I know, I'd get nuked instead. But until then—I need a little light entertainment. Are you up for it?'

Catherine laughed at her cousin's phraseology. 'Up for what?' she asked, amused.

'I'm feeling lucky tonight,' said Mindy. 'How do you feel about rouletting the night away at the Forest Lodge Casino? We don't need to gamble all night. Just sit and drink coffee, have a sandwich, watch the tables. It'll cheer us both up.'

Catherine shrugged. 'Okay. Why not?' She agreed with Mindy—they both needed to get out of the vicious round of family feuding and bitter rivalry that had held them spellbound for the last few days.

'Great. I'll be round in an hour or so.'

Mindy hung up, and Catherine put the telephone back on it's smooth cradle, stubbing her cigarette out at the same time. Going upstairs, she ran a bath and laid out her clothes on the bed ready to wear when she had bathed.

The bath warmed her bones, the scented oil made her skin feel slippery smooth. Steam rose in damp tendrils, settling on her black lashes like perfumed tears, and she brushed them away, relaxing, head back on the cold blue fibreglass bath.

She wondered why Isabelle wanted to meet her again. Was this a move on her part to bring the two families out of the last quarter century of darkness? If so, she doubted that it would be successful. One reason Catherine had agreed to go was because she was interested to see what Isabelle's real thoughts about the family situation were. After all—Isabelle Managhan had been the catalyst for the hatred that had sprung up and tortured two generations of Managhans and Skeltons. How did she actually feel, knowing she had caused so much despair through one action, one grand folly?

In reality, it was important for Catherine herself to find out how all this had really happened, from Isabelle's side now, now that she had heard it from everyone else's side. After all—Isabelle's behaviour had had far-reaching consequences on all of their lives—Catherine's too. It could even be said that Isabelle Managhan was directly responsible for ruining Catherine's life.

So even if Rory had not been so charming this evening, Catherine knew she would have accepted the invitation. How could she possibly have refused it?

CHAPTER SIX

CATHERINE stacked five chips on number 7, and backed it up with a few random bets scattered around the green baize table. It had to come up sooner or later. The dull red lights glowed warmly on her arms as she settled back on the black leather stool and waited. Mindy caught her eye, then on the spur of the moment stuck a solid black chip in number 7 and grinned.

'It's bound to come up,' she explained and Catherine laughed.

'Watch it! I'm getting fixated on that number.'

The croupier gave her a kind smile as he span the wheel. The silver ball clattered on the polished wood and silver. Arms stretched forward in a sudden mad rush to cover as many numbers as possible.

'No more bets, please!' The croupier said indifferently, his gaze flitting over the table to check all bets were neatly in line. The silver ball click clacked into a neat red slot. A ripple of irritation went around the players.

'Number thirty-six, red!' The croupier put the silver-red marker on 36 and leant over to scoop masses of coloured chips. They clattered into the sorting hole, leaving only a pile of black chips on the number. They were Mindy's and she grinned excitedly as the croupier started to pay her.

'Good old thirty-six!' Mindy said, eyes glittering as a stack of chips were pushed towards her.

Catherine looked down at her diminished pile of red chips. 'I hate number seven,' she muttered under her breath.

Mindy giggled. Breathless, she stretched out to stack chips on almost every number. Catherine watched her with amused disbelief. She could hardly lose!

She listened to the clatter of chips falling into the sorting hole, the spin of all the roulette wheels. In the corner, a noisy game of Punto Banco was going on. Chinese gamblers shouted and hooted as the dealer flipped cards from the shoe. Pontoon went on quietly nearby. Someone hit the Double Jackpot on a slot machine and money jangled out in a steady stream while someone laughed with delight. An old grey-haired man lost all his money on a turn of the card in Blackjack. The low murmur of gamblers went on at every table as suspense gripped them, all hanging on the throw of a dice, the turn of a card, the spin of a wheel. It was all pure luck. Thousands were won and lost every night at the Forest Lodge Casino, lives were ruined, marriages destroyed and fortunes made in ten minutes.

Catherine played restlessly with her chips. Cash in or carry on? Biting her lip, she stared at number 7. It *had* to come up. Heart thudding too fast she reached out and stacked everything on it, then sat back, pulses throbbing.

Mindy watched her. 'God, I hope it comes up for you,' she murmured.

Catherine started to bite her fingernails, then stopped, irritated by her own tense frenzy over number 7. Drumming her fingers on the table, she lit a cigarette, her nerves stretching tighter as the croupier span the wheel.

The silver ball span, circling the numbers. Her throat tightened, pulses drumming at her wrists and temples. She flicked ash nervously into the ashtray nearby, biting her lip. Silence descended on the table. Everyone strained forward, hanging on the spin of that wheel.

A man's broad shoulders brushed hers. Out of the corner of her eye she saw the crisp outline of a powerful male body in a black dinner jacket. Her heart leapt violently. A long tanned hand stretched forwards and Catherine felt every inch of herself respond in recognition. It was Rory.

He threw a hundred pounds on the table. 'Put it on number seven.' The smoky drawl at her ear made her pulses drum and clamour.

Looking up, she met his eyes and gave him a shy smile. Rory smiled back, hard mouth twisting. She didn't quite know what to say, so she said nothing, turning back to look at the tables instead, aware that everyone around their table was looking at her and Rory in speculation. They all knew who she was, of course, and by now must be able to recognise Rory's Managhan's distinctive features on sight.

The silver ball clattered neatly into the slot and a ripple of amazement ran through the players who had watched Rory's gamble on the same number.

'Number seven, Red!' said the croupier with a smile, eyes flicking to Catherine and Rory. He knew who they were, too. Sleuhallen was a small town.

He placed the silver-red marker on number seven and began to push Catherine's winnings over to her, because her stake had been the smaller of the two, and the smallest win was paid first. Then she watched as five stacks of gold chips were pushed towards Rory, but one stack toppled and spilt on the green baize table, shimmering under the red lights.

'Oh, that's unlucky!' said an old lady in a puce-coloured dress, a heavy gambler who sat at the tables night after night, smoking restlessly and destroying her marriage while everyone watched.

Rory laughed, and Catherine slid him a quick look beneath her lashes. She was overwhelmingly aware of his presence beside her.

'Not for me,' Rory drawled with amusement. Deliberately, he laid a hand on Catherine's bare shoulder, 'Luck is my lady tonight.'

Catherine coloured furiously, aware that every pair of eyes was staring at them with open curiosity. Why had Rory done that? It would cause trouble for her, for them all. He must surely realise that.

Rory looked over at the croupier. 'Let it ride on seven,' he drawled and the players caught their breath, watching the chips replaced on the number.

'You must be crazy,' Catherine said under her breath, 'It'll never come up again!'

Rory assumed a philosophical air. '"What is life but a series of inspired follies!"' He quoted, resting one hand on the table edge, the other on his lean hip as he watched the croupier take the wheel and spin.

Catherine darted a nervous look at her own pile of chips still on number 7. Quickly, she reached over and withdrew them, saying, 'I'm not pushing my luck, even if you are.'

Rory's fingers tightened on her shoulders. He frowned. It had been a bad move, Catherine realised suddenly. Almost a public slap in the face. She looked down, irritated with the whole situation. People were now watching them instead of the game, and Catherine felt uneasy, angry with Rory for doing this. Whatever he was doing in the Casino, he shouldn't have come up to her like this. It would only rebound on her when it got back to her father.

The ball click-clacked neatly into the slot and Catherine almost fell off her chair in surprise. So did everyone else around the table, except Rory, who merely looked self-satisfied, which irritated her even more.

The croupier laughed. 'Number seven, Red!' He placed the marker on the number with a flourish, and began counting out Rory's astronomical winnings before scooping all the other coloured chips that had lost off the board and into the circular sorting hole.

Rory's fingers slid from her shoulders as he took his chips off the table, counting them out with a smile. 'Ah . . .' he murmured, wickedly amused, 'Good old Number seven!'

Catherine stood up, now intensely uncomfortable under the scrutiny of the other players. A large crowd had gathered in the space of five minutes. Everyone had recognised Rory's bent black head as he played the number, and Catherine had been recognised as soon as she arrived. Each on their own would have caused only mild interest. Together they caused speculation, but when he put his hand on her shoulder the Casino had almost become electric with avid interest.

Putting her chips in her bag, she walked quickly over to the cashier, her face cool because she did not wish to acknowledge any of the stares directed at her. Pushing her winnings through the glass partition, she waited while the cashier sorted them out and handed her a bunch of notes which she put in her hand-bag. She turned to leave the Casino.

'Excuse me!' she said coolly, bumping into Rory's muscled chest.

'Not so fast,' he murmured, hand curling around her wrist. 'I think we should talk. I didn't mean to upset you back there. I'd forgotten how small a town Sleuhallen is.'

Catherine blinked, but refused to look at him. She stared across to the Punto Banco table in the corner where the gamblers were shrieking noisily as each card was flipped over. They had won, she deduced, from the way they cheered as the bank began paying them out.

Rory pushed his chips through to the cashier, keeping hold of Catherine while he waited for them to be changed. He put the roll of banknotes in his jacket pocket a moment later and turned to her.

'Where's Mindy gone?' Catherine asked, frowning as she looked across at their roulette table.

'Home,' said Rory, cool as a cucumber.

Catherine did a double-take. 'Don't be ridiculous! Mindy wouldn't have gone home. She came here with me—she's driving me back.' Frowning, she looked around the crowded Casino, but there was no sign of Mindy among any of the faces. 'Maybe she's in the nightclub,' Catherine mused. The hotel also housed a nightclub, Brandy's, just opposite the Casino in the foyer, and one tended to flit from one to the other if one planned a long sojourn at the Forest Lodge Hotel.

Rory pursed his lips. 'She told me she was going home.' He studied her, and shrugged broad shoulders. 'But you can look in Brandy's if you want. I'll come with you.'

She gave him a cool look. 'Thank you so much,' she said with dry sarcasm.

Rory smiled wrily, escorting her out of the packed and noisy Casino, into the foyer, towards Brandy's which pulsated with noise and life. The bass throbbed, drum beat crashed from the disco inside. Catherine and Rory walked together, reflected in the full-length mirror at the door of Brandy's. Cool night air flicked her red-gold hair back, flying across Rory's dark shoulder.

Rory halted his step, hand sliding to her waist. 'Remind you of anything?' he murmured smokily at her ear, directing her eye to the dark smoked glass mirror that reflected them both.

Catherine drew in her breath, eyes widening. In the darkness, flashing lights to one side, she stood half-turned towards Rory, her body strained towards him. As she stared, he bent his head, deliberately, pressed his hard mouth to her throat and made her lips part as her breath caught.

It was uncanny. The photograph, thought Catherine, staring. The cool night wind blew strands of red-gold hair across Rory's black jacket, his white evening scarf fluttering slightly.

His mouth trailed from her throat to her mouth and she met his eyes. They stared at each for a long moment in the darkness. The white heat of a strobe-light lit his eyes, turned them silver. Catherine drew in her breath sharply, heart thudding as fast as the leaping bassline of the loud fast music they were playing in the disco.

'We must look for Mindy,' Catherine said huskily, trying to turn out of his arms.

Rory held on to her. 'We may as well have a drink while we're here,' he pointed out. His hand was at her waist as he led her to the bar where there was quite a crush of young people dressed in outrageously colourful clothes, all looking vibrant and healthy, sun-tanned, hair sticking out in assorted colours.

Rory bought their drinks and led her over to a table, seating her beneath a small Tiffany lamp with the word Brandy's written in gilt on the glass, a stained-glass pattern of a beautiful silhouetted couple kissing just above it.

Catherine's skin felt overheated in this noisy heated atmosphere. The damp sweat of night-dancers clung to the air. Smoke drifted in ribbons around their heads. The stage was crowded with dancers cloaked in dry-ice smoke which gave it an eerie glamour among the pulsating lights.

'I can't see her anywhere!' Rory shouted in her ear above the thumping music.

Catherine leant torwards him, shouting, 'Neither can I!' She sipped her drink thirstily, feeling it slide coolly down her throat. Mindy was definitely not in here, she realised. Rory must have been telling the truth when he said she had gone home. But how could Mindy have done that to her? Leave her stranded at the Forest Lodge Casino at one o'clock in the morning?

Rory suddenly took her hand as the melodic strains of 'I'm Not In Love' came flooding through the loud speakers. 'We may as well dance while we're here!' he told her, and lead her up on to the stage while she looked at him apprehensively.

Rory stopped on stage, tall and exciting in the darkness, silver eyes glittering at her. He took her sensually in his arms and held her close, beginning to dance slowly to the romantic music. Catherine's heart thudded faster as he pressed her gently against his body, his thighs moving against hers as they turned slowly, clinging to each other.

Dry ice seeped out from the stage, shrouding them, cloaking them with it's heavy scented smoke, heady as opium, damp against their hot skin. Catherine rested her head on his broad shoulder, her mouth dry.

'I'll have to get a taxi now,' she said softly as the music came to an end.

Rory looked down at her. 'I'm staying here,' he said into the sudden silence, 'You can use the 'phone in my room if you like.'

It made her breath catch. They stared at each other for a long moment. 'Isn't there a 'phone in the lobby?' she asked.

He held her eyes. 'No,' he said, and they both knew he was lying.

Catherine allowed him to lead her out of the crowded disco, just as the music began to thud and pound again, fast music replacing the soft haunting love song they had danced to.

I must be crazy, she thought in sudden panic as they stepped into the lift in silence. Once outside the nightclub she felt sanity return, and wished she had refused his offer when she had the chance. Now they rode up in the lift in a tense silence, unable to speak to each other, the only sound that of the lift sliding up to the top floor.

The air crackled with anticipation as Rory unlocked the door to his suite, leading her into the pale green and gold room. He threw the keys down on to the telephone table, watching as she closed the door and came in, her heart thudding.

'I need a brandy,' he said casually, 'How about you? Do you have time?'

Catherine flushed. 'Well, just a small one,' she murmured, embarrassed because they both knew exactly what they were doing. She watched him pick up the 'phone and ring down for a couple of brandies. Catherine felt like a schoolgirl, unsure of herself and on edge. She walked across the room to study a painting which hung over the fireplace in one corner.

Behind her, Rory put the 'phone down and the silence rang in her ears. She continued staring at the painting with pretended interest, but her heart thumped.

He walked slowly over to her. 'Striking isn't it?' he said casually, looking over her shoulder as though they were strangers at an art gallery.

Catherine nodded. 'I've always loved the pre-Raphaelites. They're so colourful aren't they?' Studying *La Belle Dame Sans Merci*, she reacted strongly to the vivid imagery and colour. A ravishing golden-haired lady sits in a flowing scarlet dress, twining her hair gracefully while a knight in gold armour lies dazed at her feet, surrounded by lush green meadows and a sea of dancing poppies.

'She looks a little like you,' Rory murmured.

She flushed, looking down. 'Thank you.' Her voice

was husky. She felt far too aware of his presence, her heart thudding a steady pace.

Rory continued staring intently at her. 'But then,' he said softly, 'I see your face everywhere I go, anyway.'

Catherine froze, pulses drumming, but unable to reply.

Rory watched her, continuing. 'When you left New York I went through hell.' He slid his hands in his pockets slowly. 'I used to come home hoping to see you on the doorstep waiting for me. I couldn't bear to go to all the old places, because I always hoped you'd walk in to a bar, or a café, or a theatre. In the end I just stopped . . .'

'Don't Rory!' Catherine broke in huskily, turning away, unable to believe what he was saying.

His hand caught at her arm. 'Why not? It has to be said.'

She looked at his face. 'But I don't want to hear it.' She stared at him for a long moment, heart thudding, then slowly broke away, walking silently over to the couch, sitting down on the pale green silk cushions, and watching as he too came over, joining her in silence.

'Cigarette?' Rory held the gold cigarette case out to her, and she took a filter-tip awkwardly. She was grateful he had not pressed the point.

Rory held a gold lighter towards her, the flame leaping. He cupped his hand and the long fingers brushed hers like an electric shock. Their eyes met. She looked away quickly. I must be out of my tiny mind, she thought, heart twisting. She could feel herself getting involved with him very very fast, and her head was almost spinning with it.

'Did I tell you how beautiful you look tonight?' Rory said and a husky catch in his voice made her heart thud violently.

She looked into his eyes. Her pulses drummed.

'You always look beautiful,' Rory continued huskily, 'You take my breath away.'

Catherine swallowed, mouth dry, aware of too much happening between them at once. Her gaze dropped to his mouth. She remembered that mouth. She remembered the way he could kiss her and send her blood rocketing. She remembered how badly he had hurt her. She couldn't bring herself to remember anything more.

Rory's eyes were on her mouth too, intent, fixed, disturbing. 'Cathy, I still want you,' he said hoarsely, and her pulses hammered.

Blindly, she tried to stand up, shaking, desperately needing to get away from him before he made her fall under that tantalising spell of his, but Rory moved quickly to stop her.

His hand caught her wrist, jerking her back down on the couch beside him. 'Don't run from me anymore,' he whispered, moving closer to her, 'You can lie to me all you like with your voice, but your body tells me how you really feel. I know you too well.'

She put her hands to his chest, eyes widening in panic as she saw his black head start to swoop towards her, trying to kiss her while she held him off with trembling hands.

'Too much has happened, Rory,' she said shakily, 'We can't go back. You must know that.'

The grey eyes burnt into her. 'Then why did you come up here?' He took her hand, held it to his chest and forced her to feel the unsteady thud of his heart, 'You still feel it too, don't you?' His hand went to her breast, holding still while he felt the violent thud of her own heartbeat. 'God yes, I knew you did.'

The black head swooped, and with a gasp, she turned her face, preventing him from kissing her. But

Rory did not draw back. Instead his mouth went to her throat, firm lips trailing over her skin, making shivers ripple through her body.

'Don't Rory . . .!' she began in hot protest, but he knew how to make her respond, and his mouth fastened hungrily on her throat with a flare of passion that made her head spin, shivers rippling through her body like shock waves of heat until her body throbbed with violent response.

'Your neck always did drive me crazy,' he muttered hotly at her neck, 'You're so sensitive there. Just one touch and you go up in flames . . .' and he slid his mouth to suck hungrily at her throat until her pulse hammered beneath his tongue and teeth.

Lids closed, heart pounding, her hands slid to his head, cupping it, hands thrusting into the thick black hair, silky and soft to the touch. She could barely breath, the touch of his mouth was making every nerve-ending light up, her breasts swelling, nipples erect, her thighs trembling.

Rory pushed her back against the cushions, sliding her legs up on to the couch and lying beside her full length, pressing her body hard against his, his hands sliding to her waist and hips, making her body temperature shoot up even higher.

Catherine struggled not to sink under the onslaught of his mouth.

'Lie still,' he muttered, pushing her back when she tried to get away, and Catherine felt totally helpless as she felt his hands slide to her breasts, cupping them with long fingers while arrows of sexual excitement shot through her. Her breasts felt hot and heavy beneath her clothes and she badly wanted him to free them, expose them to the air, to his mouth and hands.

The passion between them still surprised her. It also frightened her. Twisting her head away from his mouth she said in a voice that throbbed with panic;

'You're going too fast for me, Rory!'

He raised his head to look at her, and she saw that his skin was flushed dark red, his eyes glittering with desire. 'I have to knock you breathless Cathy,' he said hoarsely, 'It's the only way. You won't listen to me, so I have to make you.'

His mouth fastened on hers with an urgent flare of passion and she heard herself moan helplessly, twisting beneath him as they clung together in a heated embrace.

A knock at the door made her jump, startled. Shaking, she pushed him away from her, face flushed, breathing hectic. 'The door . . .' she said breathlessly when he refused to stop kissing her.

Rory sat up with a muttered expletive. 'Damn them!' He thrust a hand through his black hair, pushing it back. Catherine looked at his throat, saw a pulse throbbing there beneath the tanned skin. She saw the red flush beneath his tan, saw it at his cheekbones, his throat, his chest.

He swung his legs off the couch, standing up with fluid grace and going over to the door. She watched him go. She remembered that lazy walk. She remembered everything about him, from the way he made love to the way he slept soundly all night long, black lashes flickering on his cheekbones. It made her heart twist painfully.

Shaking, she lit a cigarette, staring at the glowing tip, the silver ribbon of smoke from it as though she had never seen one before. She heard Rory open the door, watched the waiter walk in balancing two ballooned brandy glasses on a silver tray. It was almost unreal. What the hell was she doing here alone with him? Rory Managhan, the one man who could both send her to ecstasy and despair.

Making a quick decision, she stood up, picking up her evening bag and cigarettes and preparing to go.

Rory shot her a narrow-eyed look. 'Catherine . . .?' he began,

'It's getting late,' she said tightly, flicking a nervous look at the waiter who stood waiting while Rory pressed some money into his hand.

Rory stared in surprise as Catherine started to walk towards the door, fur coat rippling over one arm. 'What the hell do you think you're doing?' he muttered under his breath, catching her by the waist as she walked across the floor.

She felt her heart thud fast. 'I have to go now, Rory.'

'But I thought——' he began and Catherine cut in sharply to say;

'I know what you thought—and you were wrong.' Taking a deep breath, she watched the waiter silently leave the room, leaving the door open for her as she stood beside it. Sliding her arms into the magnificent sapphire grey mink coat, she said; 'I have to go now. It's late.'

Rory watched her, shaking his dark head. 'I'll drive you home.'

'You won't!' She backed away from him as he took a step closer, her red-gold hair shimmering beneath the lights, like a mass of fire. 'Look—I can only presume you're bored here. Sleuhallen is a small town, I know. Not many single women for you to play around with. But if you look a little harder, I'm sure you'll find someone to——'

'Stop it!' he said bitingly, eyes suddenly angry.

Catherine jumped, startled by his tone.

'Scared you, did I?' he said grimly, 'I'm glad to hear it. I ought to slap your face for what you just said!'

Catherine reddened. 'I'd better go,' she said under her breath, turning to leave the room. But his body blocked her way, and she found her eyes level with the powerful muscled wall of his chest.

'Not just yet,' Rory said tightly, 'what in hell did you mean by that little lot?'

Catherine couldn't look at him. 'You obviously need female company,' she began, mumbling because she knew what she had said had been unfair, but she had had to say it because she was plain scared to stay in the room alone with him.

'I'm not that desperate,' he said tightly.

She fiddled nervously with the clasp of her evening bag.

'Don't fidget,' he said irritably, one hand closing over hers, 'You know it drives me crazy. What's the matter with you? Why can't you ever drop that front of yours?'

Catherine looked at him then, angrily. 'Will you stop hassling me?' she burst out, eyes a bright angry green.

He was silent then, watching her intently.

She looked away, heart thudding a steady rhythm. Sighing, she said, 'I'll see you tomorrow night, Rory. Pick me up at eight.'

Rory hesitated, about to say something else. Then he nodded, abruptly, and stepped out of her way. Eyeing her, he murmured, 'Good night.'

Catherine looked at him through her lashes. 'Good night,' she said huskily and left the hotel room, breathing a sigh of relief as she walked along the deserted corridor to the lift and pressed the call button, leaning against the wall.

Going up to his room had been a monumental mistake, and she wished to God she'd never done it. But it was too late for second thoughts. It was over and done with now. All she could do was hope that tomorrow would not turn out the same. At least Isabelle would be there to prevent him from trying to seduce her again. But, oh, how she wanted to be seduced by him, and how in God's name was she ever to be safe from him when the danger lay in her, not him?

She still wanted him, she knew that. Ever since she had seen him on his return to Sleuhallen, she had wanted badly to reach out and caress his neck, touch that thick black mane of hair. And now that she had, she knew she wanted to even more. The taste of his mouth was still on hers, the scent of him still fresh in her nostrils. He was intoxicating, and she knew she was under his spell just as strongly now as she ever had been.

Catherine got into the lift, heart thudding fast. The question was—did Rory himself realise quite how strongly she felt about him? She hoped not. He could be ruthless when it came to what he wanted. If Rory wanted her badly, he would use any weapon he found at hand—including Catherine's own feelings. She hoped desperately that he would never stoop to that. She couldn't bear the thought of being hurt and abused by him again. The first time round had cost her far, far too much.

Catherine dropped in at the Skelton House at lunchtime to see how everything was going. The house was deserted when she pulled up in her Ferrari, and unlocking the door, she went around to the rooms to peer inside, but they were all silent and empty. Frowning, she went through to the kitchen when she at least heard movements.

'Hallo, Mrs Tandy.' She watched the housekeeper busying herself at the kitchen table chopping salad, 'Where is everyone?'

'In the garden, mainly.' Mrs Tandy greeted her with a smile, and sliced a red pepper into slivers, 'Your father's at the Works though. Battling with that Managhan man, I shouldn't wonder.'

Catherine glanced out of the open kitchen door.

Sunshine poured in and the sound of birdsong made the early afternoon sound very cheerful. A large bumble bee droned around the enormous flowers which grew close to the house.

'Is Stephen around at all?' she asked, leaning against the door, and feeling the peace of the countryside sooth her.

'Out by the stream, I think. Lovely day for it, too.' Mrs Tandy tossed her head, looking most put out, 'Can't say I'd mind being out in the garden too, but some of us have to get on with our work, even if others don't.'

Catherine gave her a sympathetic smile. 'Poor you!'

Mrs Tandy nodded in agreement. 'My ankles always swell up in the heat, anyway,' she confided, 'So I shouldn't complain.'

Catherine pretended interest. 'Do they? Maybe you ought to sit down more, relax a little.'

Mrs Tandy looked round, smiling merrily. 'Why don't you have a nice glass of my homemade dandelion and burdock?' she suggested, immediately fussing over Catherine, and going to the fridge to get a bottle out, and fetching a drinking glass.

Catherine looked at the foul-smelling liquid in horror. 'Oh, heavens—is that the time?' she glanced at her watch, 'I'd better speak to Stephen fast and get back to work.'

Mrs Tandy advanced, grinning hideously, holding out a glass of evil-looking brown liquid to her, 'Just time for one, surely?' she said, reminding Catherine of a wicked witch in a fairy story.

Catherine turned pale. 'Well, just a quick glass, then,' she said, feeling sickly. She took the glass, smelt it and almost died on the spot. Bravely, she held it to her mouth and sipped a little, swallowing with great difficulty.

Mrs Tandy eyed her closely, waiting for a verdict.

'Mmmmm!' said Catherine bravely, 'How delicious!'

Mrs Tandy stepped back, satisfied, hands on her tea-towel as she looked at Catherine. 'Always been a favourite with our family,' she told her. 'My grandchildren love it.'

They're still alive, then, thought Catherine, licking her lips and pretending great enjoyment. 'I'll go and finish it in the garden,' she said with a polite smile, stepping out of the kitchen. 'See you later!'

Mrs Tandy waved her tea-towel merrily. Catherine escaped, pouring the vile and unspeakable dandelion and burdock on to the flower bed. I hope it doesn't poison the flowers, she thought worriedly, almost waiting for them to wilt in unison.

Across the manicured sweeping lawns, she saw Stephen lying down on the grass beside the laughing brook that ran across Skelton Land. He looked half asleep, but a cigarette burnt in one hand, so she presumed he was awake.

Walking to him, she stood over him, shadow falling across his body lying prone on the grass, head propped on the back of his hands, legs crossed in a relaxed sleepy way. He looked as though he'd just stepped out of a scene from *Brideshead Revisited* dressed all in white. Strawberries and cream, champagne and cigarettes were spread beside him on the lawn.

'Hi!' he said without opening his eyes.

'Working hard, I see!' Catherine drawled.

He grinned. 'I've decided to become a dilletante. I never was much good at doing anything, so I've decided to lie around all day and eat strawberries and drink champagne.'

'So I see,' said Catherine drily, eyeing the empty glass beside him, the few strawberries left in the ornate little bowl.

Stephen stretched and sighed. 'This is the life for me.'

Catherine sat down beside him, plucking a stem of grass. 'Dilletantes are never rich and famous, though. I thought that was your original plan for life?'

'Ah . . .' he sighed, 'Such is my dilemma.' He opened his eyes slowly, eyeing her with amusement, 'Don't you think I'm remarkable enough all on my own? I do. I ought to be famous just for being myself.'

Catherine studied him, smiling. 'Idiot!' she said gently, and tickled his nose with the end of the blade of grass she held in her hands.

Stephen laughed. Eyes mischievous, he started to sing, 'Who were you with last night? Out in the pale Casino . . .'

Catherine stopped short, studying him. 'God, have you heard already then?' She hadn't realised it would get around that fast. Or perhaps it had been Mindy who told Stephen—after all, Mindy had been there when Rory first arrived. In fact, Catherine wanted to see her cousin. She had a bone to pick with Mindy.

'Word travels fast,' Stephen said grimly, 'This is a one-horse town.'

Catherine sighed. 'Be serious. Does Daddy know yet?'

Stephen sat up suddenly, brushing grass from his white cashmere sweater. 'God knows. He hasn't mentioned it to me. Went off to work in a filthy temper though—gave me the day off. I think he thinks I'm useless. Do you agree with him?'

'Yes,' she said impatiently. 'Was he absolutely furious about my having lunch with Isabelle and Rory yesterday?'

Stephen stubbed his cigarette out on the grass. 'Not with you,' he told her, 'With Isabelle, mainly. He thinks she'll corrupt you. What's she like anyway?'

Catherine looked down at her fingers. 'Beautiful,' she said softly, 'And very charming.'

'I'd love to meet her,' he mused, lying back, hands behind his head. 'I've got some news for you, by the way. Are you ready for it? It may be a bit of a shock to you.'

She looked at him then, frowning. 'News? What news?'

Stephen met her eyes. 'Rory Managhan has bought the Old Manor.'

She stared in disbelief. 'You're kidding!' The Old Manor was on the outskirts of town, beside Old Hallen's wood. A big rambling Tudor mansion, it had fallen into disuse over thirty five years ago. Now the stately peaks of it's towers were used by the birds as nesting ground. The once beautiful gardens were overgrown, full of choking weeds and creeping vines, the path cluttered by dying flowers. The huge iron gates that creaked and stuck, could not open. The windows were cracked and old, the doors cluttered with dust, cobwebs and vines.

Stephen shook his head. 'Amazing, isn't it? But Rory's bought it, and intends to restore it to it's former glory. I'll be interested to see what he does with it.'

Catherine stared at her brother, amazed. 'How can you be so calm? You know that's where Daddy and Isabelle held their engagement party!'

Stephen nodded. 'Well of course!' He laughed, sitting up again, 'That's the whole point, isn't it? Buy the Old Manor and set the history books right again?'

Catherine sighed. 'Daddy will be livid when he hears.'

'Too late. He knows already.' Stephen lit a cigarette, smoke trailing off in the open air. He offered Catherine one and she lit it, watching the smoke drift off into the calm spring afternoon.

'I suppose Isabelle will be pleased,' Catherine mused. 'She only agreed to marry Daddy to save that house, didn't she?' Isabelle's parents had once owned the Old Manor, but had lost all their money in the Depression, and had moved to Tinker's Cottage when Isabelle's father went bankrupt. When Isabelle got engaged to Jed Skelton, he bought the Old Manor for a pittance and threw their engagement party there. When Isabelle eloped with Damian Managhan, the Manor had been sold again, but the owner had simply let it rot and decay, until now it was a ghost-house, a shadow of it's former self.

Stephen nodded. 'Poor Isabelle. I wonder if she dreamed it would all end like this? I mean—when she first eloped with Damian? It's been an amazing story, hasn't it? Her disastrous choice . . .' he smiled, resting his head on one hand, 'I can't wait to finally meet her.'

Catherine didn't want to hear him rambling on about the woman who had caused so much trouble. Anyone would think she was his heroine. In fact, she had caused a great deal of trouble, upset many different lives, and still apparently, did not intend to take a back seat in life.

'I'd better get back to work,' she said abruptly, standing up.

Stephen looked surprised. 'Oh? It's not that late, surely?'

'No.' Catherine looked at her watch, 'But I have a few things to do before two o'clock. I'll see you later.'

'Okay.' Stephen lay down again, closing his eyes, 'See you.'

Catherine left quickly, by-passing the kitchen and Mrs Tandy to go round to the front of the house without having to bump into any other members of the family. She got into her Ferrari and revved the engine, spinning around on the drive, throwing gravel up from the tyres before roaring off down the drive and out on to the main road.

So Rory had bought the Old Manor, had he? Catherine thought angrily, driving back into the valley of Sleuhallen towards Kendal's. He obviously intended to stay here for good.

She felt her heart twist with icy pain. She could not stay in Sleuhallen if he was living here too. It was simply out of the question. One of them would have to leave town, and it patently would have to be her. But where can I go? she asked herself, sadly. New York? Too many bad memories. London? She hardly knew anyone there, although she could always stay with Mindy until she made friends of her own.

She sighed, resting her chin in one hand as she waited at a set of traffic lights on the main road into Sleuhallen. Rory had bought the Old Manor as a deliberate snub to her father—in fact her entire family. It was well known that the Old Manor had been the setting for the most outrageously expensive engagement party that Sleuhallen had ever seen.

Isabelle and Jed had been the glittering young couple of their day. She had been so very beautiful, so enchanting, and Sleuhallen had adored her, especially when she became engaged to Jed Skelton, the fast-rising success story of the village.

It had seemed the perfect match. Jed Skelton's young Irish partner Damian had been chosen as best man. The wild, dark and passionate young man had had other ideas though. He had insinuated his place as Jed Skelton's best friend, betrayed his friend and partner. He had stolen the ravishing Isabelle from underneath Jed's nose, and had run away with her to Paris the day before she was to marry Jed.

It had caused a mind-blowing scandal at the time. The people of Sleuhallen had gathered in hatred of the Managhans, and had encouraged Jed when he set out to ruin Damian Managhan and his young bride. By the time Damian and Isabelle returned from Paris six months later, it was to bankruptcy. Jed Skelton had invested all his partner's money in bad stocks and had systematically ruined him.

Isabelle's beloved Hallen Manor had been sold off, her parents reinstated in the tiny, damp and dank Tinker's Cottage, and Jed Skelton had married Anne and settled into the big white house on the top of the hill.

Catherine wondered whether Isabelle had talked Rory into buying the Old Manor back again for her. Her lips tightened. Suddenly, she was not looking forward to tonight's dinner anymore. Damn them both! she thought angrily.

If Rory and his mother wanted to totally humiliate her family—let them. But Catherine would do everything she could to hit back at them. This buying of the Old Manor would be the final blow to her father's already shattered pride, and Catherine simply could not sit back and watch any longer.

She would have to do something, anything, to help her family.

CHAPTER SEVEN

RORY lounged against the shiny black limousine, watching with cool grey eyes as Catherine walked out into the early summer evening, sunlight glinting on her red-gold hair, a light tan making her eyes seem a brighter green. His eyes skimmed over the white silk dress she wore.

'You look ravishing,' he drawled with a crooked smile.

Catherine gave him a cool look. 'What time is Isabelle expecting us?' she asked, refusing to bow to his flattery.

His eyes narrowed. 'Any minute now.' Opening the car door for her, he watched her slip into the luxurious seat, then slammed it, going around to his side and sliding in beside her, long legs stretching out beneath the steering-wheel.

Catherine looked out of the window as he pulled away, heart thudding a little as it always did when he was near.

Rory shot her a quick sideways glance. 'Why did you leave so soon last night?' he asked suddenly.

She hesitated, pulses thudding. 'I—I didn't want it to get out of hand,' she said, then could have kicked herself for making it so personal.

His brows shot up. 'You mean you were scared?'

Catherine flushed. 'No. I just know you too well, Rory. If I hadn't left, you wouldn't have stopped.'

They took the narrow country road to Tinker's Cottage. A rabbit ran across their path and dodged into the hedgerows a moment later. Rory almost braked, but then accelerated again, the engine smooth and consistent.

'Like I said,' he drawled, eyes lazily amused, 'you were scared.'

Catherine gave him an angry look. 'Why must you always put yourself in the winning position?' she asked with sudden honesty, 'Does it ever occur to you that life isn't just another backgammon game?'

He slid a cool grey-eyed glance at her as they stopped at a junction. 'Isn't it?' he said, point-blank.

Catherine's mouth compressed. Now how had this happened? she asked herself irritably. She had come out tonight intending to hit back at Rory for his latest scheme to hurt her family, and he had twisted it already into a battle between them.

Rory played every game to win. It never entered his head that not everyone had the killer instinct, the thirst for victory. He saw his life as one long race to conquer all the injustices he had been dealt in his childhood—and there were many, she couldn't deny it. But she personally had always played life for pleasure. She hated it when Rory turned everything into win and loss.

Tinker's Cottage looked beautiful in the late evening sunshine. Catherine got out of the car and stood for a moment drinking in the warmth and tranquility of the brightly flowering garden. Fat bumble bees droned busily along the row of wallflowers, the scent of freshly cut grass filled her nostrils.

'Shall we go in?' Rory was behind her now, and lifted the latch of the cottage door. The house seemed more welcoming tonight, warmer. A vase of freshly cut daffodils stood in the polished wood hall, the blue-white Turkish rug was soft underfoot.

From the kitchen they could hear the oven door shutting with a clang, trays being set out to cool. A delicious smell filled her nostrils and she looked at Rory, brows raised;

'What's that gorgeous smell?'

Rory laughed. 'Home-made bread,' he drawled. 'My mother is an excellent cook.'

Catherine did a double-take. 'Isabelle? Home-made bread?'

He nodded, eyes dancing. 'I suppose it doesn't quite fit your image of her, does it?'

He was quite right. Somehow, she had pictured tonight's dinner as rather more formal, with the beautiful Isabelle presiding like an exiled queen. But as they walked into the airy kitchen, she saw Isabelle poking a fork into the perfectly risen bread. Standing in front of the open kitchen door, sunlight pouring over her lustrous dark curls, Isabelle wore a sunshine-yellow silk dress with white lace at collar and cuffs.

'Hallo.' Isabelle greeted them warmly, doe-brown eyes smiling, 'It's awfully hot in here, I'm sure I shall wilt!' She fanned herself with one slender hand, then extended it to Catherine. 'I'm so glad you could come. I was worried you would refuse.'

Catherine felt unaccountably shy. 'Rory persuaded me!'

Isabelle laughed lightly. 'My son is very charming,' she agreed. 'I'm quite proud of him.'

Rory opened the fridge with a smile, taking out some ice and a long glass. 'Have you got a drink, Mum? Or shall I pour one for you?'

Isabelle glanced at him. 'You know spirits are bad for my skin, darling. I think I shall just stick to wine tonight.' She smiled at Catherine, 'But you have something refreshing, Catherine. Rory will get it for you.'

Catherine clasped her hands in front of her. She felt quite inelegant beside Isabelle. Even though Isabelle Managhan was now over fifty years old, she still retained impeccable grace, and her skin was truly remarkable, still dewy and fresh. Perhaps she sleeps in a fridge, thought Catherine irritably.

Isabelle studied her, dark eyes thoughtful. 'You're the first member of the Skelton family to step in friendship inside Tinker's Cottage,' she said slowly.

Catherine frowned. 'Oh? But Aunt Katie was here before me.'

Isabelle smiled, shaking her dark head. 'That's different. Aunt Katie has watched this since it first began, thirty-six years ago. She has always been an impartial observer.'

Rory took her into the living room a moment later, leaving Isabelle in the kitchen to continue with the dinner. It was much cooler in here, Catherine thought with relief. The thick stone walls faced the shadows on this side, and cool air touched her heated skin like icy fingers.

Rory poured her drink. Catherine watched, eyes focusing on his hands. He had such male hands. That gold watch strap, the dark hairs, the lean tanned fingers. Those hands could hurt, but they could also be gentle.

'I dropped in to see Stephen today,' Catherine told him casually.

Rory handed her her drink, and their fingers brushed. Her heart fluttered but she met his eyes with a cool expression. 'And?' Rory asked.

'He told me something very interesting,' Catherine said, sliding one hand in the pocket of her white dress, watching Rory very carefully. He hadn't mentioned Old Hallen's Manor to her yet, but he must know she would be angry when she found out. Why was he so damned secretive?

The grey eyes flickered. He sipped his whisky.

Catherine met his eyes. 'You've bought the Old Manor, haven't you?'

There was a little silence. Rory watched her closely,

as though trying to figure out what was going on inside her head before he replied. Catherine heard the sounds of summer outside the house, the sounds of Isabelle serving dinner in the kitchen.

Rory nodded his dark head, slowly. 'Yes. I bought it for Isabelle.'

'I'm aware of that,' Catherine said sharply. 'But that wasn't the only reason, was it? That wasn't the only motive for spending all that money on a ghost-house that'll need thousands before you can even live in it?'

Rory was taken aback by her sudden outburst, staring at her for a long moment. Then he firmed his lips, sipping his drink and saying, 'You're referring to the history of the Old Manor?'

'Damn right!' Catherine muttered. 'You know as well as I do just what happened at the Old Manor. My father——'

'Your father wasn't the only one who was there!' Rory sniped at her, slamming his drink down on the table. Ice cubes clinked noisily. A little whisky spilt over the rim of the glass on to the polished oak. The house was silent and still. Even Isabelle had stopped moving about in the kitchen. She's probably listening, thought Catherine irritably.

Rory sighed suddenly, raking a hand through his black hair. 'Must we argue, Cathy? Again?' He studied her through thick black lashes, 'Just for tonight—can't we call a truce?'

Catherine looked down at her drink, fingers shaky. 'Why do you insist on trying to patch things up between us?' she asked in a low angry voice, and her lips tightened. 'Why? Why can't you leave it as it is?'

'I wish I knew!' he said angrily, 'I must be out of my mind. You're the most infuriating woman I've ever met.'

Her eyes flashed bright green. 'And you're perfect, I suppose?' she enquired on an acid note.

'No! I'm not perfect!' he shouted, then studied her angrily, muttering, 'I sometimes think I must be a masochist. Or verging dangerously close to it. Why else would I put up with your behaviour?'

Catherine felt her mouth firm. 'And just what is wrong with my behaviour?' she asked, voice taut.

Dark brows rose. 'Do you want a catalogue of all your faults? Or shall I just start work on Volume One?'

Catherine reddened. 'Go ahead. My faults could fill a volume—yours could fill a whole library!'

She took a cigarette pack from the pocket of her white silk dress, tipped one out and lit it, her hands trembling with unleashed anger. Deliberately she did not offer one to Rory, a fact he noted with an ironic expression, his eyes on her as she thrust the cigarettes back into her pocket.

Rory sighed, picking up his whisky and taking a sip from it, one hand on his lean hip, the dark jacket pushed back showing his tight waist.

'Dinner time!' Isabelle's cheerful voice broke the tense silence, and they both turned to look at her in surprise. Isabelle watched them carefully, her dark eyes guarded.

Rory looked wry. 'Shall we go through?' he murmured, and one hand slid to the small of her back as he guided her into the dining room next door.

Isabelle had served roast beef and Yorkshire puddings for dinner, and it was home-cooking at it's best, Catherine realised as they sat around the misshapen dining table. The room was sparsely furnished. An old grandfather clock ticked sonorously in the corner, a blue-plate-lined Welsh dresser stood along one wall. There was no carpet on the polished floor, just an old Turkish rug that must once have been very beautiful and very expensive but time had worn it bare. The French windows were open, the birds still sang outside, and the garden was filled with the scent of summer's approach.

After dinner, Rory lit a cigar, and the heady opiate scent of smoke drifted out into the stillness of the evening outside. The table was cleared, the coffee cups now empty, and Isabelle was talking in a light voice of days gone by.

'It seems my whole life has been split into before Damian Managhan and after Damian Managhan!' Isabelle was saying with a soft laugh, 'Which is rather nice. At least I had a landmark—many people just drift endlessly.'

Catherine watched her, the faded beauty who had destroyed so many lives with one reckless action. At least it was for love, she thought with a sigh at least Isabelle had not simply been selfish. She had seen her life staring her in the face and had taken it, ignoring the consequences.

Leaning forward, Catherine asked, 'But surely my father knew what was happening? He must have noticed how you and Damian felt?'

Isabelle sighed. 'I met Damian at the engagement party. Jed had kept me all to himself until then.'

Catherine was taken aback. 'You met him at Old Hallen's Manor?' she asked, voice breathless.

'Of course!' Isabelle gave her a warm smile, 'Why else do you think Rory has bought it for me?'

Catherine shot a glance at Rory, feeling her skin redden. No wonder he'd been so angry.

'Catherine thinks I'm being selfish, Mum.' Rory drawled coolly, and the grey eyes flicked to her face. 'She believes every breath I take is motivated by revenge.'

Catherine went scarlet. 'That isn't fair!' she burst out, 'I only——'

'Oh please don't argue again.' Isabelle said anxiously, leaning forward, her eyes worried, 'I sit and watch you both, and I see what you're doing to each other. Can't you take time out for each other? Just for once?'

Catherine looked away, embarrassed. 'I don't know what you mean,' she muttered.

'I think you do,' Isabelle said softly, 'Try to pretend your families don't exist. It's the only way.'

'Mother——' Rory began irritably, skin flushed beneath his tan.

'No, Rory, it has to be said,' Isabelle was firm. 'There are problems all around you, and because of them you've lost sight of each other. Stop looking at your own——'

'I need a brandy!' Rory said tightly, standing up and leaving the room. They heard him push the living room door open, slam the drinks cabinet down and take brandy and two glasses out.

Catherine sat, heart thudding, unable to look at Isabelle. There was a short uncomfortable silence. Is it so obvious? Catherine thought bitterly. What Isabelle said was right. Surrounded by family hatred and revenge, confusion had hit them both, and although Rory was obviously trying to get through to her again, they were finding it impossible to clear all the obstacles around them. She sighed, eyes troubled.

'It happened to me, too,' Isabelle said quietly, and as Catherine looked at her she saw, suddenly, the lines of strain around the other woman's mouth. 'I tried to please everyone around me. But you can't do that. You never can. You must simply take what you want and to hell with everyone else.'

Catherine laughed bitterly. 'I wish I could think like that!'

'If it's important enough to you,' Isabelle said, 'You'll do it.'

Rory came back with two brandies. Face tightly shuttered he handed Catherine a glass. She took it, heart thumping. Their eyes met. Rory looked away, black lashes flickering on his cheekbones.

There was a short, tense silence. The clock ticked. Catherine sipped her brandy. It burnt her throat, brought tears to her eyes.

Isabelle shifted in her chair. 'Have you ever had your tarot read?' she asked brightly.

Catherine looked up, puzzled. 'What?'

'Draw the curtains, Rory.' Isabelle stood up, going to the dresser and taking a pack of cards wrapped in black silk. 'My tarot was read just before I eloped with Damian. It was all predicted. I knew what would happen when I saw the Lightning Struck Tower.' She came back to the table, handing Catherine the cards. 'Here—shuffle the cards, and while you do, think of the question uppermost in your mind.'

Catherine stared at the cards, uneasy. Slowly, she shuffled them, her mind concentrating on Rory. When they felt right, she handed them back to Isabelle, and watched as she laid them out in a celtic cross, flipped the two top cards upwards. The room was dark, the atmosphere suddenly tense as they all studied the cards in silence.

'Your present position,' Isabelle studied the central cross, 'is Love opposed by Disaster.'

Catherine looked at the two cards opposing each other, the Two of Cups blocked by the Lightning-Struck Tower. She shivered, risking a quick glance at Rory, but his face was impassive.

Isabelle pointed to the card above. 'If you go ahead with your present plan . . .' she flipped the card face upwards, 'you will be the Fool.'

Catherine blinked, wishing she had stopped this before it had begun. It was uncannily accurate so far and she didn't like it one little bit. What was her present plan, anyway? To hit back at Rory, yes, of course—what else could she do?

'In the Distant Past I see . . .' she flipped the card and smiled, 'The Lovers. In the recent past—The Moon; deception, false truth and lies.'

Catherine watched her in stunned silence as she carefully flipped over the next card. It was Death, grinning skeletally, one bony hand holding a scythe over the desert-land it stood in.

'Oh dear!' Catherine said with forced humour.

Isabelle smiled. 'It doesn't mean you'll die, don't worry! Death symbolises the end of a cycle, that's all. An end and a beginning. Birth after Death.' She looked at Catherine, 'And that is in the immediate future.'

'Oh,' said Catherine, frowning. What on earth was coming next? There were still four more cards lined up.

'This card represents you,' Isabelle turned over The Devil and her brows rose, 'Confusion, a crisis of faith.' She looked at Catherine, 'Is that how you feel, my dear?'

Catherine lit a cigarette, refusing to answer. Rory cleared his throat watching with interest.

'Other people's opinions of your situation . . .' Isabelle flipped the card, 'The Ace of Swords. Strength, conflict, a battle—the Ace of Swords generally shows a strong male influence.'

Surprise me, thought Catherine irritably.

'Your secret hopes and fears,' Isabelle continued, looking at the next card. She laughed lightly, eyes sparkling, 'Good Heavens! The Ace of Cups! Well, what more can be said?'

Catherine's brows jerked together. 'What does it mean?' she asked, leaning forward, looking at the card, the huge jewel-encrusted cup dominating the white card.

Isabelle smiled. 'Marriage,' she said softly.

Catherine flushed hotly, looking away.

'And the eventual outcome,' Isabelle turned the last card over, and smiled again, 'Ah . . . the Knight of Swords.'

Catherine flicked ash into the gilt ashtray. 'And what does the Knight of Swords mean?' she said, smiling wrily, 'Or daren't I ask?'

Isabelle looked amused. 'A brave man rushing headlong into the unknown. A chivalrous man, a man with energy and determination.'

Catherine didn't know quite where to look, so in the end she just kept her eyes downcast, her face deliberately blank. Don't ever have your tarot read again, she told herself with an angry smile. That had been far too accurate for comfort.

There was a little silence in the room after the tarot had been cleared away. All that could be heard was the solemn tick of the grandfather clock in the corner. Catherine drew sharply on her cigarette, felt it bite her throat. Picking up her wine glass, she drained the last of the blood red wine. The tarot reading had been uncannily accurate and she didn't particularly want to discuss it with either of them. If I ever see a fortune teller again, she thought, I shall run like hell in the opposite direction.

Rory drove her home at midnight. Isabelle waved from the doorway of Tinker's Cottage until they were out of sight. Catherine kept that image in her head for a while, the slender shape, the bright yellow silk dress that looked so exquisitely feminine, and the tumbling curls. Isabelle was still startling.

They drove up through White Bridge, towards the black hills, then Rory doubled back to cross the valley to her own house. Catherine was silent on the way home, her mind still on the tarot reading. The Ace of Cups lingered in her mind. Secret hopes and fears, Isabelle had said, and the Ace of Cups apparently symbolised marriage. Catherine decided it was absolute

rubbish. Okay, she still cared a great deal for Rory—
but marriage was *not* on her mind.

Rory pulled up outside her house ten minutes later,
switching the engine off. The car was silent and dark,
she heard his breathing. He was very close to her.
Awareness of his body sprang up in her, making her
heart thud a steady rhythm.

'Did you enjoy tonight?' he asked coolly, eyes
hooded.

'All except for the tarot!' Catherine said with a dry
smile, and Rory laughed.

'God, yes! I never go near them if I can help it. I
prefer to think of them as superstitious nonsense.' The
grey eyes were amused as he added; 'The last thing I
want is to let her prove otherwise to me! It's
sometimes a little too close to the nerve.'

Catherine flushed. 'It wasn't tonight,' she denied
quickly, 'Most of it was wrong.'

'Oh?' He watched her, half turning in his seat, and
the movement made her body taut with awareness. 'It
seemed pretty accurate to me.'

Catherine looked away, not wanting to answer that
one. Looking at her watch she made an exclamation of
pretended surprise at the fact that it was gone
midnight.

'Is that the time? I have to be up early for work.'

Rory laughed, white teeth flashing in the dark
interior of the car. 'That's a poor excuse!' he drawled.

She gave him an irritated look. 'Why is it?'

He eyed her intently. 'You used to stay up till dawn
with me, Cathy. Or have you forgotten?'

Heart thudding, she looked away. Yes, she remembered it, only too clearly. Stepping out of his
car at daylight, barefoot, evening sandals slung
casually over her fingers as they walked along hand
in hand to the beach house. Rory in a dinner suit,
waistcoat unbuttoned, shirt unbuttoned at the throat,

black silk tie hanging loosely at his neck, hair ruffled and untidy.

'I haven't forgotten,' she said huskily.

Rory studied her. 'We could talk, then. Really talk.' The lean fingers slid to her shoulder, touching her gently, making her heart thud. 'Now we're so full of preconceptions and bitterness that we can't even look at each other anymore.'

Catherine laughed, eyes glassy. 'Well, that's just the way it is.'

He was silent for a moment, grey eyes cool. 'You're full of rubbish,' he said abruptly. 'You know that? Where the hell do you get these phrases from? Your father, I suppose.' He gave a harsh laugh, 'Jed Skelton, Oracle of the North.'

Catherine's mouth tightened. 'We can't change what's happened, Rory. It all started too long ago.'

Rory's eyes flashed an angry silver. 'Will you listen to yourself?' he said harshly, 'You sound about ninety-two! Where's the woman I fell in love with in New York? She didn't give up on life. She rushed into everything without even thinking.'

'Fell in love with?' she echoed, because that phrase had struck her full in the chest, hurting her, making her eyes an angry green as she stared back at him, 'You lying bastard. You were never in love with me! How can you keep up all this pretence? Now, when it's all out in the open, when everyone knows exactly what you were——'

'Oh, for God's sake!' he snapped, hand biting into her arm as he gripped her, making her gasp, 'Don't trot out all the old ifs and buts!' He held her tightly, staring at her, his dark face all angles and shadows in the darkness, street-lighting glowing on his hair, his cheekbones, his hard mouth.

Catherine felt herself shiver, heart thudding. 'I'm not,' she said shakily, 'I'm telling the truth. You just can't face it——'

'*Cathy!*' Anger flared in his eyes, 'Look at the bottom line, for God's sake! Get everything else out of your mind. Forget your family, forget mine. Forget New York.' He stared down at her, his mouth a firm line, 'Just forget everything but me.'

She trembled. 'How can I?' she asked in a low angry voice, 'It's always there, every time I think about you it all comes flooding back. How can I forget any of it?'

Rory muttered something under his breath, his hand shot out to capture her chin because she was looking away from him, and it made his temper flare a little more.

'Look at me!' he muttered, and his hand jerked her chin hard, 'Look . . .' he stopped short as she turned her face to his, eyes wide.

They studied each other at close quarters in the darkness of the car. Silence touched them both, made their heartbeats accelerate. Catherine felt confused and disturbed. There was so much between them, so much to pull them together, and yet also so much to pull them apart.

The black lashes flickered on his handsome cheek. 'Don't you see?' he muttered, 'It's like hating me for the colour of my eyes.'

She shook her head slowly. 'No, Rory. You're wrong.'

His jaw tightened. 'Why must you be so obstinate? Can't you——'

'No Rory!' she broke in, voice trembling. 'I hate you because you hate my family, and they're a part of me. Now can't you understand that?' Her eyes darted wildly, heart thudding, 'Can't you just get that through your thick skull?'

His nostrils flared with anger and for one moment she thought he might strike her, but instead his muscles tightened with iron self-control. He gave a harsh sigh, releasing her chin with a sharp movement.

The grey eyes roved slowly over her with a contempt that hurt. 'So,' he said with icy cynicism, 'we're back to family.'

Catherine couldn't bring herself to look at him. 'It's always going to be there, Rory.'

He gave a harsh laugh. 'That's junk, and you know it! You're not your bloody family, you're yourself. You just happened to be born into the Skelton family.' He laughed again, his eyes angry, 'Which was tough luck on me and tough luck on you.'

Tears pricked her eyes. 'They made me what I am!' she said defensively.

His head swung to look at her. His mouth twisted sardonically. 'Yes,' he drawled, and that one word held volumes more biting irony. It made her flush slowly, to her hairline, and she could no longer hold that biting glance, so she looked away, speechless.

Rory flicked his headlamps back on with one swift movement. 'Get out of the car, Catherine,' he said icily, staring out at the dark street without expression.

Numbly, she fumbled for the door handle and stepped out. Cold air rushed to engulf her. A breeze blew strands of red-gold hair across her face, made her white silk dress ripple softly. The door was slammed shut behind her. The engine flared into life, making her jump.

She stood watching as the red-tail lights disappeared into the distance, leaving her alone in the quiet street, with only the sounds of the leaves and the wind-ruffled bushes for company.

Catherine turned, alone, walked to her door, unlocked it and went inside the house which was empty and cold.

She made herself a cup of hot chocolate and climbed the stairs to bed, lost inside her thoughts. Her heart was still beating fast, and she relived his kiss in her memory, feeling every nerve-ending respond to his touch as though he was still with her.

Slipping into her white night-shirt, she got into bed, long tanned legs crossed in front of her, resting her head on her knees and staring blankly into the long mirror opposite. Red-gold hair curled in tangled disarray.

I'm still in love with him, she thought. Green eyes stared back at her. Her heart hurt. She swallowed, hands tightening around her knees. Would he haunt her forever? she asked herself slowly, or was it possible to forget? The thought of living an entire life, loving a man she could not have, was too appalling to even consider. Did other people forget? she wondered, hurting inside, or did they just make the best of it, carry on as though it had never happened, when underneath that pain would always burn, ready to spring to the surface at the slightest mention of a lover's name, a face that resembled his, a reminiscent scent, a song playing on a lonely evening, anything that could trigger off, unwanted, a memory of your lost love.

Catherine closed her eyes, and felt silent tears squeeze out from behind her lids.

Catherine felt dull and quite moronic the next day. It had been impossible for her to sleep all night. Tossing and turning till the early hours of the morning, she had finally fallen into a sluggish sleep at five a.m. It had seemed only moments later that her alarm had shrieked at her to wake up and go to work. Consequently, her whole body felt as though it was made from lead. Her head was thick and foggy, and she couldn't concentrate.

At lunchtime, she decided to take a brisk walk Leaving the shop, she wrapped herself up in her sheepskin coat and walked along the High Street as briskly as she could. She'd read somewhere that brisk exercise released endorphines in the brain; chemicals which produced euphoria. Well, she thought with a dull smile, I could do with a little endorphine induced euphoria today! The question was—would it work? Or am I beyond help, she thought, half amused.

Grey clouds were pressing down on the valley. The mountains were wreathed with mist, long silk-white lines of mist circling the dark hills which surrounded Sleuhallen. Catherine glanced up at them, cold wind biting her face.

There was a legend about the mists of Sleuhallen, she remembered. Frowning, she tried to place it. Her father had told her of it when she was a little girl, and she and Stephen had often played it out when the mists fell.

The Giant Sleu, Lord of the Valley of Sleuhallen, was supposed to drape his cloak over the valley in times of danger, to protect his sheep from thieves and villains. Catherine smiled painfully, staring up at the black hills. The Giant Sleu had probably seen Rory Managhan coming, because if ever the valley needed protecting, it was now.

A car hooted at her, made her swing round, startled. Wind rippled her hair, making it fly in a mass of red-gold tangles behind her. The cold knifed into her breast and she shivered, clutching the dark brown collar of her coat closer to her.

Stephen's dark blue Stag pulled up with a sharp screech of brakes. Engine running, exhaust fumes poured out into the atmosphere as the car waited a few feet ahead of her. The small orange indicator winked on the left-hand wing. Catherine walked slowly towards the purring sports car.

Catherine bent her head to the partly-open window. 'Hi! Why aren't you at work?'

Stephen studied her with cool brown eyes 'Dad

wants you at home right away,' he told her, one ringed hand playing with the black gear stick absently. 'Aunt Katie just rang. She's coming to the house for lunch.'

Catherine was taken-aback, eyes widening. For a moment she had thought he was breaking more bad news about Rory, and that would have been hard for her to take after the argument last night with him. He was already becoming the centre-point of her life again, and it hurt as much as it pleased.

Stephen watched her, wind whipping her hair across her white face. 'Get in,' he held the door open for her, and she got in beside her brother.

Stephen gunned the engine. 'I'm really not looking forward to this,' he told her and pulled away from the kerb with a screech of brakes that attracted attention from people in the street. The Skelton's eldest son, she could almost hear them say as Stephen roared past in the speeding car.

Catherine sighed. 'It had to come,' she pointed out. 'How is Dad taking it? He's not in a temper, I hope?'

Stephen shook his head, eyes on the road. 'He's calmed down a heck of a lot since it first happened. I think he's just about ready for whatever's coming now.'

Fields flashed past them. Stephen drove much too fast, but then, he always had. Reckless and light-hearted, he wanted nothing more than pleasure from daily existence. He was not one of life's builders, and didn't want a long list of achievements behind him. Perhaps as the years flew past he would change, as so many people do. But for the moment, he took pleasure from simple things.

Stephen rested one arm along the open window. The wind whipped his black hair. 'Have you seen Rory lately?' he asked.

Catherine blinked, surprised into silence for a moment. Stephen had always been very outspoken, and the ordinary custom of privacy meant nothing to him. Sometimes, it was refreshing to know someone with his open approach to life. But at times like these, Catherine wished he would keep to society's conventions a little more.

'I saw him last night,' she said shortly, not looking at him.

Stephen whistled. 'Did you?' He grinned. 'Well, well, well!'

She felt herself flush a little. 'Meaning?' she asked, irritated with him because she could see from the look on his face exactly what he was thinking about her and Rory.

Stephen overtook a tractor at eighty miles an hour. 'Well, come on Cath!' he said with a quick smile, 'I visited you in New York that summer. When you were seeing Rory. That was the last time I ever saw you looking happy.'

Catherine froze, hot with embarrassment. How could he come out with something like that, knowing the history and complicated background of her relationship with Rory? She looked out of the window in silence, staring at the blackening clouds, dark windy moors.

Stephen glanced at her. 'Rory brings you alive, Cathy—I can spot it a mile off. Why are you so obstinate?'

Catherine gave him a sharp look. 'Stop treading on my toes, Stephen!'

He made a face. 'Some people just want to be unhappy.' He swung the car off the main road as they reached the long tree-lined drive to the family home. The tall white Georgian mansion rose up before them on the windswept hill. He took the drive at a reckless sixty miles an hour. The wheels spat gravel, the circle of pine trees bowed against the wind. Rain began to fall in a steady wet drizzle, almost a fine mist across the gardens, making them smell clean and freshly-washed.

Stephen screeched to a halt outside the house. 'You can't draw up a contract on happiness, Cathy,' he informed her, which annoyed her immensely, as she watched him switch the engine off. 'You just have to take it, when it comes.'

'How profound!' she said with heavy sarcasm, and got out of the car.

Stephen got out too, undeterred and continued; 'Happiness is a moment. A glass of sparkling water on a sunny beach.' He warmed to his subject, following her into the house as she unlocked the door.

'Oh, put a sock in it,' Catherine said irritably, trying to ignore him.

'Happiness,' Stephen continued, oblivious, 'is climbing a tree at midnight. Happiness is a lazy afternoon watching cricket. Happiness is——'

Catherine tuned out, refusing to listen as he continued droning away in the background. She walked through the hall and into the kitchen, ignoring Stephen who was walking behind her, waving his hands around as he enthused on his pet subject.

'What's he talking about?' asked Mrs Tandy, eyeing Stephen suspiciously as he walked into the kitchen, arms spread wide, extolling the virtues of the simple things in life.

'Happiness,' said Catherine shortly. She picked up a ripe-looking apple and gave it a vicious bite.

'He's got a mind like a performing flea,' Mrs Tandy observed, and hit him with her tea-towel. 'That's enough of that, young Stephen. Happiness is bad for the digestion. Ask your father.'

Catherine left the room before she was dragged into any more personal discussions. What Stephen didn't seem to realise was that he was treading on her feelings when he started talking about Rory like that. God, couldn't he see how impossible it all was? It didn't help matters to have her own brother start reminding her of exactly what she had lost. If Rory had not been a Managhan, they could have made fireworks together. But their families had not only come between them, they had destroyed them forever. Catherine knew that. She didn't want to hear it again and again.

Glancing into the dining room, she saw it was empty. The table, polished until it shone, was lined with the best silver and crystal glasses. The clock ticked silently, tiny gold figurines staring out at the family dining room, the huge glittering chandelier overhead tinkled softly in the breeze from an open window. Rain was coming in, spattering on the polished mahogany ledge. Catherine went over and pulled it shut.

As she turned back in silence, she felt waves of *déjà vu* wash over her. Have I been here before, she asked herself with a sad smile. Staring at the magnificent, glittering dining room, she felt the years rush past, seeing a hundred important meetings taking place here. She and Stephen, hiding on the stairs, watching the well-to-do guests arrive. Dinners and balls, cocktail evenings; all the guests glittering with diamonds like frost, carriages riding up to the front door, music and laughter going on through the night, spilling out into the famous Skelton Gardens.

And now it's all over, she thought sadly. Rory Managhan has seen to that. The days when the Skelton family were the Lords of the Manor were over. A dynasty was collapsing.

The door opened. Catherine's head turned.

Jed Skelton stood in the doorway, watching her. The cold blue eyes narrowed on her. His face still held indomitable spirit, an arrogant thrust of jaw, a firm uncompromising mouth and a body with enough strength to knock a man off his feet still.

'I know what you're thinking, Cathy,' Jed said harshly. He closed the door, blue eyes flicking across the stately dining room. 'And I've been thinking it too. I never believed it would end like this.'

Catherine felt her heart tug. She sighed, arms folded as she leant against the window sill. 'I wish there was something we could do.'

Jed laughed, shaking his head. 'Aye—put a bullet through Rory Managhan's head!' He shot her a sideways glance, 'Nice idea. But they're not the rules. I'm not a man to cheat at cards, and I won't cheat at life either. He's beaten me fair and square. I was a fool not to see it coming.'

Catherine watched her father walk slowly across the room, his lean body still slim and whipcord strong. He ran his weather-beaten fingers over a gold figurine on the mantlepiece. He was a tough man. Rory had just been that little bit tougher.

'You've been seeing a lot of him,' Jed studied her with those penetrating blue eyes. 'Do you think that's wise?'

Catherine felt herself flush slowly. 'It isn't what you think,' she told him in a quiet voice, unable to look him straight in the eye for once in her life.

'No?' He eyed her, 'You're still in love with him. Aren't you?'

'Daddy!' she mumbled incredulously, sliding her hands in the pockets of her black trouser suit. How could he be so outrageously direct about these things? It was one thing after another today, she thought. First Stephen and now her father.

Jed laughed. 'Do you think I've forgotten what it is?' The blue eyes stared unseeingly at the ornate gold clock on the mantelpiece, 'How can I? One woman gave me my destiny. After Isabelle, nothing was the same. She changed my life.'

Catherine looked away, embarrassed.

Jed shot her a dry glance. 'Don't take that to mean I still love her. I was lucky. I met your mother soon after.' He thrust his hands in his pockets, frowning. 'Life's a bag of surprises. One minute you're up, the next you're down.'

'You'll get it back, Daddy,' she said quietly, watching him with sadness, 'You're a fighter.'

That made him laugh, and his face changed when he smiled, it lit up, made his eyes crinkle at the edges. He must have been awfully good-looking when he was young, Catherine thought with a fond smile. She had seen photos of him from his youth, but they were faded, difficult to see properly.

'Aye,' he said quietly, smiling, 'I'll get it back. That's one thing life has taught me, Cathy. You never know what's around the next corner.'

There was a knock on the door, and they both turned to look at it.

'Come in!' Jed called, his voice curt.

The door opened slowly, and Mrs Tandy's brown head appeared around it. She looked at them both with a smile, her face obviously excited. Mrs Tandy was the sort of person who built everything, even in other people's lives, into a grand drama, and at the moment, life was one drama after another for her. She looked fit to burst with the excitement of it all.

'Old Mrs Skelton is here, sir,' she said, nodding, 'Just driving up in her car, she is.'

Jed's face stiffened. He darted a glance at Catherine, and she wondered what he was thinking because he looked quite distracted for a few moments. He looked back at Mrs Tandy.

'Bring her in here. Keep lunch until I'm ready for it.'

Mrs Tandy nodded and disappeared, closing the door behind her.

Jed looked back at Catherine, frowning deeply. 'I

wanted to talk to you before she got here,' he said slowly, 'There's something on my mind, I've been meaning to tell you for a long time now.'

'What is it, Daddy?' Catherine asked, but she felt suddenly breathless, as though she already knew. Voices broke out in the hall. The front door was opened. Catherine heard her Great Aunt Katie's voice ringing out in the hall.

Jed looked restless suddenly, his eyes darting as he frowned. 'Damn!' he muttered as footsteps approached the door.

Catherine studied her father's strong face with a fast thudding heart. He was thinking about Rory Managhan, she knew that. He had been about to tell her something important. Her pulses hammered. She stared at him in sudden dawning awareness. Her eyes flicked to the door, aware that Great Aunt Katie was about to come in. But she knew she had to find out what he had been about to tell her.

'Tell me quickly,' she urged, putting one hand on his arm, and he looked down at her, hesitation in the blue eyes.

The door burst open.

Jed continued looking at Catherine. He shook his silver head. 'I'm sorry, Cathy,' he said in a slow, quiet voice, and Catherine's heart thumped violently. She stared at him. Rory loved her. That was what he had been about to say. She could feel it in every nerve-ending of her body. But it was ridiculous, absurd. How could Daddy possibly know whether Rory's heart was involved or not?

Aunt Katie stood in the doorway now, ram-rod straight as she stared Jed Skelton down with her determined eyes. She wore black. In her hand she held the silver-topped cane, fingers curled over it tightly.

'Well, Jed,' Great Aunt Katie said imperiously, 'Are you pleased to see me?'

Jed studied her, face cold. 'Catherine, leave the room!' he said without taking his eyes off Aunt Katie's grim face.

Catherine started to move, trying to get past her aunt in the open doorway. Her mother stood outside, watching, her face worried, one hand pressed to her throat where the silver necklace she always wore lay.

'The girl stays,' Aunt Katie said firmly, and placed one hand on Catherine's arm, preventing her from leaving. 'What I have to say concerns her as much as anyone.'

Jed's eyes narrowed quickly. 'Don't give me orders in my own house, Katie,' he said in an angry voice, 'I'm still master here.'

Aunt Katie waved that aside with one gnarled old hand. 'You'll be master of nothing if you don't do as I say.' She thrust her chin out like an angry pekinese dog and stared at him, bolt-eyed, 'Now will you let the girl stay—or shall I leave without saying my piece?'

Jed watched her with a tight-lipped expression for a long moment, but he could see that the old woman meant every word she said. So he was silent for a moment, then gave a curt nod, stepping back into the dining room while Aunt Katie shooed Catherine inside too and shut the door, leaving all other members of the family outside, staring in interest.

Catherine felt instinctively that important news was about to be broken, and she simply allowed herself to be pushed back inside with them, unable to resist hearing what she had so obviously been waiting to hear for years.

CHAPTER EIGHT

CATHERINE walked across the room in silence, sitting down on one of the high-backed chairs around the long dining table. Where was Rory now, she wondered. Did he know that Aunt Katie had finally decided to confront Jed with her reasons for destroying the company? He probably does, she thought sadly, because Rory Managhan had always been a man to have his finger right on the pulse of every situation. Nothing missed his attention.

The old woman who had for years been the backbone of the family, stood in the centre of the luxurious room, facing Jed with a calm expression. She looked older, or was it just that Catherine always thought she looked older? The heavily lined face was soft and looked paper-thin, her cheeks hollowed out, her eyes sunken. But there was an inner strength that radiated from her slight frail body, something that was strong enough to hold her steady and command respect from all who knew her.

'It had to be done, Jed,' Aunt Katie said quietly, the breeze from the small window lifting her white hair a little. 'What happened between you, Isabelle and Damian was your affair. But I couldn't sit back and watch you interfere with Catherine's life as well.'

Catherine's head came up sharply, she felt her eyes widen as she looked at her father, amazed to see an obstinate red stain spreading across his hard cheekbones.

'I didn't interfere,' Jed muttered, mouth firm, 'I just stopped Rory Managhan from hurting her——'

'He wouldn't hurt a hair on her head,' Aunt Katie interrupted, but her voice was quiet, still, as though she knew Jed would sit and listen, even though he seemed angry. 'And you knew it. You knew it then and you know it now.'

Catherine felt her skin go hot, her heart start to pound. What were they saying?

'He's a Managhan, isn't he?' Jed said sharply, but his face belied his words, because his expression was rather more that of someone on the defensive than of someone in a strong attacking position. That worried Catherine, she had never before seen an expression quite like that on her father's face.

Aunt Katie gave a soft laugh. 'Aye, he's a Managhan,' she agreed, 'And fate has decided that he should fall in love with your daughter.'

Catherine bent her head, cheeks burning because she neither believed any of this, nor wanted to hear it. Her eyes were wide as she studied her hands, folded in her lap.

Aunt Katie looked across at her, aware of the turmoil inside her. 'Catherine—did your father ever tell you what happened when he went to New York?'

Catherine did not look up. She simply shook her head, wishing that they would stop talking about her and Rory as though they were the prime reason for all of this happening. But perhaps they were, she realised with dawning awareness, although even the thought of that was too painful to face.

'Tell her now, Jed,' Aunt Katie directed, 'Before it's too late. You've made many mistakes in your life, but none so serious as this last one. Put it right while you have the chance.'

Jed sighed, raking a hand through his silver hair. For a moment he didn't speak, and as the silence grew, Catherine raised her head, looking through her lashes at him to see a troubled expression on his face, the hard mouth tightening as he steeled himself to speak to her.

He stood up suddenly, thrusting his hands in his pockets. 'I flew to New York as soon as I saw the photograph,' he said abruptly, 'But I went to see Rory before I came to your apartment.'

Catherine's eyes widened in amazement. 'Why didn't you tell me before?' she asked softly, because both Aunt Katie and Rory had told her as much but she hadn't been able to believe them. Her loyalty to her father had stood in her way and now she felt the growing awareness of having been a fool.

Jed looked uncomfortable. He didn't answer her question. He simply continued, 'I told Rory I'd found out about you both, that I wasn't going to let him get away with it. Then I came to see you, and——'

'No, Jed,' Aunt Katie said quietly, but her voice was firm and the refusal to give in made Jed sigh irritably.

'All right!' he muttered, turning back to Catherine. 'Cathy . . . Rory was in love with you. He would have moved hell and high water to marry you. He told me to give you a message . . .' Jed broke off, reddening.

Catherine held her breath, feeling the dizzy effect of her blood pounding fast round her body. 'What was the message?' she asked, and her heart hurt as she waited to hear it.

Jed came over to her, looking down at her apologetically. 'He said "Tell Cathy I'll leave it up to her. If she loves me, she'll stay in New York with me. If she doesn't, I never want to see her again."'

Catherine stared, icy cold. She could hardly breathe, her heart was beating too fast, the sudden realisation that she had been put through two years of unbearable pain and loneliness through one selfish act of her father's was too much for her to bear. She heard herself give a short husky cry, and one hand flew to her mouth. She bit her knuckles, unable to believe that she had heard him properly. How could he have done such a wicked thing to her?

Her mind span dizzily back to the night he had visited her New York apartment. She had been alone, Mindy had been out at another party, and Rory had told her he would call for her late that evening. She had been getting ready as usual, spending hours in her bedroom choosing an outfit that would please Rory, enjoying the intensely feminine ritual of dressing for the man you love.

Jed had arrived after seven, and had shocked her with his complicated web of lies. She had had no idea that Rory was one of the Managhans of Sleuhallen, his accent had been more Anglo-American than anything, without even a trace of North Country. But as her father had gone on with his story, little things had begun to add up about Rory that until then had been unexplained. His reluctance to talk about his family, or his early roots, or even his childhood, when he had spoken at great length to Catherine about hers.

That evening had been frozen into her mind like a sick caricature. The beautiful New York apartment in the height of summer, the white carpet and furniture all glittering in the early evening sunlight which shone through the wide fifth floor windows. The sound of traffic below on the fast street, and the cold reality of love's illusions slipping from her eyes.

Catherine swallowed, eyes shutting tightly as she imagined how Rory must have felt when she left New York that very evening without even speaking to him again, or leaving any form of communication. She had simply gone, back to Sleuhallen with her father.

Lifting her pain-filled eyes to her father now, she whispered, 'How could you have done it?'

Jed had the good grace to look ashamed. 'I'm sorry, lass. I thought it would blow over. I believed he loved you—I admit that. But I thought you would forget him in time.'

Catherine was incredulous, her heart thumping.

'You thought I would forget him ...' she repeated, eyes wide.

Jed sighed, frowning. 'You were only young. It could have been just infatuation. I gambled on your youth.'

Rage spiralled in her mind. 'You had no right!' she said angrily, 'You had no right to gamble with my life! How could you have done such a wicked thing?' She stared at him, eyes burning, 'How *could* you?'

Aunt Katie watched them both with a tired expression, then slowly sat down her old body weary now that her work was done. She sighed, studying father and daughter as they faced each other with a truth that should have been told a long time ago.

Jed looked impatient. 'Cathy, I had to decide what to do for the best ...'

'You can't just decide these things!' Catherine said angrily, standing up with a thudding heart, her skin heated, 'Not for other people. You cold-bloodedly ruined my life. And if it wasn't for Aunt Katie, you would never have admitted it,—would you?'

Jed looked away, his blue eyes uncertain for once, which surprised Catherine, but also made her anger fan higher because she could see that what was being said was the truth. Her father had deliberately smashed what she had with Rory for the sake of a petty blood feud that had absolutely nothing to do with either Catherine or Rory. They had been completely innocent of all the wrong in the past, yet Jed had selfishly allowed his feelings for Rory's mother to stand in the way of Catherine's happiness.

Looking over at Aunt Katie, Catherine said quickly, 'Where is he?'

Aunt Katie gave a grudging smile. 'Up at the Manor. You've heard he's bought it?'

Catherine nodded. 'Yes—and I'm going up there now.' She couldn't suppress her feelings for Rory any longer, now that she knew exactly what had happened back in New York. It was almost unbelievable that her father could have behaved so selfishly. When she thought of the pain and sheer misery of the last two years, she could quite happily kill him. It had been a wicked thing to do, and she doubted now whether she could ever forgive him.

'Catherine, love, don't——' her father began, standing up.

She shot him a damning look. 'Don't you try to stop me.' she said tightly, about to turn and leave the room when a sudden rush of cold anger hit her, and made her turn round again to look at her father with new eyes.

'What you did was unforgiveable,' she told him in a cold voice. 'You've watched me these last two years, and you've seen how unhappy I was. But you didn't lift a finger to help me. You just sat back and watched.'

She was shaking now, she could feel it, could hardly contain the tremor in her voice as she spoke. Her father stood watching her too, shame in the blue eyes, a look of pained resignation on his face which did not move her one jot. She could no more forgive him for his selfishness than she could stop loving Rory. The words ran round her heart like a song, made her feel exhilarated, alive. She could admit it now, not only to herself but to Rory, to everyone around her. She could wear her love like a shiny new badge, with pride, instead of hiding it away in a black cave and trying not to see it even on cold lonely nights when she faced an empty future and could not see her way clear of the desert she thought she was living in.

'I left Rory because I believed you,' she continued, voice shaking, 'It never entered my head that you could lie. You're my father—how could I doubt your word? And you used that. You used it to hurt me.'

Jed stared, blue eyes burning into her. He looked

white now, shaken. 'I thought I was acting for the best,' he said uncertainly, 'Isabelle——'

'I don't want to hear it!' she said angrily, pressing her hands to her ears for a moment in self-defence. When her father was silent again, she took her hands away, looking at him coldly. 'I'm going now. Don't try to stop me. I don't even know if I'll ever come back.'

Catherine pulled the door open, going out into the hall. Her mother stood outside, her face ashen. She had obviously been listening, Catherine realised as she halted in her step, staring at her. Her mother made a helpless little gesture with her hands, her eyes worried. She knew all along, Catherine thought with sudden distaste, eyeing her. Catherine didn't want to speak to any of them. She pushed past her mother, going to the front door where Stephen stood.

'What's happening?' Stephen asked, pushing away from his position, leaning against the wall beside the front door where other members of the family also stood, all waiting to find out what was being said in the dining room.

Catherine sighed. 'Ask Daddy. Can I borrow your car? I have to go out.'

Stephen hesitated, studying her closely. Then he slowly took the keys from his pocket and handed them to her. 'Sure. Just bring it back in one piece! You look a little . . . off colour. Are you okay?'

Catherine laughed, nodding her head. Tears pricked the back of her eyes. 'Oh, I'm fine!' she said, bitterness in her voice now, and took the keys, going out of the front door before he could say another word.

She revved the engine of the shiny blue Stag, twisting the steering wheel fast and veering off down the drive. What would Rory think when she told him what she had found out? She wouldn't blame him in the least if he despised her for her weakness. The strength of their relationship in New York should have been enough to make her question anything her father said against Rory, but it hadn't. Catherine knew that it had been the depth of her feelings for Rory that had prevented her from confronting him with her father's accusations. Hearing someone say 'He doesn't love you' had just hurt her too badly. When Catherine felt hurt, she always ran for cover. She always had and she always would, she saw that now, clearly. She had been running from her pain for two years, and very possibly would have continued running for the rest of her life.

The thought made an icy shudder run down her spine. She drove with one hand on the wheel, the other pressed to the gear stick, fingers frantically tapping as she prayed that Rory would still be at the Old Manor when she got there.

Thank God Aunt Katie had stepped in. Had Jed told her, Catherine wondered with a frown? He must have done, must have either confessed guilt feelings to the old woman, or even—an unpalatable thought— bragged about it to her. Catherine couldn't believe, even now, that her father was that cruel. He had probably had second thoughts over the last couple of years and had confided them in Aunt Katie.

Driving up into the black hills of Sleuhallen, Catherine saw the twin towers of Old Hallen's Manor rising above the trees which surrounded it. Her heart thudded wildly. Was Rory still there? And what would he say when she arrived. Her heart twisted at the realisation that he could very well tell her to go to hell. She had hurt him badly. Misused his trust, broken what they had together and denied him when he tested her love. The thought of having lost him altogether made her go icy cold with fear.

Pulling up outside the rusty iron gates, Catherine stopped the engine. All was quiet. Only the wind and

rain broke the silence. Stepping out of the car, she
walked on the broken path to the old gates. Looking
in, she saw the long black limousine parked close to
the manor, rain beating down heavily on it's shiny
roof.

Her heart leapt. At least he's here, she thought,
hands wrapped round the rusty iron bars of the gates.
She pushed one gate hard, it creaked, moaned and
started to move, scraping the path as she pushed it.
Wet leaves flew up in a sudden gust of wind that blew
strands of hair into her face whipping her wet skin.

Catherine got back in her car, soaked to the skin,
and drove slowly up to Old Hallen's Manor. The
windscreen wipers scraped steadily on the glass. Rain
beat on the roof like a thousand needles. She pulled
up beside the long black limousine and switched the
engine off, sitting in silence for a moment, hearing her
heart thud as she steeled herself to get out and face
Rory.

Glancing up at the old crumbling manor house,
Catherine saw a movement in one of the upper storey
windows. Her heart leapt. Rory? She swallowed on a
dry throat, opening the door and getting out, her legs
shaky. He must still love me, she told herself,
frightened in spite of the fact that she knew she had to
go through with this.

Wind and rain drove into her as she walked to the
huge Elizabethan doors of the house. Pushing her wet
hair back, she hunted for a bell, and saw an old bell
handle beside the door. She pulled it, and heard it
jangle noisily inside the house.

Footsteps approached, cool and assured, telling her
it was Rory. She would recognise his tread anywhere,
she realised with hammering pulse. Everything about
Rory Managhan was burnt into her mind and heart as
though branded forever.

A bolt thudded back. The door was pulled open.

Rory stood in the doorway dressed in black, the grey eyes narrowed on her, his tanned face devastatingly attractive. It made her blood pound faster.

'I saw you drive up,' he said deeply. 'What are you doing here?'

The deep voice wound its way into her consciousness. Let loose, her feelings were beginning to swamp her. They had been suppressed for two years, now they threatened to engulf her.

'I had to see you.' Catherine stammered, suddenly unsure of herself.

The black brows rose in an arch. 'Oh?' he said sardonically, 'Last time I saw you, you couldn't wait to get rid of me. What brought the sudden change, I wonder?'

Catherine flushed, shivering as rain tricked down her spine. 'I'm cold.' she said quietly, and sniffled as if to illustrate the point, her nose pink and wet.

Rory studied her with a wry smile. 'You poor thing,' he drawled, but did not invite her in, deliberately, she thought as she looked at him, standing there dressed in black jeans and sweater, resting one muscular arm on the door handle.

Catherine sneezed, eyes shutting tight. Looking at him accusingly, she said, 'You'll never forgive yourself if I catch pneumonia out here!'

Rory laughed, eyes creasing. 'You little blackmailer!' he exclaimed, and pulled the door open for her.

She went in, exaggerating her shivers as he closed the massive oak door behind them. Her trouser suit was soaked through to the skin, and she felt little droplets of rain drip from her to the stone floor as she stood in the baronial hallway.

Rory watched her for a moment. He frowned. 'You are wet, aren't you?' he said, and reached out one hand to touch her cold cheeks.

She felt that touch in every nerve of her body. It

made her heart skip two beats, then rapidly make up for it with an overload of ten.

Their eyes met. 'You'd better come into the kitchen,' he said abruptly, as if he had felt off-balance by that touch, too. 'It's the only warm room in the house at the moment.' He turned on his heel and lead the way through a maze of high-ceilinged rooms, saying as he went, 'It's got an old-fashioned rayburn oven in it. It's a pain in the neck to keep it going, but it certainly heats the room up.'

Catherine listened to the sound of their heels clicking on the stone floors, the empty rooms holding that cold hollow feeling that a new house always has, as if ghosts of the previous tenants were watching a new life begin in their house. She looked around carefully as she followed Rory. The rooms were magnificent, some with criss-cross black and white stone floors, others with one or two bare-looking tapestries still hanging from the walls.

Rory pushed open a door and waves of soft heat wrapped themselves around her. The long spacious kitchen was deliciously hot, the rayburn oven crackling and spitting in the centre of one of the walls as the fire burnt inside it.

Rory indicated a wooden chair at the long wooden table. 'Coffee?'

Catherine sat down, nodding. 'Please.'

He opened one of the cupboards and took out a large shiny saucepan, giving her a quick, wry smile. 'I haven't got a kettle yet,' he told her, filling the pan with cold water, 'I have to boil it up in this!'

Catherine smiled, eyes lighting up. 'I used to do that,' she said cheerfully, 'in my first flat. We never remembered to buy kettles, sheets or electric fires.'

Rory grinned. 'So you're an old hand at using the oven as central heating?'

She nodded. 'Put all the gas jets on and leave the

doors open,' she agreed, remembering those days when she and her old sixth form friends had lived in a small flat over one of the shops in Sleuhallen.

Rory put a lid on the saucepan and left it to boil. He came back to the long sparse wooden table and pulled out a chair opposite Catherine, the legs of it scraping the stone floor.

Catherine didn't look at him. Instead, she studied the kitchen walls with interest, watching the long rows of copper utensils shining in neat lines behind them. The two windows at the far end were cracked and dirty, a few plants growing along the ledges which were now rain-spattered.

'So——' Rory studied her coolly, 'What did you come to see me about?'

Her heart skipped a beat with nerves. She looked down at her hands. 'Aunt Katie came to see my father today,' she said quietly, hoping that he would guess why she'd come. He must know that Aunt Katie had been told the whole story.

Rory arched his brows. 'I see,' he drawled, 'And what exactly was said at this little confrontation?'

Catherine bit her lip. Why did she suddenly feel so nervous? 'Nothing much, at first,' she told him lightly, 'But she asked me to stay and listen, which puzzled me, I must admit.'

'I'm sure it did,' he commented, taking a pack of cigarettes from the pocket of his black jeans, a gold lighter too, and lighting one. He leaned back in his chair, studying her as cool blue smoke wreathed around his black head. 'Go on,' he prompted when she was silent.

She looked at the cigarette in his hand. 'May I have one?' she asked, throat dry with nerves.

Rory's eyes creased with amusement. 'Coward!' he drawled, studying her calmly, one long finger resting on his temple. 'I know what you're going to say, Cathy. I've been waiting for you all afternoon.'

Her heart stopped beating for a moment. She stared in surprise. 'You know . . .?' she breathed, blinking. She pulled herself together, frowning; 'But how can you possibly?'

The grey eyes were level. 'Because I knew Katie was coming to see you today.' he said, voice deep and calm. He studied her for a moment in silence while this sank in, then took a cigarette slowly from the pack on the table and offered it to her. Catherine took it, eyes on him. He held the flame of the lighter to the tip, waiting while she inhaled.

Catherine looked down at her hands. 'So you know what was said.'

He nodded silently.

Catherine drew a shaky breath. 'And you knew that I would come here.'

He shook his black head. 'No. That I didn't know,' he said coolly, 'I took a chance.'

That surprised her, and she looked up, eyes wide. 'But surely you realised that when I found out what Jed had done . . .?' she said, sentence tailing off as thoughts buzzed around her mind. Frowning, she bent forward, 'I had no idea, Rory! If I'd known the truth I would have——'

'What?' he interrupted quickly, 'Dashed round to my apartment? Deserted your father in my favour?' He laughed, 'Come off it! The minute I saw Jed Skelton on my doorstep, I knew I'd lost you!'

Rain spattered heavily on the windows. Catherine stared at Rory. 'But I loved you!' she burst out, and instantly regretted it, flushing hotly, her heart thudding fast as she realised what she had said.

Rory gave her a dry smile. 'Not quite enough.'

The saucepan started to boil, water hitting the lid noisily. Rory stood up, going over to the rayburn and lifting it off the hob. He took a couple of cups out of the cupboard, spooned coffee in them and poured the boiling water in, stirring with one small silver spoon as he did.

Catherine stood up, the chair scraping awkwardly as she did. Her legs felt shaky all of a sudden. 'Okay,' she said shakily, 'Maybe I wouldn't have come straight to see you——'

'Maybe?' he turned his head, grey eyes cold, 'Are you serious? Cathy, you run from every crisis in your life! You've got about as much fighting spirit as a rabbit.'

'That isn't true!' she said, hurt, 'How can you say that?'

He laughed. 'Because it *is* true.'

She drew on her cigarette, hands trembling. 'Look—I was being asked to choose between my family and the man I loved——'

'Very Victorian melodrama!' he drawled sardonically, and Catherine felt her lips compress with hurt anger because it had taken a lot of courage for her to drive up here this afternoon and now all he could do was make fun of her and say hurtful things.

She watched him, her mouth tight. 'You're not making this easy for me.' she said in a low angry voice.

Rory turned, eyes an angry grey. 'Easy for you?' he said under his breath and she suddenly saw the fury in his arrogant face, 'Why the hell should I?'

She stared, stunned into silence.

Threat emanated from the tautly held body. 'You kicked my teeth in. Ran away back home and left me. And for what? For a father who'd stick a knife in your back as soon as look at you.'

'Rory . . .' she began, taken aback.

'Do you have any idea what you did to me?' he said tightly, his jaw clamped hard, 'Do you have any idea how long it took me to get over you?'

Catherine backed a little as he began to advance, suddenly afraid of him. His lean body was throbbing with the threat of violence now, and all the anger that he had held in check was beginning to pulsate through him.

She swallowed. 'It took me over a year to forget you, too, Rory.' she said, voice shaky, 'It wasn't——'

'It took you nothing!' he shouted, banging the table with the flat of his hand. He was breathing hard now, anger making his nostrils flare, '*You* left me, not the other way around.'

Blood coursed through her body. 'I had to! What choice did I have, faced with what he told me about you?'

He laughed harshly, eyes brilliant silver, 'We all have a choice, Cathy. You didn't *have* to do anything. Or have you still not realised that?' He put his hands on his hips and the hard muscles in his arms flexed, 'You can choose anything you want, if you want it hard enough. There's nothing to stop you except yourself.'

'No!' she said desperately, tears pricking the back of her lids. 'There were too many other things to take into account——'

'Don't tell me about life, Cathy!' he said bitterly, and the grey eyes flashed with anger, 'I know,' he said slowly, 'all about life. And if one thing in this goddamned world is certain, it's that——' He breathed heavily, studying her, 'The only relevant thing is you, and what you want.'

Catherine felt her mouth compress with sudden anger. 'Then why didn't you follow me?' she asked in a low voice, 'Why didn't *you* take what you wanted, Rory?'

He hesitated, and the black lashes flickered on his cheekbone as he studied her. 'I couldn't,' he said abruptly, 'I couldn't face it. Come back to Sleuhallen and let the whole goddamned Skelton family laugh in my face?' He shook his black head, a tight smile touching his mouth as he gave a hollow laugh, 'Oh no. I wasn't strong enough for that, then.'

She watched him, feeling herself calm down a little. 'But you are now,' she stated, and her eyes skimmed his body with more than a little pride. She loved him still, she knew it, and she loved him for his strength as much as his tenderness. The body she knew so well was lean muscle and bone that could pack a powerhouse punch as well as move gently against her.

'Yes.' He met her eyes, 'I am now.'

There was a tense silence. Catherine swallowed on a dry throat, and drew on her cigarette, the smoke hitting her lungs with a strength that woke her up a little, made her feel more calm.

'Rory,' she said slowly, feeling her pulses hammer, 'I came to apologise, and I haven't made a very good job of it. There was so much I wanted to say——'

'Forget it,' he said harshly, mouth compressing, 'I don't think I want to hear it anyway.'

She stared, confused, 'But you must listen, I——'

'Must?' he said curtly, 'Must? There's no must in it! I don't have to do anything I don't want to.'

She sighed, hurt and impatient. 'You talk like a spoiled child.'

'That's rich,' he sniped, 'Spoiled children like you never know how to reach out and take what they want. It's always been dropped in their lap. So one day they come up against a choice, and they take whatever gets there first. People like you make the best of what they've got instead of looking for something better.'

She felt as though she'd been slapped, sucking in her breath in amazement because however much it hurt to hear it, she knew that what he said was true, and she didn't feel strong enough to face it. She'd run from the terrible decision in New York because she had never had to deal with anything like it before, so she had chosen the easy way out. Believing her father, who she had known all her life, had been easier than stepping into the dangerous unknown and putting her trust in a stranger's hands, however much she had loved that stranger.

'That's the bottom line, Cathy,' he said tautly, 'I wanted you and you didn't want me. That's the difference.'

'No,' she shook her head, certain now that however much of a coward she had been then, she was not one any longer, and whatever it took to make him see that, she was prepared to do it. She had run from the fight before, but she had only postponed the battle. Ignoring that crisis had only delayed it. Well she would face it now, however dangerously her heart was beating with fear.

'Oh yes,' he drawled tightly, 'You must always get to the bottom line. That's when you see all the garbage surrounding it for what it is. You can talk forever about family loyalty, shock and unhappiness, but when you get right down to it, it's all just——' he watched her angrily, eyes blazing, 'it's all junk, Cathy. All of it.'

Catherine moistened her lips, they felt dry and cracked, and she didn't really know what to say or where to start. But although she felt a sudden urge to turn and run, she knew she couldn't, not this time, or she would never stop running.

'The bottom line,' she said huskily, 'is that I love you.'

His mouth crooked in a sardonic smile. 'How touching,' he growled.

Tears pricked her eyes. 'I was very young, Rory. I accepted instead of questioning.'

Rory laughed. 'Welcome to conditioning,' he said drily, 'And have you changed much? Are you able to think for yourself yet?'

Her heart thudded. 'I'm here, aren't I?' she said throatily.

Their eyes met and held for a few burning seconds, and she felt the first inklings of hope because she saw his heart in his eyes, and she knew for certain that he still loved her, just as much as he ever had, if not more. Her heart flipped over.

'Well,' he said huskily, and gave a little smile, 'I guess you just can't help being a numbskull.'

Catherine felt tears slip out from under her lids. 'Oh, Rory . . .' she began, but her voice broke and she just stood opposite him, unable to move because she was so scared she might do something wrong if she did, so she just stood staring at him instead.

Rory sighed shakily, took one step forward, eyes running over her, then muttered, 'I must be crazy!' and took her in his arms, hands pressing her tight against him, pushing her head against his shoulder, cradling her in silence, his heart thudding fast against her.

She buried her face in the crook of his shoulder, eyes wet with tears. The rain pitter-pattered on the windows, the warmth from the rayburn oven had steamed them up on the inside. Catherine felt her pulse hammering as she gradually found the confidence to slide her arms around Rory and hold him close to her.

Rory ran his fingers through her hair. 'I think I've loved you forever.' he said softly, and his breath fanned her throat, made her shiver, 'I used to wake up in New York and look at you, sleeping beside me, and wonder why I'd lived without you all my life.'

Catherine closed her eyes, shaking. 'Don't . . . I'll never forgive myself for not trusting you.'

'I'm not surprised,' he said with gentle teasing, 'I almost didn't either! But even when I wanted to kill you for it, I was still too bloody scared to even set eyes on you again.'

She drew away, staring up at him incredulously. 'Scared? But why?'

He gave her a crooked little smile. 'Scared of what I would feel, I guess. Even now, everytime I see you, you look so . . . so *real*.' He frowned. 'That sounds crazy! But there's no other way of putting it.'

Catherine smiled, eyes dancing. 'Yes, real . . . I know exactly what you mean. I feel that too.'

'Do you?' he murmured, smiling, and slid one hand deliberately to her throat where a pulse beat rapidly, throbbing against his fingertips. His eyes dropped to her mouth, burning. 'Why,' he said huskily, 'so you do.'

Her heart skipped a beat. Slowly, her gaze moved down to his hard mouth, and she watched, mesmerised as it came closer, dropping a light burning kiss on her lips.

'When was the last time,' he said throatily, kissing her softly, 'that I kissed you?'

She swallowed, pulses throbbing. 'Last night?' she suggested, feeling her breathing come faster, her heart suspended as if by magic as she waited for him to fasten his mouth on hers and kiss her thoroughly.

'No, that wasn't a kiss. That was an attack,' he drawled, and his hands slid to her hips, caressing them softly with butterfly movements that made her feel weak at the knees.

'I can't tell the difference anymore,' she whispered, mouth watering as his lips played teasingly with hers, and she raised her eyes slowly to his, whispering, 'You'll have to show me.'

His heart thudded faster. 'It's a deal,' he murmured, and his mouth slid hotly over hers with breathtaking sensuality, fastening a moment later to kiss her with slow drugging movements that made her head spin.

Fingers sliding over her hips, pulling her softly closer, making her wait for the passion that was springing up in both of them as the fire burnt a slow tantalising flame. She slowly slid her hands to the back of his head, running her fingers very lightly through his thick black hair.

Rory drew back a little, studying her, his face slightly flushed. 'God, I've missed you,' he muttered, watching her through black lashes.

Her heart sang. 'Darling ...' she murmured, her voice choked with emotion, 'I've missed you.'

Rory eyed her for a moment, then groaned, his mouth fastening hotly on hers, taking her by surprise with the sudden flare of passion as he held her tightly, mouth drugging as he kissed her with fire and longing. They clung together, swaying a little as their arms tightened around each other. His tongue flicked into her mouth making her catch her breath, kissing him back with just as much passion. Her body felt hot, alive, her pulse hammering as she clung to him.

The sound of car wheels crunching the gravel drive outside made them freeze, pulling apart, faces flushed, breathing hectic. Rory looked at her with glittering eyes and she saw that his pupil was massive, a thick black circle of desire in the silver eyes.

'Who the hell is that?' he muttered, his hand sliding to catch hers, walking over to the kitchen windows to look out at the gardens.

Catherine stood next to him, fingers curling over his arm. 'My father!' she said, shocked as she saw the limousine roll up in front of the house and her father step out from behind the wheel.

'Not just him,' Rory muttered grimly, 'Look again.'

Great Aunt Katie was helped out of the Rolls Royce, but followed by Isabelle Managhan, who stepped out, shaking her head in the rain storm, her long black hair rippling unfettered down her slender back. She looked like a woodland nymph, which struck Catherine as grossly unfair, considering Isabelle was pushing fifty-five.

Rory watched with narrowed eyes as they all looked up at Old Hallen's Manor. 'What on earth is my mother playing at?' he said under his breath.

Catherine looked at him shyly, from beneath her lashes. 'Burying the hatchet?' she suggested.

Rory laughed, glancing at her. 'She'd need a whole bloody cemetery for that! This particular hatchet is big enough to worry Goliath.'

The bell jangled, echoing through the empty old manor house, and Catherine looked at Rory, biting her lip. He seemed angry to see his mother with Jed Skelton. But surely that would be a fitting conclusion to the near half century of bitterness and hatred that had sprung up between the two families? And to bring it to it's final conclusion at this house, Old Hallen's Manor, which had seen the seeds sown for two generations of hatred, and would now, she hoped see them finally laid to rest as Rory and Catherine fell in love all over again.

'Come on,' Rory said under his breath, 'We'd better go and see what they want.'

She halted him, hand on his shoulder. 'Rory . . . you're not going to do anything—are you?'

The black brows met in a bar across his forehead. 'Such as?'

'Cause trouble,' she said point-blank, 'They seem to have patched things up, or started to try, at least. You won't spoil it, will you?'

Rory studied her in silence for a moment, then stroked her hair, smiling, 'Don't worry, honey. If they really have decided to call it a day, then I'm more than happy. I just don't want to find your father coming between us again.'

Her eyes widened in dismay. 'Do you really think he'd try?'

Rory looked grim. 'Jed Skelton always has an ace up his sleeve. He taught me that a long time ago, and I haven't forgotten it. I don't intend to start losing my memory at this late stage in the game.'

He held on to her hand as he guided her back through the labyrinth of rooms that led them to the main hallway. Catherine was worried. The bell rang again just as they reached the sweeping stone hall, and walked across the black-white floor together, footsteps echoing in the flat emptiness of the manor.

Catherine shot a worried glance at Rory out of the corner of her eye.

He intercepted it. Studying her briefly, he said, 'Don't worry. We're in this together from now on.' He slipped an arm around her shoulders and held her tight for a second to reassure her.

She felt relief flood through her. Looking at his darkly handsome profile she couldn't help feeling a rush of pride. He was so attractive! And he loved her as much as she loved him, which was something worth singing from the battlements.

Rory opened the massive oak front door.

Jed Skelton stood, hands on hips, waiting. His eyes flicked from Rory to Catherine in surprise, seeing them standing linked together like Siamese twins, their faces not even defensive, but quietly at ease with each other as though the last two years had never happened.

Jed's blue eyes flicked back to Rory. 'She told you, then?' he said curtly.

Rory inclined his black head, face arrogant. 'It's all out in the open now, Jed. And not a damned thing you can do about it.'

Jed shook his head, silver hair damp from the rain. 'I'm too old to fight now, lad. I'll not stop you.'

Isabelle stepped forward, the cream silk dress she wore rippling in the wind, pearls and diamonds at her throat lending her that timeless elegance she wore so well.

'I'm so glad.' Isabelle's soft voice seemed to sing against the gentle tapping of the rain as it began to die down, 'And for it to happen in this house . . . it seems almost predestined.' She glanced at Jed, her dark eyes suddenly lit with mischief, 'Don't you think so, Jed?'

Jed stiffened, looking up at the manor, the crumbling red-brick, the overgrown ivy which clung to it's walls and the dusty old windows which were cracked and in need of repair.

Rory held Catherine closer, his arm protective. 'We'll hold our . . .' he smiled a little, eyes creasing, 'our second engagement party here.' He shot a quick look at Catherine in case she wished to disagree, but she didn't, she simply gave him a brilliantly happy smile, her eyes dancing.

Jed watched them both, eyes narrowed. 'You're going to marry, then? I wasn't sure.'

Rory nodded. 'You just delayed it by a couple of years, Jed. I suppose I ought to knock your teeth down your throat, but I don't think I need to now.'

Great Aunt Katie stood behind Isabelle and Jed, in the centre, watching Rory and Catherine with amused old eyes. Now, she rapped her cane on the cracked path, clearing her throat.

'I'm cold and wet, young man!' she said in a haughty voice, and smiled, 'I don't intend to stand out here all day. Aren't you going to give us some coffee before we go?'

Rory grinned, stepping back a little but making sure that Catherine stayed in the crook of his arm, his long tanned fingers tightening on her shoulder.

Jed was still for a moment. Slowly his blue eyes flicked to Isabelle, and they stared at each other for a few seconds, as though time flew back and all the bitterness was still to come. The rain died down slowly, the garden was silent, only the sounds of a few birds beginning to sing again after the downpour was audible in the crisp damp air.

Slowly, Jed held out his arm for Isabelle, who gave him a brilliant smile, dark eyes full of sudden affection, and slipped her hand over the crook of his arm.

Catherine frowned, hurt for her mother's sake. Surely there was no chance of Isabelle and Jed getting back together? It would destroy their family, and there was no way Catherine would just sit back and watch that begin to happen.

Great Aunt Katie caught her eye and shook her head. 'Don't worry lass,' she said, walking slowly over to Catherine, and speaking in an undertone, 'your father loves Anne. Isabelle loves Damian's memory still. They just need to start liking one another again or there'll be no peace in this town, then we'll all have to pack up and go to New York, just like Rory!'

Catherine laughed with relief as Great Aunt Katie moved away again, watching her with a wise old smile.

And so it was that Isabelle Managhan and Jed Skelton walked once more into Old Hallen's Manor, arm in arm, as they had so many years ago, but this time it was not out of love for each other, but out of love for their children Rory and Catherine, who were destined for each other, and a long and happy life in Old Hallen's Manor, in the little valley of Sleuhallen.

The door of the manor clanged shut. Isabelle, Jed and Katie walked along the empty stone floors in front of Rory and Catherine.

Rory halted Catherine, his hand sliding to her waist. 'Will you be happy here, my darling?' he murmured against her throat, lips grazing her skin, sending shivers through her body.

Catherine studied him, eyes wide. 'You plan to stay here? In Sleuhallen?'

He nodded. 'Only if you marry me, though! I'm not staying here on my own!' He watched her through thick black lashes, his eyes suddenly serious as he said deeply, 'Well? Will you?'

Catherine's heart leapt with delight, but she eyed him teasingly, 'Will I what?'

He grinned. 'Marry me!' he whispered so that the others couldn't hear.

Catherine watched him, smiling, then said softly; 'Whatever happened to the good old down on one knee?' She raised her brows, eyes dancing at him with mischief and exhilarated flirtation, 'I've always looked forward to the obligatory candle-lit dinner for two, followed by a rose and a proposal!'

Rory kissed her mouth lingeringly. 'Not until I have my answer!' he murmured, smiling, eyes so brilliant that she felt quite light-headed.

Catherine kissed his nose, grinning. 'Coward!'

He laughed huskily, 'I only gamble on winners.'

She twined her arms around his neck. 'I think you just hit the jackpot,' she murmured, and her lids closed as Rory bent to kiss her quite exquisitely.

The perfect holiday romance.

ACT OF BETRAYAL
Sara Craven

MAN HUNT
Charlotte Lamb

YOU OWE ME
Penny Jordan

LOVERS IN THE AFTERNOON
Carole Mortimer

Have a more romantic holiday this summer with the
Mills & Boon holiday pack.

Four brand new titles, attractively packaged for only £4.40.

The holiday pack is published on the 14th June. Look out for it
where you buy Mills & Boon.

The Rose of Romance

House
of Storms

Violet Winspear

New from Violet Winspear, one of Mills and Boon's best-
selling authors, a longer romance of mystery, intrigue,
suspense and love. Almost twice the length of a standard
romance for just £1.95. Published on the 14th of June.

The Rose of Romance

Mills & Boon

Take 4
Exciting Books
Absolutely
FREE

Love, romance, intrigue... all are captured for you by
Mills & Boon's top-selling authors. By becoming a
regular reader of Mills & Boon's Romances you can
enjoy 6 superb new titles every month plus a whole
range of special benefits: your very own personal
membership card, a free monthly newsletter packed
with recipes, competitions, exclusive book offers and
a monthly guide to the stars, plus extra bargain offers
and big cash savings.

AND an Introductory FREE GIFT for YOU.
Turn over the page for details.

As a special introduction we will send you four exciting Mills & Boon Romances Free and without obligation when you complete and return this coupon.

At the same time we will reserve a subscription to Mills & Boon Reader Service for you. Every month, you will receive 6 of the very latest novels by leading Romantic Fiction authors, delivered direct to your door. You don't pay extra for delivery — postage and packing is always completely Free. There is no obligation or commitment — you can cancel your subscription at any time.

You have nothing to lose and a whole world of romance to gain.

Just fill in and post the coupon today to MILLS & BOON READER SERVICE, FREEPOST, P.O. BOX 236, CROYDON, SURREY CR9 9EL.

Please Note:- READERS IN SOUTH AFRICA write to Mills & Boon, Postbag X3010, Randburg 2125, S. Africa.

- - - - - - - - - - - - - - - - - - - -

FREE BOOKS CERTIFICATE

To: Mills & Boon Reader Service, FREEPOST, P.O. Box 236, Croydon, Surrey CR9 9EL.

Please send me, free and without obligation, four Mills & Boon Romances, and reserve a Reader Service Subscription for me. If I decide to subscribe I shall, from the beginning of the month following my free parcel of books, receive six new books each month for £6 60 post and packing free. If I decide not to subscribe, I shall write to you within 10 days. The free books are mine to keep in any case. I understand that I may cancel my subscription at any time simply by writing to you. I am over 18 years of age.

Please write in BLOCK CAPITALS

Signature _____

Name _____

Address _____

_____ Post code _____

SEND NO MONEY — TAKE NO RISKS.

Please don't forget to include your Postcode.

6R Offer expires 31st December 1985

EP86

'I will not ha

house.'

Guido held her

optical half-nelson.

'You're paranoid,' Ronni said. 'I'm not a saboteur.'

He flicked a glance across his shoulder. 'So, I'm paranoid, am I?' The notion seemed to amuse him. 'Well, I suppose that's possible. . .but what I think is more possible is that I'm right.'

That figured. It was hard to imagine him ever thinking he might be wrong.

Dear Reader

Benvenuto! This month our European island is the wild, rugged, mountainous Sardinia, or Sardegna in Italian — island of history and dreams. This is very definitely a place where lovers can discover for themselves the true romance of the past, and Stephanie Howard's story blends this distinctive atmosphere with a passionate romance of the present. We hope you enjoy it!

The Editor

The author says:

'When on holiday I love to go off the beaten track, and Sardinia is definitely off the beaten track! It's still relatively wild and undeveloped as far as tourism goes, and it's still possible, especially in the mountainous inland region, to find villages where no tourist has ever trodden. The island's rugged dry landscape also appealed to me — parts of it are almost desert-like — and it was fascinating to be able to find villages where the way of life has changed little over the centuries. And I have never seen water bluer than the water of Sardinia!'

Stephanie Howard

★ TURN TO THE BACK PAGES OF THIS BOOK FOR *WELCOME TO EUROPE*. . .OUR FASCINATING FACT-FILE ★

CONSPIRACY OF LOVE

BY
STEPHANIE HOWARD

*First published in Great Britain 1993
by Mills & Boon Limited*

© Stephanie Howard 1993

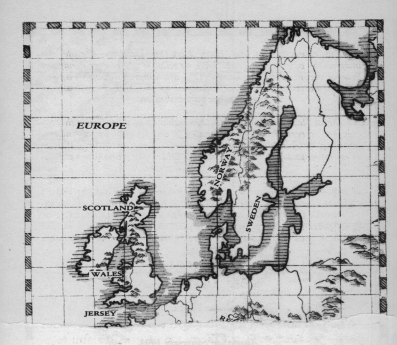

MILLS & BOON LIMITED
ETON HOUSE   18–24 PARADISE ROAD
RICHMOND   SURREY   TW9 1SR

CHAPTER ONE

'GOOD grief! Who on earth is that gorgeous-looking man?'

Ronni turned round from gazing at the figure on the jetty as her brother, manning the outboard motor behind her, responded with a snort of disapproval.

'That gorgeous-looking man is your new employer,' he told her. 'And I'd advise you to reserve judgement on him till you get to know him a little better!'

'That's Guido Falcone?' Ronni blinked at Jeff in amazement. 'You mean that's the monster you've just been telling me all about?'

Her short blonde hair whipping round her face in the breeze, Ronni turned back to fix her eyes on the jetty, which was drawing ever closer as Jeff's motor boat approached it, and focused with growing interest on the imposing tall, dark figure who stood there in the bright Sardinian sunshine.

In his early thirties, he was very tall — and growing even taller the closer they got to him! — with a shock of curly black hair that framed a deeply tanned face whose fierce, uncompromising features appeared chiselled from stone. And his lean, strong body with its broad shoulders, tapering waist, narrow hips and long muscular legs exuded a virile, potent energy that seemed to crackle almost audibly.

He was standing quite still now, arms folded across his chest, the dark eyes beneath the dark brows fixed on the approaching motor boat, but Ronni found herself reflecting that that hard muscular body, dressed now in white trousers and a faded blue T-shirt, would only be seen at its best in motion.

He would move, she guessed, with the supple grace of a panther. Unexpected excitement flickered inside her at the thought.

Her brother Jeff was guiding them alongside the jetty now. Ronni turned to glance at him, smiling her surprise. 'Well, if that's Guido Falcone, he's definitely not what I was expecting.' From Jeff's description, she'd been expecting horns and cloven hoofs!

Jeff didn't have a chance to answer. At that moment the figure on the jetty above them spoke.

'You're late.'

The accusation was directed at Jeff. But such was the power of those two softly spoken words that Ronni found her head jerking up to look at the speaker, barely aware of her brother's muttered response as he hoisted her cases up on to the jetty. And as she met the dark gaze of Guido Falcone, her breath caught as though a fist had connected with her solar plexus. In that instant she knew that standing before her was the most exciting man she had ever met.

As she tore her gaze away, Jeff helped her to disembark. 'See you later, sis,' he told her as she stood there, slightly stunned. Then he was turning the boat around and speeding away.

'*Maledetto!*'

There was another soft verbal explosion behind her, as Ronni paused to watch the boat disappear. Composing herself, she turned. 'I'm sorry I'm late,' she said. 'My flight was delayed.'

Guido's gaze was fixed seawards, watching the disappearing boat, and he did not turn round immediately to look at her. Grateful to be spared the unsettling power of that dark gaze, Ronni took the opportunity to study him for a moment.

He was quite astonishingly good-looking, she decided, though there was nothing tame or soft about the beauty he possessed. The features that had appeared fierce and uncompromising from afar, here, from a mere metre away, were even more so. The line of his jaw, the curve of his proud nose, the sweep of his high, intelligent forehead proclaimed a strength of mind and character that was almost tangible.

There was a wildness about him, too, seen in the thick black hair, just a touch on the long side, that curled over his ears. And those eyes that seemed to dance and scowl at the same time from beneath their fringe of long dark lashes gave him a restless, unpredictable air. One would never know which way he was going to jump next.

'What did you say?'

Suddenly, he had turned to look at her—simultaneously surprising her and proving her theory. And in that instant, as his eyes fixed her, another thunderbolt shot through her.

'I said I'm sorry I'm late.' To her chagrin, Ronni blushed, as a wave of sudden confusion rushed through her. 'My flight was delayed. We got in late.'

'You got in over two hours ago.' Black eyes sparked down at her. 'Even allowing for the journey from the airport, you ought to have been here long before now. Unless, of course, you encountered some other delay?'

'Not really.' Ronni smiled an apologetic smile, wishing her heart would stop thumping so hard. 'But we did stop off on the way for a cup of coffee.'

'A cup of coffee?' The jet-black eyebrows soared. Every line of his face spelt disapproval.

Ronni made a face. 'Yes. I'm sorry. I didn't realise I was keeping you waiting. You see, I was thirsty after the journey.'

'You couldn't have waited half an hour — that's all the journey from Olbia takes — and saved me the inconvenience of having to hang around for almost an hour?'

'I really am sorry.'

Ronni felt a flicker of guilt. His complaint, she couldn't help feeling, was perfectly justified. Though the stop for coffee hadn't been her idea. Her thirst could easily have waited. It was Jeff who'd insisted that they stop off for a drink. 'It'll give me a chance to fill you in on the situation,' he'd told her. She'd had no idea that her new employer was waiting!

But no doubt Jeff had, she decided, suddenly feeling torn between her sense of guilt for what now seemed like unnecessary rudeness and her automatic instinct to defend her brother.

She killed two birds with one stone and offered apologetically, 'I really was terribly thirsty.'

'In that case, what can I say?' Guido smiled suddenly, once more taking Ronni by surprise — and at the same time displaying his perfect white teeth. 'We could hardly have our new tutor dying of thirst,' he added.

With that, he reached down to grab up her suitcases. Then he was turning on his heel. 'The car's over here.'

Ronni followed behind him, her eyes on his back, watching the way his muscles rippled beneath the T-shirt. She'd been right, this man was made for motion. When he moved he had the supple, easy grace of a big cat.

Immediately, she dropped her gaze away, feeling torn once again. Her feelings of admiration — even her inclination to see his side of things — were surely totally out of place? After what Jeff had told her about Guido Falcone, the only feelings she ought to have for him were disapproval and dislike. It was most unsettling to discover that that was not the case.

They had reached a flame-red Alfa Romeo convertible, parked in the leafy shade of a fig tree. The top was already down and Guido dumped her cases in the back seat, then pulled the passenger door open for her.

He flicked her a glance. 'Get in,' he said.

Ronni got in, feeling a welcome dart of annoyance at the way he had issued that curt command. Maybe Jeff was right that the man was insufferable and she had simply been bowled over by his formidable good looks and by that quality of heady excitement he exuded. More fool me, she decided, slipping him a narrow glance, as he climbed into the driver's seat beside her.

'Is this your first trip to Sardinia?' Guido had switched on the engine, and now, with a soft purr, the car headed out on to the road.

'As a matter of fact, it is. Though, of course, I've been to Italy before.'

'Of course?' His tone was mocking. 'Why of course?'

'It was just a figure of speech.' Ronni scowled across at him, feeling another, even more satisfying, dart of annoyance. 'I was simply saying that I'm not a total stranger to your country.'

'Ah, but you are, if you've never been to Sardinia before.' Guido smiled, momentarily disarming her again. 'This island and mainland Italy have very little in common. Different landscape, different people, different culture, different everything.'

At least he was right about the landscape. Ronni detached her gaze from his in an effort to hold on to at least some of her displeasure and paused to glance curiously about her as the car sped along a dusty highway through a bright summer vista of parched scrubby fields. There was none of the green lushness of mainland Italy here.

She could even sense it in the air. This island was wild and different. The ragged mountains off in the distance were dark and mysterious, the equally ragged coastline full of secrets. She felt a flash of the excitement she had felt initially when this three weeks in Sardinia had been so unexpectedly sprung on her. For the past week she'd literally been counting the days.

'You know, you're very like your brother.' Suddenly Guido spoke. Ronni felt him flash a glance across at her. 'Same blonde hair, same blue eyes. I would have picked you out anywhere as being his sister. Were it not for certain agreeable female attributes, you could very nearly pass yourself off as his double.'

He let his gaze drift over those agreeable female attributes—the swell of her breasts beneath the simple cotton blouse, the curve of her hips currently sheathed in blue jeans. Then, lazily, he returned his gaze to her face again. 'You're virtually as alike as two peas in a pod.'

'I know.' Ronni smiled and hoped the flush in her cheeks could pass for a simple flush of pleasure. For she was pleased, just as she always was when people pointed out how much she looked like her adored older brother. Older by only nine months — they were virtually twins!

But the current flush in her cheeks had rather more to do with the boldly appraising way that Guido had just looked at her. That look had caused her blood to tingle!

She turned away and added, addressing the landscape, 'People have always said we look alike.'

'You certainly do.' His tone was light as he turned his attention back to the road again. And he seemed to be concentrating on his driving as a minute or two ticked by in silence. But then he elaborated in a tone that had a sudden edge to it, 'Let's just hope that's where the similarities end.'

'I beg your pardon?' Ronni swivelled round to look at him, her stomach tightening at the sudden dark note in his voice. A frown touched her brow. 'I'm sorry, I don't know what you mean.'

'I mean I hope all resemblance is purely physical. I hope you're not like your brother in other respects.'

'What other respects?'

'All other respects.' Guido flicked her a look. 'Particularly temperament.'

Ronni was taken aback. 'I don't know what you mean. What could you possibly think is wrong with my brother's temperament?'

'Everything.'

Ronni's eyes widened. 'Give me an example,' she challenged.

Guido smiled a small smile devoid of humour. 'I could give you a dozen different examples,' he told her, 'but here's a couple, just for starters. . . He's bolshie, he's unreliable and he's totally irresponsible.'

Ronni had never been able to hear a bad word against Jeff without leaping instantly to his defence. She did so now.

'I've never heard such nonsense! I can assure you my brother is none of these things!'

'Oh, yes, he is. I can assure you he's all of them.'

'You're just saying that because you don't like him!' Suddenly, she was remembering what Jeff had told her. 'You're just saying it because you've got it in for him!'

Guido smiled a grim smile. 'If I've got it in for him, it's because he's irresponsible, unreliable and bolshie.'

Then, before she could protest again, he turned to her and added, his eyes like steel traps in the dark lines of his face, 'And what at the moment is causing me some concern is one very simple but crucial question — are you bolshie, unreliable and irresponsible, too?'

'No, I'm not — no more than Jeff is!' Ronni glared at Guido. 'And, if you thought I might be, why did you hire me in the first place?'

At that moment, as she faced to him, waiting for an answer, Guido swung the steering-wheel round to negotiate a corner, barely bothering to decelerate at all as he did so — so that Ronni suddenly found herself lurching towards the dashboard. She glowered at him disapprovingly. Now who was being bolshie?

He flicked her a cool glance. 'If I'd known in time, I wouldn't have. Hired you, I mean,' he added in a steely tone, as she sat back into her seat again, thankful for seatbelts. 'But, unfortunately, this undesirable side to your brother's character only came to light *after* I'd hired you. You were virtually on your way over.'

'I see.' Ronni nodded. Things were falling into place. What Guido had just told her coincided with Jeff's story. It was only in the last week or so that the two of them had fallen out. But it had been a serious falling out. Bitter and acrimonious.

She felt a sudden flash of doubt, remembering the things Jeff had told her, and thought again what had occurred to her over that fateful cup of coffee. This assignment that, initially, had seemed simple and straightforward was turning out to be no such thing.

Perhaps she should just forget it and fly straight back to London. But how could she do that when she needed the money?

Ronni looked at Guido now from beneath her lashes, taking in the strong, mahogany-dark profile and remembering the story that Jeff had told her.

'Why do you disapprove of my brother's relationship with your cousin?' she asked him. 'Is it because she's from a rich family and my brother's only a mechanic?'

Guido did not answer her. Instead, he did another trick with the steering-wheel, making her lurch forward again as they turned off the road, between a pair of high wrought-iron gates, and headed up a tree-lined gravel driveway towards a fabulous, sprawling, red-roofed villa.

Ronni's jaw dropped open. Was this where Guido Falcone lived? She had never seen anything so magnificent in her life!

They came to a halt outside the front door flanked by huge stone urns overflowing with red geraniums. 'This is it.' Guido climbed out and snatched her cases from the back seat. 'Let's go in and meet my cousin, your pupil.'

The next moment Ronni was being led inside, into a huge tiled entrance hall with a round central table weighed down by an enormous vase of fresh flowers. Guido dropped her cases and strode across the tiled floor.

'Silvia!' he yelled. '*Silvia, dove sei?*'

For a moment there was only the echo of his voice, then there was a sudden shuffling sound as, through one of the open doorways, appeared the black-clad figure of a grey-haired woman. Ronni regarded her curiously. This was obviously not Silvia, Guido's cousin with whom Jeff had so unwisely fallen in love!

She watched as the woman muttered something in Italian and Guido responded with a couple of sharp questions. And she found herself smiling at the stark contrast between the two figures—the small passive figure of the elderly servant and the dynamic, vivid figure of the dark-haired man.

But then anyone would look passive—even a little lifeless—she decided, when placed in the shadow of a man like Guido. And, though she did not want to, again she felt a shiver of excitement. In spite of herself, as she watched him, she felt dangerously drawn.

As the woman shuffled off again, Guido spat an oath. Then he rounded on Ronni, as though she were to blame. 'Silvia's not here. I've been told she's gone into the village. If she's gone to see that brother of yours, I swear I'll break her neck!'

He looked as though he might. Sparks flew from his eyes that were suddenly as black and threatening as thunder.

'I can meet her when she gets back.' Ronni smiled a light smile, seeking to pour oil on troubled waters. 'Please don't worry on my account. It doesn't matter.'

'It does matter. I told her to be here! She had no business going off!'

'Maybe she got tired of waiting. After all, I was late.'

'She ought to have waited, just as I did.' Guido paused and the dark eyes seemed to pounce on her suddenly. 'Why are you defending her? Do you know something I don't? Do you know, for example, that she's gone off to meet your brother?'

Ronni shook her head. 'I don't know anything. And I wasn't trying to defend her.' She blushed suddenly. The only thing she'd been trying to do was calm Guido down and defuse the situation. Though why she'd been trying to do that, heaven only knew. She'd have done better to snap back at him the way he'd snapped at her!

Guido too obviously found her motives suspect. The dark eyes flayed her. 'Come with me,' he commanded. 'You and I should have a little chat.'

He swung on his heel then and strode across the hall, his steps a sharp tattoo against the polished tiles. Ronni followed in his wake, wondering what was coming next. Though there was one thing she was even more certain of than ever — this was no simple, straight-forward assignment she'd taken on. Anything but. It was a veritable hornets' nest! And again she wondered: would she be mad to stay?

'Take a seat. Would you like a drink?'

Suddenly they were in a huge, enchanting sitting-room, with the sun pouring in through the open French windows that gave a magnificent view out over the bay.

Only a stretch of exotic gardens separated the villa from the beach.

Guido was inviting her with a wave of his hand to take a seat on one of the sofas — there were four, all in soft pastel colours and piled with cushions. As Ronni chose one by the nearest window, he repeated his question. 'I know you've recently had a cup of coffee. . .but can I offer you a drink?'

His eyes held hers with a kind of taunting amusement. Then he surprised her. 'I can imagine what the real purpose of that coffee break was. . . No doubt to brief you in your role as romantic go-between.'

Ronni looked back at him blankly. 'I don't know what you're talking about. I understood my role here was supposed to be as a tutor, not as a romantic go-between, whatever that is.'

As he turned to face her, Ronni was suddenly wishing she hadn't sat down quite so hurriedly. Standing over her the way he was, he seemed far too imposing, far too dominant, far too overwhelming.

She straightened, stretching her neck as far as it would go, meeting his eyes, if not levelly, at least unwaveringly, as he answered, 'A romantic go-between is someone who helps set up romantic meetings. Someone who relays messages and passes on little notes. In short, *signorina*, a saboteur.'

'Sabotaging what precisely?'

'Sabotaging my expressed will. And I will not have a saboteur in this house.'

He held her gaze for a moment in an optical half-nelson. As he turned away, it took Ronni a moment to catch her breath and get her eyes back into focus.

She watched him as he crossed to a table where an

assortment of bottles and glasses were laid out. 'You're paranoid,' she said. 'I'm not a saboteur.'

He was pouring something. He flicked a glance across his shoulder. 'So, I'm paranoid, am I?' The notion seemed to amuse him. 'Well, I suppose that's possible. . .but what I think is more possible. . .' He turned and headed towards her, carrying two glasses. 'What I think is more possible is that I'm right.'

That figured. It was hard to imagine him ever thinking he might be wrong. All the same, Ronni insisted, 'I've come here solely as your cousin's tutor.'

Guido was standing over her now in that dominating way he had, making her sit up even straighter and stretch her neck even more.

He said, 'Since you failed to tell me what you wanted to drink, I've poured you a Cynar. I trust you like it.'

Ronni sniffed the dark brown brew. 'I've no idea,' she answered. 'And I was about to say I'd like a glass of mineral water.'

'Then you should have spoken up sooner. It's too late now.' With a look of satisfaction, he sat down on the sofa opposite her. 'She who hesitates, I'm afraid, just has to drink what she's given.'

'Or not, as the case may be.'

With a toss of her blonde head, Ronni laid her glass down pointedly on the coffee-table that stood between them. And again she found herself thinking that maybe Jeff had been right and Guido was simply an insufferable bully, the type of man it would be all too easy to fall out with.

Guido took a mouthful of his Cynar and seemed to savour it for a moment. He smiled across at her, seeming to guess what she was thinking and clearly not the least put out. On the contrary, Ronni sensed he relished this clash between them.

Then he laid down his glass. 'So, what was I saying. . .? Ah, yes. . .' He smiled again. 'I was accusing you of being a saboteur. . .'

'And I was telling you that such a suggestion was utter nonsense.'

As their eyes met and held across the coffee-table, Ronni felt a sudden sharp *frisson* go through her. There was something almost physically pleasurable about the sudden tension between them. Pleasurable and almost frighteningly exciting.

She pushed the feeling from her, for suddenly it did scare her a little. Then she told him calmly, shifting her gaze slightly, 'I can assure you I'm here for one reason and for one reason only. . .in order to help your cousin with her English.'

'Ah, yes, that's the pretext. I'm well aware of that. But I have a feeling you actually plan on doing very little tutoring.'

'You mean you think I'm out to cheat you? To take my fee for nothing? You think I intend to spend all my time passing love notes back and forward?' Ronni exhaled an impatient breath. 'That's not only ludicrous, it's also insulting!'

Her little outburst brought a smile to Guido's lips. He regarded her suddenly flushed, angry face. 'To listen to you, anyone would think you really took your job here seriously.'

'I do take it seriously. Of course I take it seriously. I'm an English teacher. That's my profession! It would be a little discreditable of me if I didn't take it seriously!'

'Discreditable. Yes, it would be.' He reached for his glass again. 'So, you really are a proper professional teacher? At least that's something in your favour.'

'And what is that supposed to mean?' Ronni glared at him. 'Didn't you know I was a proper professional teacher? Surely my brother told you that before you hired me?'

'Oh, yes, he told me all right. . .'

'But you didn't believe him?'

'No, I believed him. Otherwise, as you say, I would never have hired you. But I believed him *before* I found out about him and Silvia. *After* I found out, I wasn't so certain.'

'But Jeff would never have recommended me if I weren't a proper teacher! And I wouldn't have come. Neither of us is that irresponsible!'

Guido took a deliberately unhurried mouthful of Cynar. All the while his eyes never left Ronni's face. Then he swallowed and leaned back against the cushions of the sofa, stretching his long, white-clad legs out in front of him.

He's as relaxed as a cat, Ronni thought to herself, looking at him. But, like a cat, every muscle in that perfectly honed body of his is permanently coiled in perfect readiness to spring.

She watched him in reluctant fascination as he put to her, 'When it comes to being irresponsible, your brother, I'm afraid, has already proved himself to be in the top league.' He paused and sat forward ever so slightly in his seat. 'He tricked me into employing him to look after my boats simply in order to gain access to my cousin. And then he likewise tricked me into employing you as her tutor in order that he could continue to divert her from her studies.' He smiled a grim smile. 'But he will not succeed.'

'I find this all rather insulting, as I've already told you.' Ronni sat slightly forward in her own seat to face him. 'The reason I'm here is because my brother phoned me and told me your cousin was in urgent need of a tutor. The one you'd booked for the summer had apparently dropped out.'

'Dropped out, indeed.' Guido did not sound pleased. 'And just a week before she was due to start.'

Ronni nodded. That was precisely the story Jeff had told her. 'Jeff told me he'd had a word with you about me and told you I had lots of experience teaching English to foreign students and that you wanted me to come and do the job.'

She paused and fixed Guido with an irritated look. 'My brother said nothing to me about acting as a romantic go-between. All he seemed concerned about was finding a new tutor for Silvia.'

Guido treated her to a long look between narrowed dark eyes. 'And did he also by any chance happen to tell you that he and Silvia were romantically involved?'

'You mean before I came here?'

'Yes, before you came here.'

Ronni shook her head. 'No, he didn't,' she had to confess. 'He didn't mention anything about that before I arrived.'

'I see.' Guido seemed to think about that for a moment. 'So, he waited till you were here before telling you the whole story.' He smiled a tight, dark, un-amused smile. 'Now I know what passed between you over that cup of coffee.'

He was spot-on about that. Ronni couldn't deny it.

During that half-hour coffee break Jeff had told her all about Silvia and about how Guido was trying to break up the romance.

'But that was all that passed between us,' Ronni hastily assured Guido. 'He didn't try to talk me into acting as a romantic go-between.'

'Are you sure about that?' Still he did not believe her.

Ronni flared with annoyance. 'Yes, of course I'm sure!'

'Absolutely sure?' His eyes drove through her.

'Absolutely sure!' Her eyes drove right back at him.

There was a silence as they glared at one another across the coffee-table. Then Guido said softly, 'OK, let's say I believe you. . . Let's say I believe that he's said nothing to you so far about the part he's hoping you'll play. . .' He leaned closer towards her, his elbows resting on his thighs, causing Ronni to flatten back a little defensively in her seat. 'The fact remains that, sooner or later, he will approach you. . .'

'That's nonsense. Jeff's not like that. If he loves Silvia the way he says he does, he'll want her to study, not skive off and waste time!'

'How little you know about love.' Guido paused and smiled a crude smile that suggested that the same could never be said about him. Then he continued, his tone scathing, 'You can take my word for it, the kind of love your brother feels for my cousin is the selfish kind that demands she spend every moment with him. He doesn't give a damn about her studies. Wasting her time is precisely what he has in mind for her.

'And I will not allow it!' He rose to his feet abruptly. 'I've promised her mother that Silvia will continue with her studies while she's staying here on holiday and pass the exams she's already failed once. And I intend to keep that promise.'

'And that's what I'm here for.' Ronni looked into his angry face. 'To help her pass these exams is the very job I've come to do.'

'Yes, it is. At least, it's the job I'm paying you to do.' Guido paused, holding on to his anger for a moment. Then he smiled, a smile Ronni found oddly chilling. 'I've had an idea,' he said. 'Here's what we'll do. . .'

He circled the coffee-table and came to stand before her. 'Since you claim that your objectives are the same as mine, and that you're not here to work against me, as I'd supposed, I'm going to put you in charge, as it were. . .make you responsible. . .'

Ronni swallowed, suddenly nervous. 'Responsible for what?'

'For Silvia's studies, and for her passing her exams. These are to be your twin responsibilities. If she doesn't study, you don't get paid. Not a single penny.'

That didn't sound fair. Ronni said so. 'I don't like the sound of that at all.'

'Don't you? Then try this.' Guido cast a harsh look down on her. 'Not only will *you* not get paid one penny, but your darling brother will lose his job — and, into the bargain, never work in Italy again.' He smiled down at her coldly. 'I can do that,' he told her.

Ronni did not doubt it. She felt a shiver go through her. Without thinking what she was doing, she reached for her glass and took a swig of the bitter Cynar. She was still grimacing from the shock of it as Guido swept from the room, announcing over his shoulder, 'So, you'd better deliver the goods — or else I will!'

CHAPTER TWO

'I DON'T see why I should be held hostage over your quarrel with my brother!'

Ronni had followed Guido from the room, running to keep pace with him as he headed across the hall. His naturally long strides, she suspected, he was deliberately making even longer in order to make it difficult for her to catch up!

She was breathless when she did catch up with him outside on the front doorstep. Between snatched breaths, she told him, 'I can't accept these conditions of yours. They're totally unfair. I demand to be paid for the hours I put in, whether your cousin passes her exams or not!'

'My, you're out of shape.'

Guido had come to a halt, turning round to face her so that she almost ran right into him. And from this close Ronni could see that the lashes that framed his eyes were as thick and sooty as a chimney-sweep's brush. He ought to have a licence for eyelashes like that!

It took a considerable effort to rip her eyes away. 'What did you say?' she demanded, still gasping a little.

'I said you're pretty out of shape.' Guido had thrust his hands into the pockets of his white trousers. He was looking down at her with a superior, amused smile on his face. 'You only ran five metres and you're panting fit for the knacker's yard.'

'I am nothing of the sort! That's a gross exaggeration.' Then Ronni conceded as her chest continued to heave, 'I may be just a little out of breath.'

'English understatement.' Guido laughed at that, and he had the most musical, most delightfully appealing laugh, Ronni thought. 'I would say it's quite a while since you did any exercise.'

'I suppose it is.' She could not dispute it. And, frankly, she hadn't realised just how out of shape she was!

'It's that unhealthy London life you lead.' Guido flicked his gaze over her as he leaned against one of the geranium-filled stone urns. 'All that sitting behind desks and riding around in tube trains. . .it's not good for you. You should take up some form of exercise.'

'Should I?' Ronni folded her arms across her chest and tried to fix a disapproving scowl to her face. Who was he, after all, to tell her what she ought to do?

But it was hard to scowl, she found, when her heart was suddenly skittering at the way the dark eyes were quite openly smiling as they continued to focus on her now lightly rising bosom. In truth, she felt like smiling back.

Then he looked into her face, folding his own arms across his chest—arms that against the faded T-shirt were mahogany-dark. He said, 'At least in that respect you're not like your brother. Jeff is one of the most sporty guys I know.'

'He always has been.' As she said it, Ronni frowned. Once, she had been as sporty as her brother. She wasn't quite sure why that had changed. Maybe it had something to do with Arnie.

'Never mind,' Guido was saying, 'this is the perfect

place for you to get in a bit of physical training. You can sail, you can ride. . .snorkel, swim. . . You can even do a bit of water-skiing if you fancy it.'

'Sounds good.' Ronni did smile then. Then suddenly she remembered. More soberly, she added, 'But who said I'll be staying?'

'Why, aren't you?'

'I may not be.'

'And why might that be?'

'I told you, I find your conditions unacceptable. I won't be held hostage to your quarrel with Jeff.'

'You're not being held hostage. No need to dramatise.' Guido smiled, lifting one eyebrow, and watched her for a moment. His curly dark hair gleamed even darker and glossier against the backdrop of red geraniums. It was the glossiest, darkest hair that Ronni had ever seen.

He continued. 'All I'm demanding is that you be the guarantor of your brother's good behaviour. You seem so certain he has only my cousin's best interests at heart. It seems a perfectly good arrangement to put you in charge.'

'It doesn't seem so to me.' Ronni tilted her chin at him. 'Why should I agree to only being paid if your cousin passes her exams?' That's ludicrous. I can't agree.'

She meant that absolutely. But she was bluffing as she added, 'I'd rather just go home.' How could she just go home when she needed the money?

'Don't you believe in payment by results? That's the way things operate in my line of work. If I don't deliver the goods, I don't get any money, In business you get paid for results, not for the hours you put in.'

Ronni looked at him. On the evidence, he was good at getting results. According to Jeff, he was one of the most successful businessmen in Italy. And this villa was certainly a testament to that. Nobody lived like this on a hired hand's hourly wage.

'But teaching's different,' she told him. 'Sometimes one doesn't get results, or at least sometimes the results are hard to measure. If teachers only got paid for pupils passing their exams, there are some pupils who'd never get any education at all. No teacher would want to take them on.'

'Are you saying that's why you don't want to take Silvia on? Because you think she may not be capable of passing her exams?'

Ronni shrugged. 'For all I know, that might very well be the case.'

'Well, it isn't. I can assure you she's a very bright girl. All she needs is a few weeks of expert tuition.' Guido paused and shifted his weight slightly against the stone urn. 'Maybe it's you who's not up to it? Maybe that's what you're afraid of?'

Ronni had the distinct sensation that she was being cleverly manipulated into a defensive little corner. She narrowed her eyes at Guido. Yes, he was clever all right. No wonder he got such spectacular results at business!

She said, regarding him levelly, her tone not at all defensive — all she was doing was stating a simple fact, 'No, I'm not afraid of that. I'm a damned good teacher.' She took pride in her expertise. She'd worked hard to achieve it. 'I'm a teacher with a very good record of getting results — even though I don't get paid on the strength of them.'

'*Touché*!' Guido smiled. 'Then you've nothing to be afraid of.' He straightened away from the stone urn and slipped his hands back into his trouser pockets. 'I may even give you a bonus if Silvia does well in her exams.'

'I don't need a bonus. If she does well, it'll be because she's worked for it. All I require is the payment we agreed on.'

'Does that mean you're staying?'

'I didn't say that. I'll agree to stay when you lift these stupid conditions.'

Guido shook his head slowly as he looked back at her. 'So you keep saying, but I think you'll stay anyway.'

'And why would I do that when I find your terms unacceptable?'

Guido smiled. 'Because you need the money.'

'Who says I do?' She felt suddenly at a disadvantage. It was perfectly true, but she hadn't known he knew.

Still smiling, still watching her, Guido reached unhurriedly behind him and detached a stem of bright red geranium. He said, 'Your brother told me. He said this job was a godsend for you, that you couldn't have managed financially without it.'

Jeff and his big mouth! Ronni scowled at Guido mutinously, as he raised the red geranium to his nose. 'I could have managed perfectly well without it.'

That was not strictly true, though she might have scraped by if she'd been prepared to go into debt. The summer school job that she'd been relying on had been cancelled at the very last minute and other temporary jobs were a bit thin on the ground. She'd been close to panicking when Jeff had phoned her about the Sardinia stint.

Guido rolled the red geranium stem between his fingers. 'Jeff told me you promised your parents that you'd treat them to a holiday this autumn in celebration of their twenty-fifth wedding anniversary — but that now you're starting to worry about how you're going to pay for it. It seems you find yourself rather short of funds. . .' He raised one eyebrow. 'Have I got the story right?'

'Yes, more or less.' Damn Jeff for snitching! 'I suppose that's more or less how it is.'

Guido continued to watch her. 'I would say that was rather —— '

'Bad planning. I know.' Now she did sound defensive. 'It was rash of me to promise when I'm constantly so strapped for cash.' That was what Arnie had said and Arnie was right. She flicked a look at Guido. 'I know what you were going to say.'

'Well, I wasn't going to say that.' Guido twirled the geranium, both eyebrows lifted now as the dark eyes watched her.

'Well, what were you going to say? Something equally damning, no doubt.'

'What I was going to say was that I think that's rather sweet of you. That's a very generous thing for a daughter to do for her parents.'

Ronni was taken aback. He didn't appear to be joking. 'They deserve it,' she muttered, as he suddenly leaned towards her, holding the red geranium to her nose.

'Smell that,' he told her. 'Doesn't it smell good?'

Suddenly, Ronni seemed to freeze. She couldn't

smell a thing. Well, she could, but it certainly wasn't the geranium. All she could smell was the clean masculine scent of Guido's skin. It seemed to rush up her nostrils and enter her bloodstream.

'Not the flower, the leaves,' he was saying. 'They're scented. Can you smell them?' He continued to hold the stem to her nose. 'Go on, take a good sniff.'

Ronni took a good sniff. 'Yes, I can smell it.'

Guido smiled. 'It smells almost as sweet as you.' Then, still smiling and holding her confused startled gaze, he brushed her cheek softly with the head of the flower, almost as though he was bestowing a caress, before leaning forward and tucking the stem behind her ear. 'There. Now you look like a Botticelli nymph.'

Ronni's tongue all at once was glued to her palate. She was aware that her heart was clattering inside her, racketing against her ribs like a demented steam train. Her skin was burning where his fingers had touched her. Her legs were threatening to give way at the knees.

'So, you really have to take this job, as I see it.' Guido leaned back against the stone urn again. 'You can't disappoint your parents and renege on their holiday.'

'I can find some other way of paying for it, however.' He was cornering her again and she didn't like it. Ronni pulled herself together and looked him in the eye. 'For a start, I can find something where payment is guaranteed.'

'Payment is guaranteed on this job — if you deliver.'

'You mean, if I agree to play the gaoler. I'm sorry, but I don't find that a very attractive prospect.'

'And if you deliver, you'll also be guaranteeing your

brother's job. Let's not forget about that aspect as well.'

Ronni hadn't forgotten. 'I can't take that responsibility. And I shouldn't have to,' she added sharply. 'Jeff's job shouldn't depend on your cousin passing her exams.'

'Perhaps it shouldn't, but it does.' He was immovable. 'You see, if she fails, it'll be down to Jeff—and you.'

'No, it won't. It'll be her own fault. She's not a child.' Jeff had told her Silvia was nineteen, only four years younger than herself. 'She's old enough to know what she's doing.'

'She was until a short while ago, until she met your brother.' Suddenly, abruptly, Guido's demeanour had altered. 'But these days—and heaven knows why!—all she thinks about is Jeff!' With the toe of his shoe he kicked a loose pebble on the path, sending it spinning and ricocheting over a nearby flowerbed. 'I wish I'd never employed him in the first place!'

Ronni looked into his angry face and felt a rush of defensiveness for Jeff. 'I imagine you employed him,' she rebuked him tightly, 'because he happens to be a first-class mechanic.' She straightened. 'He's also an extremely nice person, which is probably why your cousin fell for him.'

'An extremely nice person!' Guido's tone was dismissive. 'Well, he's here to look after my boat, not to go sniffing around my cousin!'

There was something about his tone that lifted Ronni's hackles. 'What have you really got against my brother? Is it because he's just a mechanic? Do you think he's not good enough for your cousin?'

'I think he's got no damned business playing around with Silvia. She's cut out for better things than wasting her time on some blue-eyed, grease-stained English Romeo.' He kicked another stone, which went rocketing after the first one. 'Damn him!' he muttered. 'Why did he have to come here?'

As Ronni watched him, jolted a little by this show of anger, she reflected that it was a blessing this wasn't Jeff's only job. Her brother earned his living by hiring himself out to whoever needed his services on the island. Fortunately, he didn't depend on Guido Falcone.

Then she remembered Guido's threat that he could stop him working anywhere in Italy, and suddenly she didn't feel quite so relieved any more.

She decided to try a more placatory approach. In an even tone, she told Guido, 'I don't know why you're getting so upset. All it is is a harmless holiday romance. What's the matter? Don't you approve of romance?'

'I don't approve of romance that's misguided and inappropriate.' His eyes were suddenly as sharp as daggers. They cut through her impatiently. 'I suppose you do?'

Ronni shrugged. 'Who are you to tell if it's misguided and inappropriate? Only the people involved can tell.'

'How very touching.' Guido's tone was cutting. 'Romance is all, is it? Is that what you believe? You'll be telling me next I'm wrong to interfere.'

'Maybe you are. Maybe at this point in her life what your cousin needs is a bit of romance.' Her previous placatory approach had failed, so now she might as well just say what she believed.

'Maybe her studies ought to wait till another time,'

she added. 'You might even be doing her harm by trying to interfere.'

'You think Jeff's a more worthwhile investment of her time than her studies?' Guido shook his head. 'Sorry, I can't agree.'

'I'm not talking about investments — except maybe in an emotional sense. Not everything comes down to monetary profit and loss, you know.'

Guido smiled and shook his head. 'My, you are a romantic.'

'And you're not, I suppose?'

'Definitely not. Not guilty. I would say I have a more practical turn of mind.'

'That sounds like a euphemism.' Ronni felt oddly disappointed. 'It sounds as though you really do believe that everything comes down to monetary profit and loss.'

'We can't all be starry-eyed romantics like you.' Guido paused for an instant, then added, smiling, 'I expect that's why your personal monetary situation is rather more loss than profit at the moment — because you invest so much of your time in romance?'

Ronni laughed at that, then wished she hadn't. She was aware of the speculative lift of his jet-black eyebrows. And her reaction had been rather revealing, she was thinking. And not only revealing, a little disloyal. What was Arnie if not a romantic investment?

She said quickly, covering up, 'My monetary situation is due to the fact that I'm a poorly paid teacher. I'm afraid it really is as simple as that.'

But Guido ignored that. 'You surprise me. I've been told you have a steady boyfriend. . . I would have thought romance would take up a lot of your time.'

'Would you?'

'But it would seem not. Why on earth is that?'

'Well, it does and it doesn't.' Ronni felt uncomfortable. The subject of Arnie was not one she wished to discuss with Guido. Guido would never understand her relationship with Arnie.

She added a little tightly. 'I've known Arnie for ages. We don't have one of those starry-eyed relationships.'

'I see. The gilt's worn off?'

'I didn't mean that. I just mean we have a relaxed, easygoing sort of relationship. We don't live in each other's pockets. We give each other space.'

'Space to do what?'

'To do whatever we please.' As one dark eyebrow lifted, she added hurriedly, 'Within limits, naturally. We don't cheat on one another.'

'Well, that's something, I suppose.' As a smile touched his lips, it was hard to figure out what he was thinking. Then suddenly his expression changed. 'So, though there are no stars in your eyes, you consider yourself beyond temptation?'

In that moment what was in his mind was written clearly in his eyes. Or so, at least, it seemed to Ronni. An invitation. A challenge. That was what she saw. And what she felt was an instant answering rush in her blood.

A little shocked at herself, she quickly snatched her gaze away. But not before she had answered in a firm tone, 'Definitely.'

The next moment, thankfully, they were interrupted.

'*Guido*! *Eccoti*! *Ti ho cercato dappertutto*!'

Suddenly, through the front door came bursting like a tornado the lithe, dark-haired figure of a girl in a blue mini-skirt. She came to a skidding stop in front of

Guido and Ronni, her lovely bright-eyed face breaking into a huge smile.

'You're Ronni! Jeff's sister!' She reached out for Ronni's hand and shook it. 'Wow! You're so like him. The two of you could be twins.'

Ronni shook her hand warmly, instantly liking her. 'And you must be Silvia. I'm very pleased to meet you.'

Then Guido spoke. 'You said you were looking for me.' His tone was censorious, putting an instant damper on the moment. He straightened and confronted Silvia. 'What did you want?'

Silvia tossed back her dark hair, a gesture that was openly defiant. 'I wasn't really looking for you, I was looking for Ronni.' She turned back to Ronni. 'I want to apologise. I should have been here to meet you, but you were late arriving and I had an appointment in the village.' She smiled a seductive smile. 'I'm really sorry.'

'That's OK. It was my fault for being late.' Ronni cast a quick, knowing glance at Guido, expecting to meet a pair of scowling dark eyes. But his eyes were far from scowling. They were turned on Silvia and they were filled with a look of oddly vulnerable concern. It was a look that caused Ronni's heart to tighten. He obviously loved his young cousin very much.

'I can't get over how much you look like Jeff!' Silvia's eyes were dancing as she looked into Ronni's face. Then she laughed, 'You're his double — apart from the red geranium! I can't say I've ever seen Jeff with a geranium stuck behind his ear!'

Ronni had entirely forgotten about the red geranium that Guido had slipped behind her ear. She reached for it now in sudden embarrassment, her cheeks turning as red as its flaming petals.

'How silly I must look,' she muttered, removing it.

'It didn't look silly at all. It looked beautiful,' Silvia protested.

'I already told her it made her look like a Botticelli nymph.'

As Guido spoke, his eyes met Ronni's, making her blush deepen. He had spoken the compliment as though he really meant it, just as he had the first time he'd said it. Ronni wouldn't have minded if it had been a less gracious compliment. It would have been rather nice if it hadn't just been a joke.

'Come with me.' Silvia had taken her arm. 'Let me show you the house and where we're going to be working. I'll show you your room, too, if Guido hasn't already.'

'No, he hasn't.' Ronni hesitated and caught Guido's eye. You and I, she reminded him silently, have unfinished business. We still have to work out the terms of my contract. For, though she wanted to take the job on now that she'd met Silvia, she was still not prepared to acept Guido's conditions. As Silvia led her away, she told him over her shoulder, 'We can continue our conversation later.'

Guido simply winked back at her and told Silvia with a smile, as he headed off across the garden, 'Be sure to show her the games room while you're at it. She's very keen to get in shape while she's here.'

Impudent devil, Ronni thought to herself, as she headed with Silvia towards the villa. But she was smiling, an amused, lightly tolerant smile. And in her hand she was still holding the red geranium.

* * *

'And this is your room. Do you like it?' Silvia perched herself with a broad smile on the edge of the bed. 'I picked it for you because Jeff told me that blue's your favourite colour.'

'It's a gorgeous room. I absolutely love it.' Ronni stood and stared round her, eyes wide with pleasure. 'And you're right, blue is my favourite colour.'

Here in this room was virtually every shade of that colour — from the cobalt-blue draperies, scattered with little hyacinth flowers, to the sapphire-blue cushions scattered over the bed and the powder-blue carpet, thick and soft beneath her feet.

It was a dream room, she thought — as well as a room to dream in. But then the entire house, with its views out over the bay and the stunningly wild country-side, was a dream.

'Note the double bed.' Silvia patted the hyacinth bedspread and giggled as she gave the mattress a little bounce. 'I thought you ought to have a room with a double bed, for when your boyfriend comes to visit you.'

'Arnie? Oh, he won't be coming.' Ronni flushed to her hair roots, as Silvia continued to bounce and grin across at her.

'Not coming?'

'No. He's teaching summer school in Bradford — that's a town in the north of England.'

'And he won't be coming to see you? Not even for a weekend?'

'I shouldn't think so.' Ronni shook her head. Then she added, 'Well, I'm only going to be here for three weeks.'

'I don't know how you can bear that.' Silvia's grin

had vanished. She was looking at Ronni now in stupefied horror. 'I couldn't bear to be separated from Jeff for three weeks. A couple of hours is almost more than I can stand!'

'Well, it's different for Arnie and me. We've known each other for two years.' Ronni smiled. This was a rehash of her conversation with Guido, only now she didn't feel uncomfortable touching on the subject of Arnie.

She added sagely, 'Arnie and I are used to separations, and we know nothing's going to happen just because we're apart for a while.'

'But don't you miss him?'

'Of course I miss him.' As Silvia continued to inflict on her that look of pained horror, Ronni folded her arms and assumed a school-teacherish expression. 'But neither of us allows our feelings for the other to get in the way of all the things we have to do. That's why he's in Bradford right now and I'm here in Sardinia— because each of us has to make a living.'

She kept her eyes fixed on Silvia and smiled a mock-stern smile. 'Just as you're going to have to endure being separated from Jeff every day—at least for a few hours, while we do our English lessons.'

'I want to talk to you about that.' Silvia jumped up from the bed. 'Guido says I have to do six hours every day. Three in the morning and three in the afternoon.' She made a face. 'Don't you think that's too much?'

'Quite frankly, I don't.'

At least on this she agreed with Guido. Silvia's spoken English, as she had heard for herself, was excellent, but she'd had dreadfully poor results in her

written papers. She was going to need every moment
of tutoring over the next three weeks.

Ronni told her, 'I think you're going to need six
hours a day.'

Silvia threw her a pained look as she came to stand
before her. 'I think it's too much.' Then she smiled
seductively. 'Look, Guido will never know whether
we're studying or not. He's so preoccupied with his
wretched speedboat race. . . Every afternoon he's out
at sea doing practice runs. . . That's all he ever thinks
about these days.'

Little minx, Ronni thought, as she looked into
Silvia's cajoling face. So Guido hadn't been entirely
wrong, after all!

She said, 'It doesn't matter whether Guido knows or
not. I'm contracted to tutor you for so many hours a
day, and I'm afraid I must insist on fulfilling my
contract.'

Then she added, suddenly curious, 'What's this
speedboat race Guido's involved in?' Jeff had mentioned it to her fleetingly, but hadn't gone into details.

Silvia made a face. 'The qualifying trials are in three
weeks' time — the day after my wretched exams, would
you believe? The race itself is a couple of weeks after
that.

'It's an annual thing,' she continued, 'organised
locally. Guido's won it for the past two years and he's
absolutely desperate to get a hat trick — though some
of his rivals are equally desperate to see that he
doesn't.'

Ronni listened with interest. So, this was something
else to add to the list of things that Guido cared about.
In addition to getting his own way, monetary profits

and his cousin Silvia, he also cared about winning races. She found herself wondering, curiously, what she would discover next.

Silvia was glancing at her watch. 'Look, I've got to go now. I'm meeting your brother in half an hour.' Then she bent down suddenly. 'Oh, look, you've dropped this!' She stood up, holding aloft the red geranium that had somehow slipped from Ronni's hand.

With a laugh, Silvia leaned and slipped it behind Ronni's ear. 'Don't forget you're having dinner with Jeff and me tonight.' Then she deliberately held Ronni's eyes for a moment. 'Think about what I said about the lessons. I'm sure we can come to some arrangement.'

Then, before Ronni could say a word, she was heading, laughing, for the door. 'Guido was right, you look just like a Botticelli nymph!'

Ronni stood and watched the empty doorway for a moment, feeling a little as though she'd just encountered a whirlwind. Then with a sigh she sank on to the hyacinth-coloured bedspread, feeling the soft springs of the mattress bounce beneath her weight.

'What have I got myself into?' she wondered aloud. 'I'm going to be piggy in the middle between Guido and Silvia. I'll never make it through the three weeks in one piece!'

She slid the geranium from her ear and stared at it for a moment, then shifted her gaze to her still unpacked cases by the door. Perhaps, in spite of the fact that she did need the money, what she ought to do was just catch the first plane back home.

But that was when a shadow suddenly fell across the

doorway. Ronni glanced up to see Guido standing there watching her.

'I want to speak to you,' he told her brusquely. 'Be down in the drawing-room in an hour.'

CHAPTER THREE

'WELL, have you got settled in OK? Unpacked your bags? Made yourself at home?'

Guido was standing by the bar table when Ronni walked into the drawing-room, pouring himself a generous measure of whisky. He paused to glance at her over his shoulder. 'I can see you've at least done some unpacking. That's a very pretty dress you're wearing. The colour suits you.'

Ronni fought back a blush. The compliment had foolishly pleased her. 'I'm having dinner with Jeff,' she said. 'Jeff and Silvia.'

'I see.' Guido took a mouthful of his whisky, his eyes scanning her amusedly over the top of his glass. 'How very disappointing. I thought your efforts were for me.'

'For you? Good grief!' Ronni felt thrown for a moment. Had he really thought that or was he joking? Then she tossed her head at him. 'No, I'm afraid not. Though I can see why you must find that disappointing. . .' she let her gaze drift over his white trousers and faded T-shirt, the same white trousers and faded T-shirt he'd been wearing earlier '. . .after all the trouble you've gone to changing for me.'

Guido laughed at that. 'Do I detect a hint of criticism? Perhaps you feel I'm slacking in my role as host? Allow me to make amends.' He waved a hand at the bar table and the array of bottles and glasses laid out there. 'Tell me what you'd like to drink.'

This time Ronni didn't hesitate. She had learned what happened to those who did!

'A glass of wine, please,' she said.

'Red or white?'

'Dry white, if you have it.'

'Of course I have it.' He paused and smiled at her. 'And, even if I didn't, for you, *signorina*, I'd immediately send down to the cellar to get it.'

He was joking, half flirting, stirring an intimacy between them that had sent a flickering response, like warm fingers, down Ronni's spine. It was an effort to sound scathing as she remarked, 'How very gallant.'

'A national characteristic.' Guido poured her wine and held it out to her. 'Like all Sards, I'm well known for my gallantry.'

Ronni took the glass, carefully avoiding his fingers. All at once, though she was fighting it, she was overwhelmingly conscious of how dark and wild-looking and exciting he was, with his black hair spilling in curls over his ears and forehead, the short-sleeved T-shirt exposing the mahogany of his arms and the slim white trousers moulding the muscular lines of his legs. His vibrancy and the way he drew her took her breath away.

And it struck her that he was indeed a son of this wild island, which she had glimpsed so far only briefly, yet which had struck her so vividly. And it was this untamed quality, not his gallantry, that seemed to her characteristically Sardinian!

She said, once more trying her best to sound scathing, but sensing strongly that she was only half succeeding, 'I'm glad to hear you have some redeeming features.'

'Oh, I have many.' Guido seated himself on the arm of a nearby armchair and looked at her with amusement in his eyes. 'Thought I can't say that redemption is something that preoccupies me greatly.'

'No, I don't expect it does.' It hardly needed saying. He had the shamelessly sensuous look of a man for whom being saved from his sins was the last thing on his mind.

Ronni took a mouthful of her drink, suddenly dry-mouthed at the thought of that. 'Why did you want to see me?' She glanced at her watch nervously. 'I don't have much time. I'll be going out soon.'

'Not with Jeff and Silvia, you won't.'

'Yes, I will. Jeff's going to call me.'

Guido shook his head. 'I very much doubt it. I'd forget about dinner with those two, if I were you.'

'And why do you say that?'

'They'll be too busy consoling each other and agreeing with each other about what a bastard I am.' He took an unconcerned mouthful of his whisky and rolled it in his mouth as he smiled and told her, 'Alas, you see, your brother and I have crossed swords again.'

'You've had another fight? What about? About Silvia again?'

'No, not about Silvia again. Silvia's not the only thing we fight about. Your brother and I fight about just about everything.'

'That must be your fault. Jeff's not a quarrelsome person. I've never had a quarrel with him in my life.'

'That's because you're so much like him.' Guido stretched his legs in front of him and crossed his canvas-shod feet at the ankles. 'Although, in spite of that fact and in spite of my initial fears, I think that you and I can probably manage to get along. You're definitely less bolshie than your brother.'

Ronni wasn't quite sure how she felt about that judgement. In a way it made her feel like a traitor to her brother. Was she being overly accommodating with Guido, she wondered, because of this strange effect he had on her? Had he grown to think she would meekly do his bidding? Well, he had another think coming if he did!

She proceeded to show him she could be bolshie when she wished. 'The problem of our getting along may not arise,' she informed him. She straightened where she stood and regarded his feet critically. They were placed now just a little too close to her own. 'It may not arise because I may not be staying.'

Guido swirled his drink and took another mouthful. 'You have to stay. You need the money.'

'Not that badly.' In truth, she was still undecided. She looked down into his face with its hard dark lines. 'I'm only staying if you *guarantee* that you're going to pay me.'

'We've been over that already. I do guarantee it — just so long as Silvia passes her exams.'

'And we've also been over the fact that I can't accept conditions. I have to be paid whether she passes her exams or not.'

'Absolutely not.' Guido shook his head. Then he shifted and leaned back against the back of the chair. 'You've met Silvia now. You can tell she's a bright girl. If you're a half-decent teacher, she should have no difficulty in passing.'

'Yes, if she studies.'

'It's your job to see she does.'

'I'm a teacher, not a gaoler. She has to want to study.'

'And you're not convinced she does?'

As his eyes fixed on her, Ronni hesitated for a moment, uncertain of how to combine honesty and diplomacy in her answer. She'd taken a liking to Silvia and had no wish to betray her and get her into trouble with her quarrelsome cousin. For, after all, though she'd talked about 'coming to an arrangement', Ronni had no reason to suspect that Silvia wasn't serious about her studies, and it would be wrong of her to give Guido that impression.

So she said, 'I haven't had a chance to make up my mind yet, but I have no reason not to give her the benefit of the doubt.'

'She hasn't got to you yet, then?' Guido leaned forward. 'That was why I wanted to speak to you — to find out, if during your time together, she'd managed to corrupt you.'

'No, she hasn't.' Ronni looked back at him and was aware of a flicker inside her as she suddenly caught sight of those wonderful eyelashes. Seen from above they were twice as wonderful, seeming to sweep across his cheekbones like silky black feathers. They're extraordinary, she reflected. She longed to reach out and touch them.

She resisted the urge. She said, 'Anyway, I'm incorruptible.'

'Even for the sake of love?' Guido sat back a little, mercifully obscuring his eyelashes in shadow. 'I thought you believed love should be allowed to flourish unrestrained?'

Ronni shrugged. 'I suppose I do.'

'So, you're not sure any more?'

'I didn't say I wasn't sure. I just wonder what you're getting at.' She fixed him with a look and shifted her weight. 'I think you're trying to trip me up.'

'Trip you up? Good heavens, no. I'm just trying to find out to what extent I can trust you to keep my cousin's best interests at heart. And, by best interests, as you know, I mean her studies, not her love life.'

He held her eyes a moment, drained his glass and laid it down. 'You see, if I decide I can't trust you, I'll have to resort to certain measures.'

'Certain measures?' That sounded ominous. 'What sort of certain measures?'

'Very simple. I'll have to keep an eye on you. A very close eye indeed.'

'Meaning?'

'Meaning that *I'll* have to act as gaoler, clocking my cousin in and out of lessons, even sitting in on your classes should that prove to be necessary.'

Ronni blinked at him. 'Would you really go to such lengths?'

'If I thought I had no choice. Silvia *has* to pass those exams of hers. I've given my word to her mother that I will see to it that she does—she wouldn't have been allowed to come here on holiday otherwise, she would have been shut up in her mother's apartment in Rome.' He smiled grimly. 'And I intend to keep my word.'

He uncrossed his feet and began to stand up. 'You see, the problem isn't that I don't want to pay you your salary. I want you to have that money as much as you do. I want Silvia to pass those wretched exams of hers.'

Then he paused as he stood there, dark eyes looking down at her. And suddenly he smiled, his expression softening as he reached out to brush her cheek with a long brown finger. 'And I want your parents to have their holiday.'

Ronni felt her heart give a sudden leap inside her. She could barely focus as she forced herself to look back at him.

'And there are two ways we can do it.' His finger still lingered, scorching the soft skin of her cheek like a hot iron. 'I can either trust you and allow you to take charge of the whole business, or I can decide you're not to be trusted and take charge of things myself. I've told you what that would involve, and I don't think either of us really wants that.'

His finger slid down under her chin and tilted her head to look at him. He held her eyes. 'So, which is it to be?'

Ronni swallowed. 'You can trust me.'

'You're quite sure of that?'

'Yes, you can trust me.'

'And, if you have any problems, you'll come and tell me?' Still he held her chin. 'Can I trust you to do that, too?'

'If it means the difference between being paid and not being paid, of course you can. I have no desire to be watched over as though I were a child—but I promise I'll let you know if I have any problems.'

'Good. So, that's settled.' At last he released her. He stepped away with a smile. 'I feel much happier now.'

Ronni couldn't quite say the same. She felt reassured, but deeply unsettled. At last it looked as though her fee was guaranteed—even if it might mean being constantly shadowed by Guido. But suddenly she was filled with another fear—about the wisdom of staying on in such close proximity with him.

It wasn't right the way her heart had leapt when he'd touched her. And the way her skin had smouldered, and continued to smoulder, even now.

She cast such thoughts from her. 'Yes,' she said, 'it's settled.' She felt a flickering sense of danger as she spoke the words.

'So, what are you going to do now?'

'Now?' Ronni looked at him. She was still having difficulty gathering her thoughts together.

Guido glanced at his watch. 'It's now half-past seven, and I can't see any sign of your phone call from Jeff.'

Ronni had forgotten about her phone call, but now she remembered. 'There's plenty of time,' she said, reflecting to herself that she'd expected to hear from Jeff long before now. She took a mouthful of her wine. 'He'll ring any minute.'

'I'll bet you anything he won't. I already told you, he and Silvia will be far too busy consoling each other over me.'

Yes, he had told her that, but Ronni dismissed the idea. 'He said he'll call, so he'll call,' she insisted.

Guido laughed. 'He said he'd pick up a spare part for me today, and he hasn't, which is why we fell out earlier and why I'm on my way now to pick it up myself. So, if I were you, I wouldn't put too much trust in what he said. He has a habit, as I keep telling you, of being unreliable.'

'No, he hasn't. You just can't see any good in Jeff because of Silvia.'

'I can't see any good in him because there's not a great deal of good to see.'

He threw the statement like a challenge at her. Ronni caught it and threw it back at him, impatient of his criticism.

'If he's such an unreliable, untrustworthy individual,' she put to him, 'someone whom you obviously have no time for, how come you employ him? How come you don't fire him? Surely that would be the sensible thing to do.'

'I may fire him, as I've told you.' Guido did not bat an eyelid. 'If he causes my cousin to fail her exams, I will indeed fire him.' Then he smiled a malicious smile. 'But not just yet. I'll fire him after the speedboat race is over. I won't need him after that.'

Ronni felt faintly shocked. 'What do you mean you won't need him?'

'I mean that the only reason I keep your brother on is because he's an absolute wizard with engines.' He raised one hand and kissed the tips of his fingers in a gesture of unambiguous admiration. 'No one understands my speedboat the way your brother does.' He smiled, unrepentant. 'That's why I need him.'

So, Silvia had been right; he really cared about winning that race. Ronni glared at him. 'Does Jeff know how cynically he's being used?' Then, when he simply smiled in response, she added, 'It would serve you right if Jeff walked out on you. If he left you in the lurch when you needed him most.'

'Thank you for that kind thought, but I don't think it's likely.' Guido smiled a smug smile. 'You see, I pay him too much.'

'Money's not everything.' Ronni glared at him. 'I know my brother. My brother has principles.'

'Good for him. I hope they'll pay the rent for him

when he eventually finds himself out on his ear.' Guido straightened and thrust his hands into his trouser pockets, snatching a quick glance at his watch as he did so.

'In the meantime, as I told you, I have an errand to do, then I plan to stop off in the village and have a bite to eat. Since you've obviously been left stranded, you're free to join me, if you wish.'

'Thanks, but no, thanks. Anyway, I haven't been left stranded. Jeff's just a little late in calling, that's all.'

'I'll give you one last chance.' Guido was smiling amusedly down at her. 'This is Bruna's night off. If you don't want to go hungry, I suggest you accept my invitation.'

But Ronni was insistent. 'No, thanks. I'll wait for Jeff.'

'Happy waiting.' Guido turned on his heel. 'Tell me all about it when I get back.'

Then, with an uncaring smile, he strode off through the open doorway.

It was just after nine-thirty when the telephone rang. Almost faint with hunger by now, Ronni rushed out into the hall to answer it.

'Hello? Jeff, is that you?' she demanded.

She could hear a lot of noise in the background before a voice spoke. Jeff was obviously calling from a public place.

Except that it wasn't Jeff.

'Still waiting, I see.' Ronni felt her empty insides curl with annoyance as she instantly recognised Guido's voice. 'Never mind,' he continued. 'Your dinner's on its way. I've asked the restaurant to bring you round a takeaway. It should be with you in about ten minutes.'

Then, before she could protest, he was saying, 'Got to go now. Mustn't let my coffee get cold. *Bon appetito*,' he exhorted her. And then he hung up.

Ronni was still fizzing with indignation — how dared he make fun of her? — when, sure enough, a car arrived at the front door, laden with dishes dovered in tin foil.

Ronni carried them indoors and laid them on the kitchen table, scarcely able to bear the mouth-watering aromas that were escaping from beneath the tin foil.

'I ought to throw them in the bin,' she told herself tetchily, casting one final plaintive glance in the direction of the telephone. 'That would be treating them with the contempt with which they were given.'

But, as her stomach gave another helpless rumble of hunger, she sank down weakly on to one of the chairs and unceremoniously began ripping off the tin foil.

Jeff made up for his neglect by taking Ronni out for both lunch and dinner next day.

'I'm sorry, Ron,' he told her, kissing her when they met. 'I had an absolute hell of a day. I got stuck on a job at Olbia. It took hours longer than I thought. And then——'

'And then you had a row with Guido.'

As Ronni finished the sentence for him, Jeff made a face. 'How do you know? Did he tell you?'

Ronni nodded. 'It sounds like it's a regular thing.' She might have added that Guido had also told her that Jeff would end up breaking their dinner date. But she decided not to. That had just been a lucky guess. And a rather malicious lucky guess to boot.

So, instead, she said, 'If all you do is fight with him, why on earth do you go on working for him?'

'Because he pays damned well.' Jeff grinned as he said it. Then he added as Ronni responded with a scowl—don't say Guido had been right yet again!—'But, more importantly, I stay with him because I respect him as a seaman. He's got the best boats in the whole region, and he doesn't stint in looking after them. And, what's more, he's an expert when it comes to sailing them. He's the most professional boat owner I've ever worked for.'

That was praise indeed coming from Jeff. Ronni nodded, glad to discover that Jeff hadn't sold out.

Silvia joined them halfway through lunch and had dinner with them in the evening. They sat outside at a table overlooking the bay, with the twinkling lights of the harbour beyond, the big yachts and the smaller boats bobbing at anchor in the moonlight.

'It's down to work tomorrow,' Ronni observed, glancing across at Silvia, as the waiter cleared away their fruit plates and brought them coffee. Guido had said she could have a day off, just to get acclimatised, but he'd been firm that the lessons should start immediately after that. And, quite frankly, Ronni was keen to get started anyway.

'We agreed on three hours in the morning and three in the afternoon. I suggest we start at nine,' she told Silvia.

'That's no problem.' Silvia smiled brightly. 'Nine in the morning's OK with me.' Then Ronni was aware of a look passing between her and Jeff before she continued, 'The problem is the afternoon. I always go out with Jeff in the afternoon.'

'That's right,' Jeff piped up, throwing his sister a soothing glance. 'She comes out in the boat with me when I'm going round on other jobs.'

Ronni sighed. So, once again, Guido had been right. She sat back in her seat and looked across squarely at the pair of them. 'We have to do three hours in the afternoon, to make up the six I'm contracted to do. If I don't, I'm in trouble with Guido,' she said plainly. She fixed her gaze on Jeff. 'And you will be, too.'

'Been making threats, has he?' Jeff scowled. 'Well, that's only to be expected. He always enjoys throwing his weight around.' He shook his head. 'But don't let it bother you.'

'But I have to let it bother me. I need the money. And besides,' Ronni added, 'when I agree to do something, I do it. I don't like taking something on and then failing to deliver.'

'Don't take it so damn seriously.' Jeff made fun of her. 'You'd think somebody's life was at stake the way you're speaking.'

Ronni narrowed her eyes at him. Now, that did sound irresponsible!

'No one's life depends on it, but someone's future might — the future of someone you claim to love.' She shook her head. 'I'm surprised at you, Jeff.'

But as Jeff dropped his gaze away, Silvia cut in, 'Look, I know these lessons are important. I need them to get me through my exams. But all I'm suggesting, Ronni, is that we be a bit flexible. We don't have to do three hours in the morning and three in the afternoon. We can juggle the hours around a bit to fit in with other things.'

Ronni was far from convinced. 'How?' she demanded.

'Well, we could start earlier in the morning and fit in more hours before lunchtime. We could slip in an hour in the evening. We could just juggle things around.'

'But it has to add up to six hours a day. In the midst of all this juggling we don't want to lose any hours.'

'Sure. We don't have to.'

'I must insist on that.'

'We won't lose any hours. I promise you, Ronni.'

'I don't know. . .'

As Ronni continued to ponder for a moment, Jeff leaned across the table. 'Come on, Ron. Don't be stuffy.' He threw her a wink. 'You've got nothing to worry about. Besides, who can you trust more than your very own brother?'

Ronni shook her head and smiled, finally won over. 'OK,' she agreed. 'We'll be flexible.'

Just four days later Ronni was regretting her decision. Silvia had stuck to her promises for the first couple of days, but then had followed a catalogue of excuses and cancelled lessons that had left Ronni feeling angry and on edge.

There'd been yet another cancelled lesson only today and Ronni was feeling even angrier and edgier than ever as, just after lunchtime, she made her way down the garden towards the villa's private little jetty, a corner she hadn't explored before, to try and calm herself with a breath of air.

But she almost turned and fled as she came round a corner and found herself face to face with Guido.

'Good afternoon.' He glanced up from what he was doing. 'What brings you to this quiet little corner?'

He was bent over the prow of a little wooden sailboat — he was obviously having a rest from speed-boat practice today — and was busily tightening something with a big screwdriver. And he was dressed only in faded jeans, his torso quite bare, his dark curly hair falling over his forehead.

He pushed it back as he turned to look at her, and Ronni was aware of following every movement — the cursory flick of dark-tanned fingers through his hair, the accompanying tightening of one muscular shoulder, the sinewy ripple across his broad back.

Good grief, she thought faintly, forgetting all her worrries, what a perfect visual feast he is. He had the sort of body women dreamt of getting their arms round!

But she pushed that thought from her. 'I was just taking a walk.' She had to control her breathing as she looked into his face. In the couple of days since she had last set eyes on him she had forgotten the virile power of that face.

He said what she was thinking — or at least a part of it! 'Long time no see. Where have you been hiding yourself?'

'I haven't been hiding anywhere.'

Ronni stuffed her hands into the pockets of her pink Bermudas, which perfectly matched her pale pink T-shirt. What she'd been doing was missing breakfasts and lunches and dinners in an effort to accommodate Silvia's erratic time-keeping — and still failing to do the stipulated six hours a day, she thought to herself with a dart of misery. It wasn't surprising that her path and Guido's hadn't crossed.

She glanced at him guiltily, remembering her promise to confide in him if she had any problems. But she would not tell him yet. Silvia had made a hand-on-heart promise that they would make up all their lost hours this evening and this coming Monday, and Ronni in turn had promised to give her one more chance.

Forcing herself to sound as confident as she was trying to feel, she told Guido, 'I've simply been busy, that's all.'

'I thought maybe you'd been avoiding me.' He smiled an amused smile. 'I hope that isn't the case? I'd be most upset.'

He was teasing her and, had he been anyone else, Ronni had no doubt she could have thought up some smart retort. But it was hopeless; that smile of his seemed to mesmerise her. 'Why should I be avoiding you?' was all she could think of to say.

Guido shrugged. 'I don't know. Your brother sometimes tries to avoid me.'

'Maybe he gets tired of all the rows. Anyway, I'm not my brother.'

'No, you're not.' He surveyed her. 'And thank heavens for that. You're much nicer than your brother. Much easier to get along with.' His eyes drifted over her, making her shiver. 'I'm rather glad that you and I don't have rows and fall out.'

He'd said something similar once before and it had made Ronni feel a tiny bit guilty. She felt guilty now and a little uneasy. She was being far too easygoing with him, she was thinking, too bowled over by his charm. She ought to be a little less susceptible to this man who was causing her brother so many problems.

Ronni took a step back. The easiest way to deal with that was simply to remove herself from his presence.

She glanced at the screwdriver he still held in his hand. 'I'll leave you, then. I wouldn't want to interrupt.'

'Oh, you're not interrupting, but I suppose you ought to get back.' The dark eyes fixed her for a moment. 'It'll soon be time for your afternoon lesson.'

Ronni could have just said nothing. She could have just nodded and turned away. But she wouldn't allow herself that deception. After all, there was no reason why Guido shouldn't know the truth.

So she told him it. 'We're not having an afternoon lesson today.'

'Oh?' His expression grew curious. 'And why is that?'

'Because we've made an arrangement. We've decided to be more flexible about how we organise the lessons.' There was no reason why he shouldn't know this, too. Ronni would probably have told him before if she'd seen him. 'But don't worry,' she added quickly, guessing what he was thinking. 'I'm not forgetting the number of hours we agreed.'

'That's OK, then.'

He nodded his satisfaction, and, to Ronni's chagrin, a guilty blush touched her cheeks. She bit her lip. It's not a lie, she told herself. We'll be making up the lost hours tonight and on Monday.

Guido was still watching her and he had seen her guilty reaction. His eyes narrowed. 'You're not having any problems, are you? Remember what you agreed if there were any problems?'

Ronni nodded, fighting back the colour in her

cheeks. 'No, I haven't forgotten, but I have nothing to tell you.' After all, there was no real problem. Yet. And she'd promised Silvia she'd give her this last chance to keep her word.

She reassured Guido now, 'Don't worry about it.'

'Oh, I'm not worried. You're the one who ought to be worrying.' As he spoke, Guido tossed the screw-driver aside, and, still watching her closely, took a step towards her. 'It would be most unwise of you to forget what I warned you. If you were to forget that, then I'm afraid we would fall out.'

Ronni felt her heart leap and shrink simultaneously. Suddenly, he was standing right in front of her.

'You won't forget, will you?' The black eyes burned into her. She could feel them pierce through to the back of her head.

'Of course not.'

She swallowed. Her heart was clattering inside her. What was he about to do to her? she wondered dimly. For suddenly she knew he was about to do something. And yet in spite of that — or maybe because of it — she could not move one single frozen muscle of her body.

They seemed to stare into each other's faces for a very long time. Ronni could feel her skin tingle from her scalp to her toes. All at once, she was a helpless rabbit trapped in the headlamps of a car.

Then, at last, Guido broke the deadlock. Suddenly, he reached out for her. He smiled a smoky smile. 'Come here,' he said.

CHAPTER FOUR

'COME where? What are you doing?'

Ronni squeaked a puny protest, her body suddenly as stiff as a rod of iron, as Guido's hand closed around her wrist. Yet her face reamined tilted up towards his, her lips softly puckered as though to welcome a kiss. To be truthful, she hadn't a clue what she was doing.

'Come here.'

He had taken hold of her other wrist now, and was gripping her lower arms firmly in his. Then he was lifting her up, so that her feet left the ground and her breasts brushed briefly against his chest, making the blood leap in her veins.

Again Ronni asked herself, What was he about to do to her?

The next instant she knew. He was swinging her into the sailboat, then, with a broad grin, leaping in beside her. 'Let me show you what this little boat can do.'

'But I don't want to go for a sail!'

Ronni felt strangely cheated. No, not cheated, she corrected herself hurriedly — after all, she had seriously believed he was about to kiss her! What she felt, and what she resented, was that she'd been tricked!

Guido was laughing. Perhaps he knew what she'd expected. In fact, as she met his eyes, Ronni was certain that he did, and that he was enjoying her consternation hugely.

'Don't be silly. Of course you do,' he told her,

pushing off. 'How could anyone not want to go for a sail on a day like this?'

It wasn't the day, it was him and what he was doing to her. Her heart was racing with horror and excitement at the prospect of being marooned all alone in this little boat with him.

Besides, her arms were still on fire from where he had lifted her and her nipples still burned from that brief contact with his chest. All in all, she was suddenly feeling so deeply vulnerable that she was scared to death of what might happen next.

She stared at the receding shoreline and wondered if she should make a jump for it.

'Sit down or you'll tip us over.' Guido's hand was on her shoulder. To free herself of it, Ronni sat down quickly on the wooden seat behind her. Now I'm stuck, she thought in panic, as they sped off towards the horizon.

'I'll do all the work. All you have to do is sit there.' Guido was swinging the sail round to catch the light wind. 'Pay attention,' he told her, 'and you might learn something.'

'I don't want to learn something. I want to go back.' Yet, as she watched him, perched as lithe as a cat on the prow, leaning back out over the waves to balance the little craft, his splendid chest scattered with little beads of water, Ronni was aware that she didn't really mean it. Her heart was beating with excitement inside her.

She detached her gaze hurriedly and tried to slow her heart's beating. Think of Jeff, she told herself. Think of Arnie.

That sobered her a little. She informed Guido in a

cool tone, 'Learning to sail isn't going to be a great deal of use to me. I can't say I do much sailing in London.'

'You can sail on the Thames. I have friends who live in Essex.' Guido shifted position slightly, as supple as a rubber band. 'They go sailing all the time.'

'Do they?' Ronni kept her gaze averted. 'Well, I'm afraid I don't move in such elevated circles.'

'So, what circles do you move in?' He had one hand on the tiller. 'What do you do with yourself when you're not working?'

Ronni felt caught off guard. 'Why do you want to know?' she asked him. 'Is that why you spirited me off — so you could ask me personal questions?'

'I don't think I'm being terribly personal. I'm just curious, that's all.' Guido smiled and persisted. 'So, what do you do with yourself in London?'

He was right, it wasn't terribly personal, yet Ronni still felt oddly threatened. She stared at the sparkling blue horizon. 'Things,' she said unhelpfully.

'What kind of things? Be specific. London's a city that's full of diversions. I'm interested to know what you get up to.'

'I go to the cinema sometimes.'

'And the theatre?'

'Sometimes.' In truth, the last time had been over a year ago.

'And restaurants? I suppose you eat out a lot? London has a fabulous selection of restaurants.'

Ronni nodded. 'Yes, of course.' Then she bit her lip guiltily. The last time she and Arnie had eaten out they'd gone to the local curry house where they went about four times a year. That could hardly be called sampling the capital's restaurants!

'And is that all you do? The theatre sometimes? The cinema sometimes?' Guido leaned on the tiller and adjusted the sails. 'I hope you don't mind my saying so, but it sounds pretty boring to me.'

She'd known he'd think that and that was one of the reasons why she hadn't wanted to get into this conversation in the first place.

Ronni turned to deliver him a look of disapproval. 'It may sound boring to you, but it isn't boring to me. I'm perfectly happy with my lot.'

'Your lot.' Guido grinned. 'Doesn't sound a lot to me. In fact, I'd say it sounds pretty meagre.'

'It isn't meagre at all.'

Guido raised an amused eyebrow. 'In that case, there's obviously something you've forgotten to tell me. Your weekly visit to the library, perhaps?'

Ronni glared at him, but wondered, Did it really sound as dull as that? Would anyone else have mocked her, or was it just Guido?

It was just Guido, she decided, throwing him a harsh look, wishing he'd lose his balance and fall head first into the water.

'But, of course, I was forgetting.' His eyes were still on her, as he kept one hand on the tiller and the other controlling the sail. It was irritating how easily he seemed to do several things at once. 'I was forgetting about your love life,' he continued, eyeing her. 'I expect that takes up a lot of your time?'

'I expect it does.' Ronni stiffened defensively. This was another reason she hadn't wanted to get into this conversation. She'd known that it was bound to lead to Arnie.

'I expect when you're not going to the theatre — sometimes — and going to the cinema — sometimes — you're having cosy little evenings in with Arnie?'

'I expect I am.'

'Now that sounds more exciting.' He paused, surveying her. 'Except that I seem to remember you telling me that you and Arnie don't like to live in each other's pockets. What was it you said? You like to give each other space?'

'Yes, that's what I said.' Ronni was surprised he remembered that conversation by the urn of red geraniums. She watched him for a moment, wishing she didn't feel so defensive every time he broached the subject of Arnie. For, though she couldn't explain why, it somehow felt disloyal to be discussing Arnie with Guido Falcone.

As he looked back at her, waiting, she forced herself to elaborate, 'Like me, Arnie's a teacher, and he does a lot of extra-curricular work. We both do. It takes up quite a lot of our time. But we spend what time we can together.'

'It doesn't sound like much.' There was an amused smile in Guido's eyes as the wind whipped his dark hair in curling strands about his face. The corners of his mouth lifted as he put to Ronni, 'But, who knows? Maybe it's more exciting than it sounds. And if you're happy, why should I criticise?'

And why should I care whether you criticise or not? Ronni told herself silently but firmly. Yet his remark had caused a sudden emptiness to go through her, shocking her a little, taking her unawares. And, suddenly, as she pushed the feeling from her, more than anything in the world what Ronni wanted to do was wipe that smug, amused smile from Guido's face, that smile that made her feel so exposed and vulnerable.

She lifted her chin and looked at him squarely. 'Yes, I'm happy. Arnie's a wonderful man. Maybe the life we lead isn't what you'd call exciting, but we care about each other and that's what counts.'

Ronni was rewarded by seeing his expression falter. And, just at that instant, as his concentration wavered, a side-wind suddenly caught the sail, momentarily snatching it from his grasp.

'Look out!' In the same instant he was yelling a warning. But Ronni, distracted too, reacted too slowly. As the boat swung round sharply, she toppled overboard.

She had a sensation of sailing briefly through the air, like a bird, she thought, rather enjoying the feeling. Then with a splash she was plunging into the crystal-clear water, and, an instant later, bobbing unharmed to the surface.

She was almost surprised to see Guido swimming towards her.

'Are you all right?' His face wore a look of concern.

'Of course I'm all right. Why would anything be wrong with me? All I did was fall in the water!'

He was helping her, quite unnecessarily, towards the drifting sailboat. 'You never know. I thought you might have got a fright. For all I know, perhaps you can't even swim.'

'In that case, you should never have taken me out sailing in the first place!' Ronni scowled at him, suddenly filled with alarm at the way his arm was round her waist and at the way her body longed to sink unresisting against it.

'You talk about other people being irresponsible!' she accused him, taking refuge from her confused feelings in a display of outrage. 'That was irresponsible in the extreme!'

'Ah, but I knew we had a first-class lifeguard on board.' Smiling and apparently oblivious of her alarm that was rapidly turning into panic, Guido continued to guide her towards the sailboat. 'I knew you would never be in any danger.'

'Then, if you knew so much, I wish you'd warned me that we were about to change direction quite so abruptly.' The way he was embracing her was making it difficult to breathe. The words came out in sharp little machine-gun bursts. 'It would have saved me getting my shorts and T-shirt wet!'

'They'll dry soon enough. Anyway,' he told her, 'anyone who learns to sail has to experience at least one ducking. It's all part of becoming a sailor.'

'A sort of initiation rite?' Ronni flashed a glance at him, struggling to match her expression to the staccato in her voice. But she was forced to snatch her gaze away in total disarray at the sight of the way his thick dark hair was curling in delicate wet tendrils over his forehead. It was like a thrust to the heart. He looked so utterly gorgeous.

She swallowed hard. 'I wasn't aware I was learning to sail. I already told you I don't need to learn to sail.'

'You never know. One day it might come in handy.' They'd reached the side of the boat and Guido's hands were at her waist, about to hoist her up on board. 'One day you might find yourself moving in different social circles.'

That remark sent a flash of real irritation through her, as Ronni remembered how he had laughed at her before, mocking what he perceived to be her dull life in London. Just as he began to hoist her upwards, she turned on him and snapped, 'Leave me alone! I can get on board myself!'

The sudden jerky movement rocked the boat, creating a wave that knocked them both off balance. Suddenly, to Ronni's dismay, she was falling into Guido's arms.

'What were you saying?'

The black eyes were pouring through her, amused and oddly smouldering at the same time.

'I said I can get back on board by myself.'

'I thought that was what you said.' He smiled. 'So, what are you waiting for?'

Ronni wasn't waiting for anything. She just felt hopelessly entangled in the strong brown arms that were wrapped around her waist. The eyes that burned through her seemed to hold her like rivets. It was just like before, back at the jetty, only this time it was a hundred times worse.

Then he smiled again and she felt his arms tighten, drawing her ever so gently against him. 'While we're waiting,' he said, 'how about this?'

Ronni felt something inside her switch on like a light bulb. It was as sudden and dramatic and undeniable as that. For the next moment he was kissing her and she was instantly realising that nothing quite so exciting had ever happened to her before.

The lips that covered hers were soft and warm and

salty. She loved the taste of them. She loved the way they felt. With a sigh, Ronni pressed her own lips against them, feeling sparks of electricity skitter down her spine.

Or perhaps it was his fingers that were having that effect. As his hands caressed her back, the long strong fingers kneaded and moulded every vertebra along the way. It was like a waterfall of sensation, sending shivers of longing through her. With a sigh Ronni surrendered to the sensuous magic of those hands.

And it was all a surrender. Not an ounce of her resisted, as he consumed her with kisses and slow-moving caresses. As their two entwined bodies bobbed like corks in the water, Ronni closed her eyes and let herself melt against him. It felt as though she'd drifted into some dreamlike watery paradise.

It wasn't until she felt his hand on her breast and experienced, like hot needles going through her, the sharp tug of responsive desire in her loins that Ronni belatedly realised what was happening.

She was being seduced by her employer, a man she barely knew — and, what was more, she was colluding in her own seduction. She was walking right into it with a smile on her face!

Ronni dredged up some sanity from the depths of her half-stunned brain, detached her lips from Guido's and pushed him away.

'That's quite enough of that!' she declared.

'Is it? Ah, well. I suppose so. For the moment.'

'No, not for the moment. That's quite enough, period!' Ronni turned away in confusion as Guido simply went on smiling, bobbing up and down unrepentantly in the water, his dark hair plastered like strands of silk to his forehead, quite obviously thoroughly enjoying her confusion.

And what confused her was the fact that she didn't really feel angry. In fact, part of her felt like smiling right back at him. She'd only pulled away because she knew what was happening was wrong, not because she hadn't been enjoying it.

'So, are you going to climb on board or do you prefer to stay here in the water? It's a perfect opportunity to have a swim.'

'With all my clothes on? No, I don't think that's a good idea.'

'You could take your clothes off—at least as many of them as you want to. Take my word for it, I wouldn't be shocked.'

That hardly needed saying. Ronni sensed nothing would shock him. She turned her back on him. 'I'm going back on board. You can stay here in the water, if you want.'

'Without you? That's no fun.' He held the boat steady, as she proceeded, less than elegantly, to clamber back on board. 'You're right,' he observed, as she flopped breathless on the deck, 'you really are incredibly unfit.'

Ronni turned to scowl at him as, with the easy grace of a pole vaulter, he swung himself over the edge of the boat. The only reason her own embarkation had been so hopelessly clumsy was because her limbs were all suddenly shaking like jellies. Delayed anger, she told herself, reassured by this analysis.

'I'm not incredibly unfit. I had a nasty experience, that's all. I'm just a little shaken up.'

'I thought you said it was nothing?' He was adjusting

the sail ropes and pulling the tiller back into position. 'I thought you said you weren't bothered about falling in the water?'

'Perhaps falling in the water——' Ronni glared at him, bluffing, struggling to get back in control of her emotions '—wasn't the nasty experience I was referring to.'

He simply smiled at that. 'I see,' he said. He let his dark eyes drift over her sodden figure, over the T-shirt, now quite transparent, which clung to her wetly, displaying a pair of nipples that stuck out like doorknobs.

He let his gaze rest there a moment. 'I get your drift. Quite clearly, as you say, something has shaken you up.'

Ronni followed his gaze and felt herself turn crimson. 'That was the cold water,' she bit at him in horror, folding her arms across her chest. 'It has nothing to do with anything else.'

'Heaven forbid.' Guido was laughing, as the little boat began to scud across the waves again. 'So, what shall we do now?' he asked her, winking. 'I must say I'm rather enjoying our little outing.'

In the event he took her round the Baia Sardinia, a stretch of dancing turquoise water nestling in the embrace of a tumbling rugged coast. Then they sailed further on, to the fabled Costa Smeralda, one of the most luxurious resorts in all the world. Where once upon a time there had only been fishing boats, now bobbed the magnificent yachts of international millionaires.

'This place was developed by the Aga Khan,' Guido told her. 'He discovered it by chance about thirty years ago, when his yacht ran in for shelter from a storm.'

And the more Ronni saw of Guido's beautiful island with its contrasts of perfect chic and untamed wild, the more fascinated and drawn to it she felt. It was like nowhere she had ever been before. It felt magical, untouched, a paradise to discover.

All the same, she felt relieved when, just before five, they finally returned to the villa again and she was able to step out of the boat on to dry land.

Alone with Guido in the little boat, she'd felt a constant sense of danger, like sitting on a time bomb that might go off at any second. For what would happen if he tried to kiss her again?

He had not tried, however, and now he was tying up the boat and expertly folding down the sails.

'So, where are you off to now?' he asked her over his shoulder. Then he added before she had time to answer, 'I expect you have an English lesson pretty soon—especially since you didn't have one this afternoon?'

He did not look at her as he said it, but there was a sudden unmistakably sharp edge to his voice that warned Ronni that the smile had gone from his face.

She hesitated on the jetty, hands in the pockets of her Bermudas—quite dry now, as was the once-revealing T-shirt! She looked at Guido. 'Yes, I expect I have.'

It was the truth, but she knew it sounded evasive and that evasiveness was not a quality that would appeal much to Guido. But his interference in this issue was making her prickly. She preferred to be left alone to handle her problem with Silvia—at least until Silvia had had a chance to keep her word.

Guido's reaction was predictable. He turned to look

at her, an expression of undisguised warning in his eyes. 'I hope so,' he said. 'I hope very much so. I hope there's nothing going on that I wouldn't like.'

Ronni bridled at that. What was he accusing her of?

Though she suspected she knew. He still believed her irresponsible. He still believed her capable of conniving with Jeff and Silvia behind his back.

She looked him in the eye and forced herself to tell him calmly, 'Don't worry. Everything's under control.'

'I hope that means what I want it to mean and not something else.' His eyes bored back at her, unblinking. 'It would be very unwise of you to mean something else.'

Ronni detached her gaze and turned away in irritation. 'Thanks for the sailboat ride,' she told him curtly. Then, without a backward glance, she headed for the house.

Back at the villa, after she'd showered and changed, Ronni spent the next hour pacing her room. Silvia had said she'd be back some time before dinner, and already the hands of the clock were nudging seven. She was beginning to feel the faith trickle out of her.

She sank down on to the bed and glanced at the writing pad that she'd tossed there after a brief effort to write to Arnie. For some reason, she couldn't think what on earth to write to him. And that was another thing that was troubling her.

Ronni sighed and lay back on the hyacinth-coloured bedspread. She'd been here four days and it was high time she wrote to him. She'd promised she would as soon as she arrived. But that was before she'd known the traumas that lay in store for her.

She gazed up at the ceiling with its painted blue flowers and wondered what Arnie was doing in Bradford. Teaching summer school, she told herself with a quick dart of guilt, not kissing wild Sardinians in the middle of the ocean. Which was something she had no business doing either!

But it had just happened. Heaven knew how. She hadn't meant it to happen. She stared hard at the blue flowers. And it would never happen again.

But, all the same, as she remembered those brief moments in the water, she felt her heart turn over with a flip-flop of pleasure. Never in her whole life before had she experienced such feelings.

She sat up abruptly, more guilt rushing through her. She was going crazy. She must be. She reached for the phone.

The next moment, with trembling fingers, she was dialling England. She got through immediately. 'I want to talk to Arnie.'

But Arnie wasn't available. 'He's got a class, I'm afraid.'

'Then give him a message, please. Tell him Ronni called—just to say hello and to give him my love. Thanks,' she added, and quickly rang off.

She sighed a small sigh, feeling a little better. That knot of tension in her had slackened a little. Then as her gaze focused unconsciously on the hyacinth-coloured bedspread, she found herself remembering what Silvia had said: 'I thought you ought to have a room with a double bed, for when your boyfriend comes to visit you'.

Ronni made a small face. Arnie wouldn't be coming to visit her. Theirs was not a relationship of expansive gestures like that. It was a quiet relationship, the sort of relationship one slipped into. For that was precisely what she'd done. She'd just slipped into it over the years.

That sounded dull and unexciting, she reflected, feeling guilty and telling herself she shouldn't be thinking such things. But what made her feel even guiltier was the simple fact that, somehow, no matter how hard she tried, she couldn't imagine Arnie lying with her in the big blue bed.

The only person she could imagine lying in it with her was Guido.

By eight o'clock there was still no sign of Silvia.

Ronni had very nearly paced a hole in her bedroom carpet. I'll have to tell Guido, she kept thinking over and over. This whole situation's getting ridiculous.

She had dinner alone — there was no sign of Guido — then went for a walk out in the moonlit garden. She would wait up till he came back and then she'd speak to him. For better or worse, she had no choice.

It was just before midnight and she was out on the terrace, staring out only half seeingly at the star-spangled horizon, when she heard the sound of a car drawing up at the front of the house. That must be Guido. She felt a dart of tension. Then she squared her shoulders and headed indoors.

But on her way to the front hall she stopped in her tracks as, suddenly, all hell seemed to break loose around her.

Silvia had just came through the front door — that car hadn't been Guido after all. But Guido was there all right; he must have come back without Ronni knowing, and he was facing Silvia in the enormous hallway, a fulminating tower of bristling black anger.

Ronni felt her heart quail as he exploded with fury, and, though he was yelling in Italian, there was no need for translation. Silvia, in any language, was being torn to shreds.

'*Bastardo*! *Ti odio*!' Silvia was screaming defiance, her lovely face as pale as the parchment walls around her. '*Ti odio*!' I hate you! she screamed again. Then she was making a dash for the huge carved staircase.

'*Vieni qua, maledetta*!'

Guido was stepping after her, like a crackle of lightning. And, as he reached for the pale, fleeing figure of his cousin, he looked like a man with murder in his heart.

And that was when Ronni made her move.

Instinctively, she darted forward, throwing herself between them. 'Leave her alone, you disgraceful bully! Don't you dare lay a hand on Silvia!' Every inch of her was shaking with outrage and indignation.

Silvia took advantage of Guido's surprise to escape up the staircase. And, a moment later, as Ronni and Guido confronted each other, there was a lond bang as Silvia's bedroom door slammed shut behind her.

'What the devil do you think you're doing?' Guido had recovered from his surprise. He scowled down at Ronni. 'Get out of my way at once!'

'No, I won't get out of your way! Leave Silvia alone!'

'I'll do what I like with Silvia, and I'd advise you not to interfere!'

'No, you won't do what you like with Silvia, and yes, I will interfere!'

Ronni's heart was roaring like a steam train inside

her. She glared into his face, all sorts of emotions pouring through her, suddenly, for some reason, very close to tears herself.

'What do you understand about anything — especially love?' she found herself demanding. 'All you care about is being boss and getting your own way. You've no idea how a young girl in love must feel. How dare you upset her and bully her that way?'

Guido's hand was on her shoulder, as tight as a steel snare. 'Get out of my way,' he demanded through his teeth.

'I will not get out of your way.' Ronni thrust her chin at him. 'Leave Silvia alone. She's already upset enough!'

The black glittering eyes seemed to tear at her like scissors. Any minute, she was sure of it, he'd thrust her roughly to the ground.

But Ronni continued to resist him. 'Say what you have to say in the morning. There's no point in doing it now. Wait till everyone's calmed down.'

'Playing peace-maker again? Silvia's faithful guardian angel.' The flicker of an ironic smile touched his lips. 'Well, don't think you're going to talk me out of having it out with her. All you're doing is putting off the evil hour.'

'I realise that. I'm not trying to talk you out of anything.'

Was it her imagination or had his grip on her shoulder grown less tight? There seemed to be a softness in his fingers now that was making her shiver.

Ronni looked into his face, feeling suddenly quite light-headed, and heard herself tell him, 'Wait until morning. Silvia's here now. She's not going anywhere. It won't do any harm to wait.'

There was a long, shivering pause. 'You reckon not?' he said at last.

Ronni snatched a quick breath. 'I think it would be better.'

His fingers on her shoulder had definitely grown softer. She could feel them move, almost like a caress, towards her neck, then flicker slowly upwards to brush against her jawline. All at once it was very hard to breathe.

'Perhaps I'll take your advice, then.' His eyes were pouring into her as his fingers lightly tilted her chin. 'I suppose it won't do any harm to wait.'

Ronni had to swallow. All at once she could not speak. Her tongue was glued to the roof of her mouth.

Guido continued to look down at her, almost making her heart stop, his fingers still lightly holding her chin. Then he smiled a fleeting smile. 'You win,' he told her. 'Just this once I'll take your advice.'

'I think it's best.' Ronni forced herself to speak, to fill the air that seemed to quiver all around them. It would be too dangerous, she sensed, to let another silence fall. 'I definitely think it's best,' she said again.

'We'll see.' Guido sighed and drew his hand away. His eyes seemed to study her for a moment. Then his expression suddenly hardened as his eyes flicked past her to the staircase at the top of which lay Silvia's room.

'But this is merely a postponement, not a cancellation,' he reminded her. 'First thing tomorrow morning that young lady's in for trouble.'

Then, without another glance at her, he was turning on his heel and striding on clipped steps across the hall.

It took a moment or two for Ronni to gather herself together, then she hurried upstairs and tapped on Silvia's door.

'Are you all right?' she whispered. 'Do you want to talk?'

'I'm OK.' At last, a muffled voice answered. 'But I don't want to talk. I just want to sleep.'

'OK. Sleep well. But if you change your mind, feel free to come and knock on my door.'

What a night! she was thinking, as she made her way to her own room. And what a morning it promises to be! Oh, well, she sighed, as she climbed into bed, it's probably all to the good. Everything will finally be solved.

But, come the morning, Ronni was in for a rude awakening. Suddenly, as she still slept, a hand was on her shoulder, ripping her roughly from her bed.

She blinked as a pair of black eyes glittered down at her.

'OK, where is she? I want to know — *now*!'

CHAPTER FIVE

'WHERE is who? What are you talking about?'

Ronni stumbled sleepily in his grip, as Guido snatched her from her bed to stand before him. 'And what right do you think you have to assault me like this?' She glared into his face, bristling with outrage. 'For all you knew, I could have been sleeping naked!'

'Don't try to change the subject.' An amused flicker touched his lips. But it had no sooner touched them than it had instantly melted away again. He gave her an impatient shake. 'You haven't answered my question. Where the hell is Silvia and where is my boat?'

'Where is Silvia?' Ronni glanced at her bedside clock to discover it was only just after six-thirty. 'At this hour I imagine she's fast asleep in bed—unless, like me, she's been ripped out of it by some hooligan!'

'Don't get cute with me!' Guido gave her another shake, holding her there by the scruff of her pyjama jacket. 'Just do yourself a favour and tell me now where my cousin is.'

Ronni tried to wriggle free from him, but he held her firmly. 'How would I know where your cousin is?' she shot back at him. Then she grew still as a sudden anxious thought occurred to her. Silvia had been in a bad state last night. Perhaps she'd done something silly.

She frowned at Guido. 'You mean she's really disappeared? You mean you really don't know where she is?'

Guido, quite evidently, did not share her anxieties. 'No, I don't,' he flared back at her. 'But I think you do.' His jaw was clenched tight and white with anger. 'And I'd be grateful if you'd just tell me without the need to shake it out of you.'

'But I don't know where she is! Have you searched the villa? Are you sure she's not just in the garden or down at the jetty or somewhere?'

'She might have been down at the jetty a couple of hours ago. In fact, she almost certainly was. She had to go to the jetty in order to steal my speedboat — though, undoubtedly, it was your brother who did the actual stealing.'

Ronni was suddenly a great deal more confused than angry. 'What do you mean? Are you trying to tell me your boat's disappeared, too? Silvia and your boat, all at the same time?'

'Yes. Silvia and the boat — *and Jeff*, all at the same time! Quite a remarkable coincidence, isn't it? Though you of all people shouldn't be surprised.' He released her with a sudden, impatient gesture, so that she slumped down gratefully on to the bed. 'You, after all, were a party to this little plot.'

'What plot?'

'What plot? The malicious little plot that you and Silvia probably hatched up last night.' He glowered down at her. 'I heard you go to her room — after so cleverly reassuring me that she was going nowhere.'

'But she wasn't! Or I didn't think she was!'

'Yes, that was very clever.' He continued as though

she hadn't spoken. 'It got me out of the way while you put your nasty little heads together!'

'But I hardly even spoke to her! She said she wanted to sleep.' With a moan of total helplessness, Ronni dropped her head in her hands. 'Whatever's going on, I can assure you I've got nothing to do with it.'

'Oh, I'll bet you haven't!' He did not believe a word of it. He reached down and grabbed her hair and snatched her head up. 'Whose idea was it to take the speedboat? Yours, I expect. That sounds just like you. And it's a great way for Silvia and your brother to pay me back for trying to interfere in their sordid little love-affair. No doubt they absolutely jumped at the idea.'

'So, that's what you're thinking!' Even through the pain in her head where Guido was holding on to her hair the plain facts of what he was saying were finally sinking in.

'You believe Jeff and Silvia have run away together, taking your speedboat with them out of spite — and you think the whole thing was my idea!'

'Yes, that's precisely what I think.'

'Well, you happen to be wrong!' Ronni glared at him fiercely and tried to loosen his grip on her hair with a punch. Then, when that failed, with all the strength she was capable of summoning, she sank her nails into his wrist. As he swore and released her, she informed him angrily, 'I can't say I'm sorry they've taken your boat.' She rubbed her tingling scalp. 'It's no more than you deserve! But neither can I claim that I had anything to do with it. I congratulate them. They thought it up all by themselves!'

Then she jumped up from the bed before he could

grab her again and darted past him to the window. 'If you lay a hand on me again, I'll cry rape,' she warned him. And then, to her own total embarrassment, she blushed.

'I never rape girls who wear such unenticing night-wear.' An amused smile touched Guido's eyes as he let his gaze flicker over the rumpled high-necked cotton pyjamas she was wearing. 'On that count, take my word for it, you're in no danger.'

Then, his smile vanishing, he shoved his hands into his trouser pockets. 'However, you're right. You ought to make yourself decent. Get dressed and we'll continue this discussion downstairs.'

'I'd rather not continue this discussion anywhere. As I've already told you, I don't know anything.'

'You've already told me a great many things, an alarming number of which have turned out not to be true. So, whether you particularly want to or not, we'll continue our discussion as soon as you're dressed.'

He turned on his heel, heading for the door, then paused and informed her over his shoulder, 'Oh, by the way, I ought to tell you I knew you weren't sleeping naked. When I came into the room, you were lying with the sheet half off you, so I had the full benefit of the sight of your virginal pyjamas.' He held her eye. 'I knew your modesty was in no danger.'

Then, leaving her unaccountably blushing again, he strode from the room, pulling the door shut behind him.

Ronni dressed quickly after an even quicker shower and ran a brush through her shiny blonde hair. What Guido had just told her was a little difficult to take in.

Not the part about Jeff and Silvia disappearing off together — though she felt angry with them for doing that, she wasn't totally surprised. The way things had been going she could hardly be that. But she was astonished, and deeply shocked, that they should have gone off with Guido's speedboat. Though in her anger she'd told him it was no more than he deserved, in reality she considered it a rather low thing to have done.

She rolled up her pyjamas and stuffed them under her pillow, before quickly pulling the bedclothes to. Then she paused and lifted the pillow and glanced down at the offending garments. What was wrong with her cotton pyjamas? she thought with quick annoyance.

Maybe the women in Guido's life were rather more accustomed to red silk nightdresses with plunging necklines and the sides split halfway up the thigh, but personally she had never possessed anything quite so racy.

I've never had any call for it, she thought with a regretful little flicker. Could it possibly be that she was missing something?

She dropped the pillow back into place and gave herself a shake. What was she doing pondering the pros and cons of pyjamas and red silk nighties when Jeff, her brother, was up to his neck in trouble?

Pull yourself together, she told herself, and hurried downstairs.

Guido was waiting for her in the hallway, his face as black as thunder. 'I want to show you something,' he told her curtly. And, with that, he proceeded to lead her outside.

Ronni followed, eyeing his broad muscular shoulders

with annoyance. 'Do you mind telling me what you want to show me?' she demanded. She didn't like the way he just snapped his fingers and expected her to follow.

'Some of your brother's handiwork.' He shot her a look across his shoulder. 'No doubt it'll please you to see just how much damage he's done.'

'Damage? What kind of damage?' They were headed across the garden, making their way down the winding palm-fringed path to the jetty where Guido's boats were kept. 'This doesn't sound like Jeff,' she told him. 'He may occasionally be irresponsible, but he isn't a vandal.'

But what jumped before her eyes a moment later, as they rounded the corner towards the boatshed, was very definitely a work of vicious vandalism.

The door to the boathouse where the speedboat was kept hung open, swaying drunkenly on its broken hinges. The lock had been forced—and with brutal, excessive force—so that the wood all around it was torn and splintered.

Ronni gasped with dismay. 'Good grief! What a mess!'

'What a mess, indeed.' Guido regarded her tightly. 'You can imagine my feelings when I discovered it this morning. I can assure you I said something a little stronger than "good grief".'

'I imagine you did. I imagine the air was blue.' And, quite frankly, Ronni couldn't blame him. He was right. 'Good grief' was a gross understatement.

'But Jeff couldn't have done this.' As they drew nearer to the damage and she could see that it was even worse than it had looked from afar, Ronni felt herself recoil at the very thought that her own brother could be responsible for such a thing. It was an act of violence that she found alien and shocking.

'Well, Silvia as sure as hell didn't do it.' Guido had turned to glance at her with a look of mocking distaste. 'This little love note required the strength of a man.'

'I can see that, but I still don't think Jeff could have done it.' She shook her head unhappily. 'He's not the destructive type.'

'Isn't he?' Guido ripped free the dangling drunken door like a man putting out of its misery a fatally wounded animal, and looked down at the broken pieces in his hand. 'Don't believe it,' he said. 'We're all capable of violence. And, invariably, it comes out when we hate someone enough.

'But I can see you weren't expecting this.' He paused for a moment and looked down into her stricken, ashen face. 'I can see he's gone a little further than even you thought he would.'

'I didn't think anything. I didn't know anything about it.' Ronni looked back at him numbly. 'Why do you keep accusing me ——?'

'Is he going to wreck the speedboat, too? Is that part of the plan?' Guido spoke across her abruptly, his eyes accusing. 'Is that a part of the plot you hatched up?'

'What plot? I've never been a part of any plot! Why do you keep accusing me of everything?'

'Because you've been a part of it from the start.' With an angry, violent gesture he flung aside the broken piece of door. 'Don't try to deny it. I know you have.'

'But I do deny it and you know nothing of the sort!'

Guido stepped towards her, making her jump back.

'You've been lying to me and covering up for them all along. Telling me that everything was under control. Keeping me sweet. Making me believe I could trust you.'

'But you could—you can! It wasn't like that.' He was making her out to be a two-faced liar.

'What was it like, then?' He glared down at her in fury, his eyes as dark and dangerous as whirlpools. 'Would you deny now that Silvia was skipping lessons—and, that you, in spite of your assurances, neglected to tell me?'

'No, I can't deny it, but I was going to tell you. I'd made up my mind that I was going to tell you last night.'

'Liar! You had no intention of any such thing! The only thing on your mind last night was rushing to Silvia's defence!'

'That was only because you were tearing her to pieces. The poor girl was upset. Someone had to stand up for her.'

Guido made a scoffing sound. 'Silvia doesn't need you to stand up for her. I can assure you she's more than capable of standing up for herself.'

Ronni suspected that was probably true and that she'd always known it. Silvia was no helpless, downtrodden flower. Which meant that something else, apart from the defence of Silvia, had provoked her own furious outburst yesterday evening. Some more personal resentment that had come from within herself. She turned away from that thought, unwilling to look it in the face.

'You know, I had actually decided you might be genuine.' Guido's eyes swept over her like tools of dissection. 'I actually thought I might be able to trust you.'

Ronni started to respond, but he cut across her.

'Not one hundred per cent, of course. That would have been foolish. But enough to allow you to go your own way. I knew Silvia wasn't doing the hours we'd agreed on, but I decided it was possible that you'd come to some other arrangement——'

'We had.' Now it was Ronni who cut across him. 'We had,' she assured him, hating his accusations of deception. 'We'd agreed that——'

'What? That she should just forget about her lessons and rush off to see your brother whenever she pleased? Was that the convenient little arrangement you'd come to?'

'No, of course it wasn't!'

'Is Silvia paying you? Is that it? Is that why you could afford to go against me?'

'Silvia isn't paying me anything.' Ronni was outraged. Suddenly, she was being accused of being a double agent!

'I know she has money. Quite a considerable sum, actually.' Guido regarded her icily. 'That's it, isn't it?'

'No, it is not! Do you really think I'd do that—take money from you for doing one thing, and at the same time take money from someone else to do the opposite?'

'People do it all the time.'

'Well, I don't. Don't insult me!'

'Don't be so damned high and mighty. Why not just admit that's what you did?'

'Because it's not what I did. I'd never do a thing like that!'

'I was right all along. The three of you are in it together. That's why Jeff brought you to Sardinia in the first place!'

'I won't stay and listen to this!' Angrily, Ronni swung away. A sudden shocked coldness was sweeping through her. How could anyone believe such a low, despicable thing of her?

But she got only two steps. Suddenly, he had reached out and grabbed her. 'Oh, you'll stay all right.' His tone would have cut concrete. 'You're not going anywhere. I haven't finished with you.'

'And what is that supposed to mean?'

Ronni had swung round to face him. And all at once the coldness that had seemed to freeze her was being swept aside by a sudden rushing warmth. His hand on her arm was sending burning pulses through her. His fingers seemed to singe against her tender flesh.

'It means you're going nowhere until you tell me where they've gone. It means you're moving not one step from here until you've told me all you know!'

'But I don't know anything!' She gasped as he yanked her closer. Suddenly, he was holding her pressed up against him, her breasts grazing his hard chest, her thighs brushing against his. And suddenly she was back in that embrace in the water. Suddenly it was as though they weren't enemies at all, but locked in a passionate, warm embrace.

Involuntarily, her eyes drifted from his eyes to his mouth. Suddenly she could feel it pressing against hers. The blood soared inside her. She felt her body sink against him. 'Please,' she heard herself murmur. 'Please.'

'Please what?'

'Please let me go.' She couldn't stand it. She could fight anything except what the nearness of him did to her.

Still holding her arm, he reached up slowly to tip her chin back. 'I'll let you go when you tell me what I want to know.'

'But I don't know where they are. I have no idea. I was never a part of any plot with them.'

She looked up into his face. Some of the harshness had gone now. There was a soft, cloudy light at the back of his eyes. His grip on her seemed to slacken a little.

He said, 'Are you sure you're telling me the truth?'

'I am. I swear I am.' Ronni dropped her gaze away. That soft, cloudy light in his eyes unhinged her.

She swallowed. 'Look, you're right about the lessons. We weren't doing the hours that I'd agreed to do, and Silvia and I had come to a sort of arrangement. . .'

Guido did not move a muscle. He said quietly, 'Continue.'

Ronni took a deep breath. She wanted to move away from him, but she seemed to have lost all sensation in her limbs. The only parts of her anatomy with any feeling in them were the parts that were pressed against the harder parts of Guido. It was as though all of her nerve-ends had flown to these spots.

She swallowed. 'We agreed to do the same number of hours. . .' She glanced into his face quickly. 'I wasn't trying to cheat you. . .' Then she glanced away again, equally quickly. She would drown in them if she allowed herself to look into those eyes.

Again she sighed, in an effort to steady herself. 'We arranged to spread the hours differently from the original agreement, working extra in the mornings and in the evenings. . .' She shook her head miserably. 'But it wasn't working out.'

'I would say it definitely wasn't.' There was no sympathy in the statement. 'So, now we come to the crucial bit. Why didn't you come and tell me?'

'I was planning to. I really mean it.' She did look up at him then, pleading with her eyes to be believed. 'If that row with Silvia hadn't happened, I would have. I swear to you. I was waiting out in the garden for you to come back.'

'But I'd been home for two hours when Silvia got back. Why were you waiting in the garden?'

'I don't know. I didn't hear you. I thought you were still out.' She flushed now, remembering how she'd realised last night that he must have returned without her hearing. It was a flush of confusion and shame and despair, for she could see in his eyes that that stumble had condemned her. He did not believe a single word of her story.

Guido released her and stepped away, and where there'd been warmth there was suddenly coldness. All the points of her body that had been pressed against him were suddenly touched with fingers of ice.

He said, dismissing her explanations as worthless, 'I'd rather not hear any more stories. All I want you to do now is tell me where they are.'

Ronni sagged. 'I don't know. I keep telling you I don't know. Please don't keep on at me. I'd tell you if I knew.'

In a flash his hand had reached out to catch her chin again. He jerked it up, forcing her to look at him. He fixed her with a look. 'Would you really?'

The impact of his eyes caused her to blink almost defensively. They were as hard and intractable as bars of iron. And suddenly she felt fierce anger flare up inside her at the way he continually misjudged and denied her and seemed to reject every good and decent thing about her.

She glared at him. 'Suddenly I'm not so sure I would tell you!'

'That's what I thought.' Again, dismissively, he released her. 'But don't worry,' he added, 'I'll get it out of you. If it's the last thing I do, I'll get it out of you.' His eyes sparked at her like firecrackers. 'You can count on that.'

'Is that supposed to be a threat?'

'More of a promise.'

'And how can you make me do something that I have no power to do?' Ronni glared at him, hating his arrogant self-assurance, as he stood there looking down at her as though he ruled the world. 'How can you make me tell you something I don't know?'

'Perhaps I'll jog your memory. Perhaps I'll remind you that it's not a good idea to play games with me.'

'More threats?'

'No. More promises.' He thrust his hands into his pockets. 'And I would be grateful if you would come to your senses sooner rather than later. I need the boat back by the end of the week to get it in shape for the pre-race trials.'

He threw her a final black look and proceeded to storm past her, then paused at the edge of the path that led back through the gardens. 'I need your brother back even sooner than that — though perhaps I'd better not say what fate I'm planning for him.'

Death by a thousand tortures, Ronni imagined, if the look on his face was anything to go by. When he caught Jeff — and he would, she didn't doubt that for a second — her poor foolish brother would have hell to pay.

Well, he's brought it on himself, she couldn't help thinking, and I don't see why I should stick around and be made to pay too.

As Guido stepped on to the garden path, Ronni stepped forward and called after him, 'I won't be staying on now, whatever you threaten! I don't know where Jeff is and I have no more business here now that your cousin's disappeared as well!'

The words sent a huge wave of relief pouring through her. She smiled to herself. It would be an absolute blessing to get away from here and back to quiet sanity. Back to England and back to Arnie.

Guido barely turned to look at her, but his message was unmistakable. 'You're not going anywhere. I've already told you that. You leave here when I've finished with you and not a moment earlier.'

'I'll leave here tomorrow, as soon as I can book a flight.' Ronni glared at his arrogant, retreating back. Who the devil did he think he was? 'And you can't stop me!'

He swivelled round then to look at her. Oh, no? his eyes challenged. Then, as though no further communication were necessary, he turned and strode quickly up the path.

'Pig!'

Ronni fumed all the way back to the villa. She had allowed five minutes for him to get back ahead of her —

she'd no desire to go trailing in his arrogant footsteps! Then on determined steps she made her way up the path, cursing and swearing under her breath.

'I'll show him!' she told herself. 'I'll damn well leave tonight!'

Back at the villa, Ronni went straight to her room, closed the door behind her, sat down on the bed, picked up the phone and quickly dialled. She must get this phone call done before Guido could interrupt her.

The operator answered. '*Pronto*?'

'Do you speak English?' Ronni cursed her lack of Italian. 'Can you get Olbia airport, please? Reservations.' A minute or so later she had been connected and the reservations clerk was asking for details of her ticket.

Ronni reached for her bag, which was lying on a nearby armchair. 'Just a minute,' she said, scrabbling inside it. 'Just a minute. I've got it right here.'

But she couldn't find the ticket. She laid the phone down. 'Hold on,' she told the clerk. 'I'll be with you in a second.'

Starting to panic, she turned her bag upside-down — and the situation was a great deal worse than she'd first feared. Suddenly, from head to toe, she was starting to feel cold.

She picked up the receiver numbly. 'I'll have to call you back.'

The next minute she was leaping up from the bed, striding across the room and snatching the door open.

'Guido!' she yelled furiously. 'Guido! Where are you?'

'I'm here.'

She was startled by his calm reply. Suddenly, he was

standing at the top of the staircase, apparently on his way to his bedroom. He stood and looked at her with an expression of total innocence. 'Is there something you wish to say to me?'

'There certainly is!' Ronni was jumping with fury. 'I've just this minute turned out my bag,' she told him. 'And guess what? My tickets, my passport and all my traveller's cheques have suddenly, mysteriously disappeared!' She glared at him furiously. 'I know you've taken them! And I demand that you give them back this minute!'

To her dismay, Guido smiled. 'I'm sorry, it can't be done.' Then, hands in pockets, still smiling, he swept past her. 'You see, I was right. You're going nowhere,' he said.

CHAPTER SIX

FURIOUSLY, Ronni stormed after him.

'Do you think I'm going to let you get away with it? You must be joking! I want my things back!'

'You'd better find them, then.' Guido turned and paused to confront her with a smile in the doorway of his bedroom. 'After all, you won't get very far without them.'

'I won't get anywhere without them! That's why you took them!' Ronni glared at him, her blue eyes sparking. 'You probably took them this morning while I was sleeping, or maybe right now, before I got back from the jetty.'

'You're right. The possibilities are endless. Perhaps I sneaked into your room in the middle of the night, while you were lying there dreaming in your cotton pyjamas.' He cocked his dark head at her in amusement. 'I wonder what you were dreaming about? Were you dreaming about Arnie?'

'I was probably dreaming of seeing him again somewhere far from here!'

Ronni shot her response at him like a reflex action, a little guiltily aware that it had rather less to do with the truth and rather more to do with her sudden need for a shield. Guido's totally unexpected reference to Arnie, and the way he'd cocked his head at her and smiled as he'd said it, had thrown her and made her feel totally vulnerable.

She added, drawing her shield more closely about her, 'That's probably what I was dreaming of. It's what I dream of all the time.'

'So, you're missing Arnie?'

'Of course I'm missing him.' She kept her gaze steady, suddenly feeling safer.

Guido said nothing for a moment, but simply watched her. Then he observed in a flat tone, 'What a tragedy, in that case, that you won't be seeing him for a while.'

'Because you've taken my things. I notice that at least you don't deny it!'

'I neither confirm nor deny anything.' Guido smiled a relaxed smile, slipping his hands into his trouser pockets, and leaned more comfortably against the door-jamb. He looked, thought Ronni, like male arrogance on legs. 'But that's not the point. The point is you're stuck.'

'I know I'm stuck. But I intend to become unstuck.' Ronni thrust out her hand to him. 'Give me my things back.'

In response, Guido simply smiled more widely. 'Find them,' he taunted. 'Search anywhere you like.' He made a gesture to indicate she could even search his bedroom. 'Feel free,' he told her. 'I won't stop you.'

Ronni found herself glancing beyond his broad shoulders to the half-shuttered, sumptuously furnished room beyond, with its rug-strewn floor, picture-covered walls and vast, deeply unsettling canopied bed.

What on earth does he need a bed that size for? she wondered. Then, as the obvious answer occurred to her, she became doubly uncomfortably conscious of the dynamically virile physical presence of him. She took a half-step back, smothering the blush that warmed her cheeks.

'It would be pointless me searching. You've probably locked them in some safe. I doubt very much they're hidden under your pillow.'

'Check if you like.' With a mocking smile, he stood aside. 'But I confess you're right. You won't find them there. As a rule, I don't keep passports and money under my pillow.'

This conversation was centring too much on bedrooms and pillows, and Ronni was finding it increasingly hard to handle. Wanton images kept flashing across her brain of Guido with some ladyfriend in the vast double bed engaged in the vigorous pursuit of fleshly pleasure. Somehow, it was the easiest thing in the world to imagine, though it definitely wasn't her habit to go around imagining such things!

She pulled herself together. 'Let's stop playing games. Just give me my things back — *now*, if you don't mind.'

'Or?' The black eyes danced at her.

'Or I'll go to the police. I imagine that even you are not above the law?'

'Certainly not.' He shrugged. 'Then go ahead.'

'Does that mean you won't give me them?'

'Yes, I guess it does.'

'OK.' Ronni swung round angrily. 'Then you leave me no choice.'

Inside, she was suddenly filled with helpless frustration. What hope would she have with the local police when the issue came down to her word against Guido's? For, of course, he would deny everything to the police, and, though she knew she was right, she didn't have a shred of evidence.

But she had only gone two steps when Guido spoke again. 'Why are you in such a hurry to leave, anyway? You've only been here a few days. You've scarcely had time to see a thing.'

'I didn't come to sightsee.' Ronni delivered a scathing glance. 'I came here to do a job of work, and since that quite clearly is no longer possible—I can hardly tutor a pupil who isn't even here!—I can see not the slightest reason to stay. Particularly,' she added cuttingly, 'since the few days I have been here I have found disagreeable in the extreme.'

'As your host, I'm sorry to hear that.' The dark eyes surveyed her, but he did not sound inconsolably sorry. 'But that's all the more reason to stay on and take the opportunity to redress the lamentable impression you seem to have had of my country.'

'Oh, it's not your country I have a lamentable impression of.' Ronni fixed him with a look that required no interpretation. 'On the contrary, what I've seen of your country I rather like.'

'Good. Then you'll enjoy seeing a little bit more of it.' A look crossed his eyes, almost like a warning. Then he seemed to change the subject as he continued, 'You surely don't think I plan just to sit around and do nothing about getting my speedboat back, not to mention my cousin? The police are on to it, but that's not enough for me.'

'No, it wouldn't be.' Ronni scowled at him. 'I wish you success.'

'I think you'll do more than just wish me success. I think what you'll do is help me to find them. You may not know exactly where they are, but I still think you know more than you're telling.'

Ronni gritted her teeth in silence as he went on, 'It's in your interests as well that I find them quickly. The sooner you have your pupil back, the sooner you can resume your tutoring—needless to say, without any little "arrangements"—and the sooner you can get on with earning that money you need.'

He paused. 'I feel sure you'll agree to co-operate.'

What he was saying made sense, yet Ronni was reluctant to concede. She continued to grit her teeth in silence. But then another thought occurred to her and she said, 'OK. For Jeff's sake I'll agree to help you.'

'For Jeff's sake?'

'Yes, for Jeff's sake. I know he deserves to be punished, but when the time comes I'd like to be around to stick up for him.' She'd decided at first that her brother deserved what was coming to him, but on reflection no one deserved to be thrown at Guido's mercy.

Guido smiled now. 'So, you think you can persuade me to be lenient?'

'I can try.' She spoke without much conviction. When had she ever had any influence over Guido?

'So, that's settled, then. I have your co-operation.' Guido straightened slightly as he went on to observe, 'I'm sure we'll succeed more quickly working together—and you'll have a chance to see more of this country you like so much. . .'

He paused just long enough to ensure he had her full attention before going on to deliver his thuderbolt.

'I expect our journey to track down Jeff will take us to areas you haven't seen.'

'*Our* journey?' Ronni blinked. 'What do you mean *our* journey? I'm not going anywhere with you!'

'Oh, yes, you are.' There was a definite warning in his eyes now, as he stood away from the door-frame and folded his arms across his chest. 'Like you, I hope our journey won't take long, but, however long it takes — hours or days or weeks — we're going to cover every centimetre of this island until we find them!

'And our search starts right away!' His eyes blazed down at her, as he proceeded to issue his final order. 'So, kindly pack a bag. We leave within the hour!'

Ronni wondered, as she flung some T-shirts and things into a bag, if she ought to have put up a stronger fight against Guido.

Maybe she ought to have carried out her threat to go to the police. Maybe if she had she would now be planning her escape from Sardinia. After all, though she wasn't quite sure how she would have done it, she could have found some other way to lay hands on the money she needed.

But she knew she couldn't have gone and left Jeff in such a fix. What he'd done was wrong, but he was her brother. She owed it to him to be on hand when he needed her. And there was nothing surer than that he was going to need her when Guido finally caught up with him!

She pulled the zip of her bag shut and glanced around the room, checking that she hadn't forgotten anything she would need. So, it was really thanks to Jeff, she thought, that she was being unwillingly forced to join Guido in his search for his boat.

She shivered elaborately at the thought, then, unexpectedly, caught a glimpse of her reflection in the mirror and was utterly horrified and shocked at what she saw.

Her cheeks were pink with excitement, her eyes shiny and bright, as though she was getting ready to go off on some adventure. She didn't look unwilling in the slightest.

It's just the thought of seeing more of the island that appeals to me, she told herself firmly, hefting her travel bag across her shoulder. That's the only reason I'm looking so pleased.

But as she left the room she had to make an effort not to hurry with excitement down the stairs. She felt a warning twinge of alarm deep inside her, as she very deliberately slowed her steps.

Was she taking leave of her senses? What was happening to her?

But, no matter how hard she fought to squash it, a flicker of excitement continued to torment her, like the buzz of a mosquito that just wouldn't go away.

'I thought we'd be going by boat.'

'Well, we're not, we're going by car. The car is faster and, in case you're forgetting, I'm in a hurry.'

'I wasn't forgetting, and I'm in a hurry, too. I have no desire for this ordeal to last any longer than need be.'

It made Ronni feel a great deal better to say that. Saying it helped to quell that flicker of excitement.

They were out on the villa forecourt and Guido was loading the car, the same racy-looking open-top red Alfa Romeo that he had brought her to the villa in on the day of her arrival.

Ronni took the opportunity to make a scathing comment — which she was aware had the effect of adding to her sense of well-being.

'Fast cars, fast boats. . .' She met his gaze with disapproval. 'You seem to have an unhealthy obsession with speed.'

'Do I?' He met her gaze with his customary amusement, which dented her sense of well-being slightly. 'I can't say I've ever thought of it as an obsession. And certainly not as an unhealthy one.'

'No?'

She watched as he dropped their bags into the boot and slammed the lid shut. He had changed into a cotton shirt with the sleeves rolled back and a pair of faded black jeans that hugged the contours of his body. And she reflected that even his body was built for speed. Aerodynamic. Powerful. Honed to perfection.

She felt aggrieved at that thought and the accompanying flare inside her. Banishing both, she said, 'Well, it sounds obsessional to me. You don't seem to be interested in anything that doesn't involve going fast.'

'I don't play bridge, you mean?'

'No, I didn't mean bridge.' Trust him to go to the other extreme. 'You don't involve yourself in ordinary, leisurely sports. Like tennis, for example. Or golf.'

'I'll take up golf in my old age.' He had opened up the passenger door for her. He smiled. 'That is, if I've slowed down enough.' Then, as she climbed in and he slid into the driver's seat beside her, he turned to look at her.

'OK. Where are we going?'

'How would I know where we're going? You're supposed to be in charge.'

He gave her a meaningful look. 'Where are we going?' he repeated.

He really did believe she knew something she wasn't telling. Ronni sighed, once more about to protest her innocence. But maybe it was the way he was looking across at her with those all-seeing predatory jet-black eyes of his, or maybe it was the way she felt just a bit claustrophobic at being shut up beside him in the narrow confines of the car and the desire that sparked in her to have this ordeal over quickly, but all at once an idea popped into her head.

She said, 'The other day Silvia said something to me about going to Alghero.' She shrugged. 'I don't know, but maybe they're there.'

Guido seemed to think about that for a moment. 'I know Jeff has a couple of clients in Alghero. Even if he's not there now, I suppose it's possible they might know something.'

Then, as Ronni watched him, he decided, 'OK, we'll try that lead first.' He flicked a quick smile in her direction. 'Alghero's on the other side of the island. We'll cut across and let you see a bit of inland Sardinia.'

A moment later, tyres spitting gravel, they headed out of the forecourt.

Guido turned to her with a grin. 'Let's see how fast we can go.'

They drove speedily but safely along the main road that headed west through the mountainous inner regions of the island, skirting villages where blackshawled women sat in doorways, past almond groves and fields full of woolly black goats.

'This is the real Sardinia,' Guido told her. 'These mountains are the soul of the island, and the people who live here are its heart.'

Ronni could believe that without difficulty. As they wound along the twisting tarmac, she had a sense that this was what the island was all about. She could taste its remoteness, its ever-present wildness. It was a sanctuary, untouched by the mad modern world.

'What are these?'

Suddenly, as the road narrowed, she raised her finger and pointed to what looked like a hedge of tall cactus lining one side of the road.

'They're prickly pears. Haven't you ever had one?' Guido drew up abruptly at the side of the road. 'You can't be in Sardinia and not try a prickly pear.'

He was so impulsive, Ronni thought, watching as he climbed from the car, then, snatching a wad of tissues from the box in the back seat, proceeded to pick half a dozen of the greeny red fruit. It was an aspect of his character that she found deeply appealing. He didn't seem to stop and ponder, he just went ahead and did things.

He was returning to the car, holding out his booty. 'You can eat these later, once we've disarmed them,' he told her, wrapping them in more tissues and laying them on the back seat. 'They're lethal if you try to eat them as they are.'

Ronni glanced at the back seat and instantly saw what he meant. 'I can see they're not called prickly pears for nothing!' For the surface of each one was covered, like a sea urchin, in long, rather nasty-looking spikes.

'They can be a devil,' Guido told her, climbing back into the driver's seat. 'The spikes break off under your skin and you can't get them out.'

As he gunned the engine, Ronni looked across at him. 'It's so kind of you to have my welfare at heart. I would have thought it would quite amuse you to see me with my hands full of spikes!'

'Amuse me?' Guido raised one curved black eyebrow. Then he shook his head. 'No, that wouldn't amuse me.'

As he looked at her, Ronni was aware of a tiny curl of pleasure. Don't say he was actually capable of feeling compassion towards her?

But he proceeded to disabuse her, smiling wickedly as he did so. 'Such a sight might not altogether displease me, but I certainly wouldn't find it amusing. I pride myself on having a slightly more sophisticated sense of humour than that.'

As they screeched off down the road again, Ronni felt duly chastened. So much for her rash assumptions of compassion!

But what had really struck her in his remark was that word sophisticated. It was a word that, up until that moment, Ronni had never thought to associate with Guido. But now she suddenly realised it fitted him like a glove. Beneath that wild, impulsive exterior lurked as sophisticated a character as she was ever likely to encounter.

She found that realisation deeply intriguing. There were many layers to this man, she was fast discovering.

They stopped for lunch at a wayside trattoria and

were shown into a shady courtyard at the back, where half a dozen tables were set out under the trees.

All of them were occupied, but, without even a word from Guido, the proprietor snapped his fingers, and even as they were being led towards it an extra table was being laid.

'I see you're known here.'

Ronni cast him a glance, as they seated themselves at opposite sides of the table. She was feeling perfectly relaxed, almost carefree, she reflected, a mood that had unfolded in the course of their journey. It's because Guido hasn't been picking on me, she decided. He's been too preoccupied with his driving.

'I've been here once or twice.' He seemed relaxed, too, as he turned to the beaming waitress and ordered water and a carafe of wine. 'It's very flattering that they should recognise me,' he added, addressing Ronni again, as the woman bustled off.

Only once or twice? Ronni wondered if he was joking. From the welcome he'd received, she'd assumed he was a regular. But it could well be true. He was a man anyone would remember, she reflected with a flicker of admiration.

The restaurant was one of those informal places where there was no written menu and the waiters simply told you what was on offer. As the woman returned with their carafe of wine and their water, she proceeded to reel off in rapid Italian the various dishes of the day.

Guido turned to Ronni and quickly translated. Then he told her, 'I insist you try the *porcheddu*. It's a local speciality and I'm sure you'll love it.'

'If you say so.' Ronni was prepared to take his word

for it. 'In fact,' she told him, 'I'll have whatever you suggest. I'm in your hands. You choose the entire meal for me.'

'Such faith.' He held her eyes and smiled that careless smile of his, causing a quick warm blush to touch her cheeks. Then he turned and reeled off their order to the woman.

Ronni watched him from beneath her lashes. Had that sounded a little too cosy? she wondered. That 'I'm in your hands'. . . Ought she not to have said that?

But she was being silly, she decided, continuing to watch him. A man like Guido would have no problem with such a small intimacy. And he would probably rather enjoy looking after a woman, even one he had as little time for as her. She found that thought warming and rather appealing. It was a novel situation for her and she definitely liked it.

They had pasta to start, delicious home-made shells served with a piquant wild mushroom sauce. Ronni had rarely tasted anything quite so delicious.

'That was heavenly,' she told Guido, mopping up her sauce with a lump of bread. 'I'll say one thing — you Sards certainly know how to cook.'

'We Sards know how to do a great many things.' Guido held her eye with an amused smile for a moment. 'And what we know how to do we know how to do well.'

I'll bet, thought Ronni, interpreting the sensuous smile and feeling a warm little shiver go through her. She remembered those kisses they'd exchanged in the water. He certainly knew how to kiss pretty well!

As he finished his pasta, Guido sat back in his seat, touching his napkin briefly to his lips. 'So, what do you reckon the boyfriend's doing right now? Do you reckon he's with some young lady, enjoying an al fresco lunch?'

Ronni shrugged. 'I suppose he might well be with one of his female colleagues.'

As she said it, she managed to look back at him levelly, though she'd had to suppress a dart of guilt before she spoke. Had she, she wondered, been enjoying Guido's company a little too much for one who had a steady boyfriend back home?

Nonsense, she decided. And if Guido was trying to get her back up by suggesting that Arnie might be enjoying some romantic peccadillo, he would have to look for another way to upset her. Arnie, she knew, was as faithful as a Labrador.

Guido continued to watch her, toying with the salt cellar, his long tanned fingers very dark against the white cloth. He said, 'Silvia told me he might be coming over.'

'Silvia's got romance on the brain.' Ronni shook her head at Guido, remembering how Silvia had said the same thing to her. 'I can assure you Arnie definitely won't be coming over.'

'Got better things to do, has he?'

'Not better. He's working.'

'Him over there. You over here. Why couldn't you arrange to be together?'

Ronni shrugged. 'That's the way it happened. There's no big deal about it. Arnie and I often end up teaching in different places. Last summer he went to Scotland and I stayed in London.'

'That's a bit unsatisfactory, isn't it?' Guido continued to finger the salt callar. To her annoyance, Ronni found herself watching the long tanned fingers and remembering with a start how they had felt against her flesh. She was rather glad that at that moment the waiter brought them their *porcheddu*.

'It's roast suckling pig,' Guido told her as she took a mouthful. 'I'll bet you've never tasted anything like it.'

Ronni hadn't, and it was melt-in-the-mouth delicious. She nodded with enthsiasm. 'Scrumptious,' she assured him. 'I'm glad I left the choice to you.'

'I'll bet Arnie doesn't look after you as well as this.' Guido raised his glass and drank. 'Go on, admit it.'

Ronni felt faintly put out by this further reference to Arnie — especially since the allegation was perfectly true. Arnie had never looked after her in the way Guido meant, performing the sort of small but pleasing acts of chivalry that seemed to come so naturally to him. But then Ronni had never expected that of Arnie.

'What's your sudden fascination with my boyfriend?' she put to him.

'I'm intrigued, that's all. Why? Does it bother you?' He laid down his glass and looked across at her.

'No, of course not. Why should it?'

'I've no idea. But it appears to.'

'It doesn't bother me. I just find it strange that you should be so fascinated.'

Guido shrugged. 'It's not so strange. Human relationships fascinate me. And most people enjoy talking about their relationships, anyway.'

'Then you talk about yours.' Ronni narrowed her eyes at him. Discussing Arnie with Guido didn't appeal to her in the least.

She might as well have addressed her request to the tablecloth. Guido continued, sitting back in his seat and watching her, 'Is this all part of your practice of giving each other space? He goes to Bradford and you go to Sardinia?' He chewed on a mouthful of *porcheddu*. 'You do your thing and he does his?'

'You make it sound rather cold and rather uncaring.' Ronni's tone was defensive. 'And that's not the way it is.'

'Isn't it?'

'No.'

'It rather sounds that way to me.'

'That's because you know nothing about it. I care a lot for Arnie and I know he cares for me.'

Guido seemed to consider this. He said nothing for a moment. Then he leaned towards her and narrowed his eyes at her. 'Would Arnie mind if he knew you were here with me?'

'Of course not. What's to mind?' But she felt a guilty flare inside. She sat back in her seat, distancing herself a little. 'Arnie's not silly that way. He wouldn't object to an innocent lunch.'

'I suppose not.'

As he watched her, Ronni held his eyes, but she was aware that her heart was suddenly racing inside her. It was appalling the way he could affect her like this. She held her breath on another quick dart of guilt.

There was a pause. A taut, ticking silence flowed between them.

Then Guido said, 'But somehting strikes me as not quite right. You're too composed, you and Arnie.' Dark eyes flashing, he leaned closer. 'See that couple over there? Now, they look right. There's nothing tight and composed about them.'

Almost with relief Ronni snatched her gaze away

and turned in the direction he had nodded. And what she saw was a handsome dark-haired young man who sat laughing with a girl in a bright green dress.

And Guido was right. Ronni could see instantly what he meant. Even from this distance of a couple of tables away one could sense the crackle of electricity between them. They looked vital, alive, anything but tight and composed.

'I don't think he would like it much if she was having lunch with another man. Do you?' Guido added, as Ronni turned to meet his gaze.

Ronni suspected he probably wouldn't, but before she had time to answer Guido elaborated, 'But little wonder. She's an extraordinarily attractive girl.'

And at that moment, as he turned to look at the girl again with a glint of admiration in his eyes, Ronni was aware of a reaction deep inside her. It was so sudden and so fierce that she could not deny it. Instantly, she thrust it from her as though it were the plague.

It was after they'd finished their *porcheddu* and the conversation had switched to other things that Guido suddenly excused himself. 'I have something I have to do.' Then he was rising to his feet, beckoning to the waitress and heading towards the main part of the restaurant.

He probably had to make a phone call or something, Ronni decided, her eyes following him as he disappeared inside. She sat back in her seat contentedly. It had been a splendid meal. He certainly knew how to feed a woman!

She didn't notice Guido's return just over ten minutes later.

She only glanced up when she felt his shadow fall

across her. And, as she raised her eyes, Ronni broke into a smile as she caught sight of the plate he was holding out to her. For on it lay the prickly pears he had picked for her earlier, now denuded of their spikes and cut into quarters.

'Why, thank you!' she exclaimed as he laid the plate before her. She felt an almost silly surge of pleasure rushing through her.

'Don't mention it.' Guido was seating himself opposite her again. Then he added with a wink, clearly teasing her, 'But all the same, I'll bet Arnie doesn't look after you like this.'

'No, he doesn't.'

This time Ronni admitted it, feeling a little like a traitor at the confession — and at the sense of pure delight she felt at Guido's gesture. Her heart had turned to liquid inside her.

It was at that moment that the couple whom Guido had pointed out earlier finished paying their bill and headed out to the car park. As they passed Guido and Ronni's table, just for an instant Guido turned and seemed to smile directly at the girl. And that was when, for the second time, Ronni felt a fierce jolt inside her.

She dropped her eyes to the tablecloth, suddenly confused and deeply ashamed of herself. Not only, she was thinking, didn't Arnie look after her the way Guido did, but, far more alarming, there was something else he'd never done.

Never in the entire two years she'd known him had he inspired in her such a hopeless rage of jealousy as she'd experienced when Guido had looked at that girl.

CHAPTER SEVEN

THEY were on the road again just before four, when the fierce pin-point sun had lost some of its bite. Yet a soporific stillness hung about the air, as though the dusty dry land was still enjoying a siesta. There was scarcely another car on the road.

'We'll be there in about an hour or so,' Guido told her, as Ronni sat by his side stiffly, staring out the window.

'Where are we going, exactly?'

She did not look at him. To look at him filled her with too many confusing feelings. She was still recovering from the shock of that earlier bout of jealousy. Nothing even remotely similar had ever afflicted her before.

'We're going first to some friends of mine — Filippo and Agnese. Jeff does a bit of work on their boat from time to time. If he's been in the area, they may know something.'

Then he paused and swivelled round to look at her. 'That is, of course, if you were telling the truth and Silvia really did say something about going to Alghero.'

'Of course I was telling the truth.' She did glance round then, and was shocked, as her eyes met his, by the jolt of her heart. Just for a moment she felt totally winded.

'Let's hope so.' He had turned away, leaving her

tight and shaking. The blood seemed to be driving in great swoops through her head.

I must get a grip on myself, she told herself firmly. This is ridiculous. And more. It's shameful and dangerous.

She'd always felt drawn to him. She could not deny that. Something in her had responded to him from the first moment they'd met. But that had been just harmless, meaningless attraction. It would seem her feelings were now turning into something else.

If I let them. But I mustn't, she told herself firmly. I mustn't and I won't. I would have to be mad.

They arrived at Alghero a little before five and headed straight for the home of Guido's friends.

'Their house is on the seafront,' Guido told her. 'They have one of the most spectacular sea views on the island.'

That was no exaggeration, Ronni soon discovered, as fifteen minutes later they were winding their way through the narrow, colourful streets of the walled city of Alghero to climb a hill to a cliff-top where they were suddenly confronted by a breath-taking panorama of endless blue sea.

Ronni blinked down at the glittering sea that was divided from the craggy landscape by a broad silken ribbon of glittering pale gold sand. 'Wow! This is almost as beautiful as where you live!' she exclaimed. 'This island is just full of beautiful places.'

'And full of surprises, too. How's your Spanish?' Guido asked her.

'Spanish?' Ronni blinked at him. 'No better, alas, than my Italian. Why do you ask? Are your friends from Spain?'

Guido smiled. 'No, they're locals, born and bred. But in this part of Sardinia the local tongue is a version of Catalan. Six hundred years ago it was settled by Spaniards — just as the south part of the island was settled by Moors and Turks.'

As Ronni's eyebrows rose with interest, he added with a wink, 'I keep telling you we're a complex and fascinating people.'

Ronni couldn't argue with that. 'And what about you?' she asked. 'Where did your ancestors come from?'

'Italy, Spain, North Africa, Turkey.' Guido smiled. 'I have a bit of everything in me.'

And the best of everything, Ronni found herself thinking, though wishing with all her heart that she hadn't thought it. She also wished he didn't sound so damned exotic. It simply added to the fatal pull he had over her!

His friends' villa, set in sprawling gardens, had a distinctly Spanish air — with its balconies decorated with wrought-iron scrollwork and a pretty bell tower in one corner. At the end of the wide driveway Guido drew to a halt, and instantly the blue front door burst open and a brightly smiling young woman appeared.

'*Guido Falcone*! *Che diavolo fai qui*?' What the devil brings you here? she laughed, rushing towards him.

The next minute Guido was out of the car and the young woman was in his arms, kissing him on both cheeks, obviously delighted to see him.

Ronni climbed from the car, hating the dismay that suddenly filled her. It wasn't sexual jealousy that was afflicting her this time, for it was obvious that the woman was just a good friend. Instead, she felt frozen by a sense of desolation that she would never be on the receiving end of such a display of warmth from Guido. That suddenly felt like a terrible thing.

He was turning towards her. 'Agnese, this is Ronni. She's Jeff Cole's sister — and Silvia's English tutor.'

'I ought to have guessed!' Agnese held out her hand to her, her lovely green eyes shining at Ronni. 'You're your brother's image. I've always thought he was good-looking, but that blonde hair and those blue eyes look even better on a girl!'

She laughed as they shook hands. 'Welcome to Alghero.'

'Thank you.' Ronni was instantly ashamed of her jealous feelings. Agnese was charming. No wonder Guido was fond of her. She had the kind of warm personality it was impossible not to be drawn to.

Agnese was leading them through the front door into a cool tiled hallway, strewn with locally woven rugs and sweet with the delicate scent of freesias.

'So, what brings you here?' she asked Guido, then glanced at Ronni. 'We'll speak English for Ronni's sake, unless of course you speak Italian or Spanish?'

'Only a few words, I'm afraid,' Ronni answered. 'Just about enough to order a coffee.'

Agnese laughed. 'What a splendid idea! Let's all have coffee out on the terrace!'

Fifteen minutes later they were doing just that. Coffee had been brought in a huge white porcelain pot and matching white cups arranged around the white-painted table that stood at the edge of a huge paved terrace overlooking the endless sparkling blue sea. And miraculously, too, a dish of sandwiches had appeared and another one piled high with disgraceful-looking cakes.

'Help yourselves,' Agnese invited.

Ronni tried to control herself, but the temptation was too great. She reached out and helped herself to an almond pastry.

It took a long time to get round to the subject of Silvia and Jeff. Guido and Agnese had so much to talk about, and Ronni found herself included with perfect ease. In fact, she was feeling so relaxed that she ate a second pastry.

'You know, you timed this visit perfectly,' Agnese suddenly revealed. 'Filippo and I are throwing a bit of a party this evening. All pretty informal—we only decided last night. I phoned to invite you this morning, Guido, but of course you weren't there.'

She, too, helped herself to an almond pastry. 'It's just a small celebration in honour of the fact that it's six years to the day tomorrow since Filippo and I met——' She broke off and giggled. 'We met in a car park. I'd just made rather a good job of denting his back bumper.'

Ronni looked into her smiling face and felt a sudden stab of envy. Dredge her mind as she might, she couldn't even begin to remember the moment that she and Arnie had met. And that had been just two years ago. She ought to remember.

She heard Guido say, 'I remember Filippo telling me that story. He said it was the most expensive accident he's ever had. It ended up costing him a diamond engagement ring.'

As Agnese laughed delightedly, Ronni's eyes drifted

to Guido. But she wasn't really thinking about what he was saying.

What she was thinking was that, unlike her memory block with Arnie, she couldn't imagine ever forgetting the first time she'd laid eyes on Guido.

That moment when she had seen him standing on the jetty, a tall dark figure against the bright sun, would remain locked in her memory foever. That thought brought a sob of pain and pleasure to her heart.

'No, we won't stay for the party,' Guido was saying, as Ronni fought to shake the feeling from her. 'We're here on an errand. We're looking for Jeff and Silvia. I wondered if you might have seen either of them or heard from them over the past few days.'

Agnese shook her head. 'I haven't seen either of them.' She was plainly curious, but too polite to ask what was going on. 'But then I very rarely come into contact with Jeff. Filippo would know better than me if either of them have been here.'

'Is he out on the boat? When do you expect him back?' Guido was glancing at his watch.

'He should be back any minute. He's just gone for a sail.' Agnese grimaced across at Ronni. 'These men and their boats!' Then she laughed. 'He'd better be back pretty soon. He promised to help with the preparations for the party!'

In fact Filippo appeared just as they were clearing away the coffee things.

A lean, dark-haired man with a smile as bright as his wife's, he appeared delighted at the sight of Guido. 'You're a little early for the party,' he joked. 'Unless you've come to lend a hand with the preparations?'

Guido explained what he'd told Agnese earlier, that

he was looking for Jeff and Silvia. 'I was told there was a possibility they might have been here yesterday,' he explained, carefully avoiding glancing at Ronni.

Instantly, Filippo nodded. 'They were here yesterday, both of them. Jeff had a small job to do on the boat. But they left about five o'clock in the evening.'

'I see.' Guido nodded, and then glanced across at Ronni—and she was surprised at the look of open apology in his eyes. She felt a sense of giddy relief rush through her. At last he knew, and had acknowledged, that she wasn't a liar.

Guido continued, looking back at Filippo, 'Have you any idea where they might be now? Did either of them mention anywhere they might be going?'

Filippo shook his head. 'I understood they were going back home.'

Then he frowned and seemed to consider for a moment. 'But I do remember something. . .' He paused to rack his brains. 'He was speaking to himself rather than to me at the time, but I recall Jeff muttering under his breath something about having to go to the mainland soon. . .'

'To the mainland?' Guido frowned. 'Did he mention what for?'

'No. As I said, it was just a passing mumble. I'm not even sure if I heard him correctly.'

'Do you mind if I use your phone?' Ronni could see that Guido's brain was whirring. 'I'd like to make a couple of calls.'

'Of course. Help yourself. You can use my study.'

Guido disappeared for nearly half an hour. When he re-emerged, the others had adjourned to the kitchen, where Ronni was helping Agnese arrange stuffed salami slices on a plate, while a couple of young girls, specially recruited from the neighbourhood, busily chopped and whipped and blended, and Filippo polished a mountain of crystal glasses.

'I'm glad you're back.' Agnese grinned at Guido. 'You can help Filippo with those glasses.' Then she added more soberly, 'Did you have any luck?'

'Yes and no.' To Ronni's astonishment, Guido picked up a tea towel and proceeded to polish glasses. Did he know what he was doing? she wondered, smiling. He certainly was looking a little distracted.

'I got on to a friend in Civitavecchia who seems to think that some mate of his saw Jeff this morning down at the harbour.' Guido scowled. 'But I can't get hold of the mate in question. I spoke to his wife and she said to try later this evening.'

'So, you're staying, after all.' Agnese beamed with pleasure. 'Now, just keep polishing those glasses while I go and check the drinks.'

As Agnese bustled off, Ronni was dying to ask what connection Jeff could have with Civitavecchia. It was a port town not far from Rome. She knew that, but not much more. Why would Jeff and Silvia have taken the speedboat there?

But for the moment she kept her questions to herself. Guido was being mercifully discreet about what Silvia and Jeff had done to him, when she had thought it would be more his style to rant and rave in anger.

Though, on reflection, she realised she'd been silly to think that. As she was already aware, Guido had many complex layers. And one aspect of his character she ought to have guessed at was his total loyalty to family. He wouldn't blab, even to close friends, about family problems.

She liked him and deeply respected him for that.

The party was due to kick off about half-past eight.

'You'll stay overnight, of course,' Agnese had decreed, when it became obvious that they would indeed be around for the party.

But Guido shook his head. 'We may not be staying long. It depends what happens when I get through to that guy in Civitavecchia. We may want to make a dash straight back to Olbia so that we can catch the first ferry across in the morning.'

Ronni felt a sharp stab of disappointment. Though she had nothing remotely suitable with her to wear to a party, over the past hour or so, as she'd arranged salami slices and stuffed olives and listened to Agnese and Filippo's bubbly chatter, she'd found herself slipping into a party mood. It would be lovely, she'd been thinking, to be at a party with Guido.

Which was maybe a good reason why it probably wouldn't happen, she told herself sternly as she stuffed another olive. She ought to be hoping instead that they *did* go to Civitavecchia and finally sorted out the mystery of Jeff and Silvia. To be thinking about partying was downright frivolous!

But it began to look as though they were destined to attend at least part of the party. Guido returned from another phone call attempt just after eight, looking doleful.

'Still no luck,' he said. 'I've got to try again in a couple of hours.'

'In that case. . .' With a firm hand, the redoubtable Agnese, by now all done up in a slinky black number, proceeded to take charge of Ronni. 'In that case, it's time you got changed, young lady.'

'But I've nothing to change into.' Ronni frowned. 'Only another T-shirt.'

'You can borrow something of mine. We're about the same size. And you can have one of the spare rooms to get yourself ready in.' She glanced at Guido who was watching with wry amusement. 'As for you, if you want to make yourself pretty, you can borrow the blue room.'

The two women giggled all the way upstairs to the bedroom. 'The trouble with Guido,' smiled Agnese, flinging the doors of her wardrobe open, 'is that he's far too pretty to begin with.' She sighed. 'If I wasn't a happily married lady, I'd envy you having such a gorgeous partner.'

Ronni blushed to her hair roots. But Guido's not my partner! She wanted to say it, but she didn't. Somehow the thought was too delicious just to reject instantly. She wanted to savour it for a moment.

But already Agnese was leaving her. 'Take whatever you want. The guest room's two doors down the corridor. It has its own bathroom if you want a shower.' She glanced at her watch. 'And now I've got to dash. The guests will be arriving any minute.'

In the end, after much hesitation — all Agnese's stuff looked so expensive! — Ronni selected a blue silk jersey dress the colour of her eyes that clung to her in all the right places and looked sensational, and a pair of matching blue sandals that, miraculously, fitted.

She grinned at her reflection in the mirror. 'Yes, you shall go to the ball!' she told herself, giggling. Suddenly, she was brimming with happy excitement —

which had nothing whatsoever to do with Guido, she kept telling herself. He'd probably spend all evening making phone calls anyway.

By the time she appeared, the party was in full swing. A band was playing out on the huge terrace and one or two couples were lazily dancing. The rest seemed to be engrossed in animated conversation, filling the sweet night air beneath a huge pale moon with the sounds of laughter and happy chatter.

Ronni stepped out on to the terrace feeling elated with excitement. All her instincts were telling her this was going to be a fabulous evening.

But then, like a balloon encountering an unexpected thorn, there was a loud pop in her heart as all her good spirits were blown out of her. For there, at the other end of the terrace, standing far too close to a girl in a pink dress and deep in conversation with her, was Guido.

He was wearing a pair of his customary white trousers and a plain white shirt, rolled back to the elbows, with a black belt at his waist and a pair of shiny black shoes. And Agnese was quite right — he looked far more gorgeous than any mortal had right to.

Ronni felt her heart roll over and die at the sight of him. And again, too, she felt the merciless lash of jealousy.

She turned away abruptly and snatched up a glass of champagne as a waiter passed by with a tray of brimming glasses. Then, a moment later, Agnese appeared.

'Ah, there you are. Come with me. There's someone over here I'd like you to meet. He's a professor of English. He and his wife have a house in London.'

As Agnese proceeded to steer her across the terrace, Ronni stole a glance at the spot where Guido had been. But he was no longer there, and neither was the girl. She felt a plummet of misery. They weren't on the dance-floor, either. Where had they gone and what were they up to?

The professor and his wife were charming people. In other circumstances Ronni would have been delighted to chat with them. As it was, she made a good show of appearing delighted. But she kept thinking of Guido and the girl in the pink dress.

'I used to have a tutee who lived there,' she responded brightly when the professor's wife told her in which part of London they had their house. 'It's a lovely area. So close to the park.'

'Just a stone's throw,' agreed the professor. 'We absolutely love it.'

The waiter was coming by with more glasses of champagne. Ronni knocked back the remains of her first glass and reached for another. Drunken oblivion, she thought cravenly. That would suit me nicely.

But her fingers never quite made contact with the glass. She froze as a hand suddenly slipped round her waist.

'Let's dance,' murmured a voice. 'They're playing our tune.'

Ronni whirled round, cheeks flushing, recognising his voice instantly. 'Guido!' she gasped, feeling her stomach disappear, as she looked into his smiling, handsome face. Then, making their apologies to the professor and his wife, he was whisking her off towards the dance-floor.

'You look sensational.'

Thank heavens the band was playing a waltz and not a rumba. Ronni looked into his eyes and smiled at the compliment, inwardly shuddering as he took her in his arms and proceeded to lead her in time to the music. Suddenly she wasn't looking half as sensational as she felt.

She nodded her head at him. 'Thank you,' she said.

'What were you talking to the professor about?'

It sounded almost proprietorial. Ronni flushed with inward pleasure. 'London,' she said.

'Ah, yes, he has a house there. I'd forgotten. Richmond, isn't it?'

'Yes, it's Richmond.' But Ronni wasn't thinking about Richmond. She was thinking how delicious the hand at her waist felt and how she longed to let her body sink against it and luxuriate in its gentle, virile strength. With an effort of will she resisted the temptation.

'Do you know it?'

'Know what?'

'This Richmond we were talking about. This place where the professor has his London house.'

'I know it a bit.'

Ronni was suddenly grateful that just a moment ago she'd already had this conversation. It meant she could answer without thinking, which was an infinite mercy, for suddenly she was quite incapable of thinking. She was too busy fighting another temptation.

It was her hand that lay decorously on his shoulder. Suddenly it was taking every atom of her will-power to stop that hand from doing what it longed to do — namely rise up and tangle with the silky black hair that curled so invitingly round Guido's left ear.

She swallowed hard. Pull yourself together, she told herself. 'I used to have a tutee who lived there,' she told Guido.

'A tutee.' Guido laughed at that. 'Little miss school-mistress.' Then his hand seemed to tighten against her waist, making her judder and catch her breath. 'Well, you definitely don't look like a schoolmistress tonight.'

'Don't I?'

'Definitely not.' His hand tightened a little more. Suddenly, Ronni was finding it difficult to breathe. 'Tonight you look far too beautiful to be locked in a classroom. The only place you ought to be is locked on this dance-floor with me.'

It was a line. Ronni knew it. But it still turned her knees to water. Oh, to be locked anywhere with him, she was thinking foolishly.

He paused and looked down at her. 'There's only one thing wrong. . . One small thing that doesn't fit. . .'

'What doesn't fit?'

Those wicked dark eyes of his were lifting her up into another planet. Ronni felt as though her heart was floating on starlight.

'Nothing that can't be fixed. . .' Then, 'Wait a minute,' he interrupted himself, unclasping his left hand that had been holding hers, and reaching out to brush her hair.

'A bit of acacia blossom,' he told her. 'It gets everywhere.'

Ronni wished an entire treeload of acacia blossom would fall on her if she could just experience again the thrilling touch of that hand. Where he had touched her

her scalp was prickling like a porcupine. Her hair felt
as though it was standing on end.

But he was continuing. 'As I was saying, there's just
one thing wrong. . .'

'Oh?' She started to ask what, then swallowed
instead.

For the hand that had set her scalp alight was now
doing the same to her hand. Before, he had held her
hand lightly, so that she was barely aware of it, but
now, making her heart skitter, he was lacing his fingers
with hers. Ronni felt a sear of heat right up to her
shoulder.

He said, 'It's nothing that can't be fixed.' Then he
smiled. 'Only your name.'

'My name?' Ronni blinked. 'What's wrong with my
name?'

'Nothing serious.'

With a small smile playing round his lips, he drew
their two hands with the intertwined fingers into the
space between them and leaned them lightly against his
chest. Ronni almost fainted as she imagined she could
feel the beat of his heart.

He went on, black eyes watching her, smiling down
at her, 'How can I call the most beautiful woman at
this party by a name that sounds as though it belongs
to a man? Tonight you most definitely do not look like
a Ronni.'

Ronni's heart was thumping at at least twice its
normal rate. 'It's short for Veronica,' she told him.
'My real name's Veronica, but I've always been called
Ronni.'

'Not tonight, you won't be. Tonight you'll be
Veronica. It's a beautiful name.' His eyes poured into

her. 'A woman as beautiful as you are deserves a beautiful name.'

Ronni was dying with happiness. 'No one's ever called me that,' she said. 'I was Ronni to everyone before I could even walk.'

'Well, not any more.' He smiled. 'Veronica.' The way he said it made the name sound like orchids and honey. 'Tonight it would be a sin to call you Ronni.'

He raised her hand to his lips and kissed it, then continued to hold it against his lips. 'Why didn't you tell me you had such a beautiful name?'

Ronni shook her head helplessly, sensing it would be wiser not to speak. If she were to try, she would only end up gabbling something silly, for the heat of his lips against her fingers had sent her brain into a kind of mental tailspin. She felt incapable of putting two sensible words together.

And anyway, who needs words? she told herself blissfully, as they continued to float across the dance-floor together — though Ronni wasn't on the dance-floor, she had both feet in heaven.

But then, to her dismay, she realised the music had stopped. Some couples were moving away while others waited for the band to strike up again. Ronni held her breath, wondering what her fate would be. Was this the end or would he want to dance some more?

'I enjoyed that. That was almost as good as swimming.'

He was smiling down at her, dark eyes twinkling, making a warm blush fly across her cheeks. Then, to her dismay, he released her and glanced quickly at his watch.

'However, I'm afraid I have to go and make a phone call.'

'Of course.' Almost weeping, Ronni slid her hand from his shoulder. 'I'd forgotten. You have to call Civitavecchia.'

'It shouldn't take me long.' He was leading her to the edge of the dance-floor. 'Shall I leave you in the care of the good professor?'

Stupidly, that hurt. It felt as though she was being off-loaded. There was certainly nothing even the least bit proprietorial about *that* remark!

'That won't be necessary,' she said, drawing away from him, speaking a little more sharply than she'd intended. 'Just you go and make your phone call.'

He held her eyes a moment, but his gaze was oddly shuttered. There was no way of telling what he was thinking. Then as a waiter passed by bearing a laden tray, he reached out swiftly and snatched up a glass of champagne.

He handed it to Ronni. 'I think this is where I came in.' Then, throwing her a wink, he turned and moved off into the crowd.

At first Ronni didn't look as he headed back towards the villa. She tried to keep her blurred eyes focused on the sky. Then at the last minute she swung round, her heart bursting inside her, just in time to see him disappear through the terrace doors.

And suddenly she felt as stiff and cold and fragile as the champagne glass that was clutched in her shaking hand.

I'm done for, she thought. Wiped out. Finished.

What on earth is to become of me? I'm in love with this man.

CHAPTER EIGHT

IT WAS all too much to bear. Ronni had to escape. Still clutching her champagne glass, she hurried from the terrace and made her way along a path through the garden towards the sea.

At last, she reached a wall, waist-high, stone-built, below which stretched the shore, as pale as a seashell in the moonlight. With a sigh, she leaned against it, laying down her champagne glass, then closed her eyes and forced herself to breathe deeply and slowly.

Surely it wasn't possible, she told herself in horror. Surely she couldn't really have been so foolish as to fall in love with Guido Falcone?

He was a man whom, by rights, she ought not even to like. He was a tyrant, a bully, and he'd stolen her things — which made him a thief into the bargain!

Ronni opened her eyes and stared at the moon, feeling her poor heart quiver inside her. He was all of these things, but somehow none of it seemed to matter. All that mattered was that he was the most exciting man she'd ever met in her life.

She thought quickly of Arnie, feeling deeply disloyal, but she couldn't help the feeling of elation that swept through her as her thoughts flitted instantly back to Guido. He made her feel alive. He'd lit a bonfire beneath her, releasing in her all sorts of wild emotions that she had never, even fleetingly, experienced before. He had taken her heart and given it wings.

But that was the problem. Instantly, she sobered. In truth, he had given her nothing but dreams. As he had flashed into her life, so he was destined to flash out of it again, leaving her heart and her dreams turned to ashes.

'So, this is where you've got to?'

Ronni swung round with a start to find Guido standing just a few feet away from her. And in that instant her heart seemed to burst with love inside her and simultaneously shrivel with grief and helplessness. Her fairy-tale prince, so handsome that it hurt to look at him.

'What are you doing down here?' He was stepping towards her, taking a mouthful from the champagne glass in his hand as he came. 'When I couldn't find you I thought maybe you'd run off with the professor.'

He smiled as he said it, that careless smile she loved so much. But, though she tried, Ronni found she couldn't smile back. It was so obvious that he wouldn't have cared in the slightest if she really had run off with the professor. On the contrary, he'd simply have found it amusing.

She half turned away and stared at the horizon. 'I felt like a walk. A breath of fresh air. You really needn't have troubled yourself to come looking for me.'

'Needn't I? I disagree. I wanted to find you.'

Ronni understood then. She turned back quickly to look at him. 'You got through to that man, then? The one in Civitavecchia. I suppose you've come to tell me you want us to go straight back to Olbia?'

'And if I have?' He had come to stand alongside her,

leaning one hip lightly against the stone wall. 'Would you be sorry to leave the party?'

Ronni kept her gaze fixed seawards as her stomach leapt inside her, remembering that dance they'd shared together. To dance with him again was a prize she'd sell her soul for, and tonight, here at the party, would be her only chance ever.

Yes, she thought, I'd hate it if we had to leave the party. But, out loud, she said, shrugging, 'It makes no difference.'

'Aren't you enjoying yourself, then?' She could feel his eyes watching her. Then he smiled. 'Perhaps you're missing Arnie again?'

Ronni flushed. That hurt, too, just like his gibe about the professor. It didn't bother him in the least that she might be missing Arnie. Which she wasn't, of course, she admitted to herself guiltily. She kept her eyes glued to the moon and didn't answer.

'Poor old Arnie.'

Ronni could sense his smile as he said it. She swivelled round irritably. 'And what's poor about Arnie?'

'I feel sorry for him, that's all.'

That sounded condescending. 'And why on earth should you feel sorry for Arnie?'

Guido drained his champagne glass and laid it down on the wall beside him. Lazily, making her skin jump, he let his dark gaze drift over her.

'I feel sorry for him,' he said, 'because he's not here with you. He's not here to see his beloved Veronica looking more beautiful than any Botticelli nymph.' He smiled again, darkly. 'How could I not feel sorry for him?'

It was a game, that was all. Ronni knew it in her heart. It amused him to flirt with her and flatter her and see her blush. He probably did it to countless women all the time.

But, though she knew that, she couldn't help it, her insides had turned to jelly. Humiliated by her own foolishness, she turned abruptly away again.

'Don't be so glum. What you need is some of this.' Suddenly, he was reaching past her to pick up her untouched glass. 'Champagne is very good for cheering people up. Have some. It'll help you to stop missing Arnie so much.'

Then, before she could speak, he held the glass to her lips. 'Go on,' he told her. 'Take a sip.'

'I can manage by myself.' She made a move to take the glass.

But he caught her hand and held it. 'Just keep still and drink,' he told her. 'You wouldn't like me to spill the whole lot down the front of Agnese's dress?'

Most definitely she wouldn't. So Ronni kept still and allowed him to hold the glass to her lips. She took a sip. 'Thank you,' she said, wondering why he was still holding her hand.

'You don't mind if I have some, too?' He raised the glass to his own lips and, as she shook her head, took a mouthful. 'I think there's nothing more therapeutic than sharing a glass of champagne.'

'I wouldn't know.' She could see his lips slightly wet with champagne and was suddenly seized with a desire to feel that wetness against her own mouth. At the thought she felt her insides squeeze with longing.

'Are you telling me you've never shared a glass of champagne before?' As Guido spoke, he held the glass once more to her lips. 'What an awful lot of things you haven't done.'

'It may seem like that to you.' Obediently, Ronni drank. The hand he held in his was slowly going numb from the effort required to stop her fingers curling round his. 'And I suppose there *are* quite a few things I haven't done. Yet.'

'Now, that's what I like to hear.' He raised her hand to his lips and kissed it. His lips were soft and gentle and cool. The touch of them made her heart turn over.

Then he looked into her eyes. 'Now are you feeling any better? Has the champagne helped your mood?'

'There was nothing wrong with my mood.'

'I thought you were missing Arnie?'

Ronni snatched her gaze away, discomfited by the dark-eyed scrutiny. Did he know, she wondered, that he was miles from the truth?

'You don't have to worry. I'm feeling fine,' she said.

'It nearly always works, I find, a glass of champagne.' He smiled. 'And when it doesn't, I know another trick.'

As he spoke, he held her hand against his cheek. Ronni could feel the slight roughness where he had recently shaved. A dart went through her, of hopeless, hungry yearning. This is disgraceful, she told herself. But it made no difference.

She looked into his eyes. 'Oh, yes?' she said.

He held the glass to her lips again and watched her while she drank. 'Finish it,' he told her, tipping the glass up. Then, when she left a few drops, he drained it himself before laying the empty glass beside his own on the wall.

'Yes,' he told her. 'I know another trick.'

Ronni's poor heart was galloping uncontrollably. She opened her mouth to speak and found she couldn't. She couldn't even think what she'd wanted to say.

'Come here. Let me show you.' He was straightening slightly, slipping his free hand round her waist and gathering her against him. He smiled. 'It's one of my favourite tricks.'

'I think you showed it to me once before.' Ronni's voice was thick and gravelly. She felt both shocked and outrageously delighted by the way their two bodies moulded so perfectly together. They seemed to cling and collide effortlessly in all the right places.

'Yes, I believe I did.' One hand caressed her spine, while the other still held on tightly to her hand. He kissed her fingertips again, making her shiver. 'This time, so I won't bore you, I'll show you a variation.'

Ronni felt herself smile. It was hopeless the way he charmed her. She found the gall of him delightful. Delightful and exciting. As he released her hand and slid his fingers through her hair, drawing her unresisting head towards him, she reached out at last to touch the dark curls at his ear. As her fingers made contact, her legs melted beneath her.

Show me any variation you like, her heart was singing.

A moment later her arms were twining round his neck as his lips brushed hers as soft as gossamer. Softly, gently, cruelly, he teased her, his lips alighting for a moment, then moving away again, arousing her hunger, making her blood cry out for him.

He kissed each corner of her mouth, her chin, her nose. Then he brushed her lips again, lightly, fleetingly.

'This is one variation,' he murmured against her cheek. 'Would you like me to show you another?'

Ronni sighed in response. 'Yes, please,' she whispered.

This time his fingers seemed to tighten in her hair, drawing her mouth like a prisoner against his. But it was a happy, willing prisoner. Ronni shuddered against him, her lips parting as flames of desire shot through her. This was no gossamer kiss. This was thunder and lightning. It rocked her senses and turned her soul to powder.

As his lips plundered hers, greedy, insatiable, she could taste him warm and sweet on her tongue. I could devour you, she thought, every glorious inch of you. And when I'd finished, I'd want to devour you again.

Guido seemed to feel the same. He pressed hard and hot against her, his lips echoing the hunger she could sense in his body. And she longed to unleash that hunger, that virile, pulsing craving that seemed to strain through every muscle of his hard-limbed body.

'Veronica. . . My lovely nymph. . .' He breathed the words against her ear. 'Isn't this better than champagne? Doesn't it make you forget everything. . .?' He sighed and kissed her again. 'I know it does me.'

Then, as his lips possessed her, carrying her towards heaven, his hand swept round suddenly to possess her swelling breast. Ronni felt her blood leap and burn within her as he held it for a moment, squeezing gently, then, almost as though the gesture was an afterthought, allowing his thumb to graze lightly against the burning peak.

It was just like before. Ronni jerked against him, feeling a sensation like sheet lightning root her to the spot. A moan escaped her lips. Her fingers tangled in his hair. She came very close to whispering, I love you.

That sobered her somewhat. She drew back a little. Suddenly she felt afraid of where this might be leading.

To my ruination, she thought, if I'm thinking thoughts like that. What's happening here, though sublime, isn't love, it's purely physical. To him I'm just another body.

And too willing a body. She drew back a little more. Far too willing for my own good.

He stopped kissing her and looked down at her, his black eyes smiling. 'These are all the variations I can show you for the moment.' As he spoke, he continued to caress her swollen breast, clearly sensing that she had no desire for him to stop. 'All the other variations require a horizontal position, and I can tell we're not quite ready for that.'

Ronni blushed, but smiled back at him. 'No, we're not,' she answered. It took a great deal of effort to resist adding the word 'yet'.

'So, in the meantime——' it was almost as though he'd read her mind! '—I suggest that you and I go back to the party. If they're playing another slow tune, I'd like to dance.'

'You mean we're not going to drive straight back to Olbia? You mean we don't have to leave, after all?'

Guido shook his head and laid his hands on her shoulders. 'We're going nowhere—at least, not until tomorrow. We're staying for the party and we're spending the night here.' He smiled. 'I believe your room is just down the corridor from mine.'

Then, as she blushed again, he slipped an arm

around her waist and led her back through the garden to the party.

They danced almost till dawn, till there was no more champagne and almost all of the other guests had long gone home. Ronni had never been so deliriously happy in her life.

'Time we were off to bed.' At last, Guido said it, as they stood together on the edge of the dance-floor and he dropped a kiss into her hair. 'Shall I carry you or will you carry me?'

Ronni giggled. 'I suggest we carry each other.'

'Come on, then.' He wrapped an arm around her waist and smiled as she wrapped an arm around his. Then he was leading her across the terrace and through the open doors of the villa, across the drawing-room and out into the hall.

At the foot of the stairs Ronni darted him a quick look. On the next floor lay their separate rooms, just along the corridor from each other, as Guido had already pointed out. What was about to happen now? she wondered, her stomach tensing. Would he invite her to taste his horizontal variations?

As they began to climb the stairs, arms still wrapped around each other, Ronni asked herself for the hundredth time what she would do if he did. And for the hundredth time she found it impossible to envisage saying no. For the hundredth time her insides twisted and shivered with excitement.

They reached the top of the stairs and headed along the corridor, Ronni's heart beating so loudly she was sure he must hear it. And suddenly she was hopelessly, desperately aware of the hard male body that her arm was circling. Every inch of her was pulsing and seething with anticipation.

'Did you enjoy your party?' Guido had stopped to gaze down at her. They were standing very near to the door to her room.

'It was wonderful,' she nodded. 'The best evening ever.'

'I'm glad.' He kissed her. 'I enjoyed it, too. At least for a while we both managed to forget.' He paused. 'And now, there's only one thing left to do. . .'

He slid a finger beneath her chin and tilted her head to look at him. Ronni imagined she saw a question form in his eyes and already she was forming her answer in her head.

I shall say yes, she was thinking. I have to say yes.

But then he took her by surprise. 'The only thing that's left now is for me to kiss you and wish you a very good night.' He bent briefly to brush her lips, then he was reaching behind her to turn the handle of her bedroom door. 'I'll see you some time in the morning.'

Ronni was afraid her disappointment might be showing in her face. She turned away abruptly. 'Goodnight,' she told him. Suddenly she was feeling as though she'd been dropped from a great height.

Guido was already heading down the corridor towards his own room, but he stopped suddenly and glanced back at her across his shoulder.

'By the way, I forgot to tell you. . .you're a hell of a dancer.' He threw her a wink. 'We must do it again some time.'

Later, Ronni lay and seethed in her bed.

'By the way, I forgot to tell you. . . We must do it

again some time'. If that wasn't a brush-off, she didn't know what was. There she'd been, aching for a night of passion and the best he'd felt moved to offer her was a compliment on her dancing!

Though I should feel grateful, she decided. He could have taken advantage. He could have humiliated me totally with a one-night stand.

But that really wasn't the point. She didn't want to feel grateful that the whole thing hadn't degenerated into something absurd and degrading. What she wanted was to understand why she'd misjudged the evening so totally.

To her it had felt as though something special was happening between them. Not love. If there was love, it was entirely on her side. It had never occurred to her to delude herself that it might be otherwise.

But she had been rash enough to believe he was starting to care for her. His smiles, his glances, his gentle intimacies. . .somehow they had all seemed to be pointing in that direction. She had dared to believe they might be moving towards something together.

And she had been wrong. Of course. He had merely been playing with her. Still seething with anger, she pulled the bedclothes around her. Well, she told herself, what else did she expect?

She lay there and seethed, stoking her anger. Anger against Guido and anger against herself.

But deep inside she knew she wasn't as angry as she was pretending, that anger was really only a small part of what she felt. Only it was safer, less painful, to fill her heart with anger, so that there was no room left for anything else.

For suddenly she was remembering those enigmatic

remarks he'd made, which she'd paid barely any heed to at the time. What was it he'd said? 'Doesn't it make you forget everything? I know it does me'. And then, later, 'At least for a while we both managed to forget'.

She'd thought at the time — fleetingly, without really dwelling on it — that he'd been referring to Arnie with these remarks. But now she wondered if she'd been wrong — or, at least, only partly right. Perhaps he'd been referring to someone else as well? Someone that *he* was trying to forget.

The thought sent a chill of anguish lapping round her heart, puncturing her anger, making tears rise in her throat.

Was there another element in the equation that she hadn't even considered? Was Guido in love with someone else?

It was after ten next morning when Ronni emerged from the villa, wearing a T-shirt over her swimsuit, to find Filippo and Agnese having breakfast out on the terrace.

'I thought I'd go for a quick swim before breakfast,' she told them, deeply grateful that there was no sign of Guido. Right at that moment, on an empty stomach, she couldn't have faced him.

'Go ahead.' Agnese was looking as bright and lovely as ever. She had evidently, Ronni thought, slept rather better than she had. 'There's no rush. Have breakfast whenever you're ready.'

There was a gate in the wall that overlooked the seashore — the wall where she and Guido had stood last night — with a flight of stone steps leading down to the beach. Ronni hurried down, pulling her T-shirt over her head, and ran across the warm silver sand to the sea's edge.

The water felt delicious. Ronni sighed as it embraced her. Then she struck out towards the horizon, doing a slow, leisurely crawl.

She had barely slept last night — even what little of it had been left when she had finally crawled beneath the bedcovers. Round and round in her head had gone the memory of the evening, undoubtedly the most magical evening of her life, but tarnished now by the memory of how it had ended, with Guido's crude brush-off and her belated realisation that he was in love with someone else.

For Ronni was sure of that now. There was someone he was trying to forget. In fact, the entire evening, spent flirting and dancing with her, had probably been no more than a cynical exercise in keeping his mind off someone else.

Damn him! Ronni thought, as she continued to spear through the water. Well, one thing was for sure. . .he wouldn't catch her out again!

With a sigh, she rolled over and floated on her back for a bit and did her best to talk herself out of her feelings for Guido.

I don't love him, she told herself. How could I possibly love him? I've known the wretched man for less than a week! He's just turned my head, that's all, and I intend to turn it right back again. From now on there'll be no more going weak at the knees!

She felt a pang of hunger. It was time for breakfast. She rolled over and headed back towards the shore.

It wasn't until Ronni stood up at the shore's edge

that she saw Guido standing watching her, bare feet planted in the sand.

'That was better,' he told her. 'And you're not even out of breath. I would say you're definitely fitter than you were.'

Ronni tried not to look at him and squeezed the water from her hair. In spite of all her fine resolutions, her heart had slammed against her ribs at the sight of him and suddenly she felt decidedly weak at the knees.

She said, curtly, 'How nice to know you approve.'

He was dressed in white trousers and T-shirt, his hands in his trouser pockets. 'I came to tell you I'd quite like us to leave before too long—just in case you were planning a lengthy swim.'

'You thought maybe I was planning on swimming all the way to Africa?'

Compared to his easy tone, she sounded stiff and hostile. Which was precisely the way she wanted to sound, she told herself. This man had simply made a fool of her last night.

She added, 'I wasn't planning anything quite so strenuous.'

'Good.' He met her gaze, and now his tone had altered. There was a touch of steel as he told her, 'We'll be leaving as soon as you've had breakfast.'

'Might I know where we're going?' Ronni proceeded to stride past him. Her legs felt like pokers jabbing into the sand. 'I suppose we're going to the mainland on another wild-goose chase?'

'No, we're not going to the mainland.' He was following behind her, and Ronni could feel his annoyance growing. 'It appears that won't be necessary, after all.'

'Then where are we going?' She flicked a look over her shoulder, glad to have provoked this bad feeling between them. She was suddenly feeling a great deal safer.

'I'm getting a little tired,' she added tetchily, 'of being shunted all over the place looking for your wretched cousin.'

'And your wretched brother.' His tone was a cool warning. Ronni could tell he didn't like her attitude one bit.

Good, she thought, snatching up her T-shirt from the sand. Let him see I'm no longer the pushover I was last night!

As she started up the steps, he was following her, telling her, 'The latest news I have is that they're planning to return to Olbia today. I intend to be at the harbour to meet them.'

'I see.' At the top of the steps, Ronni turned to look at him, as a sudden curious question popped into her head. 'What about the speedboat? Are they bringing that back, too?'

'There's no word about the speedboat.' Guido's eyes lanced through her. 'No one's seen the speedboat. It seems to have disappeared.'

'Oh.'

She ought to feel pleased by that, but the truth was she didn't. And those lancing dark eyes were making her heart weep. She had a sudden desperate longing to relive last night—at least, the part up until when they had said goodnight.

She said, softening her tone a little, 'It has to be somewhere.'

'Oh, it's somewhere all right.'

'Maybe they've hidden it.'

'Or sold it.'

'Surely not.' Ronni pondered for a moment. Then she shook her head. 'Jeff wouldn't sell your boat. Whatever else he is, my brother's not a thief.'

'Well, you could have fooled me.' Guido's tone was harsh and angry. 'He's made a pretty good job of spiriting off my speedboat, not to mention spiriting off my cousin.'

'But he hasn't stolen it. I'm sure he hasn't. He's only taken it temporarily. It'll be somewhere. Jeff's not a thief.'

'Don't defend him to me!' Suddenly the dark eyes were flashing. 'Your brother's an irresponsible, thieving blackguard. I'll never forgive him for involving Silvia in all this. But he'll pay for it. That's one thing I can guarantee!'

Ronni felt herself wince in the face of his sudden anger, but at the same time, finally, she understood something. It was Silvia he was really concerned about, not the speedboat. And it was his concern for Silvia that was at the root of his anger.

She frowned into his face, suddenly anxious to reassure him. 'I'm sure you needn't worry,' she started to tell him. She'd been about to add, I'm sure Jeff's taking good care of her. But before she could continue, he was brushing past her roughly, almost causing her to stagger and stumble back down the steps.

'Kindly don't waste any more of my time,' he ordered her. 'Just make sure you're ready to leave in half an hour!'

Then, like a whirlwind, he was storming off through the garden, heading back towards the villa.

When Ronni reached the terrace, there was no sign of him, but Agnese was waiting for her, a concerned look on her face.

'I just saw Guido,' she said, coming up to Ronni. 'He looked furious.' Then she laid a hand on Ronni's arm and smiled into her pale face. 'Whatever passed between you, don't take it personally,' she said kindly. She squeezed Ronni's arm. 'He's just worried about Silvia.'

Then as Ronni looked into her face, she nodded wisely. 'You've got to understand about Guido and Silvia. Guido's feelings for Silvia have always been very special. More special, perhaps, than is strictly wise. Sometimes I think that girl will break his heart.'

Ronni stared back at her with a sense of helpless inevitability, suddenly, with a shiver, putting two and two together.

She had been right in her deduction that he was in love with someone. And that someone, it now appeared, was Silvia, his cousin.

CHAPTER NINE

OF COURSE. Now it all made sense. She should have have thought of it before. That was why Guido was so against the romance between Jeff and Silvia. Because he was in love with his beautiful cousin himself.

Ronni had plenty of time to torture herself with these thoughts as they made the journey back to Olbia, barely exchanging a word the whole way. An icy distance had grown up between them. They barely even glanced at one another.

But now, at last, they had reached Olbia harbour and, leaving the car in the car park, were on their way to meet the ferry. Guido was deliberately going faster than Ronni could comfortably keep up with and she was being forced to run to avoid being left behind.

'What makes you so sure they'll be on this ferry, anyway?' Catching her breath, Ronni added, 'All this panic could be for nothing.'

'It could be, but I don't think so.' Guido had found a perfect position with a good view of the approaching ferry. 'According to my information, they're almost certainly on board.'

Ronni wasn't sure whether she hoped they were or not, as she watched the ferry dock and the landing plank go down. If they were, it would almost certainly mean a major row, but even if they weren't the prospects weren't too bright. Either way, she wasn't looking forward to what was coming next.

There was much pushing and shoving and shouting and waving as the passengers at last began to disembark. Ronni peered at the faces coming off the boat. Poor Jeff, she was thinking, you're in for it now.

And then suddenly he appeared, making her heart smile inside her, as he stood out from the crowd with his shock of bright blond hair. She felt a surge of solidarity and loyalty towards him. Even in the face of Guido's wrath, she would stand by him. She couldn't believe he was guilty of anything really bad.

She glanced at Guido and saw that his eyes were fixed on Silvia, who was following behind Jeff as they made their way down the landing plank. And there was such a look of stark relief in his eyes that his beloved cousin was safe, after all, that, just for a moment, to hide her own pain, Ronni had to drop her gaze away.

It was as she raised her eyes again that Silvia suddenly caught sight of Guido. Ronni saw her say something to Jeff and point. They're going to make a run for it, she thought.

But that was not what happened. In fact, what happened was quite the opposite. All at once, a dignified Jeff was walking towards her and Guido, looking Guido straight in the eye as though he had nothing to fear.

He stopped in front of the taller man and held up the parcel in his hand. 'I hope you're grateful for all the trouble I've just gone to,' he said. 'This is the petrol gauge part we needed for your speedboat. I couldn't get it locally. I had to go to the mainland.'

For a moment Guido just looked at him, clearly slightly thrown. He said in a flat tone, 'And where's the speedboat?'

Now it was Jeff's turn to look thrown. He paused and said, frowning, 'I presume it's in the boathouse, where it always is.'

'No, it's not in the boathouse.' Guido spoke quietly, his eyes never leaving the other man's face. 'It vanished from the boathouse a couple of days ago.'

'Vanished? You mean it's been stolen?' Jeff looked thunderstruck. His blue eyes were flashing. 'Who the devil could have taken it?'

It was at that moment, Ronni thought later, that Guido made up his mind that he'd been wrong in associating Jeff with the disappearance of his speedboat. It must have been as clear to him as it was to her that Jeff, most definitely, wasn't acting. Nobody could have faked the shocked look on his face.

And it was greatly to Guido's credit the way he proceeded to react. He laid a hand on Jeff's shoulder. 'I apologise,' he said. 'I confess that I thought you'd taken the boat. I can see now I was mistaken and I'm sorry I ever thought it.'

Ronni felt proud of him at that moment. Her heart swelled within her. As she looked at him, for a moment the icy distance between them vanished. At least no one could ever accuse him of lacking decency and moral courage.

'You thought *I* took the boat?' Jeff's eyes widened in astonishment. 'How could you think a thing like that?' Then he smiled and proceeded to make Ronni feel even prouder — her brother was a pretty decent fellow, too! 'You crazy man, I love that boat as much as you do.' Jeff slapped Guido amicably on the shoulder. 'And I'm going to help you find it. Come on,' he added. 'Let's get cracking!'

But that was when the atmosphere subtly altered.

'Not so fast.' Guido's expression had darkened. 'I haven't finished with you yet. In fact, I haven't even started.'

Scowling, he glanced at Silvia who, so far, hadn't spoken, then his dark eyes darted back to Jeff once more. 'What do you mean by sneaking my cousin off to the mainland when she's supposed to be at my place, studying? Are you totally without even a gram of responsibility?'

'He didn't sneak me off.' At last, Silvia piped up. 'It was my idea as much as Jeff's that I went with him.' She held up the sports bag she held in one hand. 'But I took my English books with me.' She glanced apologetically at Ronni. 'I've been studying every spare minute. I promise I have.'

'Well, I'm afraid that's not good enough.' Guido was unforgiving. 'You made an undertaking with Ronni to do so many hours a day and you have flagrantly disregarded that undertaking.'

'I know.' To Ronni's surprise, and apparently also to Guido's, Silvia stared humbly down at the ground for a moment. Then, surprising them both further, she apologised to Ronni. 'I'm sorry. I've behaved badly. And after you coming all the way from England. But I hope you'll forgive me and decide to stay on. I need you if I'm going to pass those exams.'

Then, with a touch of her old defiance, she turned back to Guido. 'I went off with Jeff because I was so angry with you. And that was also why I didn't leave you a note explaining what we were up to as Jeff told me to. I get sick of you always trying to tell me what to do. I really hate you when you're like that.'

Ronni was aware of a look of withdrawal touching Guido's eyes. She's hurt him, she thought. He really does love her. Agnese was right, his feelings for her are very special.

And, just for a moment, in spite of the pain that brought her, it was the thought of his hurt that tore at her heart. She couldn't bear to think of Guido suffering.

She laid a hand on his arm. 'We ought to go back. . . so you and Jeff can start trying to find the boat.' Her tone expressed the warmth that flowed through her heart as she added, looking into his eyes with a smile, 'And so that Silvia and I can start making up for lost time.'

Their eyes met for a moment and Guido smiled back at her, flooding her heart with foolish pleasure. 'You're right,' he said. 'We've wasted enough time.' Then he was turning back to Jeff and Silvia. 'I take it you came here with Jeff's boat?' he was saying. 'So I'll leave you to find your own way back to the villa. As soon as possible,' he added crisply. 'No diversions.'

'No diversions.' Jeff nodded in agreement. 'Come on, Silvia.' He turned away. 'Let's get cracking.'

Guido was silent until he and Ronni reached the car park. Then as he pulled open the door of the Alfa Romeo and invited her to climb inside, he suddenly caught her arm and looked down into her face.

'I owe you an apology, too,' he told her. 'You clearly knew nothing about what Jeff and Silvia were up to. I jumped to conclusions that I had no right to jump to.' He pulled an apologetic face. 'I hope you can forgive me?'

Ronni glanced away to hide the flush that touched

her cheeks. Didn't he know she would have forgiven him anything?

'I hope you'll agree to stay on,' he was adding. 'I have a feeling that Silvia may have finally come to her senses.'

He looked oddly withdrawn, the dark eyes shuttered. Compassion flooded through Ronni. She longed to reach up and kiss him. It must be hard, she was thinking, to see the person you love so obviously in love with someone else.

And for a moment the irony of the observation escaped her. She should save her pity for herself. Her situation was the same.

But her tone was lightly teasing as she tried to cheer him up. 'You mean I have a choice as to whether I stay on or not?'

Guido smiled and touched her arm, then, too quickly, dropped his hand away. 'After the way the Falcone family have treated you, I would say we have no right to stop you if you want to go — and, whatever you decide, I'll pay you in full. I think that's the very least I owe you.'

'Oh, yes, you'll pay me in full all right.' Ronni spoke mock-sternly. Then she softened her tone and added, smiling, 'You'll pay me in full because I intend to stay on and make damned sure Silvia passes her exams. You're looking at a lady,' she added sparkily, 'who doesn't walk out on a job half done. I like to see things through to the finish — and to see them through successfully.'

But a minute or two later, as they turned out of the car park and headed for the road that led back to the villa, Ronni gave way to the growing desolation within her.

She meant what she'd said and she intended to keep her promise — but how would she survive another two weeks of living in such close proximity to Guido, when with every moment that passed her hopeless love for him grew deeper?

She felt suddenly, confusedly, a little like a man who had voluntarily passed a death sentence on himself.

At least there was one thing to be grateful for. Silvia was as good as her word.

Over the days that followed she and Ronni dutifully worked together for at least six hours a day. And it was Silvia, not Ronni, who was the first to arrive and the more reluctant to leave at the end of each lesson.

'You mustn't overdo it,' Ronni warned her one day, amazed that such a necessity should ever come to pass. 'You'll tire yourself out. It'll be counter-productive.'

But Silvia was relentless. 'Don't worry, I can stand the pace. As long as you can?' she added with concern.

'Oh, don't worry about me. I can stand the pace all right. But you're the one who's putting in most of the effort.'

'And about time, too.' Silvia smiled a wry smile. Then she laughed. 'Right, that's enough chat. Let's get back to work!'

There was another small mercy for which to be grateful. Ronni had barely set eyes on Guido for days. He and Jeff were out most of the time, trying to track down the speedboat, for which a popular local search had been mounted, and he was hardly ever at the villa.

That's a blessing, Ronni told herself, trying not to

think how much she missed him. Maybe I'll make it through the next couple of weeks, after all.

But then, quite by accident, she made a discovery that more or less forced her to seek him out. At first, she put it off. The thought of seeing him deranged her. But then she pulled herself together. It had to be done.

And so, about a week after their last direct encounter, she found herself one evening waiting up for him, sitting with a glass of vodka and tonic in the drawing-room, long after Silvia had gone to bed.

It was well after midnight when at last she heard his car.

At the sound of his footsteps approaching down the hall, she rose to her feet and hurried out to meet him.

'Guido. . .' How bittersweet that name tasted on her tongue. 'Guido,' she said again. 'I'd like a word with you.'

He was dressed in a pair of faded black jeans and a striped blue shirt with the sleeves rolled back. And, as she looked into his face, her heart thundering inside her, Ronni wondered how she had survived without him. He was her life. Her sun. He was what made her world go round.

He seemed in good spirits and mercifully oblivious of her torment.

'Well, this is a surprise. What are you doing up so late?' He glanced at the glass she held in her hand. 'What a good idea. I could do with a drink.'

'I was waiting up for you.' Ronni followed him back into the sitting-room and stood awkwardly watching him as he poured himself a whisky. Just being in the same room with him was an exquisite torment. 'As I said, I want to have a word.'

'Oh, yes?' He seemed distracted. He dropped ice into his glass and crossed to sink down into one of the nearby sofas. Then he smiled up at her. 'We've had a breakthrough. I think we're finally on the track of the speedboat. It's beginning to look as though one of my rivals may have stolen it.'

'That's marvellous — I mean that's terrible — I mean I'm glad you've almost found it.'

Ronni's brain was tripping and tumbling inside her. She could hardly speak for the ache in her heart. An ache of hopelessly mixed-up pleasure and pain. She longed to fall into his arms and at the same time to run away.

'I'm hoping that by tomorrow we'll know something definite. But it looks as though we're on the right track at last.' Guido took a mouthful of his drink and paused in what he was saying, looking up at her with an amused, curious glint in his eye. 'Why are you standing there looking like a startled deer? Take a seat. Make yourself comfortable. Surely you don't need to be invited?'

'Of course not.'

Did she really look like a startled deer? Ronni supposed she must. It was rather how she felt. She sat down gingerly on the edge of a nearby armchair, took a mouthful of vodka and pulled herself together.

'I was just fascinated and delighted by your story,' she fudged.

'So, what did you want to see me about?' Guido leaned back against the cushions. His hair, caught in the light from the table lamp at his back, was transformed into a luminescent halo of black curls. Ronni felt another layer of her feeble defences crumble.

He said, 'I hope you're not having problems with Silvia again?'

'Oh, no, nothing like that. I can't complain about Silvia. She's working like a beaver and improving in leaps and bounds.' Ronni smiled, relaxing a little, feeling a genuine sense of pleasure. 'I think you can be sure now that she's going to pass her exams,' she added.

'I'm sure she will.' Suddenly his expression had grown sober. 'As long as we can continue to keep her away from your brother.' His eyes narrowed and a muscle seemed to tighten in his cheek. 'I'm almost sorry we're so close to finding the boat. Helping me look for it was keeping your brother away from Silvia.'

Ronni felt a thrust to her heart. Nothing had changed. He was still in love with his cousin and still against her relationship with Jeff.

Instantly, she was filled with the need to protect herself from the hopelessly vulnerable way that made her feel.

'I don't know why you're still annoyed with Jeff after the way he's been helping you.' There was a satisfying, distancing edge of criticism in her voice. 'I would have thought you'd be feeling grateful to him.'

'I am. I'm most grateful for his help with the boat.' Guido looked back at her, eyes narrowed, and took a mouthful of whisky. 'But I still can't say I'm grateful for his behaviour regarding Silvia.'

No. Of course he wasn't. And Ronni knew why.

She looked back at him and challenged him, 'What's wrong with his behaviour regarding Silvia?'

'Everything, in my opinion.'

Ronni felt her stomach tighten.

'What's the matter?' she said a little cruelly. 'Don't you like your cousin being in love?'

'Not when it's with a man who has no regard for her welfare.' To his credit, not a flicker crossed his eyes as he said it. Had she not already known, Ronni would never have guessed the truth.

Guido elaborated, 'I'm afraid I'm still a long way from forgiving your brother for his irresponsible behaviour.'

'Yes, I can see that. But you're wrong about Jeff. He may have behaved irresponsibly, but he's not an irresponsible person.'

'We shall see.' For a moment, Guido stared into his whisky. 'Personally, I'm rather hoping that the romance will just fizzle out.'

Ronni wanted to say, I don't think it will, somehow. That, after all, was what she believed. But it would have been too cruel, and she had already been cruel once, and being cruel to him didn't help her own pain.

So, instead, saying nothing, she too stared into her glass.

There was a silence. Ronni could hear the beating of her heart and she fancied she could hear the beat of Guido's, too—beating with hopeless love for Silvia. All at once, she felt driven to the floor with sheer misery.

Then, at last, Guido broke the silence. 'You said you wanted to speak to me. I take it the subject you wished to discuss was not Jeff and Silvia?'

'Oh, no.' She shook her head and smiled a wry inner smile. That thorny subject, if he but knew it, was as painful to her as it was to him.

She straightened in her seat and regarded him steadily. 'I wanted to see you,' she told him, 'in order to apologise.'

'Apologise for what?' His dark eyebrows lifted. 'I can think of nothing you need to apologise to me for.'

'Ah, but there is something.' Ronni smiled a small smile, grateful that the subject of Jeff and Silvia had been left behind, and enjoying, for once, the fact that she had him at a disadvantage. She sat back a little more relaxed in her seat. 'That business about my tickets and my passport and my traveller's cheques. . .'

As she paused, Guido nodded. 'I take it, then, that you've found them?'

'They were down the side of the armchair in my room. They must have dropped out of my bag and slipped behind the cushion.' Ronni flushed and frowned in shameful consternation. 'I'm sorry that I accused you of taking them.'

Guido smiled then, without rancour. 'We've both been doing a bit of that — accusing each other of things that neither of us is guilty of.' He gave a small laugh. 'I guess it must be something in the chemistry.'

For a moment he held her eyes with an oddly searching expression. He looked as though he was about to say something, Ronni thought. Then he shrugged instead. 'I'm glad you found them. As a matter of fact, I'd forgotten all about them.'

'So had I, oddly enough. . .' I had other things on my mind. She added that to herself while, aloud, she elaborated, 'I was fishing for a coin that I'd accidentally dropped down the back of the chair. . .and there was my passport and the rest of my stuff.'

She shook her head. 'Anyway, that's why I waited up for you. I wanted to apologise for that.'

'And your apology is accepted and the gesture much appreciated.' Guido drained his whisky glass and laid it down on a nearby table. Suddenly, the dark eyes were twinkling across at her. 'We seem to be spending a great deal of time apologising to one another these days. But I'm glad we finally seem to have got everything straight.'

'Yes. I'm glad, too.' Though Ronni knew the remark was hollow. What was there to be so glad about when nothing made any difference? Things might finally be straight, but he still didn't love her.

She glanced at her watch, all at once anxious to escape. 'Well, I've told you what I wanted to tell you, and now it's rather late.' She started to stand up. 'It's time I went to bed.'

But then, to her dismay, Guido stood up, too.

He said, 'Yes, I suppose it is rather late.'

Then he stepped towards her to stand just a couple of feet away.

Ronni swallowed. She longed to turn and walk away. But her feet were fixed with six-inch nails to the floor.

Then suddenly Guido smiled and reached out to touch her cheek. 'Tonight,' he said, 'you look like Veronica again.'

Ronni felt like weeping with the desire that flowed through her. Just the touch of his hand and she was turned to putty. She gazed at him helplessly. 'I don't know what you mean.'

'What I mean is that I wish I could snap my fingers and suddenly there'd be a band playing some soft, slow music.' He smiled. 'Then you wouldn't say no if I asked to take you in my arms under the pretext of inviting you to dance.'

Ronni couldn't bear to listen. Her soul was bleeding. She opened her mouth to speak, but no sound came out.

'Still, we could always pretend. . .'

He had moved a little closer. She could feel the heat of him pressing against her. She longed for it to swallow her. Barely breathing, she closed her eyes.

A moment later, it seemed to Ronni, she could indeed hear music. She made no attempt to move away as his arms slipped round her. With a sigh she fell against him, her heart in uproar.

The music was carrying her away as his fingers laced her hair. The slow, steady rhythm was pulsing in her veins. Then suddenly her breath caught as the tempo quickened at the touch of his fingers against the back of her neck.

'Veronica. . .'

He breathed the name against her cheek, just as he had on the night of the party. And Ronni was suddenly helpless. She felt her arms twine round his neck.

'Oh, Guido. . .!' she murmured with a strangled sob.

The next minute he was kissing her and she was kissing him back, her fingers in his hair, her breath sobbing in her throat. And all at once it was as though a fire raged between them, scorching their hungry bodies, sending sparks into the air around them.

His hand was on her breast, moulding, caressing through the thin cotton fabric of her T-shirt. Then, impatiently, he was pulling the T-shirt aside, freeing her breast from her bra and taking hold of her naked flesh.

It was what she had longed for. Ronni moaned and pressed against him, her own hand seeking the buttons of his shirt, undoing them quickly then sliding inside to press against the muscular warmth of his chest.

'Veronica, let's go upstairs.'

Suddenly, he was gathering her against him, as though he would lift her up into his arms and carry her off. And she knew it was what she wanted. She longed for it desperately. With every atom of her being. But she knew it could not be.

What would happen when it was over? No, she could not live with that.

Summoning all the will-power she possessed, she took a step back away from him.

'I can't,' she said. 'I can't. It's Arnie.'

She ought to have been struck down by a thunderbolt, Ronni thought later. No one had been further from her mind at that moment than Arnie. But desperate situations called for desperate lies. And Arnie was the first lie that popped into her head.

And to her relief and utter despair, the lie worked a treat.

'Arnie. Ah, yes. I was forgetting about Arnie.' A look crossed Guido's face as he dropped his hands away. He took a step back from her. 'How could I have forgotten Arnie?'

There was a cruel taunt in his voice that cut her to the quick. Ronni nearly retaliated, And what about Silvia? She's the one who's really standing in our way!

But, instead, she heard herself say, 'I'm terribly sorry.' Then, unable to look at him, she was turning and rushing from the room.

Up in her room with the door locked, she stood quivering and shaking, her emotions oddly dulled, unable to cry. It was as though all the pain and grief inside her was so heavy and immense that it had totally stunned her.

Good, she thought, I don't want to feel.

But then suddenly she saw it, lying on the tallboy, its petals turning brown now, withered and dry, the red geranium that Guido had picked from the urn.

She stared at it for a moment, her body feeling frozen, her heart as still as a stone in her chest. Then, like a dam bursting, suddenly she was diving across the room, a sob escaping from her lips as she reached out to snatch it up.

Just to hold it, that was all she wanted, and press its dry petals against her cheek. It was the only thing she had that Guido had given her.

But as she seized it in her hand, before her horrified eyes the dried petals fell away and fluttered to the floor, scattering like confetti at her feet.

Oh, no! Now she had nothing! With a cry of despair, Ronni sank to her knees and collapsed into tears.

Ronni heard through Silvia that the speedboat had been found.

'It was Guido's arch-rival who he's beaten into second place twice. . .he's the one who took it, and now he's been arrested.' Silvia laughed. 'He won't even be coming second this year!'

'But what about Guido. . .? Is his speedboat all right? The thief didn't do any damage to it, did he?'

'No, the speedboat's OK. At least, more or less. Guido reckons he'll have it ready for the qualifying trials.'

'Thank heavens for that.' Ronni felt a weight lift from her. It had crucified her to think that the boat might be damaged and Guido deprived after all of his hat trick.

'Don't worry,' Silvia told her proudly. 'Guido will win. There's no one in the world who can beat my wonderful cousin.'

And Guido was putting in long hours to ensure that he did win. Over the following week, Ronni rarely saw him. But she made a point of going down to the jetty one day to tell him, 'I'm really glad you found your boat.'

'Thanks.' He turned to smile at her as he answered, making her heart slam with love and helpless grief against her ribs. 'Now all I've got to do is get it in shape and make sure I pass the qualifying trials this weekend.'

'Oh, you'll pass all right, and then go on to win the race.' Just like Silvia, Ronni had no doubt about that. 'I'd lay my very last penny on it,' she told him.

'Such faith.' He smiled again, so that she had to look away. And then he asked her, 'And what about you?'

'Me?'

'Yes, you. Are you going to win, too?'

How can I do that when I've already lost? The thought seared through her brain, and then belatedly she understood. Ronni managed to force a smile. 'I'm pretty sure I'll win — or, rather, that Silvia will. I think she'll pass.'

'Then we can have a double celebration. I'll look out the champagne.'

As he said it, he held her eyes and suddenly Ronni was remembering that glass of champagne they'd shared at the party. She turned away abruptly, fighting the pain that choked her. 'I'd better leave you now,' she muttered over her shoulder. 'You've got things to do and I've got a lesson.'

Then, head bent, she was hurrying back to the villa, suddenly knowing in her heart what had to be done.

She said nothing to anyone until the very last moment. Then, as she and Silvia packed up their things after their final English lesson, she told the other girl, 'I'll be leaving tomorrow, just as soon as your exam is over.' As she spoke, she fiddled with the corner of her notepad.

Silvia was horrified. 'You can't!' she protested. 'You'll miss Guido's test run! You'll miss the celebrations!'

'I know. But I have to go.'

'Why, for heaven's sake? I thought you didn't have to start work again for another three weeks?'

'I don't, but there are things I have to do at home.' Nervously, Ronni continued to fiddle with her notepad. 'Urgent things that need my attention. And besides,' she added, before Silvia could protest again, 'once your exam's over, my job here is done. I really have no reason to stay on.

'I wish Guido all the best in the trials, of course,' she added, 'but there's only one thing that really matters to me now — and that's going home as soon as I can.'

As she said it, she stared fixedly at the shredded corner of her notepad and wished vainly, but with all her heart, that it were true.

CHAPTER TEN

RONNI flew off with a heavy and tormented heart. How could she survive knowing she would never see Guido again?

But I must, she told herself. Even when the sun goes down, the world still has to keep going round. And, somehow, I too must keep going without my sun.

It was raining when her flight arrived at Heathrow and it rained all the way back to her flat in Islington. But Ronni almost felt glad. The rain fitted her mood.

Dumping her bags in the bedroom, she sat down at the kitchen table and began to sift lethargically through the pile of accumulated mail, from time to time eyeing the phone in the hall. She ought to phone Arnie to let him know she was back, but he was the last person she felt like speaking to right now. For one thing, what on earth was she going to say to him?

She laid down her letters and stared blankly at the wall. You *have* to speak to Arnie, she told herself firmly. You have to speak to Arnie and tell him everything. Not about Guido. He needn't know about Guido. Guido had nothing to do with what she had to tell him.

For Guido, she realised, had only been the catalyst that had finally forced her to confront her true feelings for Arnie. Or rather, her *lack* of feelings, she admitted shamefully. Guido hadn't stolen her affections from

Arnie. There hadn't been much in the way of affection
to steal.

No, that wasn't quite true, she corrected herself,
frowning. She had been fond of Arnie. In a way, she
still was. They'd been friends, companions, they'd got
on well together, but, now that she knew what real
love was, she knew that she had never for one moment
loved him.

Her heart clenched inside her as she thought of
Guido and the dizzy, consuming passions he aroused
in her. That was love. Something to die for. She felt a
sob break within her. More appropriately in her case,
it was something to die without.

She dropped her eyes back to the pile of letters. It
was no good dreaming. What she had to do, finally,
was face reality. And reality meant speaking to Arnie
face to face. A letter or a phone call would be much
easier, but that was the coward's way and she had too
much pride for that—not to mention too much respect
for Arnie. He deserved to be told the truth to his face.

She brushed away the tear that she'd been totally
unaware was slowly trickling down her face. Then she
took a deep breath. I must go to Bradford right away.

The following day she caught an early train from King's
Cross station and set off on the two-hundred-mile
journey north. She'd slept badly and felt numb with
weariness and grief. The last thing she felt like coping
with was a confrontation.

But this was something she knew she had to do. This
was the urgent business she'd spoken of to Silvia.

It was a bright sunny day when she arrived in

Bradford, the late July sun slanting against the roof-tops, bathing the city in a warm, gentling light.

Ronni took a taxi to the college where Arnie was doing his summer school—she'd phoned his flat from the station and been told that was where he'd be.

At the college gates, she got out, preferring to walk across the campus. Putting off the evil hour, she suspected. Gathering up her courage. All the way up on the train, she'd been rehearsing what she'd say to him. She was praying with all her heart that he wouldn't be too hurt.

Groups of students and teachers were sitting on the grass, chatting and laughing in the sun. There was a feeling of high spirits and jollity in the air. Ronni felt like an executioner at a party.

And then she saw them and stopped dead in her tracks.

Her mouth fell open. Surely, it couldn't be?

But it was, there was absolutely no doubt about it. Walking towards her, yet totally oblivious of her presence, was a smiling, literally radiant-faced Arnie, one arm circling the waist of a red-haired girl.

Ronni caught her breath. Well, I never!

They were almost right on top of her before they saw her. And they mightn't have seen her yet if Ronni hadn't spoken, so totally absorbed were they in one another.

Ronni could scarcely keep her face straight. 'Hi,' she said.

Now it was Arnie's turn to stop dead in his tracks. He looked at Ronni as though she were a particularly disappointing novelty that had just fallen out of his Christmas cracker.

'Hi,' he said, dropping his arm from the girl's waist.

'Don't bother. I saw.' Ronni smiled a wry smile. And I really don't mind, she was about to add.

But Arnie cut in. 'I was going to tell you.' He looked shamefaced. 'I didn't know you'd got back.'

Ronni shook her head and laid a hand on his arm, smiling kindly at the blushing red-haired girl as she did so. 'It's OK. Don't worry. But I think we ought to talk. Is there anywhere around here where we can have a cup of coffee?'

An hour later, after coffee and cakes in the canteen, all three of them were feeling a great deal better.

'I hope we can be friends,' Arnie said, looking earnestly at Ronni. 'All three of us, I mean. I hope we can keep in touch.'

'I hope so, too.' Ronni meant it. She'd taken an instant liking to Arnie's new girlfriend, who was patently far more suited to him than she'd ever been. And she bore Arnie no hard feelings. On the contrary, she felt happy that he'd found true love at last.

She raised her coffee-cup in a toast. 'I wish you both all the best.'

Arnie and Penny, as she was called, had tried to insist that Ronni stay overnight and return to London the following morning. 'We'll take you out for dinner,' Penny suggested.

But Ronni declined. 'No, I have to get back. I've got a thousand and one things I have to do. Perhaps we can have dinner some other time.'

And, as she climbed on to the train, she was glad she was going home. She did have a thousand and one things to do, though there wasn't a single one of them that couldn't have waited. The real reason she'd wanted to leave was the harsh discovery that when you were nursing a broken heart there was nothing more painful than being surrounded by others who were happily in love.

'All mankind love a lover'. All the world but a lover spurned.

She stared at the darkening landscape as the train headed towards London, feeling that sense of numbness settle inside her once again.

And again she asked herself, How will I survive now that the sun has been taken out of my life?

The phone rang. It was Betty calling off their game of tennis.

'Sorry, I've got to take Jerry to a chum's party,' she told Ronni. 'Tony was going to do it, but he's got tied up with something else.'

'That's all right.' Ronni was understanding. 'Maybe I'll go along to the club anyway and see if I can get a game with someone else.'

As she laid down the phone, she decided she'd do that. Even if she couldn't get a game, there'd be something going on at the club, and it would be better than moping around at home. Moping was definitely a dangerous pursuit.

Over the past two weeks Ronni had done her share of moping. And her share of weeping and lying sleepless until dawn. And there'd be more to endure. Though she was learning to cope, she was a long way from being over Guido yet.

She'd managed to cope, principally, by keeping busy. She'd rejoined the sports club she used to belong to before she'd allowed her membership to lapse during her time with Arnie. And she and her friend Betty had spent long hours together, playing tennis and squash and doing a bit of swimming. Though occasionally, like now, Betty's family commitments — she had a husband and a three-year-old son — meant that she had to cancel a date.

'I got into all this sports stuff after Jerry was born,' Betty had told her. 'I needed something to get me back in shape.'

Precisely what I need, too, Ronni had thought privately. Though it's my head, not my body that needs pulling into shape. After her three weeks in Sardinia she was physically quite fit. As Guido had promised her, her stay there had knocked her into pretty good shape.

But she hadn't dwelt on that thought. She never dwelt on thoughts of Guido. To dwell on thoughts of Guido would be to drive herself mad.

She glanced at her watch now. It was just after eleven. She would go down to the club and do some keep fit for an hour, then have a fruit juice lunch and see if she could find a game of tennis.

Grabbing her sports bag, she glanced at her reflection in the hall mirror. She looked a little less hollow-eyed than she had a week ago. If she kept working on it, a week from now, she might look even better.

She slung the bag over her shoulder and stepped towards the front door. And in that very same instant the doorbell rang.

Ronni yanked the door open. Who could it be?

Then she saw and felt her heart turn to powder inside her.

Her mouth fell open. She stood there, paralysed.

'I see I just caught you. May I come in?'

'I was on my way to tennis.' Ronni looked back at him, dumbstruck. 'I——' She stopped and stared at him. 'What are you doing here?'

'I've come to see you.' He leaned one hand against the door-frame. 'Aren't you going to let me in?'

Ronni was barely aware of what he was saying. Her brain was still having a great deal of difficulty coping with what her eyes were telling her.

Was this really Guido standing before her, looking unbearably handsome in a pale linen suit? Were those dark eyes that were gazing down at her really Guido's? If she reached out to touch him, would he vanish like a ghost?

She dared not put that suspicion to the test. She remained rigidly immobile, suddenly quite incapable of moving anyway. Even her heart seemed to have stopped in mid-beat in her breast.

But dimly she heard him say again, 'Aren't you going to let me in?'

Ronni struggled from her stupor and stepped back into the hallway, her legs feeling like bales of straw beneath her. Then she heard herself say in a voice that sounded almost normal, 'Of course. Forgive me. Please come in.'

The next moment he was inside and she was closing the door behind him, then leading him along the narrow hallway towards the living-room.

He'll have disappeared when I turn round, she thought. I'll discover it was all a dream.

But to her amazement he was still there as she turned to tell him, 'Please make yourself comfortable. Take a seat.'

He looked too big for the room as he seated himself in one of the armchairs. Too big and too dramatic, with his wild black hair, copper-dark suntan and eyes as black as midnight. Too big, too dramatic and too impossibly wonderful.

She felt the love in her heart thrust sharply against her ribs. Helpless pain and longing went flooding through her.

'How have you been?'

He was looking across at her as she seated herself gingerly in the armchair opposite him. She licked her dry lips. 'Terrific,' she said.

'That's good.' He leaned back against the cushions, but there was a stiffness to his movements and a stiffness in his voice.

'I hear you qualified for the race.' Jeff had rung to tell her — and to tell her at the same time that Silvia had passed her exams with flying colours.

Even more stiffly now than Guido, Ronni leaned back in her chair. 'That's good,' she said. 'Congratulations.'

'Thank you.'

'And what about the the race itself? Did you win your hat trick?'

'The race itself is not until next week.' Guido paused, his eyes surveying her. 'Next Wednesday, in fact.'

'Oh, yes, of course.'

If she'd thought about it, of course, she'd known that. But thinking about Guido and the race were two things she'd been trying very hard not to do.

She said, 'I would have thought you'd be busy practising.' And as something flickered across his eyes, for the first time she wondered what on earth he was doing here in London. And, more to the point, what was he doing in her flat?

'Silvia and Jeff have got engaged.' It was as though he'd answered that last question. 'They made it official just a couple of days ago.'

So, he was in London on some business or other and had simply dropped by to tell her that Jeff and Silvia had got engaged. Ronni felt a swooping, irrational plummet of disappointment. What on earth else had she thought he'd come here to tell her?

She said, 'That's nice.' Then, remembering Silvia and his feelings for her, she asked him quietly, 'Are you pleased?'

'I'm coming round to the idea.' He paused, then smiled suddenly. 'Actually, I think I've already come round. I've finally forgiven Jeff and I'm delighted at the engagement.'

How could he be? Ronni frowned at him as he continued, 'I think they'll make a go of it. I think they make a very good couple.'

He certainly sounded pleased. But how was that possible when he was secretly in love with Silvia?

Ronni fiddled with her chair arm. 'I'm surprised to hear you're pleased.'

'Well, I am.' Guido sighed and seemed to relax a little, as he told her with a light smile, 'In fact, I'm very pleased. Now that Jeff's in the picture, it means I can back off a little and stop feeling quite so responsible for Silvia.'

'Back off a little?' Ronni's heart had grown still. 'What do you mean back off a little?'

Guido shrugged. 'I don't know if you know the

story. . .? Perhaps Jeff's told you. . .? About me and Silvia?'

Ronni shook her head stiffly. 'I don't know any story.' She had grown so still now she was barely breathing.

Guido gave a brief sigh. 'It all started with the accident. . .the accident five years ago when Silvia's father was killed.' He lowered his eyes briefly, as pain flickered across them, then raised them to look at Ronni again. 'He was on his way to Rome airport, coming to visit me. . . There was a terrible accident. . . He was killed. . .'

As he paused, Ronni watched him. What was coming next?

'Silvia was distraught.' Guido was continuing with his story, and again Ronni caught that flicker of pain. 'She was young at the time, just fourteen, and I suppose didn't really know what she was saying. But at the funeral, in a fit of hysteria, she turned on me and blamed me for causing her father's death. If he hadn't been coming to visit me, it would never have happened.'

'But that's outrageous!' Ronni sat forward in her seat, momentarily forgetting about everything else. 'Don't tell me you ended up feeling guilty?'

'I'm afraid I did. I know it's not logical, but I couldn't get it out of my head that Silvia blamed me. So, I tried to make it up to her in every way I could — though it wasn't easy — she went on hating me for years.'

'How absolutely terrible!'

Now Ronni understood what Agnese had meant by her remarks about Guido's special feelings for Silvia and her fear that Silvia would break his heart. And it was a million miles from what Ronni had assumed!

She frowned across at him, her heart going out to him. 'I hope she doesn't still blame you?' she said.

'I don't think so. At least, she says she doesn't. But there are still times, when she gets angry with me, that I can't help remembering, and wondering what's in her heart.'

'Oh, but you mustn't wonder!' Ronni also understood now that hurt look she'd sometimes seen in his eyes during his angry exchanges with Silvia. 'She loves you!' she told him. 'I'm sure she does. I've heard her refer to you as "my wonderful cousin"!'

Guido smiled at that. 'Thank you for telling me.' Then he paused for a moment. 'But why are we talking about Silvia?' The dark eyes flickered. 'I didn't come here to talk about Silvia.'

'Oh?' Ronni remained leaning forward in her chair. She wanted to lean back, but her muscles had become paralysed. 'And why did you come?' she heard herself ask.

Guido was leaning forward too now, dark eyes shadowed by long dark lashes. 'I came to ask you to come back to Sardinia. I want you there for the speedboat race.'

'Why?'

'Because there's no way I'll win it if you're not there.'

'You passed the trials without me.' Was that all he wanted? An extra supporter to cheer him on in his race? 'I don't see why the race should be any different.'

'I didn't know you weren't there at the trials.'

Ronni was aware of that stiffness about him again,

and suddenly she noticed too that, like herself, he had a slightly hollow look about the eyes.

'I didn't know,' he went on, 'that you'd already gone back to England. If I'd known that, I wouldn't have stood a chance.'

What was he saying? But before Ronni could wonder further, suddenly he was rising to his feet.

'I scared you off, didn't I?' He was standing over her. 'That night when I suggested we go upstairs. . . I moved too fast. . . That was why you left. . .'

Ronni gazed at him, astonished. He hadn't scared her off. It was her silly fears about Silvia that had scared her off.

But before she could say anything, he was continuing, 'You said it was Arnie, but I knew it wasn't. I was pretty certain you weren't in love with Arnie.' He smiled a small smile. 'And I gather from Jeff that I was right.'

Then all at once he was taking her hand and drawing her up to stand before him. 'Come back for the race. Come back and stay forever. I love you, Ronni. I can't live without you.'

Ronni could not speak. She reached up and touched his cheek. Her heart was beating like a drum inside her.

Then, shivering, she told him, 'I love you, too.'

There was a moment of total stillness, then suddenly he was embracing her, holding her against him, raining kissing across her face.

'Marry me, Veronica. Say you'll never leave me.' He gazed down at her almost fiercely, his voice breaking as he told her, 'I cannot endure another day like the last two weeks.'

'Nor I.'

Her heart full to bursting with love and happiness, Ronni fell against him, burying her face against his neck.

'I'll never leave you. How could I leave you? Without you I am nothing.' She looked into his eyes. 'I love you with all my heart. You are my sun.'

The marriage took place the day after the race.

'You are my prize,' Guido told Ronni. 'My prize for all my life.'

'And what if you'd lost?' For, of course, he'd won, easily, miles and miles ahead of the rest. Ronni teased him, 'Perhaps you wouldn't be so happy if you'd lost?'

But he grew serious now as they sat out on the terrace, two blissful days into their marriage, watching a blood-red sun sink into a blood-red sea.

'It wouldn't have mattered,' he told her. 'Now nothing matters. How can anything matter now that I have you?'

Ronni felt her heart turn over. 'I love you,' she told him.

He smiled. 'Tell me again. I can't hear it enough.'

Ronni obliged. 'I love you. I love you,' she repeated.

'And I love you. I love everything about you.' He smiled. 'I even love your parents.'

Ronni laughed. 'I think it's mutual. And you'd better go on loving them. It looks as though they're going to be regular visitors here.'

She felt a pang of gratitude, remembering his generous offer to provide them with a month-long Sardinian holiday, not only on their anniversary this year, but every single year to come. Her poor parents had been totally overwhelmed.

Just as I am, Ronni thought, glancing across at him, feeling her heart swell inside her with love and longing. I never knew it was possible to be happy like this. To love someone this much and to want them so badly.

Guido slipped an arm around her and bent to kiss her, then reached out suddenly to the stone urn beside them and pulled off the stem of a red geranium.

'My Botticelli nymph,' he smiled, slipping it behind her ear.

Ronni blushed with pleasure, then reached up to kiss him as, with a glint in his eye that she knew and loved well, he added, 'And now shall we go upstairs?'

Welcome to Europe

SARDINIA — 'Italy's Emerald Isle'

A unique mingling of past and present, and a glimpse of Italy as it used to be. . .an island where the shepherds still make up poetry and where a broken romance may yet be the cause of a never-ending family feud. . .a place where there's no need to visit a museum to experience history, for the past lives around you in the landscape and the culture — Sardinia is all that and more.

THE ROMANTIC PAST

Although it is the second largest island in the Mediterranean, after Sicily, before the advent of aeroplane travel Sardinia was too distant geographically from the mainland to take on the characteristics of the Italian peninsula, and in fact resembles only its neighbouring island of **Corsica**. Its large areas of bush and impenetrable landscape have in recent centuries led to countless legends of brigands and vendettas, but its colourful history actually goes back far further.

Very few of the inhabitants of Sardinia have pure Sard blood; instead they are likely to have **Spanish**, **Genoese**, **Pisan**, **Turkish**, **Moorish**, **Phoenician** or even **Austrian** ancestry. Roman soldiers gave the central mountain region the name 'Land of Strangers' without knowing how prophetic their term was to be! The island was to be fought and argued over for many centuries.

We know very little about the **earliest inhabitants** of Sardinia, but the clues to their mysterious existence lie everywhere across the island in the massive citadels of stones called *nuraghi*. These *nuraghi*, unique to Sardinia, date back to around 1300 to 1200 BC, and are generally agreed to have been dwelling-places-cum-fortresses; a *nuraghe* is like a cone with the top cut off, made of huge boulders and often two or even three storeys high, with an entrance at ground level. They are often complicated by additional towers and defence walls, and are a constant and fascinating reminder to the visitor of the island's ancient history.

Phoenician, Carthaginian, Roman and Byzantine rule followed, and in more recent centuries the squabbling over Sardinia did not cease. In 1479 Ferdinand II of Aragon married Isabella of Castile, turning Sardinia from an Aragonese province into a subject state of the newly united Spain, and the Spanish were not deposed until the 18th century.

During the War of the Spanish Succession the Austrian Habsburgs temporarily occupied the island, and by 1720 Sardinia had been given to the Dukes of Savoy on condition that they relinquish their more disputed claim to Sicily. The **House of Savoy** ruled Sardinia until Italian unity was achieved in 1861, when the then King of Sardinia, **Vittorio Emanuele II**, became King of Italy — so Sardinia was in fact the cradle of the Italian royal dynasty. Only when Italy's royal capital and seat of government transferred from the House of Savoy's mainland home city of Turin to Rome did Sardinia lose some of its political importance and revert to being an offshore island. In 1948 the island was finally given its own **autonomous regional government** within the framework of Italy.

Sardinia's **culture and customs** are strongly centred around the cycle of **birth, marriage** and **death**, as well as being linked to the religious calendar. Just as there are many local dialects, and variations in the national costume, so also the legends and rituals vary from village to village.

Engagements and **weddings** are occasions of great ceremony. One area has a courtship ritual known as the *precunta*, in which the hopeful suitor takes a friend to visit his girl's father, pretending to look for a 'lost lamb'; when they find her, the betrothal can be announced. In Gallura the bride rides on a horse, waving a staff of coloured ribbons, and in other areas the groom must recognise his bride from among a group of masked women before leading her to the altar!

For **wedding feasts** a special loaf is baked, decorated with towers and pinnacles, and a plate will be broken to ensure fertility; the number of pieces is the number of children the couple will have.

Children are considered a gift from heaven. In Gallura, as soon as a child is born the father blows on its eyes, then opens the windows and fires two gunshots for a boy, one for a girl. And there used to be an old custom in the village of Donori that the husband of a woman in childbirth would quit the house, leaving his trousers on the bed, which local women would then beat with sticks to drive away evil spirits!

THE ROMANTIC PRESENT — pastimes for lovers. . .

Sardinia is a place one visits for its stunning landscapes and fascinating history rather than for cathedrals and monuments; nor will you find much of a nightlife anywhere except the tourist-developed Costa Smeralda area.

You should begin your visit to Sardinia with a short stay in the island's capital, **Cagliari**, in the far south of the island, before visiting some of the smaller towns and villages to get a feel for the romance of the past.

Cagliari is really the only town where you might see the influence of Italy in the architecture and churches. The cathedral, in the **Piazza Palazzo**, represents in its various styles many aspects of the city's history, and contains the tombs of famous people such as **Martin II of Aragon** and **Marie-Louise of Savoy**, wife of Louis XVIII of France. The city's panoramic position in unusual natural surroundings means that flights of flamingoes, cormorants, ducks and herons are an everyday sight as they move from one lagoon to another, passing over the town. At sunset, an extraordinary pink light spreads over the walls and the old ramparts of the castle.

The best *nuraghe* can be seen at Barumini, but, going north, **Alghero** on the north-west coast is an old walled town worth stopping at for its fine cliff scenery and its stunning stalactite caves, the **Grottoes of Neptune**. At the northernmost tip of the island is **Santa Teresa**, from where you can take a boat and visit **Caprera**, a special nature reserve and location of the tomb of Garibaldi, the 'sleeping lion whose breathing makes the ocean swell', and the charming archipelago of **La Maddelena**, where a walk through the little streets and square of the old town centre, paved with granite, will pass a pleasant hour or two.

South of Santa Teresa is the flowery, green **Costa Smeralda**, whose emerald seas gave the stretch of coastline its beautiful name. This area was discovered and developed by the **Aga Khan** and fast became the holiday ground of the rich and famous. But if the jet-set scene is not for you, you might prefer the ancient city of **Olbia**, with its 11th-century **Church of San Simplicio** ; Olbia typifies the strange contrast between old and new that is such a feature of Sardinia today.

Wherever you go, you'll be bound to catch sight of at least some of the local people wearing the **national costume:** for women a white long-sleeved blouse and dark, long, full skirt for everyday wear, with bright colours including red making an appearance for festive occasions; and for men a distinctive full-sleeved white shirt and white baggy trousers tucked into black boots and gaiters, with a black waistcoat or jacket and a belted black apron worn on top.

If you like **wildlife**, apart from the birds around Cagliari you may be lucky enough to catch sight of the legendary wingless partridge, or to see a wild *mouflon*, the ringleted mountain goat alleged to have had the original Golden Fleece.

If, however, **food and drink** play a large part in your holiday enjoyment, then as well as standard Italian dishes there are plenty of Sardinian specialities to tempt your palate. **Bread** comes in an enormous variety of shape and texture, each village having its own type, and at *festa* time special loaves are baked in the shape of birds, animals or human figures.

Other delicacies include the smoked Sardinian sausage (*salsiccia*) and *cinghiale*, a type of ham made from wild boar. There are, as you would expect, the whole range of pasta-type dishes, but you might want to try the Sardinian variations on these — *fregula* or *succu*, for example, a soup containing tiny saffron-coloured balls, in place of the usual minestrone. The most typical meat dish is *porceddu*, roast suckling pig, but the more adventurous among you might like the unique Sard dish *taccula*—thrushes or blackbirds boiled whole and hung in bags full of aromatic myrtle leaves. There are some delicious, flavoursome **cheeses**, but if you don't have a strong stomach take care to avoid the *casu becciu*—a cheese so old that it is eaten with the cheese mites still alive in it! Any of these dishes would be perfect washed down with a glass or two of one of the full-bodied, strong Sardinian wines, the most famous of which is the dry white **Vernaccia** . . . or do you have a sweet tooth? Sardinia is also famous for its aromatic, bittersweet **honey**, and for the confectionery made from this, together with nuts, fruit and candied peel.

And finally, before you return, why not take home some of the excellent local **handicrafts** as presents or simply mementoes of your visit? Bright woollen **shawls** and **rugs**, hand-carved **wooden objects** and gold filigree and coral **jewellery** are among the rich and varied selection.

DID YOU KNOW THAT . . .?

* although it is the second largest island in the Mediterranean, at 24,090 km sq, Sardinia has the lowest **population** density at about 60 people per square km of any Italian region.

* the currency of Sardinia is the **lira**.

* Sardinia was called Ichnusa or Sandaliotis by the Greeks because of its supposed **sandal** shape.

* although Italian is spoken, the range of Sard dialects that come under the term **Sardo** are closer to Latin than any other language spoken today.

* the Italian for 'I love you' is '*Ti amo*'.

* despite the island coastline, **fishing** has never been a principal activity of the inidigenous Sardinians — of 2,400 Sard proverbs only 3 make any reference to the sea, and most fishing terms are expressed by Neapolitan, Genoese, Catalan or Arab words.

LOOK OUT FOR TWO TITLES EVERY MONTH IN OUR SERIES OF EUROPEAN ROMANCES:

A PART OF HEAVEN: Jessica Marchant (Bulgaria)
Falling in love with Nikolai Antonow was easy. But Mallory wasn't the person Nikolai thought she was — what would happen when he found out the truth?

CALYPSO'S ISLAND: Rosalie Ash (Malta)
On the romantic island of Malta, Caroline threw caution to the winds and fell in love. But could she trust Roman when he told her that she wasn't just a holiday diversion?

ROMAN SPRING: Sandra Marton (Italy)
Nicolo Sabatini *claimed* that his interest in Caroline was merely that of an employer. So why did he seem to be taking over her life?

LOVE OR NOTHING: Natalie Fox (Balearics)
Ruth had loved — and lost — once on the beautiful island of Majorca. But, this time, she was determined to win Fernando's heart once and for all. . .

Accept 4 FREE Romances and 2 FREE gifts

FROM READER SERVICE

Here's an irresistible invitation from Mills & Boon. Please accept our offer of 4 FREE Romances, a CUDDLY TEDDY and a special MYSTERY GIFT! Then, if you choose, go on to enjoy 6 captivating Romances every month for just £1.80 each, postage and packing FREE. Plus our FREE Newsletter with author news, competitions and much more.

Send the coupon below to: Mills & Boon Reader Service, FREEPOST, PO Box 236, Croydon, Surrey CR9 9EL.

NO STAMP REQUIRED

Yes!
Please rush me 4 FREE Romances and 2 FREE gifts! Please also reserve me a Reader Service subscription. If I decide to subscribe I can look forward to receiving 6 brand new Romances for just £10.80 each month, post and packing FREE. If I decide not to subscribe I shall write to you within 10 days - I can keep the free books and gifts whatever I choose. I may cancel or suspend my subscription at any time. I am over 18 years of age.

Ms/Mrs/Miss/Mr _____ EP55R

Address _____

_____

Postcode _____ Signature _____

MAILING PREFERENCE SERVICE

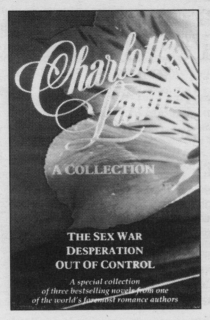

Next Month's Romances

Each month you can choose from a wide variety of romance with Mills & Boon. Below are the new titles to look out for next month, why not ask either Mills & Boon Reader Service or your Newsagent to reserve you a copy of the titles you want to buy – just tick the titles you would like and either post to Reader Service or take it to any Newsagent and ask them to order your books.

Please save me the following titles:		Please tick √
A DIFFICULT MAN	Lindsay Armstrong	
MARRIAGE IN JEOPARDY	Miranda Lee	
TENDER ASSAULT	Anne Mather	
RETURN ENGAGEMENT	Carole Mortimer	
LEGACY OF SHAME	Diana Hamilton	
A PART OF HEAVEN	Jessica Marchant	
CALYPSO'S ISLAND	Rosalie Ash	
CATCH ME IF YOU CAN	Anne McAllister	
NO NEED FOR LOVE	Sandra Marton	
THE FABERGE CAT	Anne Weale	
AND THE BRIDE WORE BLACK	Helen Brooks	
LOVE IS THE ANSWER	Jennifer Taylor	
BITTER POSSESSION	Jenny Cartwright	
INSTANT FIRE	Liz Fielding	
THE BABY CONTRACT	Suzanne Carey	
NO TRESPASSING	Shannon Waverly	

If you would like to order these books in addition to your regular subscription from Mills & Boon Reader Service please send £1.80 per title to: Mills & Boon Reader Service, Freepost, P.O. Box 236, Croydon, Surrey, CR9 9EL, quote your Subscriber No:.................................... (If applicable) and complete the name and address details below. Alternatively, these books are available from many local Newsagents including W.H.Smith, J.Menzies, Martins and other paperback stockists from 8 October 1993.

Name:...

Address:...

....Post Code:.......................

To Retailer: If you would like to stock M&B books please contact your regular book/magazine wholesaler for details.